THE WO
WH

About the author

Audrey Howard was born in Liverpool in 1929. Before she began to write she had a variety of jobs, among them hairdresser, model, shop assistant, cleaner and civil servant. In 1981 she wrote the first of her novels when she was out of work and living in Australia. There are now more than twenty.

The Woman from Browhead

When Morning Comes

Audrey Howard

CORONET BOOKS

Hodder & Stoughton

First published as two separate volumes:

The Woman from Browhead Copyright © 1994 by Audrey Howard
First published in Great Britain in 1994
by Hodder and Stoughton
First published in Coronet paperback in 1994
by Hodder and Stoughton
A division of Hodder Headline

When Morning Comes Copyright © 1998 by Audrey Howard
First published in Great Britain in 1998
by Hodder and Stoughton
First published in Coronet paperback in 1999
by Hodder and Stoughton
A division of Hodder Headline

A Coronet Paperback

ISBN 0 340 79377 5

Printed and bound in Great Britain by
Clays Ltd, St Ives plc

Hodder and Stoughton
A division of Hodder Headline
338 Euston Road
London NW1 3BH

THE WOMAN FROM BROWHEAD

For June Hall
who got me started

1

The kitchen at Long Beck Farm trembled into the nervous activity the arrival of Sarah Macauley always produced. Cook, who had been about to sit down in her favourite rocking chair, the one in which no posterior but her own was ever allowed to settle, hastily put away the mug of hot, sweet, strong tea she was sipping appreciatively and with a skilful and fluid movement which belied her years and the 'bad back' she purported to have, dipped a spoon into the enormous 'kail pot' which simmered on the fire, stirring vigorously before lifting it to her lips.

"A smidgin more thyme I think, Dolly, and mind it's no more than a smidgin. Too much can spoil a decent soup."

"Yes, Cook."

"And when you've done that get out the flour and sugar, some butter and eggs. I've a mind to make Master Reed a few biscuits. Lemon, I think, so you can squeeze me a couple while you're at it, and don't throw away the peel. He likes my lemon biscuits, does Master Reed. Oh! there you are, Madam . . ." starting visibly as the grey-clad figure of her mistress appeared at her elbow. "I didn't see you there. I was just about to . . ."

"Yes, Mrs Lewis, I can see exactly what you were doing so don't let me stop you." Mrs Macauley moved towards the fire on which the pan was kept simmering at all times, summer and winter, for there were men, her husband's shepherds and yardmen, who might be in need of a bit of something inside them, especially in the winter. Since this was her kitchen and her soup she took a spoonful and, like Cook, lifted it to her lips. She tasted it thoughtfully and the whole kitchen held its breath. If it was not to her liking she would say so, offending Cook, who was good at her job. If Cook was offended, indeed put out in any way, it would be *they* who would be made to feel her displeasure.

She was a tyrant, was Mrs Macauley who, until her husband had prospered on his farm, had been a true farm-wife, working in her own kitchen with a young maid to fetch and carry and a woman to scrub. She herself had done all the cooking and baking, the making of bread, the pickling and preserving and salting, only allowing – and that thoroughly supervised – the maid to perform the task of making the soap and the candles and any task which, in Sarah Macauley's opinion, any fool could do. Her life had been busy, hard and busy, but she had found it satisfying since she knew nothing else. The day on which her husband told her he was to entertain a wool merchant from Yorkshire had been a shattering one for Sarah since it was the last one in which she was a true farmwife.

"I don't want you fiddling about in the kitchen, my lass. Your place is at the head of the dining table. You're mistress of this house and as such you must help me to entertain this fellow-me-lad and you can't do it chained to the kitchen range. Get yourself a cook and another maid. One that can wait on at table."

"A cook! What do I want with such a thing? I can do my own cooking and I'll have you know there's not a better one in the whole of Bassenthwaite parish." She was scandalised and not only that, affronted, but her husband was adamant. He was moving up in the world and his hill farm, which stretched as far as the eye could see from his farm gate, was growing and thriving. This bit of business with the chap from Yorkshire could lead to even greater things and it would not do to have one's wife mucking about in the kitchen, running backwards and forwards, flushed and perspiring, from there to the table and back again.

It was only a step from employing a cook to having not one kitchenmaid to help her but two, then three. A scullery maid, a dairy maid and the woman whose sole task it was to scrub the kitchen floor, the pantry floor, the dairy, the buttery, the back step, the front step and the long, stone-flagged 'hallan' which led from the front of the house to the back. It had been hard, harder than anyone realised, since she was a woman sparing of words, for Sarah to 'sit about on her behind', a phrase she used only to herself, and it had altered her subtly from a woman who, though sharp-tongued and exacting was always fair, to one who was shrewish, grim, testy, fault finding and not well liked by her servants.

They all waited, Mrs Lewis the cook, her expression one of guarded effrontery, Josie the parlourmaid, Dolly the kitchenmaid and Prudence whose job it was to be everyone's slave. Even the tangle-haired woman on her knees at the bucket by the door leading to the hallan rested back on her heels. There was a child beside her, a young girl with her own bucket and brush. She was no more than ten or eleven years old, scrawny and thin-faced, and she watched, open-mouthed and with keen interest, the very evident contest of wills which was taking place between Mrs Macauley and Cook. Mrs Macauley would have the last word, the girl knew that, for didn't she always, and Cook would be furious, no doubt holding back the left-overs of food, perhaps a mutton chop or a knuckle of bacon, a spoonful of jelly or a broken biscuit which were nothing to her and which, in an off-handed kindly way she would often pass on to herself and her mother. It was a shame for they had lived on nothing but turnip bread for the last week. The juice from the turnip was pressed out, flour and salt added to the mixture and the result baked on the 'bakstone' over the fire. Tasteless and unsatisfying, but it filled an empty stomach and the hard work she and her mother did gave them a sharp appetite. And those tit-bits were a blessing on a tongue which needed something to *taste* now and again. She'd miss them tonight if Mrs Macauley got the better of Cook, which she was bound to do for this was her kitchen.

It was a big room with tables of yellow-white sycamore which stood up to years of pounding, chopping and scrubbing and from its ceiling hung hams and bunches of herbs, crates of bread, kept there since Sarah Macauley

had come as a bride to Long Beck for there had been rats
and mice then. Besides the iron pots and pans there was
a vast array of highly polished copper utensils. The walls
were whitewashed every six months for the climate in the
room was always intensely busy, blasted by fires and
ovens and rendered moist and murky by steam and smoke.
Cook and the kitchenmaids worked flat out from breakfast to supper time. It was a proud boast of Sarah's that
everything her family ate was produced in her kitchen
and dairy, and even now a leg of pork was being spit-
roasted over the open kitchen fire. The farmhouse was old
and many of the things in the kitchen had been used
by Sarah Macauley's mother-in-law and *hers* before that,
dating way back into the last century, but beside the
huge open fire which was set in the wall behind strong,
horizontal metal bars was an equally huge enclosed range,
blackleaded, glowing and dark and cleaned each morning
by Prudence.

   Set neatly on shelves attached to the spotless walls
were trivets and skillets, toasters and grills, tongue
presses and beef-warmers. There were jelly moulds of
earthenware, copper and glass, for Sarah Macauley prided
herself on her good table; copper pans, earthenware bowls
and wooden ladles, all playing an essential role in the
endless round of preserving, boiling, baking, roasting and
toasting, culinary activities which had been carried on for
the past thirty-odd years by Sarah herself. The two kitchen
dressers of oak were crowded with a blue-and-white china
tea set, dozens of cups and saucers, plates, cream jugs
and sugar bowls in a delicate willow pattern, and beside
them was blue and white dinnerware in the same design.
Enormous meat platters, vegetable dishes, soup tureens,
dinner plates and ladles. They had been in the Macauley
family for fifty years, come from the Staffordshire potters
Josiah Spode and Thomas Minton, and it was woe betide
any luckless kitchenmaid who touched any part of them
unless supervised by her mistress. About the room were
several beautifully carved and well-proportioned Windsor
chairs, again old, cherished, well polished, but not meant

for sitting on, for Sarah Macauley's servants were here to work not loll about, except for the brief period in which they ate their meals.

"Hand me that skimmer, if you please, Dolly," Mrs Macauley said, and the child on her knees held her breath for, on the action of the woman who, if only temporarily, was her mistress since Annie and Lizzie Abbott were 'casuals', depended the left-overs she and her mother would take home with them that night.

The skimmer was slid delicately into the soup. Carefully Mrs Macauley lifted it out again, scrutinising it minutely as though she fully expected a cockroach to raise its ugly head. Cook watched her, her face devoid of all expression, but in her eyes was a gleam which said if looks could kill her mistress would be lying dead at her feet. Cook was a woman in her late fifties, too old to be taken on now in any of the grand houses in which she had once worked and where she had received her training. She was an experienced and imaginative cook and though she was not awfully sure *why* Mrs Macauley seemed to have it in for her, since it was Mrs Macauley who had employed her in the first place, she was well aware that her mistress did her best to find fault.

The skimmer came out clean and fatless. There were tiny, plump onions, shreds of cabbage, slivers of beef, slices of mushroom and carrot in the skimming spoon but nothing else.

Mrs Macauley was clearly annoyed. She would have liked nothing better than to have given Cook the length of her tongue for in that way it would have bolstered her own waning belief in herself and her talents in her kitchen where, since her husband had gone up in the world, it had melted slowly with her self-esteem.

"It'll do," she said ungraciously and was vastly put out when Cook smiled complacently. "Now then, let's see to those biscuits for Master Reed."

"Nay, Mrs Macauley, I'll make them," Cook said ill-advisedly. "You go and sit yourself down and put your feet up."

Sarah was incensed. Put her feet up indeed, and to be told to do it in her own kitchen by a woman who had no right to be there in the first place, in her view.

"That'll be enough from you, Mrs Lewis, and what are these girls doing standing about with their mouths open? Have they no work to do? Really, I've never seen such an idle-handed lot in my life and likely to continue to be so, it seems to me, if I'm not here at their backs. They are in your charge, you know, and I expect you to oversee their work in a more appropriate manner."

She turned away from the thunderous face of Mrs Lewis and right behind her Lizzie Abbott's bucket seemed to leap up and catch her in the shins. She stumbled, the water slopped on the hem of her gown and it was as if a knife had struck her in her side, a knife with a serrated edge which not only sliced into her but turned its blade a time or two for good measure. It was the worst pain Sarah had ever experienced since the first one had struck her over six months ago, and it almost brought her to her knees.

"Get out of my way, woman," she screeched and in her senseless agony she lifted her hand, striking the woman – who was she? – so hard she fell sideways, her arm going up to the elbow in her own bucket. The child who knelt beside her – who was *she*? – went with her and the pair of them sprawled on the wet floor they themselves had just scrubbed. The woman began to cry weakly, the sort of tears Sarah often felt like crying herself, despairing tears, hopeless tears, but the child leaped to her feet and for a minute Sarah thought she was about to strike her, then, after carefully lifting the weeping woman to her feet, where she stood, humble head bowed, the girl ran past Cook and the astonished maids and out through the kitchen door into the yard.

The bright sunlight of the early spring day was in Annie Abbott's eyes as she scrambled over Mrs Macauley's threshwood, and across the cobbles where hens pecked and a rooster strutted. There were a couple of young Border Collie dogs fastened by a chain to the wall,

sheepdogs who were not yet fully trained to herding and
they stood up, wagging hopeful tails. This was a working
farm and up on the fell Alistair Macauley and his shepherds
were 'raking in' the heavily pregnant ewes for it would
soon be lambing time. But not Alistair Macauley's son.
Not his fine, twenty-three-year-old son, Reed Macauley.
The young, black mare he rode, dashing, wild and as
handsome as himself, skittered madly out of control as
Annie came through the kitchen door and, in her haste to
get away from her own black rage at what Mrs Macauley
had done to her mother, almost went under the horse's
hooves. The mare was tall, blotting out the sunlight, crashing her hooves in alarm on the cobbles and rolling her eyes
in fury as the child and the hens scattered about her.

Reed Macauley scarcely seemed to notice Annie
Abbott. She might have been no more than a wisp of straw
which had blown from his father's stable. She was there
in his vision but of such little consequence he did not see
her. His vivid blue eyes looked directly into hers but his
gaze moved on impassively as he guided his restless animal
towards the open stable door.

"Albert," he shouted, "rub Victoria down, will you, and
give her a handful of oats," then he was gone.

It was their first meeting.

It was October, six months later, when she saw him
again, and as at the last time he rode by her with as much
interest as he would show a kitten which frolicked in the
grass. The track at the back of Browhead led up to Long
Beck and he and his mare moved easily along it, his gaze
passing over her and her father as if they did not exist.
Annie watched him go then bent down, doing her best to
lift the swill basket which was filled to its brim with newly
picked potatoes, the ones she herself had lifted that morning, and though she heaved and strained until the sweat
broke out on her childish brow and ran down her cheeks,
she could not move it. She straightened up, rubbed her
hands together as she had seen her father do, spat on
them then bent down again, gripping the basket at its rim
where holes had been left to fit each hand. The basket,

crafted by her own mother for this very purpose, was not heavy in itself, being made from split hazel rods woven with white willow, but its contents weighed over twenty pounds and were too much for a child.

"Will tha' never learn sense, girl? Can tha' not see tha' load's too big? Tek some out an' put 'em in a pile then shift what's left down to t' barn. *Then* come back for t'others. Think girl, think! I don't know why the Good Lord made women so half-witted. Tryin' to lift a bloody basket it'd tek me half me time to get off t' ground. Lighten it, girl, an' look lively."

"Yes, Faither."

"An' tell thi' mother I'm waitin' on me dinner whilst tha's down there. I've never known a woman so feckless as she is. Bugger it, it's gone noon an' I'm parched. An' I don't want no cold tea, neither. A jug of ale'd go down nicely."

"Yes, Faither." Annie had obediently emptied half the potatoes, piling them neatly on the ground.

"Off tha' go then an' don't tha' drop that swill or I'll 'ave summat ter say ter thi'. Them potatoes is money an' we've none o' that ter be chuckin' about an' don't come back empty-handed. Fetch me some o' that manure in tha' empty swill."

"Yes, Faither."

The neat rows of healthily blooming plants stretched out at the backs of the man and child in the walled field behind the farmhouse, each row exactly twenty-seven inches from its neighbour, each set, or plant, twelve inches from the next. They were erect, tall, branching, their tops crowded in a spreading confusion. The stems had a pink tinge and the flowers were a lovely red-purple but Joshua Abbott was not concerned with their appearance, except in so much as it was a healthy one, only with the smooth, oval-shaped harvest which grew at their root. He and the girl had planted them in late March. They had been well fertilised with the manure from his farmyard, the child's job again since it was within her capabilities and now they were to be lifted and those not needed for the family's winter requirements would go to market.

She was back within five minutes and behind her, carrying a basket which was so heavy it caused her to shuffle lop-sidedly, was Lizzie Abbott. She was obviously pregnant. Though both she and the child who staggered beneath the weight of the swill basket and its stinking, steaming contents were making heavy weather of their loads Joshua Abbott made no effort to help them. He was digging. Glancing round as they approached he threw down his spade, took off his battered and stained felt hat, wiped his sweating face with his forearm, replaced his hat and sat down, his back to the drystone wall which surrounded the field.

"An' about time too," was all he said, his tone peevish.

"I'm sorry, Joshua. I got took badly." Lizzie Abbott put her hand to her distended belly. Her thin, worn face was vastly apologetic just as though she had been caught junketing about the yard with Natty Varty who sometimes gave Joshua a hand at harvest or lambing. "I can't seem ter get over this sickness . . ."

"Aye, well, set basket down, woman." Joshua was not in the least concerned with his wife's pregnancy, nor with the details of its progress, only with its outcome. Married eighteen years and nothing to show for it but this one girl, though by God, he'd done *his* best. A bairn every year he'd given her and a few times she'd gone full term but always it seemed, again as though the blame was hers, contrary madam that she was, bringing forth some sickly infant, three of them boys, who had not lasted a month. One girl! A fine girl, strong and biddable, cheerful too, and if only she'd been a boy which was all he asked for, one boy, Joshua would have been content. It wasn't too much to expect, was it, out of eighteen pregnancies? But no, soon as it was in her belly where surely it was not too difficult to hang on to, *she'd* let it go, time after time, except for the girl. Other men had sons. Look at Jem Mounsey from Upfell Farm. Two daughters certainly but a fine lad going on twelve years now and so big and strapping, like Jem, he could do the work of a grown man. Upfell was small, like his own farm, not in the class of

Alistair Macauley's place up at Long Beck, but between
them Jem and Davy Mounsey managed it nicely with no
need of paid help like Natty Varty, or at least only in
the most dire of emergencies. Of course at ploughing or
harvesting, lambing or clipping time, every farmer and his
family helped every other. A 'boon' clip, or 'boon' ploughing, when a day would be set aside and neighbours would
come with a plough or a horse or their shears when there
were sheep to be sheared and at the end of it there would
be a tatie-pot supper, with dancing in the barn, the fiddle
played by Dobby Hawkins who was odd-job man at Long
Beck. A 'merry-neet' right enough but what had Joshua
Abbott to be merry about with no son to take over when
he himself was six feet under? If only the girl had . . .
well, brightening a little as he studied his wife's thickening
figure . . . 'appen it wasn't too late. He was only thirty-
nine himself and had many good years in him to pass on
to a lad all that he himself had learned from his father.

Browhead farmhouse and its surrounding acres had
been in his family for generations, he was not awfully sure
how many. Unlike many small farmers who had been
forced off the common land with the Enclosure movement,
his grandfather, or was it his great-grandfather, had
managed by dint of great hardship to himself and his
family to buy the land which had been freely held by the
Abbotts, or so they had imagined, from time immemorial.
Not a great deal by the standards of the wealthy
landowners such as the Macauleys but still theirs, and
though they had never managed to do more than 'hang on'
from harvest to harvest and from lambing to lambing, it
was still theirs. Still Abbott land. Joshua Abbott's land and
if he could just get himself a son to pass it on to he'd die
a happy man.

The girl sat down beside him and Joshua's sheepdog
crept up to her, leaning fondly on her shoulder, eyeing
the oatcake she had taken from the basket.

"An' don't let me see tha' feedin' that dog."

"No, Faither."

"Ruined he is an' all because of tha' mollycoddlin' ways.

See, woman, tek 'im down wi' thi' an' fasten 'im to t' chain in t' yard. I don't know what comes over the two o' you, pettin' 'im like he was some lap dog. A workin' dog he is an' when he's not workin' he stays in t' yard. Is that clear?"

"Yes, Faither."

"Yes, Joshua."

"Did tha' fetch me ale, woman?"

"Yes, Joshua, 'tis in t' basket."

"Well, then, there's no need for thi' to hang about here, is there. There's bound ter be summat for thi' ter do in tha' kitchen."

"Yes, Joshua," and, obedient as a trained animal, his wife moved off in the direction of the farmhouse which stood slightly lower down the sloping field so that its roof was on a level with where the man and the child laboured.

"Don't forget bloody dog, woman."

His wife turned in a flurry, her face anguished at her own foolishness. What was she thinking of? Day-dreaming, he'd say, though her dreams were not dreams at all but galloping worries on how she was to manage the next four months with the burden she carried . . . oh, please God, don't let me lose this one . . . I must not give way to despair . . . but a boy, a healthy boy so that *he* will leave me alone. So that he will cast off the bitterness and harshness he shows to the girl, smile a little . . . all that work the child does and her not twelve yet . . . all that I do . . .

It was hard to believe that she had once been pretty Lizzie Bowman from Cockermouth since those who had known her then could not remember it and her own child had never seen her other than timid, hard-working, patient, dumb, thin and anxious of face, her skin and hair a uniform greyish-brown. She was thirty-four years old. Her life and that of her daughter was one of unremitting labour from early dawn until they fell into their beds at dark. A hard life which was restricted not just to herself and Annie but was the lot of farm women everywhere in Cumberland. There was the clapbread to be baked, the ale to be brewed, pickling and bottling, baking, cooking and cleaning, rush making, cheese and butter making, the pickling of beef and mutton, the drying of the meat in the smoke of the chimney. There was washday when water must be brought from the spring ready for boiling. There was the vegetable garden, the herb garden and when all that was done there was the spinning of the yarn from the fleece of Joshua Abbott's Herdwick sheep and the weaving of it into the hodden-grey wool from which most of their serviceable clothing was made. She and her daughter milked cows and collected eggs, killed the pig, salted the meat and wrung the necks of chickens. They fed the cattle wintering in the cow shed. In the light of the rush lamps they themselves had made they all three knitted hosiery, fashioned birch-twig besoms and swill baskets to be sold at the next market. They both worked like men at lambing time, cut peat and stacked it for drying, helped at the 'boon clip' and at backend, as winter approached, helped to bring down the flock from the high fells and the moors to the lower 'inlands' which were fenced by dry-stone walls.

Between the three of them, with the occasional help of Natty Varty who hired himself out as casual labour, they ran the farm of Browhead and now, with the growing child within her, already she was beginning to tire before the day was half-way through. She needed to rest, put her feet up now and again with a nice hot cup of tea to steady her but how was she to manage that with the hundred and one jobs that were to be done every day on the farm? You'd think with him being so desperate to have a living son he'd find some way to get her a bit of help but no, she must work just the same, just as hard and just as long and if anything happened to the unborn child it would be her fault.

The dog, she musn't forget the dog, but in her effort to appease her husband, to keep him from venting his spleen on the child, from becoming more irritable than he already was, she lunged awkwardly, tripping on the long skirt of her grey woollen dress. She righted herself but in doing so she knew she was going to step heavily on

Joshua's sturdy potato plants and though it would do them no harm since the potatoes ready for lifting were still deep in the soil, she had a horror of arousing his uncertain temper. The child in her womb fluttered feebly and, unbalanced, with her hand on her belly, she fell heavily. She was up again at once, as light as a feather rises, smiling to let him see there was no harm done, though the awful, familiar sinking in her womb told her it was too late.

"Tha's a clumsy beggar," he said, the ale he was slurping down his long, muscular throat making him good humoured.

"I know, Joshua, that's me. Well, I'll get meself home then," turning, desperate to get to her kitchen, to sit down, to lie down in an effort to hold on to what she carried.

"Tha's goin' wi'out dog now, woman. Bloody hell, it beats me how tha' manages ter get through t'day. Tha's in a maze half the time."

"Tha's right, Joshua." She had the dog now, leading him by the scruff of his neck until she reached the gate which led into the yard, flapping at the anxious animal with her apron until he was through. She chained him to the wall, even managing to tell him to 'be a good boy, then' whilst all the while the liquid flowed down her leg and into her wooden-soled clogs as the child she carried drained away from her on a tide of blood.

"I'm sorry, lass," she said later to her daughter who, being a child brought up on a farm, though she was only eleven years old, knew exactly what had happened to her mother five months ago when she had conceived in the bedroom next to hers, and understood the miscarriage she had just suffered in the very same bed.

"It's all right, Mother. Me an' Faither'll manage," Annie answered stoically.

"But how's tha' to do that, child, wi' me stuck up here in me bed? Tha' can't do milkin' an' butter an' cheese an' tha' faither'll want them ter go ter market at week's end."

"Mrs Mounsey'll help me."

"Aye," sighing weakly. "An' 'appen I'll be up afore long."

And so she was, for Joshua was not a man to sit with his knife and fork in his hands waiting for his supper and the girl was too busy in the fields and thé dairy to be of much use in the kitchen. He said nothing, not even in recrimination, when it became apparent he was not to have his son, at least this time, and when in the next eighteen months his wife, despite his nightly assault on her, failed to conceive he began to realise, and to accept that Annie was to be all that he would have. His bitterness was intense and he eyed Jem Mounsey's lad with a jealous loathing he found hard to contain.

It was the day before Annie Abbott's twelfth birthday that he dropped his bombshell, though he gave no reason for his decision since that was not his way. He knew why he was taking this course of action and that was enough.

Annie and her mother, their fingers busy with the rushlights they were making in readiness for the long winter nights ahead, froze in their seats when he spoke, their mouths falling open in astoundment.

"Tha's ter go ter school, girl. Next week. Mornings. Jem Mounsey's lasses go so you might as well an' all."

Annabelle Abbott, Joshua and Lizzie Abbott's fifth child, stood up and the rushes she was coating with mutton fat fell to the floor as Joshua, slinging his hat to his head, set off for The Bull in Gillthrop without another word.

She found her voice at last. "Does he mean it, Mother?"

"Tha' faither never ses owt he don't mean, Annie."

"But . . . *why*?"

Lizzie looked at her daughter, marvelling for the hundredth time on how she and Joshua, despite her own subdued prettiness as a girl, could have between them made a child quite as bright and lovely as Annie. What ancestor had bequeathed to her that look of a thorough-bred, of pedigree that neither the Bowmans of Cocker-mouth nor the Abbotts of Gillthrop had in their line? Tall she was, already half a head above other girls of her age and though she was far from plump the flesh on her was firm and without blemish apart from the endearing scatter of pale golden freckles across her nose. Lizzie cut her hair regularly since her father said it was unsightly to have it 'all over the bloody place' – his words – but it was thick and springing, a mass of corkscrew curls which stood in a cheerful tangle about her well-shaped head. A bright copper, depending on the light, sometimes russet but, when the sun caught it, so vivid it hurt the eye to behold. It fell about her white neck and ears and over her eyes no matter how often Lizzie hacked it off and she knew it would not be long before Joshua ordered her to bind it up in a length of cloth. There was just so much of it, and then there were her eyes. Deep and enormous, bright with intelligence in her pointed face, almost the same colour as her hair sometimes and at others a pale golden brown which could have been yellow. They were set between lashes which were long and thick, brown at their roots and tipped with gold. Her eyebrows were fine and delicate and her skin was the colour of the buttermilk Lizzie produced in her dairy. She was cheerful, good-humoured and willing, as yet unspoiled by her father's oppression. All flame and brilliance and would it be quenched one day when she was wed to some stolid labouring chap which she knew Joshua hoped to get for her in the absence of a son? Mind, she had a stubborn streak in her which Joshua did his best to curb, succeeding so far, for the child was young, but it could become wilful and when it did what would happen to Lizzie Abbott who would be caught in the middle of it? How would *she* survive?

The girl had begun to twirl, her skirts clinging to her slender legs, her bare feet stamping on the flagged floor of the kitchen. She was going to school, she exulted, she was going to school. For some reason known only to her father she was to be sent to school. She would learn. She would be able to read and write and be somebody for was not an education the key which opened the door to all the dreams she had ever dreamed? She would be a scholar, as good as them up there at Long Beck where her status in life had given Mrs Macauley the right to hit Annie Abbott's mother as though she was nothing but a dog.

Though she could not have said why, nor even tried for she was not quite twelve years old, the picture of the tall and haughty figure of Reed Macauley on his fine black mare moved stealthily across her enchanted, simmering mind.

2

Annie Abbott was not quite fifteen years old when she fell ecstatically in love with the handsome young actor in the travelling company which played at the splendid theatre recently built in Keswick. The year was 1843 and the play was *The Outlaw of Sicily* in which the handsome young actor had the leading role.

On that day Sally and Mim Mounsey were picking blackberries in the lane which led from Browhead to Upfell where their father farmed.

"A nice blackberry 'n' apple tart, that's what tha' lad needs ter pick up 'is appetite," their worried mother had said at breakfast time. "Tha' knows 'ow our Davy do like a blackberry 'n' apple tart an' wi' a dab o' cream from that lot I've just put in t' crock it'll slide down a treat."

Davy Mounsey's strange lack of appetite this last day or two had been a source of mystery to his mother and an irritation to his father who could not abide a 'finicky lad' and especially one who said he 'hurt all over' and could not get out of his bed. A bit flushed he was and not his usual self but it was the Tup Fair at the weekend and how was Jem to get his lambs to Keswick and the tup he meant to hire, back again without the help of his son, he beseeched his wife to tell him?

"'E'll be right as rain by then, you'll see," she answered stoutly, more to reassure herself than Jem. "I'm mekkin' 'im up an infusion of angelica. Sally gathered me some from t' woods, didn't tha' lass, an' wi' a cupful o' that inside 'im 'e'll soon pick up. A rare good tonic is angelica an' it settles the stomach. 'E'll soon 'ave 'is appetite back. 'E needs a bit o' summat tasty inside 'im . . ."

Aggie Mounsey's cure for all ills was a 'bit o' summat tasty' and a good swig of one of her herbal remedies. "That blackberry 'n' apple tart'll do the trick, you just wait an' see if it don't," she added hopefully.

Sally and Mim, quarrelling half-heartedly as they always did, more from habit than ill-feeling, had reached the gate to Browhead having picked indolently for the whole of the October morning at a speed which would have incensed Joshua Abbott. Both big girls, Sally the same age as Annie, Mim a year younger, but in his opinion allowed to do as they liked by the indulgent Jem. As long as they helped their mother when she needed it in the dairy or the kitchen, or in any task she set them such as the blackberry picking, their father didn't concern himself overmuch with how they did it or how long it took providing it suited his Aggie. Good-natured, the lot of them, feckless Joshua would have said, but Upfell farm thrived where Browhead did not so how to explain it? He could not, unless it was his own lack of a son. He did not consider the almost inhuman amount of work his own daughter did each day worth mentioning.

She was trudging up the lane from Hause drawing the sledge which Joshua had made behind her, the harness about her shoulders, the leather straps cutting into her flesh and thrusting forward the young swell of her breasts. She leaned into it, her clogged feet feeling the track for purchase since the load on the sledge was heavy. Her face was dewed with sweat and it soaked the armpits of her shabby grey bodice. Her hair was tied up in a length of cloth, allowed to grow now that it was covered, drawn back severely from her pinched face and braided about her head which the cloth covered. On the sledge were two enormous sacks of milled grain which she had just collected from the miller in Hause.

She stopped when she saw Mim and Sally, her breath scraping from her lungs in great heaving gasps, and drawing off the harness she threw herself down on the grass verge, wiping her face with the sleeve of her bodice.

"Watch out fer me faither, Sal, will tha'? I'll 'ave to 'ave
a breather. Them straps are cuttin' inter me summat cruel.
Look . . ." She pushed down the neck of her bodice and
on her white flesh were two bright red weals from her
shoulders to under her armpits and both sisters drew back
in horror.

"Eeh Annie, them's nasty. Can tha' faither not fetch
grain 'imself. That there load's too 'eavy fer a lass."

"Try tellin' 'im that, Sally. 'Tha's a big girl now, our
Annie,' 'e ses ter me, besides, 'e's up rakin' fells for t'
sheep an' 'asn't time. Me mother offered ter come wi' me
but yer know 'ow it is wi' 'er."

Oh, aye, they all knew how it was with Lizzie Abbott,
poor soul. Sad, oppressed Lizzie Abbott who, with her
daughter, led the most miserable of lives. A life on the
level of an animal, their mother said indignantly though
there was nothing *she* could do about it. And like an animal
Lizzie bred every year, or had done until three years ago
when her overworked body had given up the struggle and
simply refused to conceive again. She had strained at every
task her husband put her to, overburdened and doing her
best to protect her child, taking jobs from her which were
beyond the child's strength but now it was the other way
around as Annie grew tall, taller than Lizzie and though
slender to the point of leanness, strong.

They chatted for a while, the three girls, sitting on the
sun-warmed grass verge, idly eating the blackberries Sally
and Mim had picked. The sweat dried on Annie's face but
it was very noticeable that she was not relaxed, that her
head constantly swivelled from side to side, her eyes on
the look-out for her father who could, though he never
hit her, reduce her to trembling, rebellious fear, calling
her a lazy young varmint, his words cold, his jibing voice
filled with his contempt, his hard nature venting his spite
on her for his lack of a son. She who was a mere girl. She
knew he was up on the fell but the habit of a lifetime
was so strong in her she could not throw it off but must
have eyes in the back of her head on guard for his silent
approach.

"We're goin' ter Keswick, me an' Mim, ter see the players. I don't suppose there's any chance tha' can come wi' us?" Sally put a good-hearted hand on Annie's bare brown arm just where it disappeared into her sleeve. The difference, as the sleeve rose a little at Sally's touch, in the skin which had been exposed to the sun and that which had been covered, was startling. A deep honey colour suddenly becoming a pure, alabaster white. Her face was the same, and her throat, but where the open neck of her bodice began it became an almost translucent white. She worked in the open fields or on the fells for much of the day, every day, when she wasn't at school and the constant exposure to sun and wind, to the wild elements which more often than not prevailed in the Lakeland district was, as she remarked mournfully to her mother – for who wanted to look like an old man when you were going on fifteen – making her as weatherbeaten as her father.

Annie laughed shortly. "Don't be daft, Sal. How can I get away from t' farm? Faither knows where I am every minute o' t' day an' night. Besides, even if I could get away, which I can't, where would I get money fer such a thing?"

"It's only threepence ter stand at back, Annie."

"Maybe, but it might as well be three guineas 'cos I 'aven't got it."

"What about tha' mother? 'Asn't she got a bit put by?" as *her* mother had, for the egg and butter money was traditionally the perquisite of the farmwife since she did the work.

"Don't be daft, Sal," Annie said again, but less caustically, with less certainty. There was nothing in the world she would love more than to go to the playhouse with Sally and Mim. To be as carefree, as *free* as they were allowed to be, even if it was only for a few hours. She went nowhere that was not connected with the farm except for the year in which she had been allowed to go to school in the village. She had been twelve then and had known nothing, but in those twelve months she had absorbed

more than Sally and Mim had learned in three years. She
could read and write and add up and do 'take-aways'. She
had learned a smattering of history and geography, for
the teacher, finding Annie wanted to learn and was not
just passing the time as Sally and Mim and most of her
other pupils were doing, had shown an interest in her and
had even lent her her own precious books. *Sense and
Sensibility* by Miss Jane Austen and Mr Charles Dickens'
Pickwick Papers. These had given Annie a taste, not, alas,
fulfilled, to read more, to see more, to know more and
how was she to do that, labouring round her father's farm
until she was married when, she presumed, she would do
the same round her husband's. William Shakespeare was
a great writer of plays, so her teacher at the Dame school
had told her and perhaps it might be one of his that was
to be shown in Keswick.

"What's on?" she asked abruptly.

"On where?" Mim answered, popping another blackberry in her mouth.

"What play is it?"

"'Tis called *The Outlaw of Sicily*."

"Did a chap by the name of William Shakespeare write
it?"

"Nay, don't ask me. Who is 'e, anyway?" Mim was
clearly unimpressed, and anyway, did it matter?

"He's a great play writer."

"Well, I don't know if 'e wrote this 'un, but it says on
the playbill that there's to be dancin' betwixt each
part."

"Dancin' . . ." Oh, how she loved to dance. Not that
she'd done much but at the last 'boon clip' she had twirled
in the 'Cumberland Square Eight' with Davy Mounsey, to
the music of Dobby Hawkins' fiddle and to her astonishment her father had allowed it. The speculative gleam in
his eye had gone unnoticed by her as she stamped her
foot and threw back her growing hair, again, amazingly,
allowed to hang free, though Lizzie Abbott saw it and so
did Aggie Mounsey, both aware of its significance.

"What time you goin'?"

"Mid mornin'. Faither'll give us a lift to Keswick but we've to walk back."

"Threepence, you say?"

"Aye." Sally clasped Annie's hand, gazing earnestly into her face, seeing for perhaps the first time what no one had perceived before. Annie had always been scrawny, with her collar-bones looking as though they were about to break out from beneath her delicate white skin. She had thin, square shoulders, an extreme boyish slenderness, brittle and fine-textured, all hollows and angles with a pointed face in which her eyebrows flew rejoicingly up or ruefully down depending on the mood of her father. She had the rich, woodland colouring of a fox, her eyes just as golden and hunted but now, with her expression one of growing excitement, she seemed to light up, come alive, to crackle with anticipation and she was quite incredibly lovely.

"Will tha' come then?" Sally felt her own excitement begin to snap.

"If me mother'll give me threepence. That's if she 'as it, an' that's if Faither's up on t' fell again an' if 'e's to be there all day, an' if . . ."

It seemed Lizzie did have threepence to give her daughter and more besides which of course no one knew about, saved painfully over the years, a farthing here, a farthing there, stolen, Lizzie supposed it was, whenever she could do so undetected, from the egg money, the butter money, money that passed through her hands in the transactions over besoms and swills, most handed over faithfully to Joshua except for what was hidden behind a certain loose stone in the cow shed.

She had been aghast and yet, looking into her daughter's pleading face, a face suddenly lovely and bright with hope, she could not find it in her heart to refuse since the child had nothing in her life but hard work from cock-crow to nightsong. Giving in to the only impulse she had ever known since the one she had succumbed to when she had accepted and married Joshua, she pressed the threepence into her daughter's hand, kissed her cheek and told her

to be back before her father returned from Middle Fell.
Her face worked painfully as she watched the light, dancing
feet of her child, almost fifteen, run down the track
towards the farm gate where Jem Mounsey and his girls
waited for her. She had on the dress Lizzie herself
had been married in, carefully stored in lavender in the
press in the bedroom, a light shade of tawny brown which,
on Annie, as it had not done on Lizzie, looked exactly
right. It was too short and a mite too tight across the
breasts, causing a pang of misgiving in Lizzie for, with her
glorious hair brushed until it stood out from her head
and down her back in a brilliant copper cloud, Annie was
enough to catch the eye of any man which worried Lizzie
even more. But how could she resist that pleading face,
those vivid eyes which, after all, were asking for very
little? So innocent. A ride into Keswick with a perfectly
respectable family to see the players which evidently
Jem and Aggie Mounsey thought fitting for their girls
to see.

As Annie turned to wave rapturously, Lizzie's eyes
looked up towards Middle Fell and she prayed lustily that
Joshua would remain there until nightfall.

They stood at the back of the playhouse, Annie and
Sally and Mim, their young minds enchanted, their young
eyes bright with the joy of it, for they were no more than
children and did not see the tawdry costumes, the artificial
deportment and speech of the actors, the triviality of the
story. They were transported into fairyland, the land of
myth and legend and imagination, and with the rest of the
unsophisticated audience they cheered and howled, wept
and laughed, loving every minute of it. In the first interval
between parts, when Annie felt a tap on her arm, she did
not at first recognise the young man beneath the appalling
stage make-up as the leading male player she had just seen
on the stage. He was quite alarming close to with his
drawn-on black moustache, his gypsy ear-rings, his boots
and his cutlass and for a moment all three girls shrank
back.

"Ladies, forgive me. I had not meant to frighten you,"

he said, smiling his wicked 'outlaw's' smile. His voice was
soft, deep and completely irresistible and his chocolate-
brown eyes gazed into Annie's. He took her hand and
raised it to his lips and the girls, all three, stared at him,
hypnotised by his beauty and his charm, like three little
rabbits which have suddenly come across an extremely
handsome fox.

"I saw you from the stage," he went on, "and could
not resist coming down to greet you. I could tell you
were enjoying my poor performance and . . . well . . .",
his smile deepening to reveal two engaging clefts – in a
woman they would have been dimples – at each side of
his mouth. "I could never withstand a pretty woman and
when there are three of them it seems the challenge is
tripled."

The word 'pretty' would have been enough but to be
called a 'woman' when one is only fourteen was heady
stuff and Sally and Mim began to preen. In sharp contrast
Annie's face appeared to pale. She became still and hushed
as though in the presence of some being who is truly from
another world, a world in which gods lived, for surely this
could only be one of those. Her hand had remained in his
and her eyes, enormous, clear and incredibly lovely as she
fell headlong into the pit of love for the first time, did not
even blink. He kissed her fingers again and she could feel
his lips burn her flesh and beneath the bodice of her
mother's wedding-gown something quivered. It was the
most delightful feeling but at the same time it hurt her.
She felt a great need to put up her hand and draw this
man to . . . to . . . She was not sure what it was she
wanted, or what to do about it since, apart from her
father, when she was a child, she had been touched by
no man.

"The music has begun. Will you not dance?" he asked
her softly. Her heart knocked frantically and her mouth
was so dry she could not have spoken if her life depended
on it but her limbs worked independently of her mind as
he led her down towards the stage. Her cheeks burned
with a bright flame as, with the practised ease of the

accomplished seducer he put his hands gently about her
waist and whisked her away in the lively, noisy reel 'The
Circassian Circle'. She had seen it performed and had
tapped her foot longing to join in on many occasions and
she found that her body did the dancing for her while her
benumbed mind dwelled in the rapture Anthony Graham
had introduced her to.

"Won't you tell me your name?" he whispered in her
ear before he returned to the stage for the second part of
the play.

"Annie . . ." The first word she had spoken since he
had burst into her life like a shooting star across an empty,
navy-blue sky.

"Wait for me at the end of the performance, Annie," he
pleaded, kissing her fingers again, holding her hand for a
moment before he sped away to his role as the Outlaw of
Sicily.

"I see you have another little chicken all ready to be
plucked," his ageing leading lady said acidly.

"And why not since there's nothing here to excite one's
interest."

"They get younger in every town," she replied
sneeringly.

"Which is more than can be said of some I could
mention."

Sally and Mim were persuaded by Anthony to walk
ahead of himself and Annie as the four of them sauntered
up Market Place.

"We can't 'ang about, Annie," Sally managed to mutter
into the unheeding ear of her friend who was drifting along
in the direction of Greta Bridge and the road to Hause on
the solicitous arm of The Outlaw of Sicily. He had not
stopped to remove his make-up nor change his costume
in his eagerness to catch Annie when the performance
ended.

"I . . . don't mind if you go on, Sal."

"No, you go on . . . er . . . Sally, is it? I'll see Annie
to her door."

Sally eyed him doubtfully. Did he know how far it was

from Keswick to Hause? Did he even know that Annie lived up that way or even where it was and how long it would take him? His queer get-up looked even queerer in the broad light of day. Though she had initially fallen under his fascinating spell, as Annie and Mim had done, she was not quite so bewitched as Annie appeared to be and her reason told her that no man, particularly one as handsome and silver-tongued as Anthony Graham, would walk a girl like Annie a distance of ten miles just for courtesy's sake. He had another performance that evening, he said, and Sally knew he would certainly not be back in Keswick by then, and anyway, Annie was her friend and she couldn't just walk off and leave her with a perfect stranger, could she?

"'Tis five miles or more ter Hause," she said resolutely.

"Five miles!" Anthony came to an abrupt stop, seemingly unaware of the comically disbelieving faces the townsfolk turned in his direction. "I thought you lived in Keswick, Annie." For a moment his face was thunderstruck, then he gently pulled her round to face him, a winsome smile softening what had almost become petulance.

"But you'll come again tomorrow, won't you? There's no afternoon performance so you and I could spend some time together. You could take dinner with me at my lodgings at The Packhorse before I go on in the evening. Please say yes, Annie. I would be devastated if I thought I was never to see you again."

So would she.

"Please, Annie." He whispered her name, softly, lovingly, and in a tone no one, not even her own mother, had ever used. He gazed longingly into her eyes and she thought she would swoon with the sheer joy of it. He held her hands to his chest and she felt the strength, the warmth, the absolute masculinity of him as his heart beat against her hand. Nothing had prepared her for this, this thrill of quivering excitement, this trembling his touch set in motion and which ran deliciously through the whole of her body, right down to her knees. They felt as though they were made of jelly and her face was on fire with it. Her skin prickled and yet at the same time glowed and she could refuse him nothing, her eyes told him.

"Tomorrow at noon," he said encouragingly.

"Yes." Her eyes held stars but it meant nothing to his well-hidden and self-seeking heart.

Sally and Mim hurried, but Annie Abbott floated, light as thistledown along the five miles of lake road from Keswick to Hause, past the darkening mass of Dodd Wood on the right, the quiet beauty of Bassenthwaite Lake on the left. The sun had almost gone from the sky and the shape of Broom Fell across the water was dark and featureless but the glory of it had leaked into the lake itself, turning the flat surface of the water to a burnished golden-orange. The fells on the far side were reflected in it, a perfect mirror-image and a dark trail of cloud, golden-edged, poured across the water and the sky, one silhouette duplicating the other. From over the meadows which lay between the road and the lake, a tiny light burned in the windows of St Bridget's Church, and from those of the farms and scattered houses, looking like golden stars in the deepening darkness.

Annie could not have hurried had she tried. She had just lived through the most exciting experience of her young and drab existence and she still dreamed in it and in the dazzling remembrance of the man who had captured her innocent heart. She would see him tomorrow. She was to 'take dinner' with him at The Packhorse. She hadn't the faintest idea how she was to manage it since her father knew her every movement, or at least he did until today, but she would do it somehow, she told herself airily as she skipped along the last bit of track which led to the farmgate of Browhead.

"Wheer's t'girl?" her father had asked her mother. The men of Lakeland were thrifty, not only with their emotions – of any kind – and with their cash which was more often than not in short supply, but with their words.

"She'll not be far away, Joshua," her mother had faltered placatingly and when Joshua Abbott had demanded to know

exactly where that might be, Lizzie Abbott could not tell
him for after twenty years of marriage to him, twenty
years of servitude and uncommunicative constraint to his
dour and unbending will, indeed ever since she had come
to Browhead as a trembling bride of sixteen, her mental
processes had become severely hampered by her fear of
him.

Her mind had gone dead as Joshua waited for an
answer. Her tongue had stuck to the roof of her mouth
and though he had never struck her or their daughter,
she had cowered away from him as though expecting a
blow.

He was waiting for Annie where the farm track ran
down to the road. He hit her for the first time that
evening.

"Where've tha' bin, girl?" he wanted to know, and who
with? which were the words he most wanted to speak for
since the night of the 'boon clip' when she had danced in
such a lively fashion with Davy Mounsey, his dejected and
faltering hope of a son had risen like air. Not a son, of
course, but the next best thing. His farm and Jem Mounsey's allied in marriage and a man who has land, even if it
comes with a bride attached to it, will look after it. He'd
tie it up, naturally, so that it would still be Abbott's farm,
Abbott's land, with his grandchildren working on it, but
now, in the space of a day, since he had left this morning
feeling more optimistic than he had for years, she had
threatened the tentative dream he had allowed himself and
set it to shaking and crumbling like a weakened drystone
wall. All dressed up in some flibbertigibbet's gown – not
even recognising the dress in which his own wife had married him and in which she had looked as pretty as a hedge
rose – she had been off somewhere on her own and
returned so flushed and brilliant he could only suspect the
worst.

She refused absolutely to tell him since she did not want
to involve her mother who was grovelling by the fireside
like a whipped dog and when Joshua opened the door and
pointed silently out into the yard she had gone, her head

high and defiant, her cheek swollen, the flesh about her eye already beginning to change colour.

"Tha'll sleep in t' barn tonight, girl," he said to her, "wheer't th'animals sleep an' in t' mornin' thee an' me'll 'ave summat to say to one another. Think on it an' remember this. No one defies me in me own 'ouse. Now get out theer an' get some sleep fer there's a field ter be ploughed tomorrow."

The walk back to Keswick was long and dark and her clogs blistered her bare feet. She did not weep nor did she do much thinking except to repeat the words which had sung in her head ever since Anthony had winked audaciously at her over the footlights and stolen her innocently beating heart.

'I love him, I love him, I love him,' the song went and the rhythm of it moved her tired body along the deserted road. The night was inky black. She could see nothing, only her country senses keeping her on the track where she might have blundered into the dangerous and densely packed tree trunks of Dodd Wood on her left or down to the rippling, deep and equally dangerous waters of the lake on her right. Stones chinked beneath her feet and an owl hooted close by, the suddenness of it making her heart leap in alarm. A farm dog, sensing her passing, or perhaps scenting the fox which was raiding the hen-coop, barked hysterically, then stopped in mid-voice as though a heavy hand had persuaded him to do so.

She reached The Packhorse at midnight, just as Anthony and the troupe of strolling players who were drinking with him were becoming deep in their cups. They were singing some bawdy song, crashing their ale pots on the table and the landlord, whose wife did not care for such 'goings-on', being accustomed to a less vigorous class of customer, shepherds and farmers and the like, was about to remonstrate.

The whole of the bar-parlour fell silent as Annie hesitated in the doorway. She had the look of a weary child about her, pale, delicate with great smudges beneath her wide, frightened eyes. The bruise her father had given her made her appear even more vulnerable and when Anthony Graham saw her hovering there his masculine body surged towards her in ferocious and uncaring need. He stood up triumphantly, then moved across the room to take her hands, bringing them to his lips in the gallant gesture for which her girlish heart had craved on the long walk from Hause. He turned for a moment to wink at his friends who whistled and clapped their hands and stamped their feet in perfect understanding, but Annie was too tired, too love-struck to know what it meant.

"Come," he whispered smilingly, leading her away from the noisy group and up the stairs until they reached the door of the room he shared with three others. Guiding her through he locked it behind him and within five minutes, less, Annie's trembling and virginal body was revealed to his lecherous gaze in all its naked innocence. He did not speak nor even kiss her. What was there to say? She was already his with no need of pretty speeches or persuasion.

It was all over within minutes. She was laid on the bed with scant interest in her half-hearted protests since she wanted to tell him how much she loved him; to hear how much he loved her and desired nothing more than to spend the rest of his life with her. That was why she had left Browhead, because of their love but he didn't seem to want to know. He pulled painfully at her breasts and bit her belly, leaving teeth marks which would turn black by morning. He forced her legs open and thrust himself inside her with such force and rapidity she scarcely knew what was happening until the pain knifed her between her thighs and the blood flowed.

He fell asleep on top of her. Her breasts hurt and her belly was on fire, as was that part of her body that had no name. The softness and gentleness he had shown her . . . where had it gone? . . . and where was the man she had loved so devotedly for the past twelve hours? Was this it? Was this love? Is this what happened when two people loved one another? Was it? Mother . . . oh, Mother . . . where are you? and Lizzie's frightened face slipped behind her closed eyelids. Is this what she suffers every night of her life . . . Oh, Mother . . .

Anthony snored beside her where she had heaved him and outside the door men shouted to be let in but gradually the noise died away and, being a tired and healthy child, she slept.

3

The girl on the bed gave one last heave and the child slid
out from her as easily as a dab of butter, the woman in
attendance was to tell Hesper later that afternoon. It lay
peaceably between its mother's thighs with none of the
new-born infant's lusty rage at being propelled head first
into a world it was not sure it would care for. It was as
though it was born with the knowledge of the precarious
state of its mother's position in life and the uncertainty of
their future together.

"A girl, me duck," Polly Pearsall said cheerfully, "thank
the Good Lord, fer there's enough o' the other damned
sort in the world already." She expertly cut the cord,
tucking everything away neatly, then lifting the baby on
to a length of clean linen, bound it up tightly and placed it
in the hesitant arms of its mother. "A little beauty an' all.
Look at them red curls, just like her Ma's an' wi' nowt
of . . ." She stopped speaking, cutting off the words with
a sharp, irritated click of her tongue for the less said about
him, the child's father, the better. Scoundrel that he was.
'Handsome is as handsome does' was one of the maxims
which fell regularly from Polly Pearsall's lips and though
he'd been full of charm and a fine-looking chap, what he'd
done to this poor child was far from fine. If Polly had had
her way he'd have been brought back and put before the
magistrate. Made to pay something towards the upkeep
of the child just born but he'd be in the next county by
now, no doubt of it, and that troupe of strolling players he
travelled about with.

She watched as Annie looked into the face of her daughter, waiting for that glow of maternal pride, that bond
which is formed between mother and child in the first

moment of their meeting. For that soft-eyed look of wonder and the awed need to touch the baby's cheek, to put a tentative finger in the curled shell of the child's hand which would instinctively grasp it. But it did not happen. Annie Abbott held her new-born baby in the awkward crook of her arm, her eyes wary, her expression somewhat alarmed. "What am I supposed to do next?" it seemed to say. She glanced up apprehensively at Polly looking exactly like a caller who has had some other woman's child put unexpectedly into her arms and, politely, is holding it for the shortest possible time before returning it thankfully to its rightful owner. Of course the babe had not been cleaned up yet. Perhaps that was it though usually, in Polly's experience, a mother will give even the muckiest of new-borns a cuddle.

"'Ere, give 'er ter me an' I'll bath 'er then you can put 'er to t' breast."

That ought to do it, she told herself. She could remember when her first had folded its pursed lips about her nipple and even now, twenty years later, the unique joy she had experienced then was something she would always remember.

"See, give yerself a wipe round," slapping a bowl of soapy water and a cloth on to the table by the bed, "an' I'll send Hesper up ter change bed an' fetch you a cup of tea. An' there's some soup I made fer the noon trade. That'll put the heart back in yer, then I'll 'ave ter be gettin' back downstairs. Seth's bin shoutin' for me, the great lummox, so I'd best get off. Yer'll be right as rain now, me duck. Yer've done well an' as far as I can see everything's fine down there," pointing in the general direction of Annie's belly. "Yer'll be up an' about in a day or two. Yer young an' strong. An' when yer up to it, later, I'll fetch them little duds our Maggie wore. Well, they all did, all my childer and Maggie was last."

All the while she talked Polly was sloshing the quiet baby about in another bowl of warm water which she had poured from the big earthenware jug on the dresser. She doused it vigorously, careful of the top of its head and the

neatly tied up cord on its belly. Again she wrapped it firmly
in the length of cloth, then put it once more in its mother's
arms.

"Give it suck now, child," she said kindly to the equally
quiet girl on the bed. "She'll need feedin', yer know, an'
there's only you can do it."

Annie held the tiny, fiercely wrapped bundle in her arms.
Hesper had been changing the soiled sheets on the bed,
holding the baby, clucking and fond, exclaiming on her
lovely red curls whilst Annie wriggled into an immaculate
nightgown, one which belonged to Polly and which Annie
herself had washed and ironed only yesterday. She had
drunk the tea and obediently spooned the thick vegetable
soup into her surprisingly ravenous mouth before being
handed the child again. Hesper, a bundle of soiled linen
under one arm and the bucket of water in the other, had
gone and Annie was left in the hushed company of the
baby who was hers, hers and Anthony Graham's.

It was a week since he had left, he and the company.
She had been with him for just fourteen months and in
those months she had learned many things, acquiring an
education in a life she had not known existed. She had
gained a knowledge of the world which was to stand her
in good stead in the years to come. The life of the strolling
company had been one of casual drifting from one town to
the next, of bookings which had been cancelled, days of
excitement and others of boredom and uncertainty, thrilling at first to the young girl to whom, in her old life, the
arrival at the door of a pedlar had been one of dazzling
intoxication. She had taken small parts in the production,
those that did not involve speaking and when Anthony, on
a whim, had taught her to speak as the rest did, she had
become understudy to the leading lady. She had passed
out handbills in every town they played. She had, because
she could sew a little, taken care of the company's wardrobe. She had learned how to slip out of town without
paying bills, how to make love to her lover's satisfaction;
how to avoid being made love to by amorous actors and
playgoers alike. How to live well when the takings were

good and how to starve when they were not. She had
been a part of them, doing what they did until her increasing girth made it impossible, and last week, as she was
doing her best to earn a few pennies, hanging out Polly
Pearsall's washing at the far end of the long back garden
of the inn, they had all slipped away without her, one by
quiet one, leaving their bills unpaid and the landlord, Seth
Pearsall, in such a state of menacing rage, Annie had
feared for her own safety.

Polly, his cheerful, uncomplaining and phlegmatic wife,
had stepped deftly between Annie and her husband's rage,
her own hefty proportions complementing his.

"'Tis no good threatening the lass, Seth. She's no money
else why should she be workin' fer me, tell me that? This
last week while them lot were jabbering their piece on't
stage in that there barn, aye, despite size of 'er, she's
worked like a good'un from mornin' 'til night so *she* owes
us nowt. Yes, I know she were with them but that don't
make 'er responsible fer their debts, do it, me duck? So
'tis no good you threatening ter fetch constable. Now, she
can go on earnin' 'er keep alongside Hesper in t' kitchen
until babby comes an' then . . . well, we'll see. We could
do wi' another body ter give a hand, me an' Hesper, so
just you calm down an' get back inter t' bar fer there's
men wi' their tongues hangin' out fer a pint."

For a week, until she was brought to bed, Annie had
filled a pail each morning, scrubbing the floor of the kitchen
and the flagged passage which led to the dining room and
bar-parlour of the inn. There was mud and grease mixed
with straw and even manure stamped into it and though
her head swam and the baby inside her kicked and
squirmed she did not falter. She washed and ironed and
heaved this and that and though Hesper and even Polly
Pearsall, who were both good souls, did their best to
save her from these heavy tasks, Annie would not hear
of it.

"Yer'll 'arm that child, Annie," Polly protested but Annie
did not care. The child was not real to her who was merely
a child of fifteen herself. What would she do with it when

it came? Perhaps it would be born dead which would be a blessing but, of course, it hadn't, and here it was.

She studied the small, round face of her daughter, the fluff on her head which was not red but a pure, golden copper, the shape and colour of her eyes which were open and seemed to be studying *her*. Her skin was like satin, clear, pale, flawless, her mouth pink and pouting and her hands, one of which had escaped Polly's binding and flexed helplessly in the air, were like daisies, perfect in every detail. Carefully Annie unwrapped the binding and the tiny body lay trustingly beneath her gaze. The child's legs jerked and bent and the small, hidden fold of her female gender was revealed. A girl. A female child who would, one day, be subjected to the hurt and fear and humiliation she herself, and her own mother, had suffered. Poor little girl. Poor baby. So quiet, so patient, it seemed to Annie, and she wondered if her own submission to Anthony Graham's mastery of her – since what else had there been for her? – had transmitted itself to the child who was inside her.

Slowly, not at all sure what the correct procedure was but hoping the baby would know, as newly born lambs did, she opened Polly's nightgown and turned the child in the general direction of her breast. At once, but with the utmost delicacy, the small rosebud mouth fastened on Annie's nipple and began to suck. It did not hurt, Annie discovered. In fact it was quite pleasant. Quite companionable really, as though she and the baby were friends and, like friends, one was doing the other a favour. The child's hand rested on her breast and Annie smiled, putting her finger inside the tiny fist. Immediately the child gripped it and it was then that it happened. A great wave of loving tenderness, a great drowning in which she and the child went down together, deep, deep, then floated in perfect harmony to the surface where they lay, fastened together by an invisible, indivisible thread which, she knew, would never be broken.

They were both asleep, she and the child, when, the rush over, Polly put her head round the door several hours later. She smiled. The child was held protectively in the curve of the mother's arm, trusting, well fed, loved, Polly could see that and her smile deepened in satisfaction. That was it then. What had not happened at once had happened now.

"She's all right now," she said to Seth as they tumbled into the great feather bed they shared.

"Why shouldn't she be?" he grumbled, reaching for her comfortable, still enticing breast and giving it a hopeful squeeze.

"She didn't take ter t' little 'un right away, not like I did wi' mine."

"Oh, aye." His hand explored his wife's ample body with greater urgency and Polly let him since, though he was a great daft lummox, she was fond of him and knew exactly how to get what she wanted from him.

"Aye, a grand lass an' a good worker, like I said. We'll keep 'er on, I reckon. Babby'll be no trouble," hitching herself into a position more accommodating for her husband's questing masculinity.

"Righto, Poll. Now then, here's a little mouse lookin' fer a hole."

"'An here's a little 'ole fer 'im to 'ide in," neither of them seeing anything ridiculous in the obviously well-used words.

She was there for six months, sleeping with the child in the furthermost attic of the inn where, Polly hoped, she would not disturb Hesper, the guests, nor herself and Seth who both needed their sleep but the baby, thriving and as pretty as a picture, even Seth agreed, was not the slightest trouble to anyone, least of all her doting mother whose hitherto untapped source of love sprang into full bloom and was lavished unstintingly on her child.

"What you callin' it?" Hesper asked interestedly when Annie was back at the kitchen sink. They worked steadily side by side in the hot kitchen, a good team, Hesper was inclined to think and she said so to Mrs Pearsall, adding that she didn't know how she'd managed before Annie came, her being such a devil for work.

Annie's hands which were busy peeling potatoes with their customary vigour, became still and her eyes turned to the basket where her child's fingers could be seen clutching the air above the rim of the wickerwork. Her feet kicked and her voice murmured some bubbling sound to the smoked hams and dried herbs which hung above her head.

"I hadn't thought," Annie answered slowly.

"She'll 'ave to 'ave a name, duck."

"Yes, I suppose so."

"There's no suppose about it, Annie. *Everyone* 'as to 'ave a name. What were yer Ma called?"

"Lizzie," and for a brief moment, hurriedly put away, her mother's haggard face flowed sorrowfully across Annie's vision. No, not Lizzie, nor Elizabeth which, Annie presumed, was her mother's true name, though she was not sure of it. She did not want her beautiful daughter to bear the name of the woman who would always, in Annie's mind, be connected with degradation and shame, with grief and pain and hopelessness. She could hear her father's voice, when he did not call her 'woman', shouting for 'Lizzie', and that made it even worse.

"No, she ain't a Lizzie," Hesper said equably. "What were yer Granny called?"

Granny? She didn't remember ever having one of those but she did recall her mother telling her that *her* mother, who had come from Scotland, had been named Catriona.

"Catriona."

"Eeh, that's lovely. Catriona. Catriona Abbott. That's nice, that be."

"We need a 'and in bar, Poll," Seth roared one night when, two coaches having come in at the same time, every passenger on board wanting a hot meal or a hot toddy, or both and at once, the place was in uproar. It was February by then, cold and damp and with no hint of spring about it which surely should be just round the corner in this Midland county.

"Well, Hesper can't manage it. She's busy with them

pies an' I'm up to me eyes with the goose. It'll 'ave ter
be Annie."

She was an instant success. Her lovely face became
flushed and lively and she found her brief training as an
actress, and as a 'hander out' of handbills, and the repartee
which was part of the job, had bestowed on her a saucy
tongue to which the customers responded, demanding
more drinks than they would normally have, just to be
served by the pretty barmaid. She was quick and light on
her feet, watching for Seth's signals on where she was
needed and the tips she received which she was ready to
hand over to him, were hers to keep, he told her, his huge
grin telling her how well she had done.

She brought in custom. She learned to be bold without
being vulgar. How to smile and tease without being coarse.
How to give the impression that each man was her especial
favourite while at the same time allowing no liberties to
be taken with her person. Which was fine and perfectly
acceptable to Polly until she discovered it was her Seth
who was the worst culprit, doing his best to urge the
red-faced and vehemently protesting Annie into the larder,
his hand already up her skirt.

Polly said nothing then, being a wise woman, merely
making an unnecessary clatter to warn them of her
approach. She and Seth had a thriving business and she
wanted no bad blood between them. He was an old fool,
but that was all. A man, like the rest of them, who could
not resist a pretty face but she was not about to jeopardise
her marriage, her livelihood, her future, over a temporary
flush of youthful lust which had come over her Seth.

Catriona Abbott was six months old when Polly Pearsall
told Annie, regretfully, that she would have to go. It was
June, the day fine and bright, the honeysuckle which
climbed up the wall at the side of the inn melting into pink
and cream, its sweet fragrance as heady as wine. Yellow
irises bloomed in the little stream which warbled through
the inn's back garden, threaded with the yellow and orange
flowers of mimulus. Linnets were nesting under the eaves
and above the sound of the stream their twittering could

clearly be heard. The washing Annie was pegging out snapped in the breeze and Annie sniffed at its good clean smell, then sighed in content.

She turned in amazement when Polly spoke at her back.

"Leave? But why? What have I done?"

"Nothin', me duck. You've bin a good, 'ard-workin' lass an' it's not your fault you've been blessed wi' that bonny face of yours, nor the shape of yer. I say 'blessed', but perhaps 'cursed' would be a better word. There's Hesper who's as plain as a plank an 'as no trouble gettin' or keepin' a job when she's not 'alf the worker you are. Willin', aye, but she's not got your . . . your way o' doin' things. All of a muddle she be wi'out me ter tell 'er what ter do, but you . . ."

"Then why, Mrs Pearsall, why?" Annie's voice was rich with passion at the injustice of it but deep down where her female instincts matched those of Polly Pearsall, there was a growing understanding.

"I think yer know why, duck." Polly's voice was sad and beneath her steady gaze Annie's face became flooded with colour. She hung her head and tears brimmed to her eyes.

"It wasn't me, Mrs Pearsall. It wasn't my fault. D'you think I want an old man like . . ." like that fat pig who is your husband, the unfinished sentence said, but Polly finished it for her.

"Like my Seth, is that what you were goin' ter say? Well, 'e's not much ter look at, I'll give yer that, but 'e's a good man really an' . . . 'e's mine, Annie. I'm fond of 'im, see, an' 'e is of me . . ."

"Then why doesn't he leave me alone?" Annie's head lifted defiantly and her eyes flashed in golden brilliance. Damnation, but this lass has got troubles ahead of her, Polly had time to think. Wherever she goes it will be the same. Men after her like dogs chasing a bitch on heat and though she doesn't ask for it, not in so many words, the very way she walks, swinging her hips and twitching that little bum of hers, lifting them fine breasts, turning her head to smile, it drives them on until all they can think of is getting their hands on it all. Since the child her figure had ripened. Motherhood – and the good food she ate – had put flesh on her, a rich, creamy flesh and all in the right places, curving her breast and hip but the hard work she did kept her waist small and neat. Her hair grew and flourished, burnished with good health to the deepest copper, unconfined in its glory even when she plaited it where it fell in a swinging rope to her buttocks. She was happy, poor little bugger, and it showed in the vivid and startling loveliness of her eager smile and they were all mesmerised by it. Like my Seth, the old sod.

For a moment her female pride and jealousy for someone younger and prettier than herself took a hold of her and she wanted to smack the silly little cow in the face and tell her to 'hop it' and ply her wares elsewhere but her own sense of fairness returned.

"'E's only a man, Annie, like them all. 'E's right fond o' me an' we rub along right well. So you see, duck, you'll 'ave ter go. An' I'd be obliged if yer'd pack yer things an' leave right now. I don't want yer sayin' owt ter Seth or Hesper. They're both busy so it'd be best. I'll tell 'em you just upped an' took off. Try over Gretton way. There's a lot of inns on that road. 'Tis a busy one an' 'appen you'll get summat. Eeh, Annie, I'm right sorry this 'appened, me duck. I've got proper attached to that babby . . . an' ter you."

She had gone within the hour, speaking to no one, stunned and speechless, her few belongings – Lizzie Abbott's wedding-dress which she kept scrupulously mended and cleaned, and the baby's change of clothing – in a wicker basket Polly gave her. There was food, enough for a couple of days and the few shillings she had earned. It would keep her going until she reached Gretton. Catriona was carried on her hip, held with a length of clean grey cloth tied over Annie's shoulder. She clung there like a small animal, her thumb in her mouth, her enormous golden brown eyes gazing solemnly at Polly who was as close to tears as she had been in years.

It was the same wherever she went and she was never,

in all her travels, to find a place so good nor a woman so kind as Polly Pearsall.

"That babby just won't do, me duck. It'll be a nuisance what with the stink of it . . ."

The *stink* of it, her sweet smelling, dewy fresh little daughter who was bathed every day and changed the very moment she soiled her napkin.

". . . an' then there's the noise. I can't 'ave it near my guests . . ."

The *noise*! That soft gurgling of laughter she and Catriona shared, the nuzzling contented sounds as she settled at Annie's breast.

". . . an' there's no doubt you'd be neglecting yer work runnin' up an' downstairs to it every five minutes, wouldn't yer?"

"No, ma'am, I wouldn't. She's a very good baby, really she is. A quieter baby never breathed. She sleeps a lot and I could feed her when I'm eating my meals. I would never neglect my duties . . ."

"Where did yer learn ter speak like that, me duck? Yer not from these parts, are yer?"

"No, Cumberland."

"Well I never. I'd no idea they spoke so posh up there."

"Would you have a job for me then? Anything . . . scrubbing, bar work . . . ?"

"Well . . ."

"I would work for very little."

"Well . . ."

For the next two years it was the same, working wherever and whenever she could, mostly in the bar-parlours of country inns where folk were kinder than those in the bigger towns. She brought trade with her lovely face and lively tongue but she also brought trouble since there was not a man who drank the pint of ale she put in his hand who did not want her as well, and not a few were willing to fight over it, with each other or with her when she would not allow what they often considered to be part of her duties. Time and again she was asked to move on, she and her child who had learned to be good and quiet in the attic rooms which were allotted them and where Annie was forced to leave her for hours on end. Catriona was to learn that she must wait patiently for her mother's return. That she must not stamp about or shout as other children were allowed to do but must play with the rag dolly Annie had made for her out of scraps of material, sitting quite still in the middle of the straw pallet. She dozed and crawled, then crept on her little faltering legs into a walk and when Annie came up, there she would be, the light from Annie's candle falling on her lovely, blinking eyes, her eager, expectant face, the riot of her soft, bright curls, so like her mother's.

"See what mother's brought for her good girl tonight," Annie would say, popping broken custard tart into her child's mouth, morsels of the daintiest food scraps she could find left over from the dining room and all the while praying that the landlady of the inn at Brigstock or Desborough, at Clipston, Naseby, Rothwell, wherever it was she had tramped to in the hope of finding work, would not blame her for the black eye Jim Sorrell had given to Harry Appleton in the yard as they fought one another ferociously over who had more right to Annie Abbott's favours.

She was in Market Harborough when she saw the newspaper. She had worked for the past week in the kitchen of The Plough in the Market Square, scrubbing, peeling potatoes by the bushel, cleaning vegetables, washing and drying the mountain of dirty crockery and glasses which came from the dining room and bar-parlour by the hour. She wore a bodice and skirt she had bought from a market stall, grey, much mended, too big in order to hide her shapely figure, and round her head she had bound a length of colourless cotton. An enormous apron made of sacking enveloped her from neck to ankle and up in the roof in a space too tiny even to be called an attic, her daughter lay apathetically on a grubby palliasse. She was almost three years old and the life she and Annie had been forced into was slowly reducing her from a placid but bright and con-tented infant who could, because she slept for a good deal

of the day, accept her restricted life, into a dull, spiritless
little ghost who scarcely turned her head when Annie crept
into the room, the cupboard in which they slept. Annie
despaired over her, rocking her in passionately tender
arms, whispering into the dazed little face until the child
responded, telling her tales about her own childhood which
now, in contrast to her daughter's, seemed rosy indeed.

But it could not go on for ever. The little girl was
growing, a baby no longer. She needed companionship,
the outside world, people, animals, beauty, stimulation.
When she had an hour Annie would take her into the
market place, telling her what the objects were on the
stalls, ordinary, everyday things which were a wonder to
the child who stared for hours on end at four blank walls.
Annie carried her out of the town and into the countryside
which surrounded it, letting her wander in the woodland,
watching her absorption with a simple cowslip, a scurrying
beetle, the cows in the fields and for a brief moment her
child would come alive. They would run, hand in hand,
and Annie would shout out loud but Catriona would put
her hand to her mouth, her eyes enormous in her pinched
face as she looked about her as though, even here, she
must make no noise.

The newspaper was the *Lancaster Herald* and was dated
several weeks ago, evidently left there by some traveller
from the North. It lay discarded beneath a table in the
snug bar, the floor of which Annie was about to scrub. It
was thick and would make a good pad on which to kneel,
she decided and then later, if she could pinch a good candle
stub, she would read it in the privacy of her room. Who
knew what great events might be taking place in the world
of which she was completely ignorant.

Catriona was asleep, her face pale in the flickering light
from the candle, her hair in a lifeless tangle on the stained
pillow. She had eaten half a pork pie, some cold potato
and a spoonful of cabbage, obedient as always, but vague
and ready, worryingly so, to go back to the heavy sleep
Annie had wakened her from.

Annie watched over her for half an hour, anguished by

the little girl's docility, then, sighing, she picked up the newspaper.

She turned the pages lethargically. What did she care if there was to be a revolution in Paris as seemed likely? Or even if it was happening in the county of Leicestershire from where, no matter how she tried, there was no escaping the drudgery and hopelessness of her life? She was about to throw the newspaper down and climb into the bed with Catriona when her own name sprang out at her from the words which were printed there. The shock of it sluiced over her like a deluge of icy water and she gasped, her breath catching painfully in her throat. Her brain became numb and her hands shook and for several moments she could not focus her eyes nor even keep the newspaper still.

'Annabelle Abbott,' it said, 'late of Browhead Farm, near Hause in the county of Cumberland . . .'

Dear God . . . she couldn't read it . . . the candle-flame flickered so . . . and her hands would not stop their trembling . . . Annabelle Abbott . . . that was her . . . her name and there could be no more than one Annabelle Abbott surely? And if there were, this one lived at Browhead . . . it was her. *It was her!*

At last she reached the end of the words, the words printed in the four-week-old copy of the *Lancaster Herald*, the words which appealed to Annabelle Abbott or anyone who knew of her whereabouts to contact the firm of solicitors, Hancock, Jones and Hancock, in King Street, Lancaster.

4

King Street was a pleasant thoroughfare in the centre of Lancaster. It led away from the Town Hall which was large, pillared and handsome and, at this time of the day, its wide shallow steps were busy with the feet of the respectable and hard-working citizens who had business there.

She and Cat had walked from Warrington where her money for railway fare had run out. They had moved in an almost straight line going northwards through Wigan and Preston and Garstang, but happily on more than one occasion they had been given a lift on the back of a cart, the farmer taking pity on the weary woman and child and inviting them to 'hop up' and sit among the crates of indignant hens and geese, the sacks of corn and potatoes he was taking to market. Annie had been grateful, smiling her glowing smile, lifting Cat up where the child would instantly fall asleep for as long as she was allowed, as she did herself at times. Weeks they had been on the road and if they did not get to Lancaster soon, what small reserve of pennies she had kept for food would be finished and she would either have to stop somewhere for a few days to earn a bob or two, or resort to begging.

It was November when they reached the town, a harsh November day which struck through the increasingly threadbare fabric of their clothing and Cat shivered as she and her mother moved along that last mile, the ancient castle which dominated the town and which had been the landmark towards which they had been inching for days, looming high in the November mist. It was a shire house and county gaol, Annie was told by a tinker who had taken it upon himself to travel with them the last few miles from

Scotforth, a sprightly Irishman who carried a pack on his back and had a merry twinkle in his eye and who offered to carry Cat as well. Annie could not refuse for Cat was nearing exhaustion and though she was afraid the man might expect some reward, and not of the monetary sort, she allowed it.

On the top of the castle stood a large tower called 'John of Gaunt's Chair' from where, the tinker told them, having been this way before, there was a fine view over the whole of Cumberland and even, on a clear day, across the sea to the Isle of Man. Lancaster was a small but splendid port on the River Lune over which a brand new bridge spanned, with five elegant arches. Market days were Wednesday and Saturday, their informative friend told them cheerfully, handing the dazed child back to her mother, smiling indulgently since he had children of his own, he added, letting her know that though his eyes admired her he had no designs on her person.

It was Wednesday and the streets were busy but, the tinker having given her directions she found her way to King Street easily enough. It was a tree-lined jumble of old houses, one of which had been made over into a doctor's consulting rooms, an architect's office and, on the second floor, the rather grand quarters of Hancock, Jones and Hancock.

The clerk at his high desk in the small front office eyed her and her daughter with the appalled air of a man come face to face with persons of the lower order, those whom, had he been at his own home, he would have ordered to the back door. Annie smiled wryly. Having been on the road for eight weeks she could not blame him since she and Cat were not looking their best. Nevertheless she kept her head high and her expression lofty as she passed him the dog-eared, practically unreadable scrap of newsprint which she had torn from the old edition of the *Lancaster Herald*. He took it between his thumb and forefinger as he might a piece of mouldy and evil-smelling cheese.

"I'm Annabelle Abbott," she said, "and this is my

daughter Catriona. I am here to see either Mr Hancock or Mr Jones, whoever is available."

"Indeed! and on what business?" ready to show her the door for her impertinence.

"My own. The newspaper cutting asked for me and I am here."

"But this is months out of date. I'm not sure . . ."

"I was in Leicestershire."

"Oh . . ." not at all sure why that was significant.

"I walked a good deal of the way so if you will tell Mr Hancock I am here I would be obliged."

"He is very busy."

"We will wait," and tipping her head regally she guided Cat towards a chair which was placed against the wall.

It was the same with Mr Hancock, whose expression of amazement matched that of his clerk. He seemed to remember something about a farm, he said, when he had recovered his composure, and the name of Abbott rang a bell though he could not quite recall . . .

"Why have I been summoned here?" She cut through his ramblings, his vague fumbling with this paper and that, his shouted orders to his clerk to fetch the . . . what was the name again? . . . turning to Annie . . . the box marked Abbott . . . yes, yes . . . and when her bald question finally penetrated his tangled mind which, it seemed, had been thrown into some confusion by her appearance, his expression was startled.

"Why?" he repeated.

"Yes. What does this mean?" indicating the newspaper cutting which the clerk had returned to her as though afraid he might be contaminated by its continued presence between his fingers.

Mr Hancock had the correct papers before him now which he studied through the thick-lensed spectacles on the end of his nose.

"Aah, yes, of course, it's about the farm," eyeing her abundant hair which, though she had done her best with it, was cascading in a rippling mass over the weary, straining cloth of her elderly bodice.

"The . . . the farm? Browhead?"

"Indeed. What else?"

"But . . ."

"Now that your mother and father are dead . . ."

The rest of his words faded away as she entered the dizzy, echoing tunnel which was long and black and shocking and when she came out of it at the other end Mr Hancock was talking of legal matters which, he said, were apparently in order and all that was needed was for her to . . .

"My . . . my parents are *both* dead?"

"Indeed, that is what I said."

"When?"

"Oh, it must be twelve months since . . ."

She scarcely remembered leaving his office, nor the few shillings which Mr Hancock – kindly now – pressed into her hand for her railway fare to Penrith, nor much of the journey either, and it was not until the man spoke to her that she came out of her shocked state.

She was arranging the child's clothing when he first noticed her, twitching its little bonnet more closely about its face, stuffing tendrils of bright copper hair beneath the brim, re-tying the scarf which already fitted snugly about its neck, but doing it so fiercely the child was pulled this way and that like a puppet on strings. She – he had decided the child was female – didn't seem to mind, accustomed to rough handling, he supposed, perhaps knowing no other. She stood patiently, submitting to being turned about for the woman's critical inspection; to a general smoothing down of the drab, ankle-length skirt; to a forceful tug at the equally drab shawl which was crossed over her narrow chest and tied at her back, the last ministration nearly taking her from her small feet. Then, bringing a glowing smile to the child's face, the woman knelt down and planted a hearty kiss on her upturned cheek. The gesture was so spontaneous, so full of irrepressible and loving warmth the man felt his own lips twitch in a smile.

It was a scene with which he was very familiar though

not one he had experienced for twenty years. His own mother had treated him thus before he set off on his short-legged fell pony across his father's land which lay up beyond the splendour of Dash Falls. From there he had dropped down the packhorse route which skirted Lonscale Fell to Latrigg and on to Keswick where he had attended the grammar school.

"Now then, Reed Macauley," she would say in her broad-vowelled but rhythmic Cumberland dialect. She always called him by his full name when she wanted to impress upon him the importance of what she was about to utter. "Now then, Reed Macauley, mind tha' keeps tha' scarf tight round tha' neck. There's a fair bottom wind blowing' down t'valley an' I'll not have thi' tek cold for the want of a bit o' sense."

As if he would, her expression said. Her son! He'd never had a cold in his life, no, nor any of the childish ailments which afflicted other weaker boys, but she had to have her say nevertheless, for it was only in this way that she could demonstrate her deep and abiding love for him. He was the apple of her eye, the darling of her heart, the centre of her universe but if her life had depended on it she could not have told him so. Instead she would fuss about him, her work-worn hands at his neck fixing his scarf to her own satisfaction beneath his chin. His cap would be jammed down on his head until it met his scarf. His durable hodden-grey jacket, the wool from which it was made spun and woven by her from the fleece of his father's own sheep, smoothed down briskly, his buttons checked to make sure they were all done up as she liked them to be.

Her pride in her only son, her only remaining child, was enormous but it was kept well hidden beneath her own snow-white, cruelly starched apron bib where her heart lay. Any physical or emotional manifestation of how she felt about him was beyond her. Die for him she would and right gladly, to save him a moment's hurt, but to kiss him, as the woman had just kissed the small girl, to put her arms about him would have seemed a foolish and wasteful embarrassment to a woman of her practical nature.

So she made sure he was warm, well fed, that his clothes were of matchless quality, laundered and immaculately pressed; mended when he tore them in the endless scuffles lads of his age engaged in. That his boots, the best his father's money could buy, were well polished. In short, that Reed Macauley, her son, wanted for nothing.

The engine of the Lancaster-to-Carlisle train standing at the platform of Penrith station and from which he had just alighted gave a mighty shriek and several horses in the station yard tossed their heads nervously. The noise and the sudden confusion which it caused brought him sharply back from the past and he straightened himself to his full height. He was a tall man, lean of waist and belly and hip but with strong muscled shoulders which filled the roomy, sleeved cloak of navy cashmere he wore. His hair was thick and a rich, dark brown, ready to curl vigorously from beneath the brim of his tall beaver hat. He was amber-skinned and clean-shaven and his eyebrows frowned above eyes which were compelling in their narrowed watchfulness. A vivid blue they were, in which the clear northern light had put the brilliance of a sapphire. They were framed by long black lashes. He could not be considered handsome, though many women thought so, since he was too fierce, his chin too arrogant but there was about him an observant, mocking humour which allowed him to view those of his acquaintance with something less than the serious application they often thought their due. There was in the casual stance of his long, lounging body and the insolent lift of his dark head, a sure belief in his own infallibility and the sense that here was a man who was diverse, complex, a man with many shades and nuances to his nature which no one had ever been allowed to penetrate.

His obvious and complete masculinity did not prevent him from dressing in a way which in another man, particularly one from these parts, might have been considered dandified. The men of the lakelands of Cumberland, his own father among them, wore what their fathers and

grandfathers had always worn. Homespun of hodden-grey
made from the mixed wool of their own sturdy Herdwick
sheep. Serviceable, durable and warm, jackets, breeches,
gaiters and sturdy boots, for the climate of the lakes was
damp and chill for a good part of the year. Not for them
the immaculately tailored dove-grey trousers Reed
Macauley had taken to wearing after the death of his
father, nor the fine worsted, plum-coloured coat, and as
for the cloak which was lined with fur of some sort, well,
what kind of man went in for such fripperies and more to
the point, what would become of him? Certainly not the
taciturn, blunt-spoken, independent men who were Reed
Macauley's neighbours and business associates.

He removed one of his buff-coloured kid gloves and took
out his pocket watch, a magnificent gold hunter, flicking
open the case to check the time before returning it to his
waistcoat pocket. A thick chain hung across his chest and
on the smallest finger of his hand a diamond sparkled. He
took out a cigar case, selected a cigar, lit it and breathed
in the smoke with a lingering pleasure which was almost
sensual.

He had been lounging against the station yard wall waiting for the lad from the inn to bring his horse which had
been stabled there, when the woman and the child had
caught his attention. The clattering of the animal's hooves
on the cobbles, the barking of several dogs which were
bristling and snarling up to one another by the yard gate,
the tuneless whistle of a coachman who waited beside his
mistress's carriage, the nervous whinnying of the greys
which pulled it, all these sounds penetrated Reed
Macauley's state of unfocused abstraction and he shivered
slightly as though the ghost of his mother had touched him
as she moved back into the past.

The groom led the tall black mare towards him somewhat gingerly for she was of a highbred disposition and
had been known to bite at the hand which held the bridle.
A beautiful animal with a coat like satin, rippling as she
stepped daintily across the yard, her head tossing, her
eyes rolling, eager to be away and at the gallop for she

had been stabled at The Fiddler's Arms for three days whilst her master attended to some business in Lancaster. It took all the groom's strength to hold her.

"Theer she be, Mr Macauley, sir, an' a right bugger she were an' all. She's not 'ad much exercise seein' as 'ow theer's none cares to get on 'er back an' theer's none she cares to 'ave on 'er back, neither. Jake led 'er up t'road a piece an' into t' field at back o t' church but a right to-do-ment it were."

Reed Macauley smiled. He threw the butt of the cigar to the ground, stepped on it then took the reins from the lad's very willing hand. He patted the animal's arched and quivering neck, gripping her mane, then smoothed his gloved hand down her nose, blowing into her distended nostrils, his lips close as he murmured something to her deep in his throat.

At once she quietened, standing passively beneath her master's touch, her luminous eyes looking into his, her head beginning to nuzzle affectionately against his shoulder.

Reed's smile deepened, revealing the perfect white teeth his mother had bequeathed to him with her pirits of fresh milk, the blue milk cheese known as 'wangy' cheese sliced between thick wedges of home-baked bread which he took to school with him; the fresh vegetables which she had grown in her garden and the fresh herbs she had cooked in her herb pudding. A dish consisting of alpine bisort, nettles, chives, blackcurrant leaves, barley, butter and beaten eggs, made in the spring by most housewives but served once a week on Sarah Macauley's table.

"You have to treat a horse as you would a woman, Sam," he told the groom, who looked startled, since no woman he had approached had tempted him to blow up her nose. "They like to be soothed and petted and have little bits of nonsense whispered in their ear. It's quite amazing what a man may be allowed with the female sex if he treats her kindly and it is the same with a horse I have found." He winked engagingly at Sam who began to grin. "They are strange but delightful creatures and cannot resist flattery, can you, my beauty?" running his hand along the mare's flank, "so you must tell them how splendid they are at least a dozen times a day at the same time stroking them as I am stroking Victoria here. Isn't that so, Victoria?"

The mare actually nodded her head, the groom told Jake later when he was recounting Mr Macauley's amazing words, what he could remember of them since many had been too high-flown for his understanding and just plain bloody daft anyway. Mind you, Mr Macauley's reputation with the ladies was legendary, his exploits in that direction – and the results of them, most with eyes the colour of deepest blue – discussed wherever men gathered as far afield as Borrowdale and Rosthwaite at the southernmost tip of Derwent Water, to the east to Penrith and west to Whitehaven. So perhaps what he advised with the mare, and women, was not as barmy as it sounded. Maybe Sam'd try it next time he coaxed Maggie Blamire out from behind the bar counter of the inn and into the pitchy darkness of the long garden at the back of the privy.

"Try it, Sam," Mr Macauley said as though he had read Sam's mind. "Now then, Victoria, let's be off home. It's a fair ride to Long Beck and I don't fancy the fells after dark."

Placing his foot in the stirrup he leaped lightly into the saddle with the fluid grace of one who has been on horseback from the day he could toddle. He put his heels to the mare's side, guiding her from the yard and out into the busy street of Penrith's centre towards the monument which divided it, noting that the clock on the tower stood at one thirty.

"Hup Victoria," Sam heard him say as the animal broke into a canter.

Victoria! Imagine calling a horse Victoria. It was said in the dales that Reed Macauley had named the foal, given to him by his father in the year their young Queen had come to the throne, after her, which had seemed somewhat disrespectful, even insolent to the intensely public-spirited community of middle-class yeomanry and manufacturers of Bassenthwaite parish, though it had brought a wry smile to the dour men of the fells who, calling no man master, spoke as they pleased and allowed others to do the same.

She was about a mile out of Penrith on the road to Keldhead when he caught up with her, striding gracefully along beside the grass verge, her skirts swinging, her head high, her long back straight and supple, the child almost running beside her. It was just gone two o'clock by then, November, and already the short winter's day was beginning to lose its light. It would be dark within the hour and the road was not lit as those in Penrith were. So where were this young woman and her child headed? He was amazed that they had got as far as they had since last he had seen them in the station yard, particularly the child who could not have been more than three or four years old.

She did not look round as his mare approached at her back. The road was completely deserted since the folk in these parts had more sense than to tramp about, unless it was absolutely necessary, especially on a raw winter's afternoon as nightfall approached. The high banks on either side of the road topped by drystone walls were dank and squelchy with dormant winter vegetation and the remains of last year's leaves. The trees arching darkly across the road were grim and bare against the pale, rain-washed sky and the low sun was no more than a veiled yellow ball setting directly ahead of them. Clouds were moving over the fells from the west and the skies would soon be 'kessened out' as his mother used to say and if he was not mistaken, and as a countryman he seldom was, though it was unusual at this time of the year, it could herald snow. And here was this young woman stepping out with her child as though she, and it, were off on a summer Sunday afternoon stroll, the large wicker basket she carried – her only baggage – holding a picnic perhaps, which they would eat at the end of it! It was none of his business, of course, but could he call himself . . . well, a public-spirited gentleman, which he considered himself to be, if he did not enquire of her intent and destination? She might be a stranger with no knowledge of the district, which was bleak and inhospitable to say the least, or of her own danger in it. The weather could change from minute to minute and though it was clear and fine now within the half-hour she could be striding into the teeth of a howling blizzard. And not only that, there were pedlars and vagrants about, out-of-work colliers and weavers, desperate men who would throw her over the wall and have not only her purse, but her, before she could lift her voice in a shout for help which would, in any case, go unheard and unheeded.

"I beg your pardon," he said pleasantly, raising his hat as his mare drew abreast of her, for lady or serving wench he was invariably charming to the female sex, which perhaps accounted for his popularity with them.

He was considerably taken aback by his own reaction to her as she turned to stare haughtily up at him. He might have been some common fellow who had insulted her, he had time to think, before his breath caught in his throat and he felt the need to swallow convulsively. She was, without doubt, one of the most extraordinarily lovely women he had ever seen. This was the first time he had actually seen her face, hidden as it had been by the deep brim of her bonnet. Some women are beautiful, as a jewel is beautiful so that a man feels the need to look and look again, to touch, to possess. Others are pretty, as children are pretty, innocent and empty of face since they have experienced nothing, but this woman was lovely, soft and eternally female and yet with an honesty, a humour, a warmth, a strength, a young vitality about her which was, contrarily, mature as though she had known and survived hardships not suffered by many. A woman, and yet still a girl for despite her self-sufficiency, her air of being complete, her hauteur, she could have been no more than eighteen or nineteen.

"Yes?" That was all, asking him to state his business

and be off since what was he to do with them though he noticed she drew the child protectively closer to her skirts.

"I apologise if I startled you," he began, still somewhat taken aback. He frowned, amazed at his own callow need to stare for he had known many lovely women in his thirty years. None like this though, his male senses were whispering and it was true. She had turned away, continuing to stride on, the child trotting beside her as neat and fleet of foot as she, treating him as though he was a beggar who had asked her for a farthing which she was not prepared to give.

He felt the first stirring of anger and his frown deepened. Damn the woman! Let her go her own way. Let her fall by the wayside, be buried in snowdrifts, blunder about in the rolling mists which could come down at a frightening pace; be attacked by tinkers, her skirt thrown over her head to muffle her cries. What was it to him? He had meant to do no more than guide her to the nearest hamlet, perhaps, or advise her to make haste before the storm which was surely coming, devoured her and her child but if she was to take this high-handed tone with him and she no more than a farm girl or maidservant by the look of her, then she could go to the devil and take the child with her.

It was perhaps the child who restrained him and kept at bay the hot flow of temper which was very likely to take him over since from an early age he had felt no need to bridle it.

"Madam, I do not wish to impede you in any way but being familiar with these parts and accustomed to the menace of the changes in the weather, I cannot just ride on and leave you. The nearest village is over two miles away and the landscape is wild . . ."

"Thank you, but we'll be all right." She did not turn her head when she spoke to him and he felt the most foolish urge to make her do so. While there was still light enough in the sky he wanted to look at her again, to study her face, her mouth, the sweetly curving short upper lip, the full lower lip, the square little jaw, and were her eyes brown or hazel? And her hair which was completely covered by the rather ugly bonnet, was it the same bright copper as the child's? God's teeth, what was wrong with him?

He could feel his temper begin to flare even more and a slight wash of colour flowed beneath his smoothly shaved skin. He was not used to being spoken to as though he was some impertinent hobbledehoy she had come across and whom she was summarily dismissing for his audacity in addressing her. He was one of the wealthiest sheep farmers in the district with interests in coal and copper mining; in the newly expanding railways; in the manufacture of woollen goods and other lucrative business concerns in which he had become involved since his father had died. He had a fine, old, recently extended, recently modernised farmhouse set at the foot of Little Calva up and beyond Dash Falls, with gardens about it to display to those who were impressed by such things that he could afford to waste some of his land on frivolities like flower beds and lawns and even a rose arbour. His family had lived at Long Beck since the days before the reign of James I, and the union of England and Scotland. His forefathers had gained privileges, mostly of land, when they had answered the call to arms to defend the borders between the two countries and when the need no longer existed they had clung to their heritage and were allowed to retain their rights. 'Estatesmen' or 'Statemen', they were called, yeoman farmers who emerged as the most powerful social group in Cumberland, and he would not be spoken to by this country girl, for she was no more than that in her clogs and shawl, without proper respect.

"Madam," he remarked coolly, "I wish to do no more than show disquiet for your safety and that of the child but I can see I should not have concerned myself. I will bid you good afternoon."

Raising his hat once more he prepared to move on but suddenly she turned and smiled at him. Not a smile of politeness as one would show a stranger but one of genuine amusement.

"And what danger could I be in along this deserted road, Reed Macauley, tell me that? I've walked on roads such as this a hundred times, aye, and later in the day and come to no harm. Anyway you want to watch that animal of yours. She looks dangerous to me."

She grinned, showing excellent teeth and he had time to notice in the fading afternoon light that her eyes were the colour and had the glowing depths of the topaz his mother had worn on a silver chain about her neck. Transparent and luminous with a strange, almost yellow light in them. They were surrounded by thick brown lashes nearly an inch long which were tipped for half their length with gold.

His mare was beginning to dance sideways, irritated by this unprecedented stop when all she wanted was to wildly gallop her unexerted legs along the road and across the fells to her own stable. Reed spoke sharply to her, holding her tight in by the reins and when he had her under control the woman, without for a moment slowing her pace, had gone on another thirty yards. Swearing under his breath and angry with his own foolish need to find out more about this impudent female who obviously knew him, he jumped lightly to the ground and leading the restive mare, hurried after her.

"You know me?" he questioned as he caught up with her.

"Oh aye. Who doesn't in these parts?"

"You have the advantage of me then," for if he had met her before he certainly would have remembered her.

"Is that so?" and her stride seemed to lengthen so that the child was forced to break into a run to keep up with her.

He frowned. He was not a lover of children since he knew none to love. Though his mother had come from a large family residing in Maryport, and he had many cousins on her side, he himself had been an only child, the last his mother bore, those before him lying in the family plot in the churchyard of St Bridget's by Bassenthwaite Lake. Nevertheless, despite knowing nothing of children it seemed to him that the little girl was being pressed beyond her age and endurance. She made no complaint, merely increasing her speed when the woman did, her small feet almost a blur beneath the dark hem of her rough skirt. Again it was none of his business but still he turned his attention once more to the woman, surprising himself with his own words.

"Perhaps you could slow your step somewhat. That child should surely not be forced to walk so quickly. She can barely keep up with you."

"She's used to it and if she wasn't she'd soon have to learn. I had to."

"Who are you, for God's sake? Can you not even tell me your name since you seem to know mine?"

"Why? You and I won't be moving in the same circles, Reed Macauley. We didn't in the past and I can see no reason why we should in the future." She tossed her bonneted head and a stray curl escaped at the nape of her exposed white neck, the last rays of the weak sun setting it alight with bright copper tints. It was the same colour as the child's.

"Is she yours?" His voice was brusque and she turned to look at him. There was no animosity in her glance, only a cool indifference and once more he felt that disconcerting flush of warm blood run in his veins accompanied by the menace of his own quick temper.

"Yes." Again the proud lift of her head, the indignant flush of rose at her cheek-bone informing him that it was really none of his concern, but for some curious reason he could not let it go.

"And your . . . husband?"

"Aah . . . !" Her breath drifted from between her parted lips and hung in the cold air like smoke before disappearing.

"Does that mean you have none?"

"It does."

The leap of gladness in him was apparent only to himself. "Dead?"

She came to an angry stop in the middle of the road and the child stopped with her, patiently waiting for whatever was to happen next. She showed no strain except in the heaving of her narrow chest which rose and fell rapidly, due no doubt to the pace she had been forced to keep.

The woman spoke coldly. "I cannot imagine why you think you have the right to question me, Reed Macauley, nor to form judgements on . . . my behaviour which it seems to me is none of your business. I am not interfering with you in any way, nor impeding your progress. I would be obliged if you would do the same for me."

He studied her vivid face with increasing interest, wondering for the tenth time in as many minutes who the devil she was. She was dressed poorly. Clean and neat and the obvious tears in her and the child's clothing had been decently mended but the material of her skirt was rough and drab, her bonnet was old and of a style fashionable ten years ago. Her shawl, which was thin and shabby, was faded from much washing and on her feet, and on the child's, were worn, wooden-soled clogs. Had it not been for her exceptional beauty and easy, upright carriage which thrust forward the soft swell of her full breast, no man would have given her a second glance.

And where the devil had she learned to speak so well? There was a clicking vestige of the glottal Cumberland dialect in her voice but it was clear, modulated and articulate. She was no lady but her manner of speaking seemed to indicate that she did not come from the lower classes either.

"Believe me, madam." His own voice was cool and stilted. "I do not presume to judge you." For a moment he was tempted to grin since he was the last person in the world to condemn another's morals but his irritability with this stubborn female, and with his own strange reluctance to leave her here where there was so much to harm her, sent his amusement spinning away. "How could I? I do not know you."

"Precisely, so perhaps it would be as well if you got on that beast of yours since she seems likely to trample us all if you don't, and went on your way. My daughter and I are perfectly well able to look after ourselves."

"I doubt it."

"Well, that remains to be seen."

"Where are you heading?" As he spoke he glanced up at the low grey clouds which were beginning to tumble away to the west over the high peak of Blencathra and the wild fells of Skiddaw Forest. Coming out of Penrith as they had done they were still in the Vale of Eden but up ahead were vistas of wild and rugged splendour, of range after range of mountains, of cascading cataracts and deep, dark-eyed tarns, of wooded dales and windswept moors, of nature's raw and unremitting challenge. Even so, it seemed this woman meant to challenge it with as little concern as though she was to take a walk along the path of his dead mother's rose garden.

"Gillthrop," she answered casually.

"Gillthrop!" He was appalled. "But that's nearly twenty miles. You cannot possibly make that by nightfall."

"I'm aware of that and I don't intend to try." She had begun to stride on as though she hadn't a moment to spare, especially to stand gossiping with the likes of him and again the whip of anger moved in him. His eyes snapped the brilliant blue his mother would have recognised and his voice was steely.

"Are you quite out of your mind?"

"Really, can it be anything to do with you if I was?" She relented a little. "Anyway, Cat and I will find shelter in a barn at Penruddock or some farm along the way. I have money to buy food." She raised her head even higher to indicate that she begged charity from no one, evidently finding great satisfaction in the statement. "We'll start afresh in the morning."

"Even so, it's a long walk for a child."

"She's strong, aren't you, my lamb?" Her eyes were

warm and glowing for a moment as she looked down into those of the child and he noticed with a part of his mind which was not seething with frustration over this bloody woman's stubbornness that they were exactly the same colour as her mother's.

"Besides," she went on, "I shall go by the old pack route round the back of Blencathra and across Mungrisdale Common. I shall follow the track from Skiddaw Forest down to Gillthrop. It is but a stone's throw to . . . where I am going. I shall cut the journey by several miles."

"It's extremely wild up there and . . ."

"Yes, yes, I know, very dangerous. You have told me so before and I cannot help but wonder, Reed Macauley, why you're taking such an unusual interest in me and my child. We are nought to you."

"True, and I can assure you that my concern is no more than any decent man would show for the safety of a lone, defenceless woman and child," but he knew as he spoke the stiff and rather pompous words that it was not true.

"There is no need."

"So you keep telling me."

"Then why don't you ride on?"

"God's teeth, woman, I've a good mind to and leave the pair of you to your own devices. If it were not for the child . . ."

"Why should you bother about her? You and your sort are not in the habit of concerning yourselves with me and mine."

"My sort . . . ?"

"Aye. My mother worked for yours years ago and though she was not deliberately cruel she did not concern herself overmuch with my mother's feelings. And she got her money's worth, and more, from my mother's labours. From dawn to dusk and later she worked in your mother's dairy and kitchen at Long Beck and when she stopped for no more than a minute to rest, being old even then, your mother gave her a right clip round t' lug. Heavy-handed she was . . ."

"You don't have to tell me, madam. I felt it myself a time

or two," and he could not help but smile at the memory as he rubbed his ear.

"'Tis no laughing matter, Reed Macauley. 'Tis one thing to clout a growing boy especially if he's your son and no doubt deserved it but to lift your hand to another woman is not to be tolerated. I'd not have tolerated it . . ."

"No, I can see that."

"And so I'll thank you to get on your way and leave me to get on mine."

"And where is that to be? Does your family live in Gillthrop?"

"Just up along, or at least they did. My mother and father are dead." A spasm of what might have been pain shattered the composure of her face. "I'm going home to . . ."

"Yes?"

She drew a deep breath and in the last fading haze of daylight which was almost gone he saw the flash of bright anger in her eyes and the deep rose of it stain her creamy skin.

"'Tis nowt ter do wi' yoo, Reed Macauley." The dialect of her childhood returned to her tongue in her fury, "so climb up on tha' mare an' get thi' gone. Me an' Cat've walked best part o't'way from Leicestershire ower past few weeks an' we'm still alive an' lively an' all, so don't thi' go tellin' me we need tha' protection."

"Damnation . . ."

"Don't you damnation with me . . ."

"Christ Almighty, could any man do *anything* with you, woman? I've yet to meet a more obstinate, self-willed . . ."

". . . and I a more persistent nuisance . . ."

In his rage which the animal sensed, it took him a good three or four minutes of mad circling to quieten the mare long enough to mount her, and when he had done so the woman was almost out of sight along the dusky road. He put his heels to the animal's side, driving her at once into a wild gallop, her hooves thundering on the road. The woman did not even look round.

He did not know why he said it and she did not know why she answered for they were both in a surprising state of wild anger.

"You never told me your name," he shouted over his shoulder.

"Annie Abbott, not that it's anything to do with you."

5

She and Cat spent the night in a barn, wrapped about in
hay and the old blanket the brusque farmer's wife, taking
pity on them since the night was cold, had lent them. In
the morning she had sold Annie some bread and cheese
and, at the last minute, given them both a long draught of
warm cow's milk to sustain them. It was almost noon and
she was half-way across Mungrisdale Common when she
thought about Reed Macauley again. She had known him
at once, of course, though he had not recognised her. She
had been no more than a child of eleven or twelve and he
a grown man of twenty-two or so during that dreadful
winter when, besides the work she did at home in her
own kitchen, Lizzie Abbott had been forced to labour in
that of Mrs Macauley. It had been either that or starve
for Joshua Abbott's flock had perished in the scourge of
murrain which had attacked his sheep. His crops of oats
and barley had failed and they had lived for nearly a month
on turnip bread.

Mungrisdale Common was high, over two thousand feet
above sea level and the short November day had not
improved on the previous one. In the summer the walk
from where she had left the road was pleasant and easy,
crossing the Glenderamackin River, coming through the
bracken of Mousethwaite Combe, going up and up until
she and Cat were looking across the rolling upland summit.
Bent tufts of cotton grass inhabited in the summer by
sheep, and at this time of the year by only the occasional
wandering herd of wild fell ponies. She did not know it as
well as the fells at the back of her own home, the remote
and lonely High Pike, Knott, and the affable and friendly
giant of Skiddaw, but the pack routes were clearly marked,

for it was not long since they had been used by the men who had walked these mountains. Monks going from grange to grange, drovers plodding behind herds and flocks on their way to market or new grazing. Men with ponies carrying goods to outlying farms and hamlets. They said that if you listened carefully you could still hear the tinkle of the bells which warned of the approach of the pack trains. They had carried salt and wool, hides and charcoal, coal, lead, silver and iron, moving along the complex network of narrow green tracks which lay on the lower slopes or ran between the dales like the veins on a leaf.

But today was not summer and though she knew Cat was almost at the end of her child's endeavour they dare not stop to rest. It was too cold for sitting about. To the right and behind them were the rough crags of Bannerdale and ahead was the climb to the summit of the common but here was peace and tranquillity. The ground, though boggy since it was a watershed and covered by tussocky grass, made for easy walking.

"Come sweetheart, mother will carry you," Annie said to the silent child who was beginning to look strangely pale about the mouth. "Eat this, my lambkin," she added, as she picked her up, thrusting a thick piece of bread and cheese into the little girl's hand, the last of their food. "It will make you feel better."

The child did as she was told, then immediately fell asleep, her head lolling on Annie's shoulder, her white face gaining a little colour as she slept.

Annie strode on, her skirts swinging about her ankles, not at all weighted down by the basket in which everything she and her daughter possessed was carried, nor by the small girl who slept in her arms. Her bonnet had fallen to the small of her back, bouncing as she walked, and her clogged feet made a strange sucking sound each time she lifted them from the squelchy ground but she did not falter.

It was dark and beginning to drizzle when she reached the end of the pack route which ran beside Dale Beck and led down to the farm gate of Browhead Farm. Pitch black dark and had she not known every step of the way, every blade of grass, every rough and broken stone she would have lost herself and Cat a dozen times. She was no longer striding for she had been walking for nearly twelve hours this day and the wicker basket had become heavier with every long, cold mile, as had the child and now, just as she really could go no further, she was home. She was here to claim her inheritance. Browhead.

Her strong, working fingers, on which there was no wedding ring, searched for the enormous iron key where it was always hidden, where the lawyer in Lancaster had told her it would be and for the first time in four years Annie Abbott bent her head and stepped over the threshwood of the farmhouse from which her father had despatched her.

She and her child were asleep in his bed five minutes after she had locked the door behind them.

She awoke to greyness, greyness and a chill so riveting she huddled up against Cat who was still asleep. They were both deep in the – she realised it now, *damp* – feather mattress, only the tips of their noses exposed to the biting cold and they were still fully dressed except for their clogs which she remembered had clattered to the bedroom floor as she and Cat fell into bed. It was the last thing she remembered.

The pale morning light, dim and hazed as it did its best to gain entrance through the small and filthy oak-mullioned windows of her parents' bedroom, revealed the shadowed shapes on the wall of the samplers she and her mother had worked – when had they had the time, she wondered idly? – all four of them beautifully framed by her father.

'Glory be to God' one said and beneath it, 'Elizabeth Bowman is my name' and the year 1810. Another had every letter of the alphabet stitched on it, her own name and the date 1840. The third and fourth, though she could not see the words in the poor light, were embroidered with lines from the twenty-third psalm and the Lord's Prayer. The samplers were worked on plain white linen with hundreds and hundreds of tiny cross stitches in bright thread and she could quite clearly remember how her eyes had ached as she stitched diligently in the light from the rush lamp. To this day she could sew a fine seam and given the materials could have made garments of a good quality and style for herself and Cat.

The carved oak press which her mother had brought from Cockermouth as a bride and in which she kept her clothing stood against the whitewashed wall and still hanging on plain wooden pegs fixed beside the window were a jacket of her father's and her mother's hodden-grey winter cloak. On one side of the bed was a small, gate-legged table, again part of her mother's dower and on it stood a plain earthenware ewer and basin. The floor was bare, the wood of it once so highly polished you could see your face in it. She herself had had the polishing of it.

She wondered what time it was. Well into the morning by the look of the light. She must have slept for over twelve hours but was it to be wondered at, the walking she and Cat had done in the past four weeks? Whenever they could which meant when the distance they must travel was too great for the child to walk – and she could afford the fare, she and Cat had taken the railway train but they must have tramped well over a hundred and fifty miles on their journey from Market Harborough to Lancaster.

And now, here she was, lying in the bed her mother and father had shared for over twenty years and where they had both died within a few days of one another from a virulent fever of the lungs. The lawyer in Lancaster had been none too sure of the details and none too concerned with them either. His duty was done when he handed over to Joshua Abbott's legal heir, this amazingly lovely young woman who stood before him with no sign of nervousness, the deeds to Browhead Farm.

There was no money, unfortunately, the lawyer told her, and, not that he was aware, any livestock, and with his words ringing in her ears, those which told her that in his opinion she would be wise to sell, she had boarded the

Lancaster-to-Carlisle train using the money he had given her to purchase a ticket, getting off at Penrith, and here she was.

Lord, but it was cold and it would not get any warmer lying here next to Cat, tempting though the idea was. A fire first on the hearth of the deep inglenook, that's if there was anything to make it with. Peat was what they had burned four years ago, dug by herself and her mother, and she hoped anxiously that there would be a supply in the barn cut by Lizzie before she died a year last October, ready for the winter ahead. The fire had never, winter or summer, been allowed to go out. Well, it was out now and there was only one person to get it going again.

The floor was so cold it hurt her bare feet and she flinched, drawing in her breath sharply. Tucking the heavy, hand-made quilt more cosily about her daughter who had not yet stirred, she did a hasty little dash across the floor, reaching for the cloak her mother had once worn. She threw it about her shoulders, hunching it more closely to her and from its heavy folds came the smells which had always lingered about her mother and which brought back sharply the patient, pale-faced, anxiously kindly woman who had done her best, Annie could see it now, to take some of the overwhelming load which her father had heaped on her own young shoulders.

"See, let me do that, sweetheart." Annie could still hear the words her mother spoke when Joshua had stumped out of the house. "'Tis more than you can manage, so off you go and play with Sally an' Mim for half an hour. But no more, mind . . ." for if he came back and found his daughter off on some frivolous tack it would be woe betide the pair of them.

Annie lifted the durable wool to her nose and sniffed the mixture of herbs, the smell of hay and buttermilk, fresh bread and clean linen flapping in the wind, of lavender and linseed and all the dozens of aromas linked to the tasks with which her mother had occupied her days and though she had barely – to her shame – given her a thought in the past four years since she had been too busy thinking of her own and Cat's survival, she thought of Lizzie now and wanted to weep.

But there was no time. Not even now. She would weep later when the fire was going and the kitchen was warm enough to fetch Cat down, when there was something cooking in the pot hanging from the randle tree across the fire, even if it was only some 'poddish' for surely there would still be some oats in her mother's oak kist?

Picking up her clogs and taking one last look at Cat she moved down the tight winding staircase to what was known as the 'fire-house' – since this was where the only fire was, a kitchen and living room simply called the 'house'.

The most important feature of any farmhouse is the fireplace for it is around this that the social functions of the farm take place. The hearth of the fireplace occupies most of the stone wall in which it is set, an enormous inglenook above which the chimney hood rises and beneath which, it being the warmest place in the house, the family gather. All cooking and baking is done on the fire or on the 'bakstone' which was built above it, the area to the side illuminated by a small oak-mullioned 'fire-window'. Two more windows were set across the front of the kitchen and in between was the door to what Lizzie had hopefully called the garden.

Annie stood on the bottom step of the staircase and gazed about her. Opposite the fire-window at right angles to the inglenook was a stone partition called the 'heck' and this shielded the inglenook and anyone sitting in it from the draughts which can come, and usually did, through the door which led out into the yard at the side of the farmhouse. Along the heck side of the fireplace was the 'sconce', a fixed wooden bench under which the kindling for the morning's fire was stored and on the opposite side of the fire was a long, elaborately carved settle. To the side of the fire at eye level and set in the wall so that the warmth of the fire kept it dry was a cupboard in which spices and salt were stored. The door of this cupboard was carved with the initials of some long-dead Abbott. FA, it said and was dated 1701.

Nothing had changed. Nothing.

The floor of the kitchen was flagged with slate slabs. Opposite the hearth was placed Lizzie's oak bread cupboard where she had stored the Haver bread she baked. It was carved with the initials of Lizzie's grandmother who had bequeathed it to her, AB for Annabelle Bowman and the date, 1736. There were two carved oak chairs, similarly decorated and an oak table so big it had obviously been built within the house.

On the hearth was a poker, a copper kettle, a box smoothing iron and iron fire dogs to prevent the fire from falling out and to support the poker and tongs. There was a cooking spit and a dripping pan, toast dogs on an iron tripod with spikes to hold the bread which was to be toasted, an iron frying-pan, a cast-iron kail pot with a lid for boiling meat and all looking exactly as though Lizzie Abbott had put them there before she went to bed in readiness for the next day's work.

Which she probably had, her daughter thought as she stepped slowly down from the stair into the kitchen. She had gone to her bed, probably coughing and feverish with the inflammation of the chest which was, though she had not known it, to kill her. Had anyone nursed her? Or her father? Who had died first? Questions which would be answered soon when she could get out to Upfell, the Mounsey farm, but first she must make the place warm, get some food from somewhere to put inside herself and her child. The room was filthy and draped about it, from the heavy beams, from chair to table, from hearth to heck, were cobwebs, for it was over a year since the farm had been occupied. Every object, every surface, the floor, the table, the low window-sills were thick with dust and the valley's 'bottom wind' had blown a drift of soot down the chimney which had settled wherever the draught, always present, had placed it. It was barely light though her country senses told her that it must be almost midday and when she moved to the window to peer through the veil of dirt which curtained it, a mantle of fine rain moved across her vision screening the fields and even the lake which lay in the front of the farmhouse. She could see nothing beyond the blurred outline of the gigantic hawthorn tree which stood at the right-hand corner of the farmhouse.

She remained at the window for a while and the presence of her mother crept about her again, touching her with that almost shy affection which was all she had ever shown her daughter. Defensive somehow, as though she had expected a rebuff or perhaps her husband's irritation which could not do with any show of what he would have thought of as weakness. What a sad, drab life she had led, her daughter reflected, doing her husband's bidding, working every hour of daylight and then beyond into the dark night with no thought of her own needs, or even if she had the right to any, or her own satisfaction. With no hope of reward, not even that of affection nor gratitude from the man she had married. Her home had been her life. Keeping it neat and clean and the best she could make it and she would turn over in her grave if she could see it now, Annie thought sadly.

Her clear, brown eyes became clouded as she looked back sadly at the hard and empty life her mother had led. And yet had her mother ever done anything to attempt to better it? Had she, in the beginning, when she was young and strong and pretty, perhaps able to cajole a kiss and a smile from her young husband, determined on a place for herself, one of importance in her husband's life, not that of a drudge but as an equal in the equally divided labour they shared? Had she made an effort to achieve for Lizzie Abbott and the family which she presumably hoped to have, some grasp of independence, some comfort, an identity which was hers, a knowledge of who Lizzie Abbott was, not Joshua Abbott's wife, but herself, or had life and Joshua Abbott trodden her down to the browbeaten woman Annie herself had known? Had she done her best to force her will on the harsh reality a daleswoman was destined to know, to twist it until it gave her some measure of peace, content, hope, joy? Perhaps she herself was being unfair. Perhaps there was no way a woman such as her mother could ever gain what surely was due every human being, in some quantity and which Annie Abbott meant to have. Oh yes, make no mistake about it. She had been given this farm, this chance, and she would have all the things her mother had been deprived of. *She* would have these things. She was not awfully sure what these things were but if hard work, tenacity, a resolute will, a powerful determination and a knowledge of her own individuality, her own uniqueness was a gauge to reckon by, then she would succeed. She would not be another Lizzie Abbott. She would not depend on, nor answer to, any man, as her mother had, as she herself had been forced to do when she had run off with Anthony Graham. She would get there by herself. Again she was not awfully certain where *there* was, or how long it would take but she'd reach it somehow. On her own it would be difficult. It would be doubly so with Cat. A child born out of wedlock. A woman with no man's protection. She would be hard-pressed to find a friendly smile, particularly among these taciturn, independent, moral men and women of the dales and fells of Lakeland, not one of whom would give her the time of day when they saw what she had brought back with her from the outside world.

But she had this farm, this land. She had no money, no livestock, nothing but the coppice wood standing beyond the field at the back of the house, but in which surely, with the knowledge her father had ground into her as soon as she could toddle, just as he would a son, she could make a living, something on which to feed her and Cat until she got on her feet? She would dig and plant and sow, weed and hoe and grasp sustenance from the earth as the Abbotts had always done. She would take one day at a time until the winter was over, find work, perhaps, in some other woman's kitchen as her mother had done in hard times. Anything to earn and save some money so that when spring came . . .

Spring! Dear God, here she was, her blood thinning in

her veins, her breath ready to freeze in the air about her, her bare feet shuddering on the icy slate floor, no fire, no food, day-dreaming about spring when the harsh Lakeland winter was still to be got through. She should be looking for kindling to light the fire, for the oats to make clapbread to put in her child's mouth. Oh, please, God . . . just this once . . . Dear God . . . look kindly on me . . . Let there be peat . . . and oats in the kist . . .

It was there, just where her mother had placed it before she went up the stairs to her death. The kindling beneath the sconce, plenty of it, enough to start a fire and out in the barn would be the stacked, dried peat, the tree roots and ash tops her mother would have gathered to put on the slow burning fire. On the little shelf above the fireplace was the flint and striker and next to it in the 'candle-bark' in which they were kept were the rushlights her mother had made during the long winter evenings. When she had 'nothing else to do' since to drag her weary body to bed before she had the permission of her husband would have been unthinkable.

The soot proved tricky. No matter how she brushed it, swept it, wiped it away, it lifted in a drifting cloud to settle on her hair and clothing, getting in her ears and every fold of her fine flesh. It was on her face and hands, she could taste it; she breathed it in with every breath and it made her cough and sneeze, but nevertheless within half an hour she had the beginnings of a fire and a pan of water, fetched hurriedly from the spring beside the house, bubbling gently over it, waiting for something to put in it. But what? The oats in her mother's kist had gone mouldy, she discovered, and were uneatable and besides the salt and the spices there was nothing in the house. No pickled meats in the brine vats, no salted pork. Cat was still sleeping, her face a grey smudge on her grandmother's white pillow, and Annie's only hope was that there might be a carrot or a potato, or a turnip to make turnip bread still left in her mother's vegetable garden. Obviously whoever had locked up the farm for the lawyers had removed all the edible food when they left, the smoked ham and mutton which usually hung under the chimney canopy. If there had been any!

She was just swinging the cloak about her shoulders, ready to brave the elements and see what could be found in the vegetable garden when some fist hammered lustily on the front door.

6

"Dear God in Heaven, what have you been up to? You look like some climbing chimney boy," were his first words and her amazement turned at once to irritation and, surprisingly, momentarily to a deep mortification that he should find her in such a sorry state.

"What do you want, Reed Macauley?"

"Well, first of all I would be obliged if you would stop calling me by my full name. Reed will do, or Mr Macauley. Whichever you feel the most comfortable with. On second thoughts, though, perhaps the latter might be more appropriate since we are barely acquainted." There was a wry gleam in his blue eyes. "And I can't say I care much for your attitude, Annie Abbott . . . there you have me doing it now. I merely happened to be passing on my way to the blacksmith in Hause. Victoria has . . ."

"Victoria?"

"My mare."

"Good God! What a name for a horse."

"So people keep telling me. Or at least they do until I prove to them, usually with my fists, that the name is perfectly proper since I meant it as a respectful gesture to Her Majesty in the year of her coronation, which is when my father gave her to me. Though, to be honest . . ." He grinned and she could feel her own mouth tug, ". . . my sense of humour does not appeal to everyone."

"No, I can see that it wouldn't. Now, if you don't mind I have a lot to do . . ." treating him as though he was an unexpected and unwelcome caller who hoped to take tea with her, he thought irritably, though this time he kept his quick temper in check.

"Yes, I can imagine," he managed to say mildly enough. "A bath would be the first task, I should . . ."

"Mr Macauley, since you prefer to be called that, I have only just this minute got a fire going. My child is . . ."

"Ah, yes, the child. It did occur to me that, being a somewhat . . . er . . . unconventional mother you might not have considered the state in which you would find Browhead, your parents being . . . gone, and the house untenanted as it has been for over a year. I realise it will seriously insult you . . ." again the wry gleam, ". . . being as independent as you are, but . . . yes, yes, it is none of my business you are going to say, I can see it in your expression, but I was presumptuous enough to enquire into your circumstances and as I was on my way down here anyway, I brought something over. It was my cook, you see, a good-hearted woman, so she put one or two things together and I promised her I would bring them over."

Nothing to do with him, of course, he would have her believe. Left to him she and her child could starve to death, or share a bed in the workhouse.

"Not much . . ." he continued airily, ". . . but if you . . . well, the child is bound to be hungry, or so my cook tells me, so, I will be on my way if you have nothing more to say. I am getting confoundedly wet dithering about here on your doorstep."

"Nothing more to say?" she repeated somewhat foolishly.

"Miss Abbott, you strike me as being a woman who always has something to say, more than likely on subjects which don't concern you. I am merely being polite so do not put on that aggrieved air with me and if I were you I should take this basket . . ."

"I want none of your charity, Mr Macauley." She lifted her defiant head and though the soot lay in a fine cloud about it, it in no way detracted from the beauty of her hair. Since her mother had cut it many years ago no scissors had been put near it and it tumbled in a great profusion of rich copper, the curls, so tight he wondered how she got a brush through it, falling down her straight back to her buttocks, wild, thick and springing. As defiant as she was, he thought, marvelling, needing no ribbons or ornaments to enhance its shining loveliness. She pulled her mother's old cloak about her as though it was made of velvet, ermine trimmed, and he felt her courage move him. Her clogs sounded a rebellious clatter on the wooden threshwood as she prepared to close the door but he stood his ground, no sign of the emotion she aroused in him showing in his face, his own proud head somewhat bowed beneath the low door frame. They confronted one another, neither ready to give way.

"And the child?" he asked harshly, angry at something in himself which he did not care to name. A weakness she had awakened in him twice now and which drew down his dark brows in a frown.

She hesitated then for if she was prepared to starve rather than accept Reed Macauley's largesse could she condemn Cat to the same fate? Neither of them had eaten a really decent meal for weeks ever since she had left the bar-parlour of The Plough in Market Harborough. Bread and cheese mostly, which was cheap and filling, a hot potato from a stall, milk, warm and frothy straight from the cow on the farms they had passed.

"I haven't all day to stand here, Miss Abbott, so if you would allow me to bring in this basket I'll be on my way to the blacksmith." She was startled by the asperity in his voice. As far as she knew she had done nothing to deserve it.

He stood to one side revealing a hamper in the yard behind him, a hamper so large he could scarcely lift it. But lift it he did, humping it past her with little ceremony and placing it carelessly on the haphazardly swept oak table from which a cloud of soot rose once more into the air coming to rest on his snowy white, immaculately ironed white frilled shirt cuffs. He brushed at it fastidiously.

Dear Lord, there must be enough in there to feed her and Cat for a month, she thought exultantly, though not a sign of it showed in her face. He might have emptied a

cartload of horse manure on her table, by the expression
on her face, though she bowed graciously enough.

"It is most kind of your cook, Mr Macauley. Thank her
for me, won't you? Cat will be most obliged."

"And not you, Miss Abbott?" he asked ironically.

"Oh, my mother has . . . had a well-stocked vegetable
garden. I dare say we would have managed well enough."

"I dare say you would." Again his voice was filled with
irony but he managed to smile in her direction. A smile of
genuine humour this time, one that said he knew that had
she been hollowed out with hunger and ready to faint with
it, but with only herself to consider, she would have
twitched her skirt aside, tossed her head and told him to
go to the devil.

He tipped his tall hat sardonically in her direction. He
looked pointedly at her from head to toe, studying her
soot-coated hair and face with especial care then he
grinned suddenly, surprisingly and turning on his heel left
the house, banging the solid door to behind him.

She let out her breath on a long, wondering sigh, then
sank slowly into the carved oak chair in which generations
of Abbotts had sat, wearing the seat into a shallow
depression. Her mother had rested in it, that is if you
could call the constant work her busy fingers had occupied
themselves with, resting. The sewing and darning, the
knitting and rushlight making, always employed at some
task, never simply sitting. Doing nothing. Day-dreaming
in a square of the rare sunlight which eased its way through
the small windows and into the house.

The idea made her smile sadly, then, turning her mind
from the preoccupation with her mother which she had
seemed prone to since she returned home, she studied
the bounty which had just come her way.

Would you believe it, because she couldn't. Mr High
and Mighty Macauley hauling the enormous hamper which
loomed over her on the table, all the way down the grassy
slope which lay beside Dash Beck from his house up at
Long Beck and on that skittish animal she had seen him
on yesterday. How on earth had he managed it? she

marvelled, but then Reed Macauley, from the little she'd seen of him, would not let a small thing like a frisky mare interfere with what he had in his mind to do. And of course his tale about his cook insisting on 'putting one or two things together' just as though she had the running of his house was just pure nonsense. It was her guess that *he* was the master of his own domain and that on some pretext or other he had ordered his footman or his butler or his housekeeper, or whoever it was wealthy gentlemen of his sort employed to see to their needs, to inform Cook that he needed a good, nourishing hamper of food packed. A hamper fit for the needy and poor of which there were a good many, and to have it at the front door within the hour. That would be more his style. A man such as he would feel no need to explain himself to a servant. Why should he? He paid their wages and they were there merely to obey his orders. She could imagine the consternation in the kitchen when the order came, the conjectures on who it was who would receive the hamper of food and no doubt before the day was out it would be known in every village and hamlet between Hause and Keswick and, innocent as the whole thing was, they would, naturally, put two and two together and make it come out five. Her reputation which was already suspect since she had run away from home four years ago, leaving her poor mother and father broken and bereft, would be in tatters even before the folk in the neighbouring farms and villages had clapped eyes on Cat.

Well, it was no good sitting here sighing on the lack of her reputation since it would be gone soon enough as it was. Never look a gift horse in the mouth had been a favourite maxim of Polly Pearsall, and of hers in the past three years and this one was certainly welcome even if it had offended her to accept it, especially from him, though why she should feel that way was not clear to her. The fire was going nicely for, as she had suspected, there was enough peat and wood in the barn to keep a dozen fires burning. Should she go and awaken Cat before she opened the hamper? Make a celebration of it, for the poor lamb had had little enough in her young life to celebrate. Or should she take a peek herself? It might contain tea and there was nothing she would like more in the world at this moment than to drink a cup of hot sweet tea, not with milk, of course, since there was no cow in the byre, but steaming, fragrant tea, in a dainty bone china cup, just like a lady. To have for a few minutes the illusion of ease and plenty, of warmth and leisure, as ladies did, before she tackled the daunting task of putting the house and her life in order. Her stomach was rumbling and churning in the most distracting way and yes . . . she felt curiously light-headed, but then was it any wonder when she remembered that it was at least twenty-four hours since she had eaten, and had taken no more than a handful of icy cold water from the River Caldew as they crossed it yesterday at noon.

"Mother?" an anxious voice questioned at the foot of the stairs. Annie turned, her warm smile ready, her arms held out and, reassured at once, the child ran into them, her bare feet making no sound on the slate floor.

"I didn't know where I was, Mother," she said in her childish and yet dreadfully adult way. Contained, as she herself was contained and Annie wanted to swing her round and round, make her squeal with delight and the simple joyous fun of being three years old. "You weren't there and I didn't know where I was," she went on solemnly.

There had been so many times in her life when Catriona Abbott had not known where she was. When she had awakened in a strange bed, a room she had never seen before, a view from a window she did not recognise. Many's the time she had gone to sleep in one place and woken up in another, her infant days and nights spent moving along the path on to which her mother's own youthful and innocent indiscretion had forced her. Rooms in which the only furniture had been a frowsy blanket, a chair and a bucket. Sometimes in a cellar with others who could afford no more than a few feet of straw-littered earthen floor on which to rest. Several times, when her mother had appeared to be well settled in some low, smoke-blackened, ancient bar-parlour, they had occupied a snug room together, alone and sheltered and allowing themselves – at least Annie did – to think that they had at last found a safe haven, but it had never lasted.

So off they would go again, the regretful words of the landlord, or more likely his wife, ringing in their ears but wherever they went, wherever they 'ended up', never, not once, had Cat Abbott failed to find her mother beside her in the bed they shared. Though she had not known where she was, she had always known who would be beside her.

"We're home, lambkin, that's where we are, and if there is in this basket what I think there is then you and I are going to have our first meal in our own home beside our own fire. What do you think of that, my little love?"

The child looked into her mother's face, her own still serious, then, with a smile brightening across it like the sun shining on the still waters of the lake which she had not yet seen and which lay beyond the door, she turned in her mother's arms, perhaps for the first time in her life with the spontaneous and natural excitement of a child towards the hamper.

"Can we open it, mother, can we?"

They had eaten their fill of the 'one or two things' Reed Macauley's cook had 'put together' for them. Even as she unpacked them, passing each napkin-wrapped packet to the entranced child, the hand of the man who had given it to her was very obvious in the choice of much of the food. A dish of apricot soufflé, evidently meant for dinner guests expected that night and which Reed Macauley's cook would have to re-make. Roast duck, glazed and decorated with slices of orange; an enormous concoction of meringue and chocolate, rich with cream, the sight of which widened Cat's eyes to the size of saucers. Annie could just imagine him stalking through the kitchen where, in all probability, he never set foot from one year's end to the next since what was that part of his house to do with him, as long as it provided him with superbly cooked and imaginatively planned meals whenever he required them? What would he care how they came about? 'Send this and this' he would have said to the flustered and indignant cook, her feelings on the matter kept hidden from him naturally, pointing to the delicacies in her pantry, not concerned with her opinions, her labour. No matter how unsuitable nor how difficult to replace, if it took his fancy to send it, send it he would. And when it was learned where it had all gone, Annie Abbott would be the talk of the valley which would do her no good. Make all the more difficult the task she had set herself when she had learned that she was the owner of a farm and the land which went with it.

Ah, well, that couldn't be changed now. It was no good worrying over spilled milk, as Polly used to say, and at least she and Cat would have full bellies for the next few weeks. There were other things in the hamper, sensible, durable things which could be stored away for future use, flour and salt, tea and sugar, oats for clapbread and hasty pudding, potatoes, carrots, onions, cabbage, a saddle of dried lamb to make 'crowdy'. A smoked ham, pies of minced mutton, eggs, butter, cheese, a quart of fresh milk, a drop of which went into that first cup of tea, alas not in a bone china teacup but the pewter mug she and her family before her had used for generations. There were jars of pickles and preserves and what was evidently Reed Macauley's cook's home-made jams.

They were children, both of them, laughing with the hysterical excitement which can soon turn to tears, the excitement of those who have been set down in wonderland and told to take whatever they fancied of the delights on display. It took all Annie's good sense and restraint, and the caution she had learned in the past four years, a caution which urged her to put something away for that rainy day which was sure to come, to stop herself and Cat from eating until they were sick.

"No more now, sweetheart. We must put all these lovely things away in Grandmother's bread cupboard and then we shall have something to eat tomorrow, and the next day. You understand that, don't you?" and the child, accustomed to frugality and the need to think to the future, even at the age of almost three, nodded her head sagely, helping her mother to place their treasures safely away in Grandmother's bread cupboard whilst Annie explained to her about Grandmother and Grandfather who were in Heaven, wherever that might be.

The rain had stopped and a glint of sunshine pushed through the veil of mist which had shrouded the farm-house though the fells amongst which it was set were still hidden at their topmost peaks. It was cold, raw, with that November dankness which can insinuate itself through layer after layer of clothing, through the very flesh to the bone and even into the veins, making the blood move sluggishly. There was a great fire roaring up the chimney now but Annie felt the need to get out for half an hour, to stand in her own fields and touch the trunks of her own trees. To look about her at the acres of land which was hers. To simply breathe in the damp air which, because it moved across her farm, her land, belonged solely to Annie Abbott. To drink it in and get tipsy on it since its intoxication would be bound to go straight to her head.

"Come on, lovely, let's wrap up warm and walk down the fields a way. Mother wants to show you your new home."

The child, used to instant obedience, stood up at once and allowed her mother to bundle her in her old worn shawl and put on her rough clogs.

"Wait a minute, sweetheart, let's see if Grandmother has any stockings in her chest," and there they were, just as Lizzie Abbott had left them, newly knitted, some of them, carefully darned those that were older, far too big for the child but pulled up her thighs to her drawers they were warm and sturdy inside her footwear. A pair for Annie, the thick, hodden-grey cloak woven from Joshua Abbott's own Herdwick sheep, no bonnet, either of them, and they were ready to step out, hand in hand on to the roughly cobbled path which led through Lizzie's bit of a garden to the rough track going between two fields to the road gate.

Though the farmhouse was small it was sturdily built
with walls three feet thick and a heavy blue slate roof
which had been fashioned to defy the strong winds and
driving rain, the icy cold and measureless snow which
played a large part in the lives of the farmers of Cumberland. A white, roughcast exterior which was an efficient
method of weatherproofing, two cylindrical chimneys, one
at each end of the building for the kitchen and the parlour,
and small, oak-mullioned windows for the farmers were
more concerned with warmth than with a view. There
were four across the front of the farmhouse at ground
level and two above. The porch, designed to keep out
draughts, was low, and let into the floor was an oak
beam four or five inches high known as the 'threshwood',
securing the walls on either side of the door. Nailed
to the side of the threshwood was a horseshoe, said to
keep out unwelcome spirits, and a withered sprig of rowan,
no doubt placed there by Lizzie Abbott twelve months
ago to bring good luck to the house. Much good it had
done her!

The building was extended to the left beyond the dairy,
by the cow house and stable, above which was a loft. A
long, low farmhouse then, set snugly with its back to the
rising fields and wooded ground of the fell. A quiet and
lovely fold of the hills, remote and separate, protected
from the bleak and often wild conditions which prevailed
in this part of the world. To its back and surrounding
it were the majestic heights of Cockup, Broad End and
Skiddaw. In the summer it was a place of smooth, heathery
uplands and low-lying green pastures, wild roses, rasp-
berries ripe in the hedges, purple vetch, small grey farms.
Quiet woods with trees which cast long shadows across
patches of still sunlight. Paths rough with ling and little
golden brown tufts of wood-rush and the spear-like
hog-rush. Deep peaty dykes filled with water over which
larches hung and where grew thrift, heartsease, sandwort
and scented thyme. The waters of the lake cold as ice and
the hot, bleached stones around it, which burned the bare
sole of your foot as you stepped from it. Buttercups in

the meadow, and the wind continually stirring the cotton grass.

But it was the winter which was ahead of them where the same wind could be so strong you could lean on the gusts and not fall over. Flurries of hail whipped like gravel into your face. Great grey curtains of it sweeping violently across the shadowed fell moving the waist-high bracken to a menacing fierceness. The storm-wracked sky from which, without the slightest warning, could come a white vortex of blinding snow to bury the unwary, those who did not heed the fell's warning. Days of hard frost, brilliant sunshine, crackling snow ruts, crusted and deep, heather with icy stalks sparkling and winking. The sky, gold flecked, and whooper swans sailing over the low fields and when the sun disappeared a fine half-moon with a single star above a silent, crisply white world.

A beautiful, treacherous, hard world. Her world and one which she intended to conquer, as her father had never done. And it was to the sloping 'inlands' which lay in front of the house and on which her father's few poor sheep had pastured, and perished, that Annie's eyes were drawn. Down across neatly walled fields to where, beyond hers, sheep were wintering, a slow moving carpet of pale grey against the lush, well-watered green pasture land. Jem Mounsey's flock whose fields lay side by side with hers. Hers which were empty now but one day, she promised herself as she stood at the door, they would be filled again with the flock, her flock which, when she had acquired them, would be brought down from the high fells each winter.

A fell farm has three sections. The high ground across the summits, over two thousand feet up, where the sheep spent the summer; the 'intakes' which are big, grassy slopes fenced by drystone walls and the 'inlands', small, rich enclosures spread about the farmhouse itself where the sheep winter. And one day her sheep would cover this land. One day!

She could see the head of the lake from where she stood. Bassenthwaite, not the most beautiful in this county of beautiful lakes or so she had heard since she had seen only this one and Derwent Water which joined it near Keswick, but to her it was loved almost as much as she loved her child. Instinctively a part of her, as Cat was a part of her. She had known it at all seasons. The angry clouds chasing one another across its surface, the wind patterns ruffling and lifting the waters to dash them against the shore in miniature waves. Veiled in fine curls of mist, flat and mysterious, clear and motionless. Frozen and white and empty of all but sliding ducks and the odd, fearful young lad who had been 'dared' to go out on to its frozen surface. Blue as the skies which were reflected in it, surrounded by leaning slender birches, their leaves shining like golden sovereigns ready to dip into the water which lapped gently, benevolently about their feet, a fine haze of summer midges dancing on its textured expanse.

Already over the fells to the west the dying sun was sinking to its bed, no more than a sliver of it peeping through the high misted summits. Down the valley towards the lake half a dozen wild duck were silently zig-zagging above the water and from down by Chapel Beck several dogs were barking.

Cat had squatted to examine a tiny clump of reindeer moss growing in the shelter of the drystone wall which ran across the front of the house, separating it from the field. She was absorbed with it, studying it with the delight and amazement of a prospector who has discovered a rich vein of gold. Annie watched her, her arms resting on the Cam stone at the top of the wall. She lowered her chin to her arms to stare out across the fields to the lake and when she heard her name called she was disorientated, just as though her mother had suddenly come from the farmhouse doorway, telling her it was time for supper. It took her a long moment to return from that dreaming state into which the familiar and yet new scene had drawn her.

"Annie? Annie Abbott, is it you?" the voice asked hesitantly and when she turned about she did not at first recognise the plump young woman who stood further down the path. She had evidently come up the farm track, the sound of her sturdy clogs muffled by the grass which grew in its unused ruts. The track, which led up from the road, ran at the back of the farmhouse, and then on to farms further up the valley.

"Yes . . . ?" She was as tentative as her visitor. The woman had a look about her that was familiar, bonny and round-cheeked but she was full-bosomed and wide-hipped and much older than Annie, she decided. She had a baby in her arms, as apple-cheeked as herself, and a toddler at her skirt and, Annie noticed, was very evidently near her time with a third.

"'Tis me, Annie . . . Sally," the young woman said, a certain shyness in her, it seemed to Annie, though the Sally she had known had never been shy.

"Sally? Sally Mounsey?" She began to smile, stepping forward in glad recognition.

"Aye, though 'tis Sally Garnett now. Has bin these three years." She preened just as though what she had achieved was worthy of great admiration, a success evidently not granted to the girl who stood before her by the look of her ringless hand. But there was a look about her of being pulled down, of bearing a burden which sat uneasily on her despite her youth since she was the same age as Annie, an expression of weariness and vexation of spirit well known to Annie for had she not seen it in her own dead mother?

"You never married Bert Garnett?" she exclaimed incredulously, then could have bitten her tongue for the glad and welcoming expression on Sally's face at once became truculent.

"Well, at least I got married," she snapped, then just as suddenly the rancour left her and she sighed. Her shoulders sagged and she shifted her burden to her other hip.

"I'm sorry, Annie, I didn't meant to . . . but aye, I did, God help me. An' all I ever get from 'im is childer, 'ard work an' a clout round t' lug every Saturday when he's the ale in 'im. Our Davy died, did tha' know? No, well, you wouldn't, then me faither, so . . . it seemed sensible to marry a lad what knew farmin'. Bert moved in wi' me an' Ma an' Mim. 'E's a hard worker but . . . well . . . I could o' done worse, I reckon."

"Sally . . . oh, Sally, I'm so sorry about Davy, and your father, but all the same it's lovely to see you, and the children, but won't you come in and have a cup of tea. The kettle is on . . ."

"Aye, we saw tha' smoke from t' chimney. That's why I come up. Ma said she'd spotted Mr Macauley come along track on that black devil of 'is. She thought 'e'd bin 'ere, she said. Why don't tha' go up an' find out what's what, she said. I'm not as lish as I was, bein' so near me time, but I come anyway. There's bin rumours . . ."

"Rumours? About what? About me?"

"Aye, that tha' was ter come 'ome. That lawyer chap that'd bin seein' ter tha' faither's place 'ad come round a time or two, lookin' in ter things, 'e said, so we reckoned tha' must be on tha' way, or someone was, an' when I saw tha' smoke . . ."

She faltered then, her eyes going slowly to Cat who had stood up and crept close to her mother's skirts, shy and ready to hide her eyes in the presence of these strangers. Sally had not noticed her but now, as she did, her jaw dropped in slack consternation and her pale blue eyes widened. The likeness between mother and daughter was quite remarkable and when Annie put out her hand, drawing her child closer to her in loving maternal tenderness, the truth was plain.

"This is my daughter, Catriona, Sally. She is almost three years old."

You could see it in Sally's eyes, the slow working out of the dates and the years between. Sally, good-natured and uncritical, generous and warm-hearted could barely add two and two together despite her three years' schooling but she knew what had happened to Annie Abbott for here was the three-year-old proof of it. Perhaps she had been wrong about the ring . . . perhaps . . .

"Your . . . husband?" she gasped painfully, hopefully, since she liked Annie Abbott, always had done and would have been glad to renew their friendship.

"I have none, Sally." Annie Abbott, though she could have done so, would not lie, even for Cat's sake.

"Glory . . . oh, good glory . . ." and without another word Sally, her face as scarlet as the geraniums in her mother's window bottom, turned tail and ran like a monstrous, overburdened cow, dragging her whining toddler so fast down the track behind her, he or she, it was hard to tell its sex, almost lost its balance.

Annie sighed deeply, sadly, then taking Cat's hand in hers led her back into the glowing warmth of her kitchen. At least she had that. A warm kitchen, and Cat. It would have been nice to have a friend though. She'd known this would happen, of course. When they heard. When they heard about Annie Abbott's disgrace, her shame, her dreadful fall from grace which had resulted in the one thing most girls would rather die than suffer, and sometimes did. A bastard child. It would be all over the valley, like the news of the hamper, by morning.

The knock on the door five minutes later took her by surprise, as did Sally Garnett's face when she opened it.

"Bugger 'em," was all she said, thrusting her child in before her as she moved heavily over the threshwood. "I'll 'ave that cup o' tea after all, Annie."

7

The snow came just after Christmas, the first hesitant flake or two taking Annie by surprise; she could not have said why, since it was the season for it.

She and Cat were up in the coppice wood at the back of Browhead. The term 'coppice' meant literally, 'grown for cutting' and the trees there, oak, ash, birch and sycamore, beech, hazel and alder, evergreen holly, pine and yew, were the only crop which had never failed Joshua Abbott. A bad harvest of the oats and barley – known as 'bigg' – which he grew, one which withered in the fields, caused great hardship since it meant that the food which would have seen them through the year had to be found elsewhere. That the fodder for the cattle who were hand fed in the cow house where they had been brought to winter was not available. The beasts, of which Joshua never had more than one, could be fed in an emergency on bracken cut from the fells, but humans needed more than bracken. It brought disaster to many a small farmer, men who had nothing to fall back on as Joshua had in his coppice wood. One acre of well-grown coppice was capable of producing 10,000 poles at every cutting. This was raw material for bark tanneries, swill baskets, grommets, hoops, charcoal and bobbins although naturally, Joshua was not concerned with all these industries. But he could sell his poles to those who were and the crop which was not sold he and Lizzie and Annie had made into swill baskets and birch-twig besoms – somewhat like a broom – to be sold at Keswick market.

Bark for the tanneries was cut in early summer when rising sap in the coppiced oak trees allowed the bark to be stripped off more easily. Of course this year no bark had been peeled and it was too late now to do anything about it but next year Annie meant to contact Natty Varty who did casual work for any man who needed an extra hand and would pay him, to fell and peel the bark from the oak. As her father had taught her when she was a girl she meant to turn her hand to making swill baskets and peddle them either from door to door at the outlying and remote farmhouses on the fells, or take them to market.

The actual felling and splitting of the coppice poles was hard and laborious but she was strong and who better than herself knew about hard labour? There were many processes through which the wood must go before she had the materials for the swill baskets which were used in many industries, farming, coal mining, charcoal burning and which went to many parts of the country, even as far as Liverpool where they were in common use on coaling steamers. A good workman could make seven baskets a day but Annie meant to work during the evenings since she would be busy on the actual farm the rest of the time. The farm she intended to build from the ashes of the one her father had worked so desperately to keep going.

And then there were the birch-twig besoms with which Lakeland housewives swept their floors and yards. She and her mother had made hundreds of the things and if they brought in only a few pence, it all helped and she would need every resource she had to begin to build the dream she dreamed of. She had already made two dozen or so, helped by Cat, and the neat bundles were piled in the barn even now, ready for selling at Keswick market.

There was the knitting of hosiery, the weaving of the wool and the spinning of the yarn on the loom and spinning-wheel which her mother kept in the parlour and which Annie had carefully cleaned ready for use. When she had her flock, of course! There were many crafts she could turn her hand to when the spring came but first she must earn some money to get her and Cat through the winter. If she could, she would also put something aside towards replacing the small flock of sheep her father had once owned. She had no idea what had happened to them though

Sally had spoken of debts and a bad summer harvest in the year Joshua and Lizzie had died.

"Me an' Ma came every day ter nurse them, Annie, but by the time we got 'ere tha' faither and mother were off tha' heads an' made no sense. There was no money fer doctor but we did our best. Ma made up one of 'er infusions from the root of Wood avens. 'Tis good fer fever an' colic but it were too late, she reckoned."

Sally had sighed sadly, settling her swollen body as comfortably as she could in Lizzie's chair, sipping reflectively and with great enjoyment the mug of tea Annie had brewed, her feet up to the good hot fire on the hearth.

"Yer Ma went first. Asked fer thi' times, she did. Wanted ter tell thi' summat, she kept sayin', an' Ma said she'd pass a message on, not knowin' when she'd see thi', like, but doin' 'er best ter calm 'er, but she said nowt more. She went quietly, lyin' next to tha' faither. We'd only just lifted 'er out . . . well, with yer faither still alive it didn't seem right ter leave 'er aside 'im . . . when 'e went an' all. No more than an hour atween 'em, poor souls. We did it right, Annie. A proper 'bidden' funeral they 'ad an' everyone came, even from Cockermouth where tha' Ma was born. We took it in turns ter 'laat' with 'em, me Ma an' others from hereabouts, Mrs Gunson and Mrs Strickland an' old Ma Bibby from down Scarness way, 'er bein' a friend of tha' Ma's. They was carried on the 'corpse way', so there'll be no ill omens laid on this 'ouse, Annie. Church bell tolled, nine times fer tha' faither an' six fer tha' Ma an' we 'ad a funeral feast. Ma baked the arvel bread and gave it round. Oh, it were done right, lass, 'ave no fear o' that."

"I must go and thank your mother, and all of them, Sally, and you, of course, for what you did. I didn't know . . ."

Sally sat up cumbersomely and her good-natured face which had became even rosier with the fierce heat of the fire, twisted into a horrified grimace.

"Eeh no, lass, tha' cannot go up ter me Ma's, nor to any of 'em."

"Why not? I am most grateful . . ."

"They'd not 'ave thi' over t' threshwood, none of 'em would, an' neither would Bert. He reckons 'e's head of the 'ouse now since me faither died an' he'd 'ave no truck wi' . . . well not wi' . . ." She indicated with a nod of her head and a swift glance in her direction, Annie's grave-faced little daughter who was watching with the greatest fascination Sally's boy Sammy devour a piece of Reed Macauley's cook's chocolate meringue, something he had never before come across and which he plainly found much to his liking. As he ate his eyes never shifted from what remained of it and the speed with which he ate it implied that the sooner he got it down, the sooner he could have another piece.

"You mean that because I have a child, one born out of . . ."

"Don't be daft, Annie. Yer know what they're like round 'ere. None of 'em'll 'ave 'owt ter do wi' thi. Did tha' expect it ter be any different? As soon as it's known tha's back wi' a . . ."

"A bastard?" Annie's chin rose challengingly.

"Aye . . ." sadly, ". . . an' after tha' ran away like tha' did, wi' that chap from the travelling show."

"He was ready to punish me, Sally. My father. I don't know how or what my life would have been like had I stayed . . ."

"Threw you out, the story went an' served yer right, they said. Yer'd bin seen in Keswick wi' that actor but I felt right badly about it. Like it was my fault . . ."

"*Your* fault?"

"Well, if I 'adn't coaxed thi' ter come ter t' play it wouldn't 'ave 'appened. None of it."

"No, Sally, you musn't blame yourself. I chose to go, to take the chance, knowing what my father was like, and so I must bear the consequences."

"What'll tha' do now, Annie?"

"Stay here."

"Nay, will tha' not sell?" Clearly Sally was of the opinion her friend was off her head for whoever heard of a woman living alone on a farm? How would she manage without a

man? How would she feed and clothe herself and her child?
And more to the point, how could she stay here in this
upright and God-fearing community amongst those who
would turn their faces from her? Who would have no social
communication with her whatsoever. Who would shun her
and her child, for what decent man or woman could,
without tainting themselves, be concerned with a woman
such as Annie Abbott? To accept her would be to condone
her behaviour, loose and immoral as it had been, and for
all any of them knew, still was. If she could act as she had
in the past with one man, or even more, who was to say
she could not do it again with another, theirs, in fact,
the women would tell themselves, and the men, having
daughters of their own to protect, could only look upon
her with contempt since to do otherwise might put the
idea in their daughters' heads that there was no sin to it.

"No." Annie shook her head resolutely in answer to
Sally's question and Sally watched in wondering admiration
the play of firelight in Annie's copper curls. They were
tight and shining, long tendrils hanging in coils about her
slender white neck and falling over her ears. She had
bundled it up on top of her head, skewering it with several
pins but it was far too heavy and vibrant to remain there,
slipping in bright disarray from its fastenings.

With a generosity which held no envy Sally admitted to
herself that Annie Abbott had grown into a right comely
woman.

"What *will* tha' do, then?"

"Run the farm, Sally. Work. Buy sheep when I have
the money. A cow, pigs. A horse. Plough . . . I was
hoping the men would oblige with some 'boon-ploughing'
when the time came . . ." a custom in which all the men
in the community would help one another at ploughing
time, ". . . plant oats and bigg on a couple of acres. Get
Natty Varty to do some coppicing and in the evening make
swills and besoms. Given a chance I can make this farm
successful. That's all I need, a chance, or even half a one.
Mr Macauley . . . I met him on the road yesterday . . .
his mother knew mine . . ." which was half a truth . . .

"brought over this food . . ." indicating the basket, ". . . otherwise we would have gone hungry."

She frowned at Sammy who was reaching with grubby hands for the chocolate meringue. "That boy of yours, should he be eating so much rich food?" since he certainly would not be used to it, her manner said. Besides which, what was in the basket might have to last her and Cat through the next few weeks which it wouldn't if he was allowed to make free with it. She could see that Sally was one of those good-natured, careless mothers who, as long as they were not bothering them, gave no concern to the activities of their offspring.

Sally glanced indifferently at Sammy. "Oh, 'e'll be all right. Nothin' makes 'im sick."

"Perhaps not, but I'd rather he was sick on someone else's food, if you don't mind. That's all me and Cat have until I earn some money."

"Well then, we'd best be off." Sally struggled to get out of her chair, ready to be offended, but the effort to do either was too much for her and she sank back, panting with the effort.

"Give us a 'and, Annie, an' see, Sammy, give over touchin' that cake. He's never seen 'owt like it," she explained to Annie apologetically, pushing aside the smaller child, a little girl she called Janie, and when Annie had got her to her feet and through the doorway on to the threshwood, she turned impulsively, putting her hand on Annie's arm.

"I'll try an' get over ter see thi', Annie, but with me Ma an' Bert it'll be difficult. Yer know . . ." nodding again in Cat's direction. The Mounsey farm, Upfell, ran next to Browhead, the distance between the farmhouses no more than a mile or so but it seemed to Annie that though the track was not long it might as well have been a hundred.

"You must do as you see fit, Sally." She lifted her head proudly, as she had done with Reed Macauley, for she would have no one, him or Sally, handing out favours to her, then she relented, for Sally had been good to Lizzie and Joshua. "Come if you can, Sal. I'd be glad to see

you, and your mother, but don't cause trouble at home,"
meaning with her husband, Bert.

Sally laughed without humour. "If yer thinkin' of Bert,
he don't care what I do as long as 'is dinner's on t' table
when 'e gets in from t' fell an' I'm in 'is bed when 'e goes
up to it."

Annie had not seen Sally since that day. She had seen
nobody. December had come in with a biting furious wind,
unfriendly and finding its way into the house despite the
thickness of the walls, bringing fresh soot down the
chimney and though there was plenty of peat and wood
in the barn she had tried to use it sparingly in order to
make it last thoughout the winter. The house had been
cleaned and polished and scrubbed and aired, even the
tiny windows buffed until they sparkled. Bedding had been
washed and mended and the contents of her mother's
chest searched for suitable garments from which to
remake and replace the clothing she and Cat wore. She
had sewn a new little dress for her daughter from a skirt
of Lizzie's, a dull and washed out grey, vowing as she did
so that one day she would make her one in a bright and
pretty material, but at least she was warm and her appearance was neat and clean.

She had baked clapbread and made a pan of crowdy,
finding the vegetables in what had been her mother's vegetable garden. She had managed to do some digging before
the ground had become too hard but their supplies were
getting low again, the basket of food brought over by Reed
Macauley nearly empty. She needed some money, hard
cash, since it was obvious that those with whom she might
have done a trade, had she had anything to exchange,
would not be willing to oblige her. Some of my oats for a
leg of your lamb. A quart of milk for a lump of cheese, or
butter, eggs for a hunk of bacon and though she had been
careful with the food it had been hard at Christmas time
when she had tried to make a little celebration for Cat.
No presents, of course, except for the surprising loop of
bright emerald-green ribbon she had found at the bottom
of her mother's chest wrapped about a shining strand of

copper hair which had matched Cat's and her own. Who had it belonged to? she had wondered before tying the ribbons in her daughter's curls. Someone from her mother's past, or perhaps one of her small brothers and sisters who slept in the churchyard by the lake. It had not occurred to her that the curl had been cut from her mother's own head when she had been pretty, fifteen-year-old Lizzie Bowman.

She had cut a tiny fir seedling from the coppice and decorated it with pine cones and bright red berries and ribbons of paper from about the food in the hamper, fashioned into bows and hearts. Not much, but with a Christmas carol sung as the child drowsed on her knee she felt she had done her best with the first Christmas they had shared in their own home. Next year would be different. This time next year it *would* be different.

No one came near her.

On Boxing Day she and Cat walked down the track to the road which led to the hamlet of Gillthrop where the Highthwaite pack had just set off on the traditional Boxing Day fox hunt, one of the many which took place each winter between November and April. Not a sport as it was known in other parts of the country, but a necessity since the fox was an unrivalled predator in the fields of the local farmers, attacking and taking new-born lambs when they came. The drag for the scent had taken place earlier that day and the hounds were already away, eager to follow the fox over the hostile terrain which, particularly at this time of the year, could strike without warning at a man who did not respect its moods.

A Lakeland village was not the cosy affair of inn, church and pretty cottages grouped about a village green and pond which was known elsewhere but was a line of small buildings in a thin straggle along the rutted road. Women stood in small knots as Annie walked towards them, Cat's hand in hers and as she drew nearer all conversation ceased. Almost as one they folded their arms defensively across their offended bosoms, their attitude proclaiming at once that she was not welcome and that she'd best not try her doxy's tricks here. Shawled heads turned away, eyes sliding to watch her nevertheless.

The hound pack could be heard in full cry, a rushing river of melody fading to a gentle swarming-bee sound as the dogs took flight through the bracken of Orthwaite Bank in the direction of Little Cockup as they trailed the fox. The men had gone, following the excited hounds. Farmers, the whipper-in, the hunstmen in their hodden grey. Sturdy boots and gaiters, snug breeches and woollen jackets and jaunty bowler hats. Some carried fox screws to winkle out the cunning animal should he go to ground in a borran, others had walking sticks and shepherd's crooks for they would cover a good many miles today. There were terriers trained to follow the fox into the borran and flush him out. The thrilling notes of the hunting horn rang out, carried on an echo and for a moment every head turned in the direction of the sound then all the women looked back at Annie Abbott, waiting, silent, accusing, hostile, curious for none had known a bad woman before.

She knew them all. They were decent, hard-working, quick to help one another, loyal and true friends to those who deserved it. Gillthrop was no more than fifteen minutes' walk from Browhead. She had attended the church school with their children and her mother had passed the time of day with the older ones, but none spoke.

"Good morning, Mrs Armstrong," she called out, her stride bold and graceful, not faltering. Her full skirt swung, brushing the tops of her wooden-soled clogs and revealing an inch of the thick woollen stockings her mother, or perhaps it was her father, had knitted. She wore no bonnet and the brilliant sunlight lit her hair to flame. Her back was straight, long and supple and she walked with the ease and elegance of a cat. From the inn yard of The Bull where he had tethered his mare, Reed Macauley drew in his breath admiringly.

Jesus God, but she was a rare one. It took a special kind of courage to do what she was doing. It was easy to carry a sword or a musket into battle, into the heat and fury which was generated when men came up against other men. It was easy to be brave when all about you were being brave with you, but to be one woman, one solitary soldier against so much hostility, called for the sort of valour which had nothing to do with the race of blood which carries a man through an armed conflict.

He had passed at the back of her farmhouse on more than one occasion in the past four weeks as he came down from Long Beck and on to the pack route which led through the fells to Carlisle where he had business interests. He had not called though he had been tempted to do so if only to see how she was managing. Sheer curiosity, he told himself, though why he felt the need to justify himself, even to himself, irritated him. They were neighbours of sorts, weren't they, and any decent neighbour would take the trouble to enquire after the health and condition of another, especially a woman alone who had just come back from what Gillthrop would consider wild adventuring and who would, given the circumstances, be bound to encounter hostility. The hamper had been an impulse. She was nothing to do with him, and, if she was to be given the chance she needed he would serve her best by staying away from her. She was in enough trouble as it was and needed no further gossip about what those in the neighbourhood would see as the questionable visits of a young, unmarried man on a woman of already dubious character. No, best leave her alone to swim, or sink if that was the way of it, in the turbulent waters she herself had stirred up.

But she intrigued him. He thought about her more often than he liked. She was a vastly attractive woman, of course, and promised to be . . . interesting, stimulating, with an air about her of something hidden which could prove diverting to reveal and he was not a man who would take much persuading to reveal it! If he helped her without those of Gillthrop knowing he was helping her, giving her that covert support – of a material sort – to get her through the winter and on to her first step towards independence, which he had a fancy to do, what might she be capable of achieving? She'd not do it on her own, of course. She had nothing, nothing but the farmhouse and the land. No resources, no capital with which to purchase her flock, the livestock she would need, the farming implements, the seed to plant her first crop, nothing but her own strong back and indomitable spirit.

And courage, he told himself. Would you look at her now, striding through the gathering of village women, nodding, smiling, calling her greetings as though she was as welcome as the first daffodils and getting no response whatsoever beyond sour looks and the coldly turned shoulder of every woman in the village. Not showing that she gave a damn either, head held high and a smile on her to melt the coldest heart which meant nothing to these women. Now if they were men! Ah, that would be different for what man could resist that springing step, that neat waist and lilting breast, that glowing, hatless tumble of hair which gave her the appearance of having come directly from some man's bed after an hour or two of delightful love-making.

"Good morning, Miss Abbott," he called out, stepping from behind his mare, hoping perhaps to startle her though why he should want to do so was again an enigma to him but she merely glanced coolly in his direction, nodding politely as she turned into the inn yard. The women in the street watched avidly.

"A fine morning, is it not?" he went on, moving towards her, drawn by some strange and annoying need to have her do more than nod. What? A smile perhaps, one of those he had seen illuminate her great, golden-brown eyes on the day they had met? A curl of her poppy-red lips, lifting at the corners to show her white teeth? Some words to let him know she had not forgotten the hamper since she must know she and the child would not have survived without it.

She did none of these things. The smiles she had showered on the village women were gone and her manner told him, and them, that she was a woman with whom men were not encouraged to dally. She was on some business of her own here and it was nothing to do with anyone but herself and whoever she had come to see.

Without knowing why, not meaning to since it was his intention to go with the pack on the fox hunt over the fells, he followed her inside The Bull, leaning casually, his arms crossed on his chest, against the door frame of the low-ceilinged, oak-panelled bar-parlour of the inn. Though there was a huge log fire burning on the hearth it was gloomy for the windows were small, and an aroma of ale and spirits and tobacco filled his nostrils and caught the back of his throat. It was empty but for an amiable-looking man with wide shoulders and short bandy legs standing in front of the bar. He turned from his lethargic wiping of a glass as Annie entered. At once into his eyes came that foolish, longing-to-handle expression with which Annie was all too familiar but with Reed Macauley at her back and the dreadful apparition of starvation staring into her face she had no choice but to carry on.

"Good day, landlord," she said brightly and smiled.

He smiled back, not yet sure who she was but liking what he saw.

"Good day to you." His glance fell to the child and understanding began to dawn.

"I'm Annie Abbott. I'm looking for work."

Behind her Reed straightened slowly and for a second the man by the bar allowed his eyes to drift in his direction, catching the slight nod which, in these parts, meant a great deal. Among his other business concerns Reed Macauley had substantial sums of money out at interest. And it was not only substantial sums he lent, but small loans to the small man. Perhaps a matter of no more than two guineas but for the period of time that man owed money to Reed Macauley, he was Reed Macauley's man. And the landlord of The Bull, going through a bad spell when the farmers, or the smallholders did, was in debt to the man who now stood in his bar-parlour.

Catching the landlord's shift of inattention Annie turned to look where he did though she was too late to see Reed

Macauley's nod. Her face hardened and her eyes became brilliant with anger.

"Mr Macauley, I would be obliged if you would take yourself off in whatever direction you were heading when I came into the inn yard. Mr . . . er . . . the landlord and I have some business to discuss and I would prefer to do it in private. It is none of your concern."

"Indeed, Miss Abbott, but is this not a public bar and if I want to drink in it then it *is* my concern. Mine and the landlord's."

She was confused for a moment and he grinned, but recovering at once she turned back to the landlord, her glorious head showering small ringleted curls about her forehead. Both men watched her in some fascination. Spying a door behind the bar she indicated to it with her nod of her head.

"Perhaps we could go in there, sir. I have no wish to keep Mr Macauley from his . . . whatever it is he drinks."

"Go ahead, Will. Give me a brandy and I'll just sit here by the fire whilst you and Miss Abbott attend to your business. I am the last person to stand in the way of private enterprise." His grin broadened as he threw his long, immaculately tailored leg in its superbly polished boot over the bench, leaning his elbow on the table.

Annie found it surprisingly easy. She was a very experienced barmaid, she told Will Twentyman. Strong and willing and conscientious. Six hours each evening would be fine though threepence an hour was less than she had earned . . . oh, of course, there would be tips, but by the look of the women in the village their menfolk would not be encouraged to throw their cash in her direction.

"And my supper?"

He shrugged. "There's always food here."

"And . . . my child."

He frowned. He had been given the nod by Mr Macauley to take on the girl, which was no hardship. Good-looking barmaids were always hard to come by since the respectable folk in the parish did not put their pretty daughters to this kind of trade. There was no doubt she would attract custom, not only with her looks but with her reputation. They'd all be here, the men from the village and the hill farms within walking distance to get a look at her, to try it on with her. He would himself if his old woman wasn't looking. Oh, aye, he'd have taken her on without Mr Macauley's say so, that's if his Eliza would let him but he'd not bargained for the nipper as well.

"She would be kept out of the way, Mr Twentyman, I promise. She's used to being quiet and is no bother to anyone."

Aye, he'd not argue with her about that, poor little mite, all big eyes and a solemn expression on her that would have sat well on a judge. Kept out of the way while her mother entertained her 'friends', he'd be bound and what he wouldn't give to be among that number.

"She'll just go to sleep in a corner, Mr Twentyman. You won't even know she's there. I . . . I can't leave her alone at home."

"When can tha' start?"

"Tonight?" She gave him her saucy barmaid's smile.

"Aw reet, but keep tha' bairn out o't way."

"I will, and thank you, Mr Twentyman."

She did not even glance in Reed Macauley's amused direction as she swept regally through the bar and out into the brilliant December sunshine. Her elation showed in the heightened colour of her smooth cheeks and the vivid, transparent depths of her golden eyes.

A week later, with her first week's wage of nine shillings in the tin box beneath the pile of kindling under the sconce, with the few pennies in tips jingling in her pocket, the good, solid meal she and Cat shared every night and the few odds and ends of broken tarts or a mutton chop slipped to her by Will Twentyman, she had taken that first arduous step on the road to success. She was settled. She had a job, money coming in. She was, for the moment, safe. She could, for the moment, allow herself to feel exultant, for despite all her neighbours' cold hostility, their down-right longing to see her fall flat on her face, she had shown them all that she did not need them. She had succeeded in hanging on and though she was far, very far, from what she intended, she had for the time being found honest work and had earned her first week's wage.

And when that first snow fell, starting with a sudden flurry of flakes floating in the thin air, she immediately took Cat's hand, banishing all thoughts of gathering birch twigs for the making of the besoms she was accumulating in her barn. She and Cat began to make their frantic way down the track at the back of Browhead towards the farmhouse. She had lived for most of her life in this part of the world and knew well the pitiless cruelty of the blizzards which could attack so quickly. The light was fading rapidly as the slanting snowflakes began to thicken and almost before they had left the comparative shelter of the coppice it had settled thickly on the ground, on their bent heads and bowed shoulders, on their eyebrows and eyelashes so that they were forced to blink rapidly to clear their vision. The cold was devastating and within minutes, though they were no more than a few hundred yards from the farmhouse, they were enclosed in a solid, moving, violent curtain of snow. Had she not known every inch of the way or had they been several hundred yards further from the farm she could not have found it. She was only relieved it was Sunday and the inn closed for the day.

They fell into the kitchen, a great tide of snow accompanying them, laughing and gasping, Cat, who had been ready to be frightened, laughing just as merrily as her mother. The fire was burning brightly. They had rushlights and warm clothing, a simmering 'tatie-pot' on the fire and when, later, they dozed before their own hearth, warm, well fed, Annie sighed in sheer bliss, and, in perfect imitation of her mother, Cat did the same.

8

She sighed in sheer exasperation the following morning
when daylight, what there was of it, revealed the still
solidly eddying veil of snow. It had drifted up to the
window ledges and covered the drystone wall opposite the
farmhouse door and when she opened it a waist-high
barrier of frozen, crystallised whiteness rose before her,
preventing her from going any further. Not that she
needed or wanted to go any further just yet but she was
expected at The Bull at six o'clock that evening and she
intended to give none of those in the village a chance to
mock her female weakness, as they would see it, nor her
inability to look after herself and her child. She knew they
would be betting with one another on how long it would
take her to admit she was beaten; to sell up and move
away, take her bastard child and ruined reputation elsewhere and allow them to attend to their moral and, until
she came among them, virtuous lives.

It was noon before the snow stopped falling. The beauty
of the landscape as she opened the door again took her
breath away and for several minutes she and Cat stood in
absolute silence, the door latch held in one hand whilst
she lifted the other to shade her eyes, for the sheer white
brilliance of the immaculate snow was a physical pain. She
had forgotten during the four years she had wandered the
flat plains of the Midlands, the magnificent and awe-
inspiring splendour of the Lakeland which had been, and
would be again, her home, particularly after a snowstorm
of the proportions of the night before. It sparkled and
glittered as though a careless hand had scattered millions
of diamonds across the rolling landscape. The sky was the
deep blue of a cornflower, cloudless and serene. The trees

stood proud, unbowed beneath their burden of snow, a marvel of black and white etched against the silvered lake. It was a mystical land of gentle lowlands and high, sharp-featured peaks, a land unmarked by walls or fences or gates, for they had all vanished in the night storm. It was cold but not the raw biting cold of November. This was sharp, clean, stimulating, making the blood race and tingle. A white, silent cold in a white, silent world where nothing moved and nothing could be heard but the faint bugle call of the whooper swans who came down each year from the north to winter on the lake.

"Well, Cat, my sweet, grand as it is, it's going to create a problem we could well do without."

The child nodded sagely, staring out as anxiously as Annie for even at her tender age she was well aware of the importance of work, of wages, of food to eat and a place to eat it in. She had been her mother's sole companion since she was born and had been suckled to the sound of Annie's voice musing on how to make a penny do the work of two. She had understood nothing at first as she listened to the soft murmur of the words her mother spoke, not to her for she had been an infant at her mother's breast, but to herself. Annie had found that to speak the words out loud, though there was no answer, had given her the feeling she was discussing her problems with someone; that perhaps the solution might be divulged to her, and often it had. With Cat's wide, long-lashed eyes gazing unwinkingly into hers, the child's mouth pursed on the nipple of her full breast, she had talked and talked and gradually, as Cat grew, moving on to a cup, a plate, a spoon, she had begun to understand, to listen as Annie talked to her and if she had no answer, her intense, unchildlike concern was felt by her mother, giving her comfort, and the bond between them was strong and unbreakable.

"We could dig," she offered, her eyes bright, her trust complete in this mother who had never been anything but utterly trustworthy.

"We could, darling," her mother answered doubtfully

for it was a good fifteen minutes' walk to Gillthrop and that was in the best of weather.

"Shall we put our clogs on, mother, and try?" The child's hand slipped confidingly into hers and for a second Annie felt her heart twist painfully inside her. Her daughter was so . . . so lovely, not in the visual sense, though she was that too, but in her sweet child's heart. Wanting to please and console, to help as though she was an adult, to attempt any gargantuan task with her child's strength if it would ease the worry in her mother's heart. To dig a path to The Bull if it should be necessary and would please Annie. She was far too serious for her age since she had never 'played' but her goodness and sweetness shone from her. She was strong, too, and steadfast in her love, and yet these people of the parish of Bassenthwaite wished her nothing but ill. They would shun her and teach their children to shun her and it broke Annie's heart to think about it but there was nothing she could do but go on, work hard, make a place for her and Cat, and hope. That was all she could do. *Hope.*

"Why not? You run upstairs and get mother's cloak and your shawl and scarf. Oh, and the thick stockings from the chest. I wish we had some boots," she added wistfully, "but our clogs will have to do."

The snow had already crusted. Fortunately the big, long-handled shovel Joshua Abbott had used to clear the yard to the side of the house of the manure his animals deposited there, the one with which Annie had been attempting to turn over the hard earth, was still standing just by the side door. First she must get herself out of the house and up on to the level to which the snow had fallen. To cut out steps would be the best, she thought, so that she and Cat could go up them one at a time until they stood, with any luck, at the same height as the window ledges where the snow lay, that's if the snow would hold them.

This proved easy enough and soon she had moved about ten feet from the front door, throwing the snow first to one side and then to the other, forming a narrow,

tramped-down path in which the wooden soles of her clogs
actually helped. They were sturdy and warm and providing
the snow did not seep over the sides, afforded good protection.

At the end of an hour she was hot and panting with
exertion and she had almost reached the gate which led
out to the farm track and down to the road. To the road
to Gillthrop and The Bull. Cat was behind her scooping
out snow with the lid of the tin box in which Annie's first
week's wages lay, resolutely stamping down the packed
whiteness with her little clogged feet. Her cheeks were
like poppies and her eyes great golden brown stars and
for a moment Annie paused to watch her, comparing her
with the inanimate doll she had been three months ago.
She had pushed back the scarf Annie had tied about her
head and her hair, exactly the same colour and texture as
her mother's, fell about her forehead and down her back.
Like a rippling sheet of copper it was, catching fire from
the sun. The mother and child were singing. An old song
Lizzie Abbott had sung to Annie and which she in turn
sang to Cat. It was said to be a 'cocking' song before
cockfighting was made illegal in 1835. 'The Charcoal Black
and Bonnie Grey' it was called, a ballad popular throughout
Cumberland and Westmorland, the place names mentioned
in it changed to suit the location in which it was sung.

'Come all of you cockers far and near,' it began and they
had got as far as the last verse,

'Now the black cock he has lost their brass,
And the Gillthrop lads did swear and curse . . .'
when a deep-throated masculine voice joined in, roaring
out the remainder of the song with a dash and musical
gusto which, though it silenced them in surprise for a
moment, they took up again and finished with him.

'. . . and wished they'd never come that day,
To Bassenthwaite to see the play.'

They looked at one another, she and Reed Macauley,
vivid blue eyes locking with golden brown, bewitched by
the sensation of pure joy, the feeling of exhilarating pleasure, of sheer, childlike enjoyment of the song they had

shared. It lit up their faces and in that moment, for that moment, broke the fetters which adult human beings bind about themselves and which children have not yet learned. That guarded restraint which is erected to protect dignity and hide from view that innermost vulnerable core of one's self. They looked at one another and, quite simply, fell deep in love and for the space of five seconds their eyes admitted it. She relaxed, ready to sigh over the perfection of it. Soft, her eyes became, and so did his, dazed with awe at this emotion neither had known before and certainly not expected, dazzled with the wonderment and confusion since it had come on them so blindingly, so suddenly, so amazingly. But scarcely before they had acknowledged its sweetness, as though a warning voice had whispered inside them both, at exactly the same time they became business-like, brisk, turning away to fumble with something, she with her spade, he with the sledge he pulled behind him and with the implement he had devised to push away the snow in front of him.

"I knew damn well you'd not stay home like any sensible woman, Annie Abbott." His voice was top heavy with something he did his best to hide from her. "No, not you. Up to our necks in bloody snow and more to come, no doubt . . ." heedless of the sky which showed not a suspect cloud from horizon to horizon, from high peak to high peak, ". . . and where are you and this poor child you drag around with you? Not by your own hearth where a woman with sense would keep herself but out on the damn fell digging like some damn ten-year-old making his first snowman. Could you not for once remain where you are safe from danger? A woman from these parts who is familiar with its weather should know when discretion comes before bravado."

And the strange thing was, though it incensed her beyond measure, she knew exactly why he was speaking to her in such a menacing, furious tone. The snow had stopped falling no more than two hours since and yet here he was dragging a sledge – on which there was yet another hamper – just as though he was a boy about to play the

wild games boys who had nothing better to do often play.
Pretending he was 'passing by' no doubt, on his way to
some important and not to be postponed meeting but in
reality slipping and sliding down the long, snow-drifted
track, hazardous and uncertain at the best of times, as
soon as he could from Long Beck to Browhead to see that
she and Cat were in good condition. This was not the first
time he had come to her rescue and not the first time he
had done his best to give her a hand over the rough path
life had put her on, but it wouldn't do. *It wouldn't do!* He
was Reed Macauley, wealthy farmer and businessman,
son of a prosperous and successful 'statesman' family and
she was Annie Abbott with an illegitimate child and a
derelict farm, and a way to make in the world for both of
them. It would be hard enough to make it without him to
muddy the already unclear waters of her life. To interfere
because he had a fancy, she told herself, to play the gallant
knight to her damsel in distress.

"What's it to you, *Mister* Macauley, *what* I do?" She
had to screech like this. She had to let him see, make him
see that he must leave her alone. She had to fight with
him since it seemed it was the only way to get rid of him.
The last few minutes had frightened her badly. She was
in one of the most desperate situations of her life, ready
to fall over the brink of disaster and into a heaving pit of
despair. She was holding on by a whisker, by the fragile
tips of her fingers and one false move, one tiny movement
that was unbalanced would tip her over into it and she
could not, *could not* afford to – she would not even think
it, let alone *say* the word 'love' – look at any man, not
now, not at this precarious moment in her life and certainly
not one like Reed Macauley. It had been no longer than
the time it takes to blink an eye, that gladness, that meeting, that astonishing meeting of their senses and really,
no harm had been done, not yet, and she must fight to
make sure that that tiny fraction of time in which tenderness, concern and passion had been revealed, was not
repeated. She could only do it with harshness.

"It's none of your damned business, as I've told you

before," she shrieked. "Lord, every time I turn round there you are at my back demanding to know what I'm doing and why. I've only been home a few weeks but already you've had something to say about the state of my looks," – referring to the day he had knocked on her door and found her coated in soot – "the condition of my daughter, my fitness for my work," – which was not strictly true but she did not care in her furious attempt at true rage – "and now my state of mind in trying to get to it. I have a job to do and if I don't get down to it I won't get paid, besides which I'll not have those crows down in the village say that Annie Abbott hasn't the guts to fight her way through a bit of snow to . . ."

"So that's it, is it? You'd chance this child's health so that you can prove to a stupid gaggle of women that . . ."

"Don't you speak to me of my child's health since I'm the one who has worked her fingers down to the bone, and in any way I can, to put good food in her belly and warm . . ."

"In any way you can?" He towered over her, his eyes slitted with his own rage, his mouth suddenly hard and cruel. "Yes, I suppose you would do that since it's an easy way to earn a living, I would say, and you look like the kind of woman who would enjoy her work. Tell me, are you still employed in that profession for if you are I might be persuaded to avail myself of . . ."

He was quick and strong. Had he not been she would have opened his head with the force of the blow she levelled at him. The spade was vicious and her swing true but he caught the handle and twisted it from her and from both the killing fury drained away leaving them trembling and sick.

"I beg your pardon," he said, his voice as cold as the air they breathed. "That was unforgivable. Allow me to help you with your . . . digging," and as though his life depended on it, and perhaps his sanity, he began, turning his back on her and Cat, biting into the snow with the spade, throwing it wildly from him, much further than he need.

She moved away without a word and took Cat's cold
hand in hers, hurrying the bewildered little girl back into
the farmhouse. She did not look outside again and when,
at half past five, she lit a rushlight and prepared herself
and Cat for their journey down to Gillthrop there was a
clear, well packed path from the sledge which still stood
where he had left it, to the first cottage in the village
street.

"By gum, lass, we'd not expected thee this night." Mr
Twentyman and his Eliza were the only ones in the
bar-parlour and though one or two more adventurous men
crept in later, stamping their feet and blowing on their
hands, those who lived in the village, as Mr Twentyman
remarked, there had really been no need for her to have
bothered herself. Mind, she'd got gumption had Josh
Abbott's girl and if this was an example of what determination could do, she'd go far that one would. He was
inclined to like her. A liking which had nothing to do with
the way she looked. Not that he wouldn't have said no to
a kiss and a cuddle and a little feel of those ripe and lovely
breasts but his Eliza had eyes in the back of her head so
there was no chance of that, sadly.

And she'd certainly brought in custom, even in the week
she worked in the bar, smiling warmly at anyone who
addressed her and yet not too familiarly so that none of
them could get the idea that what they saw could be theirs.
She had added something to the atmosphere which he was
at a loss to understand but which nevertheless he was
grateful for, though Eliza Twentyman could have told him,
had he asked. Annie was polite, pleasant, cheerful, interested in the men who crowded at the bar, getting to know
their names, enquiring after their families, sharing a joke
but there was an innocence about her which she had never
lost despite the life she had led and her own motherhood,
and the men liked it, and her.

Their womenfolk did not, and said so, to each other, to
their men and to Eliza Twentyman and though she kept it
to herself for as long as she could for, like her husband,
she had taken to Annie Abbott and the little slip of a thing

who was her daughter, she knew the day must come when they could no longer keep her. Eliza had to live with these women who were beginning to cold-shoulder *her*. The folk who lived in the Lakeland communities, often isolated for weeks on end, relied upon one another. They were close-knit, open-handed with those of whom they approved, intensely loyal to one another. Her husband depended on their husbands for his livelihood and though The Bull was the only inn for miles, should they turn against her and her Will they would be hard pressed to survive.

It snowed several times in January, which was the worst snow month, but again Annie Abbott got down from Browhead to Gillthrop. The snow melted partially, thawing down to a manageable level where it was possible to get about more easily. Then it froze, a cruel frost which set the world into a hard, timeless beauty. There were deep, crackling snow ruts, crusted just enough to cover the tussocks of heather on the slopes behind the farmhouse, scintillating in the brilliance of the winter sunshine. The sheep had moved down from the high fells and as they drifted in small groups towards the 'intakes' the ice which had formed on their fleeces tinkled musically. The snow buntings were picking seeds from the bent, a stiff-stemmed, rush-like grass. Grey geese flew south and the crows cruised up and down the rushing streams on the look-out for trout. Foxes, thin, nervous-eyed, starving, crept close to human habitation as they waited for spring and on February 2nd, Will Twentyman reluctantly told Annie that he no longer required her services.

She was devastated. She had worked for five weeks and, with the help of Reed Macauley's second hamper which she had seen as foolish to refuse, particularly as she could not leave it sitting on the sledge on the track up to Dash Beck, she had managed to save £2.14s.0d. but that would not buy her a flock of sheep. She had hoped to save more money from her work as barmaid and when the first market took place in Keswick and she sold the besoms she and Cat had made, the amount realised might buy her half a dozen young ewes. Put to a good ram which she would hire, they would, by next year, bring her the start of her flock. She would make swill baskets when Natty Varty had cut and peeled her poles for her at the end of April; these also would be sold at the summer markets.

Now, with a few awkward and apologetic words Will Twentyman had knocked down her precarious house of cards and brought her face to face with ruin. She needed her ewes in the spring. She could not afford to wait until her besoms or her swills were made and sold at the summer fairs she meant to tramp. She had a sledge, the one her father had made years ago. Two, in fact, for the one Reed Macauley had used to haul down the hamper still stood in her barn and short of dragging the thing up to Long Beck, which would cause even more talk, there it would stay. She needed new clogs for herself and Cat. She could cobble together clothing for her daughter from the few bits and pieces left by her mother but something for herself she could not manage, nor the clogs, not with the best will in the world. Her own garments, even her mother's wedding-dress which she still kept in the chest, were threadbare and falling apart at the seams and the only clothing in the place of any substance was that once worn by her father.

"Why, Mr Twentyman?" she asked passionately, in exactly the same way she had asked Polly Pearsall over two years ago. "I'm a good worker and have caused you no trouble" – despite the men who had done their best to engage her in it. "I've not once let you down even when the snow was as high as my shoulders."

Will Twentyman watched her mouth form the words and was fascinated by the sound which came from it. Where had she learned to speak as she did, almost like a lady? It was still possible to detect the rhythmic sound of the Cumberland dialect on her tongue, but she had lost what some might consider the ugly glottal stop of East Cumberland. She did not pronounce 'face' as 'fee-ass' or 'butter' as 'boother' and she had taught her child to speak as she did. And that was one of the reasons, he supposed, but not the main one, of course, why she was not liked, at least by the women. She was 'different'. She had 'got above herself' and though it fascinated their men-folk, it segregated her from the women of the village as sharply as though she had come from another land and spoke a foreign language.

"What is it, Mr Twentyman? Why am I not allowed to build a life for myself and my child? Why do they hate me so? Oh, yes, I know why it is you are forced to get rid of me. What is it I have done to them that turns them against me to the point where they will not be satisfied until they have driven me from the parish? I've done nothing to hurt them. Nothing to hurt anyone except myself and Cat and I'm doing my best to put that right. I only want to work, that's all. To work as men do . . ."

Aye, that was probably it. As men do, which was not the way of things in these parts . . .

". . . to earn an honest penny, to get back on my feet and be dependent on no one. I don't want to interfere with them or their men . . ." since she was well aware of what the nub of their resentment was, ". . . and I want no one interfering with me. Why are they so . . . so cruel, Mr Twentyman?"

And Will Twentyman had to admit, sadly, that he had no answer. He could only slip an extra sixpence in her hand and some left-over suet pudding his wife had made in readiness for the travellers who would, now that the snows had melted and the turnpikes were clear again, be staying overnight at The Bull.

There was an enormous winter moon, full and mysteriously beautiful hanging in the dark blue velvet sky, its light paling the intense colour about it to a silvery lavender. It illuminated the track up to the farmhouse so that every frost-spiked blade of grass could be seen as though it was noon. The great barrier of High Pike and Knott and Great Calva loomed to her left and before her was the majestic splendour of snow-capped Skiddaw. The path of the moon fell across the silken lake to her right, broad and completely still and from somewhere higher up the intakes a dog fox howled in hungry misery. The sound was taken up by another set of barking, closer and somehow different, a frantic sound in which she could detect fear and she wondered who would have their dogs, and young ones at that by the sound of it, out on a night like this.

"What is it, Mother?" Cat huddled closer to her skirts and clung to her hand as they panted up the steep track towards home, and all the while the frenzied noise of the dogs grew louder.

"It's only a couple of dogs, lambkin. They won't hurt us."

"But why are they barking so much?"

"They've probably scented the fox and are doing their duty protecting the chicken coop."

"Whose coop, Mother?" fearfully, and indeed whose coop could it be since the only dwelling between here and Upfell where the Mounseys lived was her own farm?

They were tied to the latch of her door, two puppies whose breeding, even in the light from the moon, was very evident. Black-and-white Border Collies of the sort used by shepherds and farmers for centuries in the care of their flocks. Silky of coat and lively of eye and so pleased to see Annie and Cat that it was hard to know where one puppy ended and the other began. An incredible squirming tangle of limbs, sharp baby claws and cold noses, long bushy tails whipping against Annie's and Cat's laughing, delighted faces, four bright saucy eyes, ready to love with enormous hearts these two humans who had come to rescue them.

"Where have they come from, Mother, and can we keep them? Please, Mother, see, they are so good . . ." which was not true for the moment they were let inside the house they had knocked over a stool, spilt a jug of milk brought up yesterday from The Bull and had begun to worry between them one of Cat's clogs which she had kicked off as she stepped over the threshwood.

"Sweetheart, they are not ours to keep . . ."

"Then whose are they, Mother? They were tied to our door . . . Oh, Mother, don't send them away. I love them so much and they will be no trouble . . . I will let them share my food . . ." for even in the midst of so much joy the practical matter of food and the money to buy it was not overlooked by the child. "They can sleep in my room and they will be such fun." Cat was down on the slate floor with them now. She lay on her back whilst one pup flopped on her chest and licked her face with the slavish devotion of one who knows exactly which side his bread is buttered whilst the other fondly chewed her bare toes, pricking his ears and casting his bright, intelligent eye in the direction of Annie since it seemed to him she might be the provider of food. He and his companion had already demolished the spilled milk but that did not mean he could not manage any other delicacy which might come his way.

Annie sat down, smiling in a way she had not thought possible an hour ago. She had never seen her grave young daughter laugh, even giggle, as she was doing now. A child she was, a young child playing, giddy with laughter and simple fun, her excited cries filling the room with her joy, her childish normal pleasure. And of course, who would have left the puppies here but Reed Macauley? There was not a soul in this dale or up on the higher fell farms who would give her the time of day, let alone two well-bred dogs such as these. A good sheepdog, well trained to his work, was worth his weight in gold, much prized by the farmers who would part with their wives before their dogs and these two, when she had her flock, would be invaluable to her. They would be loyal and stead-fast, as good as two men, true friends and companions for Cat, and when they were grown would enable her to leave her child alone whilst she herself worked since they would guard anything they thought of as theirs with their lives.

He had done it again. Just as she was at the edge of despair and disaster he had thrown her a lifeline to pull her back from it. She had not seen him since the day he had dug the path through the snow and glad she was of it for it made it easier for her to go on without any . . . complications. Oh, God . . . oh, dear God, let there not be complications, meaning, of course, don't let my weak and foolish woman's heart dictate to my wise and far-seeing mind, for even as she allowed him into her thoughts her pulse started to race in the most alarming way. Her stomach lurched, refusing to be still. Her eyes were full of him again and just because he had brought her two damned puppies, and she couldn't allow it. Dear God, she couldn't allow it. Not now when she had just been fired from her job and somehow must get herself and Cat through the days and nights, weeks, even months before she found another one. The bark peeling could not take place until April. Oak poles must be felled and she must 'speak' for Natty Varty who must be paid for his labour.

She must have work, but where? She could not even knock on some farmwife's kitchen door and ask for it as her mother had done, for unlike her mother whose reputation had been beyond reproach she was known from one end of the parish to the other as a 'fallen woman'.

Then you must look elsewhere, her uncompromising and logical mind coolly told her. You are strong and – so you told Reed Macauley – afraid of no one, of nothing, and certainly not of walking from here to Keswick where you are unknown to find work. There was an inn on every street corner in Keswick. When the snow had gone and it was possible to get there, and without Cat, who could then be left in the company of the two puppies, she could be in Keswick and back again in no time at all. Working her six hours and – if she could get it – at fourpence an hour, with tips and the always acceptable bonus of left-over food she and Cat would hold off that wolf from the door whilst she saved her wage for her ewes. She might pick up some bargains at the Sheep Fair, since she knew a good sheep when she saw it, but she must have them by September and the Annual Tup Fair when the rams were hired out or sold for breeding purposes. Soon the farmers would be bringing their sheep down from the fells for dipping which took place in February, to guard against lice and keds which could badly weaken a strain. The ageless cycle of gathering, lambing, dipping and clipping, of putting the tups to the ewes would begin and she must be ready to place herself in its moving orbit since its pattern must follow the course nature had planned. Each section of that course could take place only at a certain time of the year. Miss one section of it and a whole year would be wasted.

The child squealed with laughter and the puppies yelped with excitement, pulling with their sharp little teeth at the hem of her already frail skirt, digging their claws, uselessly as it happened, into the slate slabs of the floor as they hung on. They could not get a purchase, slipping and sliding with great good humour, growling in mock ferociousness, for the game they played was to their, and the child's liking.

Annie smiled and rose to her feet. She picked up both squirming bundles and deposited them firmly in a high-sided basket from which they could not climb.

"Fetch some of that dry bracken from by the side door, my lamb, and we'll line the basket for them. They can sleep in here tonight."

"And . . . tomorrow, Mother? You're not going to send them back, are you?" Cat's eyes were desperate in their pleading.

"I wouldn't know where to send them, sweetheart, so . . ."

"We can keep them, can we, can we . . ." jumping up and down in a way Annie had never seen her do before.

"We'll see, my darling."

"Please, Mother . . . please?"

"Well . . ."

"Please, Mother, I will look after them and feed them and . . ."

"Clean up after them?" smiling at a suspicious pool by the hearth.

"Oh yes . . . yes . . ."

"And what would you call them, that is if we kept them?" She drew the child to her knee and sat down beside the basket where the pups, like the babies they still were, had fallen instantly asleep.

"Blackie and Bonnie, like the song." Cat did not even have to think.

"But they are both boys."

"I don't care." And after all, Annie thought as her daughter nodded against her shoulder, where else would her lovely child find inspiration for names for her puppies? Annie had not, in her three years, read a story to her, nor even told her one since she had never had time in her desperate fight to simply keep them both alive. 'The Charcoal Black and Bonnie Grey' was the only song her little girl knew.

It was appropriate too, she mused, almost asleep herself in the warmth of the fire. He it was who had sung it with them and brought the dogs to her. Helping her but, she was sure, ready to deny it if she should accuse him of it. Not that they would be likely to meet again, she and Reed Macauley, for neither would wish to be caught in the violence of need which had trapped them for an enchanting moment several weeks ago. They must keep well apart for she knew with every quickened heartbeat and every racing pulse in her woman's body that there would be nothing more wonderful in the world than for it to be possessed by his.

9

The snow had gone from all but the highest peaks. Blackie and Bonnie had been with them for over seven weeks and were probably four months old, perhaps a bit more, she had no way of telling, when she walked to Keswick to look for work.

It was almost the end of March and in all that time she had seen only Sally, brave Sally who had defied her mother and her sister Mim, who were convinced in their bigoted ignorance that Sally would not only be the talk of Bassenthwaite parish, consorting with a woman like Annie Abbott, but would bring home some dreadful disease, the kind of disease women of her sort were bound to have. Sally's husband Bert had threatened her with a 'clip round t' lug' if she as much as looked in Annie's direction, she told Annie imperturbably, let alone entered her kitchen, but as she had to pass along the track at the back of Annie's farm, crossing Annie's land, in fact, which had been common practice for generations by those who lived further up the valley, and as Upfell was more than a mile away and hidden behind a fold in the hill, they'd not know she'd 'popped in', she said loftily.

She had her new baby under her shawl, another girl whom she'd called Emma, already shortened to Emm, but she'd left Sammy and Janie at home with their grandmother since their Sammy'd be bound to say 'summat' out of turn.

"Come in, oh, come in, Sally." Annie was pathetically glad to see her, ready to sweep the good-natured girl into her arms, for she had spoken to no one but Cat since she had left The Bull.

"Well, I can't stay long. Ma looked at me a mite peculiar when I said I fancied a walk down to t' smithy. Seth

Armstrong's mendin' some 'arness an' chains fer Bert so I made the excuse that I'd see if they was ready. Save Bert a walk, I said, which sat well wi' 'im, lazy sod. But I wanted ter see 'ow thi' were. We 'eard as 'ow you were workin' at T'Bull. Good fer 'er, I ses ter meself, right pleased tha'd got summat, though Ma an' Mim pulled their faces an' said what were the world comin' to when the likes of Annie Abbott were allowed ter mix wi' decent folk . . . Oh, sorry, Annie, I didn't mean ter . . ."

"I know, Sally, and for pity's sake don't be afraid of offending me. I'm used to them all staring and pointing and whispering behind my back and sometimes they don't even do that but say it out loud as I pass by. The woman from Browhead, they call me . . ."

"Aye, I know, tha's bin the talk o't' valley ever since tha' come home an' now tha's got sack, so Bert tells me. Pleased as punch, he were, just as though tha'd done summat to 'im personal, daft bugger. So what'll tha' do now, lass?" sitting down in the chair before Annie's hearth with a cup of Annie's tea, the last from Reed Macauley's hamper, in her grateful hand. She opened her bodice, more from habit than any need on the part of the infant who was, in fact, fast asleep, threading her distended nipple into its partly open rose-bud mouth and instinctively it began to suck. Cat stared, open-mouthed, distracted from Blackie and Bonnie who had been told to 'sit' and had done so at once. They too, it seemed, were fascinated by the sound the suckling infant made. Into the lady's mouth the tea went, Cat observed, and came out of her fat chest where the baby drank it which clearly was some kind of magic about which she would question her mother at the first opportunity. She and the two dogs surveyed the amazing spectacle with great interest.

Annie was silent, the snuffling sound of the baby, the hissing sigh of the peat fire, the panting of the dogs, both of whom thumped the floor with their tails every time anyone's glance fell on them, whispered about the warm room. It had been miraculously transformed from the hollow, dust-coated barrenness which had been its condition last November. Everything winked and sparkled, the light from the fire touching polished surfaces to a glowing smoothness. The door to the parlour was kept closed since Annie could not afford to warm two rooms but even though she and Cat did not use it the parlour was kept achingly clean and was as tidy as the neat kitchen. In the weeks since she had lost her job at The Bull she had gone through the whole farmhouse from the slate roof to the slate floors of the downstairs rooms. It was a tradition in Lakeland that spring cleaning must be done by Easter and Annie, with nothing else to do, had emptied drawers and scrubbed them, taken out the two beds and brushed and beaten them. She had boiled all the baking tins, scoured the milking cans and calf buckets with silver sand and scrubbed the butter boxes until they were as white as the snow which still capped Skiddaw and Broad End. The dairy itself and the cow house had been given a coat of the whitewash she had found in the barn and, having some left over she had carried outside as much of the furniture as she could from the kitchen and the parlour, and painted the walls of those two rooms as well.

All this had taken place, of course, after she had done what planting she could manage: some bigg, vegetables and black oat, which would see her and Cat through until next winter. Her father's barn, untouched since he died and where over a year ago he had carefully stored them ready for his planting season, had revealed a sack of seed potatoes, some gone mouldy but the rest worth a try. There were corn and parsnip seeds, turnip and carrot, onion bulbs and all of them had been sown and planted in neat, well-tended rows as soon as the frozen ground allowed.

She could do no ploughing, naturally, since her father's wooden 'stitching' plough needed a horse to pull it, but she had trimmed her hedges with his bill hook and set his traps in the hope that, now that spring was almost here she might catch a fine rabbit to go in the pot with her vegetables.

She had gone with Cat and the dogs to cut peat on the

fells, pulling it home on the sledge which, as those on the fells knew, was easier to drag about on the grassy slopes than any wheeled cart. The peat had been stacked to dry since what her father had left before he died was almost gone. She had cleaned his tools, sharpening the scythe and the sickle and the shears and even polished the leather horse-collar and harness in readiness for the day when her horse would wear them.

So, she had done what she could. Her house was in order. Her garden tended, her home sweet-smelling and well ordered, welcoming and warm. The sunlight which crept in through the small windows painted a golden haze about the domesticated simplicity of the mothers and their children, and in an old jug, chipped about its rim and therefore useless for its purpose of holding milk, Annie had arranged a great nodding bunch of golden catkins cut from the pussy-willow which grew on the edge of the lake. There was a serenity, an ageless peace in the room, a simple comfort which warmed the senses. In this house generations of Abbotts had been born, had laboured and died, none of them achieving even the status of 'small statesmen'. When other men had prospered they had been dogged by ill-luck, disease, bad harvests, the land which was theirs remaining theirs, but only just. They seemed to crowd at Annie's back, shaking their heads and wringing their hands at her foolhardiness. Sell, they seemed to be telling her. Sell and start a new life where you are unknown but she pushed them away, raising her head to stare about her defiantly as though to scatter them.

"So what'll yer do now, Annie?" Sally asked sympathetically. She pulled her nipple from the baby's mouth, the sound it made like that of a cork from a bottle.

"I'm off to Keswick but don't tell anyone, will you?"

"Eeh no, love, but what are thi' ter do there?"

"Get a job, I hope."

"What sort?"

"Barmaid, what else?" Annie's voice was calm, strong, sure. She was sitting on the sconce and she leaned forward to pull out a stout piece of wood from beneath it, throwing it to the back of the fire. The sudden flaring of the flames heightened the signs of strain on her face which seemed to Sally to be thinner than when they last met, but Annie's eyes were clear and steady.

"I wish there were summat I could do for thi', Annie," Sally sighed, changing the baby to her other enormous breast. The child suckled obligingly, its plump face as ripe and rosy as its mother's.

They chatted for half an hour, of the days when they were children, of their schoolteacher who had smelled of mothballs, of the girls in their class, most of them, like Sally, now young wives and mothers, of Lizzie and Joshua, of Mim who was courting Ben Postlethwaite, a young local farmer with a fair flock of Herdwicks up Binsey way. Mim, because of Annie's close proximity to Upfell, and her and Sally's past connection with her, was terrified that her chances of a good marriage might be dashed, particularly if Sally continued to visit Browhead.

"Silly cow," Sally added mildly as she lumbered to her feet. "Now I'll try and get down again, love, when I can," hitching the sleeping baby beneath her shawl, "but God knows when that'll be. I'll be expected to 'elp wi' dippin' which is any day now. Bert's fetchin' sheep down right now. Natty Varty's bin tekken on ter give a. . . ."

"Natty Varty?"

"Aye, tha' knows Natty. Work fer anyone, 'e will."

"I know. I was hoping to get him to come and cut some of my timber. It'll be ready for peeling and riving by May. How long will he be working for Bert?"

"Nay, don't ask me, chuck. All summer I 'eard tell. We've a fairish-sized flock, tha' knows. Natty's a good worker an' can turn 'is 'and to owt."

Annie groaned. "I know, that's why I wanted him."

"Can thi' not get anyone else?"

"Who? Nobody would work for me, that's if I could pay them which I can't until I get work of my own. Do you know, Sal, I feel as though I'm going round in circles getting absolutely nowhere. I do my best to get over these obstacles which will keep looming up in front of me but the minute I clamber over one another one appears. I suppose I'll have to try and cut the timber myself if Natty's spoken for. I know all the procedures. I learned them from my father and I have the tools, but he did all the heavy work. There was a decent stack of birch in the barn which he must have cut before he died and put there to mature but most of it's been used by now. Cat and I have made a fair amount of besoms ready to take to market, and I want to start on the swill baskets but I can't get going until the oak's cut. I need to save cash to buy sheep and I can't get cash until I work. . . ."

"Eeh love, tha's in a right pickle. I only wish I 'ad a few bob ter lend thi'." Sally's blue eyes clouded solicitously and she bit her lip as though in anxious contemplation of her own pitiful resources. Of which she had none.

"I know, Sally, but don't worry. It takes a lot to get Annie Abbott down and I'll manage this. I've been in sorrier states, I can tell you."

Sally was torn between an avid eagerness to hear what sort of 'sorry state' Annie had been in and the certain knowledge that if she didn't get home soon she'd be 'in for it', from her Ma, or her husband, or more than likely both. The life her friend had known had the fascination of the mysteriously wicked for her.

It was with great reluctance that she took her leave.

In the end Annie took Cat. She had explained to her that she would be gone all day; that Cat would be perfectly safe with the growing dogs to guard her and keep her company. That she must bolt the door and watch that the fire did not go out. That there was 'tatie-pot', sadly without meat, in the oven for her dinner and that Mother would be home before dark. She knew that Cat was a careful, sensible child, clear-headed and reliable since she had had to be all of these things in her short life. She would do exactly what Annie told her to do and really there was no need of concern but she was only just three years old last December and her eyes, though steadfast and trusting, doing their best to reassure her mother that she would be as good as gold and as safe as houses, had a small shadow of uncertainty in them. Blackie and Bonnie stood, one on either side of her, their heads cocked, their ears pricked as though they too understood the seriousness of what must be done and were well prepared for their part in it. Annie had been training them in the field at the front of the farmhouse, doing her best to remember the series of whistles and commands her father had used when he had dogs of his own. A young Border Collie will often have an inborn herding instinct at an early age and both Blackie and Bonnie did their best to 'round up' Cat and bring her back to the safety of the farmhouse door. Annie had already taught them the verbal commands of 'lie down' and 'stay' and they were accustomed to walking on a leash made of rope. She and Cat had spent many patient hours in their training but it was difficult, she told herself wryly, to train a dog to herd sheep, without the sheep!

Still, they were obedient to those commands she had taught them and would obey Cat if the necessity arose. What necessity would that be? she wondered anxiously as she stood in the doorway, three pairs of eyes looking uneasily into hers. The day was fine. Already in the valley 'inlands' the first lambs were clinging to their mother's sides, their heads lost from view beneath her heavy fleece, their tails going mad behind them as they suckled, their plaintive bleat as mother moved to find her own dinner, filling the warming air. The first purple flowers of the self-heal plant, related to the deadnettle family, had appeared on the edge of the rough, tussocky grass at the back of the farmhouse. Blue and white bugle, the red of hedge-wound wort and the creamy pink of wood sage was revealed as the early morning mists rolled away. Annie had found purple mountain saxifrage among the damp rocks when she and Cat had taken the dogs up towards Dead Crags, moving through the heather which was almost ready to burgeon into life. Spring would be here soon. It was all about her, the life, the colour, the readiness to burst forth in its annual exhilaration; the land, the animals it supported, the sustenance which supported them, and the men who relied on and laboured over it all.

She stood for several long minutes, biting her lip, then, "Get your shawl and clogs and the dogs' leashes . . ." laughing as Cat's face lit up and her eyes blazed in joy. For five minutes it was bedlam, her own face, still only that of a girl, as merry and excited as her child's, the dogs barking and whirling about, knowing of course, that great things were about to happen.

She took the lake road for though it was longer than going up and over the top of Skiddaw Forest, dropping down by Mallen Dodd and into Keswick, it was flat and easy walking for Cat. They took a short cut through the inbye fields at the front of Browhead, clambering from one field to the next over drystone walls and skirting others which were hedged with hawthorne. In a few weeks the hedges would be in blossom, a white fragrant border about each lush stretch of green, but as yet they were straggly and unkempt, still waiting for their own brief moment of glory. Annie and Cat, as they stepped out, were flanking the lower slopes of Ullock Pike, Longside and Dodd with the breathtaking splendour of Skiddaw rising up on their left and the still, gentle beauty of Lake Bassenthwaite falling away to their right. The sky was high, blue, empty, innocent and though Annie and indeed anyone born in these parts well knew it could change ferociously within an hour, today its loveliness cast a magic spell of peace and anticipation on the woman and child. The young dogs were still unleashed, ready to run wild should they be allowed, for the smell of sheep was in the air. Their nostrils contained a memory inherited from countless generations of their forbears and they were eager to be away to investigate it. Annie called them to her, looping the rope about their necks, holding them firmly to her right side since the last thing she wanted was to send Bert Garnett's flock of Herdwicks galloping mindlessly about the fields with her two enthusiastic dogs at their heels.

A man knelt by a drystone wall painstakingly fitting exactly the right size of stone, first one then another, trying each piece until he had found what was needed in the repairing of the wall. He stacked them carefully on edge, laying them at the same angle, snug and neat, with nothing to hold them in place, or together, but his own skill. The 'Cap' stones lay in vertical symmetry along the top and he had left a 'hogg-hole' about two feet square at its base to allow yearling sheep to pass through from one field to the next. The hole, when no longer needed would have a slab of stone rolled across it.

He looked up as Annie and Cat approached, ready to nod briefly which was all anyone would get from him even his closest friend, but when he saw who it was his face darkened and he resumed his task without a greeting.

"A lovely day," Annie called, undiminished by his hostility, stepping out along the turnpike road which they had now reached, passing St Bridget's Church by the lake, moving towards the close-knit greenery of Dodd Wood where the ravens were nesting and telling the whole world about it with harsh voices. In a field contained in the narrow strip of fertile land alongside the lake several men were sowing corn seed and in another others were putting in a crop of 'early' potatoes. Wherever there was a farm, sheep, dairy, arable or mixed, the annual task of beginning the year was swinging into its enduring cycle and for a moment or two Annie felt her step falter on the hard, stony path she had set herself. There was so much to do before she even began to think of farming, of actually planting her crops – apart from the pitiful few she had so far managed – of building her flock of sheep and other livestock, pigs and poultry, she intended to have. It was so overwhelmingly daunting in that savage black moment she almost turned back to Browhead where she would gather their few belongings together and use her pitiful savings for a railway ticket to Lancaster.

'Sell it,' she would say to the lawyer, 'and good riddance' but the black moment passed as quickly as it had come. Her natural resilience gathered inside her with a surge which carried her forward excitedly. Glory be, she had been back no more than four months and here she was ready to give it all up. She had managed to stay alive in that time, thanks to Reed Macauley, the honest part of her mind whispered, but she resolutely turned away from it. She had not touched one penny of the wages she had earned at The Bull. They, she and Cat, had lived through the worst of the winter. They had a few vegetables to look forward to and the good part, the best part, was yet to come. She had a friend in Sally, she had her child and a warm place to lay their heads at night. She had a beginning and she meant to cling to it, to add to it, to shape it into a bright and wonderful thing.

She began to sing as she stepped out and Cat joined in. "Come all of you cockers far and near . . ."

The sun burnished the two copper heads to a vivid, startling warmth and two pairs of golden, transparent eyes gleamed in exact replica of one another, their joy lovely to behold. Hands clasped, the woman's long stride adjusted to the child's, and beside them the young dogs padded silently, watchfully, for they did not know this part of the world and their two 'sheep' needed careful guarding.

It was just gone noon when they reached Keswick. It was market day and crowds swarmed along the length of Market Place. There were stalls laden with squares of exquisitely patterned butter, wrapped in muslin and straw, cheeses, eggs, trussed chickens, the produce of industrious farmwives whose only reward for their labours, in and out of the farmhouse, was their 'butter money', if they were allowed to keep it by their thrifty husbands. There were skinned rabbits, gingerbread and ginger ale, a stall where baked potatoes were pulled, black and smoking, from the hot coals. There were pedlars, 'scotchmen' they were called though they did not hail from over the border, calling out to passers-by to inspect their printed calico and cotton cloth, their needles, their sewing thread and bootlaces with which they tramped the pack routes, going from farmhouse to farmhouse, from village to village.

The crowds milled about them, moving on up the street between the stalls, some stopping to tap their feet and

clap their hands to the rhythmic sound of the organ grinder
and to smile at the antics of his grinning monkey. A cheerful racket which, after the peace and quiet of Browhead
and the surrounding fells, brought excited roses to the
cheeks of Annie and her daughter. They moved along with
the crowds, the dogs keeping close to Annie's skirt, their
eyes darting in some unease in the thicket of moving trousered legs and full swishing skirts of the country folk. Their
noses wrinkled in an effort to identify the mass of smells
which surrounded them and their confusion showed in the
droop of their ears and tails.

She got work in the first inn she tried. Leaving Cat to
one side of the busy, low doorway through which dozens
of men continually moved, the dogs tied to an iron ring in
the wall beside her, meant for the tethering of horses,
Annie walked purposefully across the bar-parlour and
spoke directly to the man she recognised at once as the
landlord.

"I'm looking for work," she said, doing her best to smile
her pert, barmaid's smile.

As in every room she was to enter, whatever its station
in life, conversation dwindled and died to a murmur, the
only men still conversing in normal tones those who had
not yet seen her. She held her head high though her heart
pounded against her ribs. Despite her spirited appearance
she was always apprehensive when confronted by a wall
of male faces, for on every one was that unconscious
predatory look of speculation she knew so well.

"Oh aye, an' what can tha' do?" he asked, looking
about him at the sea of interested faces and winking
suggestively.

"Whatever you like, sir, in your bar, that is."

The crowd were hanging on to every word and this last
caused a great deal of nudging and guffawing but she did
not look round. Her expression was steady, neither one
thing nor the other, neither cringing nor bold and the
landlord relented. This was no raucous pot-house full of
navvies and fist-fighters and where round the back on a
moonless night an illegal cock-fight might be held, which

was why she had chosen it. It was full of men, true. Decent
working men, farmers and farm hands, scotch pedlars and
such come to market and having a pint of ale whilst they
settled a deal, respectable for the most part, but willing,
if it could be found, or offered, to have a 'bit of sport' at
the expense of a woman who was no better than she should
be, a judgement they made on her looks and the job she
was seeking.

"You look busy, sir. It seems to me you could do with
a bit of help," she said hopefully.

"Does it indeed?" but it was true since the girl he
employed already was gathering empty pots and filling
them again with the speed and violence which verged on
the hysterical. Another woman brought a tray of steaming
meat pies through a door behind the bar which evidently
led from the kitchen, her face red and sweated, her greasy
hair hanging limply from beneath her white frilled cap. The
pies were gone in a minute and muttering that she'd fetch
another lot she clattered back from where she had come.

With a last desperate image of Cat who stood outside
the door of the inn, Annie smiled.

"Tell you what," she said saucily. "I'll give you a hand
now if you like. Just for an hour, no wages except one of
those pies . . ." which would do for Cat's dinner. ". . . and
see what you think. If I don't suit I'll try elsewhere. If I
do and we can agree a wage I'll start tomorrow night." It
had to be evening employment since, with any luck, she
would be too busy working her farm during the day.

Somewhat taken aback, not sure how his customers,
who mostly spoke in the Cumberland dialect of these parts,
would shape with the way she talked, the landlord hesitated but what had he got to lose? Only one of Aggie
Holme's succulent meat pies. And he was run off his feet,
as anyone could see.

She smiled and something in him lurched, astonishingly,
since in his trade he considered he'd seen everything,
none of it moving him to more than mild interest. Her
richly burnished hair, which she had deliberately left loose,
hung below her waist in a mass of tangled curls, tipping

her head to an angle which could only be called haughty.
Her pale golden eyes, the brown in them less noticeable
in the dim light, narrowed provocatively until the long dark
lashes which surrounded them almost meshed together.
Her skin, as rich as the cream which floated at the top of
the milk, glowed, and her mouth, too wide and full for
classical beauty, nevertheless reminded him of the strawberries which had grown in his mother's garden when he
was a boy. She was startlingly lovely and there was a
gaiety about her which he knew his male customers would
like. He was not a man clever with words, or indeed with
expressing emotion but by God, this one was . . . bugger
him . . . the only word he could think of was . . . *unusual*.

She worked her hour, tirelessly, cheerfully, fending off
with laughing good humour the hands which reached for
her, the knowing smiles, the winks, the invitations and at
the end of it, having agreed on fourpence an hour, he told
her she was to start at six the following evening.

She moved on light feet to the door of the inn, waving
and smiling at those men who had promised her they would
be there the next evening, the tips they had given her
amounting to threepence three farthings, jingling in her
pocket. Added to what she had brought with her she meant
to buy some raw wool from one of the stalls and begin the
process of spinning and weaving, ready to knit the stockings she and Cat would need, and to fashion the hodden-
grey cloth to replace their sadly lacking wardrobe.

Her daughter was exactly where she had been left and,
resting for no more than five minutes whilst Cat shared
her pie with Blackie and Bonnie, Annie took her hand and
set off along Market Place and towards the road which led
out of Keswick.

They had five miles to walk and already the afternoon
was beginning to darken. The sun had gone and the
dreaded 'messenger clouds' had begun to gather above
the rise of Black Combe, foretelling the arrival of rain very
soon and they would not be home for at least three hours.
She knew she would have to carry her daughter before
long for the little girl had already walked five miles and

had stood or strolled about the market stalls for most of the afternoon. She was visibly tired though she stepped out bravely in her ill-fitting clogs. She was growing rapidly and before the month was out must have some new ones, was Annie's worried thought.

The sound of horses' hooves on the road behind them was faint at first, growing louder as it gained on them. A wheel squeaked as though in need of a drop of oil and a man's voice 'giddupped' a couple of times to the animal. Annie stood to one side, drawing Cat and the dogs to her for the road was narrow, letting the farm cart pass her but as it drew level the man sitting hunched on the plank of wood which served as a seat, pulled at the reins, changing his 'giddups' to 'whoas'.

It was Bert Garnett. He glanced about him in the gathering gloom as though to make sure there was no one to see him, then turned to look down at her. She could see the whites of his eyes in his weatherbeaten face but no more since the light was going fast. Already the trees in Dodd Wood had run together into an almost solid impermeability, no more than a dark mass against the sky which would soon be of the same density. The height of Skiddaw Forest shaped itself menacingly above the trees and Bert Garnett fastened his eyes on the glorious, forbidden wonder of Annie Abbott. He liked what he saw. He licked his lips.

"I'll give thi' a lift if tha' like, Annie. 'Op up, an' t' nipper. Stick them dogs in t'back."

She could not have been more surprised if the Prince Consort himself had invited her to share his carriage but quickly, before he could change his mind, she 'hopped up', lifting Cat up beside her and dragging the two reluctant dogs by their ropes until they lay in the back of the cart.

"Thanks Bert," she said gratefully, wondering if Sally had mistaken her husband's antipathy towards 'fallen women' though her woman's instinct which had been fine-honed during the last four years, did not believe it.

"'Tis nowt, Annie, only neighbourly," he said, running his smile over her, a smile she knew well, a smile she had

seen on many men's faces and though he made no move
towards her – well, he wouldn't, would he, not with Cat
on her knee and the two young dogs in the back – she
was quite sure that, had it been broad daylight, Bert
Garnett would not have given her the time of day and
she was even more certain that she had just come up
against another of those obstacles she had mentioned to
this man's wife only the other day.

10

The Merle Collie ran silently at the heels of the black mare, so close it seemed in imminent danger of being struck on its nose as the lethal iron-shod hooves lifted in the gallop. The path on which they travelled was stony and well defined, snaking between the beck on one side and the growing bracken and heathery upland on the other. The horse's coat rippled like black satin across its muscled flanks and straining neck, the sunlight giving it a gloss even the hard work of its groom could not improve on and the two animals, each well bred, moved with that special grace only the thoroughbred can achieve.

The man on the mare's back was of the same breed, sitting so easily and naturally in his saddle he might have been part of the animal, his head high, his back straight and supple, his strong horseman's legs which gripped the mare's side well muscled in the thigh. He was soberly dressed in a dark grey riding coat and breeches. He wore a tall black beaver hat. At his throat was a snowy white cravat, beautifully laundered and impeccably knotted, and in its folds glittered a gold and diamond pin. It seemed to say that though he was a man dressed for the work at hand, whatever that might be in his well-cut, beautifully tailored coat and trousers, he was also a man of wealth and style.

The sound of the horse's hooves on the steep and stony path was barely discernible, obliterated by the roar of the magnificent waterfalls which pounded down the precipitous wooded ravine at the base of the Bakestall plateau from where the mare had just come. Dash Beck, issuing from the vast waste of Skiddaw Forest, leaped exultantly over the lip of the escarpment towards the gentler pastures below, plunging in a series of falls to a mighty torrent of roaring thrashing waters. Whitewater Dash, it was called. A great inferno whose thunder could be heard many miles away down the valley and whose spray shimmered like the diamond at Reed Macauley's neck in a myriad sparkling droplets over horse, rider and dog.

The track became more pronounced as the silent trio dropped down towards the valley, still desolate and lonely but showing signs of the hand of man in the appearance of a well-tended drystone wall running away from the beck and meandering through the bracken until it began to climb up the rolling slope of the opposite fell. There was a farmhouse, small and grey, surrounded by a grove of larches, with outbuildings and a yard in which pecked dozens of hens and a showy cock. A couple of dogs barked lustily on the end of chains and a man looked up from some harness he was tinkering with, nodding dourly in Reed Macauley's direction. A cart stood by the gate which led out of the yard and a small boy sat on the plank which served as a seat, flapping imaginary reins and 'gidduping' to an imaginary horse. Fresh white washing strained at the washing line to the side of the house and grey smoke was wisped in torn shreds from the circular chimney. A well-built Lakeland farm, Upfell Farm, belonging to the Mounseys and since he had married Sally Mounsey, Bert Garnett. It was as old as the fells in which it was set, or so it seemed, with its thick walls and heavy roof, its interior like so many Lakeland farms crammed with crooked doors and tilted floors and odd little staircases up and down. There were hundreds of them scattered in sheltered crannies against the fells of Cumberland, the one to which Reed Macauley was drawn but which he had no intention of visiting, none at all, even though he happened to be passing, a mile or so away towards Gillthrop. He could not get her out of his mind – that was his trouble. Three months now since he had last seen her nearly up to her waist in the snow and still, at some part of the day, perhaps for only a flashing second, she came to haunt him. She was always laughing. Though she might be imperious, her head held in that haughty, stiff-necked way she had, her grandness would dissolve into warm and lovely laughter, into the glowing love which she showed her child. Eyes long and brown and clear would narrow and melt with her emotion, her mouth wide and smiling over her perfect teeth, all brilliance and warmth, an enchantment which brought him time and again down the track alongside Dash Beck and on to the lower slopes of Great Cockup where her farm lay.

Each time he went there he would turn about impatiently and gallop off home furious with himself and his own weakness for were not women all the same? This one was no different to any of the pretty and willing females with whom he was acquainted and who were available to any man of wealth. But still he could not rid himself of her. He had been across to the inlands of his farm, the big grassy slopes which were surrounded by drystone walls and where his ewes had been brought to lamb. In winter Reed and all the other sheep farmers brought their flocks down to these safe pastures where if the weather was exceptionally bad – and when was it not, in winter? – they could be given hay to augment their feeding.

He had three shepherds who knew every inch of the terrain but still he felt the need to keep an eye on his flock. It was lambing time – April – and the ewes had been gathered for easier shepherding. The ewes were mated and the lambs of Lakeland were born later in the year than their southern cousins for up in the north where the weather was fickle and menacing, even up to the month of May, new-born lambs would be hard put to survive the fierce late blizzards which were a feature of the district. It had been known for snowstorms to linger well into May and when they were done with there was the hazard of foxes which raided among the newly dropped lambs, of ravens who would tear out their eyes and of eagles who would carry off the newly born in their strong talons. It needed constant vigilance not only on the part of his shepherds, but their sheepdogs who guarded his flocks, one of which ran at his heels today.

Bess was that most unusual of sheepdogs known as a 'Merle'. Most Collies have dark brown eyes but hers were a bright and vivid blue and it had been remarked sourly more than once among his neighbours, many of whom envied him his wealth and position that it was only to be expected that a 'fancy dan' such as he would have a dog whose eyes matched his own. Not for him the usual black and white of the Border Collie but he must have something different and Bess's body colour, though she had the white Collie marking on her face, chest, feet and also her tail tip, was of broken black and grey, giving the impression of torn patches of cloth. The two pups he had given to Annie Abbott were both 'Merles' since Bess was their mother.

He heard her voice as he drew his horse to a walk beside the singing beck and in the most alarming way he felt his heart move lurchingly in his chest. The horse he rode and the dog at his heels both pricked their ears.

"Blackie, Bonnie, come," the voice called, and as he and his animals moved over the small rise which separated the Mounsey farm from hers he saw her. Again his heart bounded and though no blame could be attached to her since she had done nothing to cause it – for could she help her own loveliness? – he felt the angry impatience rise in him. She was dressed in her usual plain hodden-grey skirt, which had once belonged to Lizzie Abbott, though he was not aware of it. Lizzie had been shorter than Annie and the hem of the skirt came barely below her calf, revealing the fragile slenderness of her white ankles and her feet which were pushed into her clogs. The bodice was low at the neck and almost sleeveless and her skin was rich and creamy, as lustrous as a pearl where the sunlight touched it. Her hair had been plaited at the back of her head, one long plait as thick as his own forearm, crisp and glowing a rich copper, swinging down her back to her buttocks where it curled vigorously at its end. She looked glorious, the plainness of her attire, the drabness even, revealing her beauty more than had she worn silk and satin and costly jewels. She lifted her hand to shade her eyes as she watched her dogs progress and her breasts rose in proud fullness, the nipples hard and pointed beneath the thin material of her bodice.

His breath caught in his throat and he felt his manhood stir enquiringly, tight and uncomfortable against his saddle. Jesus Christ . . . Oh, Jesus Christ, but she was the most . . . there was really no word . . . none.

The child was sitting on the wall at the front of the farmhouse, her own bright copper hair catching and reflecting the April sunshine, a halo of burnished curls springing about her small head which turned to look in his direction as he approached.

He had meant – or so he told himself – to ride on by the farmhouse, keeping to the track which ran behind it, but some wayward impulse, some madness – and he knew it was that – had him draw on the reins, bringing his mare to a halt. The collie who ran behind him stopped when he did, standing when he did, though her eyes were bright and watchful and her ears swivelled to listen to the commands the woman gave. They were familiar though of course the dog knew they were not meant for her.

Reed did not get down. He sat and waited for Annie to look in his direction, lounging indolently in his saddle, not at all concerned whether she did or not, his careless posture implied, though in his eyes, should anyone have cared to look, was a prick of light and a narrowed tension which belied his careless demeanour. Both mare and dog waited for a command and when none came the dog lay down, her head on her paws, the very picture of relaxed indifference though her eyes, which swivelled from side to side, gave the lie to her appearance.

Annie Abbott took as much notice of him as she would a passing sheep – less, for if he had been a sheep, she might have wondered whom he belonged to, he thought angrily. She stood, her hands on her hips now, her feet apart, watching the two young dogs as they flew up the field towards her. She let them get within ten yards of her then her voice, crisp and commanding, told them to "Lie down", which they both did at once. One of them began to creep on its belly, its eyes on her, its tail moving rapidly on the tufty grass, loving the 'game' but longing to run to her and greet her with its joyous affection but her hand stayed him and her stern eye kept him there until she spoke the words "Come here" when they both leaped forward. It took a moment or two of patient handling since they were young, no more than puppies, but she had them sitting, one on either side of her, their bright faces turned up to hers, their bright eyes asking "What next?"

"Go on then," she said, reaching to pat each fine head, "Go to Cat," and the pair of them began the frolicking to which dogs of their age are prone, leaping up at the child on the wall. Cat jumped down to them, fending off their loving tongues and exuberant kisses. Laughing and beseeching them to "Get down, Blackie, get down, Bonnie," she began to run down the field, the two dogs at her heels.

The man and woman did not speak. The tension between them was immediate and both of them were aware of it. It was ridiculous, of course, since they were nothing to each other, each was thinking, merely neighbours, and what was in that to cause this tendency to be short of breath, the reluctance to meet the other's eye, to shift about in the saddle, to shuffle on the tufty grass, as she was doing. It was in both their minds confused, angry, fearful even, and when their eyes met the impact of it was alarming.

He was already irritated by the way his heart had quickened when he heard her voice, now his alarm, since it was alarming to be so affected by a woman, when none before had done no more than stir his loins, made him sharp, cruel even.

"Those dogs are meant for sheep, not for performing tricks in a field." They were the only words he could think of to cover his own breathless reaction to her presence.

"Is that so, Reed Macauley? Well show me some sheep

and I'll set about training the dogs to them. If not, then take them back with you since I know they came from you and if there are limits to be put on what I do with them they're no good to me."

"I did not say they came from me. I know nothing of them but they were obviously bred to be sheepdogs and to have them playing the fool . . ."

"If you did not leave them tied to my door then who did, tell me that? That bitch you have there is very rare and those two are the same colourings. There can't be many Merles in this area."

"I know nothing of that. I am only remarking that it is a complete waste of two good dogs to have them performing tricks and playing with the child as they are doing."

The shrieks of laughter and the excited barking which came from the bottom of the field grew merrier, though the child and the dogs were hidden from view. The grasses were growing tall, studded with bright daisies and cowslips, and beneath the hawthorn tree which stood to the side of the farmhouse wild daffodils swayed and nodded in the light breeze. There was a smell in the air of growing things, of newness and brightness and hope, and of their own volition the eyes of the man and woman met and clung, truth in them, though not acceptance. Her anger grew for it was fed by her fear. Her lip curled, lifting over her teeth as though she would like nothing better than to sink them into some part of him which would hurt, or better yet, maim him.

"Whether they came from you or not, and I can think of no one else in this . . . this God-forsaken place who would part with them, especially to me, they are *mine* now and I shall do with them as I please."

They were not of course, arguing over his dogs but something much deeper and more meaningful.

"That is your privilege, Miss Abbott, naturally since as you say, they are nothing to do with me . . ."

"Then why are you criticising my handling of them? When I have my flock I shall train them properly, of course."

"You are expecting it in the near future, then?"

"What?"

"Your flock."

"Well . . . no, but . . . when I have the money together
I mean to . . ."

"The money you earn at the Packhorse, you mean."
There was a sneer in his voice though it was put there
not by his contempt but by something over which he had
no control.

She narrowed her eyes menacingly. Her hands clenched
into fists and she took a step towards him. He was still
mounted and the wall divided them but she looked ready
to leap it and tear at his face.

"It is money honestly earned. I do no more than serve
ale and if you are implying that . . . that . . . otherwise
. . . then you can get off my land and take not only yourself
but those two dogs as well. I want nothing from you, Reed
Macauley, nothing, neither your hampers nor your . . .
your . . . nothing. Sweet Christ, has nobody in these parts
a scrap of decency or humanity in them that they must
speak to me, treat me, as though I was dirt beneath their
feet, you included, with your filthy mouth? I am doing my
best to earn an honest shilling, a start, honestly gained,
to the farm my father left me. That's all. I don't ask for
their, or your friendship, just the right to get on with my
life uninterrupted. Do you think I want to work at the
Packhorse where every man in the place thinks he may
put his hands on me whenever he has the fancy and that
I should not object? Do you think I like to leave my child
alone at night with no one to guard her but two half-grown
dogs? Do you think I like to walk all those miles in the
dark when, as you have pointed out yourself, there are
any number of men hanging about ready to do me damage?
This world was not made for lone women, did you know
that? Of course you didn't, especially one who is as . . .
as evil as me . . ."

"No . . . not that . . ."

His voice was soft, gentle. The expression on his face
was the same and when he dismounted and, vaulting the

wall, moved to stand directly before her, she was so astounded her voice tapered away to silence.

He smiled. "I did not mean to . . . really . . . you are such a firebrand and I am . . . I chose my words unwisely. Dear God, no man could get near you to do you a mischief, Annie Abbott, not with that . . . temper of yours. I meant no offence . . ."

"Yes, you did. You insinuated that I was . . . that men were paying me to . . ." She backed away from him and in her eyes was the dreadful awareness, the sweet knowledge, the glowing warmth of what, as yet, both of them violently denied. It was mirrored in his eyes as he tried to take her hand. He meant her no harm. The gesture was involuntary. A reaching out of his flesh which longed to touch hers but she recoiled from it since she wanted it as much as he did.

"Don't . . . don't, Reed . . ."

"I mean you no harm . . . let me . . ."

"What?" Her voice was suspicious.

"Help you . . ." He shrugged his shoulders, his anger returning, the surprising, terrifying gentleness slipping away for she was looking at him as though he was the same as those men in the snug at the Packhorse. As though he would, if he could, be delighted to lay covetous hands on Annie Abbott, and of course, she was right. Her nearness, the warmth of her breath as it swept his face, the smell of lavender about her, the faint suggestion of sweat on her upper lip, her mouth, parted, sweet, moist, rosy, her breasts rising and falling with emotion, and her eyes, narrowing and darkening in a way he was so familiar with since he had made love to many women and knew the signs of need.

"How can you help me?" she asked, the words meaning nothing, just an answer, vague and automatically given, since neither was aware of anything but the physical beauty of the other, the wave of sensuality in her which was answered in him, the female and male desire which was so very apparent and which was sweeping them both on a course they ardently longed to be on. They wanted to fight it, Annie more than Reed, for had she not more to lose, but his eyes, the most vivid and compelling blue she had ever seen, between their thick black lashes mesmerised her. His lips had parted, softening ready for that first kiss and his hand was half-way to the nape of her neck. She had raised her face, flushed now, eager, her woman's body unwinding joyously its core of desire, ready even before he touched her, for his, since she was no untried girl. It was four years since she had lain with a man, the father of her child, but her body, dormant since then, concerned only with food and shelter for herself and Cat, had not forgotten.

"Hello . . . o . . . o . . ." A man's voice shouted and at once the loveliness was shattered, breaking into a thousand unrepairable pieces, gone, it seemed, and never to be repeated, for she was aware of the danger now, prepared, defended.

She whirled about, her plait flying out and across her shoulder coming to rest on her heaving breast. Within seconds she had put three yards between herself and Reed Macauley and when Bert Garnett's face appeared over the wall there was nothing left of that fragile tender beginning of what might have been between them.

"Oh, Bert, there you are." Her voice and the welcome in it was warmer than it would normally have been for, to tell the truth, Bert Garnett's unannounced and furtive visits to Browhead had become a nuisance to her during the two months since he had given her a lift back from Keswick. But his arrival at that precise moment had saved her from what she realised – now – would have been disaster. She had been ready to fall into Reed Macauley's arms and God alone knew where that would have led. Her bed, she supposed, for she had been fast in an intoxication which had taken her senses, her sense held in some spell he had cast over her, ready to move as she had vowed she never would again, into his, or indeed into any man's arms. Ready to shed her caution and sound common sense, along with her clothing, whilst her body romped, what other word could she use since what else would he want from her, with Reed Macauley's. Thank God, *thank God* for Bert Garnett, her mind was babbling as she scrambled over the wall, revealing even more of her long white legs to which the eyes of both men were drawn.

Reed was, for just a moment, still floundering in the delightful ardour into which Annie's response and sweetness had thrust him. His body was already demanding its masculine victory, glowing with that special male triumph which knows that it is about to conquer and possess. She had been ready, delightfully so, her eyes glazing, her mouth full and swollen and suddenly . . . suddenly it was gone. *She* was gone and looking over the wall was the considerably startled face of . . . what the bloody hell was his name? . . . of the man who owned the next farm up the dale and who obviously knew Annie Abbott well enough to be called by his Christian name. Married, too, Reed was well aware, to the plump daughter of the man who had owned it before he died.

He could feel the blood pump violently in his veins, grabbing at his heart and making it pound in his chest, grabbing at his temples in which a pulse began a rapid tattoo. He saw the flash of her legs . . . Dear Christ . . . and the narrowed speculative prick of male interest in the other man's eyes and for just a second, no more than a fraction of time, he knew he would kill him. Take him by the throat and choke the life out of him, slowly, of course, so that he would suffer, or perhaps he'd beat him with his fists, sinking his hard flesh into the man's stupid face, see the blood spurt and hear the satisfying sound of bone breaking and flesh splitting.

Bert was shifty-eyed and awkward since he had thought Annie to be alone but he had no choice but to say, as casually as he could the words he had come to say.

"I come to tell thi' I'm off to Keswick in t'mornin' an' if tha' wants a ride I'll pick thi' up at bottom."

"That's very kind of you, Bert. I would appreciate it as I shall have Cat with me and it's a long walk. Mr Holme has asked me to work from opening time seeing as it's

Whit Monday. The Hiring Fair will bring in a lot of custom and he will need every pair of hands he can get. He says I can take Cat with me as long as she stays quietly in the kitchen, which of course she will. And I wanted to take in some of my besoms and swill baskets, that's if you have room in the cart. A fortnight ago I spoke to a woman who has a stall there and she said she'd sell them for me, for a small commission, naturally, and I have knitted two dozen pairs of socks from the wool I purchased two months ago and have made arrangements with another stallholder to sell those for me as well. I was wondering how on earth I was to get them all to the market so your offer is a godsend."

She directed a smile so falsely brilliant at Bert Garnett his mouth flew open. He did not see the falseness, only the wide mouth, the perfect teeth, the glittering eyes, the breathless – he did not use the word feverish – way she spoke. He saw Mr Macauley as well, but not being a man of perception or indeed of any deep thought, he observed nothing strange in the wealthy farmer's presence in Annie Abbott's field. Perhaps he wanted to buy her farm since eventually she would have to sell, everyone knew that and he only wished he himself had the ready cash to make her an offer right now. It was a damn good farm lying neat as you please right next to his. A bit neglected but that could soon be put right. Why Reed Macauley should want it was a mystery since he had acres and to spare of his own but that was not Bert Garnett's concern. An insensitive man who saw nothing but what his own eyes looked at, and at the moment that was Annie Abbott's flashing white ankles and glowing brown eyes. A man shrewd and thrifty, his plain craggy features which were framed by a wisping beard, revealing these characteristics. He was known to be level headed in his working life but there were not many men whose clear sight would not be clouded by the spirited loveliness and warmth of Annie Abbott.

Reed Macauley vaulted the wall and reached blindly for the reins of his mare who was cropping placidly at the sweet new grass by Annie's wall. His dog stood up, moving her plumed tail in greeting, then sensing something not quite right in her master, pushed her cold nose into his hand. He touched her head gently and murmured to her and as though the dog had calmed something ferocious in him, he turned to Annie. His eyes were a cold, pale and distant blue and his mouth was hard, cruel.

"I will bid you good day then, Miss Abbott," he said, the words sounding more like an insult than a farewell. "I had not realised you had made such good . . . friends . . . hereabouts. But I wish you well of them." The last word a sneer which, though it meant nothing to Bert Garnett, was clearly a slur on Annie Abbott. She flushed, then turned to Bert, again giving him her glorious smile and, as she had meant it to, bringing bile to Reed Macauley's mouth.

"Oh indeed, Mr Macauley. Bert has been most helpful to me since we renewed our acquaintance a month or two back. We knew one another as children. His wife and I are old friends and our families were . . . were close."

Bert preened and moved nearer to Annie, his shoulder almost touching hers and Reed's hand jerked at the reins of his mount. The mare moved her head fretfully, not accustomed to rough handling, and he turned at once to soothe her and in that moment as he looked away, Annie Abbott's love for him, since what else could it be, she asked herself despairingly, was in her eyes and on her face for anyone, even Bert Garnett to see. He did not see it.

His grace and vigour and style were very evident as Reed mounted his mare. He was a gentleman from good sound stock, going back to the days before the reign of James I, when his forebears had supplied military service and equipment to their King; a man of wealth and position, sitting easily in the saddle, handsome, oh yes he was that, for she loved him now, and unconcerned with lesser men like Bert Garnett and women like herself. The lounging charm he showed suddenly, since what were they to him, his manner said, was light and whimsical and beneath the polish his education had given him whatever he might be feeling was well hidden. *He* was in control, of himself and of the situation and he tipped his hat quite genially to them both.

"I'm glad to hear it, Miss Abbott. And does your wife approve of your . . . er . . . friendship with *her* friend, Mr Garnett?" turning his controlled smile at Bert. "It is always handy to have one's wife's . . . permission, is it not?"

Turning his mare, calling to Bess, though she did not need it, he moved off up the dale in the direction of Long Beck five miles away. Bert Garnett, not at all sure what Reed Macauley had meant, was quite put out by Annie's sudden silence and lack of interest. He had pictured them sitting together on the wall, shoulder to shoulder, him with a tankard of the ale she had brewed recently, in his hand. They would chat and laugh and perhaps, if he could sweet-talk her, or even, being a masculine, firm sort of a chap, persuade her to a cuddle, perhaps a kiss or two and a stroke of her soft breasts which, it seemed to him, she flaunted on his behalf. Nice and polite she'd been to him when, on the quiet, of course, he'd called at her farm on some pretext or other, and always glad of a lift when he went to market. He was very discreet, or at least he had been until today, only slipping down the track to her back door when his wife and his mother and sister-in-law were busy elsewhere, but it seemed to him Annie gave him no reason to believe he was anything but welcome. Lonely she'd be, and glad of a chat with a friendly chap like himself. And she'd be short of summat else, he'd be bound, a lusty woman like her, and him only too glad to supply it. It would give him a great deal of pleasure to dip his hand down the front of her bodice and hold those lovely dumplings cupped in his hand whilst his fingers tweaked her nipples into an even more pointed firmness than they already were. She might even allow him to run his hand up those white legs, along the satin smoothness of her thighs to the joining where the damp, dark, sweet-smelling bush of her womanhood lay and when . . .

His day-dream was cruelly shattered when, with a voice as flat and cool as the lake on a still winter's day, Annie moved imperiously across the bit of garden at the front of the house and went inside. Holding the door she turned for a moment.

"I'll see you tomorrow, Bert," then closed it in his face.

11

The twice-yearly Hiring Fairs held at Whitsuntide and
Martinmas were eagerly looked forward to by the folk of
Lakeland, for they were regarded as a holiday and a respite
from the drudgery of the labours they performed on their
farms all the year round. There was no deliverance for
them on any other day of the week since even Sunday
brought the same round of chores which must be done,
but on these two occasions everyone who could be spared
had their day out. There were fairs at Cockermouth,
Kendal, Penrith, Ulverston, Egremont, Appleby and
Ravenglass but no matter where they were held, it was
an excuse for revelries. There was even a regatta on Lake
Windermere in which schooners took part in sailing events
and there were rowing matches, running, leaping and
wrestling matches and, as the poster advertised, a variety
of other amusements finishing with a ball at the Salutation
Inn at Ambleside.

But the serious business of hiring servants and farm
hands, those who were not 'stopping on' for another six
months and therefore had gathered to find a new place,
must first be got through. A straw stuck in a hat or from
the corner of the mouth indicated that a labourer was for
hire and when the deal was struck between master and
man, a handshake was all that was needed to seal the
bargain. The hired man or woman received a shilling as
'arles', or earnest money, as a token of their hiring. A
man could get between £8 and £10 for his six months with
board and lodgings included, and a woman might expect
between £6 and £7. No references were asked for or
offered, master taking man, and vice versa, on looks alone.

Though Annie had been expecting the increased

excitement and burgeoning crowds of men and women, children, dogs, horses and all the paraphernalia of this lively day, the impact as the cart, with a truculent Bert Garnett at the reins, turned into Market Place, hit her like a blow. Yesterday still clung to her like drifting cobwebs which, no matter how she strived to dislodge them, held her fast, numbing her mind and blunting her senses so that she could hardly think. The worst thing she could ever imagine happening to her, had happened, and she was twined round with her love for Reed Macauley, and would she ever be free of it? Could she function in spite of it? The heaving sea of people crammed between the market stalls only brought her fresh misery for she had to get through today and this evening, smiling and cheerfully fobbing off the often crude jokes and repartee which her customers imagined she was more than willing to enjoy. Grit her teeth and smile, tactfully remove eager hands from the different parts of her body they remorselessly attached themselves to whilst the inner being that was Annie Abbott cringed, rebelling against this humiliation which she was forced to endure. Sometimes looking at the sly admiration and . . . yes, lust, she supposed it to be, in Bert Garnett's pale, washed out eyes, she was tempted to tell him to take himself and his 'helping hand' as he described it, to the devil. She knew what he wanted in repayment for the lifts to Keswick, the vague offers of future 'boon-ploughing' and perhaps other farming activities at which he hinted. Sally didn't know he had been a time or two to Browhead and Annie didn't tell her since one day Bert Garnett might indeed be of some aid to her. She couldn't afford to insult him but she dreaded the time, which was bound to come, when he would get up the courage to tell her what was on his lascivious mind.

"I'll wait for thi' by 't corner," he said shortly. He had scarcely noticed her silence, the pale, lethargic lack of her usually bright spirits. He was too concerned with his own needs and his own offended spirits, for was he not a man of some importance in the parish of Bassenthwaite and did he not deserve more respect than the curt dismissal he had received yesterday from this woman? Laughed and joked with him for two months she had, leading him on, as he saw it, and him helping her out whenever he could – without his wife knowing naturally, for he was not a complete fool – and she'd done no more than shut the bloody door in his face and what had Macauley been doing there, answer him that? Well, child or no child, giving Cat a surly glance, he'd have more than a cool dismissal from Annie Abbott this night.

The market place and all the streets leading off it were jammed from building to building with a wide variety of entertainments. There was wrestling, slack-wire balancing, performing bears and monkeys, sad and hopeless and frightened. There were freaks such as the pig-faced lady and the hairiest man anyone had ever seen, like a monkey himself he was, coming from Morocco wherever that was, and where, the open-mouthed folk of Cumberland decided, all men must be like him, poor sods. Travelling 'doctors' sold elixirs and cures guaranteed to arouse the liver of the most sluggish gentleman; tooth pullers who always placed their booths close to the 'oom-pah-pah' of the customary brass band, since it would not do for the public, those with aching teeth to be got rid of, to hear the cries of distress from those who went before them. There was even a bull-baiting going on further along the passage which ran to the back of The Packhorse, a terrible tearing and rending as the bull, tethered on a short rope to the wall was set upon by dogs. Spectators stood around in their dozens or perched on the roofs of buildings about the passage, while the dogs roved freely round and beneath the exhausted bull, biting and nipping where they could. It was illegal of course, but the local constable, promised a fine cut of the beef when the animal was slaughtered, looked the other way. After all, it was a well-known fact that baiting the bull improved the quality of the meat.

Those who were for hire stood in patient rows, men and women apart, and moving amongst them already, for the best and strongest went first, were the masters, stopping here and there to speak to one or the other.

Annie gave them no more than an indifferent glance before entering The Packhorse, Cat beside her. She put the child in a corner of the already overheated kitchen, kissed her and told her to be a good girl and to do exactly as Mrs Holme, the landlord's wife, told her, and tying her crisp white apron about her waist, prepared herself for her long twelve hours on her feet.

She got through it. She knew she would, of course, for no matter what the state of her heart, poor weak thing that it was, her back was strong and tireless. Somehow she parried the jokes and the teasing and the greedy hands. She smiled when they demanded it, pocketing their tips and telling herself that every farthing was putting her nearer to the end of all this, to the beginning of that good, hard-working free life she planned for her and Cat. She had enough already to buy several ewes at seven and sixpence each, and by October and tup time, she hoped to have the necessary cash to hire a ram of good quality to put to them and begin the birth of her flock. She and Cat were eating well. There was always plenty of left-overs from the kitchen of the inn. Their vegetables were doing well, and the herbs she had planted, and she had even managed, with a little bit of flattery and a great deal of the smiling and dimpling which men loved, to purchase a few hens and a cock cheap from a stallholder, which had happily taken to pecking round her yard and barn. She worked hard all day, digging and hoeing, tending to her tiny crop of oats and bigg, praying for good weather, weaving swill baskets and making birch besoms. Her coppice needed attention. She and Cat went up to the peat moss to dig for peat, dragging it laboriously downhill on the sledge to be stacked in the yard. They lived off the land, except for the milk which Sally surreptitiously left twice a week for her in a can hidden beneath a tilted piece of slate in the wall by her gate. The couple of pints not missed by her mother or her husband since it was Sally's job to milk the cows. Annie meant to have her own cow one day and with her spare milk, make butter and cheese to be sold at the market, but it was enough at the moment that she was hanging on, getting there by slow painstaking, back-breaking inches. It was all very fragile of course. Just let one tiny thing go wrong and the whole meshed process of her life would topple and fall. An illness, on her part, or Cat's, which would prevent her going to The Packhorse, an accident, her crops to fail, her vegetables to rot, too much rain, too little rain and she would be finished. She needed the gods to continue smiling on her for another six months, just until she had her ewes, her ram, her oats and barley in and safely put away in her mother's oak kist. Please God . . . Oh, please God . . .

The market place was deserted of all but the serious drunkards. There were vague shifting shadows against the walls which Annie knew were the whores who did good business when the inns closed. There was a shouted quarrel at the corner of the square and several men leaned drunkenly against one another as they watched in befuddled interest. She could see Bert's cart and his loose-limbed outline slumped on the seat and from somewhere to her right, where the men and women had stood waiting to be hired that morning – twelve hours ago and, God's teeth, her legs and back ached as though it was twenty-four – there was the sound of someone whimpering. Nothing to do with her, she told herself, hefting the sleeping form of Cat close against her shoulder. It was probably some prostitute who had performed her task and then been diddled by her customer, or a woman grieving the loss of her wages gone on gin, but the sound was haunting, that of someone in deep trouble, or fear.

Dear God, she didn't want to go and find out, really she didn't. She had enough with her own weariness and the need to get her child safe home in her bed and besides which she had nearly three bob jingling in her deep skirt pocket, the tips she had earned on top of her wages which she would get at the week's end. All she wanted was to fall into bed herself and sleep the clock round. She had slipped out for half an hour at supper-time, given permission to go by Mrs Holme, the landlady, who was always pleased with the way Annie Abbott worked, 'going

at it' as she liked things to be 'gone at', as she herself
went at them, which was like a demon. She worked hard,
did Mrs Holme, and she admired it in others and besides
being pert and pretty, which drew the customers, Annie
was good-natured, hard-working and conscientious.

"O'course, dearie, you slip out for a breath of fresh air
and tek littl'un wi' thi'," and Annie had gone to the stallholder who had sold all her besoms and swills and after
giving the woman her commission, had almost another
pound, eighteen shillings to be exact, to put beside the
tips and the rest of her small savings hidden in the tin box
under the sconce in the kitchen. She had not done too
well with the stockings since at this time of the year they
were not an item women wanted, besides which most
knitted their own, but she'd save them until autumn and
try again.

A good day, a very good day and the last thing she
wanted was to be distracted by some other woman's
troubles. Anyway, the noise had stopped now so she'd
best get back to Bert who, having seen her come from
the inn, was beginning to show signs of impatience as she
dilly-dallied by the doorway.

"Now stop that, yer daft little bugger," a man's voice
said hoarsely, followed by a thud, then nothing again.
Silence. A small sound of something moving just out of
range of the light which fell from the doorway of The
Packhorse, scuffling perhaps and a grunt or two but nothing more. For some reason though, the hairs on the back
of Annie's neck rose and a peculiar dread trickled down
her back. It was nothing, she told herself. And if it was,
it was nothing to do with her, but some primeval female
instinct would not allow her to turn away and walk towards
Bert who had now jumped down from his cart and was
beckoning to her with every sign of vexed irritability.

She turned away from him slowly, trying to pierce the
shadows at the side of the inn, but the darkness was complete. There was an enormous waterbutt put there by
some optimistic soul who had hoped, one presumed, to
collect rainwater and whether it was full or empty Annie

neither knew nor cared as she peeped round its wide girth.

She could see nothing at first, then, as her eyes became used to the deeper darkness there, she became aware of movement, a shifting and twitching which meant nothing to her at that moment. There was someone there, she could make that out. Huddled against the wall and in the corner where the butt touched it, a man and woman wrestling, deep in the throes of fornication, Annie thought disgustedly, the woman's skirt well up about her waist, the man's trousers well down below his knees. There began the most awful guttural panting and the man's white buttocks gleamed in the dark corner, obscene and graceless, but as Annie had already told herself, nothing to do with her. She supposed the whores who plied their trade in the grey areas about the town must ply it somewhere and here was as good a place as any since it was dark and afforded some privacy. But suddenly the words she had heard a moment before came back to her.

"Stop that . . ." a man's voice had said, and "yer daft little bugger . . ." which were not the words a customer says to the one who is supplying him with what he is paying for.

"What's going on here?" she said loudly, commandingly, speaking before she had time to think. It was as though someone else had spoken and not her at all, the words and the way they sounded, giving the impression that she had the whole of Keswick's police force at her back. "Stand up at once," she added, "and let me see the . . ."

"Bugger off," the man snarled over his shoulder and for just that moment as he turned his head, a child's face lifted in terror beneath him, white with deep black hollows where her eyes and mouth were, her hair flung this way and that in snarled tatters across it. She was trying to scream, doing her best to convey to Annie, who stood paralysed with shock, that this was none of her doing, but the man loomed over her again, his bestial greed so great and all consuming he was deaf and blind to anything else. His great back obliterated her again so that all Annie could see were two white legs, thin and splayed, emerging from beneath his great white buttocks, the feet twitching, writhing. One was bare, pathetic in its smallness.

Annie began to scream. At the top of her voice she began to scream and so did Cat for she had been woken from her deep child's sleep to her mother's terror. Annie took no notice. There was another child whose need for protection was greater than Cat's and the only way she could think of to stop what was going on in this brutish corner, was to make a great deal of noise about it. That, and to kick.

The first one aimed with all the force of her sturdy, clogged foot behind it caught him high in the middle of his thick white buttocks but the second, now that she had her aim set square landed low between his buttocks, so low her toe fell firmly on his dangling genitals and with a scream to match her own, he fell flat across the child beneath him.

"Get off her, get off her, you bastard, you low crawling bastard. Get off her or I'll do you so much damage you'll never want a woman again . . . get off her . . . you loathsome . . ."

It was several minutes before Bert could drag her away from the screaming man and several more before she could calm herself to face the weeping, bedraggled young creature who had been his victim and who cowered like some cornered animal, on her knees in the centre of the curious but sympathetic circle of men who had gathered to see what the commotion was about. Several had put out comforting hands to her for though they were men they were not all beasts, but she would not have it, or them, curling up into herself in crazed pain and terror.

Annie shoved Cat into Bert's reluctant arms and slowly, soothingly, letting her soft female voice be heard, she sank to her knees beside the girl.

"It's all right, my lovely . . ." as she would say to Cat when she was hurt. "It's all right now. You're safe now. It's all right. He's gone now. See, stand up with me. I've got you. Put your hand in mine and let me help you up. There. It's all right now, sweetheart. Safe . . . Safe . . .

You're safe with Annie . . ." and gradually, like some small, terrified, trapped young thing which, though it is freed, cannot get up the courage to run away, the girl stood up huddling against Annie, her arms creeping about Annie's waist, her face hidden, shamed and distraught against Annie's shoulder. She allowed her disarranged clothing to be smoothed down. To have her hair brushed back from her shocked white face, all the while clinging to the only safe, female, being in her tumbling universe.

"Where are you from, sweeting? Tell Annie. See, there's no one to hurt you now," for the would-be seducer had stumbled off whilst he had the chance.

"Let me take you to your home. Where do you live? What's your name? Come sweetheart, let me help you . . ." but the girl, deep in shock now, could not or would not answer.

"Well, tha'll have to leave her here, Annie," Bert said rashly since he was eager to be off to indulge in a bit of seduction of his own, and besides, it was gone eleven o'clock and he'd hung about long enough waiting on Annie Abbott. "She'll find her way home soon enough."

"Don't talk daft, Bert." Annie's voice was quite matter of fact. "I can't just leave her here."

"What else can thi' do wi' her, tell me that."

"Take her home with me."

"Nay . . ."

"Don't nay me, Bert Garnett. We don't know where she lives or even her name and until I can get her to talk to me we'll never find out. We can't hang about here waiting, so I'll take her with me, and if she wants to, she can come back with me tomorrow night."

"What if her . . ."

"Stop it, Bert. See, there's a bundle here, probably hers. Pick it up will you and put it in the cart. Cat darling, stop crying and hold mother's hand. No, the girl is not hurt and neither are you so be a good girl . . . yes, sweetheart, I know I frightened you but this girl was even more frightened so I had to help her, didn't I? Good girl, there's my good Cat . . . Now then, let's see if we can get our new friend to tell us what her name is. What do you think? Katie, perhaps, or Molly . . ."

Her name was Phoebe, she whispered to Annie when they were alone in the warm kitchen. Phoebe what? Annie asked but Phoebe didn't know that since no one in the place had told her, she said. She'd always been called Phoebe, just Phoebe. Mrs Pike had left her in the square because she didn't want her to work at the farm any more and the man had taken the three pounds Mrs Pike had given her for her wages and though she'd stood all day with the other women, no one had hired her and she'd been so hungry and didn't know where to go or how to get anything to eat, so when the man said he'd show her, she'd gone with him and then he'd . . . he'd not given her anything to eat but had made her give him her wages and told her she'd to pull her drawers down and when she'd said no, he'd hit her. See, she had the black eye to prove it.

The words flowed from her falteringly. She was small and thin, not very clean and though she could have been older, Annie guessed she was about twelve or thirteen.

With the intuition which came from her own experiences, not of attempted rape, but of the filth with which men could coat a woman whom they thought no better than she should be, fair game in fact, for their insolent tongues and roving hands, Annie had filled the tub in which she and Cat bathed, and after putting her small, half-asleep daughter into their bed, she had coaxed Phoebe to remove her clothing and step into the warm water. There was always some heating, or being kept hot, on the slow-burning peat fire and though Phoebe had hung her head and crossed her arms across her exposed body, she had done as she was bid. Annie had bought soap from a pedlar, parting with some of her precious savings. In the past Lizzie Abbott had made her own, but having no animals or animal fat with which to do so, Annie had no choice but to buy it. It had a smell of lavender about it and taking a cloth and the soap, she gently bathed the girl, watching as, in the soft glow from the fire and the rushlight she had lit, Phoebe relaxed into the warm, cleansing water, the fear and tension gradually slipping from her.

"Would you like me to wash your hair?" Annie asked. Phoebe nodded, bending her head obediently to Annie's hands, and when it was dried, it turned out to be as dark and glossy as the coat on Reed Macauley's mare, hanging straight as a ruler to her waist.

They did not speak a great deal. After the one sudden flow of words from Phoebe, she seemed to have nothing more to say and Annie did not press her. She put her in one of her mother's clean, modest nightgowns, pushed her in with Cat and when she herself fell into bed beside the two of them, they were both sound asleep.

It was as though she had always been there, so easily did Cat, the two dogs and even Annie herself accept her. No more questions were asked and no more information of Phoebe's past life, which Annie could tell had been hard, was proffered. She was strong and, as her fright receded, cheerful and the hardest worker Annie had ever come across. She seemed to know instinctively what needed doing and without being asked, would do it, labouring from the moment her feet hit the floor first thing in the morning, until she tucked them up, last thing at night, in the little truckle bed Annie herself had slept in as a child. The area under the roof had been divided years ago when Lizzie's children had started to come since Joshua had fully expected at least a dozen, and rooms – two, one for the girls, one for the boys, must be provided for them. From the tiny landing led three bare bedrooms, one of them never used except for storing whatever surplus oats or barley Joshua might have, his hopes of sturdy boys to follow him dashed in bitterness and recrimination against the woman who could not give them to him.

So Phoebe was moved on her second night, without a word being spoken by either her or Annie, into Annie's old room and when Annie set off to tramp to Keswick and The Packhorse that night, there was no mention of Phoebe going with her. And there was no question in her mind that, thankfully, she was leaving her child in safe hands.

Later, when Phoebe had become such a part of their life, she was to wonder how she had ever managed without her. Annie had marvelled at her own lack of caution in leaving her precious child with a stranger, a young girl about whom she knew nothing. But it was as though the strong, faithful, loving bond which was to grow between them was forged and tempered on that night Annie took her from beneath the man who had degraded her. He had not – quite – raped her, she told Annie brusquely on the following morning when Cat had run off down the field with Blackie and Bonnie. She said no more than that, shuddering visibly, then, tying up her long hair and binding it with a length of wide cloth, even then as she was always to do for as long as Annie knew her, hiding its beauty from the prying lustful eyes of men, she reached for the wooden bucket, ready to begin a lifetime of devotion and servitude to the woman who had saved her and who was to become the shining light in the world of Phoebe Abbott, as she was to be known.

Bert Garnett was not best pleased several nights later when he slipped round the back of the farm with a leg of pork from a pig his mother-in-law had slaughtered, and with which he had hoped to seduce Annie Abbott, to find the expressionless face of the girl he had imagined long gone, fixing him with a level and unblinking stare from across Annie's table.

"What's *she* doin' here?" he asked truculently.

"She's staying with Cat and me. As our guest," Annie answered tranquilly.

"What the devil does that mean?" Bert was always non-plussed by the way Annie spoke, which was perhaps part of the fascination she had for him. She confused him with the way she put things, not at all like the women of her class in her manners or her appearance.

"She has nowhere to go so she is staying with Cat and me."

"What for?"

"Really Bert, do I have to explain everything I do to you? Surely you must realise that Phoebe . . ."

"Phoebe? What sort of a name's that?"

In his angry displeasure at finding someone in Annie's company when he had expected to have her to himself, and therefore defenceless, Bert was ready to vent his spleen on anything that came to hand, even the girl's name.

"Heavens, Bert Garnett. What on earth's got into you?" though of course she knew. "Phoebe . . . well, I can see no reason why she should not make her home with us, if she cares to . . ." smiling at the sudden radiance which lit Phoebe's plain features. "I am glad of her to see to Cat whilst I am working and though I can pay her no wages, and besides would not dream of considering her a servant, more a friend, she would find no better home than here with Cat and me. You have nowhere else to go, have you, Phoebe?" smiling again at the emphatic shaking of the young girl's head, "so the matter is settled. Don't you think it's a good idea, Bert? It works out well for us all. When I have to be away from the farm, Phoebe will be company for Cat, and she has already proved to be a splendid worker. Will you not try one of those biscuits? They are delicious, made by Phoebe only an hour ago . . . No . . . ?" For at the mention of the girl's name, though he had been about to take one, Bert snatched his hand back from the biscuits as though Annie had told him there was poison baked in them.

He stumped off ten minutes later taking his leg of pork with him and though Annie was glad to see the back of him she had the feeling she had made an enemy.

As though to let Annie know that she would never regret giving her a home, Phoebe stood up and busily cleared away the pewter plates and the tankard from which Bert had drunk his ale. She stored away the biscuits in the oak bread cupboard, already becoming familiar with, and revelling in, the layout of Annie's home and where everything was stored. She wiped the table, moving round the kitchen with her cloth, her eyes darting from surface to surface, as though begging for there to be something across which she could lay it. She fetched in another pail of water and arranged to her liking the kindling beneath the sconce. She rattled the fire dogs and re-arranged the shovel and the poker. The copper kettle was given a brisk polish and the kail pot in which, when better times came, Annie would boil her cuts of meat, a wipe round with her damp cloth.

Annie watched her surreptitiously, saying nothing, her fingers busy with a pair of stockings she was knitting for Cat. She knew Phoebe needed to do what she was doing. The girl had obviously been treated in her short life – wherever that might have been spent, and which one day Phoebe would surely find the peace to tell her about – as no more than a skivvy with nothing to call her own, no one to call her own and the wonder of being allowed to handle these fine things, as she saw them, of being trusted, of being called 'friend', was almost too much for her to encompass. Scrub she would, scour and polish and mop, wash down and wring out, dig and rake and hoe, cut wood and peat and even her own throat if it would please this woman who had given it all to her. If only she would ask Phoebe to *do* something, some Herculean task which was well nigh insurmountable, Phoebe would do it, her expression said, but finally, with a long, complete sigh of pure rapture, she sat down opposite Annie and fell fast asleep.

12

She heard the thunder of his horse's hooves on the stony path for several long minutes before she saw him and when he pulled his mare in and flung himself off her back, Annie could only stare at him in complete and dumbstruck amazement.

She was instructing Phoebe in the correct way to make a swill basket, sitting in a sunny corner of the flower garden her mother had made when she came as a bride to Browhead. Though the garden was wild and overgrown, the stony path crowded with sprawling plants which had not been touched for two summers now, it was pleasant, pretty with the colourful wild flowers Lizzie had transplanted long ago from the fields and hedgerows in the valley bottom about the lake. Thrift was beginning to flourish, its fragrant pink mingling with the snow white of alyssum, and against the wall of the farmhouse where it was sheltered from the worst of the weather was clematis, not yet in bloom, and yellow winterflowering jasmine. At their back were apple trees in flower, a magical floating cloud of dense blossom from which the trunks of the trees seemed to hang, and early plum trees standing between the rough flower beds and the vegetables which marched in splendid rows at the side of the house. Cabbage and carrots, turnips and potatoes, beetroot and rhubarb and onion. There were daisies pushing their cheerful way through the bit of grass on which she and Cat and Phoebe sprawled. The sun was warm and the dogs panted, their tongues lolling from their open mouths, their eyes bright and watchful guarding this 'flock' of theirs to which, recently, another had been added.

"The timber must be cut between November and May, Phoebe," Annie was saying "and the poles should be straight-grained and free of moss. Now I've peeled and split these and they've been boiled in water for several hours to make them pliable. You understand?"

Phoebe nodded to indicate that she did. She had not yet had a great deal to say for herself but her face was bright with interest.

"Now I've split them again, shaved them and trimmed the wood into these very thin strips. Next year you could do the whole process yourself . . ." Phoebe thrilled to the words 'next year'. It had a lovely sound of permanence about it which was very much to her liking. ". . . but for now we'll just concentrate on the basket. All the strips must be of the same thickness and width and then they are woven into a shallow boat shape. The rim is oval and the strips are nailed to it. See, they're like ribbons . . ." Phoebe nodded, ". . . and look very fine, but when they're woven properly they're so strong the basket will hold water. We can sell them for a shilling each to the coal mines or to the ships in Whitehaven. When we have a horse and cart . . ."

We! Phoebe felt the bursting happiness fill her, every corner of her skinny frame singing with the joy of it. *We! Next year!* It was worth what that stinking old devil had done to her to have landed up here which truly must be heaven, with this lovely lady who truly must be an angel. She would have it done to her all over again if it meant she could stay. He'd not got his 'thingy' inside her, fumbling old bugger that he'd been, but his hands had crawled all over her body, like filthy slugs, invading her private parts and bruising her tender flesh. His mouth had clamped on hers, gagging her, and his tongue had . . . Oh, dear God . . . it made her sick to think of it, her stomach heaving and her skin sweating but she'd have it done to her every day of the week . . . well, perhaps once a week, if she could continue to live with Annie . . . *Annie*. . . she'd been told to call her Annie and the little poppet who was her daughter. Loved them both she did, even the dogs, with all the pent up, dammed up love which no one, in all of her life, had ever asked her for.

She was as astonished as Annie when the chap pounded up on his great horse, astonished and alarmed for he seemed so mad about something, looking as though for two pins he was going to knock Annie for six, which of course, Phoebe wouldn't allow. He'd have to kill her first! The dogs evidently thought so too, barking furiously and standing stiff legged and menacing in the face of his threat to those they had in their care. The man's dog, who was close at his heels, bared her teeth, the warning silent and hazardous.

But Blackie and Bonnie did not back off. They stood their ground, young as they were, and it was not until the man, with a slight movement of his hand, commanded his own animal to lie down, that order was restored. The two young dogs, with the enthusiasm of youth, were still inclined to bristle, but they lay down too, one on either side of Cat, evidently deciding that, being the youngest and smallest, she was the most in need of defending.

Phoebe stood up when Annie did, the strips for the swill baskets scattering about their feet. The man was evidently under the influence of some strong emotion which he was doing his best to submerge and the only way he seemed able to do so, was by hiding it under another, that of anger. He threw himself from his horse, leaving it standing about untethered, its eyes wild and dangerous, or so Phoebe thought, glad it was on the other side of the wall as the man tore his way through the gate, almost taking it from its hinges.

"So it's happened, then," he snarled. "You wouldn't be told, would you? My warnings were completely ignored whilst you flaunted yourself about the parish as though you were invisible and therefore in absolutely no danger from the ruffians who hang about looking for women like you who are foolish enough to think they are immune to such . . ."

"Reed Macauley, would you mind telling me what the

devil you're talking about. And I'd be obliged if you'd not come charging into my . . ."

"I'm talking about you . . . your . . . dammit, Annie Abbott, can you not take more care? Do you have to stride about the countryside after dark . . ."

His face worked strangely and in his eyes was the most dreadful, haunted expression, one which Annie could not decipher. It contained anger, yes, and a curious fear, a dread which was completely foreign to his arrogant nature. There was something deep, something he was trying to hide. A different emotion to the others, soft, vulnerable, protective, *unwelcome*.

She began to understand.

"It's all they can talk about in my kitchens, apparently, and not just in my kitchens, but in everyone else's it seems, the foolish carryings-on of a woman they believe is no better than she should be and therefore, so my housekeeper informed the housekeeper of an acquaintance of mine, who told me, can it be surprising, they are saying when she gets what she asks for. Smirking he was, the man who told me . . . and . . . and . . ."

He stopped and ran his hand across his face, pushing it through his hair, the raw and naked anger in him humiliating him since he did not really understand it. His eyes glared savagely into hers. Annie had the most absurd desire to move towards him and take that hand, to bring it to her lips and brush the back of it tenderly, to comfort him and smile, as she would to a child who has been pushed too far and has lost its temper.

She must have smiled for the snarling blackness of his rage and fear became deeper. He moved closer to her so that they stood face to face.

"It amuses you, does it, madam, to be interfered with by some drunken old sot, or were you yourself so deep in your cups it scarcely registered? Two sodden toss-pots falling down behind a barrel, so I was told and taking pleasure from one another or perhaps he was a customer . . ."

He was not quite quick enough to catch her arm as she

lifted it to strike him, perhaps too incensed, too crazed
with his own boiling emotions to see the sudden ferment
of hers. The crack of her hand across his face jerked his
head to one side and brought all three dogs to their feet,
but it also brought him to his senses, and again he
controlled his older, more experienced animal with a
gesture of his hand. The violence in the air was a palpable
thing, affecting not only the animals, but the two incensed
humans.

"Down, Blackie, down, Bonnie," Annie managed to
shriek flinging out her arms to her own trembling animals.

"Take the dogs inside, Cat, and you, Phoebe, go with
her, now, go on."

Cat was crying, great fat tears rolling down her
cheeks but she allowed Phoebe to take her into the house,
each dog dragged reluctantly by the scruff of the neck
over the threshwood and the door closed firmly on the
still, cold, silent, menacing figures of the man and
woman.

Their eyes were locked, unblinking and without
expression. Neither seemed able to look away. They were
both breathing deeply as though they had been running
and whereas Annie's face was flushed, Reed's was white
and drawn except for the imprint of her hand across his
cheek.

"What did he do to you?" His voice was harsh and
painful.

"Nothing."

"Nothing? Stripped you naked and threw you down
behind a barrel, I was told. It's all over the parish and
when I came back from Lancaster, it had even reached
the inn at Penrith."

"And you believed it?"

"What else was I to do? You . . . take no care. I've
been expecting something like this ever since I first saw
you last November, striding away towards Blencathra with
nearly twenty miles in front of you . . . and . . ."

"It was not I who was . . . and if it was, why should it
concern you?"

His voice stopped its desperate tirade, cut off in mid-sentence and his mouth fell open, slack and somewhat foolish.

"What?"

"I was not the one attacked, though I dare say it suited those in the parish who wish it had been to believe it was. I was involved so therefore it must be me, the Jezebel, who got her come-uppance. No more than I deserved for hanging about an ale house late at night. It doesn't matter to them that I have to earn my living . . ."

"Not you?" In his voice was a mixture of gladness and at the same time a ferocious hostility. She was nothing to him; he had told himself so a dozen or more times. *Could* be nothing to him, and yet the anguish which had torn at his heart, moving it frighteningly in his suddenly constricted chest when her name was mentioned, with the implied word of 'rape' affixed to it, not only frightened him, twisting his sound common sense until he was bewildered by it, but ran like explosive fire, angry and uncontrollable in his veins. Why did she not stay at home – safe – where other women stayed? Quiet and self-effacing, making no sound, creating no disturbance, causing no gossip, giving rise to nothing which would reach his ears, therefore allowing him to forget her? To put her out of his life as though she did not exist. Instead she seemed to be always up to something, doing something contrary, displaying her beauty and her careless disregard for those who lusted after it, or despised it and her, so that her name seemed to be on everyone's lips. She should never have come back, they said, flaunting herself and her bastard, or if she had been forced to it, she should have sold the farm and taken herself off into obscurity where no one knew her. Instead she had been seen everywhere decent people went, begging work and showing no sign of contrition, making it quite clear she thought herself as good as anyone and equally clear that she was not only *not* going to be driven away, but was to stay and work the farm her father had left her. A hussy, and worse still, a hussy who showed no remorse and could you wonder that men considered her fair game? Even the acquaintance who had slyly told Reed of her brush with the vagrant in Keswick had thought so and had been visibly astonished when Reed, cutting through his lustful ramblings on what *he* would like to do to Annie Abbott should she cross his path, had walked rudely away.

He drew in his breath and his mouth tightened into a grim line. His jaw was set dangerously and his eyes were a pale, flinty blue, but in them was a tiny prick of warmth, soft and grateful, a thanks of some sort to whoever, whatever it was that had protected her this time. He did not know it was there but she saw it and her own face became gentle.

"It was the girl."

"The girl?"

"Phoebe. She has just gone inside with Cat. She had been at the Hiring Fair, but for some reason no one took her and she was left to fend for herself. The man demanded her money and . . . well, you can guess the rest. I happened to be handy so I stopped him."

He grinned then. It was like the sun turning the pewter-grey waters of the lake to burnished gold, light, rippling, merry. His teeth were a white slash in his brown face and his eyes became the loveliest, brightest blue. An engaging grin, infectious, making her own lips curve into a smile for she knew exactly what was in his mind.

"He won't fancy a woman for a long while," she went on and her eyes narrowed into gleaming slits of pure, golden joy.

"I bet he won't."

They began to laugh, the sound lifting on the soft, rarified air, lilting and filled with such gaiety, the dog at his feet cocked her head and pricked her ears in mystification.

"You kicked him in the . . . ?"

"I did. He should have trouble walking for a while, I should think, never mind anything else."

The door opened a crack and the white, anxious, puzzled face of Phoebe peered through it, her own pale blue eyes

round and uncertain. Annie turned and held out a hand to
her and the young girl, with Cat behind her, followed by
the dogs, tumbled over the threshwood to stand beside
her. The animals, sensing the change of atmosphere,
recognising the laughter and easing of tension, wagged
their tails, eddying about Reed and his Bess with no sign
of their former enmity.

"This is Phoebe. She will stay with us now."

"Will she indeed?" Reed scarcely looked at the plain
child, his eyes reluctant to leave the golden burnished
loveliness, the radiant smiling good humour of the woman
who minutes earlier had struck him in the face. He had
no conception of the expression which softened his own,
arrogant, compelling features and the line of his well-cut,
sensuous mouth. The joy in him was an emotion he had
never known before and because of it, he had not yet
learned to hide it. For that sweet and special moment,
that laughter-filled, bewitched moment, his relief made
him careless and he lifted his hand, needing to touch
her, to put an enquiring tender finger to her chin or
cheek, to tuck behind her ear a wild and curling tendril
of her hair. She was looking down at the girl, her own
expression gentle and she did not see it, but Phoebe
did and the tension, the fear, the wariness she was to
know with most men, fell away, for this man would
never harm this woman. Phoebe was no more than a
young inexperienced girl, but she had been brought up
in a harsh world where love, or affection, was scarce
and therefore because of its rarity, she was quick to
recognise it. It was there, warm, strong, unbreakable,
between Annie and her child. A natural love, protective
and maternal, but this was different. The same, but not
the same. She had never seen it between a man and
a woman but, because at that moment he was making
no effort to hide it, it was instantly recognisable.

"You seem to attract stray young things to you, Annie
Abbott," he said musingly, his eyes twinkling with his rare
good humour. "What are you to do with this one?" He
winked at Phoebe, who hung her head and drew patterns

on the grass with her foot, not awfully sure what to make of it.

"She will be invaluable to me, won't you Phoebe? We'll help one another. She needs a home. I need a . . . friend. I have not many of those and she and Cat will be company for one another when I'm not here. She is already a great help to me, look. I am teaching her to make swill baskets . . ."

"So I see. And do her talents run to fetching me a tankard of ale, that is if your establishment has such a thing? And if you feel the need to pour it over my head, I will quite understand."

They smiled at one another. They knew it would not last, this accord, this lightening and melting of their equally strong and wilful spirits. There was between them an unacknowledged affinity, a magnet which drew them together, whether it be in anger or fascination, a pulling towards each other of their senses which seemed to have the capacity to flare into an instant and flowing pleasure the moment they met. They did not want it, either of them, but a need, a compulsion in him drew an immediate response from her, a female thing which recognised that need and rushed to satisfy it. Her loveliness, her spirit, her defiant rebelliousness towards those who would have sent her packing, her humour, but most of all her vulnerability, called out to the male in him, bringing forth an emotion he had never before known. The need to protect, to cherish, to nourish. All these things lay between them, soft, tender and as yet fragile, but hidden beneath them was a raw and fierce desire to know, in all its glory, the sensual love which can bind together a man and a woman with bonds which are unbreakable. It was in his eyes, narrowed and watchful, even as they smiled, and in the answering curve of her parted lips. It was trembling in the air about them, muted now and subdued in the presence of the child and young girl, but ready to become clamorous and swelling with their ardour should they find themselves alone.

They sat together on the drystone wall whilst he drank

the tankard of ale Phoebe brought him. The sunshine fell
warm and benevolent about them. The air was pure and
sweet. The wild flowers grew willy-nilly in a great profusion about them, and in every crack and crevice of the
wall, filling their nostrils with a heady perfume which can
only come with spring. The grass, greening and thickening
in the field, was tufted with primroses and cowslips and
behind them, standing against the old farmhouse for as
long as the building itself, the great hawthorn tree showed
the first signs of its golden bronze foliage. Up on the
mountain pasture, the ewes and their lambs, returned
there after lambing to await 'clipping' in July, called anxiously to one another, and high in Annie's coppice, a cuckoo
sang. Larks wheeled in the deep blue of the sky above
them, their song vying with that of the cuckoo and Annie
and Reed held their breath and their own sharp tongues
so as not to disturb this sudden lovely peace which had
surprisingly overtaken them.

They talked of this and that. The troubles in Ireland
where it was thought rebellion would take place, a disaffec-
tion of the people, many of whom lived in misery and
privation, predisposing large masses of them to rise up
against it. The potato blight of several years ago had been
repeated, the crops ruined and the people starving, so
could you wonder at the unrest which prevailed there and
the influx of the hundreds of thousands of starving Irish
beggars who were leaving to escape it, many of them to
the north of England.

There was also trouble in France, rebellion again
amongst the poor and destitute, where it was said Louis
Philippe, King of the French, the 'Citizen King' as he was
called, was in danger of losing his head as a Louis before
him had done, and last month here in England, Feargus
O'Connor, leader of the Chartist movement, had declared
his intention of marching across Westminster Bridge at
the head of what was to have been a peaceful protest, to
lay his beloved Charter at the feet of Parliament. A pilgrimage it was to have been, involving 200,000 men from every
part of the country and with so many involved, surely it

would be bound to succeed. One man, one vote and a secret ballot was not a lot to ask for, surely, among the six points of the People's Charter?

But it was illegal for more than twenty people at one time to present a petition to the House of Commons. Of the 200,000 who were expected, nowhere near that many turned up for where was an out-of-work weaver or collier to get the fare to travel from Bradford or Whitehaven to London? There was no march. Those who did get there discovered no grand banners, nor bands to play them in and the confusion was appalling when the barricades erected by the police, expecting violence, were come up against. Special constables guarded every corner. There were many soldiers deployed and when at last those who got through arrived at the House of Commons, it all came to nothing, deflating like a pricked balloon.

"Will they not get what they ask for?" Annie's face was alive with interest and concern, for it seemed to her, had she been a man, one who could find no work and no hope of feeding his children, *she* would have marched on bare and bleeding feet all the way to London to demand it. It also seemed to her that this Chartism had a great deal in its favour if it helped the vast mass of men and women who had no voice anywhere in this great land, to speak up and be heard.

"Not this year they won't, nor next if the men of property have their way."

"Like yourself you mean. You have a vote I presume."

"I have, though the young men who march up and down in military formation do not believe I should, or if I have it, so should they. They will not let it rest, those who call themselves the 'physical force'. They will continue to meet and shout for Justice and Democracy even though they were defeated and sent scurrying home with their tails between their legs last month, and eventually, I suppose, they will get what they ask for. A vote for every man over the age of twenty-one . . . ."

"And women?"

"Women? What about women?" He turned to look at her enquiringly, his mind and senses bemused by the way the sunlight tangled in her bright hair, streaking the copper with gold. It curled vigorously about her head, a great chrysanthemum halo which she had attempted to plait but which, with a life of its own, tumbled and twisted across her shoulders and down her back. She had tied a scrap of bright green ribbon about it, dragging it back from her forehead but it only served to enhance the fine, creamy pearl smoothness of her skin, the fierce dip of her golden brown eyebrows and the deep brown concern in her eyes which refused to believe that men should have a vote and women should not.

"What about women! Our brains are as capable as yours of choosing a man, or even a woman . . ." she grinned gleefully, ". . . yes, even a woman to serve us in Parliament. A woman who would know what we need . . ."

He began to smile. A short barking laugh burst from him in sheer and absolute amusement at her effrontery, her wayward and foolish effrontery, since the very idea of a woman having any voice in anything, let alone the running of the country, was so madly absurd that he took her to be joking.

She was not. Her bright face darkened ominously and she jumped down from the wall, her short skirt swinging gracefully about her calves. She reached for the empty tankard which swung idly in his hand and, tossing her wild gypsy hair back from her shoulders she squared up to him somewhat in the manner of a pugilist who has just climbed into the ring.

"What is there to laugh about, Reed Macauley? Why should I not have a vote like you? I am expected, in view of the fact that I have no man to do it for me, to support myself and my child, and I am not the only woman who is forced to it. I have seen them on my travels, wives separated from their husbands by war or other misfortune, deserted when their men go off, as men do, to fight in some God-forsaken place in the Empire. They

have no choice but to work and decide their own lives
and though many of them can't do it and end up on the
Poor Law, many succeed in wresting some sort of
living . . ."

"Don't, Annie, there's no need . . ."

His face, which had been ready to crease into a smile
of disbelief, had become soft, transformed by his amazing
need to help this self-willed woman. The expression on it
was one his own servants, his friends, even his own
mother, would not have recognised. He did not care for
it, this hunger of hers to be independent, to be her own
master, to stand up and take her place among the farmers
of the community as she seemed intent on doing. He had
not been consciously aware of it but he had been waiting,
hoping in his secret heart that she would be overcome by
the sheer enormity of it, unable to manage, forced by
hunger and the need to succour her child, to ask for
help. His help, since no one else concerned themselves
with her except Bert Garnett and Reed was well aware
why *he* hung about Browhead. And Reed would be there
when she did. When she needed him. He got no further
than that. He did not think in terms of what he might gain
from Annie Abbott's delightful dependence on him, but
he was a man, was he not, and would not turn away
from any show of gratitude she might think it politic to
offer.

"Don't struggle like this, Annie. Don't . . . fight so. Can
you not see it will come to nought for they will not let
it. They will do everything in their power to stop you
succeeding, so won't you let me . . . help you . . . ?"

"Help me? How?" She stared suspiciously into his face,
looking for the reason behind his offer but by now his
emotions were well hidden.

"I'm sure there must be something you need, something
I have which . . . Why don't you let me . . . ?" Pamper
you, make life soft and easy, dress you in pretty gowns and
. . . His eyes became unfocused as his dreaming unspoken
thoughts and the images they evoked filled his mind. She
did not like it.

"And what would you expect from me, Reed Macauley?" Her head lifted imperiously and her eyes were a vivid, flashing topaz in her colour-flooded face. "No man gives to a woman without expecting something in return, or so I have found."

"I have not said I want anything." He vaulted from the wall to stand before her and down the field, at the sound of the raised voices, Phoebe and Cat turned to stare, their hands busy with the buttercups and daisies which they were weaving into collars for the two dogs. The dogs stood up uncertainly.

"Can you not accept help without looking behind every offer for an ulterior motive?" he continued, thrusting his hard, uncompromising face into hers.

"No, I can't," and she did not back away. "Experience has taught me . . ."

"Experience! Jesus God, this life you have led has made you suspicious of . . ."

"Everybody, Reed Macauley. Everybody who wears trousers and that includes you. A favour here and a favour there and having accepted them, then I am in your debt and no doubt you would be riding down here on your fine horse to collect your dues . . ."

"Like Bert Garnett, you mean."

"You have a filthy –"

"Dammit, woman, and . . . damn you. You can go to hell on a handcart for all I care, carrying that pride of yours on your shoulders and with your belly flapping against your backbone and your tattered skirt barely covering you . . . Oh, Jesus . . . !"

He turned violently away, unable to face her a moment longer so great was his anger and his . . . what? . . . What was this biting, clawing thing that ate at his guts and hurt him so badly he could not get away quickly enough? Whatever it was he did not like it and, he told himself grimly, he had no intention of suffering it. Not now, nor ever again.

He and his mare thundered up the stony path towards Dash Beck, violent and dangerous, both of them, to anyone who stood in their way, and at their heels ran the Merle dog.

Annie stood silently, impassively, or so she led herself to believe, until all sounds ceased, then, calling to Cat and Phoebe, moved back to the spilled swill baskets.

13

By September she had saved enough money to buy ten ewes and hire a ram to service them and at 'backend', the first Saturday in October, she and Phoebe and Cat set off to walk to the Keswick Tup Fair. It was tup time, that strange and mysterious moment in the shepherd's year when, with the shortening of the days, the ewe and the ram made it plain they were ready to mate. The lambs born in the spring were now almost as big as their dams. They were weaned and ready for sale along with the older ewes. But it was 'twinters', those of two winters which Annie was after, for a 'shearling' – of one winter – was too young to rear a lamb. It was barely dawn, so quiet she could hear the faint murmuring of the beck running at the back of the farm. The sun had already touched the highest peaks and was creeping down the sides of Bake-stall and Great Calva turning the gold of the rippling autumn bracken to a richness and a glory which stopped the heart with its beauty. Great swathes of heather made a patchwork of colour, dark and light, as billowing clouds formed shadows which chased one another up and down the fells. The wind made patterns on the waters of the lake and blew the swallows and lapwings helter-skelter across the patchy blue-and-white sky. It was cold, the chill of winter which came early to this high and treacherous part of the world already nipping at flesh which was reluctant to get out of a warm bed to face the cold early morning.

Annie, in a ferment of barely controlled excitement, brushed and plaited her hair, roping the plait in a thick crown about her head. They had all three bathed the night before. Their neat and much-mended clothing had been washed and pressed with her mother's old box iron heated on the fire, Phoebe crashing the thing expertly and with that vigour she put into everything she did, up and down the kitchen table until there was not a crease to be seen in any of their poor garments. They would need new for the winter, Annie especially, since nothing of her mother's was fit for anything but cutting up into clothes for Cat. She might fashion a skirt for Phoebe and a bodice or two, salvaging the least worn pieces and carefully re-sewing them to make a whole, but there was nothing from which a gown or even a skirt might be made for herself. She needed to look presentable in her job at the Packhorse for though she had carefully darned and patched the skirt and bodice she now wore, they were becoming dangerously thin. The piece of cloth she had woven from the raw wool she had bought in the spring had been fashioned into a warm winter coat for Cat. Annie had made it long and roomy, lining it with a finer piece and it should last Cat for several years.

She would buy, if she could, some more unwashed wool, perhaps a whole fleece and treat it herself in the way her mother had taught her and from it spin and weave another length of cloth to make into a winter outfit for herself. With new clogs for Cat, and her own and Phoebe's re-soled, they would manage until next spring when *her* lambs were born.

The anticipation of that day made her smile at her own reflection in the old mirror. Her lambs, her flock, and when he saw how well she had done Reed Macauley would be made to eat his words and take back all that humbug he prattled about women being incapable of fending for themselves.

Her hands became still as she allowed herself to ponder on why it should concern Reed Macauley, and indeed why it should matter to her what Reed Macauley was concerned about. She had seen him only in passing as he rode down the track at the back of her farm, nodding briefly in her direction going God knows where since the only roads at the bottom of it led to Cockermouth, Workington or

Carlisle and he would hardly ride that distance on his mare. Still, it was none of her business what he did and the rumour which was whispered about the parish, brought to her by the avid Sally, that he was to marry the daughter of some rich and influential industrialist from Yorkshire meant nothing to her. It was time he married, she told herself carelessly, since a man such as he and of his age must get himself an heir to inherit his family's wealth and position. It was his duty to carry on the name and perpetuate a line which had begun in Norman times and had brought prosperity and prestige to the name of Macauley. And naturally he could not ally himself or his pedigree with any but that which would match his. Not gentry, since he was not that, but good sound yeoman stock which was the backbone and sinew of England. A common man, a man of the people, but could such words describe Reed Macauley who was neither common nor of the masses? He was a strong man with an unshakeable belief in his own superiority. A man with a confidence and self-reliance which knew absolutely that his viewpoint was infallible. Self-assured, the undisputed master of his own life, he was not a man who took kindly to opposition. Unique, unpredictable, uncommon, since he was not merely a farmer, albeit a prosperous one, as so many statesmen had become, but since the death of his father he had entered into the realm of business, his shrewd and imaginative brain guiding him into and through the maze of investments in the many booming industries on offer to men with cash to spare: the railways, mining, coal and copper, the trades allied to wool and timber which were prolific in Cumberland.

But it was not just in his working life that Reed Macauley stood head and shoulders above his fellows. His nature was complex and many layered. It demanded satisfaction in every aspect of his life and where the men of the dales and fells, those with a guinea or two to spare, were careful with it, admiring in one another the growing size of their bank balance, Reed Macauley could see no reason to hoard his wealth. He surrounded himself with beautiful things,

luxury even, in his home, Annie had heard, and about his
person, caring not a fig for what the sensible practical
gentlemen of his acquaintance thought of his foolhardiness.
Beautiful women, perfumed and bejewelled, had been seen
on his arm. Beautiful horses crowded his stable besides
his ebony mare. A showy chestnut hunter, a pair of bay
carriage horses, a phaeton, a curricle which he drove
madly along the winding Bassenthwaite road drawn by a
dark brown gelding of a spirited nature. His body was
strong, tall, lean and completely masculine and was dressed
always in the height of fashion: impeccably tailored coats
and breeches, immaculately laundered shirts and cravats
and the expensive, beautifully polished boots he favoured.

So, he would marry then, this man who challenged her
own independence and confused her mind which needed
at this moment to be clear, steady, channelled into only
one concern and that was the holding on to what she had
gained in the last ten months and the building up of what
she intended for the future. She wanted no complications,
no distractions, and so, glad that he had the sense to
stay away from her since what would Reed Macauley and
Annabelle Abbott ever be to one another, she prepared
herself for the next step she had planned for, worked
towards, dreamed of in the last months of struggle. The
starting of the flock. Her oats and barley, the few acres
she had planted had been harvested by herself and Phoebe,
wielding the scythe her father and his father before him
had used, pausing again and again in their labours, to give
the blades a new edge with the whetstone. They had
gathered ash leaves, storing them in a large kist to feed
to her sheep in the coming winter, guarding against the
weather which might prevent the animals from foraging
on the inlands about the farm. She would hand feed them
in the farm yard if necessary for she meant to take no
chances with her precious flock.

The bracken, tall and sappy and which, if allowed,
spread like wildfire across her precious pasture, had been
cut and stored in the barn for it made splendid bedding for
stock, should she have any, and who was to tell, if things

continued to go well for her and prices were right, she might have a cow! They had, all three of them, for Cat was adept and quick to learn, cut rushes for the making of rushlights ready for the winter, peeling them and using the peelings to make besoms, brooms and 'bears', the crude matting which kept their feet from the cold slate floor. Her vegetables and fruit had been gathered, some of them dried, and the rest stored in preparation for the hungry months ahead. She was ready. Today she was ready.

They went by the rough track along the Dash Valley and up beyond Dash Beck and Dash Falls towards the Great Skiddaw Forest where oak, ash, hazel and larch stood in silent and regal splendour. They had left behind the vast withering sea of bracken covering the slopes, the fronds which had, at the height of the summer, been a glowing gold, turning as autumn came to a delicate tawny brown and shading gradually to a subtle lemon hue. The forest was still canopied with branches full of leaves capturing every shade of autumn colour from the palest brown to the brightest yellow, with orange and flame and crimson in between. The leaves were beginning to fall, drifting lazily, slowly, delicately to the already carpeted forest floor, caressing their heads and shoulders as they passed beneath them, and Cat ran on ahead, doing her best to catch one in her hand, but Phoebe as befitted her new position as friend and helpmeet of Annie, walked sedately by her side. Splashes of brilliant red revealed themselves on rowan trees and on thorn, holly, yew and juniper as the berries ripened. Annie, on impulse, plucked a sprig of rowan and tucked it into her own springing curls since it was known that rowan warded off evil spirits and she wanted none of those about her today. Good luck was what she needed and any help in that direction was most welcome.

The Tup Fair was the climax of the sheep farmers' year for it was here that the best ewes were matched to the sturdiest rams. Slight faults in either could be remedied if the right match was found, for the Herdwick sheep must be hardy and strong to withstand the rigours of a Lakeland winter. It was a small breed, lithe and agile, with a white grizzled face and long grey wool. It must be able to climb like a goat and leap like a frog. Its mutton was sweet and yet it could live on a handful of briar and shoots and thrive on it. Buried in snow it had been known to survive by chewing its own wool. For centuries it had been on the fells, proving its worth and stamina, its only fault being its real and lasting attachment to its own 'heaf' or pasture, to which it had been known to return when sold miles away.

The market place at Keswick when Annie, Phoebe and Cat turned into it had an air of great excitement about it. Through narrow, stone-walled lanes, great flocks of sheep heaved and cried, and a line of tups stood restlessly under a wall, tossing their fine curling horns which sprang, creamy white, from the base of their heads. They were held in by a hawthorn bush as potential buyers and hirers had a closer look. In every alleyway there were pens jammed from wall to wall with a moving, nervous sea of fleeces, for already the wool clipped in July was beginning to grow again. In the tup ring horny feet pattered on the cobbles and sharp horns clashed and scraped, for the close proximity of so much female flesh was almost too much for the male to withstand. They were ready to break out to get at it, fighting one another to do it. Farmers who had stock for sale were coaxing potential buyers into their own pens and in the circle in which the 'top' sheep were displayed a ram pawed the ground, ready to charge at anything that moved. There was a sheepdog or even two, at the feet of every man, alert, eyes brimming with intelligence, ready, should they be needed, to fetch an escaped hogg – an unsheared lamb – or twinter, or even to tackle a tup.

The only women present were at the market stalls, buying the basic commodities which their husbands' farms did not produce. Decent, well-turned-out women, plain and serviceable, who worked hard in their own homes, dairies and yards but would not dream of presenting themselves amongst the men with whom their husbands did business. The area where the tup fair took place was a strictly masculine preserve and when the strikingly lovely Annie Abbott stepped out of her place, a woman's place, and into theirs, every man in the market was instantly aware of it.

She was dressed in the best of what she had. The grey woollen skirt she wore in the snug at The Packhorse. A simple grey bodice and her old shawl and clogs, but the dull, washed out, much darned outfit made not the slightest difference to her appearance. Her straight and supple back swung gracefully; her shoulders moved as she walked and her long white neck swayed with the glorious weight of her hair. Her enquiring gaze fell smilingly on each sheep pen and she nodded graciously at each open-mouthed man who had them in his charge. A hush seemed to develop, filled only with the bleating of the sheep and the crack of the rams horns as, unwatched for a moment, they set about each other.

Annie moved calmly as though she was in her own kitchen, one hand holding Cat's, the other firmly pressed against her pocket where her precious store of money lay. Phoebe, much recovered from her ordeal and beginning to unfold into the strength of character and tenacity for endurance her new security had given her, walked stead-fastly beside her and, all about them, men, in their best 'setting-off' clothes and carrying their Lakeland 'setting-off' crooks, stared and began to mutter for though a woman might do as she pleased on her own acres, none with a shred of decency would come here where drovers thronged, drunk already some of them, rough mannered and foul tongued. Even the poorest woman with a pig or a goose for sale would do it discreetly away from the sheep market. And if she had to buy sheep could she not have found some man to do it for her, some experienced shepherd, instead of flaunting herself as she was doing in this strictly man's world. The noise and the stench was not for women's frail sensibilities and besides, men, without the presence of women, were inclined to relieve

themselves against any handy wall, as one was doing now.
A good 'larruping' was what she needed and there was
not a man here who would not be glad to give it to her,
and other things besides, some of them more pleasurable.

Annie passed by, hearing nothing, seeing nothing but
the sheep, and when she stopped by a pen in which twelve
'twinters' huddled the farmer who was selling them
was so transfixed he allowed her to venture inside and
even examine a couple more closely, before he found his
voice.

"'Ere, what d'yer think yer up to? Your man should be
doin' that, lass," he said roughly, but she turned her brilliant
gaze on him before drifting out of the pen.

"They're not what I'm looking for," she answered, "but
thank you for your time."

It was the same wherever she went. The presence of
the quiet child and the equally quiet but perfectly decent
young girl who accompanied her, lent her astonishing passage through the market some propriety, for no woman
with mischief on her mind would saddle herself with youngsters whilst she was about it. But still they stared and still
the stubborn streak which had brought Annie Abbott from
a terrified fifteen-year-old abandoned mother-to-be, to a
woman with her own farm and a pretty and bright young
daughter; to a woman with her life coming together around
her; to one with money in her pocket and a dream in
her heart which was slowly moving towards fruition, the
stubborn streak which would not allow her to falter. She
knew the supreme ewes and rams would be spoken for in
advance but that did not matter unduly since she could
probably not afford the prices asked anyway, but she would
have the next best her money could buy. The hire of a
ram for the winter was expensive, probably about ten or
fifteen shillings since it would have to serve no more than
a dozen ewes, which was all she could afford to buy this
year, but it would have to suffice. Getting them back to
Browhead would also be tricky since they would need to be
walked, probably along the lake road which, being walled,
would be easier to manage, with only herself, Phoebe and

Cat to control them. The dogs would have to be trained actually with the sheep before they could be trusted to herd them anywhere but in an enclosed field, but first things first, she told herself, her heart pumping with excitement, her eyes burning in her cream flushed face, her head high with justifiable pride.

She found exactly what she wanted about two hours later. The farmer was from Threlkeld way where women knew their place and whose truculent expression boded ill for Annie but she had good money in her pocket and she could see no reason why he should not do business with her. He would, no doubt, assume that any advantage to be had would be his. She had been right round the pens, scrutinising every ewe with an experienced eye, that of her father she supposed, since it was he who had taught her all she knew about sheep and what constituted a good specimen.

"Too slack behind the shoulder," she had remarked cheerfully to one surly fellow, causing his mouth to drop open in consternation.

"Too light in the face for my needs," she smiled at another.

"I'm looking for a better fleece I'm afraid," to a third, and word had got round that the 'hussy' from Browhead knew a thing or two about Herdwicks. The farmer from Threlkeld did not believe it.

"I'm not sure I'm ready to sell yet," he said grimly despite the fact that it was well past noon and his twinters were still mewling and pawing the ground inside his pen.

"Then may I ask what these ewes are doing here?"

"That there's nowt to do wi' thi'." He was aware that those in the vicinity were listening avidly since their ability to see and hear everything that was going on about them was not diminished by their own need to sell their stock. This was a social occasion as well as one in which business was conducted and a man spent almost as much time having a 'gleg' with another whom he had not seen since tup time last year, as he did attending to the sale, or hire,

of his stock. Many of the flocks had been driven from as
far away as the Langdales, the shepherds walking them
over the fells with their dogs at their heels, using the old
pack routes and sheep trods. Some were brought in carts
pulled by enormous plough horses and the drovers were
already beginning to head off towards Bassenthwaite,
Penrith, Rosthwaite, with sheep which had been bought
earlier, their dogs nipping and pushing at their heels, or
flying round to the sides of the restless flock at their
owner's whistle or shouted command.

But the area about Annie Abbott was curiously still.
Several pens away an ancient weatherbeaten shepherd
was counting in the old traditional fashion, the flock he
was to take away. Celtic numerals that had been handed
down from father to son, and thought to be part old Welsh,
part Cornish and part Breton, from all those lands which
were once included in the Celtic fringe, when Cumberland
had been under the rule of the great Celtic Kingdom of
Strathclyde just across the border.

"*Yan, tyan, tethera. . . methara, pimp . . .*" he droned
until he reached eleven when he began again, "*yan-a-dick,
tyan-a-dick . . .*"

Apart from the bleating of the sheep it was the only
sound as the crowd held its breath, waiting on the outcome
of the trading between Annie and the farmer.

"So you are saying these ewes are not for sale then?"

"No, I'm not . . ."

"Then they *are* for sale."

"They might be."

"Well, let me know when you make up your mind and
in the meanwhile I'll go and have a look at some others
that caught my eye earlier."

She nodded pleasantly and prepared to move away. She
had her hand on Phoebe's arm and the trembling in it,
though not evident to anyone else, moved down to
Phoebe's hand and up across her shoulder so that it looked
as though she herself was shivering.

"Please thissen. I'm not sayin' these twinters are for
sale, neither am I sayin' they're not. They might be and

then again they might not. Depends on who's askin' and on t' price I'm offered."

"What are you asking? And for that tup you have in the next pen? I presume he's for sale or hire?"

"Aye, that's right. But it's all good stock and I can't let any of 'em go unless I get right price."

"Sir, unless I know what that price is I cannot do business with you. We are just wasting time here. Time I cannot afford. You are not the only farmer with sheep to sell and so I will just move on."

Annie felt the blood race in her veins, hot and eager and jubilant for this was the moment she had worked towards for the past year. She was about to strike a bargain with this man and it would be in her favour. Shrewd he would be and careful, since most of these independent fell farmers could afford to be no other way. They had their living to make as did any man, but he would be not at all pleased to take his flock back to Threlkeld with him, nor would it suit him to hang on until later in the day when he would be forced to sell at an even lower price to be rid of them.

"Them's fine Herdwicks . . ." he began. "None better in the Keswick plain, nor anywhere else for that matter. Bred from a strong ram what belonged to old Jed Moffatt, him from Rush Farm up near Mungrisdale. Ask anyone . . ."

"I don't need to. I can see what they are, sir, knowing sheep as I do . . ."

"Oh aye, an' how's that then?"

"My father . . ."

"Where did he farm?"

"Browhead, near Gillthrop."

"Josh Abbott."

"Yes."

"I knoo 'im. Lost all un 'is, I 'eard." His unsmiling, unsympathetic mien told her he cared nothing for her father's experience, nor hers, as shepherds, since any man of worth should know how to hold on to what he had and Joshua Abbott had let his slip through his fingers.

Feckless, the farmer from Threlkeld, would have called that, deserving of what he got, which from what he had heard had been as close to a pauper's death as made no difference. And his lass about to do the same no doubt.

Stung by his contempt Annie pulled her shawl more closely about her shoulders and lifted her head in proud defiance. For a moment, the farmer's grudging attention was diverted by the lovely lift of her breast beneath the worn wool and the slipping tendril of bright copper hair which curled about her ear. Her flesh just below that ear was as white as the fleece of his sheep when it had been newly shorn, soft and vulnerable and he was horrified, since he was a man well past such things, to feel a stirring in the pit of his belly, just where the sagging crutch of his breeches divided. It infuriated him further.

"I'm not my father," Annie snapped and so did her eyes, with the bright golden lights of her temper.

"I'm not sayin' tha' are, lass, an' what thi' do wi' tha' cash is none o' my business."

"Quite so, in that case will you please tell me what you want for your twinters and if the price is right perhaps we can agree on a sale."

The farmer smiled, his craggy face splitting open into a hundred seams. The smile revealed his worn and blackened teeth and the pink gaps where a few were missing. He shook his head as though humouring the foolishness of a child who has asked for a completely unsuitable and unobtainable toy and Annie felt the hot joy begin to trickle away. The awful feeling which replaced it, slowly but surely, was a mixture of bewilderment and alarm for she was beginning to get the distinct feeling that this man was playing with her. That he had been playing with her for the past half-hour. Like an angler with a trout on his line, the bait in the trout's mouth, allowing the fish to reel out the line, believing it is going to be free, then drawing it in again before repeating the whole procedure. All about her she could feel the eyes of the other men, the farmers who still had sheep to sell and when she turned for a moment it seemed that everyone in the immediate vicinity was smirking and whispering behind their hands at the joke which was being played on Annie Abbott.

She whirled back to the farmer from Threlkeld.

"What's going on here?" she demanded accusingly.

"Nay lass, what do tha' mean?" and he deliberately winked at someone behind her back. Phoebe's hand had reached out to grasp her arm and beside her even Cat, sensing the strange tension in the air, crept close to her skirt. She didn't really know what she meant, as he smiled into her face, so she could not answer his question. She only knew she had a frozen feeling of dread.

"Will you name your price for these ewes?" she repeated, her voice firm and steady since she wanted no man to see her fear. "I've no time to bandy words with you so I'd be glad to get on. If you're not willing to sell, say so and I can go elsewhere."

"Then I'd do that my lass, if I were you, 'cos I've nothing here to sell to thi', not for any price." His words were soft and quite menacing.

"You have not heard my offer . . ."

"Tha's not enough money in world to buy this lot, girl, not from you at any rate, so you'd best get back to where tha' came from an' tek tha' . . . tha' family with thi'." His eyes fell coldly on Cat, then moved to Phoebe, before returning to Annie. "Tha's no call to come prancin' round here with tha' la-di-da manners and daft ideas of buyin' a flock for the farm tha' father left thi', if it can be called a farm." His mouth which had been smiling, twisted contemptuously, then meaning quite deliberately to offend, he spat on the cobbles at her feet.

"This part of the market is fer men, not women, an' the sooner tha' realise that the sooner tha'll come to tha' senses. These lads hereabout don't like bargaining wi' a woman. There's no need of it since there's plenty o' men to do business with. 'Tis no place for thee, lass, an' my ewes is not for thee so get thi' back home where tha' belong."

"My money's as good as anybody's and if I can pay the price you are asking . . ."

"How about ten guineas each beast then?" He turned to look about him, his face in a grim and mirthless grin of mockery and there were a few guffaws.

"Don't be ridiculous. The whole lot's not worth ten guineas."

"Is that so, then if tha' don't like my price, try elsewhere."

"I will." She turned on her heel, dragging Cat and Phoebe with her, her face as pale as ashes, her eyes like hot coals embedded in them. She allowed no one to see her panic as she moved on to the next pen but even before she had reached the grinning man, who leaned over the fence, he called out to her.

"This lots spoken for, lass," turning to wink at the farmer from Threlkeld, but there was a coldness, a cruelty even behind that wink. She went to them all, even one whose ewes were a sorry looking lot, but everywhere she met the same grim, narrow-eyed resolution which said that women had no place in their men's world and had no business to attempt entry. This part of the market was a strictly male preserve, as indeed was farming, and even wives with husbands who had come to buy from the stalls, never set foot inside it. Messages were carried by small boys from women waiting at the end of the day, to husbands who were dilatory, but it was unthinkable for one, one of decency at least, to move amongst the men who were bargaining here.

They walked the long way home in silence, she and Cat and Phoebe, going up and over the top of Skiddaw by the same route they had so joyfully set out upon that morning. She carried her child when it became evident that Cat, who had been on her feet for over twelve hours, could go no further. And she carried the bitter burden of knowing that the enmity which she had treated so lightly since how could it harm her, was a strong and ugly repression in the hearts of these people. They did not like Annie Abbott. They did not approve of Annie Abbott. She had done what no decent woman would, could do, but she had not been punished for it as harlots should be punished. Far from it, they had seen her survive, thrive even. They took no account, nor did they admire, that it was her own hard labour that had achieved it. So they had turned even more against her. Today had been their way of letting her know, if she didn't already, that she'd get no helping hand from them. They'd have no truck with her, even if they lost money as a consequence.

She glared ahead of her into the falling darkness, her expression as grim as the farmer's from Threlkeld had been.

14

It was the evening of the day Annie Abbott had gone to the tup fair at Keswick. The farmhouse at Long Beck was illuminated in every window, even the bedrooms, with the branches of candelabra Reed Macauley had ordered to be placed there so that not only would his guests be impressed by his own careless disregard for the cost of such things, but also his house and gardens might be clearly visible and easily found as those guests arrived in their carriages. The track up from Gillthrop was, strictly speaking, not suitable for such vehicles, farm carts being the usual transport finding its way up there, but with care and a good coachman, it was possible to manoeuvre up the steep track.

The name farmhouse could really no longer be used to describe Reed Macauley's home. Two hundred years ago there had been four small farmhouses and farmlands belonging to four Macauley brothers but in the generations that followed those four holdings had become one and had gone to Reed Macauley's canny grandfather, Hamish, who had passed it on to Reed's father, Alistair, and so to Reed. There had been, by all accounts, battling Macauleys among Reed's forebears who had not stayed peaceably at home on their farms but had sent their sons to fight against Holland in 1665, against France in 1690 and in Malborough's wars of 1702–1710, two members of the family falling in the Battle of Malplaquet. There was Culloden in 1746, where one had fought for Prince Charlie since their sympathy then had been with their Scottish cousins and another had been in India at the time of the infamous Black Hole of Calcutta, where after being incarcerated in a cell, of the 146 souls put there the night before, only 23 came out alive. War and disease had thinned out the Macauley heirs like young seedlings in a frost until land and farmhouses now all belonged to the one remaining branch of the family.

Beside the farm and its buildings there was ploughland, a peat moss, woodlands, pasture and dozens of small fields surrounding the house. These were the 'banks', steep but low-altitude grazing land close about the farm where Reed's milking cows were kept. The banks were rich and lush and green, studded with animals, knee-deep in clover and buttercups. Enclosed at the time of the 'Enclosure Acts' by sturdy, drystone walls which were kept in fine condition by the 'wallers' Reed employed. There was the moor beyond the banks where his horses, his bullocks, his heifers and 'dry' cows grazed, not enclosed but his just the same. And then there were the fells, high and rolling, where his sheep wandered, watched over by his shepherds and their dogs. Hundreds of acres of rich farmland and all belonging to one man. Since the eighteenth century, farming had slowed down as other industries were born and expanded, and there were fewer farms, but those that remained had become bigger and, of those, Reed Macauley's was the biggest.

The house itself had become, through extensive renovations over the recent years, more of a manor house than a farmhouse. Built in a sheltered fold of the fells, it formed three sides round a square cobbled area which had once been a yard but which was now a standing and turning place for carriages. There were flower beds against the house walls, thick with antirrhinums, dahlia, delphiniums and rock rose. There was, in season, wisteria, fragrant and blue, climbing up the whitewashed walls, and massed rhododendron. Lavender at the right time and lilac, and edging the path was boxed privet, all cared for by a gardener and two boys. The lawns were smooth and green and the trees, centuries-old oak and yew, stood in protective tranquillity about the house.

The house itself looked as though it had not been built by men, but had grown slowly and gracefully, from the very hills which formed its backdrop. Its mullioned windows were set deep in its thick walls, not one the same size as its fellow. The front door was situated not in its centre, but in one of the angles of its corners, wide and solid with a fluted porch above. The roof tiles were a greeny blue, almost grey, and its three enormous sets of chimneys were cylindrical. Gracious, serene, lovely and yet strong and protective of those who lived within its walls, it had been built to withstand any of the malevolent weather conditions with which the fells and dales of the lakes were challenged. It was a house which the dour and taciturn men of the fells eyed suspiciously since they liked plain, solid, foursquare, no nonsense and in their opinion Reed Macauley's high-flown ideas of comfort, luxury even, were pretentious and unnecessary.

It did not prevent them from attending the party at his home that evening in honour of the young lady to whom he had recently become betrothed, and her wealthy industrial family. A good match of course, for would a hard-headed business man like Reed Macauley have any other, despite the fact that he had no need, financially speaking, to wed where money was? From Bradford it was said the family came, woollen cloth manufacturers, which would do Reed no harm since it would provide him with a ready-made outlet for his wool. A shrewd man, was Reed Macauley, who had always recognised and taken advantage of an opportunity when he saw it.

They stood, the newly engaged couple, her beautifully manicured white hand through his arm, just inside the doorway of what the man who opened the door to them – could he be a butler? – called, grandiosely, the drawing room. Parlour, they would have said, since, though they themselves were not short of a bob or two, that was what the living rooms in their homes were called. In fact, it was not long since the living room had been known simply as the 'house' or the 'down house'.

Reed Macauley greeted them, the 'statesmen' society of Bassenthwaite parish, with a somewhat ironic smile about his well-cut mouth. He knew what they were thinking, and of course, they were right. Though the girl beside him was devastatingly pretty, with the full-breasted, broad-shouldered figure of an Amazon princess, tall with hair the colour and texture of spun gold, and wide eyes the deep blue of a speedwell, it was not these which had drawn him to her. He would find it no hardship to take her to his bed of course, and was already looking forward to the moment when, after their marriage naturally, he would strip her of her silks and satins and have at his disposal the magnificent whiteness of her young body, but it was her money, her position, or rather that of her father, her absolute qualification to be a perfect hostess at his table and a devoted mother to his children, as she had been trained to be, which had attracted her to him. Esmé Hamilton-Brown, seventeen years old, with a dazzling smile matching the magnificent diamond on her finger, which he had given her on their betrothal. They would be married in the spring, an enormous affair in Bradford, to which the élite of the industrial class would be invited and from where he would bring her back to run his home and bring up the children they would have.

The thought afforded him absolutely no joy and for that fraction of a second when the sterile picture was in his mind, he felt ice-cold waves of despair flood his body and reach his brain. When Ezra Hodgson and his wife Lucy stood before him, Ezra's hand outstretched in congratulations and Lucy's eyes all over Esmé's superb, extremely *décolleté* evening gown of rose-coloured satin, he was momentarily paralysed. He just could not, in that fraction of time, bring himself back to reality, to the reality of who he was and of what was taking place this evening. Instead he felt the impact of two deep, laughing, brown eyes, not a true brown, more golden with luminous lights of mystery in them and a message which, though he did his best, he could not make out. They were fringed with thick brown lashes which meshed as the laughter deepened and in his heart, over which again he had no control, a spasm of real pain shivered and he was desolate. Desolate and lost for

how could he do this . . . with Esmé . . . when she . . .
she . . . ?

". . . and this is the beautiful young lady who is coming
to live among us, is it?" Ezra was saying somewhat
stiltedly since what else *was* he to do when his host, on
whose arm the beautiful young lady hung, was staring at
him, saying nowt mind, with his mouth open and his eyes
glazed.

"It is," Reed said, recovering at once, indeed so completely the strange moment might not have happened.
"Esmé, my dear, may I present Mr and Mrs Ezra Hodgson
from Penrith. Mr Hodgson and I are business associates,
but I hope, friends as well. Ezra, Lucy, this is my future
wife, Miss Esmé Hamilton-Brown. I'm sure Mrs Hodgson
will welcome you most generously, Esmé, into her home
and into society when we are married."

She would, Mrs Hodgson gushed, despite the newly
affianced young lady's rather vacant expression, her
haughty manner and extreme youth. Mrs Hodgson had
girls of her own who were the same age as Esmé Hamilton-
Brown. Indeed she had nurtured hopes of Reed Macauley
for one of them, but the girl smiled, a dazzling display
of pearl-white teeth, so she was evidently good-natured.
Superb they were those teeth, as was she and there was
no doubt she would produce superb children. She would
make a splendid adornment to Reed Macauley's table as,
when they sat down to dine, her creamy breasts proved
when they were half revealed in the candle-light. She was
rich, conventional and none too bright, Lucy decided, saying as much to Beatrice Mossop when the ladies left the
gentlemen to their port and cigars, and what more could
a man like Reed Macauley, who was not one to settle
easily to domesticity, need from a wife? She and Beatrice,
on the pretext of a hem which needed a stitch, had been
directed up Reed's wide staircase to the tranquil, candle-lit
landing off which the doors to half a dozen bedrooms lay.
The door to one was open, revealing what was the retiring
room for the ladies, and in it was Sarah Macauley's old
sewing woman, Dolly, dressed in black but with her snow-

white hair covered in an old-fashioned butterfly cap and wearing a muslin apron. She was rocking peacefully before a good fire, a bit of sewing in her hand, her face seamed and placid. She had been put there by Mrs Stone the housekeeper, to hand out pins or smelling salts or clean handkerchiefs to any of the ladies who might need them; to look after Reed Macauley's guests' wraps and cloaks, many of which were made from rich velvet, lined with fur. The other younger maids, of whom Lucy Hodgson knew, from her own maids, there to be at least five, were too busy on this important night with their duties of caring for Mr Macauley's important guests and so Dolly had been brought out of partial retirement to perform this simple task.

The big room was bright with firelight and candle-light in soft shades of cream and rose repeated in the carpet, the curtains and the bed hangings. There were several pieces of Reed Macauley's mother's furniture about the room, in elaborately carved, lovingly polished mahogany, but the walls were lined with rose-pink silk and everywhere bowls of flowers stood next to silver candlesticks supporting sweet-smelling candles. It was lovely, so warm and welcoming that both women gaped, for though their husbands had wealth, they had not spent it as Reed Macauley evidently did on luxury such as this. And this was merely a spare room, so what did those which were occupied by Miss Hamilton-Brown and Mr and Mrs Hamilton-Brown have in them? The dining room from which they had just come was low ceilinged since nothing could be done to alter that, but its dark oak-panelled walls were relieved with the light from its two windows, which were shrouded in the costliest pale green velvet. The carpet was plain, rich and creamy and surely not meant for gentlemen's riding boots, and on the two sideboards were dozens of bright silver dishes, candelabra and all the appurtenances of a rich man of taste and elegance. It was the same in the drawing room, wide velvet sofas and cabriole-legged velvet chairs, ormolu-mounted inlaid cabinets stuffed with fine porcelain and on the walls, heavy gilt-framed pictures of scantily clad nymphs which those who dined there were not at all sure they cared for. Especially with ladies present.

So this was what Reed Macauley had done to his home during the last months in preparation for his bride, the ladies whispered to one another, neither woman aware that he had not had Esmé Hamilton-Brown in his mind's eye as he did so.

The tall young man moved lightly across the yard at Browhead followed by the two dogs. He was dressed in an ill-fitting pair of breeches and stout gaiters, and on his feet were thick, hand-knitted woollen stockings, pushed into a pair of well-worn wooden-soled clogs. A loose jacket, a woollen waistcoat and a long, also hand-knitted, muffler wrapped warmly about his neck. On his head was a soft felt hat with a bowl-shaped crown and brim, very battered and evidently very old.

The dogs pranced about his long striding legs, young dogs but when he spoke and his hand made some small movement, both instantly went down on their bellies, watching, ears pricked, eyes gleaming with bright interest as he entered the barn. It was several minutes before he emerged and when he did he was pulling the sledge.

"Stay, Blackie, stay, Bonnie," and the dogs obeyed, their eyes never leaving the young man as he eased the sledge back across the yard to the side door of the farmhouse. They did not move until his hand told them they may, then they bounded after him.

"Down." The quiet command was instantly obeyed.

"Good boys, now stay."

The man entered the house and the dogs remained where they were, guarding the empty sledge, sniffing the air with keen noses, alert, bright eyed, quivering with eagerness, but remembering their duty. When the door opened again they turned their heads as one, looking towards it, their plumed tails moving slowly on the ground.

A child came out, a little girl of three or four, carrying an enormous bundle carefully tied about with twine. She placed it on the sledge. She bent to put a small hand on the head of one of the dogs and he strained beneath it, longing to leap up and play but he resisted, contenting himself with licking the child's hand with his long pink tongue.

"Good boy, Blackie," the child said, then turned to the second animal who was doing his best to remain on the ground where he had been put. He inched forward a fraction and when the girl's hand was within reach licked it ecstatically.

"Good boy, Bonnie, now stay there, NO, stay, good boy."

Another figure appeared, this time that of a young girl of about twelve or thirteen, plain but wholesome, clean and tidy but shabbily dressed in an assortment of what seemed to be layers of old bits of clothing. Her dark and shining hair was strained back from her high forehead and braided about her head. She carried a pile of swill baskets, one inside the other, which she placed beside the bundle the child had already put in the sledge. They both went back inside the house then returned, carrying more bundles, more swills and another load of neatly tied besom twig brushes. The older girl spent several minutes arranging it all to her satisfaction, making sure that nothing would roll off the cart.

"Yon'll not move now," she said determinedly, evidently satisfied with her own handiwork. "Them swills is wedged in against them stockings an' nowt'll shift 'em. I've put the besoms at bottom so they'll not roll out."

"I hope it doesn't rain," the child said dolefully, her small face turning up to look with worried concern at the grey clouds scudding from one high fell to the next, a long, threatening line of them following one another low across the sky, with alarming regularity.

"Nay, it'll not do that, chuck. Tha' can hear t'waterfall up by Dash so it'll not rain, tha' knows that," – which was true. The sound of falling water or the absence of it was often a sure indication of whether it would rain or not. Something to do with the direction of the wind, it was

said, vaguely, by those who lived hereabouts. They only
knew their fathers had said the same and their father's
father before that. There were many such predictions.
The direction in which a cloud moved, the colour of
the sky as the sun set, the certain way in which an owl
called, or at what time the cock crowed. A cold and
windy May heralded a good harvest, a warm Christmas a
full churchyard, and if Candlemas day in February was
to dawn fine and clear, there would be two winters in one
year. And it was found that these old sayings and fore-
casts and many others, had more than a grain of truth in
them.

The little girl brightened. She began to circle the sledge
touching a bundle, giving the swills a brisk pat, her small
pretty face as intent and serious as though the vehicle was
off to the wastes of the Arctic and its safety depended on
her vigilance. The older girl watched her, then spontaneously, she knelt and put her arms about her, drawing
the child lovingly into a close embrace. Her own face was
soft and pale and her blue eyes brimmed, though no tears
fell.

"It'll be all right, Cat, honest it will. Us've managed this
long, so don't thi' worry."

"But it's such a long way, Phoebe." The child's voice,
in sharp contrast to the older girl's, was clear, the words
well pronounced, concise with no trace of her northern
heritage in them.

"Ah know, lambkin, but tha's not to worry. We've both
told thi' that. Dogs are goin' along for protection and they'll
not let 'owt 'appen, tha' knows that. Good guard dogs,
they be, aren't tha' lads?" turning to put out a hand to the
animals. The dogs' ears swivelled and their heads cocked
as they did their best to understand what she was saying.

"Come on then, come to me an' Cat," she said, and
instantly they leaped up, moving to lean on her and the
child, conveying their devoted sympathy in the only way
they knew how at this sad time as though they were fully
aware of the underlying anxiety.

The child who had burrowed her head in the girl's bony

but comforting shoulder, looked up, brightening once more as two cold noses nuzzled at her soft cheek.

"That's right. Nothing can happen if Blackie and Bonnie are there, can it, Phoebe? How long will it be d'you think, Phoebe?"

"Nay lass, tha knows we've talked about it and it could be a week or two. But it will be before October's out, tha' can rest easy on that. Before the snows come but that's a long walk over to Rosley and back, pulling that thing, an' all, but as soon as all that stuff's sold and the sheep bought, they'll be home, tha' knows that. Aye, before the winter sets in, an' thee and me'll manage. There's things to be done about the place to keep us busy. An' yer know we promised we'd keep up wi' our reading an' writing like yer mam's bin' teaching us, an' then there's the sums. By heck, we'll be that busy time'll just fly by. Now wipe tha' face an' smile fer there's enough to be worried about wi'out tekkin' your tears with . . ."

"Well, that's that," a cheerful voice from the doorway said. "I think I've got everything. Just put this rug over the cart, will you, Phoebe, and tie it firmly. You've made a splendid job of loading up, but it's almost eight o'clock and I want to be well on my way to Cockermouth by midday. I can get a good start with this lot and then spend the night there, that's if I can get someone to take me in dressed as I am though I think I'll have to find another way to confine all this."

The young 'man' removed his hat and about his shoulders fell the most amazing and glorious cloak of glowing copper hair, thick and tight-curled, and both Phoebe and Cat smiled in delight as the 'young man' revealed himself to be Annie Abbott.

Phoebe would never forget that day at the Keswick Tup Fair, nor that night when, with Cat sleeping the sleep of the truly exhausted, Annie railed about the kitchen at the fates which had landed her such a savage blow. Hour after hour the storm of outrage slammed against the whitewashed walls and hour after hour Phoebe listened to it until, at last, she had had enough and she said so.

She would not allow it, she said, nor the self-pity in which, if not sternly spoken to, Annie was about to wallow. The destructive self-pity which can paralyse and render impotent even the strongest and most self-willed. Phoebe's sympathy had been immediate, and her concern warm hearted since she knew as well as Annie that their future had depended on the small flock of sheep Annie meant to have. They had food, grown by herself and Annie during the summer; they had peat from which to make a fire to warm them; a roof over their head. They were not destitute but she also knew how the thought of that flock of sheep, the beginning of a *proper* farm was the candle-flame of hope which had been lit in Annie's heart twelve months ago. Before Phoebe had come to live at the farm at Browhead.

It was the first home Phoebe had ever known. A found-ling from some poorhouse she had been, put to work from the moment she could wield a scrubbing brush in her small, chapped hands, knowing nothing but her bucket and the dozens of pairs of legs, male and female, who had walked by it. Put out to various farming families, she had learned many basic crafts about a kitchen. But girls were hired for their size and strength and though she was willing and worked herself until she could barely stand, she was always 'let go' at the end of six months because she had not the sheer physical strength to perform many of the brutally heavy tasks expected of her about the farm. She worked from five in the morning until ten at night. She could shake mats, scrub flags, fetch water – in a small pail – do a week's wash, light fires, milk cows, blacklead a fireplace, scrub a table until it was white; she could bake and cook a plain meal, but that, apparently, had not been enough and her last employer had taken her into Keswick and, putting her few shillings in her hand, told her to stand in line with the other maid-servants.

She had been shown nothing but indifference, uncon-cern, an impassive apathy to how she might feel and a total lack of interest in what she thought, or indeed, if she thought at all. She was no more than a pair of chilblained hands which took the bucket, the soap, the brush, a blank face which showed no curiosity since her brain, her mind had never been taught that such an emotion might lead to understanding.

Annie Abbott had revealed a magic, a splendour, a miraculous, exploding world of love, of laughter and beauty to the starved senses of a girl who had been blind and deaf and she had done it with nothing more than what, to Annie and Cat, was a part of their everyday world. The stunted emotion of the child, the young girl, had developed and bloomed, brought about by no more than an affectionate hug, a helping hand, acceptance into a home in which there was love. She had been shown the sweetness and loveliness of a flower, the colour of a sunset, the song of a skylark. The mists hanging low over the still lake, the call of the curlew across Skiddaw Forest, the mingled smells of the valley freshness after rain, the sound of the wind in the pines. All these things and the warmth of love, the power of friendship, the light-hearted merriment of the child and the dogs, the need of Annie and Cat for Phoebe, the security of knowing that this was where she belonged. It had caused a transformation in the young girl, creating in her a resilience and toughness of which she was made aware a dozen times a day. Phoebe would give her life for Annie Abbott and for Cat, and she was not about to let either of them go under, not if she could help it.

Annie wept for the first time in many years.

"Nay lass, cry if tha' must," Phoebe said that night, just as though their roles were reversed. "But don't tha' tell me it's not fair. I'll not 'ave it, so there, an' when tha' comes to thissen, tha'll see the sense of it. Ah knows tha've 'ad a knock an' ah knows it's put us back a bit, but we'll catch up, see if we don't. Thee an' me, between us . . ."

"Phoebe, oh Phoebe . . . you don't understand. They hate me. They want to see me go under with nothing . . ."

"Don't say nothing, tha's got me an' Cat. We . . . we love thee."

"I know that but all the work I've done, the insults and

. . . and contempt I've known . . . a whole year, and now, when I've got the cash, they won't sell me the sheep. It's not fair . . . it's not fair . . ."

"Life's not fair." The girl's voice was soft, sad almost, for who knew better than she how unjust life was to some, how kind to others, but that was something else again and at the moment she was doing her best to lift this beloved friend from the depths of her despair.

It was not like Annie to give way like this and Phoebe knew that when she'd had a good cry and a good shout at the world in general and the farmers who had turned their backs on her in particular, she'd be her old self again, well, almost. A hard and bitter blow had fallen on her and that sort always left its mark, left the victim slightly weakened, but if Phoebe had anything to do with it, Annie'd get what she wanted in the end. Annie had taken it very bad, the refusal of the farmers to sell her their sheep, worse really than Phoebe had expected, for there were other fairs, farther afield, where Annie wasn't known and where sheep might be bought. But Annie had dragged herself about as though she had come to the end of the road and met head-on a wall over which there was no climbing. It was strange really, for on the way home from the fair at Keswick Phoebe had seen the grim clamping of Annie's mouth, the resolute jut to her jaw and the gleam in her eye which meant, as Phoebe well knew by now, that her benefactor and friend had made up her mind to something. Phoebe had gloated as she watched her, knowing that Annie had a plan to put right what had happened that day at the market. They had gone to their beds silently, but, Phoebe had been positive, with hope still about them. It had been several days later when Annie had suddenly broken down and given in to what looked like despair, crying and rocking as though the blow at Keswick had only just fallen.

"Nay," Phoebe said, "it's not like thi' ter give up so easy. I've not known thi' long, but tha've never struck me as bein' someone as'd lay down an' whine just 'cos a few daft buggers . . ."

"Oh Phoebe, I know, I know. Those daft buggers as

you call them are not worth shedding a tear over, but sometimes something happens, on top of all the other misfortunes, which just seems to . . . well . . ."

"What sorta things, Annie?"

"Oh, I don't know, things you don't quite expect. They creep up on you from behind, and even though you're half expecting them, indeed you know very well they're bound to happen, they take you by surprise and . . . knock the breath from you."

Phoebe hadn't the slightest idea what Annie was talking about and the expression on her plain little face said so. She was a practical girl who understood the mischievous tricks life played on you, the calamities which you could see and feel, just like the one that had befallen them, yes *them*, since Annie's troubles were *her* troubles now, but all this business about things creeping up on you, behind your back, seemed a bit nonsensical to her. What sort of things? Did Annie mean like that Bert Garnett who was always skulking along the path from Upfell Farm and down to Browhead? Hanging about when his wife and mother-in-law thought him, she supposed, to be away on farm business, slipping into Annie's kitchen after dark on some pretext or other. His eyes were like those of a weasel fixed on Annie's breasts and he licked his lips as a cat might, which is about to lap at a saucer of cream. Oh aye, he was the sort who'd creep up behind your back, he was, but Phoebe was surprised that it should upset Annie who was quite capable of giving him a lug round t'earhole if he so much as laid a finger on her.

They stood at the gate, Cat and Phoebe, waving and waving to her as she trudged up the lane in the direction of Gillthrop. The heavy sledge creaked along behind her. The rope they had hitched to it already bit into her tender shoulders beneath the old shirt and jacket which had been her father's. The dogs kept close to her side, looking back as she did, until they had turned the curve of the lane and Cat and Phoebe were out of sight.

"Well lads," she said to them, settling her father's hat more firmly on her head, for it would not do if her hair

fell about her shoulders, "let's get going." She hitched up
the trousers making sure the braces on them were secure,
for the waist was too big for her. They felt strange, but
the freedom in walking was marvellous. No wonder men
wore them, denying the privilege to their womenfolk, she
thought, as she strode through the village of Gillthrop.
Women who stood in their doorways stared at her, aware
that they had seen the tall youth somewhere but not
awfully sure where it could have been.

She took the road straight ahead to Uldale, squaring her
shoulders beneath the chafing rope with which she dragged
the sledge, the ache there infinitely less than the one in
her heart which had begun when she had heard of Reed
Macauley's impending marriage.

15

It was the man from Long Beck, the farm up by Dash Beck, who knocked at the door, and Phoebe opened it knowing they had nothing to fear from him.

"Where is she?" he demanded to know abruptly, almost before the door was ajar, ready to push it wider and stick his foot in it, just as though he expected it to be shut in his face. He peered over Phoebe's shoulder, his frown forbidding but in his eyes was that look Phoebe had seen in them when last he was here.

"The mistress is not 'ere at the moment," she said politely, as Annie had taught her. Phoebe was not to say where she was or how long she would be, Annie had said. On no account was Phoebe to let any caller know that Annie would be away overnight, in fact Phoebe was to act as though Annie was no further away than the coppice wood, or up on the peat moor digging for peat.

"Can I give 'er a message?" Phoebe continued, her face expressionless, empty of all but her need to be courteous but at the same time close the door in the visitor's face since the biting wind was nipping smartly in through the open door.

"Where is she?" the man said again, only his barely controlled awareness of the need for restraint on the door-step of another's home keeping him from pushing past the stiff figure of the young girl and into Annie's kitchen.

"She's out just now," Phoebe shifted not an inch.

"But where, for God's sake? Is she up on the fell?" he asked, turning to stare up into the high distance of Great Cockup. He shaded his eyes with a gloved hand against the bright, cold autumn sun, then turned again to look down the sloping fields towards the lake as though Annie might suddenly appear. The afternoon sun cast long shadows as it settled behind the stand of trees by the waterside. Tall Scotch pines, dense and darkly green, and all about them and about the lake, on its far side and blazing up the fells to where it met the grey craggy rocks, was the golden glory of the drying bracken. Gold and yellow and orange melting down to the blue and purple waters of the lake where the colours mingled, rippling out from the shore in moving beauty. On the very tops of the tallest fells there was the first faint dusting of winter snow.

"Nay, I couldn't say," Phoebe answered politely, "but she'll not be long."

It was a mistake and as the words left her mouth, Phoebe knew it.

"Then I'll wait," the man said at once and before Phoebe could test her puny strength against his, he had pushed open the door and was inside. The dog at his feet was told brusquely to wait, and the door, taken from Phoebe's hand, was closed upon the animal.

Reed Macauley looked about him, ready for the affronted voice of Annie Abbott to come at him demanding to know what he was doing in her kitchen since he had not believed what the girl had told him. She was in the house somewhere he had decided, keeping her distance, unwilling to confront him, to listen to him, no matter what he had to say to her.

And what *had* he to say to her? he asked himself, as he had done ever since he had ordered his mare to be saddled and had set off in the direction of Browhead. They were nothing to one another, he and Annie Abbott. They had never, in the twelve months he had known her, touched one another, never kissed or clasped hands. They had known no physical contact, had exchanged no promises, no vows, nor even words which might be construed as loving, and yet he loved her. She loved him. He knew it and so did she and he was, in the spring, to marry another woman. So why was he here? To do what? To say what? He did not know, he only knew that the compulsion to come, now that Esmé and her parents had returned to

Yorkshire, going before the winter snows locked them in,
had been unassailable. Of course, he had heard of her
misadventure in Keswick – who in these parts had not –
and he meant to put it right if he could do so without
upsetting that proud and rebellious spirit of hers. He'd *give*
her the damned sheep if she'd let him, and if not, sell them
to her at the lowest price he was able, *if she would let
him*. That was the trouble. She was so damned high and
mighty, she was likely to take offence and tell him to go
to the devil, taking his sheep with him, even if he offered
her the pick of his flock. But he couldn't let her go on
like this, being humiliated and treated contemptuously by
everyone in the district, sneered and jeered at, working
her fingers and her proud back right down to the bone in
her determination to be successful. Jesus, he had the
power, the wealth, the influence to put a stop to it right
now for there were not many in the parish of Bassenthwaite who did not owe a favour to Reed Macauley, and
it would take but a word from him to set her on her feet
and on the path she wanted to go. Of course, if he did
that he would also give her the power she needed to snap
her fingers at him when all he wanted, all he had ever
wanted was to have her dependent on him, soft, loving,
submissive, waiting, sighing for Reed Macauley. He
wanted to look after her, not give her the means to look
after herself. Even if he married . . . *when* he married
Esmé, he and Annie could . . . many men had an . . .
arrangement to which their wives made no objection. It
was, at least amongst the upper classes, quite normal for
a man to have a mistress, providing he was discreet and
did not fling it in the faces of those with whom he was
acquainted. Ezra Hodgson and Ben Pearson both kept a
cosy nest with a pretty bird in it, Ezra in Penrith and
Ben in Rosthwaite, far enough away not to offend the
sensibilities of their wives, but near enough to ride over
when they had a fancy for . . . well, what men with good,
sensible, but unresponsive wives, needed.

His eyes roamed the room as he waited for her to
appear, noticing the shining, fragrant cleanliness of the

homely kitchen. So had his mother's looked years ago
when he was a boy and the Macauleys, though well set
up farmers, had not had the wealth, nor the need for the
luxurious living he now enjoyed. His mother had worked
in her kitchen, directing her maids in the making of soap
and candles, bread and all the good food she had stuffed
into his father and himself. A true farmwife, who thought
nothing of spinning and weaving the cloth for their clothes,
in between her many other household chores. Now, *his*
wife had no need to do more than adorn his drawing room
when her callers came, sit at his table and make small talk
when his guests dined, make herself available in his bed
when he needed her, and produce his children which a
well-trained nurse and governess, or tutor, would bring up
for her. Not for her this gleaming, glowing, well-polished
comfort, the good smells of nourishing food which *she* had
cooked in her nostrils, and the sight of her children about
the kitchen table, busy on their primers, as Annie's child
was, dogs sprawled by the fire and . . . dogs . . . where
were the dogs? . . . The dogs were not here so where in
hell had Annie got to where she needed her dogs with
her? She had no sheep so why had she . . . ? Where had
she . . . ? Where *was* she . . . ? The two girls round the
table . . . reading apparently . . . two places set with
plates and cutlery . . . not three . . . two . . . so where
the devil . . . ?

"Where is she?" he said for the third time.

She had reached Caldbeck within the week. Though as
the crow flies it was no more than ten or so miles from
Gillthrop, the roads were winding and tortuous, simply no
more than rutted tracks in some parts, high and treacherous, and she had made many detours as she moved from
farm to farm, village to village, cottage to cottage, in the
selling of her besoms, her swill baskets and her long woollen stockings. Though most of the farm women made their
own, her goods had sold well in the villages and the small
towns of Uldale and Caldbeck. Women there did not have
the materials to make such things themselves, relying on

pedlars to bring them to the door or the market stalls at fair time. The stallholders at the fairs in the cycle of trading had bought the goods they sold from the farm women and, of course, wishing to make a profit for their trouble, had put a penny or two on the price, and the tall, good-looking young man with the soft voice was welcome with his cheaper and better-quality goods. She had spent three days in Uldale, moving with her sledge to every house in every narrow street, the dogs one on either side of her. Blackie and Bonnie were uneasy, quick to alarm, should something they did not care for threaten their mistress. They were not accustomed to people, to other dogs, to cats, horses, carts and carriages and every one seemed to them a menace with which they must deal. It took Annie's sharp commands to keep them from lunging at all and sundry. The men who passed her by, though they could not have said why, stared at her, curious and strangely ill at ease with the young man who had the graceful gait of a female which sat awkwardly on his tall, long-legged frame.

She had pulled the sledge, lighter now and easier on her chafed shoulders, through Longlands, Greenhead, Branthwaite and Fellside, going up and up, higher into the rolling peaklands towards Caldbeck Fell, where she could have taken a short cut over the tops had she not wished to go on to Parkend, Whelpo and Caldbeck itself. It was in Caldbeck she knew she would find, as she had done in Uldale, many customers for her wares. She had spent the nights in tiny inns, taking the cheapest room, alone of course, since to sleep in a double or triple, sharing with other men, though cheaper, would have caused no end of trouble; she smiled to herself as the thought came to her.

It was getting colder. The days were shortening and soon the last fortnightly cattle market would be held at Rosley, which was her destination. She had already gone past files of slow-moving cattle, and some sheep, winding their way along the passes and the fellsides, some on their journeys to new pastures and some to the cattle fair.

Whitsuntide was the time of the largest fair at Rosley Hill when travellers with their beasts came from all points of the compass to sell their goods and their animals. Rosley was on the main drove road from Scotland to the north of England and it attracted thousands of men, and women too. Its influence reached across the Solway and into Annan and Dumfries, mile after mile of gentle greenery and lush enclosures which housed the cattle and other animals as they made their way there from the Solway Plain and beyond. To the east of Rosley was the grazing ground of High Hesket, which meant that the market was set in exactly the right place to meet the needs of man and beast. Foot passengers from Carlisle and Penrith as well as Scotland found the going easy. Travelling people such as the young actor who had seduced fourteen-year-old Annie Abbott were drawn there. Pot-selling women came balancing enormous baskets of pots on their heads, the basket resting on a weather-bleached hat braided with ribbon. They wore long gaudy gowns with a blue flannel petticoat showing at the front. They smoked a short pipe for they cared nought for any man's opinion and usually had a horde of youngsters about them who carried baskets on their hips. There were carriers and collectors of news, since it was hard to come by up on the rolling fells of Hesket Forest and Westward. There were men dealing in rags and skins, women who told fortunes, vagrants and Irishmen in increasing numbers who came from Ireland into Whitehaven on coal vessels, making their way to wherever there was a promise of work, and beneath it all was a vague and shifting underworld of organised gangs of thieves and pickpockets, waiting to pounce on the unwary.

But there were none of these about as Annie Abbott approached The Drover's Rest two weeks after she had left Gillthrop. It was too late in the year for the 'fair' people, those who came to beg and entertain at the great Whitsuntide Fair. There were about her the last of the men selling what remained of their cattle and sheep and none took any interest in the tall youth who pulled an old and empty sledge and at whose heels two silent dogs trailed. Except one!

He was leaning against the inn wall, a pint pot of ale in his fist, one heel resting on the stones behind him, one hand deep in the pocket of his narrow corduroy trousers. He was tall, young and lean and straight as an arrow. No bulk about him, but a taut whipcord strength which seemed to promise toughness. He had brown, curly hair and grey, cat-like eyes set in a clever face. His mouth had a humorous twist to it, as it dipped into the ale and his grey eyes were watchful, everywhere at once, keen and alert as though he was not only guarding his back but planning his route ahead.

His eyes stopped moving as they came to rest on the figure of the tall young man and a puzzled, deliberating expression narrowed them in his brown face. He watched as the youth moved gracefully across the inn yard, a sledge at his back, his stride as long as any man's, his shoulders slightly hunched, his head set somewhat awkwardly on his shoulders, just as though he was doing his best to hide something.

But what? He was a perfectly ordinary young man, tall and slim and very shabby, but then so were many of the travellers who entered and left the inn. It was a working man's inn, cheap and clean, where dozens of drovers stayed as they took their masters' cattle and sheep, to and from the fair. He studied the young man as he leaned to put a slim hand on each of the heads of the dogs and they both lay down next to the exceedingly fragile-looking sledge. He went inside and the man leaning on the wall drifted after him. He did not know why.

"Have you a room?" he heard the youth say in a low voice to the innkeeper.

"We 'ave that, lad, at least a bed if that's any good to thi'."

"I'd like a room to myself, if you please." The landlord looked surprised.

"Nay, lad, this is t'last fair an' I'm pulled out wi' drovers. Tha's lucky to get thi' a bed to thissen, which tha'll have,

I promise thi', but not a room. See, there's only one other in't room an' that's this chap behind thi'. He'll not mind sharing, will tha', sir?"

Charlie Lucas smiled infectiously, raising his pint pot in the direction of the landlord, before turning to look into the softest, most incredibly beautiful pair of brown eyes he had ever seen on any human being, let alone another male, and it was then, as the strange imperceptive feeling of disquiet became stronger, that he began to realise.

"Not at all," he said, looking enquiringly at the youth, waiting politely to see if he was to share his room.

"No, thanks . . . I'll . . . No, thanks . . ."

"There's not a bed to be found in all of Rosley, lad," the innkeeper said somewhat irritably since he'd no time to stand around prattling on about beds with this strange-looking lad, especially one he could rent without trouble, and strange the lad was an' all. He'd better watch himself with some of the men they got around here who, short of a woman, didn't care where they stuck their 'John Willys'. Odd sort of a lad he was, who, had he been a girl, would have looked as pretty as a picture. Perhaps that's why he was so keen to get his own room, having had experiences of a . . . perverted sort before. Still, the other chap seemed harmless enough, the one who'd offered to share, but no, the lad was walking away, shaking his head as though someone had suggested he sleep in a bed with a dozen others and a ewe or two as well.

"No, thank you, it's most kind of you . . ." *Most kind of you!* The landlord wiped his cloth over the bar top, staring in amazement at the young man's back. *Most kind of you!* Whoever he was, he had the manners of a well brought up lass but he'd better watch himself because already several of his customers were nudging one another and staring after him.

Annie could feel the interest in her as she stepped through the doorway and into the sharp autumn sunshine. She would have to be careful what she said, really she would. She quite forgot sometimes that young men, what-ever their station in life, just did not use the same phrases as women, and she had slipped up several times when she had been selling door to door in Uldale and Caldbeck but then it had not mattered unduly since she had been dealing with women who had been inclined to like the politeness of the young man who was peddling his besoms and swills. They had not questioned it when she had smiled and remarked on the weather – when it had turned wet – and on the state of her clogs; the mud which she was traipsing on to their clean doorsteps and how sorry she was about it. How kind they were to offer her a mug of ale, she had said, but thank you, no. She did not wish to appear rude but . . . They had smiled, thinking her quite charming, thinking she was a good-mannered and well-spoken lad to be working as *he* was, but these rough men who lived the lives of nomads and vagrants, some of them, had no such appreciation of pretty manners, and walking was difficult too. It was her habit to straighten her back and shoulders, to walk tall and proud, her head held high, but this action thrust forward her breasts and to hide them she found she must slouch along with her shoulders hunched. The times she had forgotten, striding out eagerly towards her goal, which surely now was in sight, only to remember when some man studied her in puzzlement.

She spoke softly to Blackie and Bonnie as she untied the knotted rope of the sledge, looking up and down the narrow track on which The Drover's Rest stood. She could see at once that there was not another building in the area. The fairground was enormous and empty beyond it. There was a well where water was drawn to water the animals and in the middle of the fairground was a large cow pen in which many animals lowed restively. At the far end of the ground was a public quarry where possibly she might find a ledge with an overhang where she could shelter for the night but all around her was nothing but the vast expanse of Rosley Fairground and the rolling hills of Westward leading to the Solway Plain.

"You'll find nowhere in which to shelter, I'm afraid, not at least where you'll be . . . safe."

The voice was neutral, pleasant, with no accent that

she could place. The words were spoken softly, almost in a whisper and it was obvious that the man who spoke them meant no one to hear but herself.

She turned only her head and that but a fraction. Her jacket collar was up and she had wound round and round her neck one of the long knitted scarves she had fashioned herself last winter. It came up about her chin, almost covering her mouth. Her father's soft felt hat was pulled down to her ears and between the muffler and the hat, her eyes blazed defiantly. Speaking over her shoulder, her own words were as quiet as his.

"What's it to you," she said, "where I sleep?" trying to sound like one man taking umbrage with another.

"Nothing at all . . . lad. Not to me. But it will to you if it's discovered you're not what you seem."

"I don't know what you mean." Disconcertingly, in her panic, her voice rose to its normal pitch and the man at her back smiled.

"I'm sure you do and I'm also sure you have a good reason for your . . . masquerade. Believe me, I mean you no harm but there are dozens who would if they . . . found out you were . . . not as they are. Why don't you go back inside and, before someone else takes it, tell the landlord that you have changed your mind about the bed? That you would be happy to share with Charlie Lucas. Yes, that's me, young . . . sir, Charlie Lucas at your service."

From the corner of her eye Annie saw the impish smile, the slight bow, the raised whimsical eyebrows and, suddenly and for no reason whatsoever, she liked what she saw. Nevertheless she had no intention of allowing anyone, even this rather personable young man, to penetrate her disguise.

Her voice was gruff. "I've no idea what you're up to, mister, and I don't want to. I'd just as soon sleep out of doors with my dogs, than share a room with anyone, if it's all the same to you. As for being safe, I've nothing worth stealing." Her hand, of its own volition, went to the deep pocket of her father's ancient trousers where, sewn into a small bag and attached to the pocket lining was her

small hoard of savings. It had come from the sale of her
swills and besoms and stockings, and included what she
had scraped together over the past year. A tidy sum which
was to buy her sheep tomorrow.

The man noticed the movement but he did not let her
see it.

"Besides," she went on, tossing her head, unaware that
a wispy curl of shining copper had escaped over her left
ear, "I have my dogs to protect me," which, if she had
thought about it, was a strange thing for a man to say.

"Just as you like then, but before you move off into that
crowd of drovers, those who have nowhere to sleep
except where, presumably, you mean to lay your head,
and who, most of them, are as drunk as lords, I should
pull my hat more firmly over my head, or they may take
a fancy to see more of that rather lovely curl which is
falling round your ear."

Her hand went to her ear involuntarily, frantically pushing at the vagrant tendril, doing her best to get it out of
sight, but the more she tried to shove it under her hat,
the more it came down.

"Leave it," the man said gently, moving to stand in front
of her. "Now do it," and under the pretext of leaning to
pat her dogs, they both bent down whilst she adjusted her
unruly hair.

"I think you had better take that bed," he said, his voice
still gentle.

"I cannot sleep in a room with a . . . a . . . stranger, a
man I met no more than ten minutes ago." She spoke
through gritted teeth and her voice was normal. The
pretence she had kept up for almost two weeks was
abandoned.

"I'm not suggesting you do so, though you would be
quite safe, I can assure you, if you did. I take no pleasure,
believe me, from an unwilling woman." He smiled lazily.
"What I do suggest is we go up together as though we
were to share and then, later, when it is quiet, I will slip
out and leave you your privacy."

"How do I know you . . . will keep your word?"

"I have just told you. I like my women to be . . . amenable." Again the grin, sweet and wicked, and Annie could not help but smile back. Though his grey eyes told her he was vastly intrigued by her charade, and was willing to help her in it, and indeed in anything else she might allow, his slanting smile and amiable expression said she had nothing to fear from him. He would take nothing she did not give voluntarily.

She drew a deep breath, again unaware of the lift of her full breasts beneath the roomy jacket.

"Very well . . ."

"Charlie, Charlie Lucas."

"I'm . . . Annie Abbott."

"Miss Abbott." He inclined his head, his eyes twinkling. "But I had better call you . . ."

"What?"

"How about . . . Andrew . . . or Andy?"

"Very well, but I must warn you that if . . ."

"Yes, Andy?" and his smile was so innocent she could not help but smile back.

"I shall take my dogs to the room with me."

"Of course."

"They will not take kindly to anyone interfering with me."

"I can see that," he replied as he fondled the head of the grinning Blackie.

Reed Macauley was in Caldbeck when he found a woman, the wife of the innkeeper of The Flying Fox, who remembered buying half a dozen pairs of thick, beautifully knitted woollen stockings from a slim and handsome young pedlar with two sheepdogs. Oh, days ago now it was, she told him. No, she couldn't rightly remember exactly when, probably a week because her Arthur had worn one pair and they'd been in the wash already on account of him having sweaty feet. Came with standing behind the bar all day, see. His feet swelled something awful, making it worse, so these good woollen stockings would be a boon to him and she only wished she'd got another half a dozen.

Well, so beautifully knitted, and so cheap and the young chap was that polite . . . What? Where was he going? . . . Nay, she didn't know, though she'd seen him moving from cottage to cottage later in the day, pulling that there flimsy old sledge. No, she'd no idea where he'd spent the night. Certainly not at *her* hostelry where a better class of person than pedlars were accommodated. No, he *hadn't* said where he was off to next, sir, and really there was no need to shout. She wasn't deaf and if he was going to be abusive she'd be forced to call her husband. Very well then, she'd ask her husband if *he'd* spoken to the lad if the gentleman insisted, but really, it would do no good to question those in the bar because . . . oh very well, if he insisted she'd make enquiries . . . What? . . . Well . . . as it happened they did have a room for the night seeing as how one of their gentlemen had sent a message to cancel a regular booking . . . a lawyer he was who always came up to Caldbeck every . . . very well, Nancy will show you to your room and your horse will be attended to . . . well, did you see that, Nancy? . . . not so much as a thank you after all she'd told him. I mean to say, she couldn't be expected to know the direction taken by everyone who came to her back door. Could she?

16

Annie fell asleep almost before her head touched the sleazy pillow. She and Charlie had eaten a meal together in a corner of the bar, surprisingly good, consisting of thick wedges of bread in an enormous bowl of rabbit stew, pickles and cheese, again with bread and a tankard of ale apiece. The dogs had dined, lying beneath their feet, on hefty bones on which there was a fair amount of mutton left, and no one took the slightest interest in either her or Charlie Lucas.

They went up to the small attic room, the dogs pattering silently at Annie's back and when Annie sat down on the truckle bed, they lay across her feet and stared, flat-eyed, flat-eared, at the man who closed the door behind him.

"I have to stay until the bar empties, you do understand."

"Yes." Her eyes were on his face, her stiff manner saying that despite her instinct that told her she could believe this engagingly smiling young man when he said he would not harm her, her logical brain said she was quite insane to trust a perfect stranger just because he *seemed* all right.

"I meant what I said."

"Very well, but I would like to . . . to wash and . . ."

"I'll see if I can get you some hot water."

"Won't it cause . . . curiosity when you do? I believe gentlemen of the road don't bother with such things."

He smiled. "I am a gentleman of the road and, on occasion, I like a hot bath."

"Oh, I don't mean to bathe," she said hastily, the idea of removing *any* of her clothing in this room, which, she had already noticed, had no bolt on the door, quite horrific.

"Of course not, but if I was to . . . return to the bar for a last pint of ale you could . . ." he paused delicately, "the dogs would . . ."

The jug of water was hot and though she had no more than a brief wash, hurriedly shrugging herself back into her jacket and waistcoat before Charlie Lucas returned from the bar, she felt a lot cleaner than she had since she left home. She had brushed her hair which had become tangled beneath her hat and was just about to re-plait it when he tapped gently on the door.

"It's me," he murmured, but when she went to the door and opened it, her manner still stiff and constrained, he simply stood in the doorway as though a giant hand held him firmly rooted to the bare, unpolished boards.

"Good God," he whispered. His grey eyes had narrowed to deep grey velvet slits and his lips parted in a half-smile of wonderment. He shook his head. "Good God," he said again, "it's as well none of those men below saw you like that." His eyes moved from the flowing curtain of her hair to the delicate loveliness of the white skin at her bare neck, the soft curve of her mouth, the tilt of her fine eyebrows and the slanting set of her deep, golden eyes. How in hell's name had any chap who had clapped eyes on her, even in her man's clothing and the wide-brimmed soft felt bowler which she had jammed down over the glowing magnificence of her hair, believed that this, this glorious woman, was a *man*? Her jacket and waistcoat were still unbuttoned and the proud jut of her lovely breast strained against the coarse grey woollen shirt she wore. The belt about her tiny waist was drawn tight and her hips flared, womanly and infinitely desirable, beneath it.

"Good God, Annie Abbott," he said softly, "how have you got away with it?"

She stepped back, then swung about, her hair flying round her in a swirl of glowing copper, the light from the candle deepening it into rippling shadows. Grabbing the ribbon from the bed she thrust it under her hair at the back of her neck and with deft, sure fingers, tied it fiercely, straining it from her face. She began to plait it, bringing it over her shoulder and when it was done she wound it round the top of her head and secured it with several pins.

"Don't you get any ideas, Charlie Lucas," she hissed, "or my dogs will tear you to pieces." She picked up the hairbrush which she had thrown on the bed and held it threateningly in front of her, and the dogs, catching her fear, stood up, their hackles rising, their tails stiff and straight. From both throats came a growled warning.

"May I come in for a moment? If anyone was to come along this passage they would find it quite fascinating to see me pleading to enter my own room. Please, Annie . . . Andy, the bar is almost empty and I can slip out in half an hour or so."

"Where will you sleep?"

"Oh, I have found a cosy corner in a shed at the back of the inn. I had a reconnoitre whilst you were washing."

"Very well, but I warn you . . ."

"I know, the dogs will tear me to pieces."

She woke just as daylight crept in through the attic window. The room was dim, shadowed, the sparse furniture, a press for clothes, a chair and dresser, merely darker shapes in the gloom. The dogs slept peacefully beside her and in the other bed, Charlie Lucas slept also, one arm flung out defencelessly, the other under his head. His deep breathing was as peaceful as the dogs. He was fully dressed.

She smiled and stretched, amazed at her own unconcern.

It was whilst they were breaking their fast that it happened.

"Porridge oats," the landlord told them, "an' there's eggs for those who can pay."

"Porridge and eggs, Andy?" Charlie asked, his face innocent and smiling, the night they had just spent in the same room, though it had not been planned since he had meant what he said about the shed, concerning him as little as it seemed it had Annie. She had fallen asleep, exhausted, putting her trust in him, and he would not abuse that trust, he had told himself, despite her desirability and defencelessness. But his own weariness, as he waited for the bar to clear, had been his undoing and when he awoke, she was pulling her hat well down over the top knot of her hair.

"All right?" she had asked, indicating her appearance, making no more of it than that.

"Fine. A real broth of a boy you look."

So now they were tucking into a great bowl of steaming porridge oats whilst she told him how she meant to buy a decent flock of sheep, only small, 'twinters', if she could get them, and the price was right, leaving them here to winter, paying some trustworthy farmer to look after them for her.

"And where will you find such a man?"

"I don't know but I will. I can't drive them home on my own." She spooned the delicious porridge into her mouth, not with the rough eagerness of the men about her, but with the delicacy of the woman he knew her to be, and again he marvelled on how she had got away with it. Now that he knew himself, he was amazed that none of the other men at the inn could tell. Though her hands were brown and rough, they were slim, long-fingered, her wrists, where they poked from the rather short sleeves of the jacket, fine and slender. She wore her muffler again but when she bent her head to spoon the porridge into her mouth, her white neck was partially revealed, as smooth as silk, as white as alabaster. She was lovely, feminine, and the men's clothing only made her more so, at least to him who knew.

Disaster struck as she bent down to take the rope which held Blackie and Bonnie. Blackie stood up at once, catching her unawares and as her head struck the table when she straightened up, her hat was dislodged, falling away and rolling into the centre of the room, just in front of the bar, where it came to rest. Several eyes followed it, then turned to smile at the lad who had lost it. But not only had the hat taken a blow. Pins showered about her and slowly, so slowly – it was as though her womanhood was making a declaration and wished no one in the bar to miss it – her plait unravelled and her glorious hair fell about her like a cloak. The weak sun coming through the window struck it to a living, curling mass which reached to her waist. There was a warm, lively glow to it, which made every man in the room want to bury his face in it. Suddenly she was a woman, glossy, rounded, they could see it now, rosy mouthed and comely.

The silence in the room was unparalleled. From the kitchen at the back of the bar a woman's voice squeaked in tuneless song and there was a great clatter of pans. A boy's voice shouted that he'd fetch some more eggs from the run and the woman stopped her caterwauling to tell him to look lively. In contrast the quiet in the bar was appalling as those who had not seen the hat fall but who had been nudged by those who had, turned to stare in absolute silence at the woman who had miraculously appeared in their midst.

The landlord did not know what to do. He simply stood there, his jaw sagging, his brain paralysed, and when it came to life again, he still did not know what to do. No crime had been committed, as far as he was aware. Was it illegal for a woman to dress as a man? He didn't know. And what about the chap with her? They had spent the night together but again, that was not against the law, was it? Still, he didn't like it and now, as his reasoning and his power of speech returned, he was about to tell her so.

"What's goin' on 'ere?" he asked truculently, and every man's eye, as it had done in Keswick Market, turned to Annie Abbott, and as she had done then, she felt something die of shame inside her. Dear God . . . oh, dear sweet God, was she never to be allowed to draw her life together, to make the most of it, what she had? To better her life, and Cat's? She had been forced to this subterfuge by men such as these who would not countenance doing business with a woman, striking a deal with someone of the opposite sex. They were entrenched in the ways they had always known, the moralistic, male notion that a woman's place was in the kitchen and the marriage bed and by God, that was where she would stay. None of

these men who gaped at her knew Annie Abbott. None of
them knew she had an illegitimate child but still she could
feel their hostility and their salacious thoughts were very
evident in their expressions.

Charlie stood up on the opposite side of the table. He
walked casually across the room, stooping to pick up her
hat, brushing it down with his sleeve and handing it to her
as if it was a task he did every day of the week.

"Put on your hat, my dear, and let us go and look at
those sheep we promised ourselves."

She did as she was told, shoving it on to the back of
her head and from it her hair flowed and rippled down her
back. Her beauty was stunning, unique, indescribable, and
there was not a man there, thunderstruck and silent, who
dared to speak a word in disapproval. Not that she would
have cared if one had. She was looking for no one's
approval any more. Let them think what they liked, the
damn lot of them. She was doing her very best. The best
that Annie Abbott could do, and if it was not to their liking,
or indeed to anyone's liking, then they could go to the
devil. *She* approved of herself. She thought she was pretty
damn smart and that was all that mattered. She'd get
there. She would.

She stood up, her hat set at a devil-may-care angle on
her shining hair. She lifted her chin, shoved her hands
deep in the pockets of her father's baggy old trousers,
thrust foward her breasts and swaggered to the door,
followed by Charlie Lucas. His eyes were narrowed in
smiling admiration.

"Right, Charlie," she said for all to hear, "let's go and
see what's on offer."

Reed could hear them singing before they were in sight.
Two voices, one male and one female and he knew at once
that the female was Annie.

He had spent the night at The Flying Fox in Caldbeck,
setting off at early light on the road which led through
Rotten Row and up the gentle hill, just under a thousand
feet high, which led across Broad Moor to Rosley. He had

been on the road for no more than an hour, the summit of the hill just ahead of him when the words of the song rose in the crisp autumn air and at once the memory of when he had last heard them came to him. She had been singing them then.

"Come all of you Cockers far and near . . ."

He reached the top of the slope as they came towards him.

There were about two dozen ewes, twinters, his experienced eye automatically told him, and one fine ram. Two dogs were working them, Merles, both of them, and though they were young and eager, they were obeying the whistles and commands of the tall young man who strode at their heels. The inborn herding instinct which all good sheepdogs have, showed in the way they kept up with the galloping sheep and, at a word from the youth, shot ahead, one to each flank, to slow the small flock down when it would have gone careering down the rough track.

"Come by, Blackie," and "Away to me, Bonnie," and Blackie kept to the left, Bonnie to the right. "Steady . . . steady," and the two dogs moved the flock along at a reasonable pace.

There was another man who, though he kept up with the flock, gave the appearance of strolling. His hands were in his trouser pockets. His good broadcloth coat was open and pushed back and the wind ruffled his brown curly hair. He and the first youth continued their song, their heads thrown back in unison, their young throats arched, and the empty hills seemed to echo with the sound of their song.

It was Annie who saw him first and at once her throat closed up. The sheep continued to trot towards him and the dogs ran silently from side to side at the back of them. Annie stopped dead on the track and the man with her, who had walked on a couple of steps, turned, surprised.

"What is it, Annie?" Reed heard him say, his voice educated, cultured even, with none of the flat, long-drawn-out vowels of the Northerner. He turned then to stare where Annie did and Charlie Lucas and Reed Macauley looked into one another's faces for the first time.

The sheep had reached Reed's tall mare, parting like the waters of a stream round a rock, and the dogs, with no voice to guide them, continued at a growing speed down the slope. The track to Rotten Row and Caldbeck branched to the left just beyond Reed's mare but, as Annie stood, silently rooted to the bit of stony path on which she had stopped at the sight of him, the sheep overshot it and the dogs followed. They were doing what Annie had trained them to do, herding what was in their care but with no commands from her, the band of animals would soon be out of control.

"You'd best speak to your dogs, Annie Abbott," he said, and though his voice was mild, his eyes were colder than a blue winter sky and there was a thin white line, livid and very noticeable about his mouth.

Still she stood. She had plaited her hair as she and Charlie began the drive down the fell from Rosley, though she had worn it carelessly tied with its ribbon and spilling down her back as she and Charlie had bartered for the sheep she wanted. She had been disagreeably aware that had it not been for Charlie's presence, she would have been as unsuccessful as she had been at Keswick. They did not want to do business with her. Her 'femaleness' got in their way. They could not tear their gaze away from her shining eyes, the soft flush of excitement on her creamy skin, the rippling amazement of her hair across her shoulders and back and the very evident fullness of her breast as she strode, straight-backed, among the pens. How could they make a sale and a profit, if their shrewd minds were plagued with her beauty? And so they would have turned their backs on her as they had at Keswick, but she let Charlie bid for her and it seemed they had no objection to that. He was a man, after all. She showed him the sheep she wanted and, keeping an eye on her as she nodded or shook her head, he bought them for her.

There are crags, bracken and bogs on the fells and the

Herdwicks she chose were the only breed of sheep to do well there. The strain had proved itself for centuries where she came from. They were small, wiry and agile as goats. They had deep, round bodies and rough white faces. They were thick-boned, sweet-fleshed with a massed fleece which was hard to shear, but they could survive in the harshness of Lakeland winters. The ram she had hired had fine curling horns, creamy white in colour, springing from the back of his head, and in May, after he had serviced her flock, she was to return him to his owner at Rosley Whitsuntide Fair.

She found her voice at last, tearing her eyes away from Reed Macauley's terrible anger.

"Come on, Blackie, come on, Bonnie," she called and with a flurry of excited nippings which, with the part of her mind not concerned with Reed Macauley, she made a mental note to train from them, they turned the flock and began to drive them back towards her. It took several long minutes to quieten sheep and dogs alike, but eventually the dogs lay on the grass, their noses on their paws, their eyes first on the flock, then on Annie, the sheep cropping placidly. The ram was already doing his best to mount a willing ewe and again the farmer in her made note of it, thinking hysterically that her flock would have grown by a couple of lambs before she got them back to Browhead.

Charlie moved to stand beside her and though he still lounged in that casual way he had, he was clearly ready to protect her, should it be necessary, from the black-browed horseman who seemed about to spring from his mare and attack her. He said nothing.

"What d'you want, Reed?" she asked quietly enough.

"I came to bring you home." He could barely speak through his gritted teeth.

"Don't be ridiculous." Her voice was low and, it seemed to Charlie, had a deep sadness in it.

"It is you who are ridiculous, Annie. Or rather foolhardy. I don't know who this . . . this . . . gentleman is beside you and I don't care. There will be time for that later. If you would be good enough to climb up behind me, I will take you home where you belong."

She laughed, a short sharp bark and put her hand to her brow as though in deep perplexity. She looked down at her clogged feet which had tramped so far in the last two weeks then up again at him. She saw the terrible fear in his eyes. She saw the wildness, the anger and the love, the deep and tearing love in him for her and her voice was gentle.

"Go home, Reed. I am in no danger. Charlie here . . ." smiling at the man beside her, ". . . is a friend . . ."

"When did you meet?" The words tore out of him, the sound like the ripping of calico.

"When? Why, yesterday. Was it only yesterday, Charlie?" smiling again.

"*Yesterday!* You develop your friendships very easily, Annie Abbott, and very quickly too. This time yesterday you had not met and today you are the best of friends. Is that it?"

"Why . . . yes, that is it, Reed. It just so happens . . ."

"I have no wish to know what happened so if you will bid your friend goodbye, we will be on our way."

"Now look here . . ."

"No! You look here, Annie. I am tired of hearing your name mentioned wherever I go, usually in connection with some damn fool escapade that no sane person, man or woman, would be involved with. You trip lightly here and there, dressed in . . . in . . ." He could barely speak, so great was his emotion, ". . . whatever that outfit you have on is . . . with no thought nor care for your own safety or reputation, men about you like flies to syrup . . . look at you . . . Dear sweet Christ, have you any idea what . . . what men would do to you if they found you alone up here . . ."

"I am not alone . . ."

"You have been. That is if you only made the acquaintance of . . . of this jackanapes yesterday. Or are you being honest with me? Have the two of you been tramping the fells together for the past two weeks? I thought Bert Garnett was your . . ."

"Stop it, Reed . . . stop it!"

". . . but I can see any man will suit . . ."

"I'd be obliged if you'd get down from that horse and apologise to Miss Abbott, and failing that perhaps you would care to remove your coat and insult me instead of a lady who cannot, at least with her fists, defend herself."

Charlie stepped forward, placing himself in front of Annie, gently urging her away, but her two dogs, sensing danger, stood up and at once the flock began to eddy this way and that, one or two heading back up the track in the direction from which they had come. The confusion grew. Blackie was clearly of the opinion that his loyalty lay with his mistress and began to growl threateningly, not quite sure which man should be his target, whilst Bonnie moved to circle the remaining flock, at the same time casting anxious glances at those who had escaped him. He did not know what to do, and he yelped for an order.

"Dear God, will you stop it, both of you, Charlie, please, it's all right. Mr Macauley and I are . . . we know one another and he seems to have the idea that . . . Reed . . . please . . . go home . . . go home to your . . . your fiancée . . . oh, yes . . . I know of her and . . . your . . . What I do is my own affair . . . oh, please . . . dear God! . . . I cannot . . . I cannot bear it . . ." Her eyes were deep and burning in her white face and both Reed and Charlie were frozen by the anguish in her. Charlie, sensing that there was more between these two than he had at first been aware, stood awkwardly to one side. Inside him was a need that grew with every moment since he had met her, to go to her, to put his arms about her, as a friend if that was all she needed, to comfort, protect, shield her from the black and savage anger of the big man on the horse.

Before Charlie could move, Reed leaped from his mare, moving swiftly towards Annie, but she put up both her hands, palms towards him, holding him away from her with the gesture. Her mouth worked and her eyes glared and she shook her head violently.

"No . . . don't come near me. Not now, and not ever.
Go home to your bride, to your life and leave me to lead
mine. What I do does not concern you and what you do
can have no interest to me. I don't know where you got
the idea that you have the right to . . . to interfere in what
I do. I don't need you, nor your protection . . ."

"You ate my food, took my dogs . . ." His tender
concern for her which had replaced his anger, melted
away again and he stepped back as though in loathing.

"Take them . . . take them back with you . . ."

"They are of no use to me, Annie Abbott."

"Then go and don't come near my farm again."

"Believe me . . ."

"I wish I could, I wish I could," she moaned.

She turned to Charlie her eyes entreating him to . . .
to do what? He did not know but, instinctively he moved
to her side and when she turned her face into his shoulder,
his arm rose to hold her to him.

Reed Macauley's face closed, tight as a clam, grim and
ugly with his hatred of them both. His eyes were terrible,
a glazed and icy blue in which there was nothing now of
what he felt for Annie Abbott. Only hatred, venom, a cruel
and savage wish to hurt in any way he could. To hurt as
he was hurting, to tear at flesh and heart and mind, as his
flesh and heart and mind tore into agonising shreds.

His breath gasped from between his thinned lips.

"So that is the way of it, is it, Annie Abbott? Not only
Bert Garnett and whoever came before him, there is
another man with his hand up your skirts now. What they
said about you is true then, and I was fool enough to
believe that you were . . . innocent. My God, I've wasted
my sympathy, I see. They were right and I was wrong.
Well, whoever you are . . ." turning his violence on
Charlie ". . . I wish you luck of her since you will need
it . . ."

He was provoked beyond the state where he knew what
he was saying, making no sense, his virulence spilling out
of him in a tidal wave and Charlie had a moment's sympathy
for him since to love as Reed Macauley loved Annie Abbott

was surely not an emotion any man would care to be burdened with. And the trembling violence of the woman in his arms told him she felt the same.

"I should take my leave if I were you," he said calmly to the wildly shaking figure of the man. "Get on your horse and go. There is nothing for you here."

It was as though the quiet words had poured a soporific over Reed Macauley's inflamed brain, soothing, or freezing it, into numbness, so that for the moment the pain went, allowing him to think, to reason. She was standing in the arms of another man so what did that mean? In Yorkshire Esmé Hamilton-Brown wore Reed Macauley's ring, so what did that mean? Only one thing, of course. His brain moved sluggishly along the track and he knew that he must go, go home. Go to his bride-to-be and put her, *her*, this one, out of his mind. "There is nothing for you here," the stranger had said, and it was true. *There never had been*, so . . .

He climbed on to his mare, weary and old, or so he felt and without looking at her, knowing she did not look at him, he put the mare to a quiet canter down the track.

They got back to Browhead three days later. Without the diversions she had made on her journey out to Rosley, to sell her besom brushes, her swills and her stockings, she and Charlie, her small flock, herded more efficiently by Blackie and Bonnie now, moved almost in a straight line from Caldbeck, skirting the high Caldbeck Fells, moving along Parkend Beck, through Longlands and dropping down into Gillthrop on the third day. They had slept in barns, keeping clear of farms, Charlie buying the necessary food from farmers' wives with Annie staying out of sight. They no longer sang. They strode out together side by side, speaking occasionally but only when it was needed. Charlie realised that Annie was in active pain, deeply grieving for Reed Macauley. That her lively and dashing spirit was struggling to survive the slashing words he had aimed, deliberately and accurately, at her heart. She ate when he handed her food. She spoke to her dogs and watched her flock but the brave excitement had gone from her and he was saddened by it. She did not question him, nor ask him where he was going when they reached Browhead. He was gentle with her and she appeared to be grateful. He knew nothing of what was waiting for her at the end of her journey and he did not ask. He watched her as she slept and when she woke he was on his own bit of straw in his own corner of the barn.

The people of Gillthrop came out of their cottages to stare at Annie Abbott as she tramped behind her bleating flock of ewes and the prancing ram. Her dogs were in full control and there was no need for her, or the man she was with, to give them anything but the occasional low word.

She took off her hat as she strode through the village and shook out her curtain of hair, allowing it to cascade down her back. Her legs in her father's breeches were long and supple and the men and women gawped, open-mouthed, silent and forbidding. She began to smile then, turning to Charlie to draw him into some delight she felt. She took his arm, and taking a cue from her, he strutted by her side, bowing from left to right as though it was a royal procession he and Annie were in. This is what it's about, he remembered thinking. This is what she is doing. Showing *them* and Reed Macauley that Annie Abbott is a person worthy of respect and admiration for she is surviving when she should be going under. But why? Why does she need . . . ?

The answer came running down the track, flying, her small feet barely touching the ground, her long copper curls streaming out from her small head, her great golden eyes snapping in lovely excitement.

"Mother . . . Mother . . ."

"Cat . . . oh, my lovely Cat . . ."

And mother and daughter ran joyfully into each other's arms.

It was Whitsun and the ram Annie had hired was due to go back to Rosley.

"I'll take it," Charlie offered. He looked round the table smiling, his eyes moving from Cat to Phoebe and lastly to Annie, remaining there, as they always did. "I could just manage a good day out. In fact, why don't we all go?" He sat back in his chair, grinning engagingly, his eyes gleaming like those of a schoolboy who has just suggested a wicked prank. He was twenty-five now, though he had mentioned it to no one when his birthday came in February, and the hard work he had done at Browhead had added some breadth to his shoulders. He still had on the old, threadbare coat he had worn when Annie met him in October but beneath it was a beautifully knitted long-sleeved jerkin Annie and Phoebe had created for him between them. A design of Phoebe's who had knitted the sleeves whilst Annie had done the back and front. Cat had sewn on wooden buttons which Annie had found in her mother's sewing basket.

"Tha' cannot go about wi' nowt' on but that old coat, Mr Lucas," Phoebe had told him, horrified when he had attempted to set off up the fell on a day of biting December wind and a hoar-frost so thick his boots sank in it. Not that the boots were much better than the coat, good boots once but now badly scuffed and in need of a cobbler's hand. "See, ah'll knit thee a waistcoat with sleeves in it. Annie'll give me a hand, won't tha'? Thou shall have it on by weekend." And he did, along with a muffler, from Cat, and a pair of the thick woollen stockings Annie and Phoebe knitted whenever they had a moment to sit down.

The room was cosy and the fire glowed red and orange

in the inglenook. It was May now and the weather, though warmer, was still cold, but here in the kitchen a small sanctuary had been created in the vast, windblasted confusion of black rock, gloomy gills, fan-shaped screes and rippling streams which was Skiddaw in the winter. The weather was still inclined to be fickle, showing the face of spring on a soft and lovely morning and by noon, clouds would be chasing one another across the torn sky with a wind so strong you could lean on it. Beyond the small, oak-mullioned windows the grass in the pasture moved in flattened waves and the sound of the rushing air could be heard in the branches of the hawthorn tree to the side of the house.

The two dogs, along with a pretty marmalade kitten which had been found wandering alone, piteously mewing behind the farmhouse, lay dozing in a tangled heap in front of the fire dogs, set to prevent the logs from rolling out of the slightly raised hearth stone. All three had coats glossy with health, contrasting sharply not only with one another, but the scrubbed slate of the flagged floor. The randle-tree fixed to a beam above the fire supported several pots not quite touching the glowing peat. In one was the 'poddish' made from oats which they were eating for breakfast and which was keeping warm for those who wanted another helping and in the other was 'crowdy' again made with oatmeal in which beef stock had been mixed. In the third was Annie's Easter-Ledge Pudding consisting of young green leaves, not unlike dock leaves, boiled with barley and mint sorrel, to be served with dried beef. It was said to have great medicinal powers, especially in the cooling of the blood.

On the table round which they sat was a platter of 'clapbread', freshly baked that morning. It had been rolled into a ball in Phoebe's hands, then 'clapped' until it was as thin as paper, put on an iron plate and set on the fire until it was baked crisp. They drank tea, hot and sweet, but without milk since Annie could not yet afford a cow.

She and Charlie sat in two carved oak chairs dated 1742, come, she supposed, from better days and in which she

could remember her mother and father resting, but Cat
and Phoebe sat side by side on a rough wooden bench.
The enormous oak table, which had never been moved
for the simple reason it was so heavy it could only be lifted
by six strong men, was set under the window. A big jar
of lavender was placed in the centre of it, filling the room
with its fragrant scent. In the window bottom was a vast
copper bowl planted with winter hyacinths which were still
blooming.

Annie looked doubtfully from Charlie's good-humoured
face then out and beyond the window to the field of rippling
grasses and the wind-driven silver waters of the lake. The
flock with the new lambs had been herded up on to the
fell only two days before. The ploughing had been done
in March and so there would be a brief respite in the farm
work, but the weather was uncertain today and Annie was
not sure the walk to Rosley and back was within Cat's
strength.

"Oh, Mother, may we?" the child breathed ecstatically,
jumping down from the bench and running to lean against
her mother's shoulder. "May we? Phoebe says there are
all sorts of wonderful things to see at a fair. Clowns and
acrobats, and fat ladies and monkeys. And puppets too,
aren't there Phoebe?"

She turned her great velvety brown eyes to Phoebe
who looked alarmed for she had told the child only of what
she herself had spied from the corner of her downcast
eyes as she was hurried by her last mistress to the Hiring
Fair in Keswick a year ago. She had not meant to fill Cat's
head with a longing to see them, only to entertain the little
girl as they worked side by side at one of the many tasks
they shared. It was not as if she had seen anything properly
herself, though, if she were truthful she would dearly love
to.

"Nay, lambkin," copying Annie in her use of the endearment for she loved the child as though she was her own.
"Ah didn't mean ter say that . . ."

"And merry-go-rounds and . . . and . . ." Without waiting for Phoebe to finish her stumbling sentence, the little

girl put her face close up to Annie's, childlike, begging to be allowed this treat which Charlie had suggested.

Charlie smiled disarmingly. "It can do no harm, Annie, and if you are thinking of the distance we could take the sledge with a blanket in it and if Cat here gets tired she could sit on it while I pull her."

"But the weather, Charlie. You know it can be fickle at this time of the year."

"There are shelters, Annie. Every farm has a barn and no farmwife would refuse a child."

"But what of the cost of a night's room?"

"You and Cat and Phoebe could share, and I can sleep wherever I fall. A few pence, that's all."

Cat looked from one face to the other, as the two adults discussed it, her own luminous with her yearning to see the fascinations of which Phoebe had told her. Her hands clung around Annie's neck and her soft young mouth trembled as her breath quickened.

"Oh, Mother, please . . . please . . . ."

At last Annie looked down into her daughter's face and her own was soft. She had been nowhere in her life, Catriona Abbott, that could be called 'a treat'. She had trudged at her mother's skirts for more than half of her baby days in weather as inhospitable as any the fells could manifest, if not quite as dangerous. Without complaint she had done it. Not for her the tantrums and whining Annie had seen in other children, like Sally Garnett's boy, for instance, who, on the few occasions he had been in her kitchen, had grizzled and clamoured for his mother's attention the whole time they had been there. Cat had nothing, no toys, none of the 'sweeties', the indulgences other parents gave to their children, and it was only this last year that she had found safe refuge, warmth, security and the growing knowledge that these, surely the right of every child, were to continue. She had known only one thing which had been a continuing, everlasting, element in her young life and that was Annie's love. It was time she had *fun*.

Cat held her breath, her eyes never leaving her

mother's. They were no more than six inches apart, as though the child, with her fixed stare, hoped to hypnotise her mother into acquiescence.

Charlie and Phoebe both sighed in pleasure as Annie nodded her head, but Cat, surprisingly, did not jump for joy or cry out her gladness. She laid her cheek against Annie's breast, burrowing herself into her mother's arms like a young chick, thankfully settling beneath the hen. She was too enraptured to speak, it seemed, her childish heart overcome with this miracle which had been allowed her. Above her head Annie's eyes met Charlie's. She smiled through her tears, her throat too full to speak.

They might have been going to Australia, so great was the planning of this mighty expedition in which, Cat was adamant, even the marmalade kitten was to be included. They must be adequately dressed, of course, with a good supply of warmly knitted stockings and mufflers, and the jerkins, now that Phoebe had the hang of it, she made for them all. Food, stuff that would keep in case there was none to be had on the road, blankets for Cat and 'Dandy' the kitten, and a hurried visit by Phoebe to the cobbler in Hause to get their clogs resoled.

Annie almost changed her mind on the morning they were to go. There was a pattern of clouds, low and light, the higher ones like a sheet, broken, divided, and below them were the rain clouds, ragged, uneasy and dark in the sky. The rain already seemed to hang down, a trailing rain, which did not quite reach the ground but certainly would do so as they moved higher up beyond Gillthrop towards the village of Longlands. They would not touch Uldale, of course, going on the most direct route up to Whelpo, Caldbeck, and on across Broad Moor to Rosley. There would be many travellers en route, for the Whitsun Fair was the biggest cattle market of the year.

But the animals' way – and the unthinking humans' way – even if there are no obstacles, does not go in a straight line. Man and animal will move slowly from one point to another by much the same route, which then becomes a path. Such a path becomes a track if many use it, and so it was with the tracks and sheep trods which criss-crossed the dales and high fells of Lakeland and which they were about to take.

"I don't like the look of the weather, Charlie," Annie said more than half a dozen times between Browhead and Longlands, only to be outnumbered by Charlie, by Phoebe and Cat, none of them knowing the menace of the fells as she did. The 'messenger' clouds which moved ponderously over their heads foretold rain soon, she said, and where were they to shelter out here in the open? It was well known that there were more wet days on the fells than dry ones and with so many people on the roads, coming from every direction towards Rosley Fairground, would there be a place for them to lay their heads?

"Now stop it, Annie. You'll spoil it for Cat. Just see her striding out with Phoebe, the pair of them so filled with glee they might be off to stay the weekend with the Queen and her family. Look at their faces, Annie. Have you ever seen such delight? Phoebe seems no older than Cat in her excitement."

"I know that, Charlie. I'm not disputing it but if it gets any worse up there ahead and we get caught in the open, don't blame me. And this damned tup's not helping, wanting to go every way but the one we want to take. Blackie and Bonnie are doing their best but the thing keeps butting them."

"Let me see if I can bring him into line. He's a rogue but he's certainly given you some fine lambs so you must not malign him or his masculinity will be quite devastated."

Charlie grinned down at her endearingly then, taking her hand, pulled her to him. His grey eyes were warm and filled with his own almost childlike delight with this adventure he had conjured up for them. He would have had to go to Rosley anyway with the ram, but the joy of having Annie with him, almost a renewal of the days they had spent together last autumn, put a glow in them which she did not recognise. He had been so good to her, to them all over the past six months, bringing a merriment into the farmhouse which, though it had always been a snug and contented home, had never known such laughter as Charlie awoke in it.

He produced his own kind of music, teaching Cat and Phoebe how to play on a 'comb and paper', beating the rhythm on two spoons, introducing them to simple tunes and songs which he had known from childhood. The comical, often out-of-tune noises they produced would reduce all four to the kind of laughter they had never before known. A sense of 'silliness' which is infectious and, as Charlie said, as good for you as any medicine the doctor might prescribe. They sang and laughed together whilst Annie and Phoebe knitted and when they were quiet he would read aloud to them from one of the few books it was found he had in the pocket of his broadcloth coat. *Pickwick Papers* by Mr Charles Dickens. *Pride and Prejudice* by Miss Jane Austen and *Masterman Ready* by Captain Frederick Marryat. Only these three, but when one was finished, another would be started and when they all three had been read, he had promised to begin all over again. Their evenings were made lively, for his blithe nature would not allow for dejection or brooding, which he often saw in Annie's face, and of course, he knew why. He had made himself a part of the family, not only in the work he did, but with his humour, his patience, his quicksilver lightheartedness and his ability to turn an ordinary, everyday event into something fascinating and therefore fun.

She had the feeling there was some hidden meaning in what he was saying to her and his eyes still had that wicked gleam in them but she could not help but smile back, allowing him to put a comradely arm about her shoulder as they strode out along the track and across the stone bridge which forded Parkend Beck. Charlie dragged the old sledge which had done such sterling service ever since its first run to Rosley, and perched on the blankets within it was the marmalade kitten, its tail twitching in alarm. Once it had jumped off, stalking behind them haughtily as though the mode of transport was far beneath its feline dignity. But as Charlie said, knowing where its comfort lay and finding it was being left behind, it ran to catch up, jumping back thankfully.

"What a circus we are. We only need a monkey and a parrot and we could have our own side-show at the fair," Charlie joked, his eyes sparkling into hers.

The wind became more biting the higher they got and it was not long before Cat sought the shelter of the sledge and the blankets where, snuggling down with the kitten, they both fell asleep. The fells soared dramatically on either side of them, rising from the narrow green strips of the fertile dales on which, as they marched, they saw falcons spiralling, keeping an airborne eye on the flocks which sought the sweet herbs and grasses growing among the dark rocks. Narrow strips of order and productivity, where rowan-shaded becks ran and whitewashed farms capped with Lakeland slate nestled under craggy buttresses. Men tended sheep on a neighbouring peak, the dogs beside them silent and alert, and Annie breathed a prayer to safeguard her own new-born lambs from the scavengers which preyed on the weak and defenceless.

Despite her misgivings about the weather, though it was cold, the wind, or so it seemed, coming straight from the plains of Siberia, the rain kept off and when night fell the farmwife who opened her door to their knock and whose husband was 'only in't back yard' she said, eyeing them suspiciously, relented when Cat smiled at her, her face beaming in the light which fell on her from the rushlight, the kitten in her arms mewing plaintively.

"Tha' can sleep in' hay barn, Missus," she told Annie, whose strange and masculine garb was not immediately apparent in the light which fell from her doorway. "An' if tha wants some milk for t' bairn, tha's welcome to a pint or two from Buttercup. She's in t' barn now. Tha' *can* milk, I tek it?"

"Oh, yes, and thank you. You are most kind." Annie smiled.

The farmwife, somewhat taken aback by the way her caller spoke, smiled back, despite herself. They seemed a nice enough little family, taking the hired ram back to

Rosley, and it cost her nothing to let them sleep in the barn. They had their own blankets, they told her, *and* food, they said, but they'd be glad of a pan of hot water if she could spare it and very grateful for the milk they were.

"Aye, well then, send tha' husband ower for t' water. Tha'll be snug enough in that hay."

Cat and Phoebe were asleep, curled together with Blackie and Bonnie and the kitten under one of the blankets. They had all washed in the basin of hot water, one after the other, a somewhat sketchy toilet, and Charlie said they would have to put up with him looking like a brigand since there was not enough for a shave. They ate cheese and bread, beef pies Phoebe, who was becoming a very handy cook, had made, pickles and draughts of warm creamy milk from the obliging Buttercup. There was to be no fire, of course. The farmer, on returning from the 'back yard', had been across to make sure about that, telling them so in his blunt, taciturn way. They seemed all right but you never knew with some of these tinkers and vagrants what sort of daft things they got up to. Not that his missus would allow such through the farm gate, never mind in the barn, but the sight of the peacefully sleeping children, the watchful dogs and the quiet husband and wife reassured him.

But it was cold. There were cracks in the door of the ancient stone-built barn and the wind whistled constantly, a low whining which bit at the flesh and tore at the ears, and there was only one blanket left.

"You have it, Annie. I'm as warm as toast in this hay."

"No . . . no, Charlie, I won't have it. We can make a bed of hay and then lie back to back with the blanket over us. It's going to get colder in the night, I can tell, and we must keep warm . . ."

"I *am* warm."

"No, you're not. I can see you shivering from here."

"No, you can't. Look I'll lie down next to the dogs and be as right as rain."

She looked astonished. "For God's sake Charlie. What

do you think I'm going to do to you whilst you're asleep? Seduce you? Don't be a fool. See, we'll lie with the others and you shall lie beside me and the blanket will cover us both."

"I could share with Cat and Phoebe."

"Dear God, man, don't be so ridiculous. Come over here and lie next to me. We shall all keep one another warm. It's the only way, Charlie." She tutted irritably and shook her head. "I don't know why I let the three of you talk me into this. It's far too cold to be sleeping out in the open . . ."

"Hardly in the open, Annie." Charlie shuffled about in the hay next to her, leaving a gap of at least six inches between them.

"Don't argue, Charlie, and for heaven's sake, come a bit closer. Even if you don't feel the cold, I do, and I'd be glad if you would put your back against mine. There . . . that's it, now isn't that better?"

"Indeed . . ." Charlie's voice was strange and muffled but Annie, with his warm back against hers and already half asleep, did not hear it.

The darkness was as thick and as black as pitch when she awoke, and as she opened her eyes to stare into it, she was aware, in that confused moment between sleeping and waking, that something was wrong. The warmth which had enveloped her and soothed her to sleep was no longer there. In its place was a feeling of tension, of great strain, of a presence taut and strung up, with an emotion she did not recognise. An unknown presence which alarmed her. She was aware that Charlie was still there, the warmth of him just out of reach, but from him came a sensation of . . . of . . . of what? What was it? Anger, was that it, or was it pain?

"Charlie, what is it? Is something wrong?" she said softly, not wanting to wake the others. Charlie did not answer. She turned towards him, putting out her hand to touch his shoulder and was shocked to find it rigid, unmoving, almost ready to flinch away she would have thought had the idea not been so ridiculous.

"Charlie? Are you ill?" She sat up and leaned over him, but with an oath he sprang up and without speaking a word, stumbled towards the flimsy barn door. In the corner Buttercup shifted, then lowed softly.

"Charlie? What's the matter?" She was about to stand up and follow him, for surely there was something wrong. Charlie was so good-humoured, smiling and sweet-tempered with never a cross word for anyone. Too light-hearted by far, she sometimes thought. So careless about life and the serious consideration one must take of it, that she was often irritated. So what was troubling him now that he could not even respond to her anxious concern?

"Really, Annie, cannot a gentleman answer a call of nature without explaining what he is about?" His voice from the dark was flippant as he opened the barn door. "Now go back to sleep, there's a good girl, I won't be long."

He was not there when she awoke to the dawn chorus of the birds which nested in the trees about the farmhouse, but when she stumbled to the barn door there he was walking back from the farmhouse with a pail of water.

"Good morning, lazy bones," he said smilingly, none of the tension she had sensed in him during the night apparent now. "I've been up for half an hour. You were sleeping like babes, all of you, even Blackie and Bonnie declining to come with me so I went and begged some water from our benefactor. She even gave me this," and with an endearing grin, he produced an enormous jug brimming with tea.

"Charlie, you angel."

"I know," Charlie's impish smile changed to one of smugness. "That's why she gave it to me, I suppose, because she knew I was not your ordinary sort of a fellow. She could not resist my charm."

"I don't blame her. Now if Buttercup could spare us a drop of milk . . ."

"Just what I was thinking, but as I got the tea, don't you think it's only fair that you should get the milk?"

They were both laughing when Cat and Phoebe peeped

from their nest of hay and blankets. The kitten blinked its wide eyes and the dogs wagged their tails, and it was as though the strange moment in the night, if indeed anything strange *had* happened in the night, might never have been.

They reached Rosley Hill by mid-afternoon, the great multitude of those who were on the same road as themselves, and indeed on every road leading to the fairground, cheerful and excited, most of them, for this was the greatest event in their humdrum year. The actual grounds of the fair covered forty acres. It would be another fifteen years before dealers bought their cattle straight from the byre, but in the meanwhile this was where the drovers displayed them for sale and not only cattle but sheep and horses as well.

They could hear the sound of the brass bands as they approached the fairground, a spirited 'oom-pa-pa' which lifted the head and squared the shoulders and infected those who heard it to step out in a grand style, just as though a procession were under way. The Drover's Rest was surrounded by a hurrying mass of men, some seeking a bed for the night, which was, of course, impossible, others doing a bit of business, shaking hands on a deal, or shaking their heads in refusal. There were horses tethered in the inn yard, the stables being as full as the beds. Carts and carriages vied for position with donkeys, ponies and any four-legged beast that could carry or pull a load to this great fair and market. Stalls were set up on the roadside, those belonging to pedlars and housewives for whom there was no longer any room in the actual fairground, the housewives selling eggs and gingerbread, the pedlars shouting of gauze from Italy, ribbons and lace from France, hats and caps, cloaks, brooms, beehives and baskets. Whips cut the air as horses were driven along the track with no concern for those in their path, the quality, who on this occasion rubbed shoulders with ruffians, jumping out of their way with the same alacrity.

The fairground was a heaving, seething confusion of men, women and children, many of the men there to do business, naturally, but the rest bent on having the best time of their lives. In one corner, a fiddler and a man with a tin whistle played a lilting merry tune and Cat and Phoebe stared spellbound as those who were able danced the 'Cumberland Square Eight', the 'Long Eight', the 'Ninepins Reel' and the 'Circassian Circle'. Country dances which brought forth loud whoops of excited merriment, much twirling and whirling with many a lad glimpsing more than he should of his lass's ankles and sometimes, as she was swept from her feet, her drawers. The tent beside the dancing and which held the circus was so well attended the barker was begging people to be patient since they would all get in eventually and in the meanwhile, why did they not view the 'slack-wire balancing act', 'the pig-faced lady' or 'the hairy man' from Morocco who were absolutely free.

Charlie stopped to watch the Pugilists who were displaying their skills in a ring set up for them, accepting bets from any amateur who fancied his chances against them.

"I could take that chap on," he said to Annie, his eyes bright with that look of anticipation a man assumes at the thought of pitting himself against another. Annie was doing her best to keep her eye on Cat and Phoebe, who were like a couple of sleepwalkers who have wandered into some fairy-tale dream and are mesmerised by it. They moved, hand in hand, their mouths gaping, their eyes wide and marvelling, as they studied the spectacles on every hand, marionettes and musicians, singers, rope dancers, coconut shies and a great sad shambling bear, its muzzled face anguished, as it did its best to dance to the pipe of a gypsy's whistle.

"No, you couldn't Charlie. They're fighting with bare fists," Annie answered tartly.

"But they're betting a guinea, Annie. I've done a bit of bare knuckle fighting in my time. I'm sure I could beat him."

"*You*, Charlie?" Annie eyed Charlie's lean frame disbelievingly.

"Yes, I fought at my own weight of course."

"Well *he's* not your weight, Charlie Lucas. Look at him. He weighs twice as much as you, besides you haven't a guinea to bet with, and if you had, I wouldn't let you."

"That fellow's going to try."

"More fool him, then," and fool he was for the fight was short, crude and bloody, the stalwart young country lad who had climbed into the ring being carried out by his fellows with a face like a piece of raw meat.

The dogs were bewildered and alarmed by the press of people, anxiously doing their best to divide themselves between Cat and Phoebe, who, in their eagerness not to miss a single exhibit, forged ahead of Annie and Charlie who were studying stalls on which there were for sale such marvels as shepherds' bells and leather gaiters, bridles, saddles, whips and padlocks and saws. A travelling salesman, standing on the tailboard of the cart in which his weary horse was still harnessed, begged them to try his 'Balm of Gilead' which would cure them of all that ailed them from warts to the coughing sickness.

A musical farce was being performed by a company of players in another tent. *The Spoiled Child* was its title and Annie was carried back quite ferociously to those precarious months she had spent with . . . with . . . My God, she could not even remember his name, the name of the man who had fathered her lovely child. The thought horrified her for surely she should carry not only his name but the picture of him inside her for ever? But no matter how hard she tried, she could not bring him to mind. Charlie's hand held hers for they were in great danger of being separated as they moved across the track which led from the gate to the camphouse where many of the drovers and dealers had a bed. Behind it was the gigantic grazing ground in which were enclosed the plunging, bellowing cattle and through which ran a stream. Even the valley bottom below the hill was crowded with beasts, the air filled with the grunting and squeaking of pigs, the bleating of sheep, the cries of hawkers, with shouts and oaths and whistles.

Annie was dressed as she had been for the past six or seven months, in the jacket, trousers and gaiters her father had once worn. She had carefully plaited her hair and Charlie had helped her to stuff it beneath her hat which was then jammed down on her head almost to her ears. She could barely see from beneath its brim, but it at least hid much of her female features. If anyone thought it strange, or even noticed in the vast crowd, that two men, herself and Charlie, held hands, there was too much commotion to dwell on it. The ram had been returned to the farmer who had hired it to them. Charlie pulled the sledge at his heels and in its nest of blankets the kitten cowered, its mews of astonishment unheard in the hubbub. Annie was creased and crumpled from sleeping in her clothes, as was Charlie, but he looked decidedly worse for wear than she did, since he had almost two days' stubble on his chin. He never wore a hat as he did not own one and his hair hung over his collar and ears in a wild, uncombed tangle. They looked slightly disreputable, she was well aware, but what did that matter since there was no one she cared about here to see it.

"Phoebe, Cat, don't get too far ahead," Annie called out, her voice lost in the strident tumult. They did not hear it but the man coming towards her did and when he stopped dead where he stood, the beautifully dressed young lady on his arm almost fell over. Charlie had not noticed them, walking on ahead of Annie, their hands still clasped and for a moment the two couples, Charlie Lucas and Annie Abbott, Reed Macauley and his beautiful young wife, became entangled in wild, appalling confusion.

No one spoke. Charlie's eyes ran swiftly over the couple, particularly the man, and his hand tightened on Annie's, drawing her protectively to him. Reed Macauley instinctively steadied his wife, who was looking quite astonished that two such ruffians should have been allowed to impede the way of a lady like herself and her husband, who, or so she thought, should have had them instantly arrested. Such *strange* young men too. One attractive in a rough sort of way, the other . . . well . . . how could you describe him? She certainly could not, averting her eyes, for they seemed to he *holding hands*.

"Reed," she squeaked, as her husband of three months turned violently and began to run with her across the uneven ground towards their carriage, and when she was able to see the look on his face, it so frightened her she was glad to cower back in her seat and head off towards Carlisle and the luxurious hotel in which they were staying.

18

The weather broke as Annie had foretold it would as they made their way back across Broad Moor and down the track which would lead them to Caldbeck. Across the fells a procession of dark clouds whipped, angry and boiling, moving on at first, one after the other from the North towards Skiddaw. But just as though there was no more space to accommodate them beyond the heights of Caldbeck Fells they piled up on one another, low and glowering. A torrent of rain fell suddenly, shaking loose from the greyness and moving in a heavy curtain through which it was barely possible to see. It fell relentlessly, drifting in a cold, steady stream before them, and the noise it made was a constant, rhythmic thrumming against the grey rocks and sodden ground. Great blinding sheets, lifting and shifting, parting now and then to reveal the rough tussocky grass, the water-logged track which was dangerous with stretches of slippery stones.

Annie had removed her hat as they left Rosley since its weight on her head was more than she could bear, she muttered, tossing it into the sledge beside the startled kitten. Charlie watched her anxiously as they slithered down the track and though it took all of his strength and attention to keep the sledge upright, he could not help but be fascinated by the way the rain fell on her bare head. As it touched the darkened russet of her hair, a mass of tiny curls sprang upon her forehead. Droplets of moisture slipped to the end of each wet tendril, falling on to her brow. They touched the arch of her eyebrow, running smoothly to hang upon the ends of her lashes. She blinked to clear them and they dropped to her cheeks and ran to her parted lips where she licked them away, her pink tongue moving in an unknowingly sensual gesture which lit a small but growing flame in the pit of Charlie's belly.

She was not aware of it, of course, nor of the rain, the cold and searching wind which accompanied it; the violent lightning flashes splitting the dark clouds on the high peaks, nor the thunder which roared and cracked amongst the crags. She was not aware of her child who had been huddled by Charlie and Phoebe beneath the rapidly soaking blankets beside the kitten, nor of Charlie and Phoebe themselves. Her pace lengthened and quickened as she endeavoured to get away from the pain which the sight of Reed Macauley and his new young wife had gouged into her, and Charlie Lucas's heart despaired for her, and for himself.

She had been quite devastated by the encounter, her face ashen, her eyes wide and senseless as though she had seen some ghastly apparition which had taken her mind. He had felt the tremble in her hand at first, a quivering of her fingers as they clung to his, then, as the spasm took her, moving to her arm, her shoulder, her neck, her whole body, until even her teeth chattered and she shook as though she had been attacked by the ague.

"Take me away, Charlie," she had managed to say between her clenched teeth, her hands, both of them now, clinging to him as though his lean, strong frame, his male strength, his caring, cheerful endurance was all she had to keep her upright.

"Hang on to me, sweeting." She did not question his immediate understanding. Why should she? She knew nothing of his true feelings, only seeing the smile he smiled, the device that he used to hide what was inside him. A complex man who protected his heart and emotions beneath the layers of flippant geniality he had wrapped about himself ever since he had met Annie Abbott.

They reached the farm where they had stayed the night before but it was still daylight and the farmwife, at first surprised but not displeased to see them for they had been no trouble, got a good look at Annie and the men's clothing she wore. Her eyes, flinty as the rock which rose behind the farm, moved from Annie's white demented face and her tangled hair which was plastered to her skull and down her back, to the jacket she wore and the long shape of her trousered legs. The jacket was open for what did Annie Abbott care about anything at that precise and agonising moment, and the rain had sculpted her shirt to her breasts, the nipples of which stood out like cherries.

"May we shelter in your barn again, madam?" Charlie said in his scrupulously polite and engaging way, doing his best to signal to Annie to close her jacket. Indeed he had tried to persuade her to wait at the gate, knowing full well what the reaction of the farmwife would be. "My wife and . . . and child are so very wet and the weather shows no sign of abating, does it? We would not trouble you . . ."

"Indeed, tha' won't 'cos tha's not stoppin' an' if tha's husband to . . . to . . . that . . . woman tha' should be ashamed to let her be seen by decent folk dressed like that."

"Madam, really, does it matter? The child is soaked to the skin . . ."

"That's nowt ter do wi me."

"But you allowed us to stay here last night and we are the same family . . ."

"Nay, tha's not. Ah thought tha' was a respectable family, tekkin' t'tup back to t' fair, but ah can see ah was wrong. Ah want no . . . vagabonds in my barn so tha'd best be on tha' way."

"We are not vagabonds, madam. Annie . . . my wife . . . and myself have a farm near Gillthrop . . ."

"Then tha'd best be on tha way to it for tha've a long walk."

"Please, madam . . ."

The farmwife did not like to be called 'madam', nor did she like to be hoodwinked, which she considered she had been. The woman on her doorstep who looked as though she'd seen an apparition, was a different one to the pleasantly smiling person of the night before. She had no right to be bothering honest, virtuous folk with her flagrant disregard of the proper way for a woman to dress, and

she'd have no truck with her, nor any of them. She kept
her eyes firmly from the bedraggled figure of the child,
who was doing her best to shelter from the downpour
beneath the blanket on the cart, lest she weaken.

"Be off," she said, "or ah'll call my husband."

They went, moving slowly along the farm track until
they got to the gate, turning left towards Caldbeck and
the long, wet road to home. At every farm they tried up
to and beyond Caldbeck, they got the same answer from
the stiffly disapproving women who came to the door,
eyeing the strange figure of Charlie's 'wife' and it was not
until, nearly dark, they came to a derelict hut, used for
what purpose Charlie could not imagine, in a dip beside
the track, that they found some kind of shelter. The wind
still howled in their faces and the rain pelted down in a
heavy swaying veil and when they got inside they were
so wet they might have all been hauled from a nearby tarn.
No one spoke. Charlie handed out what was left of their
food, even the ravenous and pathetically unkempt kitten
condescending to a morsel of Phoebe's two-day-old beef
pie. Annie refused everything, even the rain water the
others drank, then lay down where she was told on a
scrap of relatively dry ground, Phoebe and Charlie on the
outside, the silent child and her equally silent mother in
the middle. Phoebe knew, of course, what had happened
without being told for she had seen the retreating back of
Reed Macauley and the young lady he dragged on his arm.
She had not questioned Charlie's abrupt statement that
they were to return home at once though Cat had cried
broken-heartedly. She could not understand why this
miraculous outing should be curtailed when it had scarcely
begun, she wept, though not in those exact words, and
for the first time in her young life she turned on her mother
and beat at Annie's trouser leg in angry disappointment.
She might have been no more than a troublesome fly for
all the notice Annie took of her.

The fire was out when they got home and it was an
hour before any warmth crept into the cold kitchen from
the one Charlie kindled.

"Take them both upstairs, Phoebe," he said to the young serving girl, who was half dead with cold herself, but the only one on whom he could rely. "Strip them both and rub them down then put them in dry clothes and bring them here to the fire. I'm sorry Phoebe, to put this on your shoulders but . . . well, I cannot do it, for obvious reasons, so I will see to the fire. Wrap them both up well in blankets or anything else you can lay your hands on and then do the same for yourself. The fire will be going by then."

"What about thissen, Mr Lucas?" Phoebe answered through teeth which were held rigidly in her locked jaw.

"I'll be all right, lass, I'm used to it. Now off you go. See poppet . . ." to the dreadfully quiet child, ". . . go with Phoebe." He sighed, "I think you'll have to carry her, Phoebe." He turned to Annie: "Annie . . . darling . . ." – the endearment slipped out unnoticed, certainly by Annie – ". . . go with Phoebe . . ." and when Annie simply stood there, dazed and mindless with cold and despair, "You go up Phoebe . . . I'll bring her". And somehow, together, Phoebe and Charlie pulled the little family together, got them warm, including themselves, wrapped about in quilts and blankets before the steadily leaping fire on which Charlie had heaped half a dozen stout logs. Tea was made, and porridge, though again Annie refused both. The dogs steamed at their feet and the kitten lay on the hearth almost in the heart of the fire, licking himself angrily, his haughty expression saying quite plainly that he would never forgive them, any of them, for what he had suffered.

Annie sat where they had put her on the settle beside the fire. The quilt Phoebe had draped about her slipped from her shoulders revealing the long flannel nightgown that had been her mother's. Modest it was, high necked and long sleeved, but Lizzie Abbott had been shorter than her daughter and Annie's bare feet and ankles stuck out from beneath the hem, white and fragile, strangely defenceless. She had gained some colour. It touched her cheeks, high on the bone, and her eyes which stared into the fire were brighter though still unseeing.

"I'll tek little 'un up, Mr Lucas," Phoebe said quietly, "and I reckon her an' me'll share a bed tonight. I want to keep me eye on her though I don't think she's tekken much 'arm. She et that porridge . . ." She eyed Annie anxiously but Charlie put out his hand to touch her arm affectionately. He was in Joshua's nightshirt, and had a coarse grey blanket which had once served Joshua's horse, about his shoulders. His feet were bare, like Annie's, and they tingled painfully as the warmth returned.

"I'll get her up, Phoebe. You're exhausted so off you go. Can you manage Cat? Right then sleep well, and Phoebe, thank you."

"Ah need no thanks, Mr Lucas. And Annie . . . well, she's not . . . she's down now but she'll be right as ninepence when . . . well . . . tomorrow, or the next day. She's 'ad a shock so . . ."

"I realise that, Phoebe, but you know she'll be all right with me."

Phoebe did. She had no idea what Mr Lucas had in mind for Annie but whatever it was she prayed it would bring her from the shocked desolation, the desert of emptiness into which the sight of Reed Macauley and his beautiful young wife had toppled her. A lovely man was Mr Lucas and if he . . . meant to . . . be *with* Annie, well, Phoebe went no further than that for it was none of her business. Only if it hurt Annie did it become Phoebe's business, and Mr Lucas wouldn't harm a hair on Annie's head.

Charlie took Annie's unresponsive hand between his own. They were sitting side by side on the settle. The animals had fallen into the deep contented sleep which comes with full bellies, warmth and shelter, and he wished it could be as simple as that for Annie Abbott. At that moment he hated Reed Macauley with every fierce and furious beat of his heart. He could feel the loathing creep insidiously through his veins, heating his blood to boiling point, and all he wanted was to rampage up to Long Beck, take the man by the throat and squeeze it until the breath in his body was stopped forever. God, if he could only crash his fists into that bastard's arrogant face, feel the flesh break and the blood flow, but what good would that do the empty-faced, empty-eyed woman who grieved for him?

"Come Annie, let's get you to bed."

She stood up and the quilt about her fell to the floor. Her lovely breasts stood taut and proud beneath the thin stuff of the nightdress and Charlie groaned in real pain. Her hand was warm in his, hot even, and dry, and from her he could feel a wave of warmth emanate. She looked at him listlessly though her bright eyes did not really see him and with a sigh which was heated with the vapour from her body, she fell against him.

"Oh, Annie, Annie, what has that bastard done to you?" he murmured into her hair as he lifted her into his arms and carried her to her bed.

He and Phoebe nursed her for a week before she recognised them. Between them they tended to her every need, neither feeling embarrassment as together they stripped her soiled nightgowns from her, bathed her naked body and put her in another. She was burning and freezing in turn, her hands to her head as it was wrenched in two, she muttered deliriously, by an iron claw. There was a knife in her chest she said, looking from one to the other accusingly, not seeing them at all.

"She's strong, Phoebe, so don't alarm yourself." It was not Phoebe Charlie was reassuring, but himself. "She'll come out of this, you'll see. By morning she'll be sitting up and shouting for her 'poddish'."

"Aye, that's right, Mr Lucas," but Phoebe was watching in horror the smooth roundness of Annie's cheeks as they melted and sank into the bare bones of her face. The fierce, dry heat of her seemed to be swallowing her before their very eyes and though they did their best they could not make her drink.

"Sweeting . . . Annie . . . oh, my dearest heart . . ." he murmured to her when they were alone, for Phoebe was needed elsewhere, attending to Cat who fretted to be with her mother. She was a rock to whom they all clung, himself included, as she quietly went about the business of cooking hot nourishing meals for them, and washing the piles of soiled linen from Annie and her bed, of caring for the animals and the newly planted vegetables, of doing the cleaning and mending and making sure that the home Annie had given her ran as smoothly as she knew Annie would have liked. There was only one relief in their routine, which moved from sick room to kitchen to the needs of the farm, and that was that the lambing was over and the ploughing done. The planting of oats and barley could wait a day or two until he could get to it, Charlie told Phoebe, as they covered the fretfully tossing body of Annie for the hundredth time.

They took it in turns to sit with her, dozing fitfully in the chair beside the bed, but when Phoebe, on the third night, fell asleep with Cat on her bed, sliding into a state which was almost that of unconsciousness, Charlie did not waken her. She was barely beyond childhood herself. She had borne stoically the hard task of looking after them all, of nursing Annie whilst he himself had an hour's sleep, of even, he had noticed from Annie's bedroom window, hoeing the vegetables when she had a spare moment. Now she was done in and could she be blamed?

Annie moaned and tossed, fever glazing her eyes, her lungs wheezing agonisingly in her rapidly rising and falling chest and for the first time Charlie faced the appalling fact that she might not survive. She was thin, her body bare bones and hollows for he had seen it, looking at it not with a lover's eye but with the detached concern almost of a doctor. He had seen men like this on the long marches he had made beside them in the cause of Chartism, through wet and cold nights, men with fever, with the coughing sickness and many had slipped silently away before the cause they espoused could come to fruition.

He loved Annie Abbott and had done for over six months now. She was an extension of his own body and spirit. Part of himself which no one knew of and now she lay wasting away before his eyes and he could do nothing about it. The full horror of losing her, though he knew he did not have her, was more than his anguished heart could stand and he leaned over her, putting his face in the curve of her neck beneath her chin. His lips touched the hot flesh of her throat and he murmured her name.

She seemed to quieten, sighing as she turned towards him.

"Reed . . ."

Dear Christ! *Reed!*

Again she said that hated name and her arm fumbled beneath the bedclothes which he had just tucked about her, as though searching for something.

"Annie . . . I'm here . . . I'm here, my darling." Lifting her head gently, he put his arm beneath it, drawing her close to him and though she still fretted and mumbled, her hot and feverish body seemed to strain towards him.

"Reed . . ."

He wanted to weep. He could not contemplate the world without her bright defiant spirit, her lovely glowing smile which lit her eyes to golden glory, her unshakeable belief that she would win through, her dauntless heart, brave and strong, and yet was he to nurse her back to health only to see her forever yearn for that blackguard up at Long Beck? And if he did . . . Oh, Christ . . . *if* he did? What was he thinking about, lying here next to the woman he loved, deliberating on what was to happen if she survived. She *must* survive no matter what she did in the future. The flame of her must not be allowed to go out, not if he could help to keep it flickering.

Again he lifted her head, replacing it on the pillow, moving away from the bed for a moment or two, and at once she twisted and turned, her breath rasping like a rusty saw through the clogged filth in her chest. When he had removed his outer clothing he climbed into the bed and took her in his arms, holding her burning body close to his.

"I'm here, sweetheart, I'm here," he murmured, his hands caressing her shoulders and back, stroking her tangled hair away from her face, his kisses sweet on her chin, the arch of her brow, her parched lips.

"Reed . . . aah . . . Reed." She turned to him, her

fever-racked body not knowing, her senseless mind deep in the loveliness of Reed Macauley's arms.

He awoke to a great drenching sweat which poured from Annie's body, soaking himself, her nightdress, the bedclothes. She was asleep, a quiet natural sleep which seemed to him to have a healing about it. He held her for a few more minutes, savouring the sweetness of her arm across him, her cheek on his chest, the tumbled mass of her hair in a drift across his face, then quietly lest she wake, he moved from the bed and it was as though his heart tore from his body, the pain of it so unbearable he bent his head, steadying himself for a moment on the back of the chair. She was better, sweating still, but peaceful, her mind and body soothed to that condition by her dream of Reed Macauley.

He dressed quickly, not taking his eyes from her sleeping face, then knelt beside her to study her, for he knew he would not share Annie Abbott's bed again.

It was another three days before she was completely herself again, weak as a new-born kitten and skinny as a post, she said ruefully, but yes, she thought she might eat a mouthful of 'poddish' and if her body remembered the night she had spent with Reed Macauley, her mind told her it was dreams and that Charlie and Phoebe had nursed her back to health.

Charlie watched her from the chair where he sat, one leg thrown carelessly over the arm of it, his usual expression of easy-going smiling insouciance on his thin face. Annie Abbott was not the only one to lose weight that week. The days moved on and she was improved, continuing to do so rapidly, the day at Rosley Hill not mentioned and if sometimes there was a pensive sadness in her eyes and a strain about her soft mouth, she did not allow it to interfere with the plans she had for her farm which she discussed with her good friend Charlie Lucas and the dreams she had for her daughter which she also shared with her good and dearest friend, Charlie Lucas.

"She's four now, Charlie, in December, which God

forgive me, I let slip by me as though it did not matter. That child has had nothing."

"She's had you, Annie."

Annie turned to smile at him, her hand reaching out to take his. Charlie was always saying things like that. He was such a blessing to her with his mischievous good humour and wit, his wicked, often ribald sense of fun, his easy, shared companionship. He took nothing seriously except the work he did on the farm and even that was done as though he found it all extremely amusing, something which suited him at the moment to perform. He would smile endearingly and raise self-mocking eyebrows before taking himself off to weed the acre of oats and barley he and Phoebe had sown at the end of May, whilst she herself recovered from the illness.

"Well, I'd best be off to pretend I'm a farmer," he would say, his step jaunty, his hands in his pockets, a whistle on his lips as though for two pins he would throw himself down on the grass and read his book, and yet she knew he did the work of two men though he tried to give the impression he was doing none. She knew very little about him for whenever she tried to question him on his past, he always laughed and said he had known a misspent youth and a wild young manhood.

"My family despaired of me. I broke every young lady's heart in the neighbourhood and my mother was forever in tears for I showed no inclination to settle down to marry one of them."

"And where was this, Charlie? Which part of the country do you come from? Certainly not Cumberland."

"Oh, further south than that. You will not know it."

"I have been as far as Leicestershire so I'm not exactly untravelled," for by now Charlie had heard of *her* past since she felt no need to keep it from him.

"My word, *Leicestershire!* You *have* seen the world have you not, Annie Abbott," he teased her.

"Never mind me, tell me what you have done since you grew to manhood. I know you had a university education but what did you do after that?"

"Oh, I moved about here and there," he said airily.

"Here and there, *where* and doing *what*? Don't try to play the mystery man with me, Charlie Lucas."

"That is exactly what I am and mean to stay. A mystery man. Don't you think it makes me more exciting? Look at Phoebe's face. You can see she is wondering what I've been up to and am I a wanted man. Isn't that so, Phoebe?"

"Nay, not me, Mr Lucas. I mind me own business I do, an' I tell no one mine," which was endearing really for what had Phoebe to tell, or hide?

"Quite right, Phoebe, that's what I always say."

And by means of teasing, making jokes about his reckless past, changing the subject cunningly so that one minute they were discussing him and then something else entirely, they knew barely more about him than on the day he had entered their lives.

"So what am I to do about Cat, Charlie?"

"You want her to go to school?"

"I do, but how will she fare in the village, even if they would take her? It is only a dame school which cost my father a penny or two a week."

"You certainly benefited from the experience."

"But Cat is far cleverer than I ever was, Charlie. All I learned there was to read and write and sing hymns."

"Is there not a 'monitorial system' in the North? In Almondbury, which is close to where I come from, there was a reverend gentleman, a curate and headmaster of the Grammar School there, who opened up his school for use as a Sunday School. Above its doors were inscribed the words of George III: 'May every child in my Kingdom be able to read the Bible,' it said but the Reverend Walter Smith did much more than that. In ten years fifty-one boys and thirty-five girls, each paying threepence a week, were taught by two teachers, but then those who were taught became 'monitors' teaching others. That is the 'monitorial system'."

"It sounds a wonderful idea, I would give anything to send Cat to a grammar school where she would learn more than reading and how to add one and one. Already she knows a little Latin and French that you taught her but a girl has not the chance a boy has."

"I will willingly teach her all I know, Annie, but is there not a grammar school, perhaps in Keswick or Carlisle, which will admit free pupils of poor means, girls as well as boys?"

"I don't know, Charlie, perhaps." Of course there *was* a grammar school in Keswick for had not Reed Macauley been educated there? Had she not seen him on his new, highstepping, black mare when she was no more than five or six years old and he perhaps sixteen? Lordly, he had been, riding easily in his saddle, arrogant even then as he galloped past her father's old horse and cart, those that had gone in the year the murrain wiped out Joshua Abbott's flock. She had been perched in the back of the cart, wedged against the evil-smelling fleeces Joshua Abbott had hoped – vainly – to sell at the market, a small silent girl whom her father had done his best to turn into a boy. The haughty youth had not even seen her, only coated her with dust, as his young mare, a recent present from his father, stirred up the dry track with its wildly galloping hooves.

It all came back to *him*. Every thought, however diverse, came back to him. To Reed Macauley. Every conversation, now matter how far removed, seemed to lead her in the direction of the pain he had wrought in her and though she knew she must bear it, sometimes it could not be borne. He was married now. She had seen him with his wife on his arm and though, naturally, she had been well aware that there could be nothing between her and Reed Macauley, in hearts that love there is always nurtured that tiny, unseen, unrecognised really, seed of hope.

"What is it, Annie?" They were sitting on the drystone wall at the front of the farmhouse. It was a June evening, Midsummer's Day and Annie was completely recovered from the illness which had laid her so low. The wall on which they sat was a riot of wild flowers which had seeded in every crack and cranny. The vibrant blue of speedwell, sea lavender, and a patchwork of pink and white where lady's smock had taken over. Up the wall of the farmhouse behind them was a demented blossoming of sweet rose briars, pink and profuse and scenting the evening air with their aroma. Daisies grew thickly at their feet, with buttercups and clover and down in the pasture Phoebe and Cat called to the dogs whilst the marmalade kitten, much grown now, stalked behind, its tail in the air, pretending a great indifference.

Charlie put his arm about her and drew her head down to his shoulder. She could smell the tang of the sharp soap he used, bought at the market from a housewife who made her own. It had a lemony fragrance and mixed with it was the good smell of earth and new grass. She did not answer his question and he did not repeat it, for of course, he knew what ailed her. He knew of her love for Reed Macauley and he would not press her. Charlie, dear Charlie, on whom she relied so much. What would she do without him? She leaned on him, depended on him, cared for him and about him. He was her friend and dear companion. He made her laugh and taught her patience.

Charlie. What would she do without him?

19

There had been great excitement in the parish of Bassenthwaite when Reed Macauley brought his bride home from the honeymoon they had spent in Italy. Italy, of all places, which no one in the parish, nor indeed in Cumberland, had ever been to, but trust Reed Macauley to do things in style. Though it had taken place in Bradford, where his bride came from, the wedding was said to have been a very grand affair, since the bride's father was one of the wealthiest men in the county of Yorkshire. Wool, of course, and all that went with it, which was enough to buy his daughter a wedding gift of the most magnificent diamonds anyone in the parish had ever seen. Not that her husband couldn't afford to do the same since he was not short of a bob or two himself and, naturally, with the dowry that came with her, he had made himself even wealthier.

They had been married in February and when they returned to Long Beck in May, just before Whitsuntide, it was soon whispered, as these things were, in such a close-knit community, that young Mrs Macauley was not yet pregnant. Disappointing for Reed Macauley who'd be looking for a son within the year, but there was time yet. Mrs Macauley was a fine young woman, tall, deep bosomed, broad shouldered, full hipped, the sort of woman made to bear children they would have said, and Reed Macauley would be doing his best, since he was that sort of a man anyway, the ladies whispered amongst themselves. Not coarse, nor even earthy, but very masculine in his ways.

All of Bassenthwaite parish and beyond, those of the upper and wealthy classes, landowners, manufacturing gentlemen, men whose money came from mining, were invited to the first dinner party the Macauleys gave. Mrs Macauley proved to be a splendid hostess. It seemed she had taken to running her husband's home with an efficiency which was a credit to her mother's training.

A placid, even docile, young woman was Mrs Reed Macauley. One with whom Reed Macauley would have no trouble and when the subject of Mrs Lewis was brought up by the new bride to her husband, no one could have been more surprised than he was himself.

Mrs Lewis had been cook to Reed Macauley for many years and he had been perfectly satisfied with what she had sent to his table. But it seemed that Mrs Reed Macauley was not, she told her husband, one morning at breakfast. Mrs Lewis and Reed Macauley's housekeeper, Mrs Stone, had run his home between them, uninterfered with, ever since his mother died, for though their master was exacting, demanding the best, it seemed that what they did was perfectly acceptable to him. Not to *Mrs* Macauley, who needed, she told Mr Macauley innocently, of all things, a French chef who could prepare the epicurean bonne-bouche she had, in her father's house, been used to.

"I am not at all satisfied with the standard of Mrs Lewis's cooking, Reed, and I'm afraid she will have to go. Mother, who has been in London, has interviewed one or two likely persons for me, persons with style and experience in the kind of cooking I want. French chefs since the people I mean to invite for weekend parties are used to certain standards, and I'm afraid Mrs Lewis has proved she cannot provide them."

"I beg your pardon," Reed Macauley lowered his newspaper slowly and the breakfast room became hushed.

"We have been home a month now, Reed, and though what she sends to the table is . . . adequate, she cannot manage many of the dishes I have asked her to prepare. Mrs Stone is also really in need of pensioning off to some cottage which I am sure you could provide, since she is past doing what I require of her, and of course, we must have a proper butler. That man who comes in when we have guests is all very well . . ."

The three housemaids who stood about the room, known as Peg, Jenny and Josie, before the coming of their new mistress, but now called Askew, Hall and Baxter, at least by her, since it seemed she was not in the habit of calling her servants by their Christian names, did their best to blend into the wallpaper, their eyes like saucers in their rosy country faces.

Reed regarded the smooth and equally rosy face of his wife, wondering wearily for the hundredth time in the last four months how he was to season himself to the realisation that this artless, innocent, young woman was to be his companion for the rest of their lives together. That from now until one of them died she would sit opposite him at the breakfast and dining table; that she had, as it seemed she was now intent on doing, the right to fire or hire his servants as she pleased. She was not silly, nor even empty-headed. She had been brought up to be the wife a man like himself needed. Not clever, for if she had shown signs of it, it would certainly have been erased from her childish mind years ago. She had been moulded from birth for her place in life: to extend a wide-eyed, unquestioning docility to her husband, as she had to her father. Embroidery, a few scales on the piano, French verbs and a prayer or two in English. That was all she knew. To sing and smile and take part in the small-talk thought suitable for a lady, and the understanding that man was the master and she his weak and female shadow. She could deal with servants, run her home with the efficiency a man of shrewd business sense would not despise, but she had no thought in her head which was not put there by her husband. Except in her own domain, which was her husband's home.

She was smiling at him in perfect innocence, anticipating no argument, merely showing him the courtesy of telling him what she intended doing in the running of their home, which was, after all, her job. To make it as comfortable as she could for him, for their children when they came, and for their guests, who would, since he was a man of business, and she a woman with friends, be many.

He sighed, doing his best to be patient since none of this was her fault, this disaster he had brought upon himself. He waved his hand at the maids, indicating that they should leave the room, praying that they would not go blabbing to Mrs Lewis and Mrs Stone, and that if they did, which seemed likely, he could smooth it over without undermining his wife's new authority.

"Esmé, Mrs Stone has been in this house ever since my mother died and Mrs Lewis before that. My father employed them to look after us and when he went I saw no reason for change. Mrs Lewis is a splendid cook and Mrs Stone, though I dare say she has had her own way and has become used to it, will quickly adapt to what you need of her. They are neither of them old enough to be pensioned off. Mrs Lewis is not yet fifty and Mrs Stone only a few years older. That is not ancient, you know."

It was to eighteen-year-old Esmé Macauley, but she waited politely for her husband to finish what he had to say before starting, sweetly, to explain.

"I agree that Mrs Lewis is splendid, Reed, as you say, but only with the provincial dishes she is used to preparing. She cannot manage French cuisine. You will, I'm sure, want the gentlemen with whom you do business and who will be dining with us, to have the very best you can give them, and I, as your wife, can only supply it if I have the proper servants. I intend to begin house parties as soon as I have the staff since my friends from Yorkshire, from Cheshire and Leicestershire, where I have often hunted and been their guest, will wish to be mine. And now that the weather is warmer, I thought it would be charming to have champagne picnics, like we did at home. I shall need another carriage or two to carry the ladies who do not ride and then, at the proper time, a harvest ball, perhaps with a marquee on the lawn for the tenants . . ."

"Tenants?"

"Why, yes, that is what my friend Lady Harrison of Edenthwaite does every year. Her husband's estate . . ."

"This is not an estate, Esmé. This is a working farm."

"Oh surely more than that."

"Shepherds, I employ. Men in the yard and the fields. A gardener or two, stable lads. There are no tenants, only those who live in cottages on my land."

"Very well, no marquee for the tenants, but a ball nevertheless and a hunt ball at . . ."

"We have no ballroom Esmé. This is a farmhouse."

"But the salon is large."

"Salon?" since he was not aware he had one.

"The drawing room then. The carpets could be removed and chairs set about . . ."

Her voice tripped on, light and silvery, and for several minutes he let it flow over him. She was so very pretty. She wore a simple morning gown of sprigged cream muslin, the neck high and frilled, the sleeves long and tight fitting. About her eighteen-inch waist was a broad sash of cream silk tied at the back in a bow. The bodice of the gown was tight, showing off her magnificent breasts, and the shoulders were sloping. Her hair was immaculately arranged with a centre parting and cream velvet ribbons threaded the side curls in a golden cloud over her ears. Her cornflower-blue eyes were wide and clear with nothing in them but her desire to please and her complete ignorance of what was in her husband's mind. She looked utterly enchanting, composed and unruffled, at eight o'clock in the morning, turned out by the lady's maid she had brought with her to a faultless perfection which, though it spoke of hours of effort, had, he knew, taken no more than the half-hour in which he himself had bathed, shaved and dressed. There was not a sign of the night before in which he had made love to her with the despairing strength of a man who fears he is losing his mind and who is convinced that only by plunging his male body into female flesh, can he save his sanity. She had made no objection. She had made no response. He had turned her, tossed her, this way and that, studying the young magnificence of her nakedness from every angle, in every position his imaginative mind could devise. For hours on end he had caressed her, doing his best to take into his mouth, into his own body, the most intimate parts of hers, going into her again and again, since if he could get her with child, at least some good might come of the charade they played out. He had exhausted himself, falling asleep with his face pressed into her flat, empty belly. He felt bruised, weary, drained this morning and she looked as though she had never known a man's hand in her life. Perhaps that was because, in a way, she had not. Like a doll she had been. Acquiescent, submissive, dutiful, *doing* nothing. There, beneath his hands, his lips, his worrying teeth, his body, but not . . . not with him. Not as . . . as *she* would have been.

At once Annie Abbott's vibrant laughing face swam into his vision and the room, the bright sunshine which streamed through the window, his wife's smooth face, his wife's tinkling voice all dissolved and vanished. Eyes, deep and golden brown as the waters in the high tarn and just as gleaming. Eyes which had melted to a rich warm chocolate on that day, long ago now when she had almost, almost moved into his arms. The day he had heard she had been interfered with and he had gone rampaging down to Browhead, only to find it had been that wisp of a child she had taken in. She had hit him, he remembered, though he could not bring to mind why, then, later, when he had drunk the tankard of ale she had given him by way of apology, if Annie Abbott could be said to apologise to anyone, there had been sweetness for a while, a hint of what might have been between Annie Abbott and Reed Macauley. Then they had argued again and he had ridden off in high dudgeon, his temper a furnace within him at her defiant stubbornness.

As he had the last time, the day on Rosley Fairground, the last day. The day he had seen her with her hand in that of another man's. The day she had looked into his eyes and held the man's hand and . . . he had run . . .

Reed Macauley had run away from her . . . It had been an agony, a pain so great even now it festered and bit deep inside him and would not let him rest. Dear sweet God, if he could only escape it, and rest. She was as ingrained in him as though she was a living part of his body. As much his flesh, his muscles, the arteries which pumped his blood, his mind which dwelled on her every hour of the day, the heart which beat and beat and grieved for her. All these elements were contained in Reed Macauley and so was she, a living extension of himself, which could no longer be complete since she was missing from his life and always would be. For weeks he had hated her. Through the winter when tales of her doings had come to him he had hated her so much the bile had come to his mouth and choked him. She was just as they said she was, brazen and unblushing, indecent in her shamelessness, a woman of easy virtue, who would use any man to achieve her own ends. They said all these things of her and he agreed, and yet, deep in his heart, which knew Annie Abbott for what she truly was, a small voice to which he refused to listen whispered that if she was all these things, why had she not used Reed Macauley? Surely, of all the men in the parish of Bassenthwaite, he was the one who could have given her the most. She had known she could have it. She had only to put out a hand to him and comfort, security, love, could all have been hers without doing a hand's turn to achieve it. A house somewhere, for herself and her child, money, jewels, clothes, his protection. Anything she wanted, needed and yet she chose to work herself and that girl she took in, into the ground to keep her independence. Putting herself in danger, dressing like a man, tramping the fells alone but for her dogs, in her eternal search for what she was after.

His wife's voice interrupted his painful thoughts and, though they were painful, they were also precious and guarded and he wanted to strike out at Esmé for ripping them apart.

". . . so I will summon Mrs Lewis first and give her a

month's notice. I think that is fair, don't you? I shall of course give her a glowing reference since she . . ."

"And where in hell's name do you think she is to go at her age? After all these years of devoted service, where is she to go, Esmé? A woman of forty-five thrown out in the street just because she can't manage bloody French cuisine . . . ?"

"Reed . . . oh, please, Reed," Esmé's face crumpled in distress but Reed Macauley did not see it, or if he did, he did not care. His mind was battered with pictures of a woman, any woman really, who is forced by circumstances to struggle in this cruel, man's world, to survive on her own. To stoop to tasks which were beyond her, physically and emotionally. Humiliated and cast out to fend for herself after all these years. He could not, would not stand for it, no, not if he had to ride over there and . . . and . . .

Jesus . . . Jesus God! it was *Mrs Lewis* who was being discussed here . . . not . . . not *her*. And he would not allow it. She had no right to even think of dismissing her, not Mrs Lewis, even if Esmé was mistress of this house now . . . Dear sweet God . . . let there be a child soon . . . a son . . . or a daughter . . . anything to ease the ache in him which wouldn't let up, anything to put Annie Abbott out of his mind, his heart, his *life*, or he would go mad with it. She was destroying him, his torment . . . his love.

"Mrs Lewis stays, Esmé." His voice was cold, implacable and his young wife shrank back in her chair as he stood up. He saw it and was sorry, but there was nothing he could say to reassure her. Not now . . . not just now when he needed to get away.

"She is . . . a member of the family . . . no, no, not related . . ." he added irritably as his wife's astonished face could plainly be seen to be dwelling on the horror of having a common cook's blood mixing in the veins of her children, when they came. "And I don't want to hear another word on it. Those with whom I'm acquainted and who have been dining here for years seem to have taken no harm from Mrs Lewis's cooking, indeed they have often praised it. Your friends I'm afraid must learn to do the same. Of course, if their fine sensibilities cannot overcome it, then they are at liberty to stay away."

Ignoring the fat child's tears which had begun to form in his wife's beautiful eyes, he strode from the room, banging the door behind him.

The long moving ribbon of sheep wound slowly down the track towards the lower pastures, a jostling, steaming throng of animals which now and then jumped as though in joyful anticipation of what was to come. The air was filled with their bleating and baaing and their hooves made a sharp clatter on the rough stones, before they reached the more profuse grass of the inlands. Two dogs worked them, as silent as shadows, moving in a sweeping blur from side to side, keeping them together, chivvying down those which were reluctant to go. At their back were Annie Abbott and Cat.

Blackie and Bonnie were experienced sheepdogs now, running as 'doubles', obeying Annie's orders with no more than a high whistle and a short command. They had gathered her ewes and the twenty or so lambs which they had dropped in May, and others besides, since any man's flock may roam freely on the high fells and sheep know no enemies amongst their own, mixing with one another as they cropped. Despite this there were not many strays. A Herdwick will stick to its own 'heaf', the pasture where it is weaned. It has in it an incredible homing instinct which fortunately had not been too deep in the ones Annie had bought at Rosley, since it had been known for a sheep sold miles away, if it is able, to return to its own 'heaf'. Annie's had not done so. There would be a 'meet' in November at a local hostelry where shepherds would gather, not only to celebrate the end of a successful farming year but where all strays, or neighbouring sheep had to be displayed by noon of the day decided, and all sheep whose marks were not in the 'Shepherd's Guide' started some twenty years ago were to be drawn into a fold apart from

the others to be inspected by all at the meeting. Those
who infringed on this rule were fined sixpence each. Every
sheep and lamb, as it was born, was branded with the
owner's 'smit' on the fleece, and all of Annie's new flock
now had her 'lug' mark on their ear. Those she found
without her mark among the sheep she had gathered must
be taken to the meet and how the farmers in the parish
who had managed over the past year to treat her as though
she and her flock, indeed her farm, did not exist, would
cope with that, she could not imagine. Nor did she care.
She had bought her flock. She had mated each ewe with
the eager ram which had been driven back to Rosley in
the spring. At lambing time the four of them, Charlie and
herself, Cat and Phoebe, and the two dogs had gone, day
after long wet day, searching out the new lambs which
stood, small and white and defenceless against the dark
contrast of their mother's bulk. The dogs even at such a
young age, knew instinctively that gentleness was needed,
driving the ewe and her staggering lamb, sometimes two,
towards Annie, where with a deft twist of her crook, she
caught the ewe, checking her udders for milk supply, since
the lamb's survival depended on its mother's ability to feed
it. The lamb was marked with exactly the same colour and
spot as its dam.

When each lamb was thriving and trotting sturdily beside
its mother, they were moved from the lambing field where
Annie and Charlie had put them earlier, on to adjacent
land, so that gradually, as a lamb was born and checked
each day, all of her flock were driven up on to the more
exposed pasture. At that time of the year, as the winter
snows melted, the streams were swollen and dangerous,
and she had lost several babies whose first staggering
steps proved to be their last. Carrion crow and foxes were
a hazard but from her twenty ewes she had bred seventeen
lambs including four sets of twins.

Today the air was clear and warm but wisps of mist
hung over the ends of the fells. Birds were pouring out
their song from throats in which the splendour of summer
was scarcely contained. A plover called to its mate, and a

curlew glided across the valley, its warbling note ending
as it touched the ground. The sun was out, her flock's
fleece was dry and ready for clipping and she felt the
peace, the content, the pleasure settle in her. All around
her was her land, not a great deal but enough to form the
small farm she had dreamed of. Her sheep streamed out
before her and when they were sheared she and Charlie
were to take the fleeces to market to sell. She would keep
the ewe lambs for breeding and sell the others at the lamb
fair at Penrith. Hire a tup to service her ewes and so
another cycle in the year would begin.

"Come bye, Blackie," she called. "Away to me,
Bonnie, steady, steady . . ."

There would be no 'boon' clipping at Browhead for who
amongst her neighbours would lend *her* a hand? She must
do it all herself since neither Charlie nor Phoebe had the
necessary skill which she had learned when her father
considered her strong enough.

Charlie would drag the sheep to her, and when it was
clipped, Phoebe would salve the shorn animal which
involved the application to the skin of a mixture of tar and
grease. The salve smelled abominable but it would not
only encourage the lamb's next fleece, making it stronger
and thicker, but would protect it against parasite. Charlie
had promised Phoebe he would fashion a harness of sorts
to attach to a ring in the wall so that each beast could be
kept still while she did it.

"Ah'll be as reet as nine pence, Mr Lucas, don't tha
fret," she had told him stoutly. Phoebe never called Charlie
anything but Mr Lucas, no matter how many times he
begged her. Cat called him Charlie as naturally as she
called Annie 'Mother', but Phoebe had seen right away
that Mr Lucas was a gentleman and as such must be shown
proper respect. She liked him well enough, for who could
dislike such a good-natured, amiable chap? Do anything
for anyone, would Mr Lucas, especially Annie. He worked
hard, though he was not much good with his hands, try
as he might. Willing, oh yes, but give him a hammer and
he hit his thumb, an axe or saw and he cut himself, or

dropped the log he was chopping on his foot. He had helped Annie to cut the oats and bigg and rye and when they had dried, he would take them to be ground by the local miller. He had cleaned and oiled Joshua Abbott's old plough and in the spring had supplied the 'horse power', laughing as he did about absolutely everything, pulling it whilst Annie guided it along the furrows. The hay was next and how Mr Lucas would fare with that there scythe didn't bear thinking about, but he had done his best. He couldn't help it if his skill lay in other directions, could he? Read anything he could get his hands on he did, always writing something he was, or talking his head off about politics, but what they would have done without him, Phoebe couldn't imagine.

She and Charlie were waiting beside the gate leading into the big field in front of the farm, both ready to give a helping hand to Blackie and Bonnie as they herded the flock through. A catching pen had been set up so that when the sheep flowed between the gateposts they were immediately enclosed in a small area which was easily accessible to Charlie as he reached in for the animal which was to be clipped. To the side of the farmhouse, just beyond the gate, was the cobbled yard and it was here that Annie had set up the special two-tiered stool which was used for clipping. She sat on the highest tier and the sheep was tipped on to its back on the lower, its head between her knees. Beside the stool were her father's shears, freshly cleaned and sharpened.

The spring, as though at last the gods were inclined to smile on Annie Abbott, had been a good one, dry and sunny. The blue sky arched away above their heads and high at its zenith a sky lark sang its heart out. The dogs, their work done for the moment, lay panting in the shade by the kitchen step, their tongues lolling from their open mouths. There were midges dancing in the warm air and in the meadow, buttercups and daisies and clover made a patchwork of delicate colour in the green of the grass.

The sheep bleated anxiously and Annie could feel the

steady rhythm of her heart quicken. The results of a
year's, no more than that, eighteen months', arduous
back-breaking labour was about to be realised. Her fleeces
would be sold, and the male lambs, and she would have
ready cash again to expand her flock. To grow! Oh, Lord,
keep my hand steady, she prayed, and my back strong,
since it all depends on me. And let me remember how to
do it!

"Righto, Charlie," she called, to the man at the gate,
no sign of the tension in her. "Bring the first."

The struggling sheep was hauled, hooves scraping,
towards her, whilst Charlie sweated and swore. The ewe's
bleats added to the growing hubbub as her frantic lamb
tried its best to go with her. The sheep stank as Charlie
manhandled it on to the lower step of the stool, struggling
to get back to its lamb, and for a moment, Annie felt a
weakness in her arms and back. She could not do it, dear
God, the thing was so enormous. Its fleece was thick,
brown, tangled . . . filthy with . . . then her father's voice
muttered irritably in her ear, telling her not to be such a
great gowk! and to get on with it, girl, and her hand
reached for the shears.

She did eight sheep that day. Sweat poured from her
so that she looked as though she had been dipped in water.
Phoebe squeaked a lot since she had had nothing to do
with sheep before, and even swore as Charlie did, but
each shorn ewe was efficiently salved against the dread
scourge of scab with rancid butter and tar, each taking her
an hour to do, and the fleece was rolled neatly into its
bundle before mother and lamb were re-united. Many of
the lambs were confused for they did not recognise the
snow-white apparition, which, once a browny grey, their
mother had now become. The bright blue 'smit' mark
stood out on her newly shorn back. Each ewe called for
her lamb, and when found, udders which had filled in the
separation were quickly emptied.

The next day it was the same, and the next, and up
beside the beck where he sat quietly on his coal-black
mare, his patient dog beside him, the man heard her laugh

of jubilation, her shout of triumph which echoed about the fell. He watched her as the man with her put his arms about her and when they capered round the yard in a rough semblance of a polka, he lowered his chin to his chest, turned the mare and began to make his slow way towards his empty home.

Charlie Lucas was a Chartist who, in April 1848, had done
his best to march with Feargus O'Connor to hand the
Chartist petition to Parliament demanding that every man
should have a vote, and that in a secret ballot, which was
the essence of their People's Charter.

The petition was not successful. It had been presented
by men who believed in peaceful persuasion and when that
failed, those who were inclined to think that 'physical force'
spoke with a voice more likely to be heard, marched with
their pikes, their green rosettes and banners through Halifax and Bradford, through Nottingham and Manchester
and other northern towns. A Chartist mob with sticks and
stones fighting against the drawn cutlasses of squadrons
of dragoons. One of that 'mob' was Charlie who, having
found that peaceful means had not achieved the justice and
equality for all men he believed they should have, had
decided to fling in his hand with the more violent sort,
though he was not a violent man.

Arrests were made, Chartist leaders who had led the
riots. The Irish Chartist, John Mitchel was sentenced to
transportation on a convict ship to Australia. Three hundred others were sent for trial and it was generally agreed
that those still at large should lie low for a while. Charlie
had fled even further north, moving from town to town,
working at anything he could find; many tasks of a menial
nature not suited to his qualifications since, as the son of
a lawyer, he was an educated man. He walked for weeks,
months, sleeping rough through the summer of 1848, the
flame of him growing dimmer, leaving only a footloose,
weary man, who, though he evaded arrest, no longer had
the fire and idealism of his beliefs to keep him going.

He had been idling about Rosley, undecided which way to go with winter coming on, north or south, east or west, what did it matter? It was then that Annie Abbott, in her threadbare, overlarge men's clothing had come striding up the track, her two dogs beside her, her fragile, lop-sided sledge behind. He had at that moment, no inclination to do anything positive, like getting on his way, wherever that might be, so he had watched her, not aware that the youth he studied was in fact female, his curiosity caught nevertheless. He had followed her into The Drover's Rest, simply because there had been nothing else to do. His grand and noble ideas had come to nought. He had dedicated himself for years to the Charter which had come to nought. He was needed by no one, until he met Annie.

On this day in October, he had been at Browhead a year and in a small way, Annie was prospering. Her lambs had been sold at Penrith and up on the fell the ewes were waiting to be covered by the fine hired tup who was butting his head in frustration in the field before the farm. In November he would be allowed to mate, but not before since Annie did not want her lambs to be dropped until April or May when the worst of the winter would be over.

The potato crop was in, the potatoes stored in clamps, long heaps in the barn covered with straw, soil and hedge-trimmings. The hay was cut, and built up into an enormous haystack, a gigantic task which had been almost beyond the three of them and next year Annie was talking of hiring some of the Irish vagrants who tramped with their families from Whitehaven having come on the coal boats in search of work. Vegetables were stored ready for the winter. Sieves had been cut and each evening the four of them had fashioned the rushlights which would illuminate the long dark nights ahead of them. Peat had been brought in and was stacked and drying in the empty cow byre attached to the house. Annie's own ewes having proved good breeders, instead of slaughtering a couple for meat, she had parted with some of her precious cash and bought two sheep at Penrith market and these had been killed

and some of the mutton pickled in brine in the huge vats
in the kitchen, the rest smoked above the fire in the inglenook. Charlie and Annie had felled timber last winter,
the straight-grained poles which, as Annie had showed
him, must be peeled, split into pieces and boiled in water
to make them pliable. They were then further split with
the 'lat-axe' and shaved and trimmed on Joshua Abbott's
'swillers-horse'. All was now ready for the winter months
ahead when the swill baskets and besom-twig brooms, the
materials for which were stored in the barn, would be
fashioned ready for market in the spring. Which market
Annie had not yet decided, she said, but Charlie knew she
had some idea brewing in her clever head. She had kept
a fleece from one of her ewes and would card and spin
and weave in the winter months, making the hodden grey
which would become garments of clothing for her and Cat
and Phoebe. She was settling, thriving, coming through,
winning!

The sky was a low, leaden canopy of grey clouds draped
from fell to fell as Charlie trudged down the track towards
the village of Hause on the edge of which stood the mill.
Behind him he pulled the sledge which, though still in the
state it had been when he had first seen Annie Abbott,
over twelve months ago now, had been used for carrying
everything from potatoes and peat, from fresh-cut sieves
to a tired child, and now the oats and bigg he was taking
to be milled. The runners had come off a time or two
causing some consternation and great hilarity when one
slid all the way down Middle Fell, scattering sheep in every
direction, until it splashed into the beck. He had followed
it, gathering speed as it did, and finishing up beside it in
the sweet tasting, icy water.

He sighed as the memories of the past year came flooding through his mind. Good, sweet memories which were
filled with Annie, with laughter and tears and worry, with
peace and fulfilment. Annie's lovely face strained so often
into deep hollows of weariness as she took on tasks which
were beyond her, but which were performed just the
same. Annie's face laughing, bright and glorious as it had

been on the day the runner came off the sledge and her tears, channelling through the birth blood which had smeared her cheeks as she had fought to save a lamb's life. Peace he had seen in her eyes as they had sat together in the dusk on the drystone wall before the farmhouse, and fulfilment as her complete flock of twenty ewes and their offspring moved placidly from one sweet tussock of grass to another. He had known her every mood, the brave goodness of her, the spirited temper, the merry humour, the bright resolve that said she would never be beaten. She was proud, defiant and independent. She was strong and beautiful and she was in love with Reed Macauley who had married some heiress from Bradford.

So what was to happen to Charlie Lucas who loved Annie Abbott? he asked himself, his eyes cast down to the rough ground before him. His good leather boots in which, with the Chartists, he had tramped the long miles from Manchester to London, moved one beside the other in his line of vision and he noted with a part of his mind which dwelled on practicalities that if he didn't get them repaired soon, they would be beyond it and he would have to take to wearing the wooden-soled clogs Annie, Cat and Phoebe wore. Not that there was any shame in that. They were warm and serviceable but somehow it seemed to him that clogs would be a symbol of his complete isolation from the class into which he had been born and the life he had known as a child and youth. A reforming family, his had been, despite their rank, taking him to reform meetings, where he had learned about Luddism and Chartism and the injustice of man against man. His father, a good man, a lawyer who had acted on behalf of many radical men on trial for their beliefs, had become bankrupt in the process, worn out from protecting other men from starvation, rarely charging for his own services, dying, as had his wife, Charlie's mother, in genteel poverty in West Yorkshire.

So Charlie had gone on the tramp, enduring what his fellow men, those with nothing, endured, moving up and down the country, speaking at Chartist meetings, passionate and ready to do whatever was asked of him in the fight for freedom and equality. It had been important to him. There had been nothing else and no one else. He had known many young women, liked them, some of them even loved a little, but lightly, good humouredly, with none of the strength and passion with which he loved Annie. He wanted Annie very badly, and how was he to continue to live beside her, with nothing more than the friendship which was all she had to give him? He slept in the snug loft above the dairy and cow byre and between his bed and Annie's was a wall a foot thick but it might as well have been thirty, or a veil of flimsy gauze, it would not have mattered, since Annie was not for him. Her demeanour told him so. She was open, generous with her friendship, her affection even, which he had seen grow as the months went by but he wanted more than that. Much more. He wanted her not only in his heart where she already was, but in his bed. He wanted her for wife and mother, to him and to their children, and her nearness, the soft curving flesh of her breasts and waist and hip, the fine delicacy of her white wrist, the sweetness of the flesh beneath her chin, her fragrance and warmth as she moved about his nights and days, were killing him as slowly and irrevocably as were the years. He had nothing to offer but himself, and his labour, and his love. She had her land, her farm, her flock. She had her child and a good friend in Phoebe and though she was not accepted into the community which lived in the Vale of Borrowdale, Bassenthwaite and Keswick, surely that would come when they realised, the people in that community, her worth. She had no need of Charlie Lucas. She would argue of course, since she could not see into his heart and would be distressed when he told her he must go. She knew nothing of his Chartist background, but if she did she would not understand, since the Chartist movement was dead so what was there for him to do, she would ask and he must think of some reason to satisfy her.

He turned at the foot of the track where it led out on

to the Hause road, looking up at the high fells where he
had lived these last twelve months. He could see Annie
and Phoebe scything the last of the bracken with long
graceful strokes. When it was cut, which must be done
each backend to prevent it encroaching on pasture land,
it would be used as bedding for any animals which were
brought inside for the winter. As yet of course, Annie had
none, but still the bracken must be cleared. They were
late with the end-of-autumn task, but the previous weeks
had been frantic with all the work which must be completed
by only three adults before the snows began.

The two women were tiny figures amongst the reds and
browns and yellows of the vast sea of withering bracken,
the fronds of which had turned over the last weeks from
a delicate tawny brown to a subtle lemon hue. In the
coppice beyond, oak and ash, hazel and larch stood regally
with branches capturing every shade of colour from the
palest brown to the brightest yellow. The leaves were
falling rapidly but here and there were brilliant splashes of
red on rowan, thorn, holly, yew and juniper as their berries
clustered. He would miss it. Annie . . .

The giant water wheel which moved the rollers inside
the mill was tumbling round at great speed since there
was never any shortage of water in these parts to turn it.
The mill was quiet but for the noise the wheels made when
he poked his head inside the door, the enormous stone
discs which ground the corn, the barley and the oats,
moving ponderously one on top of the other as they did
their work. A fine mist filled the air from the grain which
was fed through the hole in the middle of the wheels and
particles lay an inch thick on every surface. Two plump
cats were curled together on the window-sill, their size
proof of their labours as catchers of the rats and mice
which fought for a living here. There were several sacks
stacked against the wall, filled with threshed and dried
oats waiting to be ground, but little else and Charlie con-
gratulated himself on coming as early as he had. It seemed
that Annie's grain would not have to wait and neither would
he. If he left the sacks they should be ready by morning.

"Hello," he shouted. "Are you there?"

"Aye" a voice floated from somewhere above him, coming down the narrow stone steps. "Ah'll be down in a minute. Ah've just to . . ." the words lost in a jumble as the owner of the voice evidently stuck his head into some task pertinent to milling.

"Nah then, what can ah do for thee?" he was saying as he lumbered down the steps. A big fellow used to manhandling up and down them, the enormous sacks of grain brought to him.

Charlie smiled pleasantly showing his good teeth in a face which the weathers had painted a rich amber. His brown curls, long and uncut these past months, since Annie had been too tired of an evening to be barber – and could he bear her lovely touch? his heart had asked, glad of the excuse – lay over his brow and the collar of his shabby broadcloth coat.

"I would be glad of my oats ground, sir, and by tomorrow morning if I may. I seem to have come at a good time since you appear to have a lull at the moment." It had seemed impolite to imply that the miller had no work, as though the folks hereabout did not care to use him.

The miller's face had become quite expressionless, the comradely smile of welcome he reserved for his customers sliding away to nothing. He stood, already tall, towering above Charlie on the next to bottom step, both hands on his hips, his eyes cool as he looked down at him.

"Nay, can't be done," he dared Charlie to argue.

Charlie did. "And why is that?" He looked about him, delicacy gone. "You don't seem very busy."

"Can't be done, not today." The miller's bottom lip protruded truculently.

"Then tomorrow will do. I'll call back at . . ."

"Ah'm too busy. Stuff coming in this afternoon."

"I see. Then I will have to wait my turn. When *can* you do it?"

"Ah couldn't say."

"But surely you must know when you . . ."

"Nay, ah'm up to me eyes in it for weeks now. You'd best find someone else to tekk it."

"But you had no such problems last year when I brought my oats to you. Last November when . . ."

"Ah didn't know who tha' was then."

"And what has that to do with it? You are a miller who, presumably, is desirous of earning a living. I am a man with grain to grind. Why should who I am prevent us from striking a bargain?"

"Ah've had me say. Ah can't do tha' grain so tha'd best tekk it elsewhere."

"You are the only miller in these parts."

"Aye, ah know."

"Look here, this is bloody ridiculous. I have grain to be ground here and . . ."

"Bugger off. Ah'll ground no grain for thi' or for that hussy up Browhead. She'm not fit to be called owt else, trampin' about in her faither's clothes like she does. Ah knew Joshua Abbott an' poor sod'd be turnin' in his grave if he knew, an' if tha' wants a thumpin' then tha' shall 'ave it if tha' raises tha' fists ter me. Ah've nowt against you since I reckon any chap'd be glad ter get inter Annie Abbott's drawers, meself included, given a chance, so tha' can't be blamed if . . ."

Despite his size it took him all of five minutes to fling the tall, much lighter figure of Charlie out into the road. His own fists were grazed where his knuckles had connected with Charlie's nose, his eye and chin, and surprisingly he had a shiner of his own where the lad, give him his due, had landed him one.

Though he did his best to clean himself up in the beck which tumbled beside the mill, Charlie's face was a mass of contusions as he dragged his burden and his aching self back up the hill to Browhead. From higher up the fell, Annie had seen him return, waving her arm in greeting then, realising that he could not possibly have got the grain milled in the hour he had been gone, she dropped her scythe and began to run, her long legs still clad as they had been for the past year in her father's trousers, eating up the shorn stretch of bracken, the long dip of the 'inland' pasture and leaping the drystone wall as easily as any steeple chaser.

"Dear God . . . Charlie . . . dear God . . ." Her face turned white and inside her chest her heart crashed against her rib-cage in terror. Surely someone must have tried to kill him, but through the blood which refused to stop flowing from a burst lip and the agony of his eye which was already closed, he tried to smile.

"It's all right Annie. I'm not hurt."

"*Not hurt*, my God, who did this to you?" She moved towards him bringing with her the fragrance of the lavender she scattered in the chest where her clothes were kept, the smell of the bracken and the fresh, wild aroma of the Lakeland fell in which she laboured. It was her own particular fragrance, sweet and pure, and his love for her gushed through him, drowning his senses. She put her hands about his face, cupping it to hold him still and he froze in a paralysis of need which her nearness awoke in him. Her face was close to his, her eyes warm, concerned, probing and her breath was sweet.

"I got in a bit of a . . . fight," he managed to say endearingly, trying once more to smile.

"*A bit of a fight!* My God, what hit you? You won't be able to see in the morning . . ."

"I can't see now . . ." he mumbled, wishing she would go on holding him. Wishing she would put her arms about him, hold his weary, aching head to her breast and comfort him as she did Cat . . . No, not as she did Cat, but as she would a *man*. Phoebe had joined them by now and Cat had come out of the kitchen where she was at her lessons, those Annie insisted on, and they clustered about him in concern, none of them noticing at that moment the untouched sacks of grain on the old sledge.

She bathed his face and Phoebe made him tea, though quite honestly he could have done with a stiff brandy to put out the still smouldering fire of rage which had been lit in him by the miller's words. He would not tell her, of course, what the man had said. Let her think they had fought because the miller had refused to grind her oats and bigg. That he himself had been so incensed he had taken a swing at the man. He would not dirty her by repeating the man's words. But she knew, of course.

Phoebe had gone to her bed, not much behind Cat who now had her own small room between Annie's and Phoebe's. She and Cat were both tired for besides her school work, Cat collected the eggs and fed the hens which moved freely about the yard, saw to both the dogs' evening meal, brought in peat and kindling and any other light task which was within her grasp. She was nearly five years old now, growing tall and strong, her young character forming already into an image of her mother's. She was a beauty, with a sweetness in her which Charlie loved for it was so like Annie's. Not a sugary sweetness, but one which was mixed with spice and fire making it all the more palatable.

"He said something about me, didn't he? About you and me?" Annie leaned back in her mother's small rocking chair, her long legs crossed at the ankle, her feet bare and slender to the crackling fire. She had been carding the wool from her own fleece, a task which he knew gave her immense satisfaction, and the hand carder, used by her mother and her mother's mother still lay on the table. Carding involves tufts of the washed wool from the fleece being set between the wire points on the carder and 'combed' which action disentangles the fibres, loosening them ready for spinning. Next to the carder were the long combed fibres which Annie was still in the process of smoothing.

"I beg your pardon," he mumbled.

"You heard me, Charlie. Don't deny it. Nothing else would have made you set about a chap as big as Jack Bibby. He said something you didn't like and it involved you and me living here, unchaperoned . . ." She gave a snort of unamused laughter, ". . . since we can't count Phoebe. Oh, don't worry Charlie, I'm not daft. Do you think I don't know what they are *all* saying? I've seen the looks they give me when I happen to come across a shepherd on the fell, or Mrs Mounsey or Mim go past the back of the farm. Even Sally has stopped coming since . . ."

"Since I arrived. That's only because . . ."

"It's because that husband of hers has threatened her with the biggest hiding of her life if she does. They think the worst, Charlie, I'm afraid. Our reputation is ruined, yours and mine." She laughed lightly but there was deep in her voice a strange note which seemed to say it was hard being an outcast. No matter what she did, nor how innocently, they wouldn't have it. They thought the worst of her so really, what was the point of dwelling on it? She and Charlie were friends, dear friends, who supported one another as friends did. He had come into her life just when she needed one, and she had done the same for him. She gave him a home and one day, when she could afford it, she hoped to give him a wage, a decent wage, which was what he deserved.

"My reputation doesn't matter since . . ." He had been about to say since I will be going soon anyway, but the expression of vulnerability on her face, a young look of being lost for the moment, stopped him. He could not strike her with the blow which he knew would hurt her badly, just when she was suffering another. Somehow she must get her grain milled and the question was where, for there was not another miller in the parish of Bassenthwaite. But when that was done, he must go. He would tell her when all her labour was done. When she was settled for the winter, her crops in, her animals safe, her oats and bigg ground, and stored in the kist in the corner of the kitchen.

He watched her, her face pale and drawn, her weary body slumped. She was chewing her bottom lip, staring into the glowing peat fire as she worried on the question of how she was to get her grain ground and his battered face, though no emotion showed through the dried blood and bruising, was soft with his love for her.

It was noon the next day when Jack Bibby thumped on the door of the kitchen. Annie was up on the fell, scything the last of the bracken, Phoebe with her, only Charlie,

Cat and the two dogs at home. He had sworn he was able to go, and had twitched the scythe from Phoebe's hand saying she should stay at home and make him a bilberry pie from the last of the fruit they had picked from the great swathe which grew at the summit of Bakestall.

"All right then, Mr Lucas," Phoebe had said tartly. "Let's see tha' swing that scythe," and when he did the pain which had nagged him all night, flared hideously through his chest, making him gasp.

"Off with your shirt, Charlie," Annie had ordered, gasping herself as did Phoebe, at the great purple and black bruise which coloured his white skin just below his left breast.

"Oh, Charlie," was all she said, sadly, her fingers touching lightly the skin of his chest and shoulders and despite the agony he was in, he felt a stirring in the pit of his belly and the thrusting of his penis as his desire awoke.

"It's nothing really," stepping hurriedly away from her, but of course they must bind it up, they said, and did, and he must rest for a while since a rib might be cracked. So he and Cat were alone when the miller called.

Charlie stared in astonishment, his one good eye looking into Jack Bibby's one good eye. Behind the miller was a strong cart pulled by a sturdy fell pony and perhaps it was then that Charlie got the idea though it was not a conscious thought at the time.

"Ah've come for t' grain," the man said shortly.

Charlie gaped and behind him Cat held Blackie and Bonnie by their scruffs to let them know that neither they, she, nor Charlie were threatened.

"Is it handy?" the man went on, his manner truculent, his gaze shifty. Still Charlie could not speak. They both bore the scars of yesterday's fight and yet here was the miller, just as though it had not happened, enquiring for the grain which yesterday he had refused to grind.

"I don't believe this," Charlie said, his battered face a picture of bewilderment.

"'Appen tha' don't but I've no time to be standing here

whilst tha' think about it. Do tha' want tha' grain milling or not?"

The man was evidently under some strain and in his one good eye was a gleam which said he would dearly love to close Charlie's other eye but nevertheless he stood his ground.

"What the bloody hell's going on?" Charlie begged to know, wanting to laugh really, for the whole thing was so ridiculous, but not daring to, not only because of the pain in his chest which hurt each time he drew breath, but because he didn't want to turn the miller against him yet again. The man was looking over Charlie's shoulder at Cat who smiled and dropped a curtsey. For a moment his face softened and he almost smiled back then he turned to Charlie.

"Does tha want it doin' or not? Ah found that . . . well, ah've got an hour or two ter spare so ah thought . . ." he shifted uncomfortably from one big foot to the other, "well . . . mek tha' mind up."

"For God's sake man, of course we want it doing. Look, I can't lift it, not after our little contretemps yesterday." He grinned painfully and the miller wondered what the hell he was talking about but he nodded and, after Charlie showed him where the heavy sacks were, lifted them easily on to his cart and drove off.

"Ah'll have 'em back first thing tomorrow. Will that do thi?" he called over his shoulder.

"Of course, splendid and thanks."

Charlie was still grinning as he closed the door. He looked at Cat and she looked at him and though it sliced through him like a hot knife, he began to laugh.

"Now what in God's name was all that about?" he asked her, scratching his head.

"I don't know, Charlie. He must have changed his mind."

"I suppose he must, but I wish he had done it before he set into me."

The miller drove the cart along the two miles of road between the gate of Browhead Farm and Hause. He had gone no more than a mile when a man on a tall, high bred, black mare which was cropping the grass verge beside the road, held up his hand for him to stop. A Merle collie eyed him suspiciously. The miller scowled, but drew on the reins.

"Everything all right, Bibby?" the man asked quietly.

"Aye, 'tis in the back."

"And you'll have it ground by tomorrow?"

The miller sighed. "If you say so, sir."

"I do say so, Bibby, and I'm much obliged to you."

The miller sighed again.

"Aye, well . . . I'd best get on."

"Of course, and, Bibby, I won't forget this."

"No sir, neither will I."

The blizzard struck at the dales and fells of Lakeland early that winter, coming with very little warning at the end of November. January was the usual month in which the big snow was expected, only a light dusting on the peaks appearing before Christmas. In December, the frost would sting hard, every blade of grass and frond of bracken decorated with a hoary fringe. The sun would shine, turning the white peaks to a delicate rose, and the sheep would move down to where the herbage survived, with slivers of ice jangling on their thick grey fleece. Snow buntings, harbinger of bad weather to come, picked seeds from the bents, and grey geese flew in formation, heading south.

But in November the wind began to blow, thin and bitter. The hedges were black and the winter trees cowered beneath the growing force of tumultuous air. The peaks turned grey under the long snow-clouds and darkness fell before three o'clock in the afternoon. A steady flurry of powdery snow danced wildly in the turmoil of the elements, violent eddies sweeping across the fells, then it became calmer and the snow began to fall thickly, steadily, a white and impenetrable curtain through which nothing could be seen. The sheep, instinct telling them what to do, found places against rocks and walls where there was shelter, settling down to wait, and farmers did the same, knowing there was nothing else they could do. To go out in it, even to check on their precious flock, was madness. Men had been known to simply vanish in the white and eerily silent world, their bodies not found until weeks later when the thaw came. In the night, the wind returned, driving the snow directly into the face of Browhead Farm.

Morning light revealed a world in which nothing could be heard except the call of the ravens high on the peaks, nor seen but great drifts of snow across the farmyard, field, dales and fell, undulating deserts in which not even a gatepost was revealed. The grey crags stood up sharply in the white world, emerging from the snow high up the fells, beginning to turn pink as the rising sun fell on them. Trees were recognisable only by the shape of them, snow laden and top heavy. It had not yet crusted and when Charlie ventured forth on to it from the back door, which, being sheltered from the full force of the storm, could be safely opened, he fell right through it up to his waist.

"I'll have to make a path up to the barn or those hens will set up a racket to wake the dead if they're not fed," he shouted, and at once Cat and Phoebe were eager to help him, though Annie's first thought was to get up to the 'intakes' to check on her flock. Thirty-two ewes now and the ram who had been put out to service them only two weeks ago. Had they survived or were they buried in drifts which, until the snow crusted, could not be checked? The dogs would find them wherever they were and even if they were not found at once, a sheep can live in a drift for up to two weeks. The warmth and the fat of its own body would keep it alive but she could not help but worry. She was surviving by a hair's-breadth, treading delicately and it needed only one small setback, just one strand of the fine network of her life to snap and the whole structure would unravel.

"Don't even think of it," Charlie's quiet voice told her, reading her mind. She had not been aware that he was there as she stood, her eyes shaded by her raised hand, staring up into the blinding whiteness beneath which her hopes and dreams were buried. For good, or only until the snows allowed her up there, her mind agonised? She turned and smiled, though, tucking her hand in the crook of his arm.

"I wouldn't be allowed, even if I was daft enough to try, would I? The three of you would set up such a cater-wauling I would be completely overruled." She cast another anxious look at Middle Fell where she had last seen her tiny flock, then hugging his arm to her, pulled him towards the sloping drift in which Cat and Phoebe were floundering.

"Come on, then, let's have some fun. We can do nothing outside once the hens are fed and the eggs collected, so let's make a snowman." She bent and scooped a handful of snow, making it into a ball, then threw it at Phoebe who turned, surprised. For a moment she looked bewildered, not knowing even yet how to play, then her own face split into a young grin of joy and she did the same, aiming at Annie who began to shriek, the sound echoing across the valley. At once they were all at it, throwing snowballs, shouting with laughter, the dogs barking and chasing the snowballs which, when they landed, they could not find. Scarlet cheeks and brilliantly vivid eyes, smiling mouths and fast beating hearts, hands and feet tingling as the blood flowed and when the game was over, the paths dug, the hens fed, the companionable comfort and warmth of the kitchen, hands cupped round pewter beakers filled with thick vegetable 'crowdy'.

The dogs found every ewe the following week when the thaw set in. Not one lost and Annie was exultant as they were brought down to the safer inlands, the grassy pastures set directly about the farmhouse where, when the blizzards came again, as they were bound to do, they could be hand fed on the hay cut in the autumn, or even on ash leaves or holly, should it be necessary.

There was a second blizzard in January, worse even than the first, and then another so that the drifts were as high as the eaves of the farmhouse, every window and the door at the front completely blocked. There was the sound of wild geese honking, a great skein moving across the brilliantly blue sky in a huge formation, the leader a little way ahead. Crows picked at the frozen streams for signs of food and ravens searched vainly for twigs since it was coming up to nesting time. Hungry foxes barked across the frozen wastes in desperate need of sustenance. The bitter cold continued, a great frost by day and night, and

the snow was crisp and beautiful and could be walked on
with ease and safety. Becks and tarns were still frozen
over and the lovely tinkling sound which was a constant
song in the ears of those who lived beside them, was
stilled, a strange silence which was quite unnerving. The
crags were covered by shimmering icicles, field gates, if
they could have been reached, were frozen and sealed.
Bassenthwaite Lake was solid to a depth so great and so
thick, people could walk their horses across it and when
the wind shifted the fine powdery snow from its surface,
it was like mist about those who skated there, twirling
across its surface like birds on the wing. Ponies pulling
sledges could be seen crossing the vast expanse of snow
about it and in Annie's 'inlands' her ewes were heavy with
their unborn lambs. From the farmyard where Annie
paused to stare in silent wonder the fells stood up proudly,
great sleeping monsters of white and blue. In the late
afternoon, angry sunsets touched the snow about the farm
and glowed across the dark frozen waters of the lake
below.

The first intimation of the thaw in March came from the
ewes themselves as they lifted their heads and sniffed
the air. There was the sound of water tumbling down the
beck's rocky course, sky clouds to the west, and lower
down the fells, a thin yellow vegetation showed itself.
Annie saw storm-cocks perched on a tree, singing of the
coming of spring and heard the sweet sharp music of a
dipper, perched on a boulder near the waterfall at Dash
Falls. The snow melted from around the plants in the
farmhouse garden and suddenly there were snowdrops,
'the fair maids of February', revealed a month late.

Easter came and went but those at Browhead were
unaware of it, cut off as they were from all contact with
those about them. Annie would not have cared had she
known since her lambs would be here soon.

"I'm walking up to have a look, Charlie," she said. "D'you
want to come? It's a grand day for it." She sniffed the air
as her sheep had done, the pungent smell of the new fern
and heather already beginning to sprout, a delight to her.

The dogs watched her intently, waiting for the command which meant she would take them with her.

"No, I'll . . . I've things to do." Charlie did not look up from the sledge which, its runners discarded temporarily, he was attempting to patch together.

"What things?"

"Well, this for a start. You really could do with a small cart, you know, and a horse to pull it."

"When I have the money Charlie, in the meanwhile the sledge will have to do."

"And what about the ploughing? It will have to be done any day now . . ."

"Charlie dear, we managed last year and we will again."

"With me pulling the plough you mean."

"Which you did last year with no problem. Look Charlie, don't be down in the dumps. Come with me and we'll look for that fell pony you've been talking about."

She squatted down beside him, trying to win a smile from him. He had been out of sorts lately, she was inclined to think, not exactly short with her and Cat and Phoebe, but sparse with words, ready to spend time in his own room above the cow byre instead of in the warm kitchen with them. The winter had been long and trying. Four people forced by the weather to spend day after day in one another's company and though they had made enough swill baskets, besoms, woollen stockings and lengths of hodden grey wool to open a shop, or so Charlie said, busy from morning to night, it had not been easy for him, she supposed, stuck in the company of three females and two dogs. He did all that was needed out of doors, feeding the hens, collecting the eggs, bringing in peat and wood for the fire which was never allowed to go out, fetching water, checking the ewes who were still on the 'inlands', but he was restless, seeking his own company rather than theirs. When he did sit down in the kitchen, he took on the job of schoolteacher, continuing with the lessons he taught Cat, the Latin and French, showing her how to write in the beautiful copperplate he himself used. She was bright, quick, and was far beyond anything Phoebe had learned,

or even what Annie could teach her. She read the Bible
fluently, could add up and subtract as quickly as Annie,
and the question of where she should go to school must
soon be addressed. But for now Annie must get her lambing over, her fields ploughed, her vegetables and crops
planted and all the other dozens of jobs which she and
Charlie shared. And the idea Charlie had discussed with
her was a splendid one and that was to catch and break a
wild fell pony, not only to pull a cart when she could afford
one, but to draw the plough. She meant to buy a cow and
a pig if the ewes did well . . . Oh, God, let the ewes do
well . . . please . . .

"You go on, Annie, I'm busy." Charlie's voice was short
and he stood up, moving away from her. She straightened
slowly, brushing her hands down the legs of her father's
trousers. She had an idea about these too, if things went
right . . . if . . . if . . .

"What's the matter, Charlie? You seem . . ."

"Nothing, really. There's nothing," but it appeared to
her that he was angry about something.

"Of course there is. Won't you tell me? Is it your ribs?"

"No, they're fine now. Mended weeks ago."

"Then what . . . ?"

"Oh, for God's sake, Annie, can you not see I'm busy?"
and he strode away in the direction of the barn, the long
muffler Cat had knitted for him streaming out at his back.

"Very well then. If you feel like that, I'll go alone."

She went directly up the track behind the house in the
direction of Middle Fell and Great Cockup, her crook in
her hand and the dogs at her heels. Her sheep were on
the higher intake land below the snowline and when Blackie
and Bonnie brought them to her it took her no more than
two hours to examine each one. They were all fat and
healthy and she smiled in satisfaction. A lamb from each
would double her flock, please God. Nearly seventy sheep
she would have, if her luck held, and with the money she
saved and would get from the lambs she sold, she could
have that cow and the pig. Her own milk. Her own butter
and, when the time was right, bacon.

Her elation carried her on and up moving through the bracken and sprouting heather towards the white-streaked Brockle Crag which was really no more than an untidy fall of rocks. There was a sheep trod leading up beyond it. A wreath of wet mist as white as the insides of a sheep's fleece rolled off the summit of Skiddaw, but she went on. The dogs, knowing they were no longer working, frolicked in and out of the growing vegetation, scenting rabbits, chasing one another, acting the fool since they were still young.

"You'd best call off your dogs, for mine is too old to fight."

His voice came at her from nowhere as she daydreamed. She had been watching the steep track on which she was climbing, her mind dwelling pleasurably on the spring and summer to come. Blackie and Bonnie had gone on ahead, bounding away towards a group of tall grey-pitted crags and as she approached them, both dogs were standing, muzzles raised, ears flat, eyes fixed on a dog which was doing the same.

Beyond them was Reed Macauley.

It was a year since she had seen him and the shock of it struck her a blow which made her gasp and almost bent her double. Her peaceful heart exploded within her, galloping wildly to a beat which threatened to choke her and she felt the blood drain away from her brain, making her feel faint. She stood rigid and paralysed, her hands which she had brought in reflex up to her midriff, clasped tight together to prevent them shaking. Her mouth dried and she could not have spoken if her life depended on it.

They looked at one another across the hours, the days, the weeks and months which separated them, to the few precious times they had met. The day on the road from Penrith. The first day as she strode out towards Browhead and her inheritance. The time he had brought her the hamper and again on Boxing Day as she had gone to find work in Gillthrop. He had dug her out when it snowed and brought her Blackie and Bonnie, denying it as though she had insulted him. The day she had been training them and he had come . . . It was as though it was yesterday when they had sat together on the drystone wall whilst he drank her ale. Their love had shone clear and unsullied between them then as it did now, and slowly her hands unclenched and fell to her side.

He was dressed in black, nothing about him of contrast except the snowy waterfall of his cravat. A great riding cloak covered him from shoulder to ankle thrown back to reveal the fine broadcloth of his jacket, his waistcoat and breeches and the glowing black polish to his boots. His hair was shaggy, not recently cut, falling over his scowling forehead and the fierce, angry dip of his eyebrows. But in his eyes was the soft blue of his love for her. His frown might speak of disapproval but his eyes did not. There were deep, forbidding lines from his nose to his mouth and across his forehead but his lips parted, not knowing whether to smile as he wanted to, or fold into grimness as he felt they should.

"What are you doing here?" were the first words she threw at him.

"The same as you, I suppose." His face had closed somewhat but there was a look of vulnerability about it which sat strangely on its strength.

"I am checking my sheep."

"As I am."

"I see none."

"And where are yours?"

"Back there . . ." indicating with her hand though her eyes never left his.

"I see, well, you'd best call off your dogs," beginning to smile at last, stepping forward, an action to which Blackie took exception, bristling and baring his teeth.

"Make them behave, Annie," he said patiently and she called them to her, patting their heads. They dropped on to their bellies, as Bess did.

"I see I have no need to worry over your safety then," roughly.

"I did not know you felt . . . worry."

"Don't, Annie. You know exactly how I feel. Do you want me to say the words . . ."

"No . . . it would be better if we both went back to . . ."

"Better? Yes of course, and back to . . . the people who concern us. My wife and your . . . whatever he is to you. Why do you not marry him? Annie?" His voice had become harsh. "Surely it would make things more . . . comfortable for you. Must you always fly in the face of . . ."

"Marry him?" She let out a short laugh. "Marry who? You don't mean Charlie, do you . . . ?"

"Charlie? Is that his name, and who else would I mean? The man who . . . shares your . . . lives with you at . . ."

He swallowed painfully and the sinews in his neck stood out. The colour beneath his skin flared, then receded, and he clamped his jaw together, his eyes flat now and lifeless.

"Marry Charlie? Why on earth would I want to do that? He and I are friends. Good friends, as Phoebe is." She was clearly so astonished Reed could feel the loosening of the painful constriction around his heart, allowing it to expand, to draw in deep breaths of joy, though of course it made no difference to their situation. None. And yet his gladness could not be contained. He lifted his head, arching his throat, his eyes on the pale blue bowl of the sky above them and the ferocious scowling threat in his face melted away as he lowered his head again to look at her.

"He is not your . . . lover?" His mouth could scarcely form the last word.

"Charlie? Of course he is not."

"Then . . . why does he stay?"

"I told you, we are friends. He needs a home. I need someone to help with the farm. That is all."

He took another step towards her, then caught her waist and pulled her into his arms.

"Annie, my dearest love." His voice shook. "Oh, my darling, I love you, I love you, I thought . . . I thought he . . ."

"Don't . . . don't . . ." She was sharp and awkward,

bitter because this man who could have spoken to her months ago, when they were both free, was saying the words she had whispered to herself on so many sleepless nights. Into the silence of her pillow she had whispered them, to him who could not hear them and now, when it was too late, they were in the air about them, soft and true, she knew that, but no longer allowed.

"Annie . . ."

"Please . . . please, Reed, don't make me . . ."

At once his arms fell away from her and she almost fell.

"You're free to do as you like, my darling, but by Christ, I cannot bear to lose you again. I've been in hell these last months, thinking of you with that . . . that man. When I saw you at Rosley Hill . . . he held your hand . . . I wanted to knock him to the ground . . . in front of my wife. I . . . I thought you were lovers . . ."

"Which if we were had nothing to do with you."

"I know." He bent his head in anguish. "I have no right to feel as I did, as I do, but a man does not choose . . . where he loves. I married when . . . I shouldn't. You were . . . with him, I thought so what did it matter? The arrangements had been made. I wanted a son . . . children and even in that . . ." He trembled visibly since it was well known in the parish that despite almost a year of marriage Reed Macauley could not seem to get his wife with child.

"Please, Reed, don't . . . don't tell me of . . . I don't want to know. I cannot bear to think of it. To see you . . . with her . . ."

Somehow they had moved toward the rocks, seeking shelter perhaps from the keen wind which blew up on the heights, or was it a place to hide, to remain unseen by those shepherds who roamed the fells in the care of their flocks. They leaned face to face against the mossy grey stone and when he took her hand and kissed it, then, turning it over, put his lips to her wrist, her pulse leaped to meet them. He wrapped his arms about her again, holding her gently, lightly, as her body knew it had always needed, wanted to be held, and she turned her face into his shoulder.

"I love you, Annie Abbott. Whether you love me or not, and you do not deny it. I love you. It is my curse to love you, my cross to want you and I shall carry it always. I am married and should certainly not be here with you, nor should I love you but I do. Everything brings me back to you. Everywhere I go I see you . . . oh yes, you have not known . . . striding about in that ridiculous outfit . . ."

"I have no other." Her voice was muffled. Her hands were clasped tightly at his back and she could feel the wonder of it, of this day, reach inside her, soothing the wounds, already healing them, those which her life had inflicted on her.

"You will of course, not allow me to buy you one."

"No."

"I thought not."

They were silent then, their bodies for the moment perfectly content to simply lean against one another, two strong people, who despite their separate strength, gained and grew together. But they were man and woman, their bodies long denied this which they had hungered for, and presently they both lifted their heads and looked for a moment into one another's eyes. Moving slowly, they drifted into their first kiss. Delicately, both of them, laying their lips against one another, closed at first, then parting gently until they were breathing into one another's mouths. Moving their heads, their lips clung and trembled and as urgency overtook them, began to suck and bite. Their tongues met and his arms pulled her closer to him. With one hand he threw back his cloak, then undid the buttons, first on his jacket and waistcoat and then hers, pulling her closer to him so that between them was only his shirt and hers. Drawing the cloak about them both, he held her in its shelter as their kisses deepened and warmed.

"Dear Christ," he gasped at last, "don't do this if you don't mean it. This is no dalliance, Annie. I want you, I want your body, but I want *you*, Annie Abbott. Jesus, I don't know how . . ."

"Reed . . . perhaps we should part now . . ." but her lips covered his neck, his smooth cheeks, his eyes, with kisses.

"Never . . . Oh, God, I cannot bear to let you go . . ."

"You must . . . soon . . . Charlie will be looking for . . ."

He pushed her away from him harshly, holding her wrists with hands which hurt and his face snapped with menace.

"Don't . . . don't mention that bastard's name in my presence. If you had not been with him that day . . . the first time when you came back from Rosley . . ."

"What?" She threw back her head angrily and her hair fell about her in living beauty. "You would not have married? Is that what you are saying?"

His eyes burned into hers, hot and hating, then suddenly they lost their madness. His chin sank to his chest. She freed her wrists, putting out her hands to smooth back his hair. Beloved hair, beloved man . . .

"Don't, Annie . . . don't let's quarrel." His voice could barely be heard. He put his face in the hollow of her shoulder resting his lips on the soft skin of her throat and she smoothed the hair at his neck. Their arms were about one another again and for several minutes they said nothing. Their ardent bodies had quietened and carefully she put a hand to his cheek. She laid her mouth on his, kissing him as gently as she would her sleeping daughter, her lips lingering there to retain the feel of his and the clean, sharp tang of his masculine flesh. To carry it home with her, to keep and hold and cherish for she might never see him again.

"I love you, Annie," he said quietly.

"I know. I love you, Reed."

"Thank you . . . for that. When will I see you again?"

"I don't know."

"But I will?"

"Yes."

She felt him relax against her, for the moment satisfied, and wondered how long that would last. He was a man used to his own way, to having what he wanted. He wanted her, but would he be content to meet her up here on the wild fells where no one could see, or would he feel the need, and the right, once he had taken her body, which he would of course, to put her somewhere safe and secret, where no one else could have her? Would he turn sour if she would not allow him to take her away from Browhead, to set her up in a house somewhere, handy of course, and in some style, so that he could visit her whenever he felt the need? Or would he be prepared to let her keep her independence, and her farm, and her way of life as Reed Macauley would continue to do? To be free and unfettered and snapping her fingers at convention, or would he, which was more likely, want *all* of her at *his* beck and call? And what about her body, which wanted his as much as his wanted hers? What of the child it might produce? Would she, because of her female fertility, be forced to live in that secret house of his, rearing her secret child, for though she had already had one, which was illegitimate, it had not been Reed Macauley's and so no slur could be attached to his name, as it had to Annie Abbott's. If it should get about the parish, even a whisper of it, that Annie Abbott was in trouble again, and the fault lay with Reed Macauley, though men might smile and nudge one another, since a man is allowed his little distractions, the women certainly would not. His wife would not. His wife who would, no doubt, one day bear him a child of her own, a legitimate child.

It was no more than a minute or so but in that time these thoughts circled frighteningly inside her head, making her dizzy, for how was she to refuse him what they both wanted, and how was she to acquiesce when the simple honest truth was that so long as they remained in one another's lives, there was no peace for either of them? She loved him. She had admitted that to herself a long time ago, admitted it, accepted it and, believing that they could be nothing to one another, had locked him, and her love, safely away in the tender recess of her heart where he would always be.

Now he was in her arms, his body quickening against
hers, his mouth moving warmly, demandingly against her
throat, his lips dipping down into the neck of her shirt
where the top button was undone. His breathing had
become more ragged as he pulled her closer into his arms.
His head rose and his mouth closed over hers and her
hands flew to his hair to pull him and his questing lips
deeply into hers.

"Dear God . . . I love you . . . want you . . . need to
take you here, now, before you change your mind and
go . . ."

"No, not here . . ." but her hands clutched at him
and the anguished thoughts of moments ago were flung
carelessly away for how could they matter when his
rough hands were invading her clothing, cupping her bare
breasts, pressing her hard nipples into his palms. He was
not gentle as he nailed her to the stone behind her, his
need to possess her, somehow, in any way he could, to
make her his, to put his mark on her, tipping them both
over the edge of sanity. He loved her so, had suffered in
his love for her, for so long that he must assuage it *now*
and hang the consequences. Their lips clung together
whilst their hands were busy with buttons and belts,
neither of them prepared for the ferocity of love and
passion, of tenderness and need which vibrated from his
body to hers, from hers to his. Folly, oh yes, but such
sweet folly, as her breasts were sweet in his hands
and hers found the silken smooth mat of his body hair
which ran down his flat stomach to where his penis jutted
arrogantly, demandingly . . .

"These bloody trousers . . ." she heard him mutter and
as the ice-cold roughness of the stone at her back struck
her violently exposed buttocks, her reason returned,
the sense and sanity and balance which, except for a
moment when she was fourteen years old, had never left
her.

"NO . . . no . . ." The cry which tore from her throat
soared high into the air above the crags and at once all
three dogs were on their feet. Blackie and Bonnie who

had been dozing, at the same time keeping one eye on the strange animal and the other on the man who was with their mistress, growled deep in their throats, sensing the danger but not awfully sure from which direction it was to come. They began to advance on Reed who had straightened slowly as Annie struggled against him and when he turned away to lean his back on the grey rock, they confronted him threateningly, waiting for a word from Annie.

She had turned her back on him, re-arranging her clothing, sweeping back her hair and thrusting it in a tangled mass beneath the old hat of her father's which she had found hanging on a nail in the barn.

"Lie down Blackie, Bonnie . . ." and they did so. Bess looked questioningly at Reed, then seeing nothing to threaten him, lay down beside them.

"You don't trust me." The words which he flung at her were bitter.

"I trust you to do what you think is right." Hers were low.

"What does that mean, for God's sake?"

She hesitated before she spoke, not looking at him.

"I know you love me. I have always known. I love you. I have always known that too. I have wanted . . . this . . . I still want it . . . but not like this. Held against a wall like a . . ."

"I did not mean to offend you with my . . . lust." He was stiff, vibrant with anger and frustrated need.

"Reed . . . try to understand. Give me time."

"To do what?"

"To . . . to think what this is to mean to us."

"I know what it means to me, Annie. I want you. I want you to be mine. To belong to me. I did not mean to happen . . . what almost happened here . . . but when you . . . allowed it . . ."

"I want it too, Reed." Her cry of love was urgent and her dogs stood up again. The sky had clouded over, brought low with the rain which threatened. The wind had freshened, sighing over the stiff grass, bending it, ruffling the coats of the dogs. She shivered and with a low groan he pulled her to him again, sheltering her in his arms, warming her chilled body with his own.

"My love, my love, what are we to do?"

In May, Margaret Mounsey, known to her family from being a baby as Mim, married Ben Postlethwaite and went to live with him and his widowed mother on their farm up Binsey way. A week later, her own mother, Agnes Mounsey, who had, from being a young girl, worked as hard as any woman in the parish of Bassenthwaite, dropped dead on her own kitchen floor, the scrubbing brush and bucket in her hand with which she had been about to 'go over it' crashing down beside her. Even at the last she carried the implements of her labour with her and her tearful daughter, Sally Garnett had the idea that they should go in the coffin with her, to which her truculent husband replied 'that any more daft remarks like that and he'd give her a clip round't lug.'

When Annie hesitantly knocked on the door of Upfell Farm it was Bert who answered it. She had told no one she was going, not even Phoebe and certainly not Charlie, who was quartering and splitting oak logs in readiness for the first step in swill making. They would both have been horrified had they known, wanting to come with her, convinced that she would be abused, spat upon maybe, but definitely humiliated in some way, for Bert Garnett made no secret of the fact that he thought Annie Abbott should be whipped out of the parish at a cart tail, especially since she had taken up with that fancy man. Over-protective both Charlie and Phoebe were since they well knew that she was thought of as a pariah in the district and was received by no one. She was still dressed in her father's clothes for it was all she had though in her chest at home she had a guinea saved with which, when her lambs were sold at backend and she felt that tiny bit closer to 'safety', she meant to purchase a length or two of good, *coloured*, woollen cloth. A rich green, or a tawny amber, perhaps a deep sapphire blue. There was a piece of hodden grey cloth she herself had woven resting in the press next to her savings and before winter she meant to make it up into a well-fitting pair of breeches and a jacket, warm and practical. But the bright woollen gown was one of the dreams she held to her amongst the many she had. In the meanwhile she continued to wear the increasingly threadbare trousers, shirt and jacket which had been Joshua Abbott's.

It was Charlie who told her of Aggie Mounsey's death. They had seen the wedding party the week before going past at the back of Browhead. A true Cumberland wedding where each of the men rode to church on his horse or pony but when the ceremony was over, raced back to Upfell with a girl, a guest of the bride's, up behind him. It was said that the young lady who rode with the winner would be a bride herself by the year's end. There was a great to-do, guests coming and going, most in the last stages of inebriation, great gales of lunatic laughter far into the night, for Aggie Mounsey wanted her girl to go off in great style. A splendid feast, singing and dancing, the party not dispersing until Mim and Ben Postlethwaite, for that one night, were in Aggie's bed. All the guests saw them there, of course, with a great deal of coarse ribaldry, standing round the bed until she had 'thrown her stocking'. She would keep her back to them casting the stocking over her left shoulder and the girl who caught it would be the next bride. It was not quite clear whether she would beat to the altar the one who had come home first on the sweating pony!

The man clattering by the back of the farmhouse the following week on his lanky raw-boned horse, who was the undertaker for the district, though he did not approve of Annie Abbott, nor of the chap who lived with her, could not help but shout out the electrifying news that, a week after her daughter's wedding, Aggie Mounsey would be coming this way in her coffin.

Bert Garnett, one hand on the door latch, the other in his pocket, his mouth falling open in astonishment, looked Annie up and down, from the rich fall of her tumbled hair which was not covered, to her slim trousered legs and wooden-soled clogs. His eyes were like small rats, running across her breasts and waist and hips, narrowing to a lascivious gleam as they came to rest on the former. His loose wet lips parted in a nasty smile and he licked them coarsely, suggestively.

"What does tha' want 'ere, Annie Abbott?" he said loudly as though to let those somewhere in the depths of the farmhouse know of his displeasure, but he continued to smile and run his eyes over her body like a farmer at the market considering a cow he might decide to buy.

Annie gritted her teeth and held the hot, flowing tide of her temper in check. Though she had little time for Bert Garnett, despite the lifts he had given her into Keswick, she remembered what Sally had said when Annie had returned to Browhead, about how she and her mother had nursed Lizzie and Joshua when they were dying. They had done everything she herself should have done, had she been there, making sure her parents' passing was peaceful, that they were not alone and when they had gone, giving them a decent funeral. They had sat with the corpses until the 'coffining'. The coffins themselves had been carried on the 'corpse road', down past Hause and along the track to St Bridget's by the lake, but it had been the woman now dead who had seen to it all and Annie could not forget that. She might be rebuffed, probably would, by those married women who would already be 'laating' or sitting round Aggie Mounsey's body, but she could not do anything else but offer the Mounsey family, particularly Sally, whatever help or comfort she might need of Annie Abbott.

"Can I see Sally, Bert?" Annie kept her voice low, courteous.

"What for?" Bert grinned, knowing that no one but Annie saw the expression on his face. He was tickled pink that his mother-in-law was gone for though Mim Mounsey,

Mim Postlethwaite now, had a small share in the farm, most of it was his, well his and Sally's, but *she* was nowt 'a pound and would do just what he told her to do. And he enjoyed the feeling of power he now had in what Aggie Mounsey had always considered to be *her* farmhouse, and in the knowedge that he could keep Annie Abbott cooling her heels on *his* doorstep. He could do as he pleased. Ask her in or tell her to go to hell, if he had a mind.

The thought made him magnanimous. He turned shouting over his shoulder.

"Sal, there's someone here to see thi'."

"Who is it, Bert?"

"Come to t' door, an' see, tha' daft cow, but before tha' does, fetch me a jug of ale."

It was several minutes before Sally's face appeared in the doorway, pale and tear-streaked, her jutting belly testifying once again to Bert's 'manhood'. Annie had heard, through the half-open doorway, through which she could see nothing but a portion of Aggie Mounsey's well-scrubbed kitchen flags, Bert's indelicate fumbling with his wife's person and the several loose-lipped kisses he had bestowed on her. She knew perfectly well it was done for her benefit and Sally's whispered embarrassment as she somewhat timidly protested since Bert did not take kindly to rebuff, was clearly heard. The flesh round Sally's mouth and chin was red and chafed for Bert wore a scratchy, three-day stubble on his chin. Sally was already in the deepest black of mourning, the dress she had on, the one her mother had worn since the day her husband, Jack Mounsey, had died. Fortunately Aggie's girth had been wider than her daughter's, but still it strained dangerously across Sally's distended stomach.

"Annie," Sally's uncertain face lit up for a moment and she was ready to reach out and draw her into the kitchen. Then her hand fell back to fiddle with her apron and she looked over her shoulder to where Bert was evidently still quaffing his ale.

"It's all right Sally, I didn't come to . . . well, I only wanted to say how sorry I was to hear about your mother.

You and she were kind to mine and my father, and if there's anything I can do for you . . ."

Before his wife could answer, the cheery voice of Bert Garnett spoke from his comfortable chair by the fire. "There's nowt this family want from thou, Annie Abbott."

"I'm offering nothing to you, Bert Garnett, only Sally," Annie shouted. She put out her hand and took Sally's. "Are the women here laating?"

"Aye, they come up from t' village this morning." Sally's woe-begone face worked convulsively and sad tears slid down her plump cheeks for how was she to stand living alone with *him* now that her Mam was gone?

"Don't cry, Sally. You still have Mim," for who knew better than Annie the nature of Bert Garnett. Though he had made no move on her when he had sat beside her on the cart, during the long ride from Keswick to Hause, nor on the occasions he had 'called in' at Browhead, she had known that eventually he would. It was in his gleaming, greedy eyes and falsely smiling mouth, and though it was very evident that Sally suffered his nightly fumblings, he would not be averse to the same with Annie Abbott, his attitude had plainly said.

"Aye, but she's up near Binsey."

"I'm only a step away, Sal. You're welcome any time, night or day." This last in a whisper.

"Eeh, that's lovely of tha', Annie, but . . . well, that chap that's with tha'. Bert'd give me what for if I was to . . ."

"I know, but the offer is always there. If ever you can get away . . ." meaning perhaps when Bert went to market ". . . come and have a cup of tea. Bring the children . . ."

"There'll be five of un next month." But Sally's eyes had brightened at the thought of Annie 'only a step away', a glowing light in the long dark tunnel which yawned before her without her strong, outspoken and resolute Mam to stand between her and her bad-tempered husband.

"I can see that." Annie's eyes went to Sally's waistline, narrowing in that gleaming golden smile which had so fascinated Sally when they had been re-united two and a half years ago. "Now don't forget."

"I won't Annie . . ."

"What the bloody 'ell are the two of thi' whispering about?" Bert jerked the door open, almost pulling his enormously pregnant wife off her feet. As the door widened the room was revealed. At the table sat four children. Annie recognised Sammy who would be nearly five now, she thought, and Janie who had been twelve months old when last Annie had seen her. There was another little girl who must be the new baby Sally had been expecting then, Emma, Annie seemed to remember, a toddler herself now, and another boy strapped in a chair, who could be no more than nine or ten months old. Dear God . . . poor, poor Sally. In her bad moments, Annie often thought there was no woman who had more to bear than herself, but surely nothing could be worse than having to suffer the nightly advances of Bert Garnett.

"Nothing, Bert. Annie was just sayin' how sorry she . . ."

"Well, she's said it so let's shut bloody door," which he did.

Annie and Reed had met three times since their dramatic reunion on the boulder-strewn slope of Broad End. Each time it had not been planned, as the first meeting had not been planned and each time they had moved, thankfully, into one another's arms as though the action, the clinging, the closeness, the simple joining and twining of their bodies against one another, gave them both air to breathe, sweet water to drink, food to eat, sun on their sun-starved faces, life. They did not make love. They had done nothing from which they could not, with honour, both withdraw. They were content, it seemed, after the wild passion of their first meeting, merely to be together, neither wishing to disturb the sudden sweet harmony which flowed between them. She was happy, blindly, rapturously happy, blissful in the sweet, secret knowledge that perhaps today, or tomorrow, when she went with her dogs and her shepherd's crook to check on her growing lambs, she might see him. And for now, that was enough. Each time they met they made no plans to meet again. They would sit together in the sunshine, Reed's back resting against a rock, hers against his chest, his arms about her, his cheek against her wind-blown hair. They talked, she could not remember afterwards what about. His lips would capture hers, but with a loving patience which confounded her, soft, gentle, so tender, so . . . so moderate, she was aware that Reed Macauley was, for the first time in his life, humbled by an emotion stronger than his own demanding need. That his love was true and selfless. He was an individualist, an opportunist, self-indulgent and arrogant, but what he felt for her had softened him and his fear of losing her had awakened a quality in him which, perhaps again for the first time, had him putting another before himself. Maybe it would not last for he was a man, and his masculine sexual curiosity, his desire, could sweep away this gentleness in the necessity of satisfying his own male loins.

"Do you need anything? Anything at all?" he asked her, begging her to want some tremendous, difficult to come by thing that would stretch him to the utmost to get for her.

"No, nothing. I am managing very well. My lambs are thriving . . ."

"I know, I've seen them." He smiled into her hair.

"Are you spying on me?" She turned to look up at him, her lips beneath his, and when he took them, she sighed into his mouth with the sheer joy of it.

"Keeping an eye on you," he said when he could. "You won't let me do anything else for you, or give you anything, not even some trumpery bit of jewellery, so I do what I can by making sure your sheep are as fit as mine. They are grazing together on the same fell after all."

"Thank you."

"Dear God, if there was only something I could do to make your life easier."

"There is."

At once he turned her in his arms, straining into her face in his passion to give her the moon, the stars, his own heart plucked out of his breast, any of these easy things but not the one thing he wanted to present her with, his name.

"What? Say it, anything."

"My daughter."

"Yes . . . ?" He leaned back, disappointed, for what was Cat Abbott to him and what could he give to her that would satisfy *his* obsession with this woman.

"I want her to go to school."

"Well, that's easy enough. There is one in Gillthrop."

"No, she is clever. Charlie has taught her . . ."

"Goddammit woman, don't talk to me of that man. Have you no heart that you must mention him in my presence?" He stood up, thrusting her from him and his dog and hers stood up with him. All three animals were still uneasy with one another and it took very little to unsettle them. They sensed the tension and anger in him and Blackie raised his muzzle warningly.

"And you can tell that bloody dog of yours to back off or I'll take my whip to him."

"You'll do no such thing, Reed Macauley. They don't like your attitude any more than I do. I'm sorry if it upsets you when I speak of Charlie but I thought, unlike the rest of this damned community, that you understood my relationship with him. I have told you before that he and Phoebe are my only friends, except perhaps for Sally Garnett. There is nothing . . . *nothing* between us. Do you think I would be up here with you if there was? I met him at Rosley when I went to buy sheep since no one at the Keswick market would sell me any. I needed a ram and he helped me. The men there are as pig-headed as those around here and when it was discovered I was female despite my 'disguise' . . ." indicating her masculine clothing, "they wouldn't sell to me either. Charlie did it for me, and helped me to bring the tup and the ewes home. And that is all."

"*All!*" He stamped up and down, his boots crushing the tussocky grass and a clump of celandine which grew there. The wind lifted his tumbled hair from his frowning forehead and he brushed it back impatiently. His eyebrows scowled ferociously over his piercing blue eyes and it was obvious that peace had gone leaving jealousy, and his own anger at suffering it.

"Dammit, Annie. You make light of this ridiculous 'get-up' you wear but can you blame men who only *deal* with other men, when they mistrust it, and you? They don't know what to make of it, or you. They are used to their women in decent skirts and bonnets, keeping their place in the home as they have done for centuries. Then you come along, so obviously female despite this . . . this bloody outfit you wear, and they are distracted from the purpose of their transaction which is to make a profit. Not only are they insulted by what they see as your immodesty, they are seriously affronted by their own need to stare at your . . . attractions. Which, by the way brings me to the subject of how they *discovered* you were a woman and not a man! Oh, yes . . ."

"It was my hair, dammit. What do you think I did? Exposed my . . . my body to them? My blasted hat fell off . . ."

"Fell off! *Fell off!* Or did you take if off to show Charlie . . ."

"What the devil are you insinuating, Reed Macauley? Are you saying . . . ?"

"Dear sweet Christ, I don't know *what* I'm saying, woman." Again he twisted and turned in his savage distress. "I only know I cannot bear to think of you living under the same roof with him, with . . . *any man*. . . no matter how innocent. *Yes! . . . Yes! . . .*" He held up his hands in acquiescence. ". . . I know it is innocent since I know you well enough by now to understand you would dishonour neither yourself, nor me, nor him. I know you love me, Annie Abbott, I can see it in your eyes. Even now, though your face is furious and you're ready to black my eye for my impudence. Forgive me . . . I cannot help the way I am, Annie . . . my Annie . . . don't let's quarrel . . ."

"You began it by inferring that Charlie and I were more to each other than friends." She slapped away his placatory hand but he grasped her forearm and pulled her roughly to him.

"Only because I'm so jealous, dammit. I want you . . ."

"You could have had me. We were both of us free."

"Aah . . . don't . . ." He bowed his head in sudden desperation and his hands fell to his side. His stance was one of such hopelessness that at once she put her arms about him, dragging him to her in an agony of remorse.

"Reed . . ."

"I know . . ." His words were muffled in her hair. His arms rose again and held her to him. "I know . . . Christ . . . do you think I have not regretted it a hundred times since. I thought . . . you were with him . . . they said you were . . . he was living at the farm . . ."

"He needed work. I needed help . . . that's all."

"He is . . ."

"That is all, Reed."

"I should have married you when I had the chance but . . ."

". . . But I was . . . who I am." Her words were soft and they said she did not reproach him.

"Do you think that would have mattered? As my wife you would have been accepted no matter what you had done." His voice was arrogant and sure. Was he not Reed Macauley? One of the Macauleys who were 'statesmen', men of standing and wealth in these parts. There would not have been a hostess in the parish who would have shut her door in *his* wife's face, or if she had, her husband might have found himself in a poor way of business. So many owed him something, money, a favour, a bit of business put their way, and it would not pay them to insult him or his wife. Under his shelter and protection Annie Abbott would have been treated as a young queen.

"Perhaps."

"There is no perhaps about it. They would not have dared . . ."

"Does it matter now, my darling? Really, does it matter? It is too late. You are committed elsewhere and I can see no . . . future for us . . ."

"Don't say that." He clasped her to him in an agony of despair pressing her face into the hollow of his neck beneath his straining jaw line. "Don't . . . don't . . ."

"How can I help it, Reed? I've . . . been so . . . happy . . . meeting you again up here. It was so . . . unexpected. I did not allow myself to think about what was to happen tomorrow, or next week. It was enough to just be with you, to touch you and hear you speak. I blinded myself to everything else and turned a deaf ear to the voice of reason which whispered that this was madness . . ."

"If you are trying to say we should not meet again I won't allow it. I will not. We can make some . . ." He paused suddenly as though aware that he must tread carefully with his next words.

She lifted her head and looked up into his strong but vulnerable face. He was unsteady with the tumult which was beginning to overwhelm him. The angle of his hard, fighting jaw jutted ominously and the taut muscles in his throat worked. The flesh of his face was tanned and smooth, but there were tell-tale lines about his eyes and mouth which she had not noticed before.

"Listen to me," he growled, his truculent jaw threatening anyone who stood between himself and what he wanted. "It's time we talked, *really* talked about the future. We *do* have one you know, whatever you might say. I need you. I need you in my life. I want to make a commitment to you . . ."

"How can that be, Reed?"

"It could be arranged, if you'd agree."

"To what?"

"Well . . . a house somewhere. You and your daughter. She could go to school as you want her to. You would, both of you, be secure. I would look after you and there would be no need for you to slave on that blasted farm.

You could sell it. Keep the money, as your own . . ."

"Thank you." Her tone was formal.

". . . invest it so that you would be independent . . ." though he would not like that, of course since Annie Abbott's total dependence on him was what he was after.

"Thank you, Reed, but I cannot accept your offer." Her voice was cool and she moved backwards, putting space and air and a certain constraint between them. He loved her. He was suffering because of it and though the day was mild, she felt him shiver beneath the good broadcloth of his jacket. He turned away from her jerkily, his face tight, moving to stand on a flat grey rock, his hands clenched in the pockets of his jacket, his eyes on the lake below. The surface of the water changed constantly, becoming ruffled where the breeze touched it. The sun stretched a path of gilt across it on which, as the water moved, an explosion of diamonds scattered and burst. He saw none of it. Its beauty and the beauty of the hazed peaks which stretched on and on into infinity, meant nothing as Reed Macauley, loving truly for the first time, struggled with the realisation that this was one woman he could not have. She could sense the tension in him even with a dozen feet between them, the tight-clenched pain and the absolute determination to overcome it, and her.

"Christ, this is bloody ridiculous. You say there is nothing . . . there is no other man in your life and yet you won't allow me into it. I cannot bear to see the way you are treated by the people in the area, nor the struggle you are having to make . . . to turn Browhead into a decent farm. Look at you . . ." He turned violently, his face black and snarling, the menace in him dangerous, his hand raised as though ready to strike her. He passed it across his face. "Look at you dressed like some confounded vagrant, your hands worse than a labourer's and your face as brown as a gypsy. And there's no need for it, Annie. I can look after you. After *both* of you, even that skivvy you took in. You'll want for nothing – servants, a carriage, fine clothes and jewellery. A house wherever you like . . ."

"Where, I suppose, you will visit me whenever it is convenient?"

"Confound it Annie, I can do no more. It would be a good life for you and the child. You could be the widow of . . ."

"I would be a whore. Your whore."

"Don't! Don't say that. I love you . . ."

". . . and if you stopped loving me? If it should become tedious to get on your horse and travel the ten, fifteen miles, or perhaps more, I would need to hide myself to keep your reputation untarnished, would you say 'Oh, to hell with it, I'll go another day!' Whilst I and any children we may have as a result of this 'arrangement' will sit and wait patiently until . . ."

"*No*, no, never. You mean more to me than . . ."

"I would be no more to you than a mistress. Loved perhaps but condemned to a life of secrecy and deceit."

"Dammit to hell, Annie."

"No Reed, *no*! I can't do it. I just cannot do it. Already I am an outcast in this parish, but despite that I am gaining a measure of success. My flock is growing . . ."

"Less than a hundred sheep." His voice was contemptuous, made so by his bitter disappointed love.

"Don't sneer at me or my efforts, Reed." She was doing her best to keep her temper, but her eyes which had shown concern for his pain, had begun to glow hotly. "I've worked hard . . ."

"There is no need for it, Annie." His voice was pleading.

"Yes, there is. I want to do this, Reed. I *must* do it. I . . . I love you . . ."

"Then let me . . ."

"I love you and had you . . . well, if things had been different, I would have gladly shared your life though how the good folk of Bassenthwaite would have taken to . . ."

"For Christ's sake, Annie, don't turn me away. Don't turn the idea down without thinking about it. What about Penrith? No one knows you there." His voice was boyish, shaking in his eagerness, and he grasped her hands, holding them between his own, then bringing them tenderly to his mouth where he covered them with kisses whilst his vivid blue eyes held hers, the love in them as soft and tender as those of a mother gazing at an adored child. He was not a man to beg. His nature was to take whatever he wanted and if he could not take it then he was prepared to pay for it, at *his price*, naturally. His nature challenged hers, willing her to give in and yet he was making a decent offer to curb that arrogance in himself that demanded his own way in all things.

"Take me seriously, my darling, for I don't give up easily. If you don't like the idea of Penrith then we could go north, or south. You see I am saying 'we'. We would go together, travel as man and wife. Make a home together. I would come back to Long Beck just as often, and for as long as it was needed, to keep the gossips away from . . . from my wife. I could run my business from wherever we went. And the farm. A factor and half a dozen good shepherds. Bloody hell, woman, do you not see what I am willing to give up for you?"

There was a long moment of strangled silence, then, with a familiar, defensive growl, he took her by the forearms and shook her.

"Godammit, Annie. Tell me you agree. I'm . . . I cannot stand this need I have of you. Say you'll come, say it . . . say it . . ." and he shook her more violently.

"I cannot." Her voice was soft.

"You can, you *will*."

"No, Reed. I cannot."

"Why, for Christ's sake, why?"

"I don't know."

"That's no bloody answer."

"It's the only one I can give you now."

He threw her from him, his violence so close to the surface it was in danger of breaking through and attacking her. Blackie and Bonnie were ready to fling themselves on him, their muzzles raised warningly, and his old dog placed herself between them and her master.

"Then there's no more to be said."

"No."

"I shan't give up."

Why was she so pleased to hear him say that, she wondered desolately as she watched him click his fingers to his dog and move stiffly in the direction of his mare. She wouldn't change her mind! Ever. What she had feared at their first meeting a few weeks ago had happened. He had not been satisfied with what they now had. He wanted more, as *she* wanted more so was it to be wondered at? She loved him so much, so much she wanted nothing more than to call his name, to open her arms and hold them out to him. To go with him wherever he wanted to take her, but she couldn't. She didn't really know why since she already had a reputation as a harlot so why not husband stealer, or even worse, but she couldn't.

He mounted his mare and inside her, just beneath her left breast the pain was unbearable where her heart broke. He did not look back at her as he spoke.

"I'll make arrangements for the child," he said, then with a soft murmur to his dog, put his heels to the mare's side and threw them both down a length of scree with an abandon so wild and dangerous the animal whinnied in fear.

Annie sank to her knees and bowed her head.

23

Why did her body ache as though she had been stricken with some dreadful debilitating illness or as if she had been given a sound beating with a cudgel, her dazed mind wondered as she staggered down the steep hill at the back of Browhead. She seemed to hurt all over, even to the roots of her hair, which was ridiculous really, since it was her heart and soul and mind which had been badly damaged this day. It was hard to put one foot in front of the other and twice she fell as she descended Broad End. The water in Barkbeth Gill was icy cold as it crept over her clogs, when she missed her footing crossing it, and though it was high summer she shivered, the spasms rippling across her skin in cold feathers.

There was no sign of Charlie in the old shed where once her father had worked on his 'swiller's horse'. Lengths of straight-grained knot-free oak saplings leaned neatly against the wall and dozens of logs had already been quartered with the lat-axe prior to placing them in the cast-iron boiler where they would stew overnight. The three of them, Phoebe, herself and Charlie had already fashioned several dozen swills and Annie meant to make the journey to the coastal town of Whitehaven soon to sell them, for the baskets were used in the coaling of ships. Thirty pounds of coal each one could hold, hauled on the backs of the crew, basket by basket until the coal hold was full. In the lull between planting, lambing and harvest, and the sheep fairs where she hoped to sell her unwanted male lambs, they could make many more baskets, selling them wherever there was a need. She was also toying with the idea of producing charcoal from the juniper trees in her coppice wood since she could not afford to waste the utilisation of any crop which might make her money. The gunpowder manufacturers of Westmorland and Cumberland would buy the charcoal from her, for it was a major ingredient in the making of explosives. Not that she had ever done any charcoal burning, nor even seen the process, but she could learn, she told herself, since she intended to leave no stone unturned, no avenue unexplored in her aim to make Browhead into a successful, profit-making farm.

Phoebe was at the table, a fine mist of flour dancing and drifting in the shaft of sunlight which came through the window and fell across her. She was kneading dough, her big-knuckled hands folding it over and over on itself, then pushing her clenched fist into its centre. She had watched Mrs Holme at The Packhorse in Keswick one market-day morning whilst she waited for Annie and Mr Lucas who were moving from stall to stall buying provisions. Mrs Holme was a good-natured woman and on seeing Phoebe's interest as she peeped through the inn's kitchen window, had called to her cheerfully to 'come inside'.

"Tha's Annie Abbott's girl aren't tha?" she had asked, bearing no ill-will it seemed towards Annie who had left The Packhorse rather suddenly a couple of years ago.

Phoebe admitted that she was and within minutes had mastered the art of breadmaking and memorised the ingredients with which it was made. Though she had found it a terrible strain, and indeed had hardly done so, to learn and retain the letters of the alphabet, Mrs Holme had only to tell her once what went into this or that dish and it was in her head for ever with no need to even write it down. She had been given a brief sketch of several of Mrs Holme's favourite recipes which Phoebe had tried out on her 'family', finding to her own amazement and their delight, that she had the makings of a decent cook. A talent for serving up the best oatcakes Annie said she had ever eaten. Her porridge was the creamiest and her tatie-pot, the tastiest, and though, as she well knew, she had no gift with words or letters or numbers as Cat did, and no interest if she was honest, she loved the creating

of some splendid dish, many out of her own imaginative
brain, with which to please Annie, Mr Lucas and Cat.

"Tha' can tekk them clogs off for I've just scrubbed
them there flags, Annie Abbott," she said tartly as Annie
came through the door, her eyes flickering from the dough
to Annie's feet and back again. "An' them dogs can stop
outside an' all." This was Phoebe's domain in the 'fire-
house' as the kitchen was still often called. She had taken
over not only the kitchen but the whole farmhouse to
Annie's relief, scrubbing and dusting and polishing, throwing open windows and filling the place with wild flowers
and her own, home-made pot-pourri, derived from the
dried petals of roses and lavender and larkspur. She burnished the copper bowls and pans to a fine glow with wood
ash, fed the basket of kittens which miraculously had been
found one morning, mewing and suckling around the complacently purring Dandy, who had turned out to be female
after all, and whenever the weather was clear there would
be a line of sparklingly white bedding and undergarments
pegged out on her line across the yard. She had a passion
for cleanliness, not only about the farmhouse but in herself,
washing, starching and ironing the aprons once worn by
Lizzie Abbott and had even taken to wearing the frilled
cap women of Lizzie's generation had worn. It covered
her dark glossy hair completely and Annie had pondered
on whether it was an unconscious defence against the eyes
of men, of *man* who had once tried to misuse her. Her
hair was her one claim to beauty.

"Nay, what's to do?" Phoebe said on seeing Annie's
face. She reached for the cloth to wipe her hands for even
in the direst emergency, her mind worked to the pattern
of cleanliness she had set herself. "What's happened to
thi'?"

"Nothing, Phoebe, I'm just tired."

"Give over. Ah've seen thi' tired when tha've clipped a
dozen sheep, an' tha' didn't look as bad as tha' does now.
Have tha' seen a ghost?"

"Perhaps I have. A ghost of what might have been."
Annie's voice was low but she did her best to smile. The

effort was agony but how could she tell this innocent, inexperienced girl of the torment of love, of bitter despairing love that reached, in one moment, the pinnacle of rapture only to be dashed on the hard, damaging crag of despair in the next.

"Nay, I don't know what tha's talking about, love."

"No, I don't suppose you do, Phoebe, and what's more, neither do I."

"But where've tha' bin?" Phoebe sat down on the settle next to Annie and leaned forward to peer anxiously into her face. "Ah thought tha' was off up Broad End to tekk a look at lambs."

"Yes, but . . . I saw more than the lambs, Phoebe. I saw my own future, and I didn't like it."

"Nay, tha've lost me, Annie. What future's that then?" Phoebe screwed up her plain little face in an effort to understand. Her own future was so bright and rosy. She asked nothing more than to be allowed to stay here in this lovely kitchen and serve her family, Annie, Cat and Mr Lucas in exactly the way she had been doing for the past two years. She often thought she had died and gone to Heaven, really she did, remembering her life as it had been with the old missus, worked her poor fingers to the bone she had, which she didn't mind in the least since she didn't exactly sit about on her bum all day long here at Browhead. But at Browhead she was needed, respected for what she did and . . . aye she would say it . . . she was loved. She and Cat thought the world of one another and as for Annie, well there was no one in the world like Annie, for she'd given life to Phoebe, and a fond affection which wrapped about her like a warm blanket in the winter.

"It's hard to explain, Phoebe," she said now, her eyes faraway and hazed, her poor face all screwed up as though something bad hurt her somewhere. Just like it had on the day that chap . . . what was his name . . . him from Long Beck . . . had sat on the wall with her and drunk a jug of ale. They'd quarrelled. Phoebe had heard them and then he'd gone clattering off on that there horse of his and Annie had . . . had . . . And what about the time when

Annie had gone to Rosley? Before Mr Lucas had come.
That there chap had ridden off with a face like thunder
when Phoebe had told him where Annie was and since Mr
Lucas had moved in he'd never been near. Phoebe had
loved no man, and never would. No man had loved Phoebe,
and never would. Phoebe was convinced of that. Just as
some women are made for loving and having babies, others
were not and Phoebe knew she was one of the latter. Not
that she hadn't the capacity for loving in her, oh no, for
didn't she love her 'family', but not for a man. But she
knew it when she saw it and Annie loved him from up
Long Beck and she reckoned, though it was said he was
married now, that he loved Annie.

"What's to do, Annie?" she asked softly, hesitantly for
she was not one to poke her nose into other people's
business, even in that of her beloved friend.

"Nothing new, Phoebe. Just some bad dreams come to
haunt me again."

"What have tha' done today, love? Did tha' meet anyone
up Broad End?" It was said diffidently. "Tell me if you
have a mind to but I'll not be offended if you don't. I'm
here should you need me." Her face was awkwardly soft
and her hand touched Annie's with a feather of tenderness.

"Oh, Phoebe . . . what am I to do?"

"About . . . him? It's . . . him from Long Beck isn't it?"

"Yes, him from Long Beck. Reed Macauley, a married
man with whom I've been foolish enough to fall in love."

Phoebe sighed in deep, deep sympathy, her pale blue
eyes fixed on Annie with the soulful look of a devoted dog.
Without being aware of it since she was still somewhat
constrained in the giving and receiving of demonstrations
of affection, she clasped Annie's slim hands between her
own. They were big-boned, wide, made for hard work,
but gentle and soothing just the same.

"I thought it were him. I've seen the way tha' looks at
one another an' he were like a man demented when tha'
went off to Rosley Hill that time. But what's happened
today? He's not hurt thi' has he?" At once Phoebe was
like a mother hen whose chick has been threatened, her

ruffled feathers wild and furious, her beak ready to peck out the eyes of the predator. If Reed Macauley had hurt Annie Abbott, which, to Phoebe, meant what that randy sod had almost done to her in Keswick, and would have done but for Annie, then he'd Phoebe to reckon with. She'd take her kitchen knife, the one she had sharpened only that morning and cut off that foolish but dangerous bit of flesh which dangled between his legs and stuff it in his mouth, so she would.

"No, he's not hurt me, Phoebe, not physically, but he's not done my heart much good."

"How's that, then, Annie?"

"He really does love me, you know." For a moment her face was transformed to an unearthly rapturous beauty. Her skin flushed to rose and her eyes were great drowning brown pools in which liquid gold ran, then it all flowed away, leaving her white and drained. "But he wants to change me. Turn me into a doll for him to play with whenever he has a fancy for it. Do you know what I'm saying, Phoebe?"

"Well . . ."

"To put me in a doll's house. Dress me in silken gowns and expensive jewels and when he has the time, he'll come calling . . ." Her voice faded away on the last word and her clouded eyes closed and from between the lids fat tears oozed, hanging for a moment on her lashes before sliding across her cheeks.

"Eeh, love, don't . . . don't . . ." Phoebe could not bear it. She just could not bear to see the pain Annie was suffering and in an uncharacteristic gesture, she swept her into her own strong arms, pulling her close, doing her best to get Annie's head to her own shoulder which was difficult since Annie was almost a foot taller than herself.

"Don't cry lass, don't cry. See, tha's none of 'em worth it, none of 'em."

"I know that, Phoebe, sweet Jesus, don't I know that. My father was a sanctimonious old bugger who worked me like a horse. Cat's father wanted nothing from me but to get into my drawers, and when he did, and made me pregnant, ran off and left me to cope as best I could. Fifteen I was . . . Dear God! Then there's Bert Garnett who . . . well, never mind, we all know what he's after don't we . . . ?"

"Oh, aye. Eyes like slugs all over thi' . . ."

". . . and the only one who has a scrap of decency in him is Charlie . . ." She spoke in a soft, broken murmur, the steady rhythm of her weeping punctuated by her desolate words. Phoebe rocked her and shushed her and patted her shoulder, even wiped her nose on the scrap of scrupulously clean linen she kept in her pocket for just such a purpose.

She wept for ten minutes but the paroxysm of grief gradually died to a muted and occasional sniffle and at last she was quiet. She still lay in the comforting circle of Phoebe's arms, her eyes on the flickering flames of the fire in the inglenook. She sighed then and sat up, tossing back the tangled brush of her hair, turning to smile at Phoebe.

"There, it's done with. I'm all right now."

"Ah know that, Annie. There's nowt much can break thee."

"Nor you, dear Phoebe."

"True, now what about a nice cup of tea."

They were sitting companionably side by side, sipping their tea, when Cat came in. The dogs got up to welcome her, swirling about her skirts, nudging her for attention and in her basket Dandy purred her satisfaction as her kittens, three marmalade and two tortoiseshell like the tom from Upfell who had sired them, climbed all over her ready to leave the basket now in their inquisitive search for adventure.

"Where have you been, sweeting?" Annie asked her as the child sat down beside her, nestling within her mother's cradling arm. Annie was still deep in the desolation her encounter with, and rejection of Reed had forced her into, and her question was absent-minded. The apathy which nature provides to protect against deep hurt was bound about her, giving her time to start the healing process, or if not that, then the strength to take up the burden life had decided her back was broad enough to bear. She loved Reed Macauley. That was a reality, a truth, that she had carried in her heart for a long time. He could never be hers. That was another reality, another truth that had to be borne. Nothing had changed from the uncertainty of what it had always been where Reed was concerned, but given time, the hard work and determined resolve towards the future which had borne her up in the past, she would survive it. There was a great emptiness inside her. She felt like squatting down on the floor, as an animal that is hurt does and putting her hands about her ears so that she might not hear her own cries of pain, but she would pull herself through this, as she had always done.

She held her child closer and put her cheek on her windblown tumble of bright copper curls. Cat smelled of heather as though she had used the springing, colourful plant for a pillow and probably had for she would often take one of Charlie's books up on to the fell and with only the dogs for company, read in the clear sunlight or while away the hours in dreams. She was getting on for six years old, slim and tall for her age, a quiet child who, probably because of her early years, was shy and liked nothing better than her own company, though she and Charlie were good friends.

"Have you been along by the gill?" Annie asked when Cat did not answer, for the bank which ran beside the tumbling waters was a favourite spot of the child's.

"Mm, we were reading."

"You and Charlie?"

"Yes." Cat did not waste words.

"And where did Charlie get to?"

"He said he would try for Yorkshire first and then if there was nothing there he'd go to London."

Annie smiled despite her grief. Charlie was a great one for jokes, for teasing, for dreams and fantasies. He filled Cat's head with them, telling her far more about himself than he ever told Phoebe or herself and was still, despite all this time, an enigma, a merry, absurdly endearing man

with an air of mystery about him which she knew many
women would find attractive.

"Really, and did he say how he would get there?"

"He said he was to walk, mother, that's if his old boots
would allow it." The child gazed solemnly up at her
mother, then sighed deeply. "I shall miss him."

Very carefully Annie sat up, disentangling herself from
Phoebe who had not yet been stricken with the curious
feeling of dread which had laid itself on Annie, a dread so
heavy it was like a suit of armour on her already weary
body. She withdrew her arms gradually from about Cat
and looked deeply into her face. Cat's gaze did not waver.
There was a tremble in her soft lips and the golden brown
depths of her eyes were troubled but she did not look
away. Phoebe, sensing something now, leaned forward.

"What is it?" she asked doubtfully.

Annie did not answer. She spoke instead to Cat.

"What exactly did Charlie say, sweetheart?"

"He said he would try for Yorkshire first . . ." the child
repeated patiently, ". . . but . . ."

"Yes, yes . . . but . . . what did he mean? Was it something you were reading together, or a story he was telling
you?"

Her heart thudded painfully out of control and she did
not know why for it was absolutely ridiculous to think
that Charlie, dear, dear Charlie, would . . . Oh, sweet
Jesus . . .

"No, Mother, he said it was time to leave now. He was
needed elsewhere and I was to tell you . . ."

"No . . . Dear God . . . no, not Charlie . . . please God
. . . not Charlie . . . I cannot manage it without
Charlie . . ."

"Mother . . ." The child drew away, frightened.

"Annie . . ." Phoebe put out a restraining hand for
surely Annie was about to do herself a mischief.

"How could he . . . it's a joke, isn't it? He's hiding in
the yard, isn't he? I'll give him his old boots, the rascal.
I'll kill him for teasing me like this . . . really I will . . ."
and she sprang up leaving Cat and Phoebe to huddle

together on the settle while the dogs, aware that some drama was being enacted, wagged their tails placatingly, ready to take the blame as long as Annie would pat their heads to reassure them.

"Charlie . . . come on in, you devil." She ran into the yard, her head turning frantically from side to side. She raced over to the wall and stared across the fields to the lake, shading her eyes for a sight of his jaunty figure. Where was he? Where had he hidden himself? In the barn, or the cow shed? Perhaps the dairy which, without a cow to produce the milk, was still not in use. Oh, dear Lord, let him suddenly jump out at her . . . please Lord. She would scream and curse and probably strike him for frightening her so but . . . she needed him. She loved Reed Macauley, but her greatest need was for Charlie Lucas, who, she knew now, had been the hand to guide her, the arm to cling to, the rock to steady her . . . Charlie . . .

"He left you this letter, Mother." Cat's voice was timid at her back but Annie did not turn. She stood in the middle of the yard and from somewhere in her head, she heard Charlie's flippant laughter, his cheerful whistle, the sound of his voice singing 'The Cocking Song' from way up on the fell, and her world tumbled down about her ears.

She did not read it until Phoebe and a tearful Cat had gone to bed.

"My love," it said. "I can call you that now I am no longer with you. That is what you are, you see. My love, my dearest love, mine, in my heart, but not mine, for I know yours beats faster, not for me, but for Reed Macauley. I have watched you turn your head to stare over the fell which divides Browhead and Long Beck and felt your pain and longing and my own has been, at times, a burden too great to bear. I love you, Annabelle Abbott, but I simply can no longer live beside you knowing the strength of your love for him. It's too much to ask of any man. I have stayed as long as I could, as long as you needed me. You are on your feet now . . ."

"No, no, I'm not, Charlie . . . I need you with me . . ."

she whispered and the words had nothing to do with Charlie's work on the farm.

". . . your flock is healthy and your crops. You have a guinea or two put by . . ."

". . . and you have nothing. You have taken nothing that rightly belonged to you, not a penny . . ." She rocked in an agony of remorse, her tears soaking the notepaper, blinding her eyes so that she could barely see to read.

". . . and can hire a man to help you at 'backend'. What a charming way with words you people of the lakes have. 'Backend' and that is what it is to me. An ending, my darling Annie. I shall never forget. I shall never forget you, Charlie."

Phoebe crept down an hour later. Annie sat where she had left her. The letter was in her left hand and her right rested on the head of Bonnie which was in her lap. Blackie's muzzle rested across her bare feet, keeping a vigil with her as she stared, dry-eyed now, into the future which would be bleak and empty without Charlie Lucas in it.

"Phoebe . . ."

"Aye, love, I'm here."

"What am I to do without him?" and Phoebe was not awfully certain of who Annie meant. Reed Macauley or Charlie Lucas?

Annie walked to Keswick the next day and when she found no trace of Charlie there, set off along the road which ran alongside the great heights of Helvellyn by the lake of Thirlmere, down to Grasmere and Ambleside and Windermere. She stopped every man and woman she met asking them if they had seen Charlie Lucas, describing him and causing a great deal of consternation among the women since they had thought her to be a young man until she spoke. There was also a great deal of ribald comment among the men, though her white, strained face and deep staring eyes soon silenced them all. She took the dogs and her shepherd's crook and on her back was the bag of food Phoebe had packed for her but she did not eat what was in it, merely carried it because it did not occur to her to put it down. She slept wherever she happened to be, her dogs close by her, but only for an hour or two before getting to her feet and moving on.

Three days later she was just leaving Windermere, a stunned and stumbling figure, dazed to the point where she could not decide which road to take since her choice was Kendal or Newby Bridge and Charlie might have gone by either. He was a man, strong and was more than twelve hours ahead of her. Perhaps he had taken the road to Penrith and south from there to Yorkshire. She just didn't know but she must press on and find him, she must . . .

"Annie." She heard her name through the fog of her own exhaustion and lack of food. There was a hotel to her left and with a portion of her mind which was still capable of thought she noticed it had the strange name of 'Elleray'. There was a great deal of activity in the yard. A coach was about to set out, its destination Carlisle, its roof piled high with boxes and portmanteaux, the horses which pulled it striking fretful hooves on the cobbles as they waited for the off. Ostlers and hotel servants shouted at one another and passengers who were about to embark on the long journey fussed and fumed as they changed their minds a dozen times over what they should take inside with them. There were dog-carts and riding horses, the hotel and the yard overflowing with men who seemed intent on fighting one another to get either in or out.

"Annie," the voice was sharp and she turned about, disorientated by the clamour. The horseman who had called her name dismounted, throwing the reins to a passing ostler who, knowing a man of authority when he saw one, caught them obediently.

"I've come to take you home, Annie," the horseman said, moving to bar her path. "Come, let me lift you up on my mare's back and . . ."

"No, no, really. I cannot. I must find Charlie." A spasm crossed the horseman's face but he did not falter.

"No, my darling, he has gone."

"No, no, he has not. He will be on the road ahead of me and I shall catch him up shortly."

"No, Annie, he was seen boarding the train at Penrith three days ago."

"He had no money for train fare."

"It seems he sold . . . a watch, Annie." Reed Macauley's voice was very patient, very gentle and for the first time Annie was suddenly aware of who he was.

"Reed . . . ?"

"Yes, my love, I am here." He put out a hand and the people passing by were astonished to see the tall, well set-up gentleman smooth back the curling tendrils of hair which fell about the forehead of the shabbily dressed youth. "It's time to go home now. Your maid and daughter were worried about you, so I . . ."

"How did you know?" She was beginning to see two of him now. Two Reed Macauleys who fused together before drifting apart again. Both had concerned faces and a pair of blue eyes brilliant with what she could have sworn were tears but of course Reed Macauley would never weep. Why should he?

"She came to my house yesterday."

"Phoebe?"

"Is that her name? She would speak to no one but me, she told them, and would not be moved until I came. A strong-willed lass and devoted to you. She said you would probably turn her out for interfering but nevertheless she could not let you tramp the length of the country looking for Charlie Lucas."

"You knew him?"

"No. *About* him. I made it my business to . . ." but the rest of the words went roaring away into a pale grey, fast moving shaft which gathered speed and became darker and darker until she fell into the blackness.

24

The face of the man at the door was familiar but for several moments Annie could not put a name to it. He was small and wiry, as lean as a greyhound but there was a look about him which spoke of strength and endurance despite his lack of bulk. His skin was heavily seamed and in each seam was a fine line of grey as though the soap and water he sketched over it, were thrown so hastily they did no more than whisk across the surface. He wore an old-fashioned soft-brimmed hat slung on his grizzled curls, a wide-cut shirt, breeches fastened beneath his knees, stockings with gaiters over them and a waistcoat so ancient its colour was unrecognisable. He carried a labourer's sleeveless smock made from sacking.

"Tha' wants a man," he said briefly, his expression taciturn, his speech the same.

"I beg your pardon." Annie eyed him from head to foot, not sure whether to laugh or slam the door in his face but his eyes were stern, steady, with an expression in them which was completely without humour.

"Does tha' want a man or not?"

"I can't say that I do," she answered and it was then that the man's name came to her. It was seven years or more since she had seen him and then it had been with the eyes of a child, a young girl who had looked at anyone over the age of twenty with the belief that they already had one foot in the grave. All the men of her acquaintance including her father had grey hair and weatherbeaten wrinkled faces. Some had bent backs and bowed legs for the loads they carried would have burdened a horse. This man had moved on the fringes of her child's world, an unseen part of the scenery, like the tree at the side of the house or the dog which had moved at her father's heels. He had had no home as far as she was aware, no family nor friends, moving from farm to farm, a man able to set his hand to any task, coppicing, shepherding, mending the drystone walls in which not a dab of cement was added, planting, ploughing and clipping sheep, his own master and man, for as long as any one could remember. Grey but unbent, born to toil on other men's land, industrious, a man who would labour until he fell dead at some other man's plough, free, stubbornly independent and working for reasons best known to himself, for Bert Garnett.

"Why, it's Natty Varty," she smiled, the lovely glowing smile which no man could resist, but Natty did. A look of deep disapproval set his lips in a rigid line and his eyebrows moved fiercely over his eyes like two small animals.

"Aye." He stood his ground, saying nothing more. He had said all that was necessary, his attitude told her, and the next move was up to her. She'd best make up her mind what it was to be, though, for he'd no time to be hanging about waiting on the word of a lass who was no better than she should be, or so he'd heard.

"Well . . . what can I do for you, Natty?" she asked politely, still ready to smile, opening her door a little more so that if he was of a mind to, he could come inside, or not, as he pleased.

"Nay, lass, tha' can do nowt' fer me. It's more what I can do for thi'."

"For me, Natty? In what way?"

"Does tha' want a man ter work for thi', or not? Speak up an let's get it settled."

"Work for me?" Her mouth fell open in bewilderment. "Why should you work for me? And who told you to come here? I've not advertised for a labourer."

"'Appen not, but I was told tha' needed one just the same."

"But you work for Bert Garnett, Natty. You have done for as long as I've been back so why should you . . ."

"Before I tek up wi' thi' let's get summat straight. I'm Mr Varty to thi', an ah'll work where ah like. An' it weren't

Bert Garnett who hired me but Aggie Mounsey an' she be dead. So if ah've a fancy to 'ave a change, that's my business. Ah was told tha' needed someone to help wi' tha' lambs, so I upped it an' come along."

Though the words were spoken with a firm resolution which defied her to argue with him – and why should she – his grim manner and plain expressionless face told a different tale. This was not to his liking, Annie could see that. It was almost time to take the sheep to market for the buying and selling of stock, a busy time on any sheep farm and good men like Natty Varty were worth their weight in gold. There was not a man at the Tup Fair who would argue with him, even if he did work for Annie Abbott. Her passage would be smoothed enormously with Natty Varty by her side and the stock she meant to buy with her small store of coins would be readily available to her. Her flock would need salving and marking, and in a few weeks the oats and barley harvested and threshed in mid-summer would be prepared for taking to the mill to be ground. Already the trees needed for the making of her swill baskets were ready for felling, a task to be carried out approximately between October and April or May. And she had still not been able to get to Whitehaven to sell the swills she and Charlie and Phoebe had already fashioned. They were piled neatly in the dairy but they could not be stored there indefinitely since, with the milk she would get from the cow she intended to buy before winter, she meant to make butter and cheese. A stall, she and Phoebe had talked it over. They would rent a stall at the fortnightly market and with Phoebe, starched and neat and eminently respectable behind it, she could sell Annie's produce which included the eggs her hens laid, butter, cheese, chickens, perhaps a swill or two and a besom brush, and steadily they would build up Annie's tiny profit. And the cow, which would be quartered for the winter in the cow shed, would need to be hand fed on the bracken which would be cut and brought down from the fell. There was some hay, of course, but that might not last the winter, particularly if it was a hard one and the sheep were brought down to the intake land. They would need hand feeding . . . Dear God, the list was endless and without Charlie . . .

"I do need a man, Mr Varty, but I can't pay much."

"I'm not asking for much."

"Name a figure."

He did and it was so ridiculously low she gasped.

"You can't live on that, Nat . . . Mr Varty."

"I'll decide that. Can tha' give me a bed an' me grub?"

There was Charlie's room above the dairy, snug and achingly tidy since he had left and Phoebe had ferociously 'bottomed' it. Bare whitewashed walls, bare scrubbed floor, a narrow bed and a press in which nothing of Charlie's had ever been stored, since he had owned only what he stood up in. His broadcloth coat rested there in the summer with his knitted jerkin and scarf and a book or two. All gone along with the engaging good humour, the impish lazy smile, the wickedly wry tongue of the man who had come into her life with the casual manner of someone who had not a serious thought in his head, not a serious bone in his body. He had worked beside her in sleet and snow and rain and storm and made light of it, giving the impression that nothing much mattered in life besides an absurd talent for laughing at it. A gift for avoiding anything which smacked of stuffiness or monotony, nevertheless, without appearing to move at any faster pace than an indolent saunter, he had done the work of three men. Without appearing to speak in any way that was not droll and teasing, he had guided her wisely, invigorated her when she was drained and weary, gladdened her heart when it was sad, encouraged and inspired her and she could not envisage a future without him in it. It was two months since he had gone and in that time there had been no word of him, no letter, nothing, and if Reed Macauley knew of his whereabouts, he was not telling Annie Abbott.

He had brought her home that day, sleeping in the crook of his arm as she lolled before him on his black mare. On that long road from Windermere up through Ambleside and Grasmere and on to Keswick where the good folk milling about Moot Hall and the market place fell silent, gaping at the sight of Reed Macauley with his arms about Annie Abbott. As bold as brass he was, raising his hat to those with whom he was acquainted, smiling round the expensive cigar he had clamped between his good white teeth, just as though there was nothing unusual in his behaviour. As though he and Annie Abbott were accustomed to riding together on his mare Victoria, and perhaps they were, for anything could be believed of that strumpet. Those appalling clothes she wore and would you look at her hair, her long thick plait all undone and a living mantle of russet falling across Reed Macauley's arm and half-way down the mare's belly. Sound asleep in the middle of the day and what could they deduce from that except to wonder how she had got in such a state? And him with a young wife of no more than a year at home. No children and could one wonder at it if he was . . . cavorting about the parish with Annie Abbott.

The valley had rocked with it, adding fresh fuel to the fire in the middle of which they would have liked to burn Annie Abbott, for surely that was what she was, a witch! Annie had woken in her own bed the next day with no recollection of how she had got there and certainly none of the ride through Keswick and if the men and women she met on her occasional walk along the lake road, and in Hause, Gillthrop or Keswick averted their offended eyes when she strode by, what difference did it make to her since they had done so for the past three years? She missed Charlie. That was the foremost ache in her burdened heart and if the village women hissed at her as she went through, she scarcely noticed.

She had not seen Reed Macauley since.

Now, two months later, here was Natty Varty offering his invaluable services to Annie Abbott and she was immediately suspicious.

'Mr Varty, there is nothing I would like more than to employ you, but I cannot understand why you are asking me to. What was suddenly . . ."

"Look lass, doest tha' want me to work fer thi' or not?

Just say yes or no. That's all that's needed. Tha' knows ah'm a good worker . . ."

"Oh, indeed, Mr Varty, but I really find it hard to believe that you should, for no apparent reason, take it into your head that you want to work for me. Won't you come inside and we can . . ."

"Bloody 'ell . . . beggin yer pardon . . ." since for some reason it suddenly did not seem right to swear in the face of this polite and lovely woman, even if she did wear trousers and a shirt. His eyes touched briefly on the thrust of her breasts then looked hastily away. "Ah said ah'd get this argument when . . ." He stopped suddenly, realising he had said too much, his discomfiture showing in the way his angry old mouth worked and it was then Annie began to know.

"Someone has sent you, haven't they? Someone has asked you to come and offer yourself . . ."

"Nay, lass, tha's talkin' daft. Natty Varty pleases hissen where he works."

"Really, then tell me this. Why are you offering yourself at half the going price a labourer would get? £8 for half a year you could demand so who is paying you the other half?"

Natty's eyes were flat and expressionless but he did not look away. His mouth was clamped in a thin white line of contempt and something else which Annie did her best to decipher. He was standing his ground, staring at her as though he would like nothing better than to spit at her feet, but something held him there on her doorstep and she had no idea of what it could be. Reed Macauley had sent him, of that she was sure, but not even Reed could make Natty Varty work where he didn't want to. So what hold did he have on this old man, as he had on many men in the district, that he could force him to go where he did not want to go? Suddenly she made up her mind. She lifted her head haughtily as she spoke.

"Very well, *Natty*, I will employ you. You will sleep over the cow shed and Phoebe will bring your meals to you there. But there is one thing. I am to be addressed as

Miss Abbott. I give the orders and you take them and I shall pay you, *I shall pay you* the full rate. You can tell the person who sent you that you do not need his bribe, if that is what he has offered you and if I hear that you have disobeyed me then I shall fire you immediately. Is that clear? Have you your own dog? Ah, yes, I see you have," eyeing the quiet Border collie which lay with its nose just beneath the closed farm gate, "then I'll be obliged if you would keep it away from mine. Now perhaps you could start by bringing my sheep down to the 'inlands' so that they will be ready for market next week. Good morning to you, Natty. If you require anything, speak to Phoebe."

Reed Macauley rode openly across the lower slopes of Cockup Fell and down the track from Dash Beck to Browhead the following day. It was almost October and a day of damp, drifting rain, light as mist but coming to rest just as wetly on collars and cuffs from where it crept insidiously inside clothing. It dripped down boots to soak into stockings and collected on the brim of hats from where it ran in a steady trickle to cling to flesh which shivered at the touch of the oncoming winter. Slender birches drooped sadly as though they too knew well what was ahead and larches, hung about gracefully with a tapestry foliage, trembled in the shifting rain. The rowans were heavy with berries. Down by the lake at the foot of Annie's farm, trees hung over the water, clinging to the sketchiest of foothold.

Beside the mare ran Reed's old dog, stopping now and again to lift her muzzle, sniffing the air with the practised ease of an animal well used to Lakeland conditions. The heather through which horse, rider and dog moved was a mass of tiny purple flowers, giving the appearance from far off, of a solid purple carpet.

"She's in t' dairy," a startled Phoebe told him and though he knew Annie must have heard the clatter of his mare's hooves on the rocky track and cobbled yard, she did not appear.

She had her back to him, her hands busy as she stacked a pile of swills, tying them neatly into a compact bundle.

Just outside the door of the dairy, standing in the rain, was the sledge, the one which had seen such service over the past years and on it, again tied neatly in two tight-fitting rows, were more swills.

"I take it you're tramping off somewhere with that sledge I see outside," were the first furious words he spoke.

She did not turn. "Yes, I'm hoping to sell them at Whitehaven." Her voice was low.

He jerked about violently, the determination he had steeled upon himself to remain calm no matter what passed between them, exploding at once in his fear for her. "Bloody hell, woman! Whitehaven? Do you know how far that is . . . !"

"Yes . . ."

". . . and you intend walking over twenty miles there and the same back dragging that damned sledge . . ."

"Yes . . ."

". . . and October no more than a week or so off . . ."

"Leave me alone, Reed. Let me get on with my life."

". . . and God knows who tramping from the ships which dock there. Irishmen on the look-out for work or anything else they can find along the way which could include you. Do you realise . . . ?"

"Yes . . ."

". . . that any one of them could . . ."

". . . Yes . . . So you have said a number of times."

"Jesus Christ, Annie, don't do this to me. Don't put yourself in danger. Let me help you. I'll find someone to buy your bloody baskets."

"Like you found Natty Varty?"

Her voice was quiet and her head was bent low as she gripped the edge of the stone slab on which, in better times, bowls of milk were left to stand for 'three meals' before the cream was carefully removed. The knuckles of her hands were white with the fierceness of her grip.

"You know I only did it to help you. That's all I want to do, is help you. To make your life easier. I can't bear to see you working yourself into the bloody ground, getting thinner every time I see you. That fellow helped you and though it tore me apart to know he was living under your roof I told myself that he was at least taking some of the load off your back. Now he's gone . . ."

"Because of you."

"Because of me?" The bewilderment in his voice was genuine and at last she turned to look at him. She wore an apron of her mother's, an enormous thing which covered her from neck to knee. One worn for dairy work where cleanliness was essential, laundered and ironed by Phoebe to a crisp and pristine whiteness. Her hair was neatly plaited, wound about her head like a weighty crown, tipping it back so that she gave the appearance of a proud young queen. She was pale, no colour in her face but in contrast, her eyes were a deep and glowing tawny brown. Warm, filled with that velvet textured softness which betrayed the depth of her love for him. It couldn't be hidden, had she wanted to hide it. Everything he did was with her welfare in mind. From that first day when he had carted down that enormous hamper to this last when he had sent – somehow – Natty Varty to labour for her, he had done his best, what she would allow, to make her life easier and if sometimes it had further damaged her reputation he had done it with the best intentions. She was aware that the last time, after what Phoebe had told her about it and the ride through Keswick, he had irretrievably damaged his own.

But he must be made to see that it would not do. He must be made to see that he could not keep on rescuing her from the results of her own mistakes. That, and the truth must be faced by him. She did not need him now. She was glad of Natty Varty and grateful that Reed had somehow made him leave Bert Garnett and come to her, but she would manage on her own from now on. She had a tiny cache of savings, pennies put by, one by laborious one, since she had sold her first lambs, her besoms and swills, and she meant to see it grow again with this year's profits. She and Phoebe and Cat lived off the land, except for the milk which, when her husband looked the other

way, Sally Garnett left hidden by the farm gate of Upfell
Farm. Annie stocked up on tea and flour when she was in
Keswick but apart from that they were self-sufficient.
They ate mutton, dried over the fire, from the sheep she
and Charlie had killed, and they managed. She did not need
Reed Macauley.

Only with her body, her anguished heart cried. Only
with her woman's body which even now surged joyously
beneath her enormous apron, beneath her father's shirt
and baggy, much patched breeches, towards Reed
Macauley. Her heart hammered until she was sure he
could see the movement of it beneath the bib of the apron.
The glow in the pit of her belly spread a filament of need
up towards her breasts and her nipples instantly hardened.
Her breath was trapped in her throat and she parted
her lips to allow it to escape and inside her she felt the
whimpers begin, whimpers which would become a moan
if she could not get a firm grip on herself.

She saw the answering need in him. He groaned in
despair, moving almost reluctantly towards her. They met
in the centre of the dairy and when their arms rose to one
another, holding, holding on desperately, clinging lest they
fall, she could hear the tremble in his voice as he spoke
into her hair.

"Sweet Jesus . . . Sweet Christ. What are we to do? I
love you . . . starve for you . . . think of you all the time.
I can't work . . . sleep . . . my mind is full of you. I'm
dazed with it . . . with the pain . . . I'm not a man for
fanciful things . . . I want a woman I take her . . . but you
are buried so deep in me I can see nobody, nothing . . .
your face . . ."

He was hurting her, crushing her, the bones in her back
and her ribs, his own body a taut, shuddering length of
bone and muscle. She lifted her head from his chest where
his heart was pounding so hard it deafened her and his lips
flattened against hers with such force she felt her teeth
break the skin inside her mouth. His gentled then, parting
hers, so sweet and soft she knew that this time . . . this
was the time . . . here, here in the dairy, wherever he

could lay her . . . on the stone bench . . . the floor . . .
she would allow him to take her . . . *allow*. . . she would
glory in it . . .

"Where does tha' want to put them besoms?" The voice
which came at them through the bright and rapturous
aureole of their love was grim and in it, even those few
words, was the realisation that had told its owner exactly
why he had been fetched here by Reed Macauley. So that
was the way the wind blew, was it, and though it was
nowt to do with him what folk did, that didn't mean to say
that he had to like it, nor would he put up with it. Reed
Macauley had promised him a cottage right up on the
edge of the fell, away from other folk, where Natty could
live out his days as he pleased. Work a bit, he would,
when he felt like it, or stop in his own place, when he felt
like it. His dog beside him, a few hens, do a bit of rabbiting,
fishing, for though Natty would admit it to no one the truth
was he was nearer eighty than seventy and he couldn't
quite do the things he had been doing since he was a lad.
Stop with *her* for a bit, Mr Macauley had said, and when
he wanted it there would be the cottage waiting for him
up beyond Tarn Nevin. But he'd be buggered if he'd be
used as a convenience whilst these two fornicated under
his bloody nose.

They whirled to face him, both for a moment looking
foolish, guilty, flushed with something Natty had long
forgotten. Her eyes were the loveliest, deepest brown,
like the ale he drank at The Bull in Gillthrop which was a
strange thing to come into his mind, but Natty liked his
ale and admired its colour.

"An' I'll be off now so tha' can get back to tha' fun
an' . . ."

He saw Reed Macauley's face turn the colour of the
beetroot he himself had only the day before yesterday
been digging up a mile away at Upfell and Reed Macauley's
roar of rage could be heard on the same farm, Natty was
sure. And he would have knocked Natty to the ground,
Natty was sure of that too, if she hadn't put a hand on his
arm. At once, mysteriously, since Reed Macauley was

known for a man of violence if crossed, he became quiet.

"What d'you mean, Natty? You'll be off where?"

"Back where I come from." His contemptuous eyes, his curling lip told her exactly what he thought of a woman like her but she did not falter or look ashamed.

"To Upfell?"

"Aye," and he shouldered the axe he carried with which he had been about to go up to the coppice to do a bit of felling.

"Why?"

"Ah work for decent folk, allus have done," and all the while Reed Macauley stood patiently by and Natty was astonished that this woman, with a light touch on his arm, could keep him from hurling Natty Varty to the ground and stamping on him for his effrontery.

"You must do as you think best, Mr Varty, of course, but I would be most obliged if you could find it within your power to stay with me for a while. I need you, you see."

"Ah knows that, lass, but ah don't need thee, or him an' his cottage," which was not true of course, and as though to emphasise it, the 'rheumatics' with which he was increasingly plagued, tweaked at his shoulder painfully.

"I see, so that's what was promised you?" and still Reed Macauley stood like he was some grey dove perched on her hand.

"Aye, but I reckon ah've bin tricked an' ah don't like that."

"In what way have you been tricked?"

"Well . . ." Well he couldn't say really, if he was honest, especially with them great big brown eyes of hers looking at him as though what he had to say was of the greatest concern to her, and suddenly, he knew it was. She *was* concerned. It really mattered to her that Natty Varty was an honest man, with ethics which said he'd have no truck with a chap who carried on an adulterous relationship with a woman . . . well . . . like her. He'd known her all her life, ever since Joshua Abbott had lost that last lad of his and he'd realised, Joshua that is, that this little lass was all that he was going to have. No wonder she dressed herself in her father's clothes since the old man had used her like a lad since she was five or six. Worked her hard he had, but she'd always been sweet-tempered. Joshua'd not broken her, and what he'd taught her had stood her in good stead, but when Natty looked back to that day when it got round the valley that Josh Abbott's lass had gone off with some chap from a travelling company, he distinctly remembered thinking at the time, "and is it any wonder?"

Now she was back, looking at him with the desperate entreaty he had once seen in the eyes of a young doe he had cornered up on Great Calva. There had been a fawn at her back, no more than a couple of hours old, and she wouldn't leave it, but her eyes, almost human, had looked like this woman's did! It was then, for the first time in his life, he changed his mind.

"Won't you reconsider, Mr Varty? Mr Macauley and I . . ."

"Nay . . ." His anger flared. ". . . I want to know nowt about that. 'Tis nowt to do with me so . . ."

"I was only going to say that . . ."

"Ah don't want ter know what tha' was going ter say so if tha'll tell me where tha' wants these besoms put I'll be off up to't coppice to see what wants felling."

"Of course, Mr Varty. Leave the besoms by the sledge and I'll pack them later. I'm to be off to Whitehaven."

"Aye, so I heard. Ah'll come with thi'. There's a tobacconist over there that sells tobacco I like . . ."

"Oh no, Mr Varty, I can get it for you."

"No, tha' can't. Tha'd only get wrong sort. Women knows nowt about tobacco."

"That's true, Mr Varty."

"An' tha' can call me Natty, Annie."

They both had a strong tendency towards hysteria, Annie and Reed, a great bubbling laughter which welled up inside them so that they turned to one another, clinging together, not in passion, but with the merriment, the foolish absurdity which comes when a great strain has ended. They were not laughing at Natty, though his paradoxical change of direction, the sudden reversal of his antipathy towards her was comical in the extreme. It was his last words that amused Annie and it was relief that made Reed lean against her whilst great gales of laughter shook them both.

"I don't know how I kept my hands from the old fool."

"No, he's not that, Reed, but what was it do you think, that made him change his mind?"

He put her from him. Not far, no more than six inches but enough to look down into her shining eyes.

"Don't you know?" The turmoil of their bodies had subsided now and there was peace and a quality of honesty between them. "Don't you know what you have? You are beautiful Annie Abbott, but rarer than that is your absolute unawareness of your beauty. And not only your face is beautiful but so is your heart and soul. It shines through and when men look at it, men who recognise it, as I do, as Charlie Lucas did . . . oh yes, my darling, I realise now why he left . . . and as even an old man like Natty Varty does, there is nothing we would not do for you. Dear God, if only you would let me do it. Which brings me to the purpose of my visit. Do you still want that girl of yours to go to school? Ah, I see you do, well you can give me a glass of ale and sit beside me on the wall while we discuss it."

The day before they were to set off for Whitehaven, the last day in September it was, Sally Garnett came running down the track from Upfell, her youngest in her arms, her face crimson, her pale brown hair in a tangle about her head and her plump figure, never given a chance to right itself between pregnancies, wobbling all over the place like a sackful of blown up balloons.

"I can't stop, I've left Sammy in charge of little 'uns but he's only five himself and Alfie's a real handful. This is Aggie, I called her after me mam."

"Come in, Sally, oh, do come in and have some tea. Phoebe's in the dairy. We have a cow now, you know, and she says the place needs a good scrubbing out every day, just as though she hasn't done it once already today, and Cat's at school . . . Oh, yes, didn't you know? Oh, please come in and drink a cup of tea with me and let me tell you all about it. Here, let me take Aggie while you get your breath," and though the baby stank like a ferret, making Annie turn her head and think sadly of Aggie Mounsey and her passion for cleanliness, she took her from Sally's arms and tried to propel Sally into Phoebe's shining kitchen.

"Oh no, I dassunt, Annie. He'd kill me. He'd kill me if he knew I was even speaking to yer. He's in a fearful temper . . ." and now, as Annie got a good look at her, she could see what Bert's fearful temper had done to his wife's eye. It was set in a deep purple socket and her cheek-bone seemed to stand out in a peak from the rest of her face.

"Sally, come in. He's obviously away from Upfell or you wouldn't be here . . ."

"Aye, market in Keswick . . ." Sally was getting her breath back now and she eyed the interior of the kitchen and the offer of a drink of tea with some longing.

"Well then, he won't be back before dark . . ."

"Ah knows that, but ah dassunt, Annie." Sally's terror of Bert's fearful temper evidently could not be convinced that even the distance between Browhead and Keswick Market would hide her from his wrath. "Ah've just come to tell thi' that he's livid about Natty Varty. Oh, Annie, I'm that frightened he'll do summat bad to thee, or to tha' farm or even that lass of yourn. He don't care how he goes about it, but he's right set on doing thi' a mischief. That's how I got this," fingering her swollen face. "I said no more than pr'aps he'd best be careful an' he landed me one that . . . well, tha' can see for thissen. He reckons tha' coaxed Natty away wi' . . . well, I'm too ashamed to tell thee what he said, an' Natty an' all . . . an old man! Bert . . . well, he knows about thee and him from up Long Beck. I'm sorry, lass . . ." putting a contrite hand on Annie's arm, watching as the soft creamy blush and the bright glow brought about by her own arrival at Browhead slipped away from her friend's face. "He says that any man what . . . Oh, Annie, lass, he reckons tha'll lie down for any man, an' it were then when he said that, that I spoke up and he clouted me."

"Oh Sally, I'm so sorry, for you and for myself. Dear God, I've been with one man in my life, no more, and then I was a child, fourteen, ignorant, in love or so I thought. He said we were to be married . . . and for that one mistake I am to suffer this. Seven years, Sally and still they turn on me . . ."

"Aye, love, ah know. Everyone's talking about yer an' that's all they'll do, but not Bert. He'll hurt thi', Annie. Can thi' not ask . . . ?" she tossed her head awkwardly in the direction of Long Beck and Reed Macauley. "Will he not protect thi'?"

"Sally, there is *nothing* between me and Reed Macauley, nothing." Annie's words came through gritted teeth.

"He'd like there to be though, wouldn't he, lass?" Sally spoke with a sad wisdom and Annie sighed.

"Oh yes, Sal, he'd like there to be."

"Buggers, the lot of 'em."

"Oh, Sally, why won't they let me get on . . . ?"

"I don't know lass, but I'd best get back. God knows what them lot's up to. But tha'll be careful, won't tha'. Watch out for Bert."

"I'm to go to Whitehaven tomorrow with Natty."

"Eeeh, whatever for?"

"To sell my swills to the coaling ships. There's a good market there. I've sold them here and there, one or two at a time, but I reckon I could get rid of the lot in one go."

"An' tha's leaving thi' lass on er own with only that girl with her?"

Annie's face lit up for a moment.

"No, that's what I wanted to tell you. Cat's gone over to . . ."

"Tha'd best tell em to lock t' door."

"Bert wouldn't hurt Phoebe, Sally. He's no quarrel with her and Cat's gone to . . ."

But Sally was sidling away, unconcerned now with anything but her agitated need to get back to Upfell and her children. She had tied Alfie and Emma to the legs of the heavy kitchen table but she wouldn't put it past her Sammy to have released them, and God only knew what devilment or danger the four of them had got up to. Dear Lord, but she missed her mam. She wouldn't have this shiner if her mam had still been alive. He wouldn't have dared lift a finger to her, not with Aggie Mounsey at his back, the rotten sod, but he'd been that incensed when Natty Varty had left, not saying where he was off to since Natty Varty was not one for blurting his business to anyone. Natty had not been settled ever since her mam died, Sally knew that. And when Bert had found out where Natty had gone, well, she and the children had cowered in the barn for more than two hours until he'd slammed out of the kitchen and set off in the direction of The Bull. He'd abused her

something awful when he got back, no doubt putting
her in the family way again, and that was when he blacked
her eye. Oh, God . . . Mam . . .

Annie and Natty were gone five days. They had walked
the shortest route, dragging the sledge round the top of
Bassenthwaite lake and up and over the top of High Side,
bypassing Cockermouth, crossing the river Cocker and
spending the night at the Beehive Inn below Deanscales.
On across Dean Moor and High Moor in an almost direct
line until they reached Whitehaven. They were lucky.
There were many coaling ships and tramp steamers tied
up in the harbour and by the end of the third day they had
sold all their swills, though short of going from door to
door, the besoms, in any number were not wanted. Annie
was uneasy. Sally had put a worm of disquiet in her mind
and the whole time she and Natty were away, she had the
strongest compulsion to do everything on the run, longing
to tell customers to hurry and make their minds up as they
dickered between this swill or that or should it be three
or half a dozen? One man on the harbour had wanted to
discuss a bit of business, saying he would take as many
of Annie's swills as she could get across to him. His ship
called at Liverpool, Belfast, Greenock and many other
ports where the colliers docked, and he was sure he could
sell them for her if they could agree on a price, he said.
There was no disparagement in his eyes or voice, or in
those of his crew, at the sight of her strange rig-out, for
these were men who had been to the far-flung outposts
of the British Empire in their time, and though they eyed
her long trousered legs and soft bowler hat somewhat
curiously they were accustomed to seeing stranger sights
than her. She was a bonny lass or would be underneath
those baggy jacket and trousers and the unflattering man's
hat she wore, but that was nothing to do with them.
Besides, the old man she had with her was sharp-eyed
and sharp-tongued and gave the impression he'd take his
sturdy shepherd's crook to any man who looked sideways
at him, or her.

She and Natty had got on quite well together, she had

decided. It seemed he had taught himself to read when he had worked on the estate of some wealthy landowner just on the border between Cumberland and Scotland, in his youth. There had been broadsheets left about in the kitchen and being a resolute lad with little to say to his fellows, he had puzzled it out until he could decipher the squiggles on the paper. The *Glasgow Herald* had been his master's particular favourite, costing the exorbitant sum of fourpence halfpenny, and the young man Natty had grown into had become used to that one newspaper, looking out for copies wherever he went. He read everything printed in it from advertisements of cottages to let or for sale, the doings of the County Sessions, the finance accounts of the treasury, reports from the House of Lords, notices to shippers and passengers on sailing vessels and even an account of Her Majesty's Drawing Room held at St James's Palace. But anything of a political nature was bread and butter to him and he liked to discourse on it to anyone sensible enough to listen. Not many were, not of his acquaintance, but he found a ready listener in Annie Abbott.

"That were a right sad do about Peel," he said shortly, right out of the blue on their first morning together. They were passing through the wooded area just north of Bassenthwaite Lake. The sun had ventured forth in a last effort to prolong the autumn but it was cold, sharp with the feeling of the winter to come. The oaks and alders, the willows weeping into the water were fast losing their leaves and the woodland floor was rich with a spongy layer in every shade from the palest cream to the darkest red, through which tiny saplings were reaching up to the light, thick as spring snowdrops. There was a cascade of silvered water running down the beck into the lake and propping up a drystone wall over which Natty clambered as spry as a boy was a huge and noble old yew tree. Natty's dog pattered at his heels. He had no name. His eyes never left Natty and it needed only a movement of Natty's hand or the click of his fingers, perhaps just a turn of his head and the dog knew exactly what was required of him. Annie had left Blackie and Bonnie for company with Phoebe.

"Oh?" she answered delicately. She had heard of Peel but she had no access to newspapers and the only people she met or spoke to were not of a mind to discuss current affairs with her.

"Aye, I reckon country'll be worse off without him." He took his pipe from his mouth, turning to look at her and seeing that she had nothing to say on the matter, clamped it between his teeth again.

"Did tha' not know he were gone?" His tone was biting as though to say what could you expect of a woman.

"Gone?"

"Aye, dead. His 'orse threw him an' he died a few days later."

"Poor man."

"Aye, poor man indeed. An honest an' true man I reckon he were. An' I reckon it were due to 'im that this country's had peace for t' last two years. Revolution everywhere, but not here. Oh, no." He shook his head wisely and his dog watched anxiously lest there were some message for him in the movement. "You'll 'ave eard of t' 'Peelers'. Well, it were 'im who founded the Metropolitan Police. Prime Minister, he were for a while in '34 and again in '41. An' it were 'im who repealed the Corn Laws which put food in a lot o' folks' mouths, I can tell thi'."

"Do you know, Mr Varty, I had not even heard of it. Do tell me more."

By the end of the journey Annie had been informed on many matters which concerned the welfare of the people, ranging from Chartism, which Natty heartily endorsed, to his opinion of the Prince Consort, whom Natty had not cared for at first, him being a foreigner, but who was proving an able sort of chap. Well, look at this Great Exhibition he was planning.

"An exhibition, Mr Varty?"

"Aye, up in London next year . . ."

He was deep in the throes of Lord Palmerston's foreign policy, as they drew near Browhead, particularly with reference to Greece and the attack on the property of a British subject who lived in Athens and who was demanding compensation. It appeared that Lord Palmerston supported him and . . .

Annie's instincts, which had been troubling her ever since they had left Browhead, sensed that something was wrong as she and Natty, still in full spate, came over the crest of the hill and crossed Chapel Beck. Though there was nothing obviously wrong – smoke came from the chimney and the hens pecked and squawked in the yard – there was an air of something out of kilter about the farm. A feeling of unbalance, of discord.

She began to run, her old hat flying off and spinning away as she did so.

Bert Garnett glowered round the tap room of The Bull, his figure somewhat indistinct in the smoke from the dozens of long-stemmed pipes which were being puffed by most of its customers. His hard brown fist was clamped about a pint pot of ale, the fifth he had drunk since he had entered the inn, not more than an hour ago. He didn't so much drink the ale as tip the pot up and pour the liquid down his throat in one great draught, hardly pausing to swallow, then thumped it on the bar, calling to Will Twentyman to fill it up again. The violence of his thoughts was kept to himself but they were very evidently of an explosive nature, as demonstrated by the way he crashed the pot to the counter. There was an empty circle about him for there was not a man there who cared to even sit next to him let alone enquire what ailed him. They knew, of course, for it had got about the valley like wildfire that Natty Varty, much in demand at the busy times of the year, had left Upfell and gone to that lass of Joshua Abbott's. Working for her he was now, leaving Bert in the lurch and Bert was not at all pleased about it, as anyone in the bar could see.

Bert smashed his pot on the counter for the sixth time and the room fell silent for a moment. Will Twentyman was a mild-mannered man but he did like a quiet house. Men didn't come here to fight. They were honest, hard-working labourers and farmers and shepherds who liked a nice peaceful pint before they ambled off to their beds and the warm back of the missus, and how long would it be before Will spoke up?

"Summat wrong, Bert?" he asked good-naturedly enough.

"There's nowt wrong, Will Twentyman, except wi' my pot which is empty."

"Right Bert, but watch what tha' doin't wi' it, will tha'?" said Will as he placed the sixth foaming pint in front of his truculent customer.

After the downing of his tenth pint, Bert staggered out of The Bull without a good night to anyone. The night was dark, a great mass of clouds as malevolent as Bert himself pressing down on the towering fells and hiding any vestige of light from moon or stars. But Bert needed no light to guide him between the high stone walls of the road down from Gillthrop, fording the beck and along the track which led at the back of Browhead towards Upfell. He'd done it a hundred or more times since he'd married Sally, though Ma Mounsey had not been pleased about it, old cow.

He could feel the dam of bitterness surge inside him as he stopped to glare at the back of Annie Abbott's farm. Bitch, bloody interfering bitch, taking the only decent labourer to be had in the district, stealing him from Bert with them tarty ways of hers, lying down, taking off her drawers, even for an old chap like Natty. But when a full-blooded chap like himself had let it be known to her that he'd be willing to accommodate her she'd turned her bloody nose up as though he was something one of his own cows had deposited and which she'd nearly stepped in. She did it for everyone but him, opened her legs and showed off that sweet bit of fluff which Bert Garnett would dearly love to get his hands on and his prick in. High and bloody mighty Macauley was sniffing round and probably getting his in an' all like the rest of them, and yet Bert Garnett wasn't given even a smile or a wink let alone a feel of her. Bitch, cow, whore . . . and not only that, she had taken the one good man everyone in the area would give their eye-teeth to have working for them. And she was doing well, it was said, that flock of hers sold and new stock added and even a bloody cow and a pig in her yard. Oats and barley in her barn ready to be milled and a store of vegetables enough to feed the Queen's army. Gone to bloody Whitehaven she had, her and Natty, to sell her swills and there was his Sal sitting on her fat arse all day with nothing to do but stuff her face and could *she* make a swill? Could she hell! She could do nowt except produce bairns one after the other whilst that bitch in her snug farmhouse . . . By God . . . !

The dam burst and any hold Bert Garnett might have had on good sense and sanity was swept away on the roaring tide of his obsessed rage. Reaching for a rock from the track, he moved round from the back of the farmhouse to the front, picking his way as quietly as a mouse, his feet finding, as though by instinct, the soft thick grass at the side of the track. There was no light showing anywhere since it was past nine o' clock but in the fire window beside the inglenook a faint golden orange showed where the fire, tamped down for the night, glowed warmly. He heard the two dogs begin to growl warningly from inside the house and he grinned as he threw the rock. Their growl became a frantic barking as the glass in the small mullioned window shattered and in a moment or two a light flickered in an upstairs window. It wavered behind the curtains and he waited. It appeared again moments later, moving behind the kitchen curtain as whoever held it came downstairs and the dogs continued to howl and bark but he did not move away. He stood in the shadows of the tree at the side of the house and again he watched and waited. He was not sure what for nor did he care much. He was enjoying himself. He was doing something to scare that bitch, even if she wasn't there. She'd know when she got home, that you didn't cross a man like Bert Garnett, and if you did, you only did it once.

To his amazed delight, the door opened. He'd not expected that. Another couple of rocks would have done him. Perhaps one through each window for good measure, but the sight of the open doorway and the figure who stood there holding a bloody candle and shouting 'Who's there?' for Christ's sake, well, it was too good a chance to miss . . .

Wait a minute though, he didn't want to get his hands mangled or his throat taken out by one of them dogs, did he? Caution was needed here until he found out what was what. He'd no idea what he meant to do, but by God, he was enjoying this and he'd no intention of moving on home until he'd wrung every drop of pleasure and satisfaction from it.

The dogs, which he had expected to rush out into the dark did not appear. He'd been prepared to leap over the wall and leg it up to Upfell or even up the bloody tree but the daft cow in the doorway swung her bloody candle shouting 'Who's there?' and it began to dawn on him that the dogs weren't *coming* out, that . . . that she must have tied them up . . . Jesus . . . she'd tied them up . . . !

It took him two strides to reach the doorway, pushing Phoebe aside and sweeping back the door until it nearly came off its hinges and in the corner where Bonnie and Blackie were tied to the fixed settle their barking was high and frantic with hysteria.

"What do you think you're doing, Bert Garnett?" Phoebe said, her eyes livid in her outraged face. She was not afraid, not then. She had seen who it was, when she'd peeped from her bedroom window and she could see he was drunk, the daft sod and Annie'd give him what for when she saw that broken window. Good job she'd tied the dogs up before she'd opened the door or they'd have gone for him.

In answer to her outraged question Bert didn't really know what he was doing. He bore Annie Abbott a deep grudge and wanted nothing more than to vent his animosity and resentment on her for her treatment of him. Chucking the rock had been an impulse and if Phoebe hadn't opened the door that was probably all the damage that would have been done. But the sight of Phoebe's spotless kitchen, the reflection of fire and candle-light glowing in the deep rich polish of the oak table and the kist, the gleaming whitewashed walls touched to gold, the copper bowls filled with branches of autumnal leaves, the lovely fragrance of Phoebe's pot-pourri, and fainter, but just as pleasing, the bread she had baked that morning, all in such direct contrast to his own slovenly hearth where his wife seemed to live in stinking chaos since the death of her mother, brought the blood of madness to his head. He knew Phoebe was on her own. It was all over the parish where Annie's brat had gone, and who was paying for *that*, they were asking themselves, and Sally had let slip that Annie was over Whitehaven way selling her swills. Bugger the woman. She seemed to be doing better even than Bert Garnett, and living in a comfortable style if this kitchen was anything to go by. By heck, it wasn't to be borne the way some folk got on, especially them that didn't deserve it. As cosy a kitchen as he'd ever seen but by God he'd soon fix that, see if he didn't.

"Shut tha' bloody gob, woman." His voice was high and incensed at the injustice of it all, and *hers* as she shrieked at him, was grating on his nerves.

"Get out of my kitchen, tha' great daft loon," she was saying, her white nightdress flapping round her skinny ankles. Her hair, dark, long, straight as a ruler and heavy, with a shine on it in which the candle-light was tangled, fell across her shoulders and back. She confronted him, her white face glaring through it and when he struck her backhanded, she was knocked, sprawling, several feet across her own shining flags. She lay on her back, winded, dizzy, for the blow had landed at the side of her head. The room was swaying as she tried to stand but she saw his boot coming towards her. She did her best to avoid it but despite her efforts to protect herself, it struck her just below her ribs. The pain rocked her back, but again she tried to get up, which was a mistake for Bert Garnett's clenched fist caught her cheek-bone. The flesh split open and the blood poured from it and when he hit her again, and then again, his fist slipped in it. She had the good sense to stay down then, watching through the curtain of her blood-soaked hair as he systematically went about the business of destroying Annie Abbott's home.

She was sitting on the settle, the only seat remaining since the dogs had been tied to it, when Annie burst in through the front door. For an horrific moment, Annie wondered who she was, for the person by the fire was unrecognisable. She had Phoebe's figure, her snow-white apron with the pretty butterfly cap on her well-brushed and neatly arranged hair, but the face beneath it was swollen, the skin scraped away, the eyes, both of them no more than puffy slits set in a deep purple bruise. There was a scabby cut down one cheek and her lips were split open like rotten plums. Sweet Jesus . . . Who? . . . What? . . . She'd known . . . somehow she had known . . . all the while she was in Whitehaven . . . she'd known . . .

"Phoebe?" She could not help the questioning note in her voice. The dogs after the first nervous inclination to bark, ran forward swirling about Annie's legs for a moment before returning to crouch defensively at Phoebe's knee as though to say this time . . . *this time*, they would be ready. Not even Annie to whom they were devoted, would be allowed near her, but Phoebe touched their heads briefly before turning to stare back into the fire.

"Oh, God, Phoebe . . . sweetheart . . . who did this to you?" But of course she knew. Who else hated Annie Abbott enough to do this to the only friend Annie had? In Annie's absence he had come to the farm and beaten Phoebe's face to pulp, smashing it with his fists. She became aware then of the damage that had been done to the room. It was neat, clean, tidy but on the whitewashed walls something – what was it, for Christ's sake? – had been smeared and where there had been bowls of flowers there was nothing. The rug was gone and many of the utensils with which Phoebe had prepared and cooked their meals, and other meagre comforts she and Phoebe had made in the long winter nights. Cushions, a hodden grey shawl, even the samplers which had been brought down from the bedroom to decorate the kitchen walls. The curtains were missing and the room, though clean, was bare, as barren as it had been on the day Annie came home. Only the heavy oak table, the kist and the settle remaining and through her rage she wanted to weep. Not only for the Phoebe who had taken the beating meant for Annie, but for the Phoebe who had painstakingly, *agonisingly*, by the look of her, put back together what was left, tidied and cleaned, even herself, where any other woman would have run screaming into the night looking for help. She had picked herself up and bathed herself, tidied herself and then started on the room, but then, where would she go for help? Who besides Sally would give Phoebe the time of day, let alone a helping hand when she needed it? She was Annie Abbott's friend, wasn't she?

The figure on the settle stirred and began to mumble through her torn lips, but it was several minutes before Annie could decipher what she said.

"Take your time, darling." She had sat down beside her and gently taken her hand. From the doorway Natty watched quietly, saying nothing but knowing, as she did, who had done this. "It was Bert Garnett, wasn't it? How did he get in? Surely the dogs . . . what happened? . . . No, take your time, your poor, poor face . . . Oh, Phoebe . . . don't fret, we'll make him pay. Natty will fetch the constable . . . we'll see that he's put away . . ."

"No . . ."

"What . . ."

"Not him . . ."

Annie bent her head, for surely her ears were mistaken. Phoebe seemed to be telling her that it was not Bert Garnett who had attacked her, wrecked every room in the farmhouse – for Annie had seen Natty run up the stairs and come down again shaking his head – which was ridiculous, for who else . . . who . . . ?

"Phoebe darling, look at me . . . I know, I'm sorry, love . . . it is just . . . it must be agony to move" – and yet she had cleaned the whole place . . . "but we must know the truth. If Bert Garnett did this . . ."

"No . . . stranger . . ."

"A *stranger*? A stranger came in here, just off the fell

and ransacked the place? You let someone in that you
didn't know . . . ?" Annie shook her head in disbelief but
Phoebe remained passive, turning her face away to stare
through the slits of puffed flesh into the fire and nothing
that Annie or even Natty could say would make her change
her story.

"No," she mumbled through her painfully cut lips. The
man had not hurt her in the way bad men hurt a defenceless
woman. He had smashed his way in . . .

"But the door was not broken, Phoebe."

. . . and hit her when she had protested . . .

"There's nothing stolen, Phoebe, so why should
he . . . ?" for everything that was missing was found,
battered, torn, wrecked almost beyond repairing but safe
in the barn where Phoebe had painstakingly put it.

. . . No, she didn't know who it was . . . no, it was
not Bert Garnett and no matter what Annie said or did,
Phoebe would not change her story and at Upfell Farm Bert
Garnett smiled to himself.

26

The school in which Catriona Abbott was enrolled, though her mother had not been inside it, naturally, was devoted to the nourishment and education of the minds of those girls and young ladies whose parents wished them to be proficient in more than how to sew a sampler, speak a word or two of French, paint a watercolour or strike a chord on the piano. Its enlightened headteacher and the owner of the school, Miss Amy Mossop, was the daughter of a clergyman, now dead. He had given his only child a sound grounding in Greek, French, Latin, the arts, geography, history, literature and mathematics, all the subjects he himself had been taught as a boy and, having no son, only this one clever girl child, to whom to pass on his knowledge, he had done so along with a house set in three acres of garden in Grasmere and a small annual income. By then Miss Mossop was a spinster of some twenty-eight years, plain, sensible and not at all prepared to sit on her hands for the rest of her life. She did not care for the idea of marriage, had the possibility been open to her, and her hundred pounds a year was barely enough for herself to live on, let alone keep the large old house and the servants needed to maintain it and the gardens.

It became the 'Mossop Academy for Young Ladies' in 1839, though many of the neighbouring gentry and those able to afford the fees asked themselves why they should trust their girls to Amy Mossop? It was, they found after all, easier than going to the trouble of finding a governess. It was also very convenient to board a sometimes . . . well . . . an awkward child knowing she would be brought up exactly as she would at home. The dormitories were bright and cheerful, the dining hall well appointed and the gardens, where girls were encouraged to grow their own flowers, were private and safe.

Catriona Abbott was one of those 'awkward' children, intelligent, there was no doubt of that, but very shy, simply dressed in the plainest of hodden grey when she arrived in the carriage of Mr Reed Macauley who told Miss Mossop that the child's mother, who was a distant relative of his, wished her daughter to be educated to the highest standard. Her mother was unable to bring her, he informed Miss Mossop crisply, due to family circumstances, but she wished the child to be sent home every Friday afternoon. His carriage would fetch her, weather permitting, returning her at eight thirty sharp each Monday morning. The uniform of the school, ah yes, he agreed with Miss Mossop that young ladies should dress identically and he would see to it this very week.

Naturally, she did not voice her suspicions but Miss Mossop took it that Catriona Abbott, though she looked nothing like him, was Mr Macauley's daughter, the outcome of some misalliance outside marriage, she supposed. It did not concern her. Catriona was not the first, nor would be the last little indiscretion of the gentry, even the aristocracy, who found their way to her tolerant and fair-minded gates.

Annie had insisted that she provide her child's outfit for the school. Reed had told her about the scholarship which was to be awarded to a promising scholar, in this case her own Cat, marvelling that her child was so clever that Miss Mossop had chosen to give it to her. It included her tuition and board from Monday to Friday, Reed had told her straight-faced, but not her clothes which he would be willing to pay for but she would not hear of it.

The length of hodden-grey wool, the one she had woven and put by to make a new outfit for herself for the coming winter, had provided Cat's well-fitting, well-made dress and jacket. The egg and butter money, her new black boots. Phoebe had knitted her stockings and the crisp white cotton lace-trimmed drawers, petticoat and chemise had come from Lizzy Abbott's beautiful bedsheet, the one her mother had made with her own hands including the lace. They had wept, she and Phoebe with their arms about one another when Reed had taken Cat away, his carriage standing for all the world to see on the road at the bottom of the track which led up to Browhead. Like a little princess, she had looked, although try as they might, they could not contrive a bonnet for her, smiling, flushed, excited at the thought of going to a real school. At the last moment she had run back to hide her face in Annie's waist, clutching at her with frightened arms. She was not too sure she wanted to go off with Mr Macauley who was very stern and how was she to bear losing Blackie and Bonnie and Dandy and the flock of kittens which pranced about the yard? She had never been parted from her mother and Browhead was the only home she had known.

Annie had knelt to look into her face, unaware of the man who stood to watch them, his heart wrenched and torn with his love for her, that love written plain on his face and in the deep blue sadness of his eyes. He was doing this for her, the only thing she would allow him to do and even now she thought it was all free. If she could have taken Cat to Miss Mossop's school herself, she would have done so, but how could she shame her child by going to this wonderful place, where Cat was to learn all that she had never learned, looking like a vagrant, clean and darned and patched, but a vagrant none the less. But Reed would take her and his carriage would call for her each weekend and so she would swallow her pride and her deep aversion to accepting Reed's help on this one thing for the sake of her child.

"Darling, this is to be a great day for you and me, you know that, don't you?" she whispered into Cat's weeping face. "You are a brave and clever girl, lambkin, and such bravery and cleverness cannot be wasted. Think of what you will be able to tell Phoebe and me, to teach us when you come home at the weekend, and then there is the farm. When it is as big as Mr Macauley's it will need a clever, well-educated brain to look after it and that is what you will have. And you will be home on Friday. We will have a little party to celebrate. Would you like that, sweetheart?" and Reed Macauley had to turn away from the glowing maternal loveliness in Annie Abbott's face. God help him if she found out it was himself who was paying the fees and for the uniform which Cat would wear for five days of the week. She was so proud that she, Annie Abbott was doing this for her daughter with help from no one. That she and Cat between them, since it was Cat's cleverness that won the scholarship, had clawed their way up from their precarious beginnings to become a woman with a small but increasingly successful farm, and a child with a promising academic future ahead of her. He could not take it away from her, her belief that it was all hers and Cat's doing. It could prove to be tricky, making sure that Annie Abbott's daughter had everything that every other pupil in the school had without arousing Annie's suspicions, but he just hoped her lack of knowledge about an establishment such as Miss Mossop's would allow her to believe that it was all free.

The first weekend she came home, her legs flailing like small windmills up the track from the road and from where Reed Macauley's carriage was just drawing away, Annie was half-way down to meet her, her face alight with her radiant smile, her arms opened wide to catch her. The child flew into them and they strained together for a rapturous moment then Annie whirled her round and round, both of them laughing and half crying at the same time. About them circled the barking ecstatic dogs and, sidling indolently behind, backside swaying, tail up and curling gracefully from side to side, came Dandy. The kittens from Dandy's third – or was it fourth – litter scrambled and danced at her rear and for five excited minutes there was happy pandemonium.

"Darling, darling . . . we've missed you so . . ."

"I know, Mother . . . but the school is . . ."

"What . . . What . . . ?"

"Oh, it's splendid, Mother. Already I have learned something called 'geometry' and Miss Mossop was most gratified, that's what she said, to know that I already had some Greek and Latin, so I explained about Charlie and she said he must be a clever gentleman and I said that he had gone to Yorkshire . . ."

"Oh, sweetheart . . ." but by now Cat was rolling on the rough grass with the animals, all vying with one another to be first at her.

"Cat . . ."

"Blackie . . . Bonnie . . . Oh, Dandy. I've only been gone a week . . ."

"Cat . . ."

". . . and just wait until I show you what I painted for Phoebe . . ."

". . . Cat . . ."

"I knew she would like it because she loves flowers so."

"Cat, darling . . ."

"Where is she, Mother? . . . Where is Pheobe? I must show her . . ."

"Cat, come here to Mother, lambkin."

"But I must show Phoebe . . ."

"I know, sweetheart, but . . . well . . ."

"What is it, Mother? Where's Phoebe?"

"She's at home, darling . . ."

"Well then . . ." and the child turned, ready to scamper up the rocky track to where she knew Phoebe would be waiting, probably with one of Cat's favourites like Fig Sue or blackcurrant tart. In fact she was surprised that Phoebe wasn't here with mother and Blackie and Bonnie and Dandy, with Cat's family, for that was what they were, all those who lived under Browhead's roof.

"Cat, come here."

"Mother, I must . . ."

"CAT, come to Mother, darling. Before we go up to the house I must tell you that Phoebe is not very well."

The child stood instantly still and the satchel she held, a present from Mr Macauley, which she meant to show, in all its glory to Mother and Phoebe and of course, the animals, fell limply at the end of her arm, dragging on the grass. Blackie sniffed at it, interestedly, and so did Bonnie, absorbing its curious scent.

"Not well, Mother? What's wrong with her?"

"She . . . had a fall, lambkin, and hurt her face and . . ." How to describe to a child of almost six the strange and silent state of a young woman, for that was what Phoebe was now, who a week ago had been their cheerful, outspoken, faithful, hard-working Phoebe. Phoebe, whose face had lit up like the sun coming over the top of Great Calva whenever Annie or Cat came into the room. Phoebe, who now, when she was not scrubbing dementedly at the walls, or bare floor of the farmhouse, sat staring into the fire in the inglenook. Her face was less swollen but it was black and purple, green and yellow with the fading bruises. Scabs had formed where her flesh had split on her cheek and lips but it was not these that worried Annie but her deep and unnatural silence, her absolute refusal to talk about the event of a few days ago, and her absolute denial that the man who had attacked her and devastated their home was Bert Garnett. Natty had set to and with his usual dexterity had repaired chairs and kitchen utensils, even replacing the samplers in their frames and hanging them on the wall. He had gathered a great bunch of grasses and fading ling, placing them awkwardly in the battered copper bowl Phoebe had loved, so that their home had begun to look as it had before it had been treated with such violence. Bed linen which had been torn and sullied with the nasty waste of the attacker's body had been washed and could be repaired and the oatmeal and barley spilled from the kist in which they were stored had been gathered up and replaced. The child would not notice now any great difference in her home, only in Phoebe.

"She's not been at all well since she . . . she fell and hurt her face, so I want you to be especially gentle with her. Her poor face it is . . . well . . . it is dreadfully bruised, sweetheart and cut, so . . . you are a good, kind girl and I know you will not mean to upset her so . . . don't let her know you are . . ."

"I will show her the picture I painted for her, Mother."

"Of course, darling, that will make her feel better. She will be so pleased and happy to see you. I'm sure she will begin to mend at once."

The little girl was hesitant at first, not at all accustomed to seeing Phoebe sitting down, doing nothing but stare at the crackling logs in the fire. She moved across the kitchen to place herself in Phoebe's direct line of vision since it seemed Phoebe was not going to turn her head to look at her and her eyes widened as she looked at Phoebe's ravaged face.

"Phoebe, it's me, Cat," she said, then, hesitation gone, she clambered on to Phoebe's lap and hugged her carefully, gently, before placing a butterfly kiss on Phoebe's bruised cheek. "There," she said cheerfully. "All better now," just as Phoebe and Annie had said a hundred times to her, and Phoebe stirred and without conscious thought her arms went round the child.

"Oh, Phoebe, I've missed you so much, really I have, but I've so much to tell you and show you. I've painted the loveliest picture for you. They're chrys . . . chrys the mums . . . well, Miss Mossop has them in her study . . . yes, a study, it's called, and she sits there at a big desk and she said I could paint them. I told her about you and me being friends and she said *of course* I could bring my paints . . ."

Her voice went on and on, describing the wonders, the marvels which had been revealed to her during the past few days. Her eyes never left Phoebe's face, but they did not see Phoebe's scars, only the shining expression of love and amazed interest which had come to Phoebe's eyes. She would repeat it all again and again for her mother, for Blackie and Bonnie and Dandy, but it was as though at this precise moment, she knew with that curious wisdom which is bestowed on the very young, that *this* was for Phoebe since Phoebe had need of it.

". . . the food is not as nice as yours, Phoebe, so I'm looking forward to a blackcurrant tart . . ."

"and tha' shall 'ave it for tha' tea, sweeting, as soon as I've heated the oven . . ."

". . . and I tore the lace on my new drawers when Alice . . . she's my new friend . . ."

". . . Alice . . . that's a pretty name and I'll mend that tear as soon as ah've a minute . . ."

". . . so I'll get my satchel . . . yes, isn't it *lovely*. . . Mr Macauley said I should need it . . ."

". . . by heck, that's grand . . . grand . . . and kind of Mr Macauley . . ."

". . . isn't it, but wait until you've seen your painting. Mr Macauley said he would frame it for you . . . there . . . now what d'you think, Phoebe, aren't the colours lovely . . ."

"Eeh, lovey . . . lovey . . ."

"Now you mustn't cry, Phoebe . . . your face is not so bad . . ."

"Eeh . . . lovey . . . lovey . . . Phoebe's missed thi' . . ."

"I know . . ."

". . . and I've never had such a lovely picture, an' all me own, an' all . . ."

Beside the doorway Annie turned away. She lifted her forearm and leaned it on the wall. Placing her face in it she wept the tears of gladness, for Cat's return, for Phoebe's return and for the deep enduring love Reed Macauley gave her.

The little church of St Bridget's which stood in splendid isolation on the shores of Lake Bassenthwaite was generally full each Sunday but on the one following Cat Abbott's return from her grand school at Grasmere, every pew was jammed to capacity and several of its parishioners were forced to stand at the back. The church was very old, no one was sure just how old, since it was rebuilt in the reign of King Richard I. The register was begun in the sixteenth century and the font bowl was dated back to 1300 and in it, thirty-three years ago, Reed Macauley had been christened. There were many graves in the churchyard bearing the name of Macauley, including those of Reed Macauley's mother and father, and several containing his infant brothers and sisters.

The church was reached by a long track leading from the road between Hause and Keswick, down which, to reach St Bridget's, those with no carriage must tramp in all weathers, but today it was sunny and crisp, November, the sky the loveliest winter blue with not a cloud in sight. There was a stretch of woodland between the road and the church but round the actual building and the walled churchyard was a lush green pasture on which sheep grazed, and beyond it was the lake, its gently ruffled surface silver and the palest grey blue. Beyond the lake rose the browning fells, on and on into the distance as far as the eye could see.

Reed Macauley sat straightbacked beside his lovely young bride. Eighteen months they had been married and still no children and not likely to be if the rumours which were whispered in every drawing room and on every street corner in Keswick were true. And Mrs Macauley so elegant and fine looking, a perfect lady in her dove-grey velvet two-piece outfit, the skirt so wide after the narrow angle of the last decade, those who were already seated were quite amazed that the church aisle could take it. Her jacket bodice was shaped to her tiny waist and flared out below it with a basque extended over her hips. It was close-fitting to her long white neck and edged with a small white lace collar. The buttons which ran from neck to waist were of mother-of-pearl. Her bonnet, also of dove-grey velvet, was tiny, slipping far back on her proudly held head to reveal the astonishing golden glint of her hair. She wore pearls in her ears, neat white gloves and extremely high-heeled dove-grey kid boots. She looked quite magnificent, aloof, unconcerned with anything other than the long and tedious sermon to which she listened intently, her cloudy blue eyes never wavering from the rector's face.

Her husband was also splendidly dressed, like her in grey, but his was a charcoal grey, immaculate and expensive with a watered silk lavender waistcoat beneath his coat. A swallow-tailed coat from which a snowy white stock cascaded. His trousers were tight, well fitted, showing off his splendid calf and strapped under his instep. He carried a tall grey top hat. His face was grim, looking neither to left nor right as he had followed his wife's wide skirt up the central aisle but during the parson's sermon had there been anyone – bar the parson – in front to see, they might have noticed he closed his eyes several times and his face clamped itself into what might have been pain.

"We shall go to church this morning, Reed," Esmé Macauley had announced after breakfast. "Do not think I intend to skulk at home, hiding my face as though I had something of which to be ashamed during this . . . difficult time. I can do nothing to stop you acting as you are doing, causing gossip of the most unsavoury sort, but I can show society that I have nothing to hide."

"You *have* nothing to hide, Esmé, and I have done nothing of which I am ashamed."

"Really, then may I ask you why you are taking so much interest in the daughter of a woman who, or so I have been told, has a reputation for being . . ."

"Yes, Esmé?" Reed's voice was dangerously quiet.

"She is not married, Reed, and has a daughter. Surely that is all that need be said."

Esmé Macauley was not quite twenty years old. She had been ready to love her handsome husband though she had scarcely known him on the day they were married. He was wealthy and influential, not quite of the gentry, but then neither was she for her father's father had been a weaver and her father was of that new class, the *millocracy*, those coming to power and wealth in this new industrial age. She had been gently reared and her governess had instilled in her all that a lady should know. It was, she had hinted, quite acceptable for a man to have a mistress providing he was discreet and if she was honest, Esmé had not concerned herself when it came to her notice that Reed was no exception. She had not cared for his rough embrace and the indignities to which he subjected her, but she wanted a child so she must, to get one, perform her wifely duties, she had thought. There was no child and it mystified and distressed her, though she spoke of it to no one and certainly not to her husband. So what was she to make of his interest in the bastard called Catriona Abbott?

She had asked him since she did not want her own position in society to be jeopardised. She tried to be reasonable, calm, remembering the teachings of her governess that a lady never, *never* showed emotion, but she had her household to consider, her friends, most of whom came from Yorkshire, Cheshire, Leicestershire since she found the wives and daughters of the local society somewhat parochial.

"I have no interest in her other than to give her a decent education."

"But why? Why should you concern yourself with this child in particular, who is, after all, from the lower orders?"

Reed clamped his teeth about the fragrant cigar he was smoking and on his face came that scowling expression she had come to know so well and which, in the past, before she had learned to control herself, had made her cry. His eyebrows dipped ferociously over his eyes which had in them the blue chill which made his wife shiver, for she was an affectionate, placid girl who had known, and needed, nothing but kindness. She wanted Reed to be as her father had been. *Exactly*. Indulgent, fond, generous, not this truculent, grim-mouthed, pugnaciously jawed stranger who was always polite, who shared her bed most nights, at least for half an hour, and who often looked through her as though she were made of glass.

"This child from the 'lower orders', as you so quaintly put it, is bright, exceedingly so. She even knows a little Greek and Latin. Can you imagine that . . . ?" smiling in a way Esmé had never seen.

Esmé couldn't, since she herself scarcely knew how to add one figure to another and as for languages or dates of battles, they would just not stay inside her head, no matter how hard Miss Humphries, her governess, had tried to put them there.

". . . she can read the Bible from cover to cover and

speaks some French and is proficient in mathematics and she is no more than five or six years old."

"But who has taught her? Not her mother, surely."

"Some chap who . . . lived with them." His face closed up tight as a clam but his wife failed to notice.

"The mother's lover?"

Reed struck the mantle shelf so hard with the flat of his hand several ornaments which stood on it jumped half an inch into the air, and so did Esmé.

"No, he was not, dammit." He glared at her so fiercely she shrank away from him but nevertheless she would not give up.

"How do you know that, Reed?"

"Because I do, confound it. She is not a liar and when she told me that they were not lovers I believed her."

He had told her all she wanted to know. She was not clever, not it seemed like the woman's child was clever, but it did not take a great intellect to see the anger, the longing, the frustration which ravaged her husband, though once again his face had become smooth, closed up, his eyes expressionless.

"You and she discussed it then?" She lifted her lovely head and her upbringing and the practical Yorkshire common sense she had inherited from her father was evident in her smooth young face. She had to be a fool not to understand and inexperienced though she was, Esmé was no fool.

"For God's sake, Esmé, what sort of a question is that?"

"A simple one, I would have thought. You and she have talked of the child and her education, it seems, and from what you tell me, of other things, I am . . . I think I am entitled, as your wife, to know what she means to you?"

"She is . . . a neighbouring farmer . . . she fell on hard times and . . ."

"You helped her out."

Reed's face took on the menacing hue and expression those with whom he did business would have recognised. He was not a man to be questioned on his actions, whatever they might be, and he was certainly not going to explain to this child, even if she was his wife, the undercurrents which eddied about his relationship with Cat Abbott's mother. He had known from the first that his carriage at the gate of Browhead, with Cat Abbott in it as they drove on the road to Grasmere, and as it drove back, his coachman at the reins, again with Cat Abbott in it, would not pass by unnoticed. His name had been linked in a vague, unformed way with Annie Abbott's for some time, but the presence of Charlie Lucas had silenced the whispers. Now they were becoming a full-throated roar and he found that he did not care any more. He was sorry if they should hurt his wife since she was no more than a child herself. A child to whom he had done a great mischief, but his obsession with Annie Abbott was running out of control and he could not seem to harness it. He wanted to cosset her, hold her, protect her, wrap her in luxury and hide her deep and safe in the love which filled his heart, but she wouldn't let him and so he must do it through the child.

"This has nothing to do with our marriage, Esmé . . ."

"It has if you are to . . . to flaunt yourself with . . ."

His roar could be heard in the kitchens and the servants froze in terror. The little skivvy who was carrying a stack of pans she had just scoured, squeaked and dropped them with a deafening clatter and the butler Esmé Macauley had employed a year ago tut-tutted angrily.

"That is enough, Esmé. I will not be told how to conduct my life. Not by you, nor anyone. You are my wife and will remain so for as long as I live, but what I do outside this house is my own concern. You have my name and my protection. No one will ever harm you or insult you, in my presence or out of it." He twisted the massive gold and onyx ring he wore on the little finger of his left hand, then turned and walked toward the window, putting as much distance as he could between himself and his pretty young wife in case his snarling anger should become unleashed. He took another cigar from the gold case in his pocket, then returned to the fire to light it, inhaling deeply before he leaned down towards her. She shrank away.

His lips hardly moved as he spoke and his eyes were slivers of blue ice between his thickly lashed lids. He was in command of himself now after that curious defence-lessness.

"But you will obey me, my girl, and you will do it with that certain style you have which marks you for a lady. You will do as you have done for the past eighteen months. What you have done well. You will look after my house and my guests. Nothing will change. I will not change it. I will go to church with you. I will be here at our table and in your bed since I want a child. I don't know why we have not had one for you must admit I do my best to oblige. I am well aware that you find the . . . procedure distasteful and when you conceive I shall bother you no longer."

Her face became crimson at his coarse reference to what went on in their bed, then it drained away to leave her white and trembling, for she was afraid of this violence in her husband, wondering frantically on the emotion which had caused it.

"There is nothing more to say. Whatever you may hear about . . . the child you are to disregard it. Contrary to popular belief she is not mine and I will not have her discussed, *or* her mother in my house. Is that clear? Very well, put on your hat and we will go to church."

"Yes, Reed," she said, and went to fetch her bonnet.

They did not see Cat from the beginning of January when
the snow began until the end of February when it thawed.
They saw no one, spending the winter months cut off from
the rest of the world by the deep snow. She and Natty
had, at the first onset of the bad weather, brought down
the flock to the intakes so that if it became necessary they
could be hand fed with the hay cut from the meadow grass
in the summer. The cow, christened 'Clover' by Cat was
housed in the cow shed, cared for by Natty in the nature
of feeding, watering, mucking out and bedding. Phoebe
milked her daily, and she was justifiably proud of her dairy
work. The actual dairy was intensely cold, set on the
north-facing wall of the farmhouse as it was, even at the
height of the summer. There was a boiler, a stone floor
with a slight slope for drainage, and the walls were lined
with a great many stone shelves. It was all spotlessly
clean, the pails and crocks scoured meticulously for it
would not do to find one of Clover's hairs in the butter or
for the cheese to become too soft. There were no second
chances in a dairy.

"That butter's a long time comin'" was a timeless lament
from Phoebe, just as though she was heartily sick of the
task and for two pins would give it all up, but Annie knew
she relished it, tickled to death with the produce of her
own labour. The upright butter churn in which a long
'plunger' was 'dashed' up and down was in use twice a
week. There was a box churn which was for when only a
small quantity of butter was to be made, and when the
churned butter was ready Phoebe 'worked' it with her own
cold, bare hands to remove the excess buttermilk. She had
cream setting dishes made of the wood from the sycamore

tree, a butter board, a hand-carved butter stamp, a butter
barrel, again made of sycamore which did not taint the
flavour of the milk, and in which the butter was stored.
She heated her cheese-making milk in a copper cheese
kettle before adding the rennet and after the numerous
and complex processes through which it went, the cheese
was put in the 'press' where it would remain for weeks or
sometimes months before it was ripe for eating. Phoebe
chafed at the bad weather which kept them from the
market place in Keswick. The eggs which were not eaten
by herself, Natty and Annie were pickled in vinegar and
pepper. The butter and cheese was wrapped in a constantly changed wet cloth kept in hay and ice, brought
from wherever it formed, and stored in the barn to keep
it fresh. On the first day they were able to get to the
market place, drawing the produce on the sledge, Phoebe
was overwhelmed by the profit that was made. "Sixpence
three farthings for each pound of cheese an' all from nowt
really," she said, discounting her hard labour and refusing
absolutely to accept the few pence Annie would have given
her to spend.

"Nay, lass, buy summat for't bairn. 'Appen she'll be
'ome at weekend," and she was, receiving a rapturous
welcome from everyone, even Natty who poked a finger
in her cheek and told her she looked 'right sprightly'.

During the winter months Annie worked on her diary,
not as one might suppose a record of her social activities
but of her farm, and the past three years she had spent
on it. Begun at Charlie's suggestion, week by week she
had put down each meticulous detail of every moment of
her busy day, from early sowing and planting, weeding,
hoeing, feeding the land to the day it was all harvested,
stored, threshed, milled and the land ploughed ready for
the cycle to begin again. Each animal she possessed,
marked with her own mark, was recorded and its progress
noted, ewes, lambs, hoggs, gimmers, twinters and the
wethers, the castrated males she was fattening for sale.
When she had bought them, and from whom, and the
quality and price she got for her fleeces. All the hundreds

of details of which her farming year was made up. Her
tiny profits after she had deducted what she was forced
to buy in the way of provisions, those they could not
themselves grow or produce.

She and Natty spent hard days, sometimes until dark,
prodding long sticks into snow drifts the height of the
stone walls they faced, their dogs helping them, looking
for the 'daft buggers', as Natty called them, sheep which
continued to wander off up on to high ground. They were
all found, with the sharp nose of Natty's dog who was
more experienced than Blackie and Bonnie, digging furiously until the wanderer was released from a snowy grave.

As they worked they could see far below, the stone
of the farmhouse standing grey against the surrounding
whiteness. A wisp of smoke curled from the chimney and
inside Annie knew Phoebe would have a hot and nourishing
meal waiting for them, 'neaps and tatties' or 'crowdy'. It
was still on this day but the skies were heavy with fresh
snow waiting to fling itself down on those who were careless in their regard for the weather signs. They had fed
the ewes with their daily ration of a pound of hay, those
that had been 'tupped' in November and were already
heavy with their lambs.

Natty worked alone when he repaired the gaps in the
drystone walls on her 'inlands'. It was a never-ending task.
Deep snow drifts piled against the walls and alternating
frost and thaw inevitably caused gaps. The gap must be
pulled right down to the base and rebuilt. The job, long
and exhausting, could only be done when spare time was
available. Natty tidied the barn and the cow shed and
spread the fields, when the snow allowed it, with manure.
To earn a bob or two and at the right time of the year, it
was his custom to help the keeper of a local landowner's
estate by acting as a 'beater' during the grouse-shooting
season, and, for a lark, and to see if she could do it without
being spotted, Annie joined him. She was inevitably
noticed since she was by now a familiar figure in her
threadbare jacket and breeches, her gaiters and wooden-
soled clogs. She wore her heavy woollen jerkin beneath

the jacket and a long muffler wound about her neck. Her soft felt hat, the brim turned down, was pulled well over her forehead but when the keeper, a man called Abel Greenwood bade her a dour "Morning, lass", she was quite astonished, not that she should have been recognised but that she should have been spoken to. More amazing still was the nod Jackie Ingham, a neighbouring cottager, aimed in her direction and the gruff "tekk the drag, lass" from another, Willy North. As she said later to an equally astonished Phoebe, you could have knocked her down with a feather. "Are they beginning to accept me, Phoebe, at last?" she asked.

"'Appen the men, chuck, but it'll tekk time wit wimmin."

Sometimes Annie felt that Phoebe was the older of the two of them. She was cheerful again now, her old self after the beating from the 'stranger' but she had an old head on young shoulders, careful and prudent without Annie's inclination towards humour. She took her position as 'housekeeper' very seriously. She was neat and exacting, brusque with Natty if he should bring muck in on to her clean kitchen floor. Big-hearted and generous, she was nevertheless always conscious of the precarious state of their world and was never careless or carefree in the way she approached each day.

At the end of March, a Friday, the burning of the heather began. There was a light wind blowing, the heather was tinder-dry, the air crisp and clean and below where Annie and Natty stood they could see more than one dale spread out before them. The heather was to be burned in strips so that the sheep and grouse who were to benefit from it could pass easily through it, seeking out the various stages of regrowth which were the reason for burning it. The breeze must be at a man's back. A handful of bracken was set alight, transferred to the dry heather and from there carried along the desired line.

Phoebe was 'pegging out' a line of snow-white, billowing undergarments, those which her lambkin had worn and brought home from school. Though the day was nearly over there was a good 'drying wind' and an hour or two would see this little lot ready for ironing. The child had begged to go up and find her mother, wanting her to see her painting but Phoebe had said no, wait in the yard, she'd not be long and here, eat this oatcake she'd made while she waited. Her satchel was still on the step and guarding it were Blackie and Bonnie for they were not allowed on the fell when the burning was in process. Natty's dog, in canine years as old as her master, had found a sliver of sun in which she dozed but suddenly, though nothing untoward had happened, at least that Phoebe had noticed, all three sprang to their feet, their hackles rising and to her horror, Blackie and Bonnie lifted their heads and howled.

Dear sweet Lord! The clothes peg she held in her mouth fell to the ground and instinctively she looked around for the child.

"Cat, where is't tha', come to Phoebe, lambkin," for whatever it was that had set the dogs to making such a din it must surely be frightful, and might it not be threatening the child?

"Cat . . . where is't tha', Cat?" she quavered but she was not there and Blackie and Bonnie were acting in the strangest way, crouched and quivering, their tails between their legs, their ears flat on their heads as they both stared up towards the line of fire on the fell.

"Tha' should've asked Jackie Ingham and Willy North to give us a hand, lass," Natty said as he struck the tinder.

"We can manage, Natty. I'll beat at this flank and you keep to the other. It's not a long line and we can easily hold it in check between us. I can't afford any more wages, you know that. Not after paying you," for she had kept her promise, giving him the full labourer's wage of £8 a half year plus his food and room over the loft.

The burning went well. The flames advanced in a long, sizzling, crackling, smoking line, leaving behind a charred dark blue mass of pungent-smelling ash. The lusty growth in front of the line of fire contrasted sharply with the charred remains it left at the back, where next year the new green shoots would show. The rotational burning of the heather was to help both sheep and grouse but it must be done before the bird nesting season began. If the spring was wet, chances to burn were few and Annie pressed ahead, allowing the line to get longer and longer, the distance between herself and Natty growing until there was a great swathe of fire in the middle which was unsupervised.

Neither of them, frantically beating to control their end of the line of leaping flames saw the small figure of Cat Abbott, nor heard her excited child's voice as she called to her mother, for the noise the flames made was loud and angry. She ran towards them up the slope, the breeze blowing into her laughing face, exactly in the centre of the line of fire which was galloping in her direction, greedily devouring everything in its dry path. She wore her hodden-grey dress and jacket, the outfit already becoming too short for her. In her hand she carried a sheet of paper, upon which was a painting of Blackie, Bonnie and Dandy and which she had finished during the past week. She had a talent for it, Miss Mossop had told Annie in one of her polite reports and she hoped Mrs Abbott would not mind if it was encouraged.

Cat Abbott stopped when she saw the line of flames leaping towards her, paralysed by the sight and the speed with which it approached. The laughing anticipation with which she had run to meet her mother was quenched in total, panic-stricken terror. Her clever brain which at the age of six and a half could cope easily with the mathematical problems Miss Mossop set her, became blank, senseless, without thought or reason as the fire flew across the dry heather towards her.

It was her mother's agonised scream and the hoarse shout which tore from Natty Varty's throat which moved her, turned her, set her little legs to running away from the conflagration but it was too late by then. She tripped at the last moment, her face pressed into the heather as the flames swept over her.

*　　*　　*

Phoebe's hand went to her mouth as the most appalling sense of dread trickled icily through her veins. When the screams began, high and demented, leaping from fell to fell and rock to rock, echoing and echoing so that women in their farm kitchens cowered and covered their ears, Phoebe began to run, the three dogs close at her heels. She was already weeping, the breath rasping painfully in her chest as her legs propelled her across the beck behind the farmhouse and up the grassy slope of the intakes and beyond to where the heather began. She could see the line of fire, badly out of control, coming towards her, but guided by the instincts of the dogs she veered off, following them round it and across the smoking, pungent-smelling carpet of burnt heather. For some reason Natty Varty was running like a hare, *away* from her, going across and up the slope of Cockup in the direction of Dash Beck but it was not to him her eyes were drawn but to the kneeling, rocking, moaning figure of Annie Abbott who cradled something in her arms. Phoebe could not immediately recognise it but when she did her cries echoed Annie's, causing the women who had come to their kitchen doors to stare, eyes shielded, up the hill, to cower back again inside, drawing their children with them. One was Sally Garnett.

It was Reed Macauley who took charge, brought from Long Beck by the grey-faced trembling old man who had once been the phlegmatic and unruffled Natty Varty. He could not speak at first, so deep was the shock he was in and Reed had to shake him roughly to bring him from the appalled and appalling state into which the sight of Cat Abbott and her deranged mother had sent him. It was Reed Macauley who had sent him to Browhead in the first place but it was Annie Abbott who kept him there. He had developed to his own astonishment, a growing admiration for the woman who employed him. For her steadfast refusal to be browbeaten, for her spirit which snapped its fingers at those who tried it, for her courage and faith and hope, her humour and loyalty and her tenacious determination and belief that she and her family, which it seemed

included not just Phoebe but himself, would find success.
She was so proud of her child, and rightly so. She worked
the work of ten men, she was beautiful and, he had
discovered, she was honourable.

There were men, those who worked for Reed Macauley
and who had followed him, for surely something of a shocking nature had occurred. Natty Varty had been incoherent
but when they saw what it was they covered their eyes
and their mouths with shaking hands and one, Jake Singleton, who was Mr Macauley's yardman with a snug little
cottage at the back of the farm with a wife in it, sent for
her and any other woman who would help, for surely Mr
Macauley would need it.

Reed brought them down from the hill, Annie and Cat
and Phoebe. Annie was so deep in shock as she stumbled
after Reed Macauley she was no trouble to anyone. The
women took her and her child and Mr Macauley stood in
the farmyard his arms still curved in the gentle cradle in
which he had carried down the burned body of Catriona
Abbott. Tears streamed across his blanched face and his
lean figure trembled as Natty's had done but when his
men, awkward with sympathy would have drawn him
towards his home since there was nothing else he could
do here, was there? he turned on them snarling.

"Leave me be, you fools. For the love of God, don't
touch me or I swear I'll kill the first man who does. I must
stay here. She might need me."

It was then he noticed Phoebe. The women, Maggie
Singleton, Jake's wife, Nell Tyson and Lily Gill, whose
husbands all worked for him in his yard and stable and
on the fells herding his flocks, had disappeared into the
farmhouse, but nobody seemed to consider the strange
and silent behaviour of the young woman who worked for
Annie Abbott. She was not *family*, merely a servant at
Browhead and so worthy of no particular attention, they
had assumed, but Reed knew better.

She was pegging out the small undergarments she had
boiled and scrubbed and rinsed only an hour ago. The
dogs, bewildered and frightened by the death and chaos

which had entered their lives, slunk about her as though the normality of her task reassured them and hovering at her back was Natty Varty as though he felt the same.

Reed moved slowly towards her, his body bent and ancient in his furious grief. His face was still wet with tears, the furrows deep in it and his mouth worked painfully as though he could not come to terms with this frightful and surely mortally wounding blow which had come to strike his love.

"Phoebe," he said gently, "will you come inside?"

"Nay, ah've things of t' child's ter see to."

"But surely one of the women will . . . see . . . here is someone." For running headlong down the path was Sally Garnett, her plump figure all over the place, her hair streaming out behind her with the force of her speed. "She will help you . . ."

"Nay, ah must see to it. Cat'll need them . . ."

"Phoebe," his voice was anguished. "Leave them . . . please."

"Ah've work to do 'ere, Mr Macauley and I'll thank thee to let me ger on wi' it."

He took her arm, or tried to but she shook him off, turning on him like a spitting cat but still he tried to draw her away.

"Leave me be. Cat'll need . . ."

"*No she won't*, Phoebe. Cat . . . is gone. She doesn't need . . ."

"So she's to be put in her coffin in them . . . in them things she 'as on then? Well, I'll not let my lambkin go off to Heaven in stinking clothes . . . all . . . black . . . an' . . . No! . . . let me be, Mr Macauley. I want this lot dry an' ironed before dark so that . . . so that . . . oh, sweet, sweet Jesus, so that she is . . . tidy an' clean. Now, get out of me way fer ah've things ter do. . . ."

It was traditional to 'bid' two people from each farm in the area in which a funeral was to take place but no such custom was carried out for the funeral of Annie Abbott's child. The small coffin was watched constantly until the day of the funeral by the women of Reed Macauley's

household, taking it in turns with Sally Garnett, who, with
a fierce bravery furnaced by her sympathy for Annie
Abbott had defied her husband's rage and left her four
children – she was still nursing Aggie – and him to fend
for themselves. Phoebe had dressed Cat in her sweet-
smelling, freshly ironed undergarments and with only her
unmarked face showing above the white, lace-trimmed
cover which lay over her, the child seemed to sleep.
Phoebe had baked the 'arvel bread' which would be served
to the men and women who would walk the 'corpse way'
with the coffin. She had put herself and the silently distant
figure of Annie Abbott into the black dresses Mr Macauley
had produced from somewhere, Annie making no demur,
as she made none about anything but her absolute refusal
to leave her child's side where she stayed for two days
and nights. She had not shed a tear since they had brought
her down from the fell. Her eyes burned fanatically in their
sockets and when anyone spoke to her she turned them
on the speaker with what seemed to be hatred. She
addressed not a word to anyone, not even Mr Macauley
who was there day and night, going home only to bathe
and shave and change his shirt. There was hatred in her,
bitter and venomous and it could be felt in the farmhouse,
in the air they breathed and the food Phoebe cooked and
which they ate. She hated. She hated the gods or God
who had done this to her. She hated the world which had
forced her into the life she had led. She hated the men
and women who peopled it, even those who now helped
her. Where was Cat?

They took her to the church of St Bridget's by the
lake, over the corpse way, for any departure from the
recognised route would have been regarded as an ill omen.
In certain parts of the district it was necessary to remove
fencing so that a funeral procession might pass along the
traditional route and all along the way there were 'resting
stones' so that those carrying the coffin, often containing
a large corpse, might rest the coffin and themselves. No
such rests were required for Cat Abbott. Reed Macauley
was one of the bearers. Jake Singleton was the other and

behind him walked Annie Abbott and her maidservant Phoebe, side by side but not touching. Natty was there and Sally and several members of Reed's household. Will Twentyman came with Eliza for they remembered Annie Abbott's cheerful, willing labour in The Bull three years ago and the placidly silent child who was being buried today. There was a quiet woman dressed all in black who turned out to be Miss Mossop. No one else. Not a woman nor a man from Gillthrop or Hause for it was their belief that the sins of the fathers were visited on the sons, and surely mothers and daughters came into the same category.

They all went back to their homes after the funeral, leaving Annie and Phoebe beside the grave, with Natty a respectful distance behind, and lying quietly at his back were his dog, Blackie and Bonnie. Reed stood at the church gate, waiting, waiting for her to speak, to turn to him, to acknowledge his presence which, as yet, she had not done since Cat died, but when she and Phoebe went by him, neither looked in his direction. He might not have existed.

"Let me know if anything is needed, Natty," he said as the old man made to follow them. "Anything, no matter what it is. If she needs me . . . speaks of me at all . . ." since he was beyond caring now about anything but the withdrawn, hating grief which corroded inside Annie Abbott. The neighbourhood was agog with speculation, gossiping about him and the woman from Browhead, for surely his behaviour over the death of her daughter, his constant presence in the farmhouse, his purchase of mourning dresses and the bonnets – which *she* had not worn, it was said, though the maid had perched one on her dark head – his attendance as pall-bearer, meant that he was deeply involved with Annie Abbott. It had been enough when he sent the child to school and paid for her tuition but since then he had not been over the fell to Browhead himself, sending his carriage and coachman each week, when the weather allowed, to take and bring back Annie Abbott's daughter from Grasmere. The gossip had foundered and the speculation died down since it had nothing to feed on, but now, with the death of her daughter, tragic as it was, the conjecture had sprung up again. They felt so sorry for his wife, poor thing, sitting there all alone in her drawing room whilst her husband, not to mention half her women servants, spent days and nights under Annie Abbott's impure roof.

Reed Macauley shrugged his shoulders and ignored them. Not that anyone had the nerve to speak directly to him, or even, in his presence, make an out-of-place remark. They would not dare, for his temper was uncertain at the best of times. He seemed not to care at all that his reputation was finally and irrevocably in tatters.

Not a man, or woman, in the district would have found fault with him, nor thought it out of place if he had carried on an illicit affair with the 'woman from Browhead' as she was increasingly called, providing he had been discreet about it. But he had not. He had made it very obvious where his affections and loyalty lay. He had flown in the face of convention, flaunting his misdemeanours and they did not care for it.

Reed Macauley no longer even noticed their averted faces. He would stay away from her, for a while, he told himself as he watched her walk gracefully away from him as he had watched her on that first day, over three years ago at Penrith, but not because of them and what they said about him and Annie behind his back, but to give her time to steady herself. To do her grieving, come out of the shocked state into which Cat's death had impelled her; to recover a little, to accept. Natty would watch out for her and Maggie Singleton, who had turned out to be a dependable woman. Report on her progress, her health, her farm, her household. If help was needed, with her flock, her crops, he would provide it. She would want for nothing he could give her. He would wait, he loved her and his love made him patient, a characteristic he had never before known.

He turned then, striding off towards the lower slope of Ullock Pike and Longside Edge. He would walk back to

Long Beck – he would not say 'home' since his home was where Annie Abbott was – climbing over Bassenthwaite Common and Broad End and down past Dead Crags to White Water Dash waterfall. Long Beck was just beyond it. Long Beck and Esmé.

Edmund Hamilton-Brown did not like to see his little girl
in tears. He never had done and if there was anything he
could do to prevent tears from sliding down her cheeks in
that heart-rending way they had he would do it. From
being an astonishingly beautiful baby, pink and white, silver
gold and blue, he had adored her. She was the most
treasured of his possessions, and he owned a great many
of those. He had been reluctant to part with her at the age
of seventeen, even into the wealthy, important and competent hands of Reed Macauley. Of course, girls were
married in his society from the age of sixteen, transferred
from one man's care to another, always advantageously,
and he knew Esmé must do the same, but it had been the
most difficult thing he had had to do in his life. She was
his only living child, and she, and the fortune she would
inherit when he had gone, must be put in the charge of a
man who could look after both, but his house would be
empty without her. Her childish, lilting laughter, her bobbing ringleted embrace, her kisses when she badly wanted
something she thought he might consider foolish, the way
she had of snuggling on his knee and telling him of what
she had done whilst he had been at the mill, her fragrance,
her schoolgirl giggles in a corner with her friends, her
flounces of satin, her extravagance, her innocence,
her loveliness. She was the light of his life, though his
gruff Yorkshire heart would not have admitted it had he
been put to the torture. He had given her, from the
moment she could talk, everything she had ever asked
for, delighting in her delight, besotted and extravagantly
indulgent. She was a lady, in his eyes, from being a small
girl, surveying the world with a cool, charming stare, her

cloudy blue eyes, which were sometimes, depending on the light, a clear turquoise, delighting in what her Papa made it for her. She knew she was beautiful and saw no reason to learn her letters and add up a sum or two for her Papa's household made a fuss of her whatever she did, and he was inclined to agree for what did a *lady* need of these things? She would marry well, present him with grandchildren, preferably boys who would go into his mills, and his old age would be pleasantly spent introducing them into the world of yardage and quality, of profit and loss, of expansion and gain.

He had been considerably put out when she had confided to him that his dinner guest from way up in the wilds of Cumberland, a man with whom he had done business on several occasions since the quality of his fleeces had been of the best, had taken her fancy, and could Papa please get him for her? Not in those words, of course, since Esmé was gently reared, a well brought up young lady with no knowledge of the world, of men or of business and was not even aware that Cumberland was a great deal further away from Bradford than Shipley, or even Halifax. He was not at all prepared to let her go so far away though he did not say so, putting forward the charms of this young man and that, sons of nearby business associates and personal friends, but it had not done at all. She had cried, great fat crystal tears which had wrenched at his heart. Mr Macauley's affections might be engaged elsewhere, he had said desperately, and her tears had flowed the harder.

When, with what he thought was great tact and delicacy, he had approached Reed Macauley, amazingly the man had been willing, saying that he had been looking for a young, well brought up wife, and, it seemed his Esmé was exactly what he wanted.

He himself had wept in the privacy of his room when Esmé drove off in the carriage with her new husband, waving and smiling, exquisite in her happiness and he had turned away from the harrowing pictures of what Reed Macauley would do to her that night. Instead he began to look ahead to those grandchildren he would have and the visits they and their mother would pay him. Long loving visits when the house would be filled again with her high excited laughter, the pretty parcels she would have brought in from the carriage, parties, dances, dinner guests. It would all come alive again. The nursery would be filled again. With the advent of the railways, all the way from Carlisle right down into Yorkshire, Cumberland was not so far away, was it? he asked his passive wife, who counted for nothing in his life except for the bounteous gift she had given him in his Esmé. Isabel Crowther was twenty when they married and himself thirty-five and Esmé had been the last fruit of his loins, born when he was forty-six years old. There were half a dozen before Esmé lying in the graveyard. So far none of his dreams had materialised. Two years his Esmé and Reed Macauley had been wed and her still not a mother. It was hard to understand for what he had seen of Reed Macauley he would have said he was a lusty man, not a man to waste time in the getting of a family, though the image this conjured up was not one he dwelled on. Esmé's tear-soaked letter came as a bombshell in the middle of the silent breakfast he shared with his wife of thirty years. His roar of rage rattled the coffee-cups and shook the chandeliers and in her chair at the foot of the table Isabel dropped her spoon into the bowl of creamy porridge she ate each morning. It splattered up and over the bodice of her dark brown morning dress but it went unnoticed as she gaped in terrified amazement at her snarling husband. The maidservants – Edmund did not care for butlers and footmen and such fiddle faddle, the only men he employed working in the yard, the garden and the stables – cowered back against the sideboard, clutching coffee-pots and cream jugs to their palpitating breasts.

"The bloody bastard's fornicating with another woman," he roared. "No wonder he's not got my Esmé in the family way. Playing a game away from home, the talk of the bloody parish, she says . . ." brandishing the letter as though he would dearly like to smash the fist which held it into Reed Macauley's face ". . . some damned farm woman he's taken up with and he's round there from morning till night . . . an' through the night an' all, I'll be bound. Well, we'll see about that. There's no sod going to play fast and loose with my Esmé's affections, I can tell you that, woman . . ." just as though the whole thing was the fault of the open-mouthed, white-faced trembling figure who sat at the foot of his table. *His* Esmé, not hers, as she had always been. The two maid-servants, now that they realised that the savage anger of their master was aimed, not at them, but at Miss Esmé's husband, or so it seemed, relaxed their hold on one another and exchanged a glance for this promised to bring a frisson of excitement into the long tedium of their hard-working day. Wait until they got back to the kitchen, the exchanged glance seemed to say. Wouldn't they have something to tell the others? They simultaneously edged a little closer so that they would not miss anything.

Suddenly aware of them, for even in the midst of the direst emergency Edmund Hamilton-Brown was careful of his mouth, he turned on them so that they again reared back.

"And you two can clear off. I'll ring the bell when I need you."

There was nothing for it but to leave the breakfast room but they had the meat of it, hadn't they, and the rest would soon be revealed, one way or the other. Scandal always was.

"What are you . . . to do, Edmund?" his wife quavered. Edmund leaped to his feet, his wrath too much to contain sitting down. He strode to the window, flinging aside the heavy velvet curtains which were fashionable but which kept out most of the daylight. The fringed bobbled tie-backs bounced with his ferocity and his wife winced. He turned again, his wildness flaring about him, his blue eyes withering her, his mouth twitching, the saliva almost running down his chin.

"I'll tell you what I'm going to do. I'll tell you what I'm going to do, woman. I'm going up to bloody Cumberland

and I'm going to sort this lot out. No one, *no one's* going
to make a fool of my Esmé. No one's going to make my
girl cry, or if he does he'll live to regret it. I'm not without
some influence and in my years of doing business I've
come across some gentlemen who owe me a favour or
two. They'll make Reed bloody Macauley toe the line I
can tell you. I should have known. The high-faluting, ladi-
dah boyo with his fancy duds and fancy ways," his voice
became vicious, "but he'll rue the day he made my Esmé
shed tears, that he will. Now then, set them girls to
packing my bags and send that stable lad to the station to
find out the time of the next train to Carlisle or Penrith,
or wherever the nearest railway station is to bloody
Long Beck. I've a bit of business to attend to at the mill
but I'll be back in an hour. Is the carriage at the door?
Good, then jump to it, woman. I've not got all bloody
day."

Reed had kept his promise. He had not been over to
Browhead but each day he made enquiries of Maggie
Singleton, who had, questioning her closely on Miss
Abbott's health and state of mind. Was she eating, sleeping, working on the farm, or up on the fell? Maggie was
to collect the eggs, and the butter and cheese that maidservant of Miss Abbott's made and see that they got to
market. How? How did he know? There was a pony and
trap in the stables. Could she drive one? She could. Good,
and if she hadn't the time, or Miss Abbott needed her,
surely there must be some farmwife with whom Maggie
was acquainted who could take them, and of course, she
would be paid for her efforts. She was to keep him
informed. Take any profits made down to Miss Abbott's
farm, talk to Natty Varty and Jake could go with her and
any help Natty needed at Browhead, Jake was to supply
it. Now was there anything else, he asked the astonished
young wife of Jake Singleton? Anything Maggie herself
could think of to make Miss Abbott's grief less . . . well
. . . easier to bear? He was putting Miss Abbott's welfare
in *her* hands since, as yet, Maggie had no children, she

and Jake having been wed no more than six months. Jake was Reed Macauley's yardman and Maggie worked in the dairy but they were to consider themselves, for the moment, as working for Miss Abbott, was that clear? Just until Miss Abbott recovered from the dreadful death of her child.

Maggie Singleton came from Sharrow Bay on the far side of Lake Ullswater and Annie Abbott's reputation was unknown over there. She had heard tales, since she had come to live at Long Beck, of her strangeness and the odd way she dressed, but she had never seen her, and her true 'wickedness', the gossip and speculation about her relationship with Mr Macauley, were none of Maggie's concern. She was unbiased and unprejudiced and Reed could not have chosen a more kindly, tolerant young woman to keep an eye on the woman he loved. She saw Miss Abbott twice a week. Once when she slipped into the Browhead kitchen to collect the stuff for market from Phoebe, and again when she took her the money they had earned. She did not speak to Miss Abbott. The silently staring, white-faced, dead-eyed woman who sat all in black on the sconce aroused a fierce compassion in her but they were strangers to one another and she could not intrude into the grief-wracked world in which Miss Abbott dwelled.

She did not say this to Mr Macauley, poor man. He was not himself at all these days, almost as bad as Miss Abbott, she would have said, moving about the farmhouse without his usual crackling vigour, his fierce, dauntless energy which defied any man to keep up with him. From six in the morning, she had heard, up on the fells, or rummaging about the farm making sure every man who worked for him was *doing* it, ten to the dozen. Off on his wild black mare to Keswick or Penrith or Carlisle and even, Jake told her, travelling down to London on the railway train. Tireless, bloody-minded, but ready to dirty his hands, not like some, a real man and would you look at him now, drifting about the place as though he had no idea how to fill his day, only brightening when she herself approached him.

"How is she? Did you see her?" he would ask, no matter who was with him, even Mrs Macauley, who had gone as white as the driven snow at his words. She had run into the house, she had, her skirts in her hands, and Maggie had felt sorry for her, as well as him.

"She's calm, sir," was all Maggie could say, for what else *was* there to say? She's off her head with grief? She's in another world? She never speaks and only eats when Phoebe makes her open her mouth and sticks food inside?

"Calm? What the bloody hell does that mean?"

"She's grieving, sir, and still not herself, but from what I hear she's a strong woman and will recover."

"Aye . . ." he said, ready to turn away. He swung back violently at her next words:

"And she's young, sir. She's plenty of time to have another child."

"Another child! What are you blathering on about, woman? She's not even married." His face had lost its usual healthy colour during the past few traumatic weeks and now it became even more drained. His eyes were haunted but the menace in them was lethal. Nevertheless Maggie stood her ground. She had been asked to keep an eye on Annie Abbott and report back to Mr Macauley. Give her opinion on her condition and that was what she was doing.

"That could be remedied, sir."

"Remedied! What the hell does that mean?" he said for the second time.

"She's a beautiful woman, sir, with a farm which is beginning to prosper . . ."

"Prosper, prosper! A beautiful woman. Jesus Christ. She's just lost her child and here you are with her waltzing up the aisle on the arm of some fortune hunter and ready to give birth within the year. Are you mad . . . ?"

But it was not Maggie Singleton who was mad. She realised she had gone too far. She had been trying to comfort, to give him hope, though really, need she have bothered? He wanted to hear that Miss Abbott was recovering, but at the mention of the possibility that she could return to what Maggie thought of as a normal life for a woman, a house, a husband, children, he had been ready to turn on her and knock her to the ground. It was a strange job she had been given and one she did not relish. She felt a great and overwhelming pity for Miss Abbott. Though she herself had no child as yet, she was a woman, and already within her grew the seed her husband had implanted in her three months ago so she could guess, to a small degree because of it, what Miss Abbott was suffering. But what she did not care for was the way in which the other servants, knowing where she went, questioned her about Miss Abbott's home, her demeanour, just as though the poor woman was a . . . well, a loose woman and was available to every man who had a bob in his pocket. Poor woman. Gripped fast in the inflexible blackness of her mourning and them in the kitchen at Long Beck were only interested in the colour of her petticoats and the width of her bed. Prying and poking into what did not concern them. Lily and Nell, the two women who had 'laated' with Maggie before the child was buried, were more sympathetic. They had seen Annie Abbott's grief, her devastation. They had done their pitying best to contain it, but the others were 'nowt a pound' as far as Maggie was concerned.

There was a carriage, a hired hack, coming up the track towards the front of the house and Reed Macauley turned away from the troubled figure of Maggie Singleton to stare without much interest at its progress. Its wheels bounced crazily between the ruts, it was going with such speed, and when it came to an abrupt stop, the door to it was flung open with such force it hit the window of the carriage with a crash which lifted a flock of crows from the nearby trees. A man sprang to the gravelled driveway. Not a young man but expensively turned out in an impeccably cut black broadcloth frock-coat with waistcoat and trousers of the same material, the latter not quite as tight-fitting as was thought fashionable, for the man was portly. He carried a long, double-breasted chesterfield overcoat and on his head was a tall, silk top hat.

For a moment Reed was astounded. What the devil was Esmé's father doing here? In the years since he and Esmé had become engaged to be married, and since their marriage, Edmund Hamilton-Brown had been to Long Beck only once and that was on the occasion of the party to celebrate their engagement. It had been Edmund Hamilton-Brown's suggestion that it be held at Long Beck and at the time Reed had been well aware that it had been no more than an excuse for the man to inspect the house and the surroundings where his daughter would live, the servants who would wait on her, and Reed's friends and acquaintances with whom she would socialise. He had made it his business to poke here and there in every room that was available to him, noting the contents and their value, checking the service she would receive since it must be efficient, and looking over Reed's guests to ensure they were fit to sit in his daughter's drawing room. Had he found any deficiency in either the house, the service, or the people with whom she would come into contact he would, no doubt, have rectified it. Since then the only visiting done had been on Esmé's part when she returned to Bradford, and by Reed himself as business called him to that part of the world where he sold his wool.

"Edmund, this is a surprise," he called out as he moved from the side garden where he had been talking to Maggie Singleton, his hand outstretched, for despite his own misery, the civilities must be carried out, particularly to one's father-in-law.

At that moment, before Reed could reach him, the door to the house flew open, Edmund turned in its direction, dropped his overcoat to the ground and with an incoherent cry, opened his arms wide to receive his weeping daughter.

"Papa . . . oh, Papa . . . thank heavens you have come," she cried into his broad shoulder. He held her close and patted her back whilst he shushed her comfortingly, and all the while he turned an expression on Reed

Macauley which would have badly alarmed a lesser man. His face was broad and fleshy, highly coloured, for though his doctor advised against it, he drank a great deal of port and brandy and was rarely without an expensive cigar clamped between his teeth.

It was his grandfather who had begun it, the business which had made Edmund wealthy. He had been a merchant who had gone with his string of packhorses wherever there was decent wool to be had, bringing it back to independent men to be spun and woven. But as the industrial revolution, as it was to be called, had intensified he had, from the profit he made, built his own mill in which weavers and spinners, as their trade declined, worked for him. One mill, then two, as his son grew to manhood. A carding and combing mill, then another as Edmund Hamilton-Brown himself took over and though he had never known want, since he and his father before him had called themselves rich, he was, as Yorkshire men had the reputation of being, a careful man except where his daughter and *himself* were concerned. The best of everything for Esmé and Edmund Hamilton-Brown, and his appearance testified to it.

"To what do we owe the honour of this visit, Edmund?" Reed managed to say, doing his best to be polite though did he give a hang *why* the old man was here? he asked himself wearily. He had been badly shaken by Maggie Singleton's careless inference to the probability of marriage for Annie Abbott and to her bearing another child. He had wanted to hit her and tell her to shut her vile mouth. Annie belonged to him. Not bodily, not yet, but surely when she had recovered somewhat from this mortal blow which had been struck her, she would agree to let him look after her, to settle her and Phoebe in some luxurious place away from all these bad memories, to give her the soft and special things she deserved so that she could live a life of ease and never again worry her head about money. *He* would do that for her. He would love her, care for her, protect her from all hurt and if there was any child to be given, *he* would be the one to give it to her.

"Never mind that, Macauley," his father-in-law was saying, jolting him out of the pleasant dream of the future which was the only thing that mattered to him now. He cared nought for his farm, for his businesses, his investments in copper, in iron, in the railways and many other concerns, those which had made him a wealthy man. He would do again, of course, when he and Annie were together and Annie was tucked up safe and snug, but all he could think of just now was the slow worry which invaded him night and day, and the impatience he must curb until it was all over. His wife's tears concerned him not in the least. She was always weeping over something these days, moping about the house, refusing to go out or entertain, which he was glad about since the idea of engaging in small-talk at the dinner table was abhorrent to him. But it would all die down, the gossip and speculation, when Annie moved out of the district. He was a man. The men who did business with him would think him a lucky dog and wish him well of his liaison with the Browhead woman, and the women would do as they were told. As his would when he had found out what her father wanted and sent him on his way. Reed Macauley might be low, not quite himself lately, but he was master of his own home, and his own life.

"Let's get inside, my lass," Edmund said gently, his arms still about the heaving shoulders of Reed Macauley's wife. "See, you go and wash your face and have a rest. You and I'll have a nice chat later. I've things to say to your . . . . husband but it'll not take long."

"Won't you have some coffee, Papa, or a . . ."

"Nay lass, off you go. I'll have something when you come down."

He kissed her fondly then watched her as she drifted up the stairs, a tired little girl whose world, which had been so safe and happy, which *he* had made safe and happy, was tumbling about her innocent head.

"Right then, lad," he snarled at Reed when she had disappeared, "you and me have something to talk about, I think. Tell that chappie who brought me from Penrith he can get off now and have one of your servants fetch my coat in. I dropped it by the coach. And I'll have a brandy and some sandwiches. I'm taking the three thirty train back to Lancaster and I reckon you can find someone to take me to the railway station."

"Certainly." Reed's voice had become chilled. He was not used to being given orders, nor to being spoken to as though he was a schoolboy who had misbehaved. He was beginning to get an inkling of the reason for his father-in-law's visit and though he was not overly concerned he did not greatly care for the idea of being given a talk on discretion by his wife's father. Still, best get it over and send the silly old fool on his way. He had guided Edmund Hamilton-Brown into his study, indicating brusquely that he should seat himself by the cheerful fire which burned in the grate. He pulled the bell rope and when the butler came, gave the necessary orders, then lighting a cigar he went to stand by the window, looking out across the vista of his garden and beyond to the slopes of his in-land fields. They were white with his ewes which were waiting to lamb, a constantly drifting scatter, forming and re-forming into tiny groups which cropped peacefully on the lush green grass the snows of the winter had nourished.

"You know why I'm here." Edmund had found it difficult to control himself whilst his daughter moved slowly up the stairs, whilst his son-in-law nodded courteously and the butler and parlourmaid set out the decanter and glasses, the delicious sandwiches which had so quickly appeared, and the servants had barely left the room before he began. He held the brandy glass in a trembling hand and he looked ready to throw it at Reed rather than drink what it contained.

"I can guess." Reed did not turn round. His voice was indifferent.

"Is that all you have to say then?"

"What do you want me to say?"

"You have the bloody gall to . . . to carry on a filthy affair with some trollop of the district . . ."

"Be careful what you say, Hamilton-Brown." Hamilton-Brown took no notice.

". . . carrying whatever diseases she might herself have to my daughter for I don't reckon you'll have stopped paying her the attention a man pays his wife. But as if that wasn't disgusting enough, you flaunt it about the bloody district as though it concerned no one . . ."

"It doesn't."

"Is that so? Well, you're wrong, you bastard. It concerns my girl and what concerns her concerns *me*. I'll not have it, d'you hear. I'll not have her name dragged all over Cumberland and probably Yorkshire too, since news travels fast, and I'll not have her made unhappy. I've never cared to see her weep and she's weeping now and that's your fault. It's got to stop. She's your wife and I'll have her treated with some respect . . ."

"Oh, for God's sake, man, who do you think I am? Some sixteen-year-old boy who has been trifling with the under parlourmaid . . ."

"You'd get a thrashing from me if you were. That's what you need, a thrashing . . ."

"And you will give it to me?" Reed's voice was weary as he turned towards his father-in-law.

"No, not me, Macauley, but I know several men who would be only too glad to oblige."

"A threat, then." He smiled and Edmund Hamilton-Brown felt the hot blood of rage move in his veins.

"Aye, a threat. If I get another of these letters from my girl about how unhappy you're making her, or soaked with her tears as the last one was, I swear I'll make you so unhappy yourself you'll be glad to stay close to your home and your wife where you belong. Not only glad but unable to do anything else. Do I make myself clear?"

"Do you mean to say you think you can make me . . . do as you say by telling me one of your bully boys will give me a thrashing if I don't?" Reed's voice was incredulous.

"It would be more than a thrashing, lad, but you'd still be able to perform your . . . marital duties . . ."

"You stupid old man."

"Not really. I'm a wealthy man and so are you so there is little I can do to you in that direction. I realise my limitations as far as bringing you to heel where business is concerned. Besides, I want my girl to continue to live in her husband's house in the comfort she has been used to but there are other ways to make you . . . see the light, shall we say."

"Say it by all means, you interfering swine, but if you think that the threat of receiving a beating at the hands of some thug – "

"Not even if the one to be beaten was not yourself but someone you . . . might care for?"

The air in the room seemed to hang, lifeless, still, unmoving and for a moment Reed Macauley was the same, his face quite blank, his eyes staring at Edmund Hamilton-Brown with complete incomprehension, then, as realisation came, his mouth opened wide in a lethal roar of rage and his eyes narrowed to menacing gleaming slits.

"By God, you bastard. I'll kill you, d'you hear me, I'll kill you with my own bare hands if one hair of her head is harmed. D'you think I give a damn about your precious 'girl'?" His mouth twisted contemptuously and Edmund Hamilton-Brown felt his own hatred twist in his guts at the sound of it. "She's worth a hundred of your daughter, a thousand, and if she'd let me I'd bring her here and send 'my wife' back to her Papa. Oh, yes, you'd better believe it. If she'd have me I'd go and live with her at her farm and leave your precious Esmé, and all this, but she won't. She's the bravest, most honourable woman I know and I love her more than my own life. She loves me too, you bastard, though I don't suppose you know anything about that since all you seem to have experienced is the rather sickening emotion you feel for that poor child upstairs. Yes, *child*! She cannot even conceive like a *woman*. Dear God . . . Oh sweet Jesus . . . how dare you come here with your sanctimonious mouthings . . . like them all . . . they do the same, while she . . . she suffers . . . grieves.

There's not one man or woman who is worth . . . Oh God, what's the use. Get out of my house, and if you want to, take your daughter with you because she's no use to me and, perhaps more importantly, I'm no use to her. I love elsewhere, you see, and I always will."

"It were Bert Garnett what thrashed me."

They were sitting, one on either side of the inglenook, Annie straightbacked and blank-faced on the settle, Phoebe in the rocker which Natty had repaired. Natty crouched by the window. He was making a new crook, carving the head of it into some design which he favoured, and his craggy face was twisted into an expression of great concentration. At his feet lay the three dogs, their muzzles on their paws, their ears pricked for the slightest sound, their bright eyes moving from one human face to another. Blackie got up for the second time in ten minutes and went to sniff at the bottom of the door which led outside and Natty stopped to watch him. The dog would just not settle, not since the bairn had gone, restless and constantly searching for her. Bonnie watched him, his eyes so doleful they seemed to say he missed her too, and the cat jumped up on Phoebe's knee, settling passively under her comforting hand. The feeling of unutterable sadness was thick in the room and it was perhaps this, this air of finality, of ending, of hopelessness which had prevailed for the past six weeks that made Phoebe break the vow she had given to Bert Garnett on the night he had beaten her and violated their home. Besides, it made no difference now, did it? His threat to kill her lambkin if she told anyone was no longer a threat, was it? What could he do to harm any of them here in this dreary room? and it might just bring Annie from the long and black apathy in which she crouched day after day, night after night, week after week. It would destroy her soon if she did not break free of it. They had their lives to lead, that was self-evident, but it seemed that Annie had been reduced to the level where she endured hers without living it. She had drawn away from the realities of sowing and planting, of lambing time which was upon them, and had it not been for the help Mr Macauley sent down, Natty would have been hard pressed to manage. Phoebe would have gone out with him, into the fields and up on the intake lands, but she was afraid to leave Annie alone for long. She worked in the dairy and about the farmyard with the hens and the pig. She moved up to the meadow with her churn and milking stool to see to 'Clover'. Again Mr Macauley helped out, ensuring that the butter and cheese and eggs went to market, with that girl he sent down, and the few shillings they earned were put in her hand by the same girl who walked across the fell with it.

Sally Garnett came regularly, her Aggie at her enormous breast, the rest of her brood trailing behind her in a long quarrelsome line, braving Bert's displeasure and sporting the evidence of it about her sad, good-natured face. She had been pregnant again but had miscarried – thankfully, she said to Phoebe who knew nothing of such things, her tired body unable, for the sixth time in as many years, to carry its burden. She drank Annie's tea, constantly flying out to the yard to prevent Sammy from chasing the hens, the pig, the offended Dandy, his brothers and sisters, separating Jamie and Emma who, having their father's belligerent, crafty nature, fought with one another unmercifully. She addressed kind, embarrassed words to Annie who nodded politely then, without a word, would walk out of the room and through the yard and the noisy children, going up and over the slope of the hill in the direction of the burned heather where her child had died.

"Ah'll 'ave to go after 'er, Sally," Phoebe had said, suddenly frantic, leaving the open-mouthed Sally to fend for herself.

The dogs were up on the fells with Natty, checking on the ewes whose lambs would be dropping any day. When Phoebe caught up with Annie she was standing, tall, thin, gaunt in her black dress in which, for the first time, the folk about the parish of Bassenthwaite approved of her,

her eyes with that awful inward-looking expression which frightened Phoebe. She herself was deep in sorrow, badly damaged by her grieving for the child she had loved, but she was appalled by the suffering of that child's mother. Annie's despair was savage at times. She turned on them, on Natty and Phoebe, when they spoke of some ordinary thing about the farm, her eyes hollow, living, breathing, but dead inside. Though it was spring now and the snows had gone, the year had plunged into a cold, wet drizzle of rain which swept across the fells and lingered in the dales whilst all the living creatures huddled beneath tree and wall and hedge to escape its misery. It was as though the world about her mourned with Annie, keeping out of sight, birds and sheep, rabbits and all the small, wild creatures which normally squeaked and rustled in the undergrowth as she passed by.

She took to walking the fells wearing the long hooded cloak which had been her mother's, going up behind the farmhouse, turning on Phoebe with a tinge of madness in her hot-glowing eyes, sending her back, glaring, teeth bared, saying she would be alone and if Phoebe followed she would hurt her badly. She walked and climbed long, solitary miles, without, it seemed, the least purpose, or even direction, exhausting herself, punishing herself for surely Cat's horrible death must be the fault of wicked Annie Abbott? She was never alone, though she did not see Reed Macauley as he protected her, warned by a message from Phoebe, through Natty, and when she came home, her cloak so heavy with rain water she could barely stand, she would let Phoebe put her to bed where she slept like one dead.

She turned her head now to look at Phoebe and for the first time since Cat's death there was a light of reality, of sense and understanding in her eyes. Natty held his breath. They'd known, of course they had, but now it seemed Phoebe was to confirm it. He waited to see what Annie would do.

"What?"

"He made me promise ah'd not tell."

"I don't . . . understand."

It was the first interest she had shown in anything for six weeks.

"'e said e'd . . . 'urt Cat if ah was to say owt."

"Hurt. . . ."

"Aye, but now . . . well . . ."

There was a deep and terrible silence, so deep and terrible the dogs at once began to turn restlessly, sensing something they did not like, and Blackie whimpered. Natty stood up and very carefully leaned the half-finished crook against the table. It was dark beyond the window and the wind flung a handful of rain against it and blew a drift of smoke down the blackened chimney. The fire danced a merry jig, bright, cheerful and uncaring of the human conflict which was contained within the walls it warmed, and over it, hanging from the randle crook which was attached to the fire crane, the iron kail-pot bubbled with its burden of stew which was to be their dinner. On the square iron bakstone a row of oatcakes, baked earlier by Phoebe, were being kept warm. She would spread them with butter and some of the blackberry-and-apple jam she had made last backend, hoping to tempt Annie's laggard appetite.

"You are telling me that it really *was* Bert Garnett who . . . beat you? That he threatened my child . . . that you kept quiet . . . ?"

"I were afraid, lass, of what he would do to Cat."

"You need not have bothered, it seems."

"Annie . . . don't."

"She is dead anyway."

"Aye."

"And he goes scot free?"

"It weren't him what . . . killed 'er."

"I know that, Phoebe, but by God, he shall be punished just the same. If I'd a gun I'd shoot him but I haven't so . . . so . . ." She stood up slowly. Her face was thoughtful and she plucked at her lip. Her eyes were alive and burning in her white face and in them was her hatred, not only of life and the fate which had stolen the only thing of value she had, her child, but of Bert Garnett who had threatened her. He would pay for what he had done to Phoebe and for the damage to their home. She felt alive, powerful, rejoicing in the hot blood which ran through her veins where, for the past six weeks sluggish ice water had flowed. She had a purpose, a reason to breathe and she gloried in it.

Wrenching open the kitchen door before Phoebe and Natty could collect their thoughts, let alone arrange them into stopping her, she ran out into the dark. The rain flew in, patterning the stone floor and the dogs milled about apprehensively. She was across the yard before Natty and Phoebe were across the threshwood and when she came out of the cow shed she carried the horsewhip her father had used to flick in the air over the back of the horse he had once owned to pull his plough.

The wind blew more fiercely, lashing the tree at the side of the farmhouse, and the air began to shriek with its strength. Annie was wet through in a minute and in the yard she stood, teeth bared, madness in her, fighting at her pain with anything she had to hand. At last, *at last* she had something to *do*, something which would shut out that whispering voice inside her head which asked her over and over again where Cat was and how had Annie Abbott lost her? The future was too awful to contemplate now. There was no hope, no relief, no comfort, not even from Reed whose silent presence she had been aware of on the periphery of her demented mind all the while they . . . tended to Cat. But she wanted none of him, nor his love. She wanted the lashing rain and wind to drench her soul and her crippled spirit and at the end of it she wanted to wrap her father's whip about the body of Bert Garnett, to slice into his flesh, as her pain sliced into hers. For what he had done to Phoebe. For what he had threatened to do to Cat.

"Oh, Jesus . . . oh, sweet Jesus . . ." Phoebe babbled. "What have I done? Stop her, Natty . . . stop her . . ." but Annie would not be stopped by such an insignificant little man as Natty Varty. Strong as he was, she was stronger in her insane rage. Contemptuously she threw him aside, and Phoebe too, striding off along the track which led to Upfell. It was dark and the rain made the path slippery but she went on, the whip trailing behind her, and behind it stumbled Natty whilst in the yard Phoebe wept, sinking to her knees defeated, to the muddy cobbles. Even the gentle hand which lifted her did not startle her, nor did she seem surprised to see him there, for had he not always been there when he was most needed?

"Which way?" he asked.

"Upfell. She's going to kill Bert Garnett, I know she is."

She was in the Upfell kitchen when he got there. Natty was at her back doing his best to stop her but the old man stepped aside unhesitatingly to let the newcomer reach her. Bert Garnett had a stripe of running blood across his face where the whip had caught him and in front of him, where he had pulled her, was his terrified wife, her bodice open, the baby pressed against her huge, pendulous breast.

"Get out of my way, Sally," Annie was saying, for even in her demented state something stopped her from aiming the devastating lash at the woman and child.

"Annie . . . for God's sake . . . stop it . . ."

"Get out of my house, tha' bitch . . . Ah'll have thi' in gaol for this . . . see what tha's done to me face. Tha're mad, they said tha' was off tha' head an . . ."

"Annie . . . please, Annie, the bairns . . ." for in the corner of the squalid kitchen the four children huddled and wept.

The man put his hands on Annie's shoulders, strong, soothing, gentle, and his voice settled over her, as familiar as the sound of the beck above the farm, warm with his love. She knew at once who he was and the whip which was flicking like a snake about the floor, looking for an opening with which to get at Bert Garnett, dropped slowly, limply.

She turned then and looked into his face.

"Charlie . . . oh, Charlie is it really you?" She was dazed and beginning to tremble.

"Aye, I've come to bring you home, darling. You've been a long time gone and they miss you."

His arms were there to hold her as she fell into them. Neither saw the expression on Bert Garnett's face as they left, nor heard the low, vicious words he spoke, only his wife, and she didn't count.

"I read of it in the *Carlisle Patriot*, the day before yesterday. I came at once. It was an old newspaper, one the landlady where I lodge was going to use for kindling for my fire. I might have missed it . . ." He bent his head, his chin on his chest, as he remembered the wild shock and grief as the name Abbott had sprung out at him. He had read the account of Cat's death with disbelief, not willing to trust the newspaper, for how could the bright and lovely child of Annie Abbott be dead, but he said nothing of this to the woman who leaned in his arms on the settle. She had wept wild, passionate, relieving tears she had not been able to shed before, and he had wept with her. They held on to one another, sharing, drowning, together in their sorrow for the child who had been Catriona Abbott. Annie was like a wildly shaking vine, clinging to the support of a strong and steadfast tree. One which would never allow her to fall but would be there always with its roots sturdily buried in the solid earth. Charlie Lucas who smiled and teased his way through life like a whimsical summer breeze, like a drifting summer cloud, held her strongly, sustained her tenderly and would continue to do so for as long as she needed him. She talked to him as she had talked to no one, not even Phoebe, of that day. Of her guilt and conviction that she was to blame. She should have listened to Natty, made the line of fire shorter, more controllable. Hired more men to help them but in her obsession with money, with the need to save it, to put it back into the farm, to be successful, to show *them* that the woman from Browhead could be as good a farmer as any in the dales, she had sacrificed her child. Her own pride had caused Cat's death . . .

"No, no, darling, it was an accident. You can't blame

yourself. All these years I've seen you work yourself into the ground. From the moment the dawn came you were on your feet, working on the farm until the light failed and then, when other women were off to their bed, you would take up your spinning, or weaving, making swills or rush-lights and you did it not just for your own pride, as you call it, but to make a life for Cat, for Phoebe, for yourself. And if you were proud of what you achieved, what of it? You had reason to be proud. Look what your labour has provided. Look how far you have come. You have a work-ing, profitable farm, small but making its way, paying for itself, feeding four mouths . . ."

"*Four* mouths, Charlie . . ."

"Sweet Jesus, how could I . . ."

"It's . . . all right, Charlie. I do it myself. I see her everywhere. Wait for her as though she is just . . . beyond the door and will come through it in a minute. Four of us . . ."

"There will be four again, if you will allow it."

"You mean . . . ?"

"I am home, Annie."

"For good?"

"Yes . . ."

She began to mend from that moment. Would she ever be completely whole again? That was for time to reveal, but though Charlie had not yet regained that wry, lively way he had with him, that self-mocking humour which was so endearing, it seemed his presence gave them all, Natty, Phoebe, Annie, those who had *seen* what Charlie Lucas had not, a strange peace. They talked, the three of them, far into the night, while in the background, whittling on his shepherd's crook, Natty listened, saying nothing, wondering how Mr Macauley would take the return of this chap into the life of the woman he had, so to speak, put into Natty's care. It was almost a year, it seemed from what they said, since Charlie Lucas had gone.

"Did you not go to Yorkshire then, Charlie?" Annie asked him, the bright interest in her eyes a relief to Natty, who had begun to believe they would never see the return of the Annie Abbott beside whom he had worked since Charlie Lucas left.

"No, I stood on the station at Penrith and decided to toss a coin, north or south but Yorkshire is a long way and the fare to Carlisle was all I could manage . . ."

"You sold your watch."

"How did you know that?"

"I was told by . . . a friend." Her eyes became shuttered. So, it was still Reed Macauley then, Charlie's loving heart anguished, for who else would know such a thing, but then had he expected anything different? When Annie Abbott gave her love it was not given lightly, nor withdrawn easily, if at all.

"Well, I went to Carlisle and fell in with some old Chartist friends who had begun a small newspaper, one the working men, those who could read, might afford. They had gone up there to . . . avoid the law years ago. As I had when I met you."

"You were a Chartist?"

"Oh yes, and in my heart I still am. I was always one for the underdog, Annie, having been one myself on so many occasions." He grinned impishly and Annie took his hand between hers.

"Oh, Charlie," she said seriously, "I do love you."

"I know, sweetheart, and I love you, and Phoebe, and . . . I loved Cat, you know that."

"I know you did. She went to school, Charlie, did you know that? She was so clever."

". . . to school, a *real* school . . . ?"

"Yes, she was given a scholarship. Miss Mossop who was the headteacher and the owner of the school, awarded it to a girl who could not ordinarily afford her fees and Cat was chosen." Her face glowed with loving pride, though her eyes brimmed with tears.

"I knew she had it in her. She was bright beyond her years. Did Miss Mossop see her work then? How did she get to hear of Cat? Was there a judge who . . . ?"

Annie leaned back on the settle reflectively and Natty's hands stilled.

"Why, I don't know. I don't know how . . . it was . . ."

At once, his mind, quicker than Annie's who was still not completely out of the numbed state into which Cat's death had thrust her, studied the question of the scholarship which had been awarded without the work of its recipient having been glanced at, coming, of course and at once, to the truth. Not that he would tell Annie since to take away her pride in her daughter's abilities, real as they had been, was beyond his love.

"They would have seen it when she went to be interviewed," he said quickly.

"There was no interview."

"Then . . ."

"Yes, Charlie, then *how* was it revealed to Miss Mossop that there was a clever child near Gillthrop who would benefit from her teaching? Only one man . . ."

"Nevertheless, she *did* win it, Annie."

"If it existed."

"Then who . . ."

"He paid her fees, Charlie. He must have done."

There was a long awkward silence. Into the room came the tall and thrusting presence of Reed Macauley and for the first time Annie allowed it, re-living that moment when he had told her Cat was to go to school. He had lied to her, knowing she would refuse charity. He had tricked her so lovingly. Given her what she most wanted for her child, but allowing her to believe for her wretched pride's sake that he did nothing beyond ferry Cat backwards and forwards to Grasmere. And how happy Cat had been. She had thrived in those few months, leaving behind the silent, withdrawn child her life had made of her, becoming lively, vivid, fulfilled, as she soaked up the knowledge Miss Mossop poured into her receptive brain. He had given her that. He had given it to Annie, and to Cat, without looking for gratitude or reward. It had not lasted long, but Cat's short life had been enriched by it, and Annie Abbott would never forget it, or him.

She continued to wear the black dress but beneath it she had on her father's trousers and when she strode off up the fells to look at her ewes and their lambs, she tucked up her skirt into the belt, as she had seen gypsy women do, giving herself the freedom she had known for years. When she came down again, or when she and Phoebe went to the market in Keswick, her modest skirt swirled about her clogs and though she did not wear a bonnet, her hair was pulled back fiercely from her face, braided, then coiled tightly about her proudly held head. She had an air of decency about her, of respectability, and it was seen that one or two men nodded amiably to her as she went by. Her farm was thriving. She had over a hundred sheep, counting her ewes and the lambs they had dropped at the beginning of the month. A cow, a pig, hens, acres of land under cultivation and *two* men working for her.

When at the end of May it became known that Reed Macauley's wife had left him and gone home to Yorkshire with her father, the whole of the parish of Bassenthwaite rocked with it, wondering, as it held its collective breath, what was to happen now.

They had not long to wait.

He was at her door a couple of weeks later.

"She has gone," were the first words he spoke to her. She stood, her hand on the latch, her face white and thin above the dense black of her dress, but more beautiful than ever. Her drawn back hair allowed the fine bones of her face to show, the delicacy of her arched brows, the faint suggestion of hollows in her cheeks, the deep, glowing depth of her golden brown eyes. About her broad white brow tendrils of copper escaped the severity of her hair style and over her ears longer wisps fell and curled. She was not yet twenty-three years old and he loved her so much, it was all he could do not to pull her over the doorstep and into his arms.

"I've been to London to see a lawyer about a divorce. An Act of Parliament, it'll take, and plenty of money but I will have it no matter how long it takes and if it costs me every penny I own. Two bloody weeks I've been there but I came directly from Penrith. Will you marry me?"

Behind her she heard the indrawn hiss of Phoebe's

breath. They were eating their evening meal, the four of them sitting about the sturdy oak table beneath the kitchen window. The dying day cast a washed and muted light about the room which was restful, cosy with the crackle of the fire, comfortable and easy with the presence of the dozing animals and the four people who understood one another so well. Even Natty who had been Annie's friend, since that was what he was now, for only a year, was as much a part of her daily life and her affections as though she had known him a lifetime. All four had frozen in dread when Reed Macauley's mare clattered into the yard, and all four had different reasons for it. Charlie's was one of a man who sees his woman threatened, Phoebe's that of a woman who sees the composure of a dearly loved friend, one who is still frail, ready to be smashed to pieces, and Natty's, who knew exactly what lengths Reed Macauley would go to to get what he wanted, was fear, not only for Annie, but for the man at the table who was ready to stand in his way. Annie's fear was not of what Reed might do, but that she would not be able to resist.

"I'll go," she had said, standing up slowly. With the return of her senses, and her reason, had come a return of her love for the man whose thunderous knock at her door had the dogs barking in furious unison. A hurting love which had been buried deep beneath the agony of her loss. A love which she could not deal with in her damaged state so she had hidden it, but now it was back and she could not help the bright glow of gladness, the tricky leap of joy inside her as she looked, her love in her eyes, into those of Reed Macauley.

"Will you, my darling?" His voice was tender, his eyes as soft a blue as she had ever seen them and she swayed towards him, unable to stop herself. "It could be years but in the meanwhile . . ."

"In the meanwhile she's to become your doxy, is that it?"

The latch was taken from her hand as the door swung open and behind her the tall figure of Charlie loomed. He put his hands possessively on her shoulders, drawing her back against him and the physical snarling menace of Reed Macauley who did not care to see another man's hands on *his* woman, never far below the surface, surged and escaped, trampling on the aching tenderness which had bathed Annie Abbott in its glow. His eyes, which had smiled so softly into hers, suddenly held a terrible blankness but the scorching heat of his jealous rage lapped against her and she put out her hands as though to prevent him from coming nearer.

"What the bloody hell are you doing here?" His voice was harsh and he struck at his own booted leg with his riding whip, evidently wanting nothing more than to lay it across Charlie's face.

"I might ask you the same."

"That is between me and Annie. Now let go of her before I do you some damage."

"I will when she tells me to."

"Tell him, Annie."

"Reed . . ."

"*Tell him*, Annie. Come here to me and tell this . . . bastard who you belong to." His black snapping anger would be let loose in a moment and it threatened those who lived beneath her roof, he was telling her. His face was as white as bleached bone but high on each cheek a flush of scarlet had appeared. His eyes were pale blue murderous slits in the slowly deepening gloom.

"Tell him, Annie, or I swear he will suffer . . ."

"Stop it, Reed . . . *Charlie*, for God's sake, stop it. Have I not had enough . . ." She wrenched herself away from Charlie who trembled visibly in the grip of his own rage and tormented longing.

"You see, *Charlie*," Reed said, his mouth cold and hard and contemptuous, "it is not you she belongs to, whatever you might think, or hope, but me. I thought we had seen the last of you, but I was mistaken. No matter, you can go to the devil or stay and run her farm if she cares to employ you. She will not be here. She is coming to live at Long Beck with me. As soon as it can be arranged we will be married . . ."

"Reed . . ."

"Don't worry, my dearest love, you have nothing else to concern yourself with. Just climb up on the mare behind me and I shall take you home. You need bring nothing . . ."

"Reed." Her voice was very quiet. "Go home, Reed."

"Annie . . ."

"No, go home, Reed, to *your* home. Yours and your wife's. I know she has . . . gone away . . . but she will be back. She is your wife and always will be . . . *no* . . ." as he would have pulled her to him.

"No . . . don't . . . hurt me any more, Reed, please. I can take no more. This is my home. These are my people . . ."

"Annie . . ." His voice was anguished. The lethal anger was gone, and the arrogance, as his love, the strong unselfish love which had developed in him over the slow years since he met her, smoothed it all away, exposing his fear. He could not bear to lose her and he knew if he forced her, pushed her too far beyond her small reserve of strength, he would. To keep her, he must let her go, for now.

"Annie . . ." One last desperate entreaty.

"No, Reed."

"You heard her, Macauley, so get on your horse . . ."

"*Charlie*, stop it . . . leave me alone."

"I won't give up, Annie." Reed's voice was quiet, but strong. "I will have that divorce and when I do . . ."

"I know."

"Will you wait for me, my darling?"

"Go home, Reed . . ." and this time he did.

The herd of ponies browsed peacefully, cropping the short tussocky grass with strong, yellowed teeth. Their ears swivelled constantly as they listened for signs of danger, and their tails flicked in graceful, unhurried movements up and across their rumps, disturbing the flies and midges which pestered them. They were not tall, standing no more than fourteen hands, but sturdy, well proportioned and muscular. Their heads were small, as were their pricked ears. Their eyes were lively and prominent, their tails long and full and their coats varied from bay to brown, black and grey.

Any horse, whatever its breed, has such a strong sense of smell it is said that a stallion can detect a mare who is on heat from a distance of half a mile away. The wind, blowing from west to east, carried away from the ponies the scent of the two men and one woman who were creeping up on them from the east, and they continued to tear at the grass, rummaging peacefully amongst the heather shoots which grew above a thousand feet on Ullock Pike.

"Theer's a herd o' ponies up the top o' t' ridge on Ullock," Natty had declared at breakfast that morning. "An' theer's a grand 'un among them an' all. Two, two an' a half years, I'd say. Just right ter train fer t' plough. When 'tis broke, o' course." His tone was laconic and he stuffed his pipe which he had removed to speak, a long speech for him, back in his mouth.

"Can we do it, d'you think?" Annie breathed, her pale face colouring a little with excitement.

"Oh, aye, straight up th'Edge. It be but a short walk an' as long as wind's blowin' towards us . . ."

"No, I meant can we break a wild fell pony to pull a plough?"

"I told you we could years ago. D'you remember the one Jack Bibby had to draw his cart from the mill?" Charlie watched the lovely flush of rose to her cheeks, rejoicing in the improvement in her during the past weeks. It was August, five months since Cat's death, and though she still grieved, deeply and silently within herself, she was beginning to take an interest in her farm again. Not just the forced interest that is needed to fill the enormous hole left by the loss of a loved one, but a genuine concern for the well-being of what she had already gained in the years behind her.

Charlie had taken over Cat's room, sleeping in the narrow truckle bed in which Annie's daughter had slept and about the walls were the simple paintings Cat had done in the six months she had been a pupil at Miss Mossop's school. Flowers, trees, birds, a sleeping basket of kittens, all very crudely done but showing the promise Miss Mossop had hoped to foster. There was a rag doll, made for her years ago by her mother, a hairbrush on the dresser which had once belonged to Lizzie Abbott, her unknown grandmother, and in a drawer her tiny store of treasures. The books he himself had given her, a fir cone she had thought pretty, her beloved satchel, a dried wild flower pressed between two sheets of paper and placed between her freshly laundered undergarments which Phoebe washed and ironed almost every week since she did not want them to become stale, she said. It was her small, loving memorial to the child she had come to think of as her own.

Charlie would lie on the bed at night, the window wide, the stars burning a myriad holes in the blackness of the night sky and sometimes, muffled and barely discernible to anyone who was not listening for it, there would be the sound of desolate weeping but he did not go to her. He was afraid. Afraid to damage the fine thread of understanding which was growing between them and had been ever since Reed Macauley had made his devastating and foolish statement that he was to get a divorce and marry Annie Abbott. It was as though, knowing finally that there could never be more between herself and Reed than the involvement of a man and his mistress, however loving; that his desperate throw of the dice had made it plain to her how impossible anything else was, she faced the certainty of Charlie Lucas's love for her, and that a life with him would be worthwhile. Would be strong and honest and made up of a great deal which was valuable. Nothing was said but in small ways they were growing closer, more intimate. They did not touch except in the most casual, ordinary way. In the way she and Natty sat shoulder to shoulder on a wall, or she and Phoebe would link arms as they walked up the field, but it meant more between himself and Annie. She *knew* now how he felt about her. She knew what he wanted and made no objection to it and, recognising her honesty, he was aware that had she not wanted it, or him, she would have said so at once. He would wait. He loved her and would wait. He wanted her so badly. To know that she was no more than a couple of feet away from him was a constant gnawing agony to his male sexuality. Her long slender body lying in its sheath of modest nightgown which *his* masculine body badly needed to take from her; which his masculine eyes longed to look at, to study, to marvel at and love. His hands were desperate to touch and hold the naked thrusting curve of her breasts, to smooth and caress her long back, her sweetly turned waist and hips, the softly rounded satin of her belly, his fingers to investigate the moist and hidden sweetness at the meeting of her thighs. He had not been celibate in the months he had been away from her, burying his aching loins in other women's bodies but not once, as he pierced them, had he thought of anyone but Annie as he did so.

The pit of his belly flared now as she leaned back in her chair and put her hands behind her head, her mind dwelling thoughtfully on how they were to capture and break one of the fell ponies Natty had described. She and Natty had meant to spend the day 'riving' the pieces of wood into strips for her swill baskets. When the steaming pieces had been removed from the boiler where they had 'stewed' overnight, each one must be held between the knees to be split, and so she had donned her trousers and shirt that morning so as to be more comfortable. The weight she had lost had been regained and as she raised her arms the buttons on the collarless shirt strained and gaps appeared between them. She wore nothing but a thin cotton chemise beneath it but it was cut low, the two top buttons undone and the soft white skin of her upper breasts was clearly visible to Charlie as he sat beside her. He could see the rosy aureole beneath the fabric of the chemise, as big as guinea pieces and in their centre the pink buds of her nipples, small and pointed. She leaned further back and as he watched her the chemise dropped further and almost the whole of her breasts and both nipples became free beneath the shirt. They were magnificent, dark and yet rosy, surrounded by the creamy white satin of her skin. The shadowy valley between was deep and lovely, the flesh warm and full. He could not look away. His own flesh strained painfully against the crotch of his breeches and his heart hammered in his chest. His mouth became dry and with a muttered excuse he stood up and stumbled from the room into the warm, summer sunshine.

He stood for ten minutes, fastened by his pain, not just the physical pain of a man roused and refused an outlet for that arousal but the need, the strong emotional need of a man who loves honestly, truly, and is denied a means to show it. It was so unbelievably beautiful on this empty shore of the lake. There were fields between it and Browhead, and trees, but he could see the ripples on the water, shading as the breeze moved it, into patches of gold which eddied to silver. The patches grew and merged until half the lake was gold, the other half silver, two separate entities divided by a path of both colours where the sun shone across it, surrounded by a necklace of trees of every shade of green amongst which, on the other side of the lake, a small white farmhouse sheltered. There were celandines growing from the rocks on the water's edge, rough, grey rock patterned with the green of moss. Charlie loved it, loved her. They were intertwined, the beloved woman, the beautiful lake, and he knew he would never leave either, not while he lived.

They walked the wide shoulder of rough fell which turned south and climbed as a narrowing ridge to the dark and symmetrical peak of Ullock Pike before they saw the ponies. Annie strode beside him, coatless, for the day was warm and he was breathlessly aware again of her glorious breasts as they bounced, joyfully unconstrained with nothing between them and Charlie's eyes and hands but the thin stuff of her chemise and the worn fabric of her father's shirt. He could still see the outline of her nipples and he was forced to drop behind, conscious that the exquisite folly of looking at her, at her body, must in some way be curtailed.

They passed through The Watches, a strange huddle of upstanding rocks growing from the grass which were believed to be a Druids' Circle though Charlie said he was of the opinion that the formation was natural. His voice, as he spoke, sounded high and strained but Natty and Annie did not seem to notice. The ponies were above them, just before what was known as The Edge began and at once Natty signalled for them to drop down on their bellies.

"Wait here," he whispered, slithering off on some errand of his own and, shoulders touching, so close he had only to turn his head to look into her face, they lay side by side, hidden in the fragrant depths of the summer weather.

He turned his head. Her cheek was pressed flat to the earth and her brown, excited eyes smiled into his. He smiled back, the warm strength of his love for her stripping away inhibition, restraint, sense. He moved a fraction closer and with great delicacy laid his lips to hers. For a moment, an appalling moment he thought she was going to flinch away, then she relaxed. Neither of them closed their eyes. Pale grey looked into golden brown, truth between them since he knew she did not love him as he loved her and what did it matter? he asked himself for her mouth softened and opened for him and it was sweet and willing.

"My love . . . my love . . ." His breath, fresh and pure, brushed her chin and her cheek, then his mouth moved to her throat and she let him, arching her neck, lifting her chin so that his lips might move more freely towards the open neck of her shirt.

"I love you so much."

"I know, Charlie."

"My love . . ." and his mouth found hers again so that when Natty crept back they were unaware of it until he touched Annie's shoulder. They did not jump apart guiltily but turned their heads to smile at him and in Natty's eyes was a deep, glad understanding. She would be all right now.

"Theer's a fine little bay, theer, can tha' see 'im, Charlie?" His whisper was close to Charlie's ear and reluctantly Charlie took away the arm he had placed across Annie's shoulders.

"Yes, but how are we to get him away from the herd?"

"Nay lad, ah've catched many a youngster such as 'im in me day. Let's see if ah remember 'ow. Ah want thee an' Annie ter creep round t'other side of 'em so that they get wind o' thi'. Shout as loud as thi' can. They'll run this way and ah'll be ready fer 'un." He patted the length of rope he had wound about his waist.

There were sixteen of them. A mature stallion, seven mares and their foals. It was surprising to see a young male amongst the herd since a stallion will drive away any usurper when he is about eighteen months old, but the colt grazed peaceably enough though it was noticed it kept well away from the 'leader'. Several of the foals were lying down in the sunshine.

It was like a child's game and both Charlie and Annie were giggling like children as they slithered through the heather, stopping frequently to lift their heads to see where the ponies were. Once he stopped her with his hand on her arm and when she turned questioningly, he kissed her again, more deeply. It was as though he was reminding her, placing his mark on her, telling her that the previous exchange had been serious despite the lightness of their embrace. She made no objection again, lifting her face to him willingly, smilingly.

When they stood up and shouted the herd at once took flight, the foals, perhaps only months old, scrambling to their feet and following their mothers without a moment's hesitation, fast, automatic, a fundamental reaction which had been bred in them when predators such as wolves had threatened their ancestors. In the panic which ensued the ponies could barely see where they were going, and when Natty stood up directly in their path, the whistling song of his rope settled over the bay's head. It went unnoticed by the stallion, and certainly by the mares who had one ear on the disturbance and one on their own foal.

Annie looked as she had done before Cat's death. Her eyes were a brilliantly deep golden brown, clear and sharp with her joyous laughter. The colour ran gloriously beneath her skin and her mouth was wide in a great cry of excitement. She jumped up and down and clapped her hands when she saw that Natty had the bay, looking so like her own daughter in her delight, Charlie felt he could weep. For sweet, lovely Cat who was gone and for Annie who, at last, was coming alive again.

It took a long time to fetch the colt in. He squealed and stamped and kicked, his eyes rolling and wild with terror and rage, his hooves lethal as they struck out at Natty who held the rope and at Charlie who tried to throw an arm about his neck.

"Let 'im go, tha' daft bugger," Natty shouted. "Let 'im wear 'imself out fer a bit. Bye, but 'e's in a right royal temper, that 'e is."

They called him 'Royal' and those first few weeks with him were hard and sometimes dangerous, but he was basically sweet tempered and, giving in to the inevitable, gradually became tame, domesticated, not only willing to put up with the hard work and strange things which were expected of him, but becoming interested in these curious but kind creatures who had taken him from his freedom. He was accustomed slowly to what was needed from him, accepting Natty, Annie or Charlie as his leaders and companions, as he would other horses. Natty did the training, of course, for neither Annie nor Charlie had known horses. Royal became playful, almost a family pet, walking towards them with ears pricked, a 'long' nose, a jaunty prancing step and high tail, ready for fun since he was only young and Annie learned to ride him bare-backed since there was no such thing as a saddle at Browhead. It seemed to amuse him, to please him and she loved him as she loved Blackie and Bonnie.

On the day they caught him Natty and Phoebe had gone to their beds early as though by mutual consent, though nothing was said, and Charlie and Annie sat on by the fire. They could hear Royal's 'caterwauling', as Natty had put it, out in the pasture where, in case he should try and jump the drystone wall, Natty had tethered him. He sounded sad and dejected as he called to the herd but gradually his lonely whinnies died away and the dogs, whose ears had pricked in bewilderment at this strange sound, settled to doze in that half-wakeful, half-dozing state they fall into. It had turned cold and Charlie threw a couple of short logs on the fire, the flames leaping in a lively scatter of sparks up the chimney. Normally at this time of night as they made their way to bed the fire would be covered by the 'curfew', a low metal dome which kept it burning slowly, and the glowing embers would, the next morning, then have life breathed back into them with the bellows. But both Charlie and Annie knew that something must be said about what had taken place on Ullock Pike. Charlie with eagerness since he was certain that the time had come for him to stake his claim to the woman he loved. In Annie there was a tinge of dread mixed with a strange resignation since she loved Charlie and could not imagine life without him.

He lounged opposite her on the settle, his long legs stretched out before him crossed at the ankle, his hands thrust deep in his trouser pockets. He had removed his boots and his stockinged feet were close to the fire. His eyes were on her and when she looked up at him he smiled, sat up and leaned forward.

"May I kiss you again?" he asked softly, whimsically.

"You needed no permission this morning." Her own tone was light.

"I am an impetuous devil at times," but though the words were humorous the expression in his eyes was very serious.

"I noticed."

"You did not object?"

"No."

"Then . . . may I?"

She leaned towards him, lifting her mouth and he took her lips with the sweet delicacy which is the mark of the true lover. When they drew apart his eyes were steady, candid, filled with the deep and endless love which was hers for the taking. It was all there, everything she needed, just as he was always there when she needed him. He was so fine, Charlie, so fine and good. Trustworthy, making light of everything from the twelve, fourteen, sixteen hours' work he often did each day, to the poor state of his old boots, but trustworthy, honest. A man of his word. A gentleman, not just by birth, which he was, but in his very nature. He made her laugh with his droll humour but he was a man, not a milksop, and could curse with the fluency of a soldier. He was her true friend but she knew he wanted more and if she turned him away could he be expected to stay and continue as if this morning had not happened? Her heart ached with the thought of losing his friendship, the deep, satisfying companionship and support which had always been there when she needed it. He had gone away once because of her love for Reed Macauley. Would he do so again for there was no doubt in her mind, no swerving from the truth in her heart which was that she loved Reed and would do so until the day she died. Should she tell Charlie this? There should be truth and trust between friends, as there was between herself and Phoebe, but would the same apply to the man who sat opposite her? There was a great deal of difference in Charlie's masculine love to the female affection she and Phoebe shared.

"I love you, Annabelle Abbott. Will you marry me?"

"Oh, Charlie . . . !" She was taken aback. Though she had expected something, a declaration of his love, something, it had not been an offer of marriage and for one awful moment she was terror-stricken. Not marriage, no . . . not marriage for it was so *final*, so irrevocable. Reed was married but he had said . . . a divorce . . . *no, don't be foolish. . .* and if she married Charlie . . . *she would be tied*, this dreadful voice said and then if Reed got a . . . could be made free to marry her . . . *No! . . . No! . . .* it's not possible . . . *folly. . . madness. . .* and yet something inside her struggled desperately to avoid the commitment Charlie was asking her to make. But think of the peace, another voice said, the comfort, the protection, the end to the perpetual storm of Reed's love, his demanding love which, if she did not marry Charlie, and end it, would go on and on until she succumbed to it, and him.

"I had not thought of marriage, Charlie," she said slowly. Her thoughts, so many and varied, so harrowing and conflicting had taken but a few seconds and he seemed to assume her hesitation to be no more than any woman's at the offer of marriage and yet a woman who loves, in the way a woman *truly* loves a man, will not hesitate.

"I have thought of nothing else, my darling. I love you . . . so much, there are no words to describe it." He smiled, a smile of such blinding sweetness, understanding and love she felt the warmth of it, the glowing tender warmth wrap about her, hold her in safe arms, as *his* would be, but again she hesitated.

"I said once that I loved you, Charlie, do you remember?"

"Yes, but you meant . . . as a friend. I *can* tell the difference, my love, but it seems I do not care. I want you to come to me and . . . I nearly said 'to be mine' but I don't believe that one human being can possess another . . ."

How wrong you are, dear Charlie . . .

" . . . I want you to love me in any way you can. Love is such a worthwhile emotion and should not be despised if it is . . . not quite what one hopes for, but if you will marry me there is no doubt in my mind, none, that what we will have will be a worthwhile thing, Annie. Don't waste it, my lovely girl, don't waste us."

"Charlie, sweet, darling, Charlie . . ."

An appalled expression flooded his eyes. "Christ, you're going to say 'no', aren't you?" He made a small, painful sound in his throat and turned away from her to hide his fear. Bonnie, sensing the distress in him got up and came to his knee and Charlie placed a trembling hand on the animal's head. His pale, cat-like eyes were almost black in the dim light as the pupils widened and darkened.

"Charlie, I'm not ready yet, to say yes or no." You lie, the cool voice within her said. If Reed Macauley, free of all encumbrances, stood before you with an offer of marriage you would snap it up so eagerly you would take his hand off at the wrist to get at it. And yet it was true, what she had said to Charlie. She was still not the Annie Abbott she had been once. She was not in a fit state to make any decision and to take Charlie's love and twist it for her own convenience was not only unfair but cruel. The temptation was great. To thankfully fall into his arms. Let him take her to bed, now, tonight, so that in the morning she would, despite what he said, *belong* to him. There would be no looking back to Reed Macauley, nor looking forward to the foolish promise he had made. It would be irreversible, no going back or changing her mind, no more decisions to be made. She and Charlie, the farm, perhaps children . . . oh, yes, another child, a daughter . . . like Cat, but not Cat for she would have Charlie's blood in her, a son . . . a boy to inherit the farm. She would be Mrs Charles Lucas, respectable, no longer Annie Abbott, the woman from Browhead. The farm would grow and prosper. Her future, with Charlie to stand beside her, work beside her, would be secure, hard, for certain, but secure in Charlie's love. She was well aware that in the last few months she had

let her weakened state lean on Charlie, had allowed him
to anticipate perhaps, more than she intended. They had
shared secret smiles, a subtle changing in their relationship, a small degree of intimacy which had suggested,
hinted at, a growth of it in the future.

He turned back to her, his hands reaching for hers and
he did his best to smile.

"Annie . . ." He looked down at their twined fingers
and his throat worked painfully. She wanted to soothe him,
comfort him, run her fingers through his brown thatch
of curls and smooth them from his forehead. Her loving
friendship surged through her on a great tide and she
almost said it. Almost said 'yes'. She wanted to lift the
misery which had come upon him, which *she* had caused.
Take him in her arms and tell him she would be his wife
and anything else he wanted until their wedding day, but
it was not *love* that made her want to do it, but compassion.
How could she hurt him when he had given her so much?
Her sanity. A reason to live.

"Annie," he began again. "I have hoped, these last
weeks. . . ."

"I know, Charlie, and perhaps . . ."

At once he looked up at her, hopeful, ready to smile if
she would.

"Perhaps . . . Annie?"

"When I'm . . . oh Charlie, you know how much . . ."

"Yes? How much you love me? You must not say it if
you don't mean it."

"I *do* mean it."

"A man and a woman love in a special way, Annie.
Good Christ, you know that." His voice was passionate,
". . . and that is what I want from you but if you can't give
me that, then by God, I'll take anything you *can* give
me. Bloody hell, I'm not proud, Annie, I'm a man who
loves . . ."

"I know, Charlie, but . . ."

"Let it . . . lie for now, Annie. Don't say no. Think
about it. Dammit, I shouldn't be pushing you, not now
when you are still mourning . . ."

"I'm . . . I still seem to be incapable of decisions, Charlie. My mind is stunned . . . sometimes, and it . . . hurts . . . I hurt so much without her."

"Ssh . . . ssh . . . my love . . ." and without conscious thought, without the sexual ardour which had so unmanned him that morning he drew her from her chair and on to the settle beside him. His arms were round her tightly and hers crept about his neck. Her wet face pressed into the hollow beneath his chin as the devastation of her grief overwhelmed her and he rocked her back and forth. The thick plait of her hair became untwisted and it fell in a rippling, dishevelled tide about her face and shoulders, falling down her back to her waist and across her breast. His hands gripped it and his arms crushed her shivering body to him, his love, strong and incontestable, holding her secure in her grief.

"Oh, Charlie, what would I do without you?"

"There is no need to wonder, sweetheart, for I have no intention of going anywhere."

"Charlie, I lo . . ."

"No . . . no, don't say it. Not now. Not until you mean it in the way I want you to mean it. But . . . Annie . . . don't take away my hope. You know you and I could live a good life together. To be friends, to trust one another as you and I do is a fine start. The best. The rest will come, my darling. I won't rush you, though being a man of normal needs I want nothing more than to pick you up and take you to bed . . ."

"That would be . . ."

"Please . . . don't say it, whatever it is. I cannot find it in me, tempting as it is, to take advantage of your . . . vulnerability." He laughed softly. "If anyone had told me, years ago, when I was a hot-blooded youth, that I would say such a thing to a woman I would have thought them mad."

She had quietened now, lying calmly in his arms, her head on his shoulder, and he spoke into her tumbled hair. His lips touched her brow, moving softly to the smooth white flesh, pleasant but undemanding.

"But I was not in love then, Annie, and, being a male, a willing female, no matter her weakened state nor what had caused it, was fair game. I am a different man now. You have made me so. Now then . . ." he became brisk, "it's time we were in our beds . . . yes, I can even say that, Annie Abbott, though I warn you that I mean to get you into mine one day."

They were both smiling as he put the 'curfew' on the fire. She turned on the bottom stair to watch him as he opened the door to let out the dogs for the last time and unbidden, Reed Macauley's words, so like Charlie's in their content, came back to her.

"I won't give up, Annie," he had said. As Charlie had just said and though she continued to smile her heart was heavy and painful, torn as it was between two men's love.

Annie was high on the fell. It was October and time for
'raking' in the gimmer ewes for breeding, and swirling
before her in a constantly shifting pattern were her flock.
As Blackie moved away from them, coming to crouch
beside her, they formed into a long grey ribbon, one behind
the other, moving purposefully down towards the intakes.
They went at a steady pace with no need of a push and
Blackie watched them, looking out for any rebel which
might be diverted by a sweeter patch of heather. The
lambs were as big as their dams now, fine and sturdy.
They were weaned, completely self-sufficient, and when
Annie had selected those she was to keep for breeding
purposes, the rest would go to the lamb fair. The Keswick
Tup Fair would take place next week on the first Saturday
in October and it was there she would sell her surplus
stock and hire a ram for the season.

It was the real start of the sheep farmer's year. The
libido of the tups, which included the one she meant to
hire next week, was at this time in the calendar mysteriously ready to be linked to any ewe which they could heave
themselves on to, and every ewe must have her chance.
If she was not mated she could not carry a lamb through
the winter months and there would be no profit in that for
Annie Abbott.

Far below, almost out of sight, Charlie, with Bonnie a
minute speck of darker colour beside him, was herding
part of her flock into the walled inland pastures where they
would fatten up for a week in readiness for the backend
fair and, away to her left beyond Broad End and completely
hidden from her, Natty was raking another dozen or so
who had wandered that way. They were still on their own

'heaf' but in that mindless way a sheep has, a few had gone one way and a few the other. He had his dog with him, ready to take them down with the rest, and occasionally Annie could hear the faint but piercing whistle which Natty used to give it orders.

"Steady, Blackie," she murmured as the dog, one foot raised, looked up at her questioningly, waiting for her command to take the sheep down. He knew as well as she did where they were going and how to get them there and even, she often thought, why they were going. Almost four years now since Reed had left him and Bonnie tied to her door and in that time they had proved to be friend and protector and as good as any sheepdog she had ever known. A sheep will soon learn to outwit man but will seldom challenge the prowess of a well trained dog, and all the dogs asked in return for their labour and faithfulness was a good meal once a day, a decent bed and a little kindness.

"Off you go then," she told him and he went, streaking down the stripped grass, following at a distance the line of sheep, taking them towards Charlie down almost at the level of the lake and the safety of the pastureland.

Annie stood, one foot resting on the grey, moss-studded rock, her knee bent, her arms folded across it as she looked out over the loveliness of the autumn lake and its surroundings. It was late afternoon. The great sheet of water was stretched at the feet of the majestic giant, the affable and friendly Skiddaw. Dark cloud shadows crawled across the water and the quiet woods dozed about it in the last bit of sunshine. The trees cast long-fingered shade and higher up the fell the land was a riot of colour, the dying bracken fronds and red-berried rowan trees, the whiteness of the bents and the faded green of the grasses. The deciduous trees each carried an umbrella of multi-coloured leaves, robins sang, and the air was so clear Annie could hear the clatter of blackbirds in the hedgerows which lay along the lake road. The mountains all about her were going to sleep as night approached, giants crowding the sky from lilac to deepest purple before they began to fade into evening blue.

The scream of a hawk brought her from her deep reverie, echoing across the fell and bringing to absolute stillness the multitude of small creatures who lived there. She turned, lifting her hand to shade her eyes, searching the deep and darkening bowl of the heavens for the hawk's presence, and as she did so her heart gave a great and sickening leap in her breast. Standing at her back and leaning on an enormous rock as tall as himself was Bert Garnett. He had his arms crossed on his chest in a pose of casual indifference. He even smoked a pipe, looking for all the world like some weatherbeaten shepherd who stops for a smoke as he watches his flock. He was looking at her and when her gaze met his, he nodded pleasantly, then with great deliberation took the pipe from his mouth and placed it carefully on a small rock beside him before walking across the grass towards her.

She took a step backwards and almost fell as her heel caught the rock on which she had recently rested.

"Watch tha' step, Annie," he said pleasantly. "We wouldn't want thi' ter fall an' hurt thissen, would we?"

She became perfectly still, like the creatures in the undergrowth had as the hawk passed over, but her voice when she spoke was calm, cold and expressionless.

"What do you want?" she asked him, her anger icy inside her, and her pain, for in some way, though her logical mind knew it was not so, Cat's death seemed to be linked in a grotesque way to this man. She supposed it was because he had threatened Cat and now Cat was dead. Was it her turn now? Was it her turn to be abused as he had abused Phoebe? Or was it just coincidence that he should be up here when she was alone? She didn't think so.

Her alarm, which had been brought on by the sudden shock of finding him at her back and which had ebbed away when she saw who it was, began to surge again, for the expression on his face was not agreeable. Smiling, oh, yes, but overlying the smile was a patina of venom which boded ill for the one at whom it was directed. Herself. Clearly in her mind's eye she could see Phoebe's face,

that battered, split, scraped mass of raw flesh in which
Phoebe's eyes had been embedded, pale and unseeing in
her pain and shame. Phoebe had done her best to stand
up to this man but she had been no more than a thread of
a girl, tossed to one side by his cruel hands. She had
protested and, Annie supposed, threatened him with the
law but he had merely turned Phoebe's threat on her,
frightening *her* into silence with the weapon of intimidation,
of damage to the child Phoebe had loved. To Cat.

To Cat. Her darling Cat who was gone now and who
could no longer be hurt. Not by Bert Garnett. Not by
anyone. Annie had meant to punish him, not only for beating Phoebe but for using Cat to blackmail her into silence,
to lash him with her father's whip but Charlie had prevented it, taking her in his arms and guiding her from the
kitchen at Upfell, her mind dazed and stricken with her
hating grief.

The scene played itself out again. Sally with the baby
at her breast. The children seething in terrified confusion
in the corner, blood, a stripe of it across Bert's face, Sally's
screams, the children crying. They had come away, she
and Charlie, and her mind had shut itself down, enclosing
in a small portion of itself the words which had spewed
from Bert's mouth and the vicious loathing in his eyes.
That part of it had been buried, forgotten, and if she had
been questioned on it she would have been forced to admit
that she had no recollection of it.

But now, as Bert smiled, revealing the broken state of
his teeth, it was as though a curtain had been lifted, a
window opened to allow her to see the picture of his face
as it had been then. To hear the sound of his voice as it
had been then, and the words he had spoken. Wild, violent
enmity, a deadly virulence which had pledged retribution,
a hatred so thick and threatening it promised to search
her out to the ends of the earth and beyond. He would
make her pay for this, he had screamed, she remembered
it now, and for all the insults she had slung at him, at his
pride, at his manhood. Her haughty contempt for Bert
Garnett would not be forgotten, his foul tongue had told

her, though she had not listened then. She had not seen him since.

"Ah said me time'd come, didn't ah, lass?" His smile deepened, becoming even more genial but at the back of his eyes some nasty thing stirred, telling her quite plainly that he was neither amused, nor genial.

"I haven't the faintest idea what you are talking about, Bert Garnett, and I'd be obliged if you'd get out of my way," for somehow, in a cunning manoeuvre he had cornered her in the angle between the two tall rocks.

"Ah haven't the faintest idea what tha's talkin' about, Bert Garnett," he mimicked, then, making her jump violently, he put out his hands and grabbed at her. At the last moment, as she cowered away, he drew back, playing with her as a cat plays with a mouse, laughing.

"Get out of my way, Bert. If you lay one hand on me I swear I'll scream so loud I'll bring every man on the fell running up here."

"Ah mean ter lay more'n a hand on thi', Annie Abbott. 'Tis time ah 'ad my share of what tha' pass out willy-nilly. Tha' seems ter be willin' ter open tha' legs fer any man what 'as a fancy fer it but when it comes ter poor old Bert what's done more fer thi' than most round 'ere, well 'tis 'Ta-ra, Bert, see thi' termorrer,' an't bloody door shut in me face. Ah were the only one what spoke kindly ter thi' when tha' first come. Fetchin' yer ter market, tekkin' tha' swills an' besoms in me cart but was ah thanked fer it? No, not poor old Bert Garnett. All I got were a slash across t' face wi' tha' faither's 'orse-whip."

Bert's smile twisted suddenly, allowing to the surface the malice which had festered in him, smoulderingly at first, when he had been thwarted in his desire for Annie Abbott's favours, then in an eruption of hatred which had been dangerous, when she had snapped the whip about his face and body. He had seen her come and go, up the sheep trods to examine her lambs and ewes, riding her pony sometimes, working the fields about her farmhouse, striding out along the lake road or over the top of Skiddaw to the market in Keswick but always one of her household had been with her. She had finally discarded the black dress of mourning and wore instead a new outfit she and Phoebe had made between them. A well-fitting pair of breeches of the hodden-grey wool so popular in the district, which tapered to her ankle, flaring slightly above the knees in the fashion of riding breeches. A full-sleeved man's white cambric shirt over which she wore a sleeveless woollen waistcoat. Her jacket was loose and easy, comfortable for the many jobs she did about the farm and on her feet, a sure sign of the small prosperity she was enjoying, were a pair of stout walking boots. Her hair was braided and at its end was an enormous bunch of bright green ribbons, her only concession to her own femininity.

"Ah've waited fer thi', Annie. Day an' bloody night ah've waited fer thi' an' now 'tis my turn."

"Don't be ridiculous, man. You must be insane to imagine I would have anything to do with you."

"Yer were glad enough ter 'ave summat ter do wi'm me when ah took thi' ter market . . ."

"I was . . . yes . . . I was grateful but . . ."

"Well then, 'ow about tha' showin' me 'ow grateful? Let's settle oursen down on this bit o' grass . . ."

"Don't be ridiculous," she said again. "Even if we had remained . . . friends, and it is doubtful we were ever that, after what you did to Phoebe you should have been put in gaol. You damn nearly killed her . . ."

"Nay, a bit of a slap were all she got an' so will you if yer don't shurrup. Let's give over this bletherin' an' get down ter some . . ."

"Oh, get out of my way." Her voice was filled with her contempt. She could feel the violence of her own rage begin to course through her own veins, the small flare of unease his words and manner had lit in her quenched by the memory of Phoebe and the pitiful state this man had reduced her to.

"Go on, get away from me. You make me feel sick, you little weasel. Can you not pick on someone your own size to bully? Poor Sally gets a regular beating from you and how she stands you in her bed is a wonder to me. And not satisfied with knocking your wife about you had to take your fists to Phoebe. Now it seems it's to be my turn, you little rat."

Taking him by surprise with the suddenness of her movement, she shoved him hard, and he was so unprepared he retreated before her, going backwards down the trod where sheep had worn the grass down to the hard earth. He put up an arm to defend himself, mesmerised in that moment by her towering rage, by her wild and passionate beauty, as he had always been mesmerised by it. She pushed him again, spitting abuse, words she had heard in the yards of the inns in which she had worked, listening to herself in amazement, beginning to wonder if she was going mad, her heart banging and enormous in the small cavity of her chest. Like a drum it was, her pulse racing as common sense was driven from her by her hating rage.

"You touch me and I'll kill you, Bert Garnett," she shrieked. She felt ten feet tall, twice as big as he was. He slipped and sat down heavily and it was then that she should have taken her opportunity and raced off down the slope but he was up again in a second, still moving backwards away from her flailing fists and the knee she was doing her best to drive into his groin.

But he was beginning to regain his equilibrium now, dodging her blows, reaching out his own hands and when he saw his chance, grabbing her by one wrist. She tried to wrench it free, her eyes a pale savage amber in her livid face, her other fist striking him high on the side of his head but to no avail.

"Let . . . me . . . go . . . you bastard," she panted. "You put one hand on me and I'll scream . . ."

"Aye, so tha' said, Annie. Well, scream away 'cos there's no one ter hear thi' except bloody sheep an' rabbits. That sod Natty Varty's down Browhead by now an' tha' fancy man's on th'inlands. Theer's only thee an' me, lass, an' that's 'ow it should be so why don't tha' settle thissen down an' stop fightin'. We could 'ave a right good time. There's plenty ter go round, ah'd say. Him what lives wi' thi', *an'* Mr Reed Macauley, so ah 'eard, an' even owd Natty, I shouldn't wonder. Ah bet 'e's not bin missed out so 'ow about a kiss first afore we . . ."

"Let . . . go . . . of . . . my . . . arm . . ." She hissed the words through teeth which were clenched tight in revulsion but Bert had both her wrists in his hands now and though she kicked out at him with her newly booted feet the lunge she made was her undoing. She lost her balance, falling heavily on to her back and at once he was on top of her. He was big and strong and dangerous in his lust and hatred for Annie Abbott. What he wanted was here, squirming delightfully under his man's body, her every movement arousing his already aroused body to further menace. He bunched his muscular shoulders, forcing her hands high above her head, holding them both in one large fist whilst the other reached greedily for the neck of her fine cambric shirt. He knelt over her so that his knees were on either side of her writhing body and though she continued to kick her legs only threshed the air behind his back and her heels drummed ineffectually on the hard ground.

Oh God! . . . oh, dear God! . . . it was happening, just like Reed had always said it would. Even on the very first day they had met he had warned her of tinkers, travelling men who would toss her on her back, fling her skirts over her head and take what they wanted as casually as a dog mounts a bitch. But he had not thought to warn her against Bert Garnett.

His hand pulled at the fabric of her shirt. He had no time for buttons, tearing savagely at her, his filthy nails raking her skin, drawing four lines of blood from her throat to her breasts, the beast surging in him as for a moment his mouth found hers. She turned her head away in horror and his lips moved like two wet slugs across her cheek. But whilst he kissed her he could not see what his savage hand had uncovered so he leaned back for a clearer look, putting his weight squarely across her heaving thighs.

He began to grunt rhythmically, his body pounding at hers though as yet their flesh was not joined, nor even touched. His pleasure filled him and he erupted swiftly and brutally at the centre of his own body as he climaxed. At once he fell forward, his panting breath hoarse and animal-like against Annie's averted cheek and for several moments he lay, winded, replete, but by no means finished with her. Not by a long chalk. He was temporarily satisfied but he meant to do it again and again, and *inside* her. Inside her wherever he could stick it and when it was over she could crawl back down the track and blab all she wanted to that sod she lived with because Bert Garnett would be at home by then, safe in the bosom of his family where a family man would naturally be. Her word against his, that was what it would be and who would believe a woman with *her* reputation against a man, a respectably married man such as himself?

He sat back on his haunches and with great deliberation and with one hand, undid his trousers, bringing out his limp penis. Already it was becoming engorged again and he smiled as he stroked it for a moment before transferring his attention to her bared breasts. He took them one at a time into his hand. They were full and pink-nippled and he wished he had a third hand since he was forced to hold *hers* above her head which left him with only one to fondle her. Trouble was he couldn't get to that tantalising goal between her legs for the silly cow had on those daft bloody trousers. If she'd worn a skirt it would have been an easy enough job to shove it over her head. Keep her quiet an' all. 'Course, he could clip her round t' mouth, that'd do it . . .

She fought him like a tigress, doing her best to get her knee up to where it would hurt him the most, but it was *his* knee which was between *her* legs now, forcing them apart. His face loomed over hers then his mouth was at her breast . . . biting . . . Dear God . . . she was weakening . . . she could feel the waves of nausea as he relentlessly moved his mouth down her body to where the fastening at the waist of her breeches lay.

A knife of terror stabbed her again and again since he had only to cuff her across the head, stun her and in her senseless state strip her of her clothing and she would be completely defenceless. It was only her breeches and the awkwardness of getting them off that was stopping him from brutally raping her. She had only one chance. Throwing back her head so that her throat arched agonisingly, she began to scream.

Bert Garnett was displeased. He looked up, his mouth, on which there was Annie Abbott's blood, snarling like that of a crazed beast. Her voice echoed from crag to grey crag, sounding exactly like the cry of the hawk as it dives for the kill and down on the inlands Natty Varty's dog raised its head. Charlie was further down the pasture with Blackie and Bonnie. They were holding the flock for him as he opened the gate and beside them the noise of Chapel Beck as it roared over the stones in its bed, distorted the sound.

Natty Varty's dog rose to its feet and looked questioningly at its master.

"T'were only that 'awk, dog. Lie down."

But the dog turned, looking up the fell this time. Natty watched him, puzzled, for the dog was a part of himself, an extension of his own mind and body having no thought nor sense in its head but what was put there by Natty. It gave a short 'yip' and Natty's puzzlement turned to amazement. The dog *never* barked, never, and certainly his behaviour was strange. An old dog, was the dog who had no name and certainly no concerns but its devotion to Natty, its liking for the fire now that they lived this soft life with Annie Abbott, and a bit of good grub. Not flighty as Annie's young dogs could be and definitely not given to fanciful shenanigans as it was doing now.

"What's up?" he asked it, moving towards the gate which led from the inlands to the yard, but before he could open it to let the elderly animal through, it leaped, *leaped* the wall and began to run, a streak of blurred black and white, up the field at the back of the farm, again jumping the wall and on to the open fell. It disappeared then into the browning bracken and no matter how Natty whistled, the sound piercing and shrill and clearly discernible to his old dog, it had gone as completely as if the ground had opened up and swallowed it.

"Well, I'll be buggered," Natty said, scratching his head and staring up into the heights of Ullock Pike.

"What is it, Natty?" Charlie asked from behind him and then, as though they too had lost their wits, Blackie and Bonnie lifted their fine heads, sniffed the air and without a sound, their ears flat, their bodies the same, their bellies almost touching the ground, they followed Natty's dog up the field.

"Nay . . . 'appen theer's a lamb . . . ?"

"A lamb . . . ?"

"We could've missed it. 'Appen it's trapped."

"Annie wouldn't have sent Blackie down without checking."

"Annie . . ."

They looked at one another and then without a word both men surged forward, even the old man going like the wind, springing over the wall as nimbly as his dog, following Charlie who was fifty or more years younger than he was and so could be expected to get going faster than himself.

The dog, Natty's dog, raised its voice as Charlie reached The Watches, the spill of stones which was the beginning of the Edge. It sounded frantic and though already his lungs were on fire as his breath laboured in them, Charlie forced out a hoarse cry.

"Where are you, Annie . . . for God's sake . . . where . . . ?"

The dog continued to howl high up on the fell where the heather began and in a moment the sound was taken up by two more canine voices.

"Oh, Jesus . . . oh, Jesus . . . oh, Jesus . . ." Charlie kept repeating though every breath he took and every word he spoke was agony to him. His long legs crashed through the bracken, leaping every obstacle in his path, and his coat flew out behind him like bats' wings. Sweat poured from him coming from every pore in his body, bathing him in the cold slick of fear.

"Annie . . ." His voice rose to a scream as high and agonised as hers had been, the one he thought to be that of the hawk – yes, he remembered it now – and the noise the dogs made grew louder and louder though he thought he could detect a lessening in their frenzy. Jesus . . . oh sweet Jesus . . . let her be safe . . . unharmed . . . and a hundred yards behind him, his back to the breathtaking beauty of the lake and the patchwork quilt of fertile grassland which ran beside it, Natty felt the pain claw at him in the centre of his chest, exploding and extending in its fury down his left arm. It hooked him into an arch, throwing back his head, then just as violently doubling him over forwards but still he kept going.

The dogs stopped howling and the sudden silence seemed to Charlie to be as menacing as the noise.

"Annie . . ."

She was sitting, her back to the grey-pitted stone, her knees drawn up to her chest, her head bowed over her folded arms. About her, huddling close in protective formation were the three dogs. Voiceless they were now, quivering with some fierce emotion, some dangerous, barely controlled menace and for a second, as Charlie came over the rise before they recognised him, all three were up again ready to tear him to pieces.

"Annie . . . God in Heaven . . . Annie . . ." He could barely speak and his chest rose and fell in agony.

She did not look at him, keeping her face buried in her arms but as he flung himself down beside her she put out a trembling hand to him. He took it between his own, his head bent in an effort to look into her face but she seemed calm, unharmed, her hair dishevelled certainly, the heavy plait unravelled but then that was not out of character for Annie. Then why had the dogs set up such a caterwauling? They had known that something was wrong, Natty's dog at first, and then Blackie and Bonnie, their fine instincts in tune with that sixth sense which knows of disaster before man.

"Annie? Darling, what is it? Look at me. What happened? The dogs took off . . ."

She began to shake then, no more than a slight trembling in her neck and shoulders which moved her head on her folded arms, but it spread slowly and steadily down to her hands which, one held by Charlie, the other clasped about her knees, quivered and jerked dementedly. It grew worse, more violent, racing through her body and into her bent legs. Her teeth chattered and she began to moan in her throat, deep, appalling, agonised.

"Annie . . . Dear Christ . . . what happened to you?"

Charlie put his arms about her drawing her to him in a passion of love but she began to struggle, pulling away from him frenziedly, fighting him, striking out at him, deep in the grip of some emotion which seemed to him to be one of loathing.

"No . . . no . . . don't . . . please . . ." she shrieked, and though Blackie and Bonnie both rose to their feet, circling the struggling couple anxiously, Natty's dog slipped quietly away, moving off down the path along which he had come.

"Annie . . . sweetheart, it's me."

"I know, Charlie, I know . . . but please . . . let me go . . ."

Still she kept her face averted, her great heavy mass of hair falling about her in a protecting curtain but through it, now, he could see white flesh, deep claw marks, BLOOD . . . Jesus . . . blood . . . a leopard . . . wolves . . . ! His appalled mind, though it knew very well that there was no such thing up here, grappled with images of Annie in the clutches . . . or the claws . . . fangs . . . of some wild creature . . .

"Darling . . ." Putting the pictures from his mind he allowed her to pull away from him though his every male instinct shouted out to hold her close, to comfort, to protect. "Tell me what happened, Annie. Where are you hurt? Let me look . . ."

"No . . ." Her voice rose in a great cry and Blackie whimpered before coming to lean against her in sympathy. She allowed it, sinking her face into his silky fur, holding him about his neck and beginning to weep. Great wrenching cries which threatened to choke her but the dog stood rock still, his eyes sad and loving.

"Will you not come home then, Annie? Phoebe will . . ."

"Oh yes, Phoebe . . . please Charlie, get me to Phoebe." She did not turn to him but her voice changed, becoming more composed as though the thought of Phoebe strengthened her.

"Let me help you up, my lovely girl."

"No . . . no, please Charlie, I can manage."

"But . . ."

"Don't touch me, Charlie. Let me . . . please . . . take me home."

She walked, or rather stumbled ahead of him, clutching her body in her folded arms, her hair swinging about her, hiding her face and the bloody tracks across her breast.

About half-way down the Edge they came to where Natty Varty lay dead, his faithful dog crouched beside him and her cries which had swept the fells in March for her child, rose again in a growing, maddened crescendo.

The constable looked sternly from the man who stalked dangerously about the warm kitchen of the farmhouse to the woman sitting quietly in the chair by the fire and the expression of distaste on his face deepened. He stood with his hand on the latch of the door as though he was ready to be off. He was a member of the brand new police force which had been raised following the County Police Act of 1839 and though even now, twelve years after the Act was passed, there were still counties without a professional police force, Cumberland was not one of them. He had come from Keswick on his sturdy bay to investigate the ridiculous charge brought by Miss Annabelle Abbott of Browhead Farm that she had been 'set upon' – the constable's words, not hers – by Mr Bertram Garnett of Upfell Farm and wished him to be arrested and taken to the County gaol to await trial. She had been alone on Ullock Pike at the time, she said, bringing down her sheep ready for the Keswick Tup Fair and it was there that the crime against her person had been committed.

Eyeing her trousers, the man's grey woollen shirt and the waistcoat she wore over it, the constable had been hard pressed not to answer to the effect that could any man be blamed for thinking that *Miss* Abbott was not the sort of female to whom respect should be shown, or indeed, if it had happened, though she had not mentioned the word, that *rape* could be done to a woman of her character!

Mr Garnett certainly did not seem to think so when the constable, apologetically, had approached him an hour or so earlier.

"Bugger me, constable, d'yer mean ter say that trollop's

accusin' me of interferin' wi' 'er?" Bert's expression was bewildered, innocent, ready to be offended for really, should a man be accused of such gross indecency – or that was how it would be described if levelled at a *decent* woman – in front of his own wife and children? Grouped about the table they were, the children's faces given a wipe over with a sleazy cloth for the occasion, their mouths agape, their eyes round and wondering, his wife's swollen belly a handy place to perch the youngest. A respectable man with a respectable wife and what, he asked, with outrage in his voice, would he need, or want, with Annie Abbott? Mind you, she was free with her favours. Ask any man around these parts, having had an illegitimate child before she was sixteen. Take that fellow she lived with. Why didn't she marry him? Bert wanted to know and then there was him up at Long Beck. A married man with a wife any chap'd be glad to have beside him but *his* carryings on with the slut from Browhead had caused his wife's father to take her away before her health suffered. No better than a prostitute was Annie Abbott and it was well known you couldn't rape a prostitute, now could you, and as for himself, well, giving his enormous wife an affectionate squeeze, surely the constable could see that Bert Garnett had all he needed in his own cosy kitchen at Upfell.

The constable, embarrassed beyond measure, could only agree before getting on his bay and riding back to Browhead.

"Mr Garnett denies everything, Miss . . . er . . . Abbott, an' with no one ter bear out yer allegation, no witnesses, ah mean, then there's nothin' the law can do. Tha' needs a witness, yer see . . ."

"Miss Abbott has marks on her body which she has shown to Phoebe here."

"Aye, so yer said, but if she was attacked by a man, an' who's ter say it were a man, that doesn't mean it were Bert Garnett what done it."

"Miss Abbott swears it was Bert Garnett. Is that not enough? And the wounds to her body surely bear out . . . ?"

"Ah suppose tha've seen these wounds then, Mr . . .
er . . . ?" The constable's tone was insulting.

"Lucas." Charlie *was* insulted and his white face said
so.

"Mr Lucas."

"No, I have not see them, naturally, but as I have just
said, Miss Abbott's companion has. Tell the constable,
Phoebe."

Phoebe shrank back on the settle, the forbidding regard
of the constable unnerving her. She was a servant, a found-
ling brought up to believe that authority was all powerful
and to have seen what she had on Annie's breasts and
belly was hard enough without having to describe it to this
man in uniform. Charlie was nodding at her encouragingly,
but when she turned to Annie, her expression desperate,
asking did she really want it exposed – even in words –
for all the world to ogle, Annie merely continued to stare,
hands clasped in her lap, into the smouldering peat fire.
And could you blame her, Phoebe agonised, for not taking
a great deal of interest in the constable after what she had
suffered, not only this year, at the hands of men, but going
back to her childhood when her father had treated her no
better than a labouring beast in the field. There was that
bugger who had seduced her and left her with a child and
even that small and precious gift had been ripped away
from her in the cruellest way when Cat died. She had been
humiliated, shamed, spat upon, reviled and yet she had
held her head high, held her tongue still and got on with
her life, but still they would not let her be. The men!
The men who lusted after her. Not all, of course, for the
goodness of Charlie Lucas's love shone from him every
time he looked at her, which was most of the time, and
Natty Varty's devotion had been strong, impeccable,
unassailable. Poor old Natty who lay on the table in the
parlour, washed, tidy, peaceful in the deep sleep of death,
waiting for someone to put him in a coffin and carry him
along the corpse way to St Bridget's by the lake.

And who was that to be? Phoebe wondered painfully for
not one man had come forward to help, not even those

from up Long Beck. Not even Mr Macauley himself.

"Speak up, Phoebe," Charlie said gently, "tell the constable about Annie's injuries," coming to squat before her, taking her hands in his but she hung her head for how could she shame Annie by describing to this stern and hostile man what was on her body? How could she say the words, the intimate words she had spoken to no one in her life, not even another woman? It was impossible, really it was, and the worst thing about it – well, not *the* worst for that was surely what had been done to Annie – was that when the trial was held, as Charlie was determined it would be, she would have to stand up in court and say it, not to one man but a dozen. The jury in fact, and how was she, a simple country girl who could barely read, cope with that?

"Charlie, leave her alone. Don't waste your breath, or the constable's time since it will come to nothing. I only agreed to it so that . . . well, you know why."

And of course he did. Phoebe knew it too. Out of his mind, he had been, off his head and ready, *determined* to batter his way up to the Mounsey farm and with his own bare hands slowly squeeze the life from Bert Garnett's body. No, he would not be satisfied even with that, he had snarled, for it was too quick, too merciful. He would beat him to death, methodically, slowly, until Bert lay dead and bloody at his feet. His hard fist on Bert's hard bone, shattering, breaking, blood flowing, Bert screaming, his own mind empty of all but the satisfying need to have revenge, *justice* for what Bert Garnett had done to his love, the darling of his heart and not only to her, but to Phoebe. Charlie Lucas, mild mannered, good-natured, easy going had lost control, his violence exploding in a great shellburst of savagery which had the three dogs cowering away from him before slinking off into the parlour where the old man lay.

Charlie had brought him down from the fell after Annie's wounds had been seen to but it had taken all her strength of mind to make him do it since he was in such a hurry to get to Upfell.

"You will leave him to lie there until it is convenient then, will you, Charlie? Until you have attended to more important matters such as the flogging you mean to give Bert Garnett?"

"There will be no flogging, Annie. There will be a killing. I mean to . . . Dear Christ . . . I mean to make him pay dearly for . . ."

"Very well, Charlie, do what you have to do but before you go to Upfell collect your belongings and take them with you for you will never come back into my house."

"*Annie!*" Charlie's voice was anguished and the crazed dementia which had him by the throat and which was threatening to topple him over the brink of sanity, lessened a fraction.

"I mean it, Charlie. Go and get Natty, for if you don't, Phoebe and I will."

"I won't let that bastard . . ."

"I know. I shouldn't have told you about him. I could have blamed it on a tinker or a passing drover but I was not . . . in my right mind . . . after what he'd . . . after . . . then to find Natty . . . Oh, Jesus Christ, when is it to end? First Cat . . . my fault, and now . . . again . . . my pride and stubbornness . . . he said it would happen if I continued to roam the fells alone but I took no notice."

"He . . . ?"

"Yes . . . and now, because of me . . . Natty is dead . . ."

Her weeping sorrow had been inconsolable and as Phoebe rocked her in the only arms Annie would have about her, Charlie had been half-way across the yard to Upfell and would have got there had she not leaped up, throwing Phoebe to one side and gone after him, hanging on to his arm like a limpet, even when he dragged her from her feet. It was only then, when her flesh was scraped raw on the cobblestone and her voice screamed his name, did Charlie's derangement lessen, at least enough to help Phoebe get her to her feet and back in the kitchen. And to go up on the fell to bring Natty home.

The constable looked at them, waiting to see if one of the three had anything further to say on the matter. There was no doubt in his mind that the woman had taken some sort of a beating. There were bruises on her throat and a nasty cut on her lip where she had evidently been struck by a hard fist, but she was so bloody calm, so *uncaring*, just as though what had happened to her, whatever it was, was something to which she was not unaccustomed. And perhaps that was the case. This chap who lived with her, so it was said, was like a caged beast snarling about the kitchen, smacking one fist into the palm of the other, looking violent enough to flatten anyone so perhaps it was *him* who had set on her. Women were funny creatures where their men were concerned. And no one knew anything about him. Just came out of the blue, he did, a year or two back, and had stayed. There was talk of her and Mr Reed Macauley up at Long Beck, and of a certain amount of animosity between him and this chap here, and who was to say they had not fought over her? Perhaps she'd stepped between them and got caught in the crossfire, so to speak, though why she should pick on poor Bert Garnett to blame for it, who'd never caused a minute's bother in the district since he'd married the Mounsey girl, was a mystery.

"Ah'll put it before my superiors," he said pompously, opening the door on the cold, blustery wind which was sweeping across the fells and ruffling the water of the lake. The weather had taken a turn for the worse overnight, the hazed autumn sunshine of the day before hidden behind racing clouds of torn grey in every shade from pale grey to pewter.

No one answered him. At the parlour door which stood partly open, for somehow it had seemed to Phoebe that it was callous to leave poor old Natty all alone, Blackie and Bonnie pushed enquiring noses sensing a diminishing of the oppression which had so alarmed them. Natty's dog could be seen, his muzzle on his paws, his old eyes never leaving the still figure of his master on the table.

For a moment the constable wavered. It was all so . . . so quiet . . . so resigned and helpless, so *law-abiding*, so *normal*. Apart from the man, who appeared to be helpless in the grip of some awful pain, some tamped down, stamped upon emotion he was forced – for some reason – to control. The room was filled with peace, warmth, comfort even. An ordinary farmhouse kitchen where the only catastrophe to mar the day would be the failure of the farmwife's bread to rise. The woman still gazed sadly into the fire, her beautiful, tragic face – and the constable admitted it was both of these – pale as alabaster, her eyes, which he knew to be of a strange transparent brown, shadowed by her long, drooping lashes. Her hair was brushed back from her brow and braided high at the back of her head, the braid wound into an enormous coil. The other one, the little, plain one, held her hand between her own, her expression one of agonising remorse, and what he thought might be shame at her own inability to protect her mistress, if that was what she was, to speak up for her, to stand up and speak for her in this dreadful affair. Women like her were afraid of such things, afraid to make a fuss. It was believed in male circles that a female should remain in her home where she would be safe from harm and temptation and that any woman foolish enough to be out alone deserved to be molested. That the local constabulary should not be troubled with such sorry episodes. That incidents such as this were best left to settle themselves. Male violence in such cases was well known but it would not become a case if women, decent women, that is, stayed where they belonged. As this woman had not!

"Ah'll be off then," he told them briskly.

"And that's the end of it then, is it?" the man said bitterly, turning to glare at the constable. The dogs, catching his menace, turned and faced him too since he was the intruder, their hackles rising.

"Mr·Lucas, ah've 'eard what Miss Abbott 'ad ter say an' ah've listened ter what Mr Garnett 'ad ter say an' both say different. 'Tis 'er word against 'is and . . ."

"And of course you would be bound to take the word

of a fine, upstanding chap like that bastard who regularly beats his own wife and . . ."

"That's nothin' ter do wi' me, sir an' wi'out a witness ter this supposed attack there's nowt' ah can do."

"SUPPOSED . . . !"

"There's no evidence ter support . . ."

"There's the evidence of the scars on Miss Abbott's . . ."

"*Charlie!* For God's sake leave it. What would you have me do? Strip myself naked so that the constable may see for himself what's been done to me?"

Charlie was appalled. "Darling, of course not but . . ."

"Then that's an end to it."

"Is it? Is it really? Do you imagine I'm going to let Bert Garnett put his evil hands on you . . . and other things . . ." His face worked in agony as the frightful, filthy images of what Bert Garnett had done to her crowded into his fertile and imaginative mind and he turned away, his hand covering his eyes as though to block them out. "I can't allow it, Annie. I won't allow it. What sort of a man would I be if I simply went on as though it had not happened?"

Still he kept his back to the room and the constable shifted uncomfortably, not at all used to seeing such painful emotions in a man. But then perhaps *he'd* be the same if it was *his* wife or *his* girl who'd been . . . Dear God, what was he thinking of? The anguished atmosphere in the room was beginning to influence him into making judgements and convicting Bert Garnett of a crime for which there was absolutely no evidence against him. He'd best be off before his impartial concern in the matter was impaired, though of course what he thought – what did he think? – made no difference one way or the other. But she was so *sad*, there was no other word to describe Annie Abbott, the one they called the woman from Browhead.

But it seemed Mr Lucas had not yet finished.

"I only held back yesterday because you made me,

Annie. Fetch Natty, you said, and I did. Go and thrash Bert Garnett and I won't allow you back in my house, you said, so I stayed. The law is on our side, you said. He will be punished by the due course of the law and though I didn't believe it since I have seen the way the ordinary man is treated by the law on my marches to the . . . well, you will know what I mean. I realise now that all you said was merely a . . . a stratagem to prevent me taking the law into my own hands, but as you can see for yourself the law of this land . . ." turning to look contemptuously at the constable, ". . . does not concern itself with . . ."

"Now look 'ere . . ."

"No, you look here, constable. If you will do nothing to punish Bert Garnett for the horrors . . . for his brutal attacks on these two women . . ."

"TWO . . . !"

"Oh yes, not so long ago he beat Phoebe here senseless . . ."

"It was not reported."

"No, she . . . denied it was him . . ."

"Why is that then?"

"She had her reasons." Charlie turned away wearily. "Oh, what's the use? The man must be punished and it seems there is no one but myself willing to do it so if you will excuse me . . ."

"*Charlie . . . no . . . !*"

"Now look 'ere, sir, you can't tek law inter yer own 'ands. There's nowt ter prove that Bert Garnett attacked your . . . your . . . Miss Abbott an' if . . . well, sir, should 'e be found injured in any way it would naturally be assumed that you were t' culprit an' ah would . . ."

The screams could be heard only faintly at first and the constable did not appear to have heard them, his calm voice, for surely this chap needed calming, continuing to flow from him in what he hoped were soothing waves. The dogs pricked their ears and both Annie and Phoebe turned their heads towards the open door where the constable still leaned. Leaves had been tossed in by the wind, scurrying about the flags like small animals and a billow of smoke spluttered from the chimney caused by the draught the open door allowed in.

The screams grew louder and the constable turned in alarm, his face plainly showing his bewilderment. What in tarnation was up now, his expression said, on this bedevilled day? The screams were that of a woman, perhaps attacked by the same chap who had brutalised Miss Abbott, he remembered thinking, and when Mrs Garnett, whom he had seen no more than two hours ago in the rather unsavoury comfort of her own kitchen, lumbered into view, her children in a long, wailing line behind her, his face gaped in consternation.

She could not speak as she clutched at his arm. Her hair was about her like that of a mad woman's and through it her eyes peered in terror. She still had her baby under one arm, its fists flailing, its cries piteous and for several minutes it was bedlam in the kitchen as the constable endeavoured to extract some sense from the heavily pregnant woman. The two other women were calm though, putting Mrs Garnett on the settle, soothing the crying children with biscuits, brewing tea and even Mr Lucas who, it appeared to him, loathed the very sound of the name Garnett, took one child on his knee before the fire.

"What is it, Sally?" Miss Abbott was saying compassionately and the constable began to believe at that moment that . . . well, that there might be some truth in her story. "Is it . . . has he . . . ?" She could not, it appeared, quite bring herself to say his name.

"Bert, aye, it's Bert . . ."

"Has he . . . hit you . . . ?"

"No . . . oh, no . . ."

"Then what . . . ?"

The constable shut the door behind him and moved forward since it seemed to him this might be a matter in which the law could be involved. Mrs Garnett kept turning to him as though she thought so too, ignoring Miss Abbott's kindness.

"'Tis Bert, constable . . ." Her face was as white as bleached bone and her eyes looked haunted.

"What about Bert, Mrs Garnett? Has he had an accident?"

"Oh, no . . . at least . . ."

"Yes?"

"Three men come . . ."

"Yes?"

"They took 'im away. Jesus, 'e were screamin' it weren't 'im. That she'd made it up . . ."

"What? She'd made what up? Who did 'e mean?"

Sally turned her gaze on Annie but in her eyes there was nothing but a kind of sad regret.

They found Bert Garnett the next day, high on the highest point of Skiddaw where he had lain all night. A note pushed under his wife's kitchen door told her where he could be found. One of his legs was broken, and his right wrist, and when he was brought down Sally was hard pressed to recognise him. No more than a crumple of bleeding bones, his cheeks gashed, his teeth gone, his ribs broken. The painful scrape of his breath testified to damage in his lungs, the strange look in his eyes to the damage in his head.

They helped her, all the women of the parish, rallying round her as she and her mother had always rallied round them in times of trouble. But not one would stay, they told her, if she allowed the woman from Browhead across her threshwood. This was *her* fault, they said venomously, flaunting herself all over the fells and in the village causing men to . . . well, of course they were not saying it *had* been Bert who had assaulted her, that is if she had been assaulted, which they doubted, and if the constable had not been at her farm and that man of hers under the constable's nose when Bert was taken, he would certainly have been arrested for the crime. Dear Lord, there'd been nothing but trouble ever since she'd come back to Bassenthwaite and if they had any say in it, which, being women, they hadn't, she'd have been tarred and feathered and flogged out of town like they used to do in the old days.

He came that night, Reed Macauley, knocking quietly

at her door and when Charlie opened it, tipping his hat curtly before pushing past him into her kitchen. His eyes went straight to her as she stood up and in them was the deep and abiding truth of his love for her, his compassion, his fear.

"Are you all right?" he asked. The other two in the room were of no concern nor interest to him.

"Yes."

"He did not . . . ?" His voice faltered for a moment, ". . . rape you?"

"No, only . . ."

"He was telling the truth then. I thought so."

"It was . . . you?"

"Yes. Some men I know brought him to me. It was a fair fight. Just myself and Bert Garnett. I won. He couldn't be allowed to get away with it. I wouldn't allow him to."

He turned to Charlie then and though his voice was flat and quite without expression, it was very evident that the remark was aimed at him.

"You're still here then." It was not a question. His eyes were a flat, cold blue and around one of them was a deep purple bruise where Bert Garnett's fist had found its mark and his bottom lip was split. "Don't you think it's time you moved on? I can supply Annie with all the hired help she needs."

"You bastard." Charlie's voice was no more than a whisper and at once Annie went to stand beside him, putting her hand through his arm.

"Charlie wanted to thrash Bert but I wouldn't let him."

"Really." Reed smiled.

"There is no need for you to defend me to this man, my darling. I know what I should have done and wanted to do, and his opinion is of no concern to me . . ."

It seemed Reed Macauley's attention had gone no further than the endearment.

"*My darling!* My darling . . ." he snarled, his arrogant presence suddenly immensely dangerous in the small room. "She is not your darling, you insolent bastard, nor ever will be and I'd be obliged if you'd take your filthy hands off her before I give you a taste of what I gave Bert Garnett since you were too much of a coward to do it yourself. *Move away from her . . . !*"

"I have more right to her than you, you swine. Tell me, is it not true that you already have a wife?"

"Not for long. I am waiting to hear from my lawyer . . ."

"So you said several months ago."

"My wife has left me and . . ."

"Oh, please . . . stop it . . . stop it . . . Phoebe, can't you make them stop it . . ."

"Annie, come with me to Long Beck. You will be safe there from the kind of abuse you were subjected to yesterday. Let *me* protect you . . ."

"Reed, please . . ."

"Leave her alone, you bastard . . ."

"Come with me, Annie . . ."

"Reed, please . . . if you don't leave my home I will . . ."

"Yes, Annie, what *will* you do?"

"Oh, God, I don't know . . ." and before the appalled gaze of the three who loved her most in the world she slid bonelessly to the floor, putting her face in her hands and beginning to weep with the inconsolable intensity of a child. "I cannot stand another moment of this . . . can't you see . . . both of you . . . you are destroying me . . . I want peace . . . peace, not this . . . Oh, God, not this."

At once they were both bending over her but with a curt word of dismissal Phoebe was there, helping her up, holding her close, moving with her towards the twisting staircase.

"Yer like two dogs fightin' over a bone," she said through clenched teeth, ". . . an' should be ashamed o' thissen. An' what about that poor old man in there, tell me that? 'Appen if tha' was ter see about 'is coffin an' gettin' 'im along corpse way to 'is funeral it'd give 'er more comfort than thy brawlin' over 'er. That's what she needs. Comfort an' a bit o' peace."

Natty Varty was laid to rest by Charlie Lucas and Reed Macauley two days later, causing consternation in the community, for what was the hussy up to now? they wondered. They carried the coffin between them without a word, standing silently by the open grave, the two women beside them and when it was over, parting the same way.

33

The winter was hard and cold, long weeks of blizzards which locked them in the farmhouse as though they were prisoners in jail. Long weeks of freezing after that, during which Annie's main concern was for her pregnant ewes. They were quiet months in which the three of them saw no one but each other. Months of calm and peace and the slow fading away of the horrors of the previous year. Not Cat of course, she would never be forgotten, nor would the grieving and sense of loss be totally absent, but an acceptance was painfully gained day by slow day, until it was possible to live in some content and blessing.

The great white bowl of the valley glistened under a sky so deep and intense a blue it was almost the colour of the bluebells which carpeted the woods in May. The sheep had been brought down, a long dark ribbon etched thinly against the whiteness as they came in single file, each following the tail of the one in front directed by Blackie and Bonnie, though not Natty's dog, who kept close to the fire now, and at the bottom Charlie and Annie threw out great flaps of hay for the hungry sheep to feed on. The goodness of summer was in the hay and the sheep consumed it at great speed, keeping a wary eye on the dogs whilst Annie and Charlie watched in smiling silence. When he put his arm about her shoulder she moved away, pretending a concern for a ewe but he knew it was really an excuse to avoid his touch and he sighed, anguished, his hopes of last year when she had seemed to him to be ready for his love, dashed away.

He would never know who had caused it, Bert Garnett or Reed Macauley. Neither had been seen since that day in October when Bert had tried to rape Annie and Natty had died. Of course Reed Macauley was a businessman as well as a farmer, with concerns that took him to Carlisle, to London and even, it was rumoured, abroad to foreign parts, and those who had been his guests before his wife left him and who speculated on his whereabouts were in no doubt that wherever it was and whatever he was doing, he would be doing it in style. A man who enjoyed the pleasures of the flesh was Reed Macauley, a fastidious man accustomed to luxury, good living, every comfort his considerable wealth could achieve for him. It was said he had been a time or two to Long Beck checking on his assets there, making sure those he left in charge were doing their duty but he had certainly not gone near the woman from Browhead, whose name had been linked, on several occasions, with his. Speculation abounded, mouths pressed to ears that were pricked for any gossip which was fed by the interest Reed Macauley had always aroused in them. Did he see his lovely young wife? Was he trying to effect a reconciliation? Or was he, as it had been whispered last year, still pursuing that elusive something called 'a divorce' which it was said he had been seeking in London? Not one of them knew anyone who had been divorced or even how one went about obtaining such a thing, and it was certain that if one did, one would instantly become a social outcast. Divorces were granted of course, but only by a special Act of Parliament and then only after the Ecclesiastical Court granted a decree similar to that of judicial separation, which still did not dissolve a marriage, and was granted only on the grounds of adultery or cruelty and how could the lovely Mrs Reed Macauley be accused of either of these? It had been known for a man of the nobility to free himself from an adulterous wife, the law taking the view that a man such as he must be free to re-marry and get himself an heir but Reed Macauley did not fall into that category.

The winter drew to its end and in April spring flowers began to appear. There were morning mists which rolled away to reveal purple mountain saxifrage among the damp mountain rocks and the exquisite beauty of the early purple orchids which shyly raised their heads among the trees. Blue moor-grass studded the dry limestone rocks. Hellebore and bitter vetch poked their heads through last year's vegetation and in the hedgerows, purple bush-vetch, sweet woodruff, red lungwort and water-avens suddenly burgeoned, all the life-giving plants from which Aggie Mounsey had once prepared potions to ease the living and comfort the dying.

At Upfell Bert Garnett shuffled about the yard on the makeshift crutch someone had fashioned for him, his face quite blank, his eyes slow moving, his mind indifferent to the gradual disintegration of his farm. His flock, most of which had survived the winter, thanks to his brother-in-law Ben Postlethwaite, had been brought down from the high fell, and at the right time, Ben had put the tup he owned to the ewes. Upfell's inland pastures were lush and fertile, the Mounsey ewes thrived but when their lambs were dropped Bert was unaware of it.

Annie was alone in the front pasture when Sally came. Charlie was planting the oats and bigg and in the cow barn Phoebe was fondly contemplating the new addition to Annie's livestock, the calf born to Clover a fortnight ago. Clover was Phoebe's pride and joy, a handsome black-and-white Friesian, serviced by Reed Macauley's bull last year when it was walked over by Jake Singleton, and when put to the task, had obliged right willingly. It had been a part of the unspoken support Reed had ordered his men to give Annie after Cat had died, and about which Annie had been unaware. From March until the end of May when Charlie returned, and with him Annie's senses, small services had been performed by Jake and Maggie, and the calf, a heifer and, in Phoebe's loving opinion, as pretty as a picture, was the result of one of them. Of course, the calf drank all her mother's milk, that with which Phoebe had made her cheese and butter, but when she was weaned, which Phoebe meant to do when the calf was five weeks old, she told Annie importantly, for she was a strong little devil, Phoebe's butter- and cheese-making would resume. Flaked maize and bruised oats mixed with

her own mother's skimmed milk was what Phoebe meant
to give the calf, clean water and good hay and next month
when the weather turned warmer she could be turned out
in the field with her mother.

The lambing was done with, timed to coincide with the
new growth of grass, and they had all three worked for a
solid month from six in the morning until after dark, lambs
coming in an ever-increasing number, those born in the
first week marked up and ready for the fell. Taking them
up there no more than a score at a time and aided by the
two dogs, Annie had found the task immensely satisfying
as she watched her growing flock, past the first dangers
of infancy, leap enthusiastically towards the new grass and
bracken of their first summer. This was her fourth spring
since she and Charlie had brought her ewes from Rosley
and now, from that dozen, she had over a hundred, a
sturdy flock of Herdwicks which, this year, God willing,
would yield almost twice that number.

Sally's voice was hesitant at her back, and she started,
for she had been deep in contemplation of her growing
success. Blackie and Bonnie were down the field, gently
urging some recalcitrant mothers and babies towards the
gate which led to the open fell, and Annie had been sitting
on the wall, watching as they worked. She scarcely needed
to give the dogs commands now as they moved instinctively and in complete unison at their work.

"Hello, Annie," Sally said, and when Annie turned
sharply, Sally stepped back as though she would not have
been surprised had Annie struck her.

"Sally! I was . . . day-dreaming and did not hear you."
Annie threw her legs over the wall and jumped down as
light and free in her neat breeches and knitted jerkin as a
lad of twelve. Her hair was severely braided away from
her face and she looked very different from the golden,
graceful woman, her hair in a magnificent tawny tumble
down her straight back, who had captured Reed
Macauley's wilful heart almost five years ago. Still as
beautiful but in a neutral way, cool, detached, tempered.
Gone was the vital spark burning within her, the radiance

which had shimmered in her golden eyes. Remaining was a sculptured perfection of lovely bone and flesh, unwarmed by emotion. She was slender, almost but not quite thin and the wary caution with which she now viewed the world was very apparent in the way she turned to Sally.

"Sorry, Annie, I didn't mean to disturb thee."

"Not at all Sally, I'm pleased to see you."

"Really," Sally was clearly amazed and Annie smiled.

"Really. Come inside and have a cup of tea, Phoebe and Charlie are not about so you and I can have a chat."

"Eeh Annie tha's a good lass. I thought . . . well, after what 'appened last year that . . . well . . ."

Annie stopped and turned again to Sally, taking her chapped, none too clean hands in hers. Her face was serious but gentle.

"Look Sal, you mustn't blame yourself for what . . . what *he* did to me. I don't blame you and neither does Phoebe. We know what sort of a . . . well, he's your husband and . . . whatever he has done I suppose you would stick by him but . . ."

"Nay, lass, if he were in his right mind my life'd be hell but he's different now and I can't help but be sorry for him."

"Well, I'm afraid I don't feel the same, Sally." Annie's voice was cold, hard and she dropped Sally's hand, turning away, but Sally put it on her arm again, forcing her to stop.

"I know that, lass, God, don't I know it. I were never wi'out a black eye and a bairn under me pinny but that beatin' he got changed all that. Senseless he is now and crippled and if it weren't for what Mr Macauley sends down . . ."

Annie became utterly still. They had entered the kitchen. The fire blazed, the flames reflecting on all the dozens of polished surfaces Phoebe vigorously burnished each day, dancing in golden shadows on the white walls. There were bowls and jugs of spring flowers on every window bottom and in front of the fire on the rag-rug Phoebe had made especially for him, Natty's dog raised his head and thumped his tail a couple of times before resuming the doze in which he spent his old days. Dandy, the marmalade cat, was curled companionably at his back, sharing his rug, and a couple of kittens from her last litter chased a feather which had somehow got into Phoebe's clean kitchen. The kettle spluttered pleasingly, the kail pot bubbled with a tasty stew and on the 'bakstone' oat-cakes, baked that morning, were kept warm for their meal. There was a feeling of comfortable plenty, of ease and modest prosperity and Sally looked about her, not with envy, though it did remind her of how her mother's kitchen had been, years ago, but with admiration. She had always known Annie Abbott was a girl of forbearance and iron resolve. Well, she'd had to be with a faither like Joshua Abbott but she'd gone further than Sally had ever thought she could.

". . . looks a treat in here, Annie, an' it's clear tha's worked 'ard and done well for thissen . . ." she was saying.

"What did you say?" Annie's hand had been reaching for the teapot on the ledge above the fire but it fell limply to her side as she turned to look at Sally.

"I said it were a treat in 'ere, lass, especially as tha' . . ."

"No, before that."

Sally looked puzzled. "Before what?"

"About . . . Reed Macauley."

"What about him?"

"You said he was sending . . ."

"Oh, aye, 'tis true. That yardman of 'is comes down every week wi' summat in a basket. Enough to feed us all on account o' Bert not being right yet. 'Tis a mystery, really it is, for the Macauleys weren't right well known for their charity. Old Mrs Macauley wouldn't spit on yer if you was on fire. Cut a currant in 'alf, her cook used ter say an' now there's her lad sendin' great baskets o' grub down to Upfell. Don't like ter think o' the children wi'out a bite to eat, I suppose, an' often enough there's a few bob screwed in a bit of paper. Just until Bert gets on 'is feet, that Jake Singleton said, that's what Mr Macauley told him ter tell me . . ."

So he was at it again. Dispensing largesse to those in need and who more deserving of it than poor Sally Garnett whose husband Reed Macauley had crippled and from what Sally said, scrambled his brains to the extent he could no longer function as a farmer, as a man. His leg and arm broken, it was said, and his face smashed to pulp but those would mend, Annie had thought, but it seemed no part of Bert Garnett was mending, especially his mind. And so Reed . . . Reed . . .

Her heart moved painfully in her breast and a great longing to see him swept over her in such terrifying waves she had to turn away from Sally, only preventing herself from swaying dangerously close to the fire by leaning on the shelf. All these months she had shut him out, her mind closing like a trap every time a vagrant thought had eluded the tight rein she had on herself, and tried to enter it. All these months when she and Charlie might have . . . what? . . . perhaps become lovers? . . . married? . . . given comfort and love and true friendship to one another . . . to have known a certain pleasure in one another's arms . . . *he* had been there . . . always . . . lurking just out of sight and sound . . . hidden behind a rippling curtain of mist . . . unseen but *there*, preventing it, preventing her from becoming a real woman again. At first it had been Bert Garnett, a spectre of male violence, of male dominance, of the cruel, degrading, disgusting things he had done to her which had made her shrink away from Charlie's masculinity, but later, she had admitted it to herself, that had become the excuse she used to keep Charlie at arm's length. She loved Charlie so much, his hurt had been hers. He was the dearest man in the world to her, but he was not Reed. She loved Reed as a man. She wanted Reed as a woman wants her man and the simple, unvarnished truth was that her body could not contemplate the merging of itself with any but Reed Macauley's. She did not even know where he was. Presumably he came back to Long Beck to give orders to his servants and, it seemed, to dispense charity to Sally and her family. Perhaps he lived elsewhere with his wife, how was she to know, and more to the point, did it really matter? He *had* a wife whether he lived with her or not . . . Oh, sweet, sweet Jesus, but she loved him, longed to see him, to see that ironic smile . . . aah, don't . . . she could not bear to remember . . . the shape of his lips . . . on hers . . . his hands brown, hard . . . gentle on her body . . . it was killing her, this agony of feeling she didn't want, this love she didn't want. She was afraid of it, afraid of loving, not just Reed but *anyone*. It was so much easier to be detached, to be unaroused by anything more exciting than a healthy lamb, a fine crop of early potatoes, a warm fire to drowse by. Friendship, such as she and Phoebe had, demanding nothing, but not love, not *love* for when love went, when *loss* came, the pain was unendurable. She could not endure it, not any more . . . she must stop before Sally . . .

". . . so 'tis like havin' seven bairns with Bert as he is, you knew I'd another lass, didn't you? . . . *No!* . . . oh, aye, just after Bert fell ill. Kitty she's called but she'll be the last, thank God, what with Bert shamblin' about the place half-witted. Don't want me anymore, poor sod, or *can't*, an' I've to think of the bairns, haven't I? 'Tis a snug little cottage up by Binsey an' I'll be near our Mim and 'er two. Ben's mother died last backend so it all worked out right well. Ben wanted the farm hisself but it's too far for 'im ter come over an' work it, what with 'is own and he can't afford to pay anyone, an' then o' course wi' Mim to 'elp me, well, we can 'elp each other, bein' so close . . . anyway, I said to Bert . . . well, I still talk to him, Annie, even if he don't answer . . . I said ter Bert, Annie's doin' that well, 'appen she'll be interested, so I come over ter give thi' first refusal."

Sally was sitting at her ease in the chair which had been Joshua Abbott's and for a moment Annie could feel his presence in this kitchen, on this farm where he had struggled and laboured for almost fifty years as a boy and as a man and had never in all that time known true success. Blight and murrain had swept through his crops and his sheep with devastating regularity, and yet each time he had patiently, often with great bitterness, heaved himself upright and carried on. Now, or so it seemed to her stunned brain, Sally was asking her, *her*, Joshua Abbott's daughter, if she cared to buy Upfell Farm. Upfell and its splendid acres of rich inland pastures, its intakes and woodland, its snug farmhouse, all lying neatly beside her own land, twice the size of hers and if . . . dear God in Heaven . . . if she could do it . . . perhaps a loan . . . the bank . . . Mr . . . what was his name? . . . the lawyer in Lancaster . . . she would have a farm, not as big as Reed's, but bigger than most . . . a flock of hundreds . . . cattle . . . it was just too much to take in . . .

"Shall I mek tea?" Sally said sympathetically as Annie fell back on the settle.

"How much money have you got?" were Charlie's first words when she told him, and her fine and ecstatic rapture ebbed away. She felt a surge of resentment, a distinct need to stand up and stamp about in high dudgeon for how dare he spoil her lovely dream, the rainbow-coloured, star-dazzled, brilliantly glowing dream she had dwelled in ever since Sally had ambled off up the path towards Upfell. But of course the question must be answered, considered first, and answered. She certainly did not have enough to buy a farm, let alone the livestock on it but if she could get a loan . . . perhaps using Browhead as . . . what was the word? . . . collateral . . . ?

"How much, Annie?" Charlie asked again, his eyes grave, his expression withdrawn. "You know you have to examine . . ."

"I could borrow against Browhead, Charlie." Her eager face was flushed, lovely again, alive with an animation she had not known, or shown for months. It was as though she had been given a new lease on life itself, the chance to begin again, to seize hold of something worthwhile, something wonderful which she had thought would never come again.

"Who from?"

"Well . . . there's the bank in Keswick or . . ."

"Or Reed Macauley."

The silence which followed was deep and painful and in her quiet corner, Phoebe's hands stilled on the bit of work she had in them. She never sat down without something, knitting, a sock to be darned, a tear mended, a button to be sewn on Charlie's shirt, since it went against all she had been taught from the time she had been considered old enough to ply a needle, that idle hands meant mischief. That is what they had said to her, though what mischief a frightened, blank-eyed four-year-old foundling could get up to in her hard, fourteen-hour day, had never been explained to her. She looked from one awkward face to the other, seeing the confirmation she looked for in Annie Abbott's eyes, though Annie of course denied it.

"I said nothing about Reed Macauley, Charlie."

"You don't have to, Annie."

"And what does that mean?"

"It means that . . . you . . . still think of him . . ."

"Don't be ridiculous."

". . . and that you . . . because you want Upfell so badly, you would go to him for the money. He is the only man of real wealth in these parts. He lends money to . . . to those who need a loan and feeling about you as he does, a fact he made very clear when he almost killed Bert Garnett, which I should have done and didn't, he would not hesitate to further his claim, indeed he would give you the money *and you know it.*"

"That's not true . . ."

"Which part is not true, Annie?"

"Any of it."

"Do you deny he loves you?"

"Charlie . . . please . . . don't . . ."

"And by your tone I would say you still feel the same about him."

"Charlie, I beg of you, don't do this . . ."

"What, speak the truth or make you face it?"

"He is nothing to do with me, Charlie. He has a wife . . ."

"And if he had not, would I still be here?"

"Charlie, you know what I feel for you."

"Indeed I do, Annie, that is what is so sad about it. I keep hanging about like some faithful old dog hoping for a kind word, a glance, a pat on the head but really it is not enough. I am making a pathetic figure of myself and . . ."

"No, that's not true Charlie, I . . ."

"Don't! don't say you love me, Annie, truly I could not bear it if you did. I don't want what you have to give me, which is what you would give to another woman, what you give to Phoebe. I'm a man with needs of my own which have been sadly neglected over the past years as I've waited patiently for you to . . . Jesus . . . *to notice me*. I'm not a bloody machine, I want you . . . I love you . . . for Christ's sake, can't you . . . ?"

His face moved in a great spasm of self-loathing and he turned away, looking towards the corner in which Phoebe sat. She shrank from his glance, longing with all her heart to leave this room in which emotions flared and grew out of control but Charlie did not even see her there.

"I hate myself for being like this, Annie. I want to beg, to plead with you to let me . . . to let me love you . . . to love me . . ."

"I do . . . Charlie, I do."

He turned on her savagely.

"No, you don't, *you don't*. You love *him* and really, I cannot take much more of watching you do it."

"Charlie . . ."

"No . . . no . . . don't . . ."

In his headlong haste to get away from her, from the possessive love she aroused in him, from the suffering she caused him, from his hatred of Reed Macauley, from the compassion, the fascination, the tenderness, the enchantment of Annie Abbott, he almost knocked her over as she stood up. Fumbling for the door catch, he jerked open the door, crashing his head on the low frame, disappearing into the dark night. They could hear him as he vaulted the wall and the distressed bleating of the sheep as they divided before him, then it was silent.

The dogs, who had sprung to their feet, alarmed by the commotion, settled down again slowly, watching anxiously as Annie moved wearily across the room to close the door.

"He'll be back, Phoebe, he's upset."

"Aye, an' reason to be, I'd say."

"Oh, Phoebe, please don't you start on me now, I can't take much more, really I can't."

"An' neither can Charlie. For God's sake wed him or let him go."

Annie turned to stare in amazement at Phoebe who had resumed her patient stitching.

"*Let him go?*"

"Aye, or he'll never be right again. I know nowt about men but I do know what it's doin' to Charlie watchin' you fret after a chap what . . ."

"I'm not fretting over any chap, Phoebe. I have had . . . sadness."

"I'm not sayin' tha 'asnt, lass, more than most. But face the truth like Charlie said. Give Mr Macauley up. Let him make his peace with his wife 'cos he would if tha' was married to another man."

Annie bent her head and her breath left her on a shuddering sigh. She put her face in her cupped hands and her pain was an appalling menace in the room. It threatened to strike her to her knees from where she would never rise again, to bend her proud, strong back, to break it, to crush her. Blackie stood up hesitantly and moved across to her, pushing his muzzle against her knee and, when her hand dropped to his head, staring up at her with patient, loving eyes.

At last she spoke again.

"I know, Phoebe, what you say is true but . . . but I cannot marry Charlie just to keep him here, which is what I would be doing, and as for Reed . . . and his wife, that is their affair, not mine. They . . . both of them will do what they think fit, which is what I will do. Charlie . . . must make his own choices, Phoebe. I cannot say how I will feel in . . . say, six months. Last year, after Cat died, I was very close to . . . giving in . . ."

"Aye, I noticed."

"You don't miss much do you?"

"No, an' neither did Natty. We both thought that . . ."

"You and he discussed it?"

"Why not then? We're family . . ."

"Of course you are, Phoebe. You and Natty . . ."

"And Charlie?"

"Yes, I love Charlie, but not as he would want." She sighed deeply. "Well, I'd best go and look for him and make my peace."

"Don't do that, Annie. It's not peace he wants. You go ter tha' bed for if I'm any judge, tha'll be off t' bank in Keswick first thing."

She was.

The bank manager in Keswick knew her, as everyone in the parish of Bassenthwaite knew her by now. Who had not heard of her wild ways, her outlandish manner of dressing, her unconventional, outspoken behaviour, her notoriety with regard to Mr Reed Macauley, her capricious flouting of all the laws of decency and morality? Certainly not the bank manager in Keswick and would those who trusted their money and their investments in his honest and trustworthy hands, thank him for lending it to a woman such as her? She had certainly proved herself resourceful, turning her father's farm from failure to a small measure of success, but would it continue? And if it did not, how, he begged her to tell him, averting his eyes from her long trousered legs, the fine turn of her ankle in their highly polished boots, would she repay her debt?

She tried to tell him but he would not be moved. She was a woman, infamous and, more to the point, a risky one.

It was the same with Mr Hancock in Lancaster to where she took the train. Yes, he remembered her, he said kindly, looking not at what she had on for this time in desperation she wore the black mourning dress Reed's women had put on her when Cat died, but at her frail loveliness, for surely this brittle woman who looked as though she would snap like a dried twig, was not capable of running *two* farms, and certainly not of repaying a substantial loan on one of them.

A week later Upfell Farm was sold to a farmer from Lancashire. It was rumoured he had bought it for his younger son, who, having no expectations of inheriting any part of the family farm, wished to strike out on his own.

She had been shearing her sheep, her mind dazed with
how she was to get through when the shearers from Long
Beck came down.

"We've come ter do tha' 'boon clip'," one said dourly,
his short pipe clenched between his teeth.

"But . . ."

"Mr Macauley says if tha' was ter give us an argument
to tell thi' tha' can coom and give us a hand next week."

She could not help but smile though Charlie did not,
at the idea that Annie Abbott would make the smallest
difference in the shearing of Reed Macauley's 2,000 ewes
and gimmers, his yearlings and twinters and the fine rams
he owned to keep his flock pure and strong. She could
just imagine him, his eyes gleaming with sardonic humour,
giving the message to this man, knowing her and her stubbornness against taking what she would see as charity.
He had been at Long Beck for several weeks now, so they
were told, the news brought by Maggie Singleton who
could not resist her natural pride in the fine son she had
borne Jake Singleton, when she came down to Browhead
to show him off to Phoebe.

Annie and Phoebe, thankfully, both of them, left the
yard to the men who had brought their own shears and
shearing stools, and with Charlie and a boy to heave the
sheep in their direction and a couple of others to salve
those shorn, the two women contented themselves with
the women's age-old task of feeding the workers.

It was Charlie, not the presence of the Long Beck men,
who had inclined Annie to move indoors. She and Charlie
were not easy in one another's company these days and
she knew she would have to come to some decision, make

a commitment, one way or the other, either to Charlie, or to a life of loneliness, spinsterhood even, without him. He had said he would wait for ever, positive he meant it at the time, certain in his male heart and masculine pride that Annie would turn to him eventually. He may not have thought it consciously, for Charlie was not given to arrogance, but his logical mind would reason that she had no choice. She loved him, more than a friend, if less than a lover and it was pretty reasonable to assume that Reed Macauley would never be free of his pretty wife. So what other option was open to Annie Abbott? She was not fashioned for celibacy, for barrenness, for the arid life of a woman alone. She needed warmth, love, emotionally and physically, children, a woman's life in which her capacity for all these things would be fulfilled. So surely everything was tilted in Charlie's favour and soon, when her mind was at peace and the anguish of losing Cat had lessened, when her equilibrium was restored and the even tenor of their life together resumed, Charlie and Annie would be man and wife, and very well they would do together.

But he *and* Annie had not bargained on her body's stubborn refusal to consider any but Reed Macauley's, nor on her wayward female heart which, now that it was released from the icy paralysis it had known for over a year, bucked and plunged and leapt with gladness at the very mention of Reed Macauley's name.

Annie fidgeted fretfully about the kitchen that day, getting in Phoebe's way, until Phoebe began to tut-tut irritably. She had her own way of doing things, devised over the four years she had been at Browhead. This was *her* kitchen, her parlour, her dairy and cow shed and vegetable garden, and in them she worked tirelessly, methodically, contentedly, with no other woman to say her 'yea' or 'nay'. She knew very well that had the men not come down from Long Beck, a circumstance not at all to the liking of Charlie, who even now from the side door which stood open, she could see had a face on him like thunder, she and Annie and himself would have blundered on, day after day, in an attempt to get the flock clipped. An impossible task for one woman since Charlie, though he had tried to shear, hadn't the knack for it. The ewe he had started on had nearly bled to death from the numerous slashes in her skin and Charlie himself, at the end of a long struggling hour, had a cut so deep in his forearm Phoebe had threatened to stitch it up for him with her own needle and thread. He and the ewe looked as though they had just come from a slaughterhouse, slicked in the blood of both of them, Charlie grim faced, the sheep the same, the atmosphere of tension so deep and dreadful Phoebe had feared he and Annie might come to blows. He felt useless, she knew, less than a man as he was forced yet again to let Annie do the work he should have been able to do, and no matter how Annie assured him it really was of no consequence and she would manage, and though it was no fault of hers, Charlie was tight-mouthed with frustration at his unhandy ways. In the old days, of course, before this awkwardness had come upon them, he would have grinned engagingly, made a joke, laughed at himself, but not today.

Where was that lovely lilting harmony they had known a year ago, she asked herself despairingly? That lively joy and anticipation of each day they had dwelled in. Annie, Charlie, Phoebe, Cat, and later Natty, living in peaceful understanding beside one another, the future shimmering ahead of them like a silver ribbon. Natty's, short certainly, but filled with the warmth of friendship, the satisfaction and fulfilment of knowing, even at his age, that he was a trusted, *needed* member of the household. Cat had been at school and ahead of her were the days and years her splendid education would bring her, her clever young mind nourished and complete, her lovely young body giving promise of the same. Herself, here, as she had wished to be until the day she died, serving those she loved not in self-sacrifice but in joy for it was in doing so that *she* was complete. And Charlie and Annie growing closer, growing softer, growing together until their children came to complete the natural circle of love which filled this house.

Now there was nothing but strain, awkwardness, politeness, Charlie's face sad and empty, Annie's always turned in the direction of Dash Beck, or so it seemed to Phoebe who watched her. Gone were the laughter, the songs, the impish endearing humour with which Charlie had entertained them. Charlie, honest, sincere, candid and true-hearted, was becoming truculent, inward-looking, *bitter*, waiting for Annie. And how long would it be, as he waited, before he was spoiled, his love and need and sweet gentleness soured within him?

"See, get out o' me way, Annie, ah've put that milk to set and if tha' keeps movin' it it'll tek three days instead o' three meals for t'cream ter come."

"Well, let me help you with the churning."

"There's no need lass. Ah've managed it these months gone an' . . ."

"I could make the clapbread."

"An' how long is it since tha' made clapbread?"

"I've been making it since I was tall enough to stand at that table, Phoebe, which is longer than you."

"'Appen it is, but ah've got me own way o' doin' it and I can't abide havin' it messed about."

"Messed about! This is my kitchen, you know."

"No, it's not, it's mine, so go an' . . ."

"Go an' what? What do you suggest?"

"Isn't there summat in t' fields tha' can be checkin'?"

"No. The hay isn't ready to be cut yet."

"Well . . ." Phoebe tutted again, looking vexedly round her clean and shining kitchen which she could not abide having 'messed about'.

"Tek this tea out to t'chaps . . ."

"No, Phoebe . . . I don't want to do that." Annie's eyes turned to look out of the side door to where Charlie had a firm grip on a bawling sheep. They were both determined to have their own way, Charlie and the ewe, the ewe to get back to its frantic lamb, Charlie to heave it on to the shearer's stool. Charlie was soaked in sweat, his brown face grim, the muscles straining in his strong neck. With an enormous effort, he landed the ewe in its proper place, stepping back to grin in triumph and as he turned to get another, his eyes caught Annie's. Both looked away hurriedly, not in embarrassment but in an effort not to have a confrontation of any kind, even one as simple as a sympathetic smile.

"Lord's sake then, why don't tha' take Royal up to t' . . ."

"No . . ." for Charlie would see her and wonder where . . .

"Well, I don't know, but just stop gettin' under me feet."

"I'll go and cut some peat then, if that's the case."

"Aye, tha' do that." Phoebe was obviously relieved. "Sledge's at back and Charlie left the flay spade with it . . ."

"Really, it's coming to something when I have to be sent from my own kitchen so that . . ."

"Oh, get on wi' thi'! Tha' knows tha'll enjoy a walk up to t' peat moss."

She simply stepped through the back door whilst Charlie was bending over a salved sheep and before he straightened she was up behind the farmhouse dragging the loyal sledge behind her, moving through the deep tunnel of bracken towards a stand of trees and the peat moss which was beyond it.

The wood was in full summer bloom. The air beneath the canopy of trees was cool and damp-smelling, the energy of the hot sunshine soaked up by the leaves which spread above her head. The leafy crowns were so thick, barely any light got through, forming a solid mass which seemed to float above the tall, straight trunks of the graceful trees. Beech trees and oak, and growing freely beneath them were rhododendrons, their natural purple blossom gone now with the month of May. There was an open glade in the wood's centre where the sun reached, thick now with bilberry bushes, nettles, the bright yellow of celandine, the white of wood anemone, the delicate pale green fungus growing on fallen oak branches.

The silence was broken only by the droning song of a heavily laden bee and the sudden broken laugh of a jay as it was startled up from the tangle of a fallen tree when she approached. She continued upwards, moving again through bracken and gorse, following a sheep trod beside the rushing noisy waters of the beck, skirting the deep fern garlanded tarn into which the beck emptied. The sound the water made was deafening after the peace and calm of the woods but beyond it, as Annie reached the flatter area of the peat moss, the silence fell again.

It was sultry now, the sun scowling from behind the frown of a cloud. She dug for an hour, her thin cambric shirt clinging wetly to her back and breasts as she stacked the cut peat neatly on the sledge. Sweat trickled unpleasantly down her body and she thought longingly of a bath and of the jugs of cool water Phoebe would pour over her. Her hair, which had started the day braided tightly about her head, had fallen in its usual vigorous tangle across her back and shoulders and she thrust it impatiently from her face with both hands.

The man who studied her felt the hot glow begin and he shifted uncomfortably in his saddle. He was above her, hidden from her by a natural buttress of boulders which formed a screen from all eyes but that of the hawk. His face was quite inscrutable, dark and brooding, brows scowling over his darkened blue eyes and he slouched on the mare's back, one arm resting on the pommel of his saddle, both feet hanging loose from the stirrups.

He continued to watch her for several more minutes, then with a deep sigh, one of resignation to a fate which seemed greater than his own will, he threw one leg over the mare and jumped to the ground. Several sheep cropping close by twitched nervously, moving away with their heads held high and the collie dog who dozed by the mare's hooves, eyed her master in anticipation. Throwing the mare's reins over a jagged piece of rock from which she could not stray, Reed Macauley spoke quietly to both animals and then began the slow descent towards Annie. He could see her small figure in the distance all the way down the sprawling slope, but as he gazed at her, only taking his eyes from her to keep a sharp watch on the rough rock strewn track he walked, she straightened up, threw her spade on to the peat-laden sledge and began to manoeuvre it across the peat moss towards the wooded ravine a hundred feet below where she worked. There was a rocky gutter to which she kept as she went down, moving behind the sledge, clinging to the rope to prevent it from going too quickly. It was heavy, too heavy really and it took all her strength to hold it. Had the path been less rocky, it would have careered away from her. Now and again it became stuck and she was forced to go to the front and pull it free.

When she reached the tarn she was so hot and uncomfortable, she felt as though she had been plunged into a warm bath, her clothes sticking to her body like a second skin. Trickles of perspiration ran down from her hair, slipping across her eyebrows to her eyelashes. One drop kept catching at the end of her nose, and others ran into her mouth, salty and unpleasant. She paused to get her breath, bending down with both hands on her knees, gasping in the warm air, and beside the rocky path the water of the small tarn glistened deep and black. Above her the cloud had moved on, not a wisp remaining and the sun scorched down from the blazing blue of the sky. She could feel it on her back and when she straightened, pushing her heavy hair from her face, a heat haze danced, with the midges, across the surface of the pool. Dragonflies clung to the stalks of the reeds, and two delicate yellow butterflies waltzed madly in the heat. There were birch trees on the water's edge, leaning over gracefully towards it as though they would like nothing better than to dip their heads into its icy depth and beside them, crowding in great sheltering profusion were fern, flowering rush, water violets and crowfoot, green and lush and fragrant. The water ran into the tarn from the beck which careered down the ravine. It quietened when it reached the still pool, sliding sinuously round and across the satin smooth grey rocks, then moved on to the rushing drop of the waterfall and down again to follow the course of its rocky bed. A tiny breeze had stolen through the gorge to the pool. The dripping mountain plants which clung to the glistening vertical walls surrounding it moved and the dancing, tossing spray drifted across it, a million crystals shimmering where the sun touched them. The churning waters of a thousand years had carved this smooth basin from the solid rock and its peaceful beauty enchanted the mind and stole reason and good sense.

Annie hesitated for no longer than ten seconds. She looked about her, first up the path from where she had come, and then down to the wood through which she must go to reach Browhead, but there was no sign of another living human being. Kicking off her old clogs, she unbuttoned her shirt and tossed it on to a nearby clump of fern, stepped out of her trousers and the short drawers she wore beneath them and moved, trance-like, to the water's edge. Her body gleamed, white in the sunshine, clean-limbed, straight and slender, her breasts high and pink-tipped, her waist fine as gossamer, her hips curving slimly away from it. The triangle of darkness at her thighs' division had a glint of russet in it as did the fluff in her armpits and all about her flew her vibrant hair. She was glorious, glowing, polished as a russet apple and the man who watched her, drew in his breath in rapt wonder.

"Shall I jump?" he heard her say to herself, and his heart moved in him smilingly, but caution prevailed as she warily put a toe in the water.

"Dear heaven," she gasped out loud, "it's cold," and again the man felt his mouth curve in a smile. She stepped down the shallow bank, gasping with the shock of it, but at the same time her mouth widened in a delighted grin. The dark inviting depth of the water which had never known the sun's touch drew her on and beneath her white feet as she stepped on them, was the tinkle of sliding pebbles. The sound of the waters splashing and gurgling among the boulders, the roaring of the falls further on masked the sound of the approach of the man and when he reached the pool he stood between a tall clump of fern for several bewitched minutes to watch her.

"Ye gods, but it's cold," she gasped again and he could see the skin of her back prickle into a million goose-pimples. Suddenly, taking a deep breath, she plunged under the water and there was nothing to see but the ripples she left behind her.

Annie dived down and down and down between the dank walls, getting nowhere near the bottomless depths, and above her as she turned, she could see the sunlight, the green of the trees as they rushed to meet her and the tall wavering figure of a man. She broke the surface, gasping, her heart plunging in sudden terror. It was Reed, Reed Macauley. He was standing quietly by the edge of the water, his legs apart, his hands resting low on his hips. Their eyes met and clung, and could not look away, a clinging which was strong and vibrant with their suppressed emotions, suppressed these five years, but unwilling, they seemed to say, to accept it any longer. It had a sweetness about it, that exchange, a sweetness which was mixed with a sensual need so great, it was like an explosion and this time she knew she could not escape him, and did she want to? He was unsmiling, he did not speak and neither did she, though the shock of seeing him there had been severe. They had no need to speak, not now, for they had become fast in the drifting dream world of the moment, the moment towards which they had been moving ever since they had met again, as adults on the road from Penrith. He had known how it was, how it would be even then, though she had not, for she was, despite her experiences, no more than a girl, and ever since they had felt their desire grow, a desire in him which was not romantic, but was the fierce need of a man to put the mark of love on the woman who belonged to him; in her, the female need of submission to that mark.

She continued to look at him, understanding in those last few seconds what he had in his mind, and knowing that at last the time had come. Almost, but not quite, it had happened before, but now, out here where it was wild and free, uninhabited by anyone but Annabelle Abbott and Reed Macauley, was the place, the time, the appropriate place and time *for them*.

Her body gleamed white beneath the clear waters. She

moved her legs slowly to keep herself afloat and just below the surface of the water her breasts lifted gently to reveal the rock-hard peaks of her nipples. Her face was white and calm but in her eyes was the narrowed glow of sensuality. For a moment, the tick of a clock, no more, as his hands went to the belt of his breeches, her lips parted in denial and a cool clear voice inside her told her how insane this was, but when at last he stood before her, his beautiful male body, brown and hard, stripped of the packaging of civilisation, the words died within her.

"I love you, Annie," he said, almost idly, knowing full well that there would be no going back this time, but wanting her to realise all the same that this was no idle thing. He lifted his arms and dived into the water. He was gone for five seconds, no more, then he rose until they were face to face. He did not gasp with the cold as she had done, but pulled her at once against his body, his arms tight about her, his mouth on hers, her breasts against his chest, his penis questing between her thighs. There was no gentleness in him, nor in her. They almost fought one another in their hunger, and when she wrapped her legs about his waist, he penetrated her at once, the water surging and threshing about them as he moved ferociously, deeply inside her, immersed in her, loving her, the strokes of him, long, hard, insistent. She threw back her head, her arms clinging about his neck, her legs about his body and when the white-hot, ice-cold joy raced through her, she cried out loud, the sound rising and echoing about the ravine.

"Dear God . . . aah . . . my dearest, dearest love . . ." His own full-throated roar was triumphant, magnificent, silencing the sounds of the small creatures in the undergrowth, even the thunderous cascade of the waterfall dying into insignificance beside it.

For a full five minutes they remained fast together, not speaking, her face buried in his neck and shoulder, his against her wet hair. It floated about them like a rippling curtain of tawny seaweed and beneath them his legs moved keeping them both afloat.

He sighed, replete for the moment, five years of longing satisfied.

"We had best get to the bank my darling, or we shall both sink without a trace." He smiled down at her, murmuring into her dazed face, kissing it tenderly, then lifted a hand to brush back a wet, shining strand of copper hair which had wrapped itself about them both. Gently he towed her back to the bank, then lifting her into his arms, carried her to a sun-warmed patch of tufty grass and laid her down on it.

She sighed and stretched, lifting her arms above her head, deliberately displaying her proud breasts for his hands to cup, bending one knee so that the most secret part of her body was revealed to him. Her eyes were narrowed and hazy, the eyelashes tangled with drops of water, but when she smiled, the sun put a hot golden glow in their depths. He stood over her, male triumphant, his manhood a proud and flaunting thing, then, kneeling across her once again, he plunged into her until she wept with the rapture and glory of what he did to her.

The sun was setting across Bassenthwaite Lake when they kissed a lingering farewell. He had examined her body, with his hands, with his lips, his tongue exploring every inch of her, gently probing, his teeth nipping, his hands smooth and caressing, light as a butterfly until her skin shivered in delight, then hard, cruel even, making her arch her back in an ecstasy which could easily have been mistaken for pain. He devoured her, took her again and again, groaning as though he himself was in agony, and when he lay back she covered him with her own slippery wet body, moving her mouth gently on his then sliding down and down, brushing her lips across his flesh until he was roused again.

They had played in the water, two children again, young and carefree again, the years of pain tumbling joyously away, jumping and splashing one another, swimming hand in hand beneath the surface of the clear water, their bodies in lovely unison, diving down into the icy grey depths then up, moving through grey to clearest amber to a pale golden

glow as the sunlight shone through the water. They were
oblivious of time, of those who might wonder where they
were, of everything but this great and shining happiness
which had at last become theirs. They did not talk much.
The word 'love' was scarcely needed to be spoken. It was
everywhere, bathing their smooth skins, singing through
their veins, beating in their hearts and illuminating their
eyes to the glory which had come to them. They kissed
and touched and marvelled, but of course, it had to end.

"You are mine now, you know that, don't you, Annie?"
His voice was very serious. "There is no going back. I
don't know what is to happen. That is for you to decide.
You know that too. I have no intention of forcing you –
that's if I was able to – my darling, none at all. I've loved
you for so long now, with all my heart, feeling it grow
stronger inside me all these years. Have you the least
idea how much pain you have caused me . . . ?"

"Yes . . . and me."

"I know, I've wanted you for so long . . . taken other
women . . . oh yes . . . I'm a man with a man's needs and
my wife . . . well . . . I will not speak of her since she is
no more than a child and cannot be blamed . . . but you
. . . you are my companion, Annie, in the true sense of
the word, and I need you beside me . . . with me . . .
you understand what I'm saying . . ."

"Yes, my love."

"A lover to delight me, a friend to support me . . . that
is what I want in my woman . . . laughter, love . . . what
we have shared this day . . . I cannot let it go . . . nor
you, for you are that woman."

"I love you, Reed, I always have."

"And you will come to me . . . ?"

"There is so much to consider."

"I know, and we will consider it, at *your* pace, but we
will consider it, Annie. I'm getting nowhere . . . with the
divorce. She has done nothing to . . . given me no cause
. . . she, or her father, says she will come back whenever
I . . . wish it but that I must . . . well, you must no longer
be part of my life . . ." He swallowed painfully, his face

anguished for he wanted her to be the woman, he wanted himself to be the man, who would be the two halves of the Macauleys of Long Beck. It was a gift he needed to give her, and amongst all those he *meant* to give her, this would not be amongst them.

"May I come down to visit you at Browhead?" The shock of the words took her breath away. So quiet, so . . . so reasonable, the aggression, the arrogance, the overbearing challenge with which he dealt with anything which stood in his way, gone with the strength and steadiness of his love for Annie Abbott. For several moments she could not answer. He spoke for her.

"It's him, isn't it?"

"Yes." Her head bowed in pain, for how was she to tell Charlie? Tell him what? her clear mind asked and her dazed and drugged heart answered the question. Tell him that you love Reed and are to . . . to . . . *live with him* somewhere? Is that it? Has it been decided then? Have you decided, her mind asked her heart? and she supposed, somehow, that she had. That she had finally come to the realisation that she could fight it no longer. That what she had jibbed at time and time again, the submission of her will to Reed Macauley's, the acceptance of that stylish villa in Penrith or Ambleside or Carlisle, must be undertaken. She could not exist apart from him, not now, not after this enchanted afternoon but . . . there was Charlie.

"There is . . . something." He lifted her chin, forcing her to meet his gaze, smiling a little, for Charlie Lucas no longer frightened him.

"Yes?"

"The farm at Upfell."

"Yes?" Her voice rose questioningly.

"I am giving it to you. It is my first gift to you as my . . . love."

Her mouth opened and then shut again. He put a hand to her chin, beginning to laugh, ready to swing her round in a great circle of joy for at last, *at last* he could do something for her, satisfy that need in him to shower her with all the things he thought she should have, all the many and expensive things he thought she *needed* to have.

"You own Upfell?" Her voice did not warn him as it should and he continued to grin down at her.

"I do. Do you think I would let anyone have it when I knew you had set your heart on it? Oh yes, I heard of your efforts to raise a loan."

"Is there anything in this parish that you don't know about, Reed?"

"If there is, it's not worth knowing." His wide smile was like that of a child who has just been given a glimpse of fairyland, "and if I hadn't been away when you approached that fool of a bank manager in Keswick, I would have had a quiet word in his ear. Fortunately, I returned in time to get my hands on the property and now I am giving it to you. I was just waiting for the right moment and this seems to me to be *exactly* the right moment. You have enriched me with the greatest gift a woman can give today and in return . . ."

"I don't need paying for my . . . favours, Reed."

He recoiled as though she had struck him, then acting instinctively, he dragged her into his arms and held her by brute force.

"No! . . . no! . . . I will not let you do it again. *Damn* your bloody pride, your stubborn *obsessive* pride. Yes, that's what it is, obsessive. I love you, dammit, I love you and I wanted to . . . *give* . . . but, God's teeth, if it means that much, buy the bloody place from me . . ."

"Reed . . ." She was overwhelmed by the intensity of his anguish, and her own outraged pride and resentment drained away from her. She relaxed against him and he sighed thankfully.

"Annie, it's hard for me. I am a man who has, for all of my adult life, done, and been exactly what I wanted to do and be. If I had been denied in the past I have simply ridden roughshod over that denial because quite simply I did not care enough about what the other man was feeling. I've taken what I wanted and it has not been easy for me to . . . accept that with you . . . oh, Jesus . . . help me . . ."

She looked up into his face and it was haggard with the truth of what he said. His mouth was hard and tense, his shoulders slumped and weary, telling her he really could not stand it if he was to lose her again. The fatigue, the pain in him stirred her compassion and she put a gentle hand on his cheek.

"Annie . . ." he could not hide his eagerness, ". . . could we not try, start afresh, give ourselves another chance? I would dearly like to attempt it. One step at a time. The farm, the farms, for I'm sure you and I can come to some amicable agreement over Upfell." He grinned his weary grin. "They will need to be put in good hands . . . so many things . . . arrangements . . . but with care . . ."

"You mean me to live in some fine house you will build me, is that it?" Her voice was sad but resigned.

He looked astonished, then lifting his head he began to laugh, the sound again alarming the denizens of the undergrowth. He pulled her fiercely to him, tucking her head into his shoulder, his hand in her hair.

"Oh no, my darling, I am to do nothing of the sort. You are to come and live at Long Beck. You will be my wife, not legally at the moment but when Esmé, or her damned father agrees to it and I have my divorce, then we will be married. Browhead and Upfell will be yours to run as you like with no interference from me and if the folk of Bassenthwaite don't care for it, then they can go to the devil."

Day after day went by and still she had not told Charlie,
nor Phoebe. Reed would be patient for a while, but not
for ever, she was well aware of that, for no matter what
he had said to her in the rapture of that afternoon by the
pool, he was still Reed Macauley whose temper was short,
whose forbearance was the same, whose patience was
infinitesimal, whose need of her was enormous. He had
told her 'at *your* pace' but she knew that meant at her
pace as long as it went at a speed he thought suitable.

She had diverted him from his intention of calling on her
at Browhead as he had wished to do, somewhat in the
manner of a suitor paying court to his intended betrothed,
for the result of that would not only have been disastrous
but would have been a cruelty to Charlie she could not
bear to make him suffer. Instead she saw him almost every
day on the fell, slipping out of the farmhouse when Phoebe
was in the dairy and Charlie up in the coppice wood, telling
neither of them where she was going, or even that she
was to go. The weather was warm and the days golden
with sunshine and for an hour or two they would be
together in the secluded gorge in which they had first
made love, not speaking much, for as far as Reed was
concerned everything was settled and needed no dis-
cussion. Their future together at Long Beck was a fact
now, known only to themselves at the moment, and though
he found it hard, he was doing his best to bend to her
wishes, to let her settle her concerns and the question of
how to run her two farms in her own time. Not with the
best of humour since he wanted her in his bed and at his
dining table this very night, he said, but allowing it just
the same.

There was so much she wanted to do and one day, towards the end of July, when they had made love to Reed's exact requirements, which meant unhurriedly, imaginatively, erotically, until every one of his five senses was completely satisfied, and her own cries of joy had erupted from her again and again, as they drowsed in one another's arms in the aftermath of it, she began, hesitatingly, to tell him of it. She was uncertain of his reaction, knowing his need to dominate, to be the innovator, the giver, the protector, but this was a test, a gamble she must take for on this their whole life together, if they were to have one, might rely.

"Did you mean what you said about running my own farms . . . and business, Reed?"

"I did." He was satiated, replete, drained, empty and yet full of her and his voice was no more than a languorous murmur.

"No matter what I decide?"

"Mmmm."

"I will have complete control and the right to make any decision I care to, even if it does not agree with what you think it should?"

"What have you in mind?" and beneath her cheek which rested on his chest, she felt the faint tension in him. She sat up and her breasts fell forward, soft and heavy in his hand. He cupped them, smiling, his fingers smoothing her peaked nipples, his mind which had been about to become guarded, distracted from the matter of farms and 'business concerns', whatever they may be, as his male body prepared itself for another delightful onslaught on Annie's.

"You will not try to . . . take over?"

"My darling, even if I wanted to I couldn't 'take over' as you put it. Until you are my wife everything you own belongs to you. Even though we are to live at Long Beck as husband and wife . . . Dear God, Annie . . . when? . . . when? . . . it's four weeks since we decided and still you're under the same roof as . . . well, you know who I mean and I can't say I like it. Why don't you come over to Long Beck and take a look round? Perhaps you would like to . . . well, I don't know . . . move things around, re-decorate the bedroom where . . . or even choose another and make it as you want it? Anything you want to do, I don't care my darling, just as long as you are there. You must be introduced to the servants and they must accept you as their mistress and if they don't then they can find other employment. There is so much to be arranged . . . your clothes and . . . listen, why don't you and I take a trip up to Carlisle? There is a woman there, a dress maker, who is a marvel, a skilled seamstress and embroideress, a genius of design and if I pay her well she could design and make you a complete wardrobe within the week . . ."

"Reed . . ."

". . . her velvets and brocades are . . ."

Restraining her instant jealous need to know how Reed Macauley was so well acquainted with velvets and brocades and the marvellous dress maker in Carlisle, she put an imperious hand across his mouth.

"Stop it, Reed. You are doing it already, arranging me and what I should wear in the way you think I should be . . ."

"Confound it! Annie, you don't mean to wear those bloody trousers forever, do you?"

"No, but I mean to change them when Annie Abbott is ready, not Reed Macauley. In the meanwhile I want to . . . to talk to you, ask your advice . . ."

"Of course, my darling." He was at once gratified, she could see, by her female, or so he thought, dependence on him.

"I mean to . . . put in a man to run Upfell, under my supervision, naturally. No one knows it's mine yet, and of course it isn't until I have paid you what I owe. Two hundred guineas will take a lot of finding . . ."

"Annie, I don't want it."

"Reed . . . !" Her voice was forbidding.

"I'm sorry, Annie."

". . . but I should make a fair profit out of the combined

flocks of Upfell and Browhead which brings me to the question of my swills . . ."

"Swills?" Sitting up, he pressed his lips to her shoulder, his hands still at her breasts, tweaking her nipples between his thumb and forefinger. He hitched himself behind her, his legs splayed one on either side of her body and she could feel the thrust of him between her buttocks. His hands ran down her belly as his mouth moved on her shoulders and at the nape of her neck. His fingers found the sweet, moist parting of her and involuntarily she opened herself wider to allow them to slip inside. The hot fire ran from them, down the inside of her thighs, up into her belly and thrusting breasts and she arched her back . . .

With a cry of rage she dragged herself away from him, turning on her haunches like a wild cat, her eyes flaring, her teeth bared, her nails ready to claw him and he fell back.

"Jesus Christ, what have I done now?" he gasped, his face still slack with his desire, his body at the full peak of his arousal.

"Nothing, except what all men do with women."

"And you did not *want* it?" His eyes had become dangerous. He did not like to have his love flung in his face, nor did he care for the crass foolishness of his own male rejected body, which *she* had caused.

"Of course I did, but would you deal with a man in the same contemptuous way as you have . . ."

"Don't be so bloody ridiculous! It is not the same at all." He began to laugh at the very idea, ready to take her in his arms, to smooth the outrage from her naked, female body, but she would not have it. Instead she reached for her clothes and with stiff and trembling fingers, fumbled her way into them.

"Annie . . ." He was still ready to be amused, to laugh, to forgive, to continue, but she turned on him again, her wild temper beautiful and unrestrained.

"Treat me seriously, Reed," she spat at him.

"I do! By God, I do. Am I not demonstrating it by begging you to come and live with me at . . ."

"Not that." Her voice was scornful "Not that, not *us*, but me, *me*, Annie Abbott. I am to be . . . in business as a man is in business and I want respect for it. A serious consideration of how I am to go about it and I am asking you to help me. As a man who has many business connections I wish you to advise another on how to go about . . . well, all the things that will need to be done . . ."

"Could we not wait until a more appropriate time . . ."

"You mean when I am sitting prettily in your drawing room, the certainty of my life with you firmly established and the chains you have put on me, locked and secured so that I may be more easily kept at your side with nothing of my own, no one but you, dependent on . . ."

"Chains, *chains*! Christ Almighty, would that I could. If you'd let me keep you, comfortably, of course, in a room where no one, no *man*, could lay eyes on you and where . . . Annie . . . don't do this . . . *don't* let me do this to you . . . I'm sorry . . . sorry . . ." He groaned, bending his head and she was made terribly aware of how much this strong man loved her.

"Christ . . . oh, sweet Jesus . . ." and she could hear plainly in his voice the cry that meant 'I can't bear it' and she winced, for despite his strength he was very frail, weakened by his love for her.

She knelt down and took him in her arms, rocking him as a mother would a hurting child.

"Tell me," he mumbled into her shoulder, "but first let me get dressed."

She meant to go into the business of producing swill baskets, she told him, when they were both calm. She leaned in the curve of his arm as they rested their backs against a rough grey stone which grew out of the grass.

"Not just a dozen swills at a time, but a hundred, a thousand even. I have the coppicing at Browhead and now at Upfell, and could purchase more. There is a coppice wood for sale by auction in November, at Wood Top near Stepthwaite. Mostly oak of fourteen years' growth so it is almost ready for harvesting, but of course . . . well, when I have the money, that is the kind of land I will be looking for. And I will need a . . . a . . . place to work. I have the building, the barn, which could be turned into a small workshop, but I will need more, and then there are the men to make them. They are used in so many industries, the need is enormous. Coal mines, the shipping lines, farming, they could even be sent abroad. I have served my apprenticeship, Reed, so I know what I'm talking about. I could train boys, men, to be swillers, or take on men who are fully trained themselves. All it needs is someone to find the market for the swills and supply it."

"And that would be?"

"Perhaps myself . . . or . . ."

"I thought so. You would tramp about the country treating with men of business?"

"I already have a contact in Whitehaven. A sea captain who said, for a small commission, of course, that he would take my swills to Liverpool and sell them for me."

"I see."

Dear God, it was hard and would get harder, she agonised, feeling the struggle of him as he did his best not to turn and shake her into obedience and submission. He didn't like it. He was doing his best to allow her to be the woman she wanted to be, to do what she longed to do, but it went against every instinct in his masculine world which told him that she should be in his life, in his home, in his bed, safe and loved, at least by him; an instinct that detested the very idea of her being independent, free and at liberty to do as she pleased.

"Will you help me, Reed? Tell me where to start? Where you would start?"

He was silent for so long she sat up, turning to gaze anxiously into his face. He was looking out over the pool, his attention centred on the still depths of it, his face set, his eyes flat and expressionless.

"Reed?"

"I shall lose you if I don't, won't I?"

"Oh no, my darling, I love you . . ."

"I know you do, and I also know that if I let you struggle

on, unaided, you will do your damnedest to succeed, but
you will resent me. Resent my unconcern, though of
course, I *shall* be concerned. I have no choice, have I?"

"Of course you have."

"No, I knew it long ago. To keep you I must set you
free so . . ." turning to smile sadly into her eager face,
". . . let us begin. Your first lesson in sharp business
dealings . . ."

"*Honest* business dealings, Reed."

"Indeed, but you must learn that the two can run
together."

She was vaulting the wall at the back of Browhead when
Charlie rose up at her feet. Her heart was light, her face
vibrant with it, her eyes dreaming, her senses enthralled
with the marvel that was to be her future. With Reed,
with her love, with her satisfying attack on the world of
business where only men went. For that moment her farm,
her sheep, her expansion into Upfell, the life she had lived
with Charlie and Phoebe, and before that with Cat and
Natty, had evaporated as easily as the mist at the top of
Skiddaw when the sun touched it.

"Where in hell have you been?" he snarled, catching
her wrist with a cruel, savage hand, one which meant to
hurt.

"Charlie, you scared me, jumping up out of nowhere
like that. What were you doing behind the wall . . . ?"

"Never mind what I was doing, tell me what *you* were
doing, and who with, and not just today but every day for
the past few weeks? I've seen you go up there to the peat
moss and come back with an empty sledge. You thought
I was in the coppice working, as I am supposed to, as I
have been doing for the past four years, without wages
mind, whilst you crept up there on the fell, and by God,
the temptation to see for myself what you were up to has
been almost too much to bear, and only the . . . the horror
of knowing, of actually *knowing*, what I only suspect, has
kept me from it. I could not stand it you see, having the
images which torment my over active imagination, actually

come to life so I stayed away, but I knew, of course I did
. . . oh God, Annie . . . tell me I am imagining it, that you
have . . . have been . . . elsewhere . . . *anywhere* .. but
not with him . . ."

"Charlie . . ."

"Don't . . . don't try to . . . to comfort me, Annie. Don't
lie." His face was haunted. "I have never known anyone
as honest and brave and beautiful as you, my dearest love,
and I couldn't bear it if you lied to me now. I've watched
you taking on the whole of Bassenthwaite parish, all by
yourself, fighting them and their prejudices, hurting I
know, but always getting up again when they knocked you
down. You have been my pride and delight and glory and
. . . even now . . . I cannot help but love you. I have
not been celibate, Annie. It is possible to enjoy a sexual
relationship without love in it you know, but nothing, none
of them, drove you from my heart."

They stood on the high ground at the back of Browhead,
the land sloping away to the farmhouse and the patchwork
of fields beyond it, each one divided from its neighbour by
a grey ribbon of drystone wall. There was a sudden flicker
of wind straight from the fell, bringing the summer
fragrance of heather and bracken. Nothing moved, only
her painful heart as it beat for Charlie's anguish.

"Charlie, please listen." She put a warm, steadying hand
on his arm, affectionate, reassuring, but he threw it off
with a violence she had not known was in him.

"Listen to what?"

She shook her head for really all she had to tell him,
everything she had to tell him would hurt him beyond
endurance, so what was she to say? Only the truth, surely.

"Charlie . . ."

"Annie, I don't think I can bear to hear this, really I
can't."

"Charlie, you must know . . ."

"Must I? must I?"

"Yes," and she could see him freeze, become suspended
in the ice of his pain, his vitality an inanimate thing as he
did his best to find mercy. He was fighting to remain calm,

to keep a hold on hope, but his eyes told her he knew she was going to leave him. The raw pain in them burned her but she could not look away. She had kept this man here, perhaps against his will, giving him reason to believe that one day, when she was mended from all the many hurts she had sustained in her passage through life, she would turn to him in love. She had smiled on him, leaned on him, laughed and cried with him, relied on his strength, taken his strength, all the while hiding from him the honest truth which was that she could never love, or give herself to any man but Reed Macauley. He had believed the promise she had, perhaps unintentionally, held out to him, and had remained. He had tried to go away once, but *her* need had brought him back and she had used him as a crutch to get her through. Would he ever forgive her? Could she ever forgive herself?

"Charlie . . . I am so sorry. This is my fault. You made no secret of how you felt about me and I have not been honest . . ."

"Christ . . . don't . . . don't tell me . . ."

"I must . . ."

"No . . ."

"I'm not . . ."

"Don't say it, please, my darling. Don't say you're not the right woman for me, when what you mean is that I am not the right man for you. I have been mistaken in believing that you . . . that one day you would . . . forget him, but it seems . . . well, I had best pack my . . ." His voice petered away and he turned from her, stumbling on awkward legs towards the farmhouse, blinded it seemed, and her heart broke for him but she knew she must not go after him. Not now. Not this time. He must be allowed to make his own decision without the truth of her need of him to cloud his brain. She did need him. She could not imagine life without Charlie in it, as she could not imagine her life without Phoebe in it. They were her two true friends, both of whom she loved and for whom she would give her life. She wanted him to stay but she also wanted him to be happy and he could not do both. He was a decent man who deserved a decent life. A wife, children, a home, the satisfaction of a day's work well done and perhaps she could give him the latter if he would accept it.

But not now. Not at this moment when there was nothing but hatred and despair in his heart. He might, as she stood here, held fast by her sorrow for him, be stuffing his few possessions into his bag, taking his leave of a bewildered Phoebe, striding off down the track to Keswick. She might lose him for ever if he went, but she must leave him alone, for now.

He was not in the farmhouse, nor anywhere in the vicinity of it when she finally went down there. His things were still in his room. The books he had read to them years ago, those which Cat had loved so much, his woollen jerkin, his scarf and worn overcoat were all where he had left them.

"Tha'd best give Mr Lucas a shout, Annie," Phoebe advised. "His supper's on t' table, tell him, an' I've baked 'im an apple pie. I've saved 'im a drop of cream an' all. Got over two gallons of milk today from Clover, I did, which is right good, or so Maggie told me when she came by with young Jonty. He's a fine lad, that un. Six months old he be an' already tryin' to pull 'isself up. Crawl, he's like a little monkey an' into everything. I 'ad to put all me things away . . ."

"I am to buy Upfell, Phoebe."

The words cut off Phoebe's pleasant ramblings on the happenings of her contented day just as though someone had clamped a gag in her mouth. Her hands which had been busy with pans and ladling spoons, with the proper arrangement of knife and fork and plate, became still. She turned slowly her plain country face, rosy now with good health, as astonished as if Annie had said she had purchased a tiara of diamonds.

"What?"

"I am to buy Upfell Farm and almost everything in it, and on it. The farmhouse and what furniture Sally didn't want. The gimmers, wethers, ewes, the cows and a couple of pigs Sally couldn't take with her to Binsey. All the dairy utensils. What was stored in the cow barn. Wood and hay coops, the cart, horse, coppice land . . . everything. It will cost me two hundred guineas . . ."

"Two hundred . . . !" Phoebe's mouth fell open and the spoon she held dropped from her hand to the floor. Dandy drifted over to it, her sinuous body gracefully twining about Phoebe's skirts before she began to lap delicately at the cream which had splashed on to Phoebe's immaculate flagstones.

"Wheer d'yer get the money? Not the bank, nor that lawyer from Lancaster. Tha' told me that." Phoebe's words were flat and suspicious, disapproving, for hadn't she known for weeks now what Annie Abbott got up to almost every day on the fell and where else would she get the money but from the man whom she met up there?

"I haven't got it from anywhere yet. I have some put by and I shall use that as a down payment and pay the rest whenever I can. With interest, of course," she added hastily as though she knew full well what Phoebe was thinking and was determined to let her know this was a bona fide business transaction.

"I see, an' would I be wrong in thinkin' tha' intends borrowin' from him up at Long Beck?"

"No, you wouldn't be wrong, Phoebe. In fact I am to buy the farm from him up at Long Beck. It was Reed who got it from the . . ."

"Tha' knows tha'll be in his debt don't tha'? An' that he's not a man who'll be shy of collectin' it."

"What is that supposed to mean?"

"If tha' falls behind he'll mek tha' pay in other ways, lass."

At once Annie's face became brightly flushed and she felt a great need to avoid Phoebe's steady, penetrating eyes as the images of herself and Reed as they had been this very afternoon and on the many afternoons of the past four weeks, flooded her mind.

"An' what about Mr Lucas?" Phoebe went on, knowing exactly why Annie's face had flooded with colour. "He's not goin' to like it, you borrowin' money from Mr Macauley. It wouldn't surprise me if he refused ter work for thi'. It'd be like workin' for *him*, that's 'ow Mr Lucas'd see it."

"Nonsense!" Annie tossed her head in an effort to appear offended, and then suddenly letting out her breath in a resigned sigh, she moved away to gaze out of the window and down the slope to the lake below.

"What's the use, Phoebe? I cannot hide the truth from you. I have just . . . spoken to Charlie. Not about Upfell but about me . . . and Reed Macauley."

"Oh, aye, an' what's there to tell?"

"Well . . ." Somehow it was very difficult to say the words. To say to Phoebe, "I'm taking up residence at Long Beck and I shall be running both farms from there. I shall be putting in men, here and at Upfell to farm, and herd my sheep. You, of course, will come with me to Long Beck since you are my friend. You will have a comfortable life as my companion. A decent wage, pretty clothes and . . . and . . ."

Her mind tried to form a picture of Phoebe at Long Beck, sitting perhaps in a cosy chair in a cosy room, sewing, reading, or in the garden which she herself knew as a child as being extremely grand. She would ride in a carriage beside herself when they went to Keswick on business, naturally, and then . . . ?

She just could not imagine it. It just would not happen in her mind's eye and she sighed deeply for she knew it would not happen at all. Phoebe could not be made to fit into that pretty picture Annie tried to imagine her in. *This* was Phoebe, hardworking, cheerful, content to bake and darn, to scrub and scour and polish, to milk her cow and churn her butter and do all the practical, everyday jobs she had performed all her life. She would be uncomfortable in silk, in a carriage, in a formal garden, and the idea of Phoebe sitting down to read a book when there were so many more interesting things to do in the kitchen, was ludicrous.

Phoebe, if she agreed to come, and there was no guarantee that she would, could only be miserable in such a setting. But how could she leave her? her anguished mind begged to know. She had lost Cat, she had lost Natty, and there was every probability she would lose Charlie . . . if what she hoped for came to nothing. So could she bear to lose Phoebe as well? And if Phoebe stayed here, how was she to fit in with the man – who would probably have a wife – who would come to run Browhead?

"What is it Annie?"

"Charlie . . ."

"Aye, what about him?"

"Reed Macauley and I are . . ."

Phoebe shook her head testily, her patience with the vague ramblings of the woman who was usually sharp and decisive, coming to an end. Something was up, something pretty drastic if Annie's behaviour was anything to go by and the sooner it was said and done with, the better. It involved him up at Long Beck, that was very evident, for when had he not been involved with every drama which had been played out at Browhead ever since Phoebe had come to live here?

"Ah know tha's bin seein' him, Annie, so that's no surprise. Nay, lass, tha' face gives thi' away, an' if I knew, so did Mr Lucas . . ."

"Yes . . ."

"Yes, what does that mean?"

"He knew. He saw me coming down . . . just now and . . . I had to admit it . . ."

"Wheer is he?" Phoebe pushed Annie aside brusquely, peering down the field for a sight of Charlie. Royal cropped the grass contentedly on its far side, deep in the shadows cast by the tree and at the gate which led into the field, the three dogs, eyes glistening, tongues quivering, sprawled panting in the shade of the wall. It was all so normal, so as it should be, as it HAD been for the past weeks of the heatwave. Phoebe felt her heart quieten for a moment, but as though her instinct, that sixth sense which recognises danger when there is none to be seen, could sense it, little ripples of fear ran through her body.

"Wheer is he, Annie?"

"I don't know, Phoebe. He ran off down the track towards . . ."

"Wheer, for God's sake?"

"I don't know . . ."

"Tha' don't know after all that man's done for thi' . . ."

"Do you think I don't know that, but I couldn't lie to him, Phoebe. I love Reed Macauley. I had to tell him the truth . . ."

"And what else?"

"What d'you mean?"

"There's summat in tha' face that ses there's more. That tha's plannin' summat an' if I can see it, so would Mr Lucas. What is it, Annie, tell me?"

She couldn't. She couldn't tell Phoebe and she couldn't *do it*. She wanted Reed but she was afraid of him. Afraid of what a life with him at Long Beck would do to her. Was she capable of being the woman he wanted her to be? Did she *want* to be the woman he wanted her to be? If she sacrificed her independence would she, little by little, be completely possessed by Reed for he believed, quite sincerely, that the only right way was Reed Macauley's way. He would own her. She would be his completely and, though she longed for it joyfully, longed to spend each night moaning and sighing in his bed, was she able to submerge herself totally to HIS will, or was it all a dream? Had she been dreaming, living in a dream world where she and Reed would be together, sharing their lives, existing side by side in a house where his wife should be? Probably sleeping in a bed he had shared with her, giving orders to his wife's servants, taking his wife's life, the one Reed had promised to give her when he married her, and was it in Annie's power to do it? She loved him and she would always continue to give everything of herself she could offer. Gladly, rapturously, but NOT THERE, not at Long Beck, not in another woman's place. Not in his wife's place. She did not know how he would take it. Perhaps her dream would be stamped on and destroyed, for they were all in his hands. The farm at Upfell, not yet legally hers. Her plans for her basket industry which included

Charlie, if he would let her . . . Dear God in Heaven . . . so much . . . and all depending on Reed Macauley . . .

Suddenly her mind cleared and her heart became steadied. No, it didn't all depend on Reed Macauley. Upfell farm did and her intention to form a business, a swill basket industry on a scale not known before in the district, but not everything. Not everything. She still had Browhead.

Phoebe's light touch on her arm startled her and she turned abruptly.

"Annie . . ." There was a quiver of fear in Phoebe's voice but Annie smiled reassuringly.

"It's all right, Phoebe. There is nothing else. And we can do nothing about Charlie. He had to know. You told me that long ago. He had to know I could give him nothing more than my loving friendship. We cannot force him back, dearest Phoebe. He will come if he needs us and in the meanwhile everything will go on just as it always has. Nothing has changed."

"There is summat, lass." Phoebe's face was troubled.

"What is it?"

"I was keepin' it fer . . . well, when it was needed the most."

"What?"

"I know it were none of my business but I thought . . ."

"What Phoebe?"

"Tha'd best come wi' me, 'tis in the . . . well, come wi me an' I'll show thi'."

She was convinced for several minutes that he was going to kill her, or beat her senseless, or both. She was afraid, but she had been expecting it, and, knowing his strength, his ruthless determination to have what he wanted, and her own frailty against it, she did her best to let his bitter fury blow over her, bending to it, swaying with it so that it should not break her. He had been so certain of her. So convinced that finally she was to be his, not just up on the wild fell where no one could see, but here in his home, his life, where no one could fail to miss it. He wanted it acknowledged that Annie Abbott, who would one day be Annie Macauley, was Reed Macauley's woman, his wife in fact, if not in name.

"You bitch," he said, his face quite blank and holding her with one hand so that she could not escape him, he hit her twice across the face, his aim so hard and so true she felt the muscles in her neck pull in agony. When he let her go she reeled backwards, striking the wall behind her and out in the kitchen where the servants gathered in avid, breathless anticipation, the blows were clearly heard.

"Dear Mother of God . . ." Mrs Lewis, who was a staunch Catholic, sketched a hasty cross on the bib of her starched white apron. "What's he doing to her?"

"No more than she deserves," Mrs Stone said tartly. Mrs Stone had answered the door when Annie Abbott knocked on it, the elegant butler employed by Mrs Macauley long gone, and she had been so thunder-struck she had allowed the hussy, trousers an' all, over the threshwood and into the hallway before she could collect her senses and shut the door in her face.

Annie straightened up slowly, deliberately not putting

her hands to her face though she could feel the swelling coming up about her eye and taste the blood in her mouth.

"It's him, isn't it?" he said, just as Charlie had done and for a despairing moment she wished the pair of them to the devil, for how much easier her life would have been without men in it.

"No, he's gone."

"Gone? Gone where?" Still there was that terrible blankness in his eyes and she was appalled by it but she had come here for a reason and she must keep true to it.

"I don't know. I told him about you and me, and he . . ."

"You and me! You have just informed me there is to be no 'you and me', that you have changed your mind again and can no longer face the prospect of living here as my wife . . ."

"Not your wife, Reed."

"Please! For the love of God don't let's have that again. It becomes tedious after a while and I find it no longer interests me. If you will ring the bell, my housekeeper will show you out."

His manner was insulting. She was no more than an unwelcome caller, it said, not only one who was unwelcome but who had already stayed too long. He could scarcely contain his black, menacing anger and she was terribly aware for her own female frailty. He wanted to hurt her badly and was afraid himself that he might do it, so to prevent it he must get rid of her quickly, his taut, perilous expression told her.

He brought the flat of his hand down hard on the desk, setting everything on it to jumping, warning her of her danger.

"Go, Annie, get out. I don't want to see you again, and no, I don't want the money you are offering me for Upfell. It's no longer for sale . . ."

"Reed . . ."

"Don't, Annie, I'm warning you . . ."

"Reed . . . despite this . . . I love you. Can you not find it in you to understand? I don't give a damn about anybody but you. I don't care what *they* say . . ." indicating with a toss of her head those in the kitchen and even beyond to encompass the whole of the parish of Bassenthwaite. "It's me, me, don't you see? I can't live *her* life . . ."

He pushed back his chair and strode to the window then back to the fireplace where he took a cigar from a box on the mantelpiece. He lit it with a taper from the fire, then moved again to the window presenting his back to her, keeping his distance, holding in his lethal temper, barely in control of himself.

"So you have said before."

"Then may I not . . . will you not come to Browhead . . . ?"

"Now that *he* has gone I'm welcome, is that it?"

"No . . . yes . . . Reed . . . please . . ."

"Don't beg, Annie, it doesn't suit you, nor me."

"Listen to me, Reed."

"I've done nothing but listen to you for five years and I've had enough. Either you come here and live with me as my wife, *be* my wife to all intents and purposes, make a commitment, as I am willing to do, or . . ."

"Yes?" Her voice was a whisper.

"Don't expect to see me again, Annie."

She bowed her head, then lifted it, the savage marks of his hand clearly visible on her white skin. She looked at his back, his stiff lethal jealous back, then turning on her heel, left the room and the house. When she had gone he sat down heavily and stared with empty eyes into the space in front of him where she had stood.

Phoebe had found the box at the back of a loose stone in the dairy, a box so heavy she could barely lift it. She had been whitewashing the wall, 'going at it' with her usual intransigence, her unyielding determination to stand for no muck or muddle and when her brush would keep spattering her and her floor as it met a resistance of some kind in the smooth pattern of the stones, she put it in the pail and leaned forward to investigate more fully.

It had taken her no more than a second or two to discover the stone was loose, sticking out a half inch beyond its neighbours, but when she set about it, as she was wont to do with anything which was perverse enough to defy her, it would not be 'set about' but continued to shift whenever she touched it. In fact it was so loose she could pull it out and when she did she found the box.

Annie looked at it, standing away somewhat as though it contained a deadly snake which might strike her with its venom when she opened it.

"'Tis full o'money, Annie." Phoebe's voice was filled with awe. "Ah've never seen such a lot o'money."

"Did you . . . count it?"

Phoebe reared back. "Nay, tis not mine ter count, lass. Wheer d'yer think it come from?"

"I can't imagine."

"Are tha' goin' to open it?"

"I suppose I better had."

It was filled to its very brim with coins. Pennies and halfpennies and farthings, no higher value than that, but hundreds and hundreds, thousands of them which when laboriously counted out into neat piles, came to not quite three hundred pounds. There were coins with the head of their own Queen Victoria on them, coins depicting George III, George II and George I, the dates on these last, 1725. At the top of the box was a note. It was written by Lizzie Abbott and dated 1843, two weeks after Annie had fled to Keswick and the arms of Anthony Graham.

'To my daughter Annie,' it said. 'I found this when I came to Browhead. For all these generations, a hundred years and more, it seems Abbott women have saved their few pence. It weren't mine, but I added a bit when I could, as they did. It's yours now, God bless you, Annie.'

"Dear God . . . oh, dear Lord . . . Sally said my mother was trying to tell them something just before she died . . . Dear God in Heaven . . ."

She could imagine them, probably five or six generations of them, a chain, each link a thrifty woman putting by for a rainy day which, when it came was got through somehow without touching that precious hoard. A trust, a continuation, carrying on from mother to mother, to the wives of their sons, to the daughters of their sons, year in and year out, each one with a man to take care of them, to work for them, to work *for*. A picture of her mother on her knees at Sarah Macauley's scrub bucket struck her a blow which left her gasping and she began to weep, to weep for her mother and all those faithful women who had 'put by', who had been comforted by the knowledge that in the tin box at the back of the stone in the dairy was a 'bit put by' just in case. If things got too bad, each one had thought, then it was there so that her family would not starve or go clogless. 'Just in case' and not one of them had used it, nor counted it, nor even realised its value. Pennies, farthings, but which, when added up would begin a new life for Annie Abbott.

"Oh, Phoebe, women are such brave creatures. Strong and brave, faithful and yet foolish. They stay true to what they have been put to. A man, a child, a life, an idea, never wavering and yet man is supposed to be superior. The women who saved this have gone to bed hungry but not their men, not their children and they were content for they knew it was here in case of desperate need. Dear God, how desperate did my mother have to be before she dipped into this . . . Christ, she worked like a slave and yet this was here to . . ."

And what would have happened had Joshua Abbott got his hands on it, her mind, her practical woman's mind asked, as the practical minds of all the women who had gone before her, must have asked, eyeing their husbands who, perhaps, would have purchased what *they* thought was needed without a by-your-leave to the women who had saved it.

Aah . . . and now it had fallen into the hands of the only one who could, and would, if allowed, act as a man, but with a woman's careful, watchful, brave heart. It was here, in her hand, the means to do all the things she had wanted to do ever since she had come back to Browhead and the irony of it was, though she had the means now, the black, intransigent savagery of Reed Macauley's jealous will would not allow her to achieve her goal. Upfell Farm and

all its livestock, to run beside her own was what she
wanted but it was going to waste, its animals carelessly
attended to, since they knew of his lack of interest in it,
by Reed Macauley's men. The cows milked and the hens
fed, the pigs seen to. The ewes were grazing with Reed
Macauley's flock and had been serviced last backend by
his tup, the lambs born, the clipping done, the flock
expanding, but there was profit there going to waste for
want of a man, or woman, to market it, for want of a
man or woman who CARED about it. The land was lying
untended, going to seed with no crops planted. A whole
year since Bert Garnett had lost his wits in the beating he
received at Reed Macauley's hands and now, in the twisted
way life had of laughing behind its hand at human endeavour, it was all to be squandered to a man's pride. There
were other farms for sale, she was sure of it, but not in
such good heart as Upfell and certainly not as easily and
conveniently run.

"What are thi' ter do, Annie?" Phoebe asked hesitantly,
recovering somewhat from the shock of realising that – in
her eyes at least – Annie Abbott was rich beyond their
wildest dreams. She was not at all sure she liked the idea
of having all that money lying about the place but as it had
been behind the loose stone in the dairy for 125 years, or
so Annie reckoned, and nobody had disturbed it, nor even
discovered the hiding place, Phoebe supposed it was safe
enough if they put it back there and she said so to Annie.

But Annie had different ideas for it.

"No, I'm taking it into Keswick."

"Keswick? what on earth for?" Phoebe was flabbergasted.

"Do you know how much this might have earned if it
had been properly invested, Phoebe?"

Phoebe didn't, nor even what Annie meant.

"You can't just leave money lying about, Phoebe, it
should be made to earn."

Earn! What next? Really, Phoebe didn't know where
Annie got her knowledge from, nor her ideas, though she
supposed Mr Lucas, who had been an educated man and

who had talked to Annie by the hour, might have given some of it to her.

"No, this is going to the bank, Phoebe, and if that bank manager there can't suggest something, then I'll find someone who can and then, when the time is right, at least I will have a decent capital to start off my Swills Industry."

The farming year was almost at its end. The hay was in, the reaping and binding done, her stock sold and new ewes bought, the salving and marking of the sheep over with, and Clover and her growing calf housed in the byre for the winter to be fed on hay and straw. The tup was up on the fells with Annie's flock doing his joyful duty by them and the casual Irish labourers she had hired to settle her in for the winter, paid off and gone on their way. Without Charlie, she and Phoebe had managed but it had been a cheerless time of hard work, stoically borne. Her money, which Royal had dragged to Keswick in its tin box, hedged about on the sledge with trussed chickens and eggs, swills and besom brushes had been deposited with the speechless bank manager in Keswick. Yes, he could invest it safely for her, he had managed to stammer, his eyes unable to look away from the mountain of coins on his desk, astounded by her casual reference to her 'savings', and when she and Phoebe had purchased the provisions they needed for the winter, amongst which were several dress lengths of soft woollen fabric, cambric and lace, they had settled in at Browhead at the end of November to wait for spring and lambing time and what she intended would be the start of her new business. There were enough quartered logs in the barn, ready to be rived into strips to keep her and Phoebe busy making swill baskets during the winter months.

She had grieved badly for Reed during the two months since she had last seen him. He was still at Long Beck, or so Maggie Singleton innocently told them when she came down to visit Phoebe and proudly display her sturdy son and, equally innocently, to share the hope that she and Jake might be allowed to take over the farm at Upfell.

It was going to waste since the Garnetts left, she said, and Jake, who had never actually run a farm, was nevertheless a good all-round man outside and could turn his hand to anything, sheep, cattle or crops, and as for herself, she couldn't wait to get her hands on some real dairy work again. Jonty was thriving and she and Jake were no strangers to hard work. Nobody could have been more surprised than them, she confided over a cup of tea, to Phoebe, when it was discovered that it was Mr Macauley who had bought it and not some farmer from Lancashire as had, at first, been believed. Why he had kept it to himself for so long, no one could imagine, but then she supposed they should have guessed when he left instructions for Dobby Hawkins to go down to milk the cows and feed the pigs and hens, but then they had thought at the time he had been doing it as a favour to the farmer from Lancashire who must be an acquaintance of his. But no, Upfell was his, though why he had bought it and then done nothing with it was still a mystery. Anyway, somebody had to run it and why not her and Jake? She herself had a fair head for business and with her and Jake's farming knowledge she reckoned they'd do right well.

Annie had listened when Phoebe told her, saying nothing, for what was there to say? Although she went about her days with the same thoroughness and diligence to her farm's welfare that she had always applied, she felt as though there was no heart in her. As though she was a machine which functioned with the precision and power for which it has been fashioned, but a machine, though it works faultlessly, has no life of its own, no vital spark, no joy nor hope for the future. Her life had reduced itself to the level of what must be done each day to keep her farm and her animals alive, each one to be endured and got through until the time came, which she hoped to God would be soon, when she would know, if not rapture, then peace, if not love, then friendship. She had drawn away from Phoebe and Maggie with their simple and contented capacity to enjoy life, glad of the tasks which must be attended to before the long winter set in. Her eyes burned with unshed tears, her bones ached and her body felt hollow, her female body which had, for a few short weeks, been so rapturously filled with Reed Macauley's. She was haunted by the hatred she had seen in his eyes, dreaming of them, dreaming of him, existing from one dragging day which did not have him in it, to the next. She lay on her bed at night, sleepless, longing to fall into an oblivion which did not have Reed's deep blue eyes smiling in it, the reluctant but humorous quirk of his mouth, the steady strength of his arms about her for when she woke and they were gone, her heart broke again and again as it had done on the day they had last confronted one another. Was this all there was to be for her, her wounded heart pleaded? Am I to be no more than a woman who has loved and become lost because of it? Sad-eyed, sad-faced, empty-hearted, with no meaning in my days but that which can be achieved through hard work to be followed by empty nights without love.

It was Jake Singleton who brought Charlie back to them. December the first it was and her twenty-fourth birthday although no one knew of it. She and Phoebe were in the barn sorting the coppice timber into suitable lengths for splitting when they heard the dogs barking.

"Now what?" Phoebe said, clicking her tongue with every sign of the utmost annoyance, though with things the way they were at the moment any visitor was welcome if perhaps it would cheer Annie up. God knows she'd suffered these last eighteen months but without Charlie's cheerful humour to support them, Phoebe was having a hard time of it trying to keep Annie from plunging deeper into the melancholy that devil up at Long Beck had flung her in. Nearly two months now and Phoebe was worried out of her mind, really she was, watching Annie get thinner and more grim-faced with every passing day.

"Who is it, Phoebe?" Annie asked without much interest, carefully stacking the quartered logs into piles of the same size.

"Tis Jake Singleton. He's comin' up track on't cart. Now

what's he want d'you think, an' why's he fetched cart?"

"I really couldn't say, Phoebe. Perhaps you'd best go and find out," for does it really matter, her attitude asked. She continued to sort and stack the wood, her mind working methodically, despite her total lack of concern with what it was doing.

Phoebe's voice dragged her from the grey gloom, the world of shadows which still allowed her to do what was necessary but at the same time, mercifully dulled the pain her grieving brought.

"Annie, come quick . . ." Phoebe's shriek exhorted her and she turned, the shriek slicing through her apathy and quickening her step as she moved to the door of the barn.

"What is it?"

"For God's sake, Annie . . . come quick . . ."

The man was lying in the bottom of the cart, some rough sacking tucked about him, his head supported on several others folded beneath it. He was asleep, or so it seemed, for his eyes were closed in the sunken greyness of his face and his mouth was partly open as he snored, if that was what he was doing. His breath whistled in his throat and rasped hoarsely in his chest and across his unshaven face, a slick of sweat was filmed. His hair was dusty and uncombed, snarled about his head, long and uncut, and from him came the unsavoury smell of unwashed flesh.

Charlie? It *was* Charlie, wasn't it? . . . no, it couldn't be Charlie, not this crumple of old bones and foetid clothing, this stinking, gin-raddled heap of rotting human skin and sinew. Not *their* Charlie, whom they had loved and laughed with, shared their lives with, who had brought them through storm and trouble and sorrow, who . . .

"Ah' found 'im in Penrith, Miss Abbott. Ah'd tekken some stuff for Mr Macauley an' ah' were just ready ter set off 'ome when he fell down right in front o't cart. Good job I were only goin' slow on account o' t' traffic. Ah don't know why Jed didn't step on him but he's a good sensible animal an' . . ."

"Yes, yes Jake, but how . . ?" Annie was eager to get Jake off his rambling description of how the horse had avoided trampling on Charlie.

". . . well, ah' climbed down, thinking Jed 'd stamped on 'im, but he seemed all right, though ah' can't say ah' fancied touchin' 'im, ter tell truth, not the state 'e's in. Course, I didn't know it were Charlie Lucas, not then. Well, you wouldn't, would you?" eyeing the appalling condition of the man in the bottom of his clean cart. "Drunk as a bloody lord an' swearin' like a trooper 'e was. Ah don't know 'ow I recognised him really."

No, and neither did Annie and Phoebe who stared at Charlie in appalled, frozen silence.

"Well," Jake said, fidgeting about at the cart tail, "wheer d'yer want 'im put?" for the two women seemed incapable of thought and he had to get back to Long Beck before dark. He'd come out of his way to bring Charlie Lucas back to Browhead since, being a decent sort of a chap himself, he couldn't just leave a man he knew lying in the gutter could he?

It was Phoebe who took charge.

"In t' kitchen Jake, lay 'im on t' floor," which Jake did, and really, Charlie Lucas being no heavier than a half-grown lad, he could have been managed by the women themselves. Not that he minded helping, of course, for it was fair flummoxing to see what had become of the fine fellow who had once been Annie Abbott's . . . well, no one quite knew *what* his role was in her life but you couldn't deny he'd been anything else but well set up and likeable.

They stripped him down to the filth-ingrained, hollow-textured, bony, six-foot skeleton that was beneath his stinking clothing, which they tossed outside the door ready for burning. He muttered feverishly, fretfully, shrugging their hands away, his breath appalling as he wheezed into their faces. The smell of cheap gin clung to his skin as though it oozed from his pores and when, struggling with him, since it seemed he did not care to be heaved into the tub of hot water Phoebe had placed before the fire, he fell into a state of insensibility which frightened them, at least it meant he was easier to handle.

They emptied and re-filled the tub several times before he was clean. There were many things skulking in his hair and hiding on his body which, when disturbed, jumped and scurried and floated in the thick scum of the first dousings, and both women began to scratch vigorously at themselves before they finally hauled him naked up the stairs and tumbled him into the warmed bed which had been his since Cat died. They wrapped him about in half a dozen blankets for he had begun to sweat again, shivering and mumbling about being cold, his limbs trembling, his teeth chattering, the sweat turning icy on his body, a ferocious shaking which moved the bed beneath him. They could get him to take neither a sip of the broth Phoebe had simmering on the fire, nor of the milk which had come only that morning from the placid Clover.

"Oh, God, what are we to do, Phoebe? I don't like the sound of his chest. I wish Mrs Mounsey was still at Upfell for she'd know what to give him for a fever. He's not just drunk, you know."

"Ah can see that, lass, but don't thee fret, us'll get 'im right. He needs to sleep now and then when he wakes an' he's sober, a good feed."

"What's he been doin', d'you think, since he left here?" Annie agonised.

"Drownin' in gin by t'smell of 'im, an' starvin' whilst he's bin at it. Nowt but skin an' bone an' all I can say is thank God it weren't winter for he'd not 'ave survived."

Annie knelt beside the bed, smoothing back Charlie's long wet hair from his forehead. His face was bony, the flesh sunk into the skull, his eyes set in deep black circles of bruised skin, the dark straggle of his beard hiding his chin. His eyelashes, long and fine, were like those of a child and his eyebrows still quirked, one slightly higher than the other as though in humour. His mouth in the depth of his beard was vulnerable in his insensibility and on an impulse she bent down and laid her own gently against it.

"Oh, Charlie, dear Charlie, what have I done to you,"

she whispered, kneeling at his side, her arm cradling his head to her breast.

"Don't, Annie . . ." Phoebe's voice was sharp, "unless tha' means it. Unless tha' really means to give 'im what he's always wanted from thi', don't do this to 'im."

"But he's asleep, Phoebe, or dead drunk, he doesn't know . . ."

"It mekks no difference. Don't let 'im think there's 'ope, if there isn't. Even the state he's in he might know what tha's . . ."

"I'm only comforting a friend . . ."

"No, tha's not. Tha's comfortin' thissen because tha' feels guilty. Nurse 'im by all means, mek him better, or do thi' best, as I will, but don't go . . . puttin' tha' arms about 'im. Treat 'im as I do, fer if tha' break his heart all over again, ah'll not forgive thi'."

"Phoebe!"

"Tha's jittered about for the past four years between this lad an 'im up at Long Beck, leadin' them both on a bit o'string, not able to mek tha' mind up which one tha' wants, hurtin' them both an' thissen. Ah don't know what 'appened between you an' Reed Macauley at backend, and ah don't want ter know. Tha' let 'im go, so let this one go an all, or tek him for thy . . . well . . . but leave 'im alone ter . . . ter recover as best he can."

Annie stood up slowly, looking down into the thin face on the pillow, the thin face of the frail and defenceless man who was in this state because of her. What Phoebe said was true. Her own guilt at what she had done to him, her own compassion which wanted to do anything, *anything* to heal him, to make up to him for all that he had suffered at her hands, must not influence her, nor encourage Charlie, when he was himself again, to think that there could ever be a relationship between them that was anything other than that of friends. She had almost destroyed him in her weakness. Now she must do her best to rebuild his fragile strength, his endearing humour, his engaging, warm-hearted understanding, his clever, nimble mind, his peace, his life.

"You're right, Phoebe. But . . . I love him you see and I only want to give him . . . a reason to . . . go on . . ."

"Tha' can do that wi'out . . ."

"Building up his hope that one day I might . . . ?"

"Aye, love, unless tha' mean ter . . . settle wi' 'im . . ." Phoebe let the sentence delicately trail away.

"No . . . there will never be anyone but . . ."

"Right, then." Phoebe was all bustle and briskness. "I'll stay wi' 'im for a couple of hours whilst tha' sleep an' then tha' can tek tha turn. He'll need some lookin' after, will Mr Lucas. So go thi' an' tidy up downstairs first an' if ah give thi' a shout, come runnin' cos when 'e comes to himself he'll be a bit of a 'andful."

37

It was a week before Charlie 'came to himself' and in that time Annie and Phoebe took it in turns to nurse him, one of them constantly at his bedside. For six days he tossed and muttered and sweated in fever, knowing neither of them in his delirium, hallucinating about his childhood, calling Phoebe 'Mama' and urging all men to speak up for their rights. 'One man, one vote,' he ranted, fixing a stern eye on Phoebe, who patiently covered his naked body, not at all embarrassed by the tasks she must perform for him, only disconcerted when he whispered far into the night of his love for Annie, and what he would do to her in his bed. He burned in the sweat which poured from him, then was consumed in a fierce dry flame which stripped his skeleton of every ounce of fat upon it, layer after layer. Dying, Phoebe was convinced of it, parched, but unable to drink without vomiting, his body so weakened by the cheap gin he had drunk for the past eight weeks, and by the slow starvation he had subjected himself to, that she despaired of his recovery. She said nothing of this to Annie. They cleaned him again and again, scrubbing his fouled sheets, dribbling patient teaspoon after teaspoon of fresh milk or water into his mouth, exulting when he kept it down, agonising when he vomited it up again. He looked like a corpse ready for burial, his unique individuality burned away from him so that he might have been any sixty-year-old stranger they had taken in. The carefree, easy-going young man who had not yet reached his thirtieth year was gone and in his place was a human being without identity.

Annie was snatching an hour's sleep in the room next to his when he opened his eyes, eyes which had awareness in them for the first time since he had been brought back to them. Phoebe did not see it at first. The room was soft with rushlight, the curtains drawn against the keen December wind and the squally rain which lashed across the lake. They had brought the rocker upstairs and she moved it rhythmically, her feet flat on the floor her head resting on its tall back. He had been quiet for a couple of hours, seeming to sleep, and she had relaxed, almost asleep herself. His voice brought her to instant wakefulness.

"Phoebe . . ." No more than a whispered croak, but she was out of the chair and kneeling beside him, her hand on his brow, smoothing back his lank hair, her pale blue eyes shining into his with all the love she had successfully hidden, even from herself, flowing over him, ready to nurture and sustain him with every breath she drew, with her own steadfast heart, her own life if necessary.

"Aye, 'tis me, Mr Lucas." Her breath fanned his gaunt cheek as she leaned closer, afraid if she did not keep a tight hold on his return to lucidity, he might slip from her grasp again.

"When are . . . you going . . . to call me Charlie?" he asked in a faint semblance of the wry humour which was the essence of him.

"Eeh never mind that, tha' silly beggar. Tell me how tha' feel? Are tha' hungry? Can ah get thi' a drink? Ah've fresh milk keepin' cool in t' kitchen, or 'appen tha'd fancy a sip o'broth?" For whilst he was in his right mind she meant to stuff something in him before he drifted away again. He was nothing but bones, his flesh loose and empty of the strong sinew and muscle which once filled his frame. "Are tha' warm enough lad or do tha' . . . ?" She had been about to ask him if he needed to perform one of the bodily functions she herself had cleaned lovingly and without offence from him over the past week but now that he was himself again, she found the subject awkward.

"Nothing, Phoebe . . . only . . ."

"What?" Her eyes were soft, the expression in them as revealing to Charlie Lucas, even now in his weakened state, as though she had told him in so many words of her feelings. "What does tha' want? Tha've only t' say." He had wanted to ask for Annie, but with Phoebe's face so close to his, its plain intensity deepening almost to beauty in her love, he could not, at that moment, bring himself to speak her name.

"How . . . ?"

"How did tha' get here?"

He nodded, his store of strength too meagre for much more.

"Jake Singleton found thi' in Penrith. Tha' was . . ."

"Drunk?"

"Aye." Phoebe looked stern for a moment for she did not hold with strong drink, at least not with those who imbibed too freely, then her expression returned to the innocent, unrecognised love she was ready to devote to him. Not in the way a woman in love devotes herself to the man she loves for Phoebe would not have the presumption to consider herself as such a woman. She would nurse him, care for his damaged mind and body, work herself to a standstill in bringing him back to health, but it would not occur to her to even consider the hope of having her love returned. She had made up her mind long ago that she would remain as she was, nourishing those she loved, creating tranquillity and order in which to do it, devoting her life and strength and health so that those she cherished might know happiness. In this way *she* was made whole, fulfilled, satisfied. Mr Lucas had loved Annie for years. That was a fact, a truth, and to consider anything else was foolhardy, or would have been if it had occurred to her to consider it.

"But tha' was ill with a fever an' all. 'Tis bin a week now an' tha's had nowt to eat." Her anxious face begged him to consider, "so won't tha' try an take a drop of summat? Tha' always liked my broth, Mr Lucas, an it'll tek no more than a minute to fetch thi' some."

"Wait . . ."

"Yes, what is it?"

"Are you . . . alone?"

Phoebe looked astonished. What sort of a question was

that? Then comprehension dawned and she smiled, putting a work-roughened hand to his bearded cheek. It seemed somehow to find its way there all on its own, but it didn't matter, did it, since she was only checking to see if any vestige of his fever remained, wasn't she? Her hand was gentle as she smoothed the silky texture of his beard which she herself had washed only that evening. Of course, her mind reasoned, eight weeks ago he had thought Annie was . . . well, that she and him from up Long Beck were . . . well, honestly, she didn't know herself what Reed Macauley and Annie had had in their minds eight weeks ago, but whatever it was, it had come to nothing, but not before sending Mr Lucas off, half out of his mind, she supposed, driving him to the state he now was in. And naturally, him being in Penrith and drunk for most of the time, no doubt, he had no idea of the state of affairs here at Browhead.

"Annie's asleep in her bed. We've taken turn an' turn about lookin' after thi'." She sighed rapturously into his face, her breath sweet, evidently well pleased with the way things had turned out.

"Annie's . . . nursed me?"

"Aye, but see, won't tha' let me fetch tha' broth?"

Charlie Lucas sighed painfully and turned his head on the pillow, looking towards the childish paintings which still adorned the walls of what had been Cat's room. Nothing had changed. Phoebe was the same. Plumper now than the scrawny child she had been when Annie brought her home from Keswick, nearly five years ago, so he supposed she would be eighteen or nineteen years old. Her cheeks had become almost rosy but she was still plain and wholesome, like fresh new bread and as she had always been, ready to give her life in great bounteous plenty to those she loved.

And Annie. What was *her* condition? Was she still in that state of indecision into which her love for Reed Macauley had plunged her? She had been Reed Macauley's mistress in the weeks before Charlie had fled from her, he had been agonisingly aware of it. He had fled from his love for her, his passion, his urgent need of her, from the tumult of loving her so uselessly. It had been destroying him. He had been positive that she was about to tell him something of great importance regarding her relationship with Macauley, some development which Charlie had known quite definitely he could not bear to hear about, and yet she was still here at Browhead. Everything was, apparently, just as it had been then, so what had happened? Strangely, he found he could not really care a great deal. It was probably due to his weakened state, brought about by the past eight weeks of which he could remember very little. It was as though it had all happened a long, long time ago. He had suffered for love, he supposed in those weeks, pouring the cheap raw gin down his throat to alleviate his suffering, labouring at the most menial of tasks to earn the few pence to pay for it. He had not eaten a great deal, nor cared much about his condition.

And now what was to happen? These two women, both of whom loved him, would return him, he supposed, to his normal good health and then . . . ? Well, what did it matter? He was empty of all but a great need for peace, stillness, quiet, pared down to the bone, not only by the last weeks and the fever which had consumed him, but by the passion of life which he really did not think he cared to suffer again. He found that even the thought of the woman in the bed on the other side of the wall caused him no emotion beyond a flicker of surprise at the absence of it.

There was a flurry of white flannel wrapped about by a hodden-grey shawl, a swirl of tumbled hair, a drift of the lavender she kept in the chest beside the bed and there she was, Annie Abbott. He watched her come towards him, warm, beautiful, her skin as smooth and unlined as white alabaster, the weight of her hair drawing her head into that proud and haughty defiance which had incensed the outraged community of Bassenthwaite parish, its colour glowing in the light from the rush like the rich pelt of a fox, her eyes deepening to a warm chocolate brown in the soft shadows.

How lovely she is and how afflicted, he thought, amazed at his own lack of feeling, then she bent over him, her cool hands at his face, her smile radiant, her fragrance all around him. He waited for a tense moment for his own affliction to begin. For his heart to leap, his pulse to race, his breath to become ragged, but nothing happened. He was happy to see her, as he had been happy to see Phoebe, but her nearness did not unduly distress his male susceptibilities, as Phoebe's hadn't.

"The bad penny . . ." he smiled ruefully ". . . always turns up . . ." He could barely speak, he was so weary.

"Charlie . . . dear, dear Charlie."

"In . . . the . . . flesh . . ." and his eyes drooped.

"What about that broth . . ." he heard Phoebe say in an aggrieved voice, then the mist of healing sleep drifted over him as sweetly and gently as a spring shower.

He spent three weeks in Cat's narrow bed before Phoebe would allow him to set a foot out of it, lying under the warm blankets she piled on him, drowsing against the nest of pillows she arranged at his back, eating the food she shovelled into his mouth. First there were eggs beaten up in milk. Bread soaked in hot milk to put a lining on his sadly malfunctioning stomach, then egg custards until she was satisfied he could keep it down and was ready to progress to thick vegetable soup, to 'crowdy' and neaps and taties, to rich mutton stew and all the good and nourishing meals she was determined to get inside him. Apple cake and clapbread, 'poddish' with cream, oatcake with butter, cheese, minced mutton pies and all produced by her own clever hands.

"See, open tha' mouth," she would command him, "or I'll hold thy nose until tha does," and when he obeyed, resignedly, she would feed him as though he was a finicky child who knew no better.

"Here's some broth for thi'," she would say, clumping into his room, disturbing the peace and quiet he dwelled in. "Ah got some shin of beef when I was in Keswick yesterday an' it's bin simmerin' for six hours so get it in thi'."

"Phoebe, it's no more than an hour since you poured that egg and milk down me," he would protest, but it made no difference, she would stand over him until it was all gone, then off she would go, telling him to have a good rest as though he was capable of doing anything else.

But the day came when, with Annie on one side and Phoebe on the other, he was able to swing his legs out of the bed, thin white sticks, the sight of which made him snort with laughter much to Phoebe's annoyance, since she had seen them a lot thinner than that, she said, and had it not been for her good food, they still would be!

"No doubt, Phoebe, but you must admit they are foolish things and the question is, will they be able to get me downstairs?"

"You're not going to attempt the stairs are you Charlie?" Annie asked anxiously. She had his right arm across her shoulders and her left was at his back. She had not been involved as much as Phoebe with his nursing, making the excuse that she had tasks to do about the farm, which was true. The real reason, of course, was her reluctance to undermine in any way, his slow recovery by placing herself too much in his company. Might not his love for her stand in the way of his progress? she had reasoned; wound his already wounded heart and body, chafe and rankle so that his healing would be slow? Phoebe was patient and cheerful, a good cook, an uncomplaining nurse, tireless and untroubled by the complexity of emotion which gnawed at Annie Abbott and Charlie Lucas. Annie had done her share of the washing of bed linen and the nightshirts Phoebe had 'run up' from the length of flannel she purchased in Keswick market. She had done many of the manual tasks in the dairy whilst Phoebe tended to Charlie but with the best will in the world Phoebe could not be expected to get Charlie up on his feet without some help from herself.

"Why not? I feel almost myself again now and a sight of something other than these four walls will do me good."

Annie was not so sure. She had noticed Charlie's tendency to gaze into the far distance across Bassenthwaite Lake, his eyes unfocused and . . . well, not blank, exactly

but . . . not the same as they once had been. Calm, cool,
his smile was now, not the warm and wonderful thing
which had invited all about him to share his laughter. He
had an air of weary acceptance, no, it was not even that,
it was . . . an emptiness which, though she supposed it
stopped all pain, was not really the essence of the merry
and audacious man she had loved so well. But then he had
been ill, she comforted herself, and really did she want
back again, that urgent, vitally alive desire Charlie had
once felt for her? He had wanted to love her and be loved
by her. He had seen no one but her and had needed her
to look at no one but him, but now he was smiling down
at Phoebe with affectionate regard and could she be
anything but glad that he seemed . . . content?

He grew stronger each day, getting out of his bed,
sitting by the window, creeping downstairs where he was
greeted ecstatically by the dogs when they were not out
on the fell with Annie. The snows came on the last day of
the year and for five weeks they were shut up together,
going no further than the cow byre, the dairy, the barn,
only Annie moving heavily through the drifts, up to the
inlands where her flock, which numbered nearly 150 now
and would, in the spring, be doubled, were gathered.
There was plenty of hay in the barn, and with Royal to
pull the sledge up the track she had laboriously cleared,
she was able to get it to the flock. The thought of what
she would do in April when the lambs were dropped was
a constant worry to her, but by then perhaps Charlie would
be himself again and able to help her in the checking of
them and their dams. That is if he was still here. She had
no idea what he meant to do when he was completely
recovered and not wishing to appear as though she was
prying into his affairs, or giving him the idea that perhaps
it was time he moved on, she had not pressed him. Dear
God, it was hard, not for her alone, since she was frozen
for ever in her gnawing love for Reed Macauley, but for
her and Charlie since she did not want to drag up the past
by referring in any way to how it had once been.

Have you come to terms with it now Charlie? Have you

accepted that I don't love you as you wanted me to? Do you in fact love me at all, or has it all been burned out of you by its own fierce heat? Are you content? Can we live side by side in friendly companionship, you and I? Work together as once we did, or are you merely gathering your strength in readiness to move on? Am I to hire a man to help me? Not just with the lambing as I know I must do, but a shepherd to watch my flock?

She could not ask such questions of him.

The thaw set in at the end of February and the sound of the icy streams which carried the melting snow down to the lake was loud and musical. No sooner did it seem spring was on its way than winter returned, not snow this time, but a hard, cruel frost. Bright sunshine which had no warmth it in but cast itself over the sparkling hoar-frost until it hurt the eyes to look at it. It crackled beneath the feet, every ridge in the track, every furrow in the fields, every blade of grass stiff and white and crackling. The tussocks of heather up on the fell sparked and winked. The sky was blue and gold, flecked with dusty grey clouds which looked like gunbursts. The sunshine glinted on Phoebe's clean windows, burnishing them to gold, and whooper swans sailed low over the fields. At night there was a fine half-moon in the cold blue sky with a single star beside it shining on a crisp, white, silent world.

Maggie Singleton came over the fell from Long Beck in March, the first time she had been able to manage the walk since the snows first came. She had her boy on her hip, eighteen-month-old Jonty, and another one on the way, she confided smilingly to Phoebe who had willingly put aside her spring cleaning to gossip with this woman who, surprisingly, wanted to be her friend. No, Maggie went on disconsolately, Mr Macauley had not put her and Jake in to run Upfell farm, and what a sad waste it was to see that snug little farmhouse going to rack and ruin. All the livestock had been fetched up to Long Beck, the flock put with Mr Macauley's, since it seemed Mr Macauley could not spare Dobby Hawkins to run up and down the fell to see to them, he had said before he went away.

"Is he not here then?" Phoebe asked. They were alone, she and Maggie, Annie up on the inlands checking on her flock, Mr Lucas in the barn trying his hand at the swills, just making sure he could still make one, he had said. He was nearly himself again now, tall and lean and sinewy, handsome too, with his eyes so pale and cool, and his thin face regaining its amber hue. Quieter than Phoebe remembered, but content enough, she thought, and seemingly well settled back at Browhead. He and Annie were at peace with one another, none of the tension remaining which had once strained the very walls of the farmhouse.

"No, he went off with himself as soon as the snow began. I'm off to Keswick he says to Will, who is head shepherd, so mind tha' looks after the flock. My bank manager knows where I am if anything is needed. Will tha' be stayin' in Keswick, Maister, Will ses. No, ses Mr Macauley, I'm to go further than that, an' he got that funny look on his face, sort of far away as though, despite still being there, he'd gone some distance from where he started and didn't quite know where he was."

"An' what's the news of . . . Mrs Macauley? Is she to come home then?" Phoebe's voice was diffident since she did not really care for prying into other folks affairs but this concerned Annie who was her friend, at least it might do, and it was best to be prepared for any eventuality.

Just outside the door where she had bent down to remove her stout boots, Annie froze to stillness. It was not that she wanted to eavesdrop, or even wanted to know what Reed was doing, and certainly she did not want the sound of Esmé Macauley's name in her ears, it was simply that the paralysis which had gripped her at the mention of his name would not allow her to move.

"Nay, I couldn't say, Phoebe. Poor soul, what is she to do? But then she should never have left him, should she, no matter what . . . well . . ." Maggie stopped speaking, suddenly aware that she was treading on thin ice, for had not the cause, or so it had seemed at the time, of Mrs Macauley's departure, been Annie Abbott in whose home she now sat?

The boy who had been playing quietly with two pewter mugs and some smooth pebbles from the beck, putting them solemnly from one to the other, suddenly began to bang them on the stone floor, his childish delight with the noise he made bringing both women to their feet.

"I'd best be off, Phoebe," Maggie said, swooping him in her loving arms and kissing his cheek soundly; in the ensuing farewells it seemed quite natural for Annie to step inside, smiling as she did now, no sign of the pain which, though it nagged her constantly like a bad tooth, had flared in raw agony at the sound of Reed Macauley's name.

"Eeh Miss Abbott, tha's lookin' grand," Maggie said kindly, though Annie looked nothing of the sort.

"And so do you, Maggie. Your son has grown tall and handsome, and will you not call me Annie, please?"

Maggie bobbed her head in pleasure, wondering for the umpteenth time why folk in the parish of Bassenthwaite hated this woman so much.

"Well, thank you, Annie, ah will. Ah hope tha' don't mind me comin' to see Phoebe."

"This is Phoebe's home, Maggie. She may invite whoever she pleases. And I'm glad to see you. I will not forget your kindness when . . ." She put out a tentative hand to the boy, her face working, and when he beamed at her, she smiled, then turning, moved up the stairs.

"Goodbye, Maggie," she called over her shoulder, "come again soon," and they could both hear the painful tears in her voice.

The letter was delivered in May. The lambing was over and on Annie Abbott's inlands, her intakes and further up the fell where the first-born had been shepherded, her flock of almost three hundred hoggs, gimmers and wethers and their dams drifted contentedly across the new tufted grass. The ploughing had been done, the plough pulled by the patient strength of Royal and guided by the equally patient and quiet strength of Charlie Lucas. Clover and Daisy, her calf, had been put out to pasture and in her fields Annie watched the tiny new start of her crops, oats and rye and barley, which had been sown a month ago.

She had even bought a cart from the blacksmith whose forge lay just outside Hause. She had taken Royal to be shoed and had seen it, somewhat knocked about, but when she and the blacksmith had agreed a price and he had made a few repairs, Royal had pulled it up the track with herself at the reins, feeling as proud as Her Majesty Queen Victoria, she had said, grinning at the admiring Phoebe.

During the winter months, from the materials she had bought at 'backend', she had cut out and made a gown for herself, and Phoebe had done the same, sewing side by side in the light of the sieves and when Charlie had gone to his bed, trying them on, fitting one another with a pleasure which was the deeper because of the uniqueness of it. It was the first brand new dress either of them had ever owned. Phoebe's was a deep lavender blue which enhanced the colour of her eyes and contrasted becomingly with the dark brown sheen of her hair.

"Leave off that silly cap, Phoebe," Annie had told her, and surprisingly Phoebe had not argued "You're . . . pretty, Phoebe," she added, meaning it, though it was not strictly true for Phoebe would never be other than plain, fresh and sound, with the bloom of good health about her, but never pretty.

Her own gown was of wool in a tawny shade somewhere between russet and gold. It was almost the same colour as her hair, full-skirted with a well-fitted bodice down which a long line of pearl buttons ran from neck to waist. She had tied a sash of tawny velvet about her waist, an indulgence she had allowed herself, another being the pair of high-heeled, high-sided black kid boots, wondering at the time whether she would ever wear them. She had made a deep fringed shawl from the same material as her gown and with her hair twisted into an enormous shining knot at the back of her head, the height and weight of which lengthened her white neck, she looked quite, quite superb.

The letter was addressed to Miss Annie Abbott and asked her in the most courteous tones if it would be convenient for her to call in at the bank in Market Place in Keswick, where the manager had something of importance to discuss with her. He could not reveal what it was in the letter he said, since it was a matter of the utmost delicacy. She had only to call in at *any* time and he would be honoured to receive her, *any* time.

She put on her new gown.

"I think it would be appropriate if you accompanied me, Phoebe."

"Me?" Phoebe was flabbergasted. "But ah've the butter ter churn an' them potatoes . . ."

"Never mind the potatoes. They can be done tomorrow."

"But cannot tha' go on tha' own? Tha' always do."

"Not this time, Phoebe. Put on your new dress and Charlie will drive us in the cart. It's market day after all."

"But . . ."

"Don't argue, Phoebe, it's time."

"Time for what?"

"For wearing dresses," and with this mysterious answer, it seemed Phoebe must be content.

They caused a minor sensation in Keswick. It was the day
of the Hiring Fair and the market place was packed from
building to building with all the men and women who had
been there on that day, five years ago, when she had come
looking for work at the inn. They all knew her and her
notorious past. They had become accustomed to the
indecent way she dressed, to the sight of her long heavy
hair rippling carelessly down her back, to the way she
strode out with her trousered, unwomanly legs, and to
her complete lack of concern with the niceties which even
the poorest woman in the district regarded. They didn't
like it, but they had become used to it, and to her. Her
name had been sullied many years ago when she had run
off with that strolling player and when she had returned
she had deliberately, or so it seemed to them, flaunted
convention by taking in, presumably as her lover, that
well-spoken but flippant fellow from God-only-knew-
where. Her name had been linked with that of Reed
Macauley, so much so it had driven his young wife out of
her own home, and now, *he* was gone for good, some said,
and it could only be the fault of the woman from Browhead.

The cart moved slowly along the market place, Charlie
speaking soothingly to Royal who was not awfully sure he
cared for the press of people about him, towards the Moot
Hall in its centre, the lower floor of which housed the
covered market, its upper the council chamber where the
Lords of the manor held court. Their passage was slow
since those who had come to the twice-yearly hiring fair,
placing themselves where they might be studied by those
who were looking for maidservants, labourers, shepherds,
yardmen, stable lads, stood in long meandering lines down

the street. There was little interest in the cart at first for everyone in the market place was hurrying and scurrying here and there, intent on their own business or standing behind their stalls, arranging and re-arranging their wares more attractively, haggling with customers and generally engaged in the business of making a profit. There were other vehicles, a carriage or two, farm carts, passing along the street and the one carrying Annie, Phoebe and Charlie was almost at the Moot Hall before a farmwife from up Orthwaite way recognised the elegant young woman who swayed gracefully with the movement of the cart as it passed her stall. The woman in the cart was not only elegant, she was beautiful in her tawny gown and slipping shawl, her russet hair catching fire in a gleam of sunlight. Her back was straight and her head tipped imperiously with the weight of her hair and when she turned to speak to her companion, her long golden eyes narrowing in a smile, the woman from Orthwaite could only stand and gawp, her hand still held out to receive the few coppers a customer was putting in it. The customer, herself a regular visitor to the market, turned to look where the stallholder stared and her own mouth fell open. The live chicken she had just purchased squawked indignantly, and she was so startled she let go of it, allowing it to flutter awkwardly under the feet of a passing farmer. He cursed, ready to give her 'what for' but he, in his turn, followed her gaze, his eyes popping as he watched the progress of Annie Abbott along the market place.

It spread like wildfire, men nudging other men, women whispering to a neighbour, and though those who had come to hire themselves out did not know her, for many had tramped from places as far away as Penrith or Windermere, they stared nevertheless, for Annie Abbott was a woman worth staring at. The cart continued on to the left of the Moot Hall into Station Street. By now the word that some stupendous sight might be seen had reached the Royal Oak Hotel on the corner of the street, and men crowded at every window.

"It seems we are giving the good folk of Keswick

something to talk about, Annie," Charlie's voice was
laconic.

"That's nothing new, is it?"

"I suppose not. But they have not seen you dressed so
superbly before."

"No, they will be speculating on where, or how, I got
the money to buy such finery. It would not, of course,
occur to them that I earned it honestly, and with hard
work."

"Annie, don't you realise by now how much you liven
up their drab lives? They would be quite devastated if you
turned respectable."

"I *am* respectable, Charlie."

"I know that, Annie, but they don't."

Charlie, whose clothing, that which he had worn when
he first came to Browhead, had been burned when he was
ill, was dressed in the casual manner of a man of the land.
A pair of well-made hodden-grey breeches, contrived by
Phoebe and Annie who swore they could easily make a
living in the tailoring trade, they were becoming so proficient, with knee-length military-style boots. A shooting
jacket like that of a gamekeeper with many pockets beneath
which he wore a hand-knitted woollen jerkin. A 'wide-
awake' hat with a low crown and a wide brim was set at a
jaunty angle over his eyes. These had been purchased at
one of the second-hand clothes stalls which abounded in the
market, but by now Annie was paying Charlie a wage and
he meant to have a decent suit of clothing made when he
had saved enough money, he told her.

He handed them down from the cart with such a flourish
it might have been a carriage drawn by four matched
greys, and the crowd of onlookers had the strangest inclination to applaud for really, could you help but admire her,
the woman from Browhead? She had turned to smile at
them like visiting royalty, the smile somewhat sardonic,
before she entered the bank which stood in Station Street
and what, they asked one another, was she doing there?
By God, she looked well, the men told one another,
remembering perhaps, those who had been served their

ale by her at The Packhorse many years ago, the shabbiness of her dress then. The women were inclined to pull their faces since it seemed to them the wages of sin must be very high indeed.

The manager sat them down with much ceremony, wringing his hands and bowing, overcome by the honour of having them in his office, and the three of them exchanged amused glances for it seemed the possession of a little money had a magical charm for Mr Burton. By now, of course, Charlie was aware of the finding of the tin box, the contents of which generations of Abbott women had accumulated, but surely it was not enough to cause Mr Burton to bow and scrape as he was doing? Three hundred pounds was more than the majority of men in the parish saw in a lifetime but there were many wealthy farmers, industrialists and the like in Cumberland, owners of mines, and those who held shares in the new railways which brought them in more in a twelve month than the whole of Annie's savings, and which they deposited in Mr Burton's bank. So why was he so fulsome, lavish even, with his bowing and scraping?

"Now then, Miss Abbott, to the purpose of this meeting if I may," having enquired of her health, the state of her farm, the weather and everything else connected with her which came to his mind. He had before him some documents, one of which he took up, studying it for a moment before laying it carefully on his desk again. "I have here the deeds to Upfell Farm. They are in your name and have been for the past twelve months almost, but . . . well . . . I was asked not to present you with them until . . . until now. They were purchased by a certain person who wishes to remain anonymous and . . ."

"Reed Macauley." The name was spat out as though it was made of bitter fruit and Mr Burton looked up sharply.

"I am not at liberty to . . ."

"Don't be ridiculous, Mr Burton. Everyone in the parish knows the farm was bought by him and . . ."

Mr Burton held up his hand. He did not think he cared to be called ridiculous, not in his own office, and certainly not by this woman who, until today, or at least the last time he had seen Mr Macauley, had, in his opinion, been a fast hussy who was no better than she should be. His expression said so.

"Miss Abbott, that may be so but the deeds were inscribed directly from the name of Garnett to that of Abbott. The name of Macauley was never . . ."

"Where is he?" She could feel the anger, an anger so weighty and hard to control she knew she was in danger of it getting away from her. If it did, Mr Burton might be the one to carry the burden of it and it was really nothing to do with him. He was not at fault, poor man, he was merely the messenger who carried the news and could not be blamed for Reed Macauley's madness.

"Where is he?" she repeated, oblivious of Phoebe, who, feeling uncomfortable from the first in this splendid room, was now ready to stand up and get back to Browhead as soon as possible. Even her own transformed appearance had lost its wonder. She hadn't the slightest notion of what was going on, only that it was making Annie so murderously angry, she seemed about to hit Mr Burton. Charlie was saying nothing, and nothing showed in his face beyond a mild interest and a cool contempt for Mr Burton and, or so it seemed to Phoebe, all he stood for.

"Miss Abbott, I cannot divulge the whereabouts of my client. I am merely doing what he asked me to do which is to give you these deeds and to tell you that you may take up the care of your livestock . . ."

"*My* livestock? None of it is mine."

"Your name is on this document, Miss Abbott, therefore it belongs to you."

"No." She wanted to scream and strike out at him. Of course she really wanted to strike out at Reed Macauley. To strike him hard and fatally, but since he was not here, anyone would do. The heavy outraged stone in her chest which was pressed high against her lungs, making it difficult for her to breathe, would not shift and she could feel herself fighting for air. But into her mind had come a tiny probing question which asked her why she felt so angry, so overwhelmed by the need to lash out, if only he had been here, at Reed Macauley for doing what he had always done. He had given her what he knew she wanted. Ever since he had bundled that hamper of food down the track from Long Beck to Browhead it had been the same. In any way he could, whether she agreed or not, he had provided for her, protected her, watched out for her interests, and she *did* want Upfell, she had let him know it, and here it was ready to fall into her lap. She had been prepared to buy it from him but he had struck her and told her to leave his house and his life and since then she had not seen him, nor heard about him except Maggie's words telling Phoebe that he had gone. Where was he? Dear God, was she never to have peace? . . . Dear God, Reed . . . would she ever know the peace of not loving him? . . . Reed . . . Reed . . .

"I cannot accept it." Her voice was harsh. "I will not accept it."

"Then what am I to do with it, Miss Abbott? Mr Macauley was quite adamant in his instructions and I cannot just leave a valuable property lying idle with no one to care for it. I have sent instructions up to Long Beck only this morning, as Mr Macauley told me, to return the livestock to . . ."

"That is nothing to do with me."

"It is your farm, Miss Abbott, and they are your animals, therefore it seems to me that it *has* something to do with you. It is your responsibility."

"NO!"

"Miss Abbott . . ."

"Inform Mr Macauley that he must return at once and see to them for I will not . . ."

"I cannot do that. He has gone abroad and I cannot say when he will be back."

Mr Burton closed his mouth in a white line of anger, aware that he had said more than he intended, but really this splendid woman with her great dazzling eyes and heaving bosom was too much for any man to withstand. She had not deliberately gone about wheedling information out of him, as many women would, but she had got it just the same.

The silence was deep and long and into it Charlie's voice fell quite casually.

"There is an answer, of course."

Annie turned to him like a drowning sailor clutching at a piece of driftwood floating by and he wondered at the intensity of this love she had for Reed Macauley. It made her, a woman normally so practical, level-headed and thoughtful, act in a way that was none of these things. There was nothing she wanted more, he happened to know, than to run Upfell next to her own farm and yet her stubborn, illogical, proud and female mind would not allow her to accept it from a man who, it was very evident, loved her more than his own life. Reed Macauley was willing to go away, leave the life he had known since he was a boy so that she might live in peace. Or was it that *he* needed it, needed to get away from her, as he himself had needed to do six months ago? She was a flame, warm, bright, lovely but very lethal, a dangerous flame in which an unwary man could be consumed, as *he* had been, and the heat of her had burned him out, as perhaps it was burning out the essence of Reed Macauley, leaving no more than an empty husk.

"What is it, Charlie?" Annie's voice was eager and Mr Burton found he too was on the edge of his seat.

"You have some three hundred pounds deposited with Mr Burton's bank, have you not?"

"Yes, I intend to start a business . . ."

"Why do you not buy the farm instead? The business could come later."

"Mr . . . er . . . Lucas, Miss Abbott cannot purchase what she already owns."

"I presume Mr Macauley has an account with you, Mr Burton?"

"Really, that is Mr Macauley's business, but . . ."

"Surely it would be a simple matter to transfer the money from Miss Abbott's holdings to Mr Macauley's? You can put money *in*, I presume?"

"Well . . . yes . . ."

"Then what is there to stop you? Miss Abbott will then, in effect, have bought the farm. At least she will have paid Mr Macauley three hundred pounds which . . ."

"Oh, Charlie, that is a splendid idea but I believe the price was two hundred guineas. I want Upfell Farm, of course I do, but I don't want it given to me by . . . Well, I want to feel that I have . . . Charlie, really you will know what I mean . . ."

"I know exactly what you mean, Annie," and in his cool grey eyes there was a faint memory of the passionate love she had evoked in him once. He could no longer be stirred by that kind of emotion, he knew it now. It had been scourged out of him in the eight weeks he had hated her, been obsessed by her, suffered for her and had returned a different man; one remoulded and emptied of the masculine hungers he had once known. But in that moment as she turned to him in passionate relief he remembered how it had felt and he was very aware that Annie Abbott still suffered it.

As they drove jubilantly back to Browhead – at least Annie was jubilant, for Phoebe kept repeating she couldn't make head nor tail of it and therefore, as yet, could see no reason for jubilation – Reed Macauley stood beside his wife, his arm supporting her weeping, fainting figure as the coffin which contained the body of her father was lowered into the ground.

He had been about to board ship for America since he had heard there were many business opportunities to be found there and now seemed as good a time as any to go and see what they were. His affairs were all in order with men of integrity to keep them that way and his farm, efficiently run as he had designed it to be, would continue to flourish under the supervision of the factor he had employed.

The news of his father-in-law's death could not be ignored. His wife's inheritance which, by the laws of the land, now belonged entirely to him, must be put in order, the estate settled, his father-in-law's mills organised, along with his home, his servants, his wife and his daughter. His married daughter who had spent the last two years living the life of a 'daughter at home' or that of a widow, but was, in law, the wife of Reed Macauley.

Those who stood about the grave exchanged furtive glances as Esmé Macauley clung to her husband in much the same way she had clung to Edmund Hamilton-Brown, whose widow was quite overlooked. Mrs Hamilton-Brown was composed, tearless, standing somewhat apart, as though the man who had been her husband had really been nothing to do with her, the right to grieve his death belonging solely to his daughter.

The last mourner had left, the carriages following one another in an orderly line down the long gravelled driveway of Edmund's splendid house in Bradford. Reed stood, as was correct in a bereaved son-in-law, between his wife and his mother-in-law, shaking each hand which was held out to him, speaking the right words, knowing exactly what was in the curious minds of those who had come to pay their last respects to the hard-headed and ruthless businessman who had been Edmund Hamilton-Brown. There was a lot of money and how was his empty-headed daughter and his self-effacing wife to manage it without him? So was this husband of Esmé's to do it in his place? Run his mills and his home, his womenfolk, and if so were Mr and Mrs Macauley to live together again as man and wife, as, shockingly, they had not done for the past two years?

It was in Esmé's eyes as she sat down in the chair opposite the man she had married four years ago, the look of pleading, the desperate look of an animal at bay, one that knows its fate, its very life hangs in the balance and will be decided in the next few moments.

"I think I will go and rest, my dear," Esmé's mother murmured, smiling in a vague way at Reed as he opened the door for her, but in her eyes was an awareness of the importance of the next hour, not only to Esmé and her husband, but to herself since her own future lay in the hands of Reed Macauley.

"May I ring for tea, Reed, or would you prefer . . . perhaps a brandy?"

"I think brandy, Esmé, but don't trouble the servants. I will help myself."

A silence fell and still Esmé's eyes held that imploring expression. He smiled, gently, for she was so young.

"Don't worry, my dear," he said in the softest way he knew how. "I am not about to drag you back to Long Beck, nor make you do anything you don't wish to do. You are my wife and I know the law gives into my hands everything you have inherited from your father but I don't intend to use it to enforce my will on yours. Your father protected you and now I will continue to . . ."

"No, Reed, you don't understand." Her head rose proudly and her eyes were steady. What he had thought to be the entreaty of a frightened child to be told that all was well, was in fact that of a woman who is afraid that she is about to be made to do what the man who owned her, demanded that she do. "I am your wife," she went on, "and as such I must obey you, but you made it very clear two years ago that you . . . did not care for me. My father was incensed and was determined to punish you. I was . . . hurt . . . offended. I was a discarded wife and my pride was wounded. My father had made a pet of me and I had grown up believing, as he taught me to believe, that I had only to ask for something and it would be mine. Papa was a . . . ruthless man, I know that now, one who did not like to be crossed, something like yourself, and when you . . . directed your affections elsewhere he took it personally and wanted to hurt you. I . . . dissuaded him. I loved him very much and shall miss him. His death was hard for me and I shall grieve." Her eyes brimmed with tears and she dashed her hand across them in the way small children do and for the first time Reed Macauley felt a warmth towards her which he had never known before.

"I'm sorry, Esmé."

"Let me finish, Reed."

"Of course."

"I . . . do not want to be your wife, Reed, and I am

afraid that if I . . ." She took a deep breath which lifted her magnificent bosom, ". . . my mother and I are used to a certain standard of living . . ." She smiled a little, ". . . luxury I suppose you might call it, and now if you are . . . if you . . ."

"It is up to me how you, indeed IF you are to continue to live in it? Is that what you are saying?"

"Yes. It is not unknown for a man to force his wife to live in penury whilst he spends her fortune on his mistress." Her expression was defiant and Reed was made very aware that his child-bride was no longer a child but a woman of strength and maturity and he wondered on how it had come about.

"I have no mistress, Esmé." He said it mildly.

"But . . . the woman . . . ?"

"From Browhead?"

"Yes, I thought . . . that is . . ."

"No, it is all over. She loves . . . elsewhere. There is a man . . ." The look of pain in his eyes was fleeting but Esmé saw it.

"I'm sorry, Reed. I know how you must feel."

"*You*, Esmé?" He shook his head wonderingly for what did Esmé Hamilton-Brown know of love?

"You still love her?"

"Oh, yes."

"Then we are a sorry pair, Reed." She rose from her chair and crossed the rich comfort of the deep-piled carpet Edmund Hamilton-Brown had thought appropriate for himself and his family to walk on. Reed was staring sightlessly at the manicured expanse of Edmund's spring garden, *his* spring garden now, he supposed indifferently, but he turned at her words. She was almost twenty-two, a beautiful young woman, composed, elegant in her fashionable and beautifully made black mourning gown. Her skin was smooth, flawless, her mouth full and rosy and in her cornflower blue eyes was a serenity, a look of . . . of something he did not at first recognise but when he did his expression of amazement made her smile.

"Yes, you are right." Her voice was soft, marvelling.

"You . . . ?"

"I am in love, Reed, and more importantly, I am loved." She put a hand on his arm, hesitant, not awfully sure what his reaction would be since a man does not often hear his wife confess to loving another man. Though she knew he did not love her, might he not take it amiss to know that she did not love him either and might he not show his displeasure with the violence he was certainly entitled to feel?

"Esmé, I am speechless," but nevertheless he had begun to smile and she relaxed, ready to lean against him in the way she had leaned on her father. But he was not her father, he was her husband and what was to become of them? That was what she wanted him to tell her.

She said so.

"What do you want, Esmé?"

"I would like to marry him but of course, that is impossible. As you well know."

"I do indeed." His smile was weary and Esmé Macauley was saddened by the change which had taken place in this compellingly vigorous husband of hers. He was still handsome, tall, lean, hard, but the whimsical humour which he had allowed the world to see now and again was gone entirely. The brilliant blue of his eyes seemed dimmed as they gazed beyond her, beyond the room to something a great way off, remote, aloof, far removed from anything which had once concerned him. His dark hair had a dusting of grey above his ears and there were deep lines scored from his nostrils to the corners of his mouth. His eyebrows dipped in a scowl, fierce and challenging, but it seemed to her the challenge had gone leaving only the habit it had formed over the years.

"What do you want, Esmé?" he asked again.

"I want to be . . . with him but I cannot do it without your consent."

"*My* consent!" He turned to smile in amazement.

"You . . . hold the purse strings, Reed. As your wife I know I would be kept in comfort for the rest of my life even if we did not live together, but if I was to go away with . . . my lover . . . Oh, yes, he is my lover in the true sense of the word, though how I kept it from Papa I shall never know. We were discreet and I suppose lovers always find a way, and we did. He has no money, you see . . ." Her face was radiant, eager, hopeful, a quality of stillness and awe about her as though she had discovered something not revealed to other women, those who were not loved by the man who loved her. "He is the third son, you see," she went on. "There is nothing for him. He is a soldier but he intends to leave the army and then, if you agree and will . . . it *is* my father's money, Reed, and *my* inheritance, after all, but . . ." She pulled herself together, aware that her future lay in this man's hands.

"He would be content to . . . I can think of no other way to put it, Esmé, he will live on *your* money? What I *allow* you to have?"

"*You* will not refuse it, Reed, despite it being my father's, and now mine. Is there a difference? And if I was free he would marry me for it."

"And you don't mind that?"

"He loves me, but he has been brought up knowing that second and third sons of . . . his class, must marry where there is money."

"And you?"

"I love him. He loves me. We want to . . . we intend to . . ."

"What, Esmé? If I allow it, what will you do?"

"Live abroad. In Italy. We can be man and wife there where no one knows us."

"And your mother?"

"She will remain here quite happily. She and I were never close. She will scarcely know I am gone."

"I am quite overwhelmed," he said slowly, sadly, so that Esmé Macauley was left in no doubt that this quiet man who was her husband was very hurt indeed, but not by her. Damaged, weary, burdened with something he could barely lift, let alone carry. He was not at all put out that his wife not only wished to run off to Italy with her lover but that he was being asked to finance it.

Reed should have been outraged but all he felt was a small tremor of amusement. Once he would have been overjoyed for now he had the means to sue Esmé for divorce. Desertion and adultery, which were the two causes needed for a man to take his case to the courts but now, now it was too late. The woman he loved was a liar and a cheat. A woman of easy virtue who had betrayed his love. A breaker of hearts who had shared her favours between himself and the man who had moved back into her bed six months ago.

It was all too late.

Charlie Lucas moved in to Upfell Farm in August, and Phoebe, Phoebe Lucas as she was by then, went with him.

Charlie had come to Annie at the end of June, quiet and steady as he had been ever since he was brought back from Penrith. There was still a certain endearing sweetness about him, a twinkling sense of humour that shone occasionally in his pale, cat-like, grey eyes, but the lively wit, the jaunty, devil-may-care impudence which had drawn her to him at Rosley had been purged out of him and she was sorry for it. She must take the blame for it, she knew that and if there was anything she could do to atone for it, she would, and when he asked her for Phoebe, though she could not have been more astonished, she could do nothing else but agree.

"You did not know, Annie?" he asked her quietly.

"That you and Phoebe were . . . ? No, I'm ashamed to say I didn't. I have been somewhat involved in the running of two farms, Charlie, which is really no excuse since you are both my dearest friends and I should have seen it," but even as she said it she wondered why she should apologise, for nothing in Phoebe's manner, or in the way she spoke to Charlie, still calling him 'Mr Lucas', had indicated that there was anything between them other than the affectionate regard they had always known.

"She loves me, Annie."

"And you?"

"I seem to have lost my talent for grand passion, my dear, but I am left with a great capacity for friendship. Affection, if you like which is very soothing with none of the wounding effects of what is known as 'being in love'.

I think Phoebe understands this. I *know* she does. She is
. . . pregnant, Annie. I did not mean it to happen but you
have been busy elsewhere, and Phoebe and I have been
thrown into one another's company a great deal. She is a
lovely young woman, oh, not in the sense most men mean
when they use those words though I find her most pleasing
to look at. She is fresh and wholesome, strong but at the
same time gentle and wise. She . . . steadies me, Annie,
and when I made love to her . . ."

"Please, Charlie, that is something between you and
Phoebe."

"No, I want you to realise that . . . she is not second
best. You know how I felt about you but that only happens
once in a lifetime, to a man, or a woman I suppose. She was
reluctant at first, believing in some way that I belonged to
you, but when I showed her that I didn't and that I was
not merely giving in to a male fancy, that I meant her no
offence, and wanted to marry her, she . . . she allowed
me . . . *no*, she shared with me the greatest sweetness
a man and a woman can share. We both felt . . . much
joy. She is very honourable, Annie, and will go no further
unless she has your permission, despite the child, and
really, I don't know what I have done to deserve such
bounty, such a rich content as she gives me. So, we want
to be married as soon as possible. The child is due in
October . . ."

"October!"

He grinned, something of the old Charlie in him, impish,
even a little wicked, as though he knew quite well that
what he had done would not be considered gentlemanly.
Almost as though the man of the house had made free
with the housemaid whilst the mistress looked the other
way, but that had not been it at all, and Annie should know
it. He was a man, of course, and Phoebe, though he did
not, naturally, say so to Annie, was soft and pliant and
rounded beneath her prim apron and cap, and it had been
no hardship to make love to her.

Annie, who had been sitting at the table beneath the
window making up the wages for the men she had

employed to help with the clipping of her sheep, and who, now that it was finished, were moving on to a farm further north, stood up and moved to the open door. Phoebe was in the dairy and Annie could hear the regular 'thump, thump' of the butter churn. Phoebe was singing, some song the four of them had sung before Cat died and which Charlie had taught them. She was happy. It was in her voice, Annie could hear it. She was loved and wanted, *needed*, and inside her was a child. The child of the man she loved. For four months she and Charlie had been . . . Dear God, what word could she use . . . courting?, right here under Browhead's roof, it appeared, and not one whisper of it had reached her own ears. Had they slept together on the other side of the wall, making love . . . ?

For an appalling moment she could hardly believe her own . . . what was it? envy . . . outrage . . . jealousy? Was that it, a bitterness that Phoebe had what Annie Abbott would never know again? A part of her had closed down when Reed left. She had shut it away, set it in ice whilst she busied herself with her ambitious, endless plans, overburdening herself since it was the only way she could put out of her mind the totally consuming obsession of her love for Reed Macauley. She had directed an absolute concentration of will and energy into the exhausting organisation of running two farms, two efficient farms, at the same time doing her best to make a decent profit from both. She had Charlie, of course, and had he not been there, going at her command wherever he was needed, she could not have done it, and yet, behind her back . . . no, *no*! How could she say it like that, as though they had been underhand and deceitful, as though they should have asked her permission. Had she asked what *they* thought when she had gone up to the tarn on the fell to make love to Reed? Had she cared? Had she given them a thought as she had indulged in the rapture which, it seemed, was now theirs?

"Annie?" Charlie's voice broke into her reverie and she swung back to him. "We'll do very well together, you know, Phoebe and I, really we will. We . . . both need

. . . someone and . . . I hope you will agree to it but we felt . . . Lord, this is difficult, but we felt that perhaps we might take over the farmhouse at Upfell. Phoebe wouldn't hear of it at first. She couldn't leave you, she said, not on your own but . . . well . . . I cannot help but think that it would be . . . inappropriate for the three of us, four soon, to remain under one roof, can you? Not after . . ."

Annie smiled ruefully, then held out her hands to him. He jumped up and took them, smiling too, then pulled her into his arms, hugging her as a friend would, and she was made very aware that Charlie Lucas's affections and loyalty lay elsewhere now.

There was a step behind them and when Annie turned there was Phoebe, flushed, a little dishevelled, a shining tendril of dark hair wisping over each ear. She was stiff, even shy, inclined to drop her eyes since it was very evident that Annie knew. She placed the crock of butter she carried on the table and one hand fell to rest protectively on her rounded stomach as she waited.

"Phoebe, oh, Phoebe, do you know how happy I am for you? For you both?" Annie held out her arms and her tears fell, for her own sad state and for Phoebe's happy one. Phoebe moved into them and the two friends clung together lovingly.

The parish rocked with it! The banns were read in the Church of St Bridget by the lake, the woman from Browhead and her two companions there to hear them and the gasp which sighed round the church and up into its high rafters drowned the parson's voice for a full five seconds. The congregation had wondered, mouths agape, eyes wide, why the three of them should have chosen to come to church on this particular Sunday, since they had never done so before. The man was in a decent suit of good grey broadcloth, his shirt-front and stock a snowy white, his hair neatly brushed, his boots with a high polish on them. The woman who held his arm, the *other* one, was dressed in blue, a lovely lavender blue with a tiny white lace cap on her dark and gleaming hair. It was noticed that the man was most solicitous of her, placing her gently in a pew as though she was made of spun glass. Had she been ill then? they asked one another, though she didn't look ill. Far from it. She was rosy and rounded but even then they did not guess for all eyes went to her, the one who had fascinated them ever since she had come home. The woman from Browhead.

It had been – again – the talk of the parish when it was learned that *she*, the hussy, actually *owned* Upfell. That somehow or other she had got together the money to purchase the farm from Reed Macauley, or had she paid for it in a coinage of a different kind? But if so, where was Mr Macauley? Why was he not here collecting what was owed him? Dear Lord, the questions were endless, and the answers very hard to come by, and now the congregation watched her with avid speculation, as though some of them might be written on her composed face.

She wore the tawny gown which had been new on the day the deeds to Upfell Farm had been put in her hands. Her hair was tied back with a length of tawny ribbon and allowed to hang down her back in that defiant tumble to which they were well accustomed. No bonnet for her but a spray of creamy roses pushed carelessly behind her ear. No shawl, nor gloves, nor hymn book but a posy of the same roses picked from a hedgerow somewhere and which, later, she was seen to place on her child's grave.

The reverend gentleman's voice tried to rise above the sibilant hiss which moved about the congregation. It took them several minutes to convince themselves that the names he announced, Charles Edward Lucas and Phoebe Abbott, were correct! Surely he meant *Annie* Abbott? He was known to be somewhat absent-minded, but even he would not make such a dreadful error! Then it was seen that Charlie Lucas held the hand of the maidservant, smiling at her with every evidence of affection and the congregation fell silent, stunned by the realisation that Annie Abbott's lover was to marry her maidservant – and what were they to make of that? they asked one another the moment they got out of the church.

The wedding in August was attended by very few, but

those who came were Annie Abbott's good friends. She had not many in the parish but the tiny congregation which gathered for the ceremony smiled and nodded as Phoebe and Charlie exchanged their vows, the child they were to have kicking quite visibly beneath the stretched lavender blue of its mother's gown.

Sally Garnett was there, a changed woman now that she had charge of her life and the ordering of her simple-minded, harmless husband. She was clean, decent, her rosy face wearing that scrubbed and shiny look her own mother had once scoured into it, her plain brown dress tidy, her bonnet joyful with a bobbing spray of roses from about the door of her own spruce cottage. Her six children, the last born two years ago, were being 'minded' by her sister Mim who, it turned out, was a living replica of her mother, Aggie. Sally had 'pulled herself together' now, she said cheerfully to Annie, without Bert's nightly embrace and the steady stream of children which had resulted from it. She had a few sheep on her brother-in-law's intakes and a bit of land on which to grow her oats and bigg and vegetables, and with Bert, who did as he was told without a murmur, and a chap who worked for Mim's husband, to help, they did very well. What with the cash they had got for Upfell which Mr Macauley had . . . now what was the word? . . . oh yes, invested for them, and which brought in a decent little sum each month, they were doing right nicely. He'd been that good to them, Mr Macauley, sorting out all that there legal stuff and making sure that she and the children wanted for nothing and were well and comfortable in their cottage at Binsey. She seemed to bear him no ill-will for the 'heft' he had given to Bert . . . oh, aye, she and the rest of the community were well aware who it was who had beaten Bert, the community blaming Annie for the whole thing, naturally, Bert's part in it not proved, it seemed to them, but Sally knew, oh, yes, indeed! Hadn't she lived with Bert for eight or so years and who knew better than she his nasty disposition? She could well believe he had set upon Annie and he had got what was his due, the bugger. No, it had all turned out for the best, and, following Annie's example, Sally was making a fair go of it in her little cottage up Binsey way. She'd always admired Annie's gumption in running her farm and she could see no reason why she herself could not do the same.

Maggie and Jake Singleton were there, walking over from Long Beck in their best 'setting-off' clothes. They had another boy whom they had called Thomas, Tom for short, and he and Jonty crowed and laughed throughout the service to no one's annoyance, not even the parson's, for he was well aware that this was not your ordinary sort of wedding. Will Twentyman and his Eliza, in their own finery, came down from Gillthrop, defying the disapproval of their 'regulars', or at least their regulars' wives, for Annie was beginning to find favour with the men of the community for her sheer bloody-minded determination to succed in the face of all she had endured, which they were inclined to admire.

A few curious women servants from Long Beck crept into the back of the church, among them Lily Gill and Nell Tyson, the two who had wrapped Annie about in their compassion when Cat was killed. There was Willy North, and Dobby Hawkins with his fiddle and not one refused to walk over to the farmhouse at Upfell after the simple service and sample the thin, currant 'bridecake' Phoebe herself had made the day before. There was no attempt to 'throw the stocking' for it was very evident that the new Mrs Lucas was no virgin going to her marriage bed, indeed, though there was plenty of ale and a sip of port for the ladies and everyone was flushed and mellow when they bid the newly married couple a long life and a happy one before they took their leave, they could sense the strange melancholy which was in the air despite the bride's obvious happiness.

At the last moment Phoebe clung to Annie as though she really could not bear to see her go. About them was the shining wonder of Phoebe's new home and it was hard to picture the state it had once been in when poor Sally Garnett had it in her care.

"It looks like when me Mam 'ad it," Sally had remarked simply, sighing for her Mam who had once reigned in the kitchen which was now Phoebe's. Charlie and Phoebe had scrubbed and polished and whitewashed the farmhouse, returning it to the warm and comfortable home it had been years ago. A kitchen, a scullery, a tiny parlour and above them a couple of bedrooms. Phoebe had arranged the few pieces of old country furniture Sally had left behind, since they would not fit into the cottage at Binsey, burnishing them to a mirror gleam. The square fireplace in the parlour was set with logs in readiness for her 'callers' and at the window were the newly washed and ironed curtains which would keep out the vicious draughts which were a constant plague on the fells of Lakeland. The dresser in the kitchen was crowded with her brand new crockery and the glowing fire, lit even in August, had a couple of chairs placed before it in which Mr and Mrs Lucas would take their ease of an evening. Of course, 'at ease' to Phoebe would mean rush-light making, knitting, weaving, spinning, darning, for she had never in all her life sat with her hands folded in her lap. There was a basket of kittens purring like a hive of bees, their careless mother still in residence at Browhead, and beside them lay Natty's ancient dog.

"Eeh lass, ah can't bear ter think o' thi' goin' back ter that empty 'ouse. Will tha' not stay an' . . ."

"Phoebe darling, you are a married woman now with a husband to consider," laughing over Phoebe's shoulder at Charlie. "I shall be perfectly all right. Browhead is my home, you know that, and this is yours now. We are only a mile apart and no doubt you will be heartily sick of seeing me come up the hill to visit you."

"No, eeh no, Annie, tha' must come whenever tha' like, mustn't she, Charlie? Every day if tha' wants to an' ah shall be down first thing ter mek sure that . . ."

"Phoebe, you will do no such thing. You have a farm to run now, and besides, you musn't exert yourself, not with . . ."

"Oh, don't talk daft, Annie Abbott. Ah'm as right as a trivet an' if ah want ter run up an' down ter Browhead,

ah will. Ah know thee, lass. Tha'll be eating bread an'
cheese or owt else what's 'andy instead o' cookin' summat
nourishin' . . ." meaning, of course, that without Phoebe
to put a dish of crowdy, or neaps and taties or a decent
plate of mutton and vegetable stew in front of her, and
with no one but herself to be concerned about, Annie
would fade away to nothing before the week was out.
Annie was left in no doubt that even from as far as a mile
away, Phoebe would still be in complete control of the
kitchen at Browhead and whilst Phoebe was on her feet
Annie Abbott would want for nothing.

"Keep her from doing too much, Charlie," she said, as
he walked her down towards the gate which led on to the
track to Browhead. "It will take her a while to realise that
I *can* manage without her. She has been in charge of me
for so long now she cannot help but believe that the
moment she takes her eyes off me I will fall apart."

"And how will you *really* be, Annie?" He put a hand on
her arm, drawing her round to face him and his face was
filled with his concern. Yes, it said, I am married to
Phoebe. She carries my child and I will love and care for
them both with all the power that is in me, but you, you
Annie Abbott, brave, honest, humorous, loyal Annie
Abbott will always have that special place in my heart. He
rested his hands on her shoulders, looking down into her
face and she lifted one hand to rest it on his.

"I shall do very well, Charlie. Now that I know you are
settled, I shall do very well. Will it be enough for you,
Charlie?"

"Oh yes, and you?"

"I will . . . make it enough."

"I was meaning . . ."

"I know who you were meaning, but he is married. He
is committed elsewhere and I have a commitment of my
own. To this farm. To you and Phoebe at Upfell. To *us*.
The three of us will make . . ."

"I am not speaking of farms, Annie."

"I know, but I am."

There was nothing more to be said. Bending his tall

frame he placed his lips against hers. A brief kiss, soft and sweet, which said goodbye, at last, to the two people who had been Charlie Lucas and the woman he had loved.

Reed Macauley spent the last hours of 1853 in his bed with a beautiful woman whose very rich husband, twenty or so years older than herself, and no longer able to satisfy her in the ways of the flesh, if indeed he ever had, she confided to Reed, slept the sleep of the very drunk in the suite next door. There had been a ball at the splendid hotel in New York where Reed had kept rooms since he had come to America six months ago. He had danced with the beautiful woman and, briefly attracted to her sleek good looks, her smoothly chignoned black hair, the slumbrous depths of her black eyes and the half-exposed sensuality of her full white breasts, he had been drawn into the net of her undoubted charms, allowing himself to be tempted away from the dancing; out of his clothing; invited to take hers from her and spend himself in the plunging of his man's body into hers, which he had obligingly done.

She had fallen asleep and, easing his exhausted body from between her twined legs and clinging arms, he moved towards the window, slowly, wearily. As he did so he thought with wry amusement of those days, long gone now, when he could have made love to this . . . this strumpet from dusk to dawn, then, shouting for his boots gone striding out on the fell to examine his flock from dawn to dusk.

He took a cigar from the box on the table next to the window, lit it, then drew the smoke deeply into his lungs, blowing it out to wisp upwards in the dark stillness of the luxurious room. Lifting the heavy velvet curtain he looked out across the wide and handsome thoroughfare which divided Manhattan Island and which was lined with fine buildings consisting of business houses, public offices and hotels such as this one. Many had façades of white marble, testifying to the prosperity of this young and bustling nation, and it was here in this teeming city, and in others, that Reed had conducted much of his business, to do with his wool, his mills in Bradford and the many miles of woollen cloth which they produced. He had been a wealthy man when he sailed for America six months ago, even after the generous sum he had settled on his wife and her lover, but he had doubled his fortune since he left England's shores. To get money one needed money, he had often heard his own father say, and it was true for with Edmund Hamilton-Brown's hard-earned brass behind him it seemed he could do no wrong. He had lived the life of an Arabian prince, fêted and showered with invitations from America's finest society and in all that time there had not been a moment when he had not longed to go home. Home, of course, did not mean England, or Cumberland, nor even Long Beck but the particular square of earth where Annie Abbott stood.

His gaze was sombre, his face set in brooding lines as he looked back on the memories he knew full well were best forgotten, for they could only hurt him and had he not suffered enough that he should inflict pain deliberately on himself? He could see his own naked reflection in the dark glass of the window and the glowing end of the cigar as he drew on it. There were vague shadows behind him and the woman on the bed grunted as she threw herself on her back. He turned to look at her, her long white body draped bonelessly across the tumbled sheets, her hair spilling over its side like a dark and shining waterfall. She was very lovely and so had been the dozens of others with whom he had shared his nights, and many an illicit afternoon, for it seemed the cities of America were filled with wives whose husbands, busy at their desks making another million or so dollars, had not the time to love them. What was *this* one's name, he mused? studying without the least interest the slender line of her leg, bent at the knee, and the mysterious dark triangle between her thighs. He *had* known, surely, for she must at some time during the evening have been introduced to him, but he could not for the life of him remember what it was.

He turned back to the window, considerably startled

when another face took shape beside his own. A composed and serious face, exquisite in its oval flawlessness, the mouth long and tender, the nose strong and straight, the jaw set at a determined angle, the dark eyebrows finely etched above the eyes. Eyes that were a deep and tawny brown with specks of gold in them; eyes that suddenly narrowed in laughter, the soft mouth stretching over white teeth, the head thrown back with such infectious merriment he felt his own lips begin to tug into a smile and his own laughter to bubble in his chest. The image lifted a hand, pushing back the thick tangle of curls which fell over its brow and with the movement it vanished, becoming what it had always been, the misted reflection of a lamp which stood at the back of the room and which his imagination had transformed into *her*. She was gone and for a moment the pain was more than he could bear.

Where was she? he sorrowed, grieving as he had done for so long now, the death of his love. Not *his* love for her, but for the love she gave to another man. He held it at bay successfully for the most part, for he knew it would seriously embarrass those with whom he did business, those women with whom he danced and laughed and flirted, those he made love to, if they knew of the despair that festered within him. When he was completely alone he gave in to it, putting his face in his hands, holding in the flood of tears which surely were unmanly and which threatened to burst forth and drown him. He would rock back and forth, his mind bursting with all the lovely pictures he had of her, and with those of his future which was empty and stagnant without her in it.

"Annie," he whispered, his eyes on his own reflection, "Annie . . ."

"Reed . . ."

It was so real he turned about to stare into the dark shadows which, apart from that one lamp by the door, filled the room. His heart thudded, first one great leap which hurt his chest and then raced away so quickly he could hardly breathe.

"Annie . . . ?"

"Reed . . ." Dear God, what was happening to him? Was he going mad now? losing his sanity along with his hope and his capacity to take much interest in anything his life had to offer him? He made business deals with half his mind, the other half wondering on how to get through the tedious evening ahead, the long empty night, despite the woman he knew would no doubt share his bed, the next day, week, month. He managed it somehow but if he was to start imagining he could hear her voice speaking his name how could he cope with? . . . perhaps it was *her*, what's her name on the bed. Perhaps she had spoken to him but when he jerked himself across the room to look down at her she was sleeping with her mouth open emitting tiny snores.

Then? . . . He swung about, striding back to the window and, quite distinctly, as his gaze followed the slowly moving line of carriages which took the merrymakers away from the ball, though he knew without a shadow of doubt that, apart from the snoring woman on the bed he was completely alone, he felt a hand touch his shoulder, gently, *her* hand, of course, for who else could reach him over the thousands of miles which separated them?

"Dear God, Annie . . ." he groaned, the agony inside him absolutely more than he could bear and really, why did he not open the bloody window and . . . ?

"Reed . . . please . . ."

He lifted his bowed head and blindly placed his hands one on either side of the window. He glared madly at his own reflection, ready to drive his fist through the pane of glass but slowly, amazingly, he felt a great sense of peace come over him, dissolving his limbs and releasing his aching body and mind to stillness, a stillness and a resolve which astounded him.

"All right, Annie." He heard the words, the impossible words come from between his lips but they did not seem at all unusual. "All right, my beloved, I'm coming."

Sitting down in the armchair beside the window he fell at once into a deep and dreamless sleep and by her fire at Browhead, where she sat with Dandy in her lap, the dogs at her feet, her face still wet with tears, Annie did the same.

The next day Reed Macauley booked his passage on the 1100-ton Packet ship *Rainbow*, commanding a private state room. He sailed two days later, arriving in Liverpool on the eighteenth of January. It was raining so heavily the water was several inches deep on the roadway up to Lime Street Railway Station but he did not notice it in his tranced state.

He had two hours to wait before his train left and, unable to content himself with pacing the platform, he went across the road to the hotel which had been built to serve the constant stream of travellers who moved through the great seaport, by train and by ship. A brandy would settle him whilst he waited for . . . for whatever was to happen in the next days. A few brandies, in fact, for it would take more than one to calm the emotions which churned so fiercely inside him.

"Reed Macauley, where in the hell have you been keeping yourself?" a man's voice asked and somehow, in the strange, confusing, euphoric state he had been in for the past eighteen days he was not at all surprised to find himself in the company of Ezra Hodgson, the man with whom he had done business in the past and who had dined at his table on more than one occasion.

"I've just arrived from America," he answered, prepared to be polite.

"I heard you'd gone abroad, Macauley. A business trip, or is your pretty wife with you?" glancing about him conspicuously, though a lady such as Mrs Reed Macauley would hardly be seen in a bar like this. The whole parish of Bassenthwaite had held its collective breath when the news of the death of Reed Macauley's father-in-law had exploded amongst them, and speculation on whether Mrs Macauley would return to Long Beck was rife.

"No, oh no, she is . . . living in Italy."

"Her . . . health, perhaps?"

"No, her lover." Reed grinned wickedly, amazingly, or so Ezra would have said, for it was not something which would make a man smile, surely? Ezra did not quite know how to continue but he chatted on manfully, drinking the brandy Reed offered him, casting about in his mind for some topic which might stifle the embarrassment he at least felt. There was one, of course, and he grasped it thankfully.

"Of course, you will not have heard of *our* particular infamous tidings, will you? Really, you would scarcely credit it. After all the gossip and downright scandal that has been caused you will find it hard to believe, but that fellow, the one who took up with her from Browhead, you know the one I mean? Of course you do. Who doesn't? Well, if he hasn't gone and married . . . no, not Annie Abbott, but her bloody maid. Could you conceive it?" he begged Reed to tell him, "because those in the parish couldn't, though it serves her right, of course, the trollop . . ."

"I knew it, I *knew it!*" He was amazed to hear Reed shout in an exultant tone. "She was telling me . . . all those miles . . . Jesus Christ . . ."

Ezra was even more amazed when Reed Macauley drew back his clenched fist and knocked him to the floor.

"And don't you let me hear you call my future wife a trollop again or the next time I'll kill you."

40

The snow had been exceptionally heavy that winter, even by the standards of the Cumberland fells, falling silently, steadily, menacingly for days and nights on end until farms were buried up to their eaves, and flocks disappeared completely. A white curtain behind which the mountains hid as they were swept with great, tumultuous eddies of snow moving blindingly across perilous white slopes and crags, throwing deep drifts to lean against walls and gates and filling every gully and gill, levelling the 'slacks', the slight depression between hillocks so that they appeared to be compeletly flat and featureless.

For two days Annie could not get even beyond the frame of her back doorway. She made a slight hollow in the solid wall of snow which stood outside it, just big enough to allow Blackie and Bonnie to creep on to the step to relieve themselves, both bewildered by the quite alarming strangeness of it, but her main concern was for her farm animals, Clover and Daisy, who were safe enough in their byre but who would be badly in need of milking, and for Royal who was stabled in the barn. Her sheep, brought down to the intakes by her and Charlie at the first sign of the dangerous-looking snow clouds at the beginning of January would have to take their chances for there was nothing she could do about them. They had been bred for generations to winter on this inhospitable high land of the north, fending for themselves as best they could and, providing Annie could get to them with the hay in her barn before too long, they would survive. Once the blizzard stopped she would dig herself out, as she knew Charlie would be doing at Upfell and they would get through somehow.

She had plenty of provisions and a great pile of peat and logs stacked inside her kitchen door to feed the fire and so she settled herself as best her restless nature would allow to sit out the storm, taking up her knitting, doing some spinning, reading the newspapers Charlie had brought from his last trip to Keswick and, when he had read them, passed on to her.

For what reason she did not know, it seemed there was to be a war in some far-flung corner of the world she had not even heard of before. The Russian Fleet had attacked and destroyed a Turkish Squadron at a place called Sinope, all the seamen massacred, the newspapers reported and war fever was being stirred up in London and Paris. The British and French had entered the Black Sea to protect the Turkish coasts, though why it should concern *them* was a mystery to Annie, she decided, before she got up from her chair by the fire to roam restlessly again, to the bedroom to peer out from the window at the wall of snow in which she was imprisoned. The trouble was she could not even see if it had stopped falling. She knew it was night time because the quality of the light which shone through the impacted snowflakes during the day was different to the way it looked now, but beyond that she could tell nothing of what was happening beyond her own front door.

God, she wished it would let up and allow her to go about her daily round of tasks before she went mad with it. With nothing else to do she could not get Reed out of her mind. Whatever she concerned herself with, the newspapers, a frantic flurry of baking she indulged in, a positive mania of cleaning, even if it was not yet spring, she could not rid herself of the strange and yet surprisingly comforted state into which she had fallen on the day the old year had ended and the new begun.

It had been early morning, still dark and she had not slept, nor even gone to her bed despite her own tiredness. The snow had not then begun, and she and Charlie had gone up the fell to check on the sheep, looking for signs of lameness, blindness, weakness of any sort which might have been brought on her pregnant ewes by the hardness of the winter.

On the way back to Browhead, at Charlie's insistence, she had called in at Upfell to have a cup of tea with Phoebe and to admire the infant sweetness of Phoebe and Charlie's two-month-old daughter. Elizabeth, Beth for short, Phoebe had called her after asking Annie's permission, in memory of Lizzie Abbott who had, in her own way, made Phoebe's happiness possible. If it had not been for the tin box which Lizzie had guarded none of this would have happened, for Phoebe was in no doubt that without Upfell to go to she and Charlie would have been forced to move away from Browhead and the district. Could they have lived at the farm side by side in the uneasy acquiescence left by the knowledge that Charlie had once loved Annie? and deep down in the secret depths of him, hidden away from himself, still did. He cared for her, Phoebe knew it, and their baby daughter, in their life together, and was content, but the passionate love which had burned in him for so long was not easily quenched. It would smoulder for ever, unseen, like embers which burn deep beneath grey, smoking ash. Phoebe was not jealous, nor did she resent it. She was a practical woman and made the best of what she had, and in their bed at night she gave everything of herself that she had, satisfying her husband, holding him in strong, soothing arms if he should need her in his dream-filled sleep.

The baby was a plain, no-nonsense baby, like her mother, who knew right from the start what her place in her mother's scheme of things was to be. Loved, she was, and right proudly, well cared for, none better, strong and sturdy-limbed but there was to be none of the folly such as the 'grizzling' which Sally Garnett's babies had indulged in, and certainly no misconception that her mother's full breast was immediately available to her whenever Beth Lucas felt the need of it. Meals were to be taken at meal times when her hard-working mother herself had a moment to spare from her kitchen, her vegetable plot, her dairy and pasture, and if Beth soiled her napkin then, unless it was unpleasant enough to offend the senses, it remained where it was. Charlie it was who – as Phoebe tartly put it – spoiled her, lifting her up whenever she had the temerity to whimper, cradling her, kissing her rosy satin cheek, gazing into her unwinking baby eyes which were the only thing of him in her, a pure silvery grey, until Phoebe declared the placid child would be ruined. But there was a certain soft gleam in her own eyes as she said it and she made no protest, watching fondly as father and daughter forged the bond which she knew was so essential to Charlie Lucas.

Annie had nursed Beth and admired her progress on that last day of 1853, sitting before Phoebe's immaculate hearth on which an enormous log fire crackled, drinking a cup of Phoebe's tea and munching a hot, buttered oatcake, a dozen of which were wrapped in a snow-white square of linen 'fer thi' supper', Phoebe said scoldingly. It was as though she was convinced that, but for her own efforts in that direction, Annie would starve herself slowly to death and so, whenever Annie called, which was most days, either on her way up to the fell or on her way back, there would always be something in a pot, or wrapped in a neat bundle, 'to be warmed up' or 'put in th'oven fer later'.

"Phoebe, you can't keep on feeding me as well as yourself and Charlie. After all I don't pay Charlie a fortune and at this rate you'll be paupers. You should be saving . . ."

"Stuff an' nonsense! The amount *you* eat wouldn't feed a sparrow an' if ah can't give thi' a bite to eat now an' then 'tis a poor do. See, tek that custard tart wi' thi' . . ."

"Phoebe, please, I *can* bake a custard tart."

"When was the last time, tell me that?"

"Well . . ."

"Ah thought as much, so stop tha' bletherin' an' get another cup o' tea inside thi'. 'Tis a cold walk down ter Browhead."

She missed her. She missed them both as she brooded before her own fire at night with only her dogs for company. The room seemed to hold the images and echoes of the people with whom she had spent the last years, those she had loved and who had left her. Cat, sweet Cat, her bright face screwed into lines of fierce concentration as she bent over the long words in the Bible, and those in the stories of Miss Jane Austen and Mr Charles Dickens. Cat, laughing in delight as she mimicked Charlie's chanted pronunciation of French verbs. Cat, lovely, flushed with merriment as she bellowed forth the 'Cocking Song' into the lop-sided and amazed faces of her three animals. Cat, her bright face and bright smile quenched as she lay peacefully beside Natty in the lovely little churchyard by the lake.

Natty himself, brusque, exacting, testy, stubborn, his good heart shattered in Annie's defence on that last day, but his blunt presence still here in the shepherd's crook he had carved for her, in the chairs he had methodically repaired and the samplers he had wordlessly re-framed after Bert Garnett's destruction.

Phoebe and Charlie . . . Dear God, they were everywhere, smiling at her from the chimney corner as Charlie had done, winking and ready to share a joke, Phoebe standing with her arms up to the elbows in flour, labouring in everyone's service but her own, begging Annie to eat that there poddish, change her wet clothes, keep her mucky feet off the clean floor, get to her bed, sit herself down by the fire . . .

She was lonely and she didn't know what to do to ease it. She had what she had always wanted, what she had set out to get for herself, but what a price she had been forced to pay for it. She had the rest of her life . . . Dear God, she was only twenty-five . . . to get through and it frightened her for she really didn't know how she was to get through this *night*, never mind the rest of her life, this night which was supposed to be the end of something, and the start of . . . of what? . . . a new beginning? But the beginning of . . . of what? She must go on, and of course she would, but to walk a path alone was hard and dangerous, and though Annie Abbott was brave and strong for had she not been told so by more than one man, her heart quailed at the thought of doing it alone.

She sat on by her fire, not going upstairs to her bed, and it was cock-crow when she came to herself, her face wet with tears, her heart drowning in sadness, her body aching to be held by the arms she needed more than any others in the world.

"Reed . . ." she whispered.

"Annie . . . ?" The answering voice had a question in it but it was so real she turned her head, looking quickly towards the door, the yearning etched in her fire-glowed face, but of course he wasn't there. The dogs had not even stirred and yet . . . somehow . . . somehow it was as though his presence, the warm memory of his loving eyes, his smiling, whimsical mouth, his infuriating arrogance, his long-limbed powerfully masculine body, had entered the room, enfolding her in a comforting embrace, and she fell at once into sleep, her head resting on the chair back, the tears drying on her tranquil face.

Two weeks later the first snows began.

"Dammit man, you don't mean to tell me that the bloody train can go no further than this? The line is clear as far as I can see so why should the service be stopped? I have a most important engagement in Gillthrop." For a moment an expression of such blinding joy lit up the face of the speaker the harrassed station-master to whom the words were addressed was quite taken aback. He was a very tall and high-handed gentleman and he had the station-master backed up against his own office wall in the most disconcerting way. There was water on the line beyond Clifton and the track to Penrith was closed, he had already told him. Indeed it was a miracle the Lancaster to Carlisle had got as far as this, the rain they'd had recently. And, of course, the further north you got, the colder it became and there had been blizzards of such gigantic proportions, the fells of Westmorland and Cumberland had been closed to all traffic for weeks. There was no way anyone could get through.

"Is that so? Well, we'll see about that. Where's the nearest livery?" The arrogant gentleman's face was set in lines of stubborn challenge and he seemed ready to square his truculent jaw and stick his clenched fists into the handiest face he could find and the stationmaster did not care for it to be his.

"Down't street towards end o' t' village. But I doubt tha'll get Fred Strong ter allow one of his nags out in such weather," for the rain had fallen in a dense and straight curtain from the leaden skies, one that could be scarcely seen through, for days on end.

"Don't bank on it," the gentleman said, setting his jaw and narrowing his eyes before stepping out from the shelter of the station platform into the street where he instantly disappeared in the deluge which, even in these parts at the edge of the great Lakeland fells where wet days were more frequent than dry, they were beginning to talk of records and when had anyone, even old Arthur Blamire who was nearly ninety, seen weather like it?

Almost overnight the temperature rose from below freezing to a mildness which was so amazing, even the dogs seemed bewildered by it, sniffing the spring-like air and pricking their ears as though waiting for the command to go and fetch the flock down for lambing.

"No, lads," Annie laughed, watching the steady flow of melting snow cascade from about her windows in pretty, glittering bursts, followed by heavier, thundering falls as it slid down the roof and hit the ground. It was still a couple of feet deep, almost up to the window-sills but melting so rapidly it looked as though it would be gone by morning, thank God. She would be able to get up to see Phoebe and Charlie before the next lot set in for there was nothing more sure in this land of bitter winter than the certainty that there would be more blizzards before spring finally came. She and Charlie might even be able to get up to the intakes and check on the flock, perhaps fetch them down to the inlands about the farms. Four hundred sheep she had now, with those that had come with Upfell, and all the ewes were pregnant.

She had got to the distressed cows, both of them

yielding a great deal of milk and they, and Royal, were
fed and mucked out. By the time she had finished, the
earth about the barn and byre could be seen through the
rapidly thawing snow, but it was so soggy she sank almost
to her knees as the liquid mud sucked at her boots, nearly
dragging them from her feet. She could hear the sound of
water thundering down the beck as the melting snows
aggravated its usual blithe undersong to a deep throated
roar, accompanied by the steady drip, drip of water coming
from every tree and every building about her. From somewhere up the fell there was a sharp crack and she shaded
her eyes to peer upwards but there was nothing to be
seen.

But the sheep must be inspected now that her farm
animals were seen to, and whistling to Blackie and Bonnie
she began the trudge up the track to Upfell.

Charlie had gone on, Phoebe told her, and would see her
on the intakes, he had said. He'd been up since daybreak,
thankful for the early thaw, surprised by it too, for it was
not like a Lakeland winter to finish so soon. Yes, they
were all well and so were the animals though, like Annie's
Clover and Daisy, their cows had been much afflicted by
their lack of milking. And Charlie had been fretting about
her up at Browhead on her own, Phoebe admitted, smiling
without resentment at Annie. Now would she have a hot
drink before she went . . . no? . . . oh, and by the way,
Charlie had met an old friend of his the other day when
he was in Keswick, just before the snow began and wanted
to talk to her about the possibility of him, this old friend,
taking on the job of . . . well, Phoebe supposed you would
call him a travelling salesman, in the selling of Annie's
swills when she got round to it. A man from Charlie's
days as a Chartist, Charlie had said, very reliable and
accustomed to travelling. They'd gone to school together
in Yorkshire, meaning, though she did not say so, that he
was a well educated gentleman and would, because of it,
have the knack of talking to and presumably selling to, the
men with whom Annie hoped to do business. Of course,
it was up to Annie but Charlie said . . . what? . . . oh,

aye . . . she'd best get up to Middle Fell because those clouds above the lake looked like rain to her.

It began an hour later and by the end of the morning they were both wet through to the skin, rain dripping from noses and hat brims, heavy persistent rain, the water and melting snow combining to form a deluge which cascaded down the fellside in an ever-increasing torrent. They had found dozens of ewes, for the rapidly thawing snow had revealed them almost at once, most sheltering wherever there was a rock or two, a dip in the ground, even a bit of taller vegetation. They were all alive, miserable, drowned-looking creatures, their swamped fleeces crusted with melting snow, but alive.

They continued up Barkbethdale, coming to White Horse where a scatter of boulders afforded good protection and where again they found some of their flock and not only theirs but half a hundred bearing the smit mark of Reed Macauley. They were bedraggled and forlorn, all of them, but so far none seemed to have suffered any harm.

They leaned for a moment or two to catch their breath in the shelter of the rocks, some of them as big and as tall as a farmhouse. Their faces were raw and stinging and they were both shivering violently. The dogs, their coats plastered to their lean bodies, quivered at their feet, their eyes sharp and intelligent, their noses questing for the rank odour of a buried sheep for up here patches of snow still remained.

"It's getting colder again." Charlie had to put his mouth close to her ear to make himself heard. A squally wind had begun to blow, dashing the heavy rain at them with headlong speed, howling directly into their faces and no matter where they stood, moving round the tall stones, it seemed to seek them out. A racing slick of water was flowing across the squelchy grass and over their booted feet and on the slippery slope it was becoming increasingly difficult to keep from going with it.

Annie could barely see Charlie though he was standing shoulder to shoulder with her, and she felt for the first time a deepening twinge of alarm. She knew this country like her own farm kitchen and would have sworn no matter what the weather she could have found her way home. She had been out from being a small child with her father, in all weathers since Joshua Abbott would stand for no foolishness such as considering her age, her size, her gender or the state of the fells outside his farmhouse door. If he believed it was suitable to go up, up they went.

"We'd best get back, Annie. We're doing no good huddling here," Charlie shouted. "There's no way we're going to find any more ewes in this. Those we *have* found seem to be in good shape so let's hope the rest will be the same."

As he spoke the rain became even more violent, the raindrops – if the hurtling precipitation which flung itself down on them could be described as drops – had thickened, turning to hailstones. Hailstones so big and vicious they were ready to slice at any unprotected flesh.

"Jesus . . . !" Charlie turned into her, doing his best to lend his body in the protection of hers, the hailstones lashing at his back. He wore an oilskin, strong and supposedly weatherproof though the fierceness of the rain had found a way beneath it, and the hailstones hit it with a sound like gravel thrown on a pane of glass. His face had a streak of blood on it.

It took them over two hours to get down, hanging on to one another, Charlie's arm strong and supportive, clinging to any rock they could get a grip on, any tussock of grass which was not already drowned by the headlong race of water which was going in the same direction as they were. They came across another huddle of sheep, though when Blackie and Bonnie, at her command, tried to get them on the move for they would surely drown or be swept down the fell if they stayed where they were, they refused absolutely, in their senseless terror, to get to their feet. The dogs nipped and threatened but the ewes would not be moved. Annie could hear, even above the stinging slap of the hailstones against Charlie's oilskin and the drumming of it on rock and earth, the thunderous uproar of the unchained water exploding down Chapel Beck,

Sandbeds Gill, Southerndale Beck and Barkbeth Gill, all of them emptying in storm-tossed fury into the lake at the bottom of Skiddaw.

"I wish you would come to Upfell, Annie," Charlie managed to gasp when they reached the safety and comparative quiet of the Browhead kitchen. They could barely speak, either of them, bending forward, hands on their thighs as they gulped air into their tortured lungs. "I don't like to think of you here alone in this."

"In what, Charlie? This will soon let up. It's a bit unusual for the snows to thaw so early . . ."

"I know that, but this rain after the thaw is going to make it much more . . ." He had been about to say 'dangerous' but she was smiling as though to reassure him that this Lakeland where she had spent most of her life could not frighten Annie Abbott. She was concerned for her flock, naturally, but when the rain stopped there would be vegetation for them to crop and they were knowing enough to come down and gather on the inlands above the farm where she would feed them the hay from her barn. Royal would drag the loaded sledge up the slope and, before it snowed again, as she knew it would, her flock would have a nourishing, life-saving meal to see them through the next few weeks.

"I'll have to go, Annie. Phoebe will be worried."

"I know, Charlie, and don't concern yourself about me. I have plenty to eat and enough peat and wood to last a month, though I don't expect it will be that long. And these two will keep me company," pointing to the dogs who steamed before the fire.

"I'll come back as soon as I've let Phoebe know we're all right."

"You'll do no such thing. You can't divide yourself between two farms, and you must put your wife and child first, Charlie. Besides, this farmhouse has stood here for hundreds of years and will continue to do so for a long time to come. Now go on, off you go, and tell Phoebe I'll be up as soon as this lot stops."

*   *   *

Reed Macauley urged on the weary mount he had persuaded the owner of the livery stable in Clifton to sell him.
He would let no animal of his out in this weather, the man
had told him churlishly, and only when Reed had offered
to buy the beast – a somewhat ancient grey – which would
then, Reed explained, keeping his sharp temper in check,
belong to himself and would therefore no longer be the
livery owner's responsibility, had the man parted with the
sorry-looking nag.

He had moved in an almost straight line from the village
of Clifton, across low, rolling hills through the villages of
Tirril, Dacre, Hutton and Wallthwaite until he hit the Penrith to Keswick road at Burns. He crossed the River
Eamont, the waters almost reaching the arch of the bridge,
thundering down its course in full spate, carrying on its
surging torrent the flotsam and jetsam it had picked up
on its mad journey. Broken branches, great swathes of
torn-out vegetation, birds, small animals, boxes and chairs
and planks of wood which were becoming jammed against
the structure of the bridge. It was the same at the Glenaer-
amackin river and at Trout Beck, the water beginning to
overflow and flood the surrounding fields. When he
reached Keswick it was a foot deep, the Market Place
filled with frightened horses, bogged-down carriages and
carts, shop owners, their clothing plastered to their bodies
as they tried unsuccessfully to stem the inundation as it
crept over their doorsteps. Moot Hall stood like an island
in the middle of it. The Derwent and the Greta were both
in flood, pouring not only their swirling, swollen waters
into the town but all the rubbish they had collected on
their race down the high fell.

And still the rain poured out of a low and surly sky,
sweeping in a great impermeable curtain across Little Man
as Reed rode out of Keswick, blotting out the high peaks
of Skiddaw Forest until it seemed to Reed he was riding
into the skies themselves. He had exchanged his exhausted grey for a fresh mount in Keswick, paying over more
money, for though the livery owner knew him, he was
reluctant to part with a good beast, especially to hazard

it, a roan mare this time, in the elements which shrieked their furious spite on the fells.

"Nay, Mr Macauley, tha' don't mean ter ride over ter Long Beck in this, do tha'?" for you are a fool if you do, his thunderstruck expression said.

"I do, Archie Wilson, and what is it to you?"

"'Tis nowt ter me, sir. What yer do is yer own business but this animal is mine." The feel of good solid cash in his hand quietened any misgivings he might have had!

The hailstones began to hurl themselves down on him and the roan just as he reached Dodd Wood. He had decided against going up and over the top of Skiddaw when he came out of Keswick and saw the water pouring down the slopes on to the road as he inched his way beyond Mallen Dodd. If the road here was already a debris-filled swirl of water, what would it be like higher up from where it came? he asked himself. The roan was badly frightened, shying nervously at everything which brushed against her legs, flinching and rolling her eyes, difficult to handle. There was muck and mud, ripped-out heather and gorse bushes, loose scree, timber, and the bodies of many small, fellside animals bobbing madly about her and she did not like it.

When the hailstorm began Reed was forced to dismount, moving to the roan's head, holding her with both hands, soothing her terror. She was slippery with the rain, her coat giving the appearance of having been oiled, and from her mouth great lines of spittle drooped and were whipped away in the wind. The hailstones, as big as pigeons' eggs, sliced into her flesh and with a pain-filled scream of terror she broke free of Reed's restraining hands, rearing up above him, her hooves flailing, one catching him a glancing blow on the temple.

"Steady . . . steady, girl . . ." he tried to shout, the blood beginning to pour across his forehead and into his eye. He hung on grimly to the reins but even as he did so she turned towards the lake, escaping, as she thought, the tumult which crashed about them from the fell. He could not hold her and she went, vanishing in a moment as though the earth, or the lake as was more likely, had swallowed her up and Reed's last thought as he sank to his knees and then on to his face was that Archie Wilson had been right after all.

Though it was no more than three o'clock in the afternoon it was so dark it might have been midnight as the cloudburst emptied over the giant of Skiddaw. The wind had risen to a howling gale and both dogs cowered at Annie's feet. Moving to the window which rattled with every beat of her frightened heart, the dogs clinging to her heels, Annie peered out at her own reflection. There was nothing to be seen, absolutely nothing and she might have been buried in a great black hole. There was nothing from which she might get a bearing. No building, no tree, not a star in the sky, nor a shape on the ground, and the feeling of disorientation was appalling. Not in all her years in Lakeland had she seen such black nothingness and she wished now she had gone with Charlie. At least she would have had the comforting, comfortable good sense of Phoebe to sustain her and the baby's sweetness to cheer her. She had hoped she would be able to make her way over to the barn where Royal was stabled for he must be hungry by now, and probably terrified out of his wits. The cows would be easier to get to for the byre was attached to the house and she had only to feel her way along the wall to reach it but she would have left the animals to fend for themselves, really she would, if she could have crawled up the track to Upfell and the company of Charlie and Phoebe.

She was badly alarmed by a sudden thump at the back of the farmhouse, then another, the second one so violent she could feel the tremor of it in the soles of her feet as it shook the sturdy building. What was it? Had something fallen, a tree perhaps or . . . ? The thought had not had time to formulate itself in her mind when she felt the icy cold surge of water bite into her bare feet. She looked down and to her horror, seeping under the door was a dark slick which stained the floor with the sediment it contained. It moved inexorably about her feet and across the stone flags, rising, even as she watched in stupefied amazement, to lap at her ankle bone.

"Oh, dear God . . ." she moaned, shaking her head in denial, ready to wrench open the door and escape it, to run screaming up the track for Charlie and Phoebe, for *anybody* since she did not want to drown here all by herself. Not here in this dark and empty space where she existed alone. Alone because of her love for one man. A self-chosen loneliness but terrifying nevertheless and she could not bear it. Reed . . . I need you, Reed . . . I am so afraid in this cold and alien place . . . Reed . . . Oh, dear Lord . . . where? . . . where should she run to? . . . the dogs . . . Dandy, they were beginning to panic . . . to howl in fear, catching it from her and if she did not get a tight grip on herself . . . help me . . . someone . . . Reed . . .

She looked about her, fighting her panic and as suddenly as it had come, and for no apparent reason, it left her. It was as though his strong and vital presence was standing beside her filling her with a calming peace, and she was calm. As though his mind had reached into hers, giving her comfort, touching something in her, steadying her, soothing her pounding heart, and she was renewed by it.

"Come on, lads, stop that noise, Dandy," she said firmly to the animals, "it's upstairs for us. There's nothing to be done here until the rain stops. Now, let's see . . . food . . . water, rushlights, flint and striker . . . and there's the milk. Up you go, Blackie . . . aye, it's all right, boy, up you go," for even in his terror he was not sure he should move up the stairs where he was never allowed. "Good boy, up you go."

It took her ten minutes to collect as much food as she could, the hot 'tatie-pot' which had been bubbling on the fire, the last to go, and even as she moved to the bottom stair the water was already there before her and on the hearth the fire was doused for only the second time since she had returned to Browhead, its acrid smoke billowing up the howling chimney.

It was the water flooding into his mouth which brought him to his senses, choking him to consciousness, coughing and spluttering, though at first he was so confused he had no idea how he had got where he was, or even who he was.

He sat up, held fast in a violent bout of shivering, the pain at once beginning to bang agonisingly inside his skull. Dear God in Heaven, where? . . . what? . . . he was soaked through, his clothing plastered to his body like wet cement and just as heavy, but he could not seem to be able to collect his wits sufficiently to tell him how he had got into such a state. He could hear nothing but the thunder of water and the howling of the demonic wind accompanied by an occasional thud which he could not recognise though it sounded dangerous. What in hell's name? . . . where was he going? . . . how? Jesus Christ, but his head hurt, and it was as he put his hands to it, unable to bear the pain of it a moment longer that a dead sheep came to rest against his back, almost thrusting him from the flooded road and into the lake where . . . yes . . . *where his horse had gone!* He remembered that . . . his horse galloping away into that impenetrable curtain of hailstones . . . He had been on his way to Browhead . . . to Annie, when the ice particles had sliced at him and the roan he had purchased in Keswick, but how had he come to be hurt? There was blood coursing down his face, mixing with the pelting rain. He could taste the saltiness of it in his mouth, but he really could no longer sit in the rising water, pondering on how he had come to be here when he needed – with all his heart he needed – to get to Annie. She would need *him*. She would be alone now that chap had married

her maidservant and presumably taken her off to a life of
their own, and Annie would be in need of him. He knew
that with a certainty which had first come to him in New
York and had grown with every mile he had travelled to
get to her. At last, *at last*, Annie Abbott needed Reed
Macauley.

He rose unsteadily to his feet and the dead animal behind
him thudded into the backs of his legs almost knocking
him over again. It *was* a dead sheep as he had thought but
the force of its journey down the rocky fell had shorn it
of its fleece as neatly and cleanly as if it had just come
from a 'boon' clipping. He watched it in absolute horror as
it hurtled away from him towards the turmoil of the lake.
He knew the terrifying elements of the Lakeland weather,
but he could scarcely believe the forces which had been
capable of such a thing. What power had been called up
that was so fierce it could strip a fleece from a sheep and
what damage was it causing up on the mountains, and
more importantly, between here and Browhead? He must
get on. He had almost five miles of road to cover and
already he was up to his ankles in a rushing, foaming
torrent of water. His head was bursting in a pain which
almost blinded him, and the rain continued to drown him
in its vicious clutch. The wind whipped about him, lashing
the downpour into a frenzy and as he straightened himself,
turning his sightless gaze towards the head of Bassenthwaite Lake the trees in Dodd Wood, their tops whipping
and soughing like demented souls in hell, began to move
towards the lake.

"Jesus God!" he moaned. "Oh, Jesus . . ." for before
his horrified eyes a whole line of them, enormous oaks
which had stood for hundreds of years, slid slowly from
their birthplace and on to the road, the earth in which they
had stood torn cleanly away by the force of the water
which carried them. They remained upright for a moment
then slowly, painfully, lifted by the boiling, brown fury
which had convulsed down the mountain, they toppled
over.

It was terrifying, unbelievable. They were a fortress,

those trees, unassailable, invincible, and though he had seen it happen with his own eyes, Reed could not believe it. He had ridden past their enormous trunks, in the shadow of their grandeur, beneath the magnificence of their summer foliage since he was a boy on his first pony, taking them for granted, not really seeing them, or their beauty and now they were gone, humbled by a strength greater than their own, torn from their roots as though they were no more than young saplings. He felt he wanted to weep for their destruction and yet he had no time for it. He must get by them, or over them or through the jagged root system which barred his way, standing twenty feet or more in the air, tangled and clogged with earth, for beyond them was his love and there was nothing more sure in this terrifyingly unsure world than the certainty that she needed him.

Annie stood at the top of the stairs looking down them to where the pale gleam of the rushlight she held aloft showed the flood water. It gave the appearance of lying still but in reality it was creeping inch by slow inch towards her. It had reached half-way up the stairwell, black and silky and in it floated minute particles of debris which had been forced under the door by its strength. There were other things, familiar things, pots and pans and cups, the stool on which she had rested her feet to the fire several hours ago. The box in which she kept her rushlights, the rushlight holder, the one Phoebe had used, and the snuffer. They turned idly in the water where the light reached, bumping against the stairs and each other as though trying to be the first to get up to her. Which they would soon if the water continued to rise.

She had no idea of the time, nor even of how long she had been up here but she knew if the water came any higher, reaching the upper floor she would have to get out. As soon as it was as high as the top of the bedroom windows her escape route through them would be cut off. She would be trapped. She would drown and so would the animals.

She moved back into her bedroom and closed the door behind her, an instinctive action which came from her need to shut it out, to bar its entrance, that which lay behind her, though her commonsense told her there was no shutting it out. The menace was behind her, beneath her, all around her. And if she got out, when she got out, what would she do? Where would she go? The wind howled viciously beyond the window and there were constant thuds at the back of the farmhouse as, she supposed, debris was brought down from Middle Fell, from Ullock Pike, Great Calva and Skiddaw on the seething discharge of floodwater. If only she could see out into the vortex of madness which she could only imagine and which was crashing and thudding about the building, but apart from the window-sill which was revealed when she placed the rushlight up to the glass, it was as black and dense as it had been for the . . . for the? . . . how long? . . . what time of day was it? . . . or night? . . . She really couldn't seem to assemble any sensible thought into her brain for it had lost its bearings in this strange and displaced world into which the storm had thrust her. She must think . . . *think*. . . decide . . . make a plan, some action which, if it came to it, would get herself and her animals to a place of safety, if such a thing existed in this mad confusion, this violence and destruction which was threatening her. If only she had someone to talk to, to discuss the predicament she was in. Someone to whom she could say, 'what d'you think? Shall we hang on and hope the water goes down, that the deluge stops and the tempest ceases to rage, or shall we get out now, climb up on to the roof, perhaps . . . ?' She had no one, only her dogs who were whimpering at her feet, and Dandy, the straining unease showing plainly in three pairs of eyes as they looked up at her.

She sat down on the bed, the dogs huddling against her legs, the cat at once crawling into her lap. She was cold, so cold she could feel the violence of her shivering shake the bed. It was January, the coldest month of the year up here on the fells. She had no heat, only the blankets on her bed and the clothing she wore, to warm her. She was tempted to get into the bed but if she should fall asleep what would she find when she awoke? Her bed floating on the water, her nose to the ceiling . . . ?

A short, nervous laugh erupted from her. God, this was no time to be laughing, she thought, but it had the effect of steadying her. She must eat something. The tatie-pot was cold now but if she was to . . . Oh, Lord Jesus, but the thought terrified her . . . if she was to climb out of the window into the unknown terror beyond it, then she must be strong, fortified at least by a nourishing meal for the struggle ahead of her.

She stood up, moving again to the window and suddenly, as though a giant match had put a light to a rush, the moon appeared from behind a scudding cloud, shining against a backdrop of deep and silvery blue across which tattered and wind-tossed clouds raced, ragged, uneasy and dark. The light of the moon, intermittent as the clouds whipped by it, revealed the full horror of the flood and even as Annie stared at it, appalled, there was an angry roar as an avalanche of rocks, tons and tons of them leaping and tossing as though they were no heavier than a handful of pebbles flung by a child, hurtled by the end of the farmhouse and in their path was the barn.

"NO! . . . Oh, dear Lord! . . . No! . . . Royal . . ." She strained against the window, screaming out the name of the good-natured, loyal animal who had been her friend for almost three years as though in warning but even as she did so her practical mind told her that Royal was, in all probability, already dead. The waters of the flood had reached the upper level of the barn just where its sloping roof began and above which she stored her hay. Below it, and below the water line Royal had been stabled. She could imagine his terror as the water crept up his legs, up the sides of his rough flank until it reached . . . He would have kicked and kicked, doing his best to free himself . . . she could not bear it . . . the thought of his desperate, lonely struggle to escape.

Tears rolled down her cheeks and her shoulders heaved

as she wept and she turned away from the window, trying to shut out the images which flashed across her vision. Her eyes caught the movement by the door and her heart bucked in terror as the slick black waters, silent and menacing as a snake, rippled across the floor towards her. It was here . . . Reed . . . it was here . . .

The moon came out as Reed reached High Side, just where the road branched off to Hause. He had struggled through the fast flowing floodwater, at first to his ankles, then, as the level of the lake rose on his left, to his knees, the wind threatening to tear his clothes from his body, the very hair from his head, the rain pouring across his ice-cold flesh with the force and persistence of the ice-cold overflow of the waterfall where he had made love to Annie. The deluge coming at him from the fell to his right, bringing down dead cows, sheep, horses, chickens, pigs, gates, rocks, whole trees, spinning wheels, sledges and smashed carts, must be constantly watched for if anything heavy caught him he could be carried on down across the low-lying fertile pastures and into the lake. The dark had a hidden menace in it, though it was possible to see the raging shapes of the trees of Dodd Wood and the meandering flatness of the water-logged road ahead. He kept his head bent and his shoulders bowed, his eyes searching for his way, his weary legs moving slowly – too slowly – through the surging water. It deepened steadily, moving up to his thighs so that his progress became even more sluggish. He would have to swim soon if the flood continued to rise, he thought, almost idly, as if the idea of not getting there at all had not even crossed his mind. Annie was waiting for him. She was in a danger so menacing it could scarcely be contemplated and he must reach her. It was as simple as that. He could not even stop to rest, exhausted as he was, for he had waded through four miles of raging floodwater. She needed him. Annie needed him, and it was the certainty of that which kept him moving, dragging one heavy leg after the other through the thick, impenetrable water. It was like trying to walk through syrup, but no matter, syrup it was, and if it needed wading through then wade through it he would. He would not despair, *he would not*, and as he lifted his head for a moment to get his bearings the rain stopped and the moon raced out from behind a cloud. Just like that. As though a barrier had been flung across the sky, it stopped and he wanted to shout out his relief. He had been disorientated but now he could see. He had been lost but now he was found, and he was exultant for it would be easier now. He tried to remember when he had last slept, last eaten but he honestly could not bring to mind when that might have been. On the ship, perhaps? The Packet ship *Rainbow* which had brought him from New York . . . when? . . . yesterday? . . . the day before that? . . . Jesus . . . when?

God, but he was tired, and as the rebel thought whispered into his mind he glared about him, just as though someone had spoken the words out loud. His blazing eyes fell on rocks and tumbled trees, on more dead, skinned sheep, on still bundles of clothing which he did not care to investigate, and the flame in them was hot and hating for *nothing* would keep him from her this time. He thought he could be losing his mind. Many would say so, to love a woman as he loved Annie Abbott, and perhaps he was, but whatever it was she had lit in him over six years ago it would not let him rest, would keep him on his feet until she was here, held safe in his arms where she belonged, damn her.

"Give up?" he snarled into the teeth of the biting wind, as if some ghostly voice had suggested it. "Give up? Never!" and his voice was whipped back over his shoulder as he began to crawl on all fours up the slope from the road and on to the walled inlands which led to Browhead Farm.

"We'll have to go, lads. It's no use, but we'll have to go before it's too late." Her own voice startled her, it seemed so loud, and all three animals looked up at her, the dogs' heads cocked, their ears pricked. Three pairs of eyes were bright with intelligence, but all three animals cast uneasy glances at the water which was creeping across the floor towards them. Annie bent to them, fondling their ears in turn, her heart heavy with sadness. She had lost Royal tonight, she was sure of that, and was she to lose these three as well? She could not leave them here. She could only coax them, or fling them out of the window and into the water, praying to some God, or gods in which she found she could really not believe, that they would make their way to safety. She herself meant to climb up on to the roof and tie herself to one of the chimney stacks, she had the sheet torn up in readiness, and perhaps they would come with her if their fear did not panic them into swimming off into the storm water.

She was just agonising over the advisability of wearing her warmest clothing, or virtually none at all, since she would get cold and wet anyway, and perhaps clothing would drag her down, when something struck the farmhouse such a colossal blow she distinctly heard the stonework shatter and the building move. Both dogs began to bark frantically. They milled about her in terror and Dandy leaped up the curtain to crouch on the window pole, her tail lashing, and Annie felt a distinct urge to do the same. Her mind was an ice-cold, blank and senseless thing, incapable of making a decision, and she turned frantically, first to the door, then back to the window. The farmhouse was breaking up, shifting, sliding down the fields to the lake where it would come to rest in the deep waters and her with it. She had no time . . . she must *hurry*. . . the window . . . oh, please . . . someone . . . Reed . . . "Reed . . . Reed . . ." She was screaming out loud, her own voice striking at the strangely tilting walls of her bedroom . . . but she needed him . . . *she wanted him*. . . Reed . . .

She could not remember making any conscious decision but somehow she was at the deep, recessed window, dragging at the tiny half-opening, pushing it out into the teeth of the wind which still howled across the front of the farmhouse. It whipped right into her face, the spray it carried lashing against her and wetting her through before she had even climbed out on to the ledge. The floodwater was about six inches below the sill and she knew she had but minutes to spare. She could feel it behind her creeping up over her feet and clawing at her ankles and the two dogs moaned in terror, but, sensing with the natural instinct of her kind that escape was to be found only now, only here, Dandy went first, twisting her boneless body through and *up*, clawing her way on to the roof.

"Good girl . . . oh, good girl . . . now Blackie, come on, boy . . . Bonnie . . . come here to me . . ." She shrieked their names, hardly able to hear her own voice above the roar of the wind and the water it churned, but they did not move.

"Come to me, Blackie . . . come on, Bonnie . . . good boys . . . come here, come here . . ." but neither would obey her.

"I can't leave you . . . I just can't leave you . . . please . . ." She began to weep . . . "come here . . . come . . ."

Inspiration came as the water reached her knees. Both animals had leaped on to the bed, their eyes mad with fear. She knew she *must* go, *now*, for the water was nearly up to the sill. A minute, no more and it would pour into the bedroom, not only through the door, but the window, a great surge through which she would be unable to struggle.

"Come by, Blackie . . . Away to me, Bonnie." Her voice was steady and firm and at the familiar words both dogs instinctively moved, one to the right, the other to the left, swimming towards her round the walls of the room until they reached the window.

"Good boys, out you go," and without hesitation, trusting her, they jumped cleanly into the racing torrent beyond it.

"Wait for me, lads," she called. She took a deep breath and followed them, at once sinking down into the black, clogged depths of the water.

*　　*　　*

He sobbed in agony as he hung on to the gatepost from which the gate had long gone. He could see the farmhouse. It was there no more than a hundred yards away, a light flickering in one of the bedroom windows, but no matter how hard he fought he just could not get beyond this point. Three times he had crawled on his hands and knees through the boiling, mud-filled fury of the waters which howled down the fell and across the inlands, clutching at any handhold which would bear his weight, and three times he had been swept down again to the road. His clothing, but for his undergarments, had been torn from his body and he knew his flesh was bleeding from many places. His skin was scraped raw and he felt as though his hair had been wrenched from his scalp. Three times he had done it, that tiny light which he knew Annie had lit beckoning him on, and each time he had been flung down the slope again, his limbs dragged about like that of a rag doll, his head crashing and banging against shattered drystone walls, and the thousands of tons of stone which had been gouged out of the mountain by the force of the water.

He did not know how he survived it, for surely the body cannot take the punishment his was suffering, but each time he had crept to his knees and through his bitten tongue and lips, howled her name to the broken skies. All along the valley and in every farmhouse on the fells, his own included, men and women would be fighting for their lives as the deluge tore down walls, carved out new ravines, destroyed bridges, spewed out landslides which would bury farms and outbuildings for ever. Huge sections of the fellside would be laid bare as every beck and tarn, stream and river overflowed in a wild and headlong turmoil of water. He had seen bodies go by him, swept down to the lake which was at a level never before known, drowning trees at its edges which had once been tall and proud. He had seen it, suffered it, drowned in it almost, but still he would not let it stop him. Not until he was dead. Not until the last flicker of life in him, that last flame of his love for Annie was quenched, and even then his spirit would wing its way up this bloody hill to strengthen her.

He could feel the gatepost lean towards him, the strong deep roots of it which some farmer had secured for eternity, beginning to tear from the ground and he looked wildly about him for something, some anchor to which he might cling, and from there to another, and another, fighting his way until he got up to her. Dear sweet Christ . . . let me . . . please . . . she is so near, so near . . . the farmhouse, the tree beside it . . . both there, strong and safe and her within it . . . the light . . . the light . . . oh, Jesus . . . *the light. . . the light had gone.* . . No! . . . No! It couldn't be . . . not Annie . . . not his Annie . . . his love . . . perhaps she had blown it out . . . but why? . . . perhaps . . . ?

"ANNIE . . ." he roared, furious with her, ready, the moment he had her standing beside him where she belonged to let her see that he would not, absolutely *would not* be treated with this bare-faced defiance . . . why? . . . *why* would she not do as he wanted her to . . . *why?* Savage he was in his anger . . . at *her*, at Annie who had left him . . . Annie, dear God, Annie, why has the light gone out . . . why? . . . Had she climbed into her bed and carelessly snuffed the rushlight whilst he was killing himself? struggling to get up to her . . . Jesus, oh Jesus, let her be peacefully asleep in her bed . . . *why had the bloody light gone out?* He could not bear the not knowing, nor the images that darkened glow had conjured up. The possibility that . . . he could not face it . . . Annie, fighting the water . . . the creeping water . . . her lovely face contorted . . . gasping . . . drowning . . .

"ANNIE . . . ANNIE . . ." he roared again, throwing back his head in torment, feeling the gatepost drive its thick splinters deep into the palms of his clinging hands. The grief and agony in his voice seemed to stifle even the hateful roar of the waters for a moment, echoing about the devastated fells. "Annie . . ." His voice sank to a whisper and he bent his head, ducking it under the water since he no longer wanted to live . . . not without . . .

"Reed . . ." He did not hear his name on the wind.

For ten seconds he held his head beneath the raging

torrent but the instinct bred in all living creatures, to survive, no matter how the will denies it, brought him threshing to the surface, choking, demented, cursing. Well, if he could not do away with himself here where she had died, then all he had to do was let go of the bloody gatepost and let the floodwaters take him . . .

"Reed . . ."

He thought for a bewildering moment that he had actually been successful. That he had drowned and so had she, waiting for him on the other side so that they could go together to wherever it was . . .

"Reed . . ." and that was no heavenly voice calling to him to hold her hand as they met St Peter at the bloody pearly gates. It was her . . . *her*. . . *Annie* and she was coming full tilt towards him, her mouth wide and screaming, borne on a wave of scum coated water, clinging to what looked like an oak chest, its lid still tightly closed – they knew how to make a decent chest in the old days, he remembered thinking, marvelling on the ways of the human mind and its capacity to be distracted by trivia at times of great danger – then he had her in his arms, the well-built chest beneath them both, going as though it was a sledge on runners, down the long slope towards the road at the bottom.

"Hold on to me," he yelled, ready to laugh with the sheer magical joy of it, not caring really if they were both smashed to pieces or drowned in Bassenthwaite Lake since they were together, *together*. She was in his arms, clinging to him, needing him, *needing* his strength, which was suddenly prodigious, to save them both. God knew where they would end up, but by the look of it it might be in the little churchyard of St Bridget's, which was appropriate if you thought about it. If they drowned it would be side by side, and side by side they would be buried there, and if not he would take her into the church, no matter what its flooded state and extract from her her promise, give her his, force the damned words from her somehow until their wedding vows could be exchanged properly and in full view of the community of Bassenthwaite. She was here in his arms, still, both of them, in the direst of danger, but by God, she'd never get away from him again.

They came to rest by the church porch. The water still poured into the lake a hundred yards or so further on but it was slackening as the fury of the elements died away. There was debris lying all about them right down to the water, grotesque shapes only half-seen in the lightening gloom of the new day. Timber beams and walls of stone, old joists and chicken coops, stiff-legged bodies of animals wedged against one another, trees and a solid mass of mud in which a cradle was jammed testifying to the tragedies which had taken place this night.

They stood up slowly, stiffly, neither of them recognisable except to each other. They were both almost naked but for a shred or two of clothing which had not been ripped from them in the maelstrom of their flight down the fell and they shivered violently.

Annie looked steadily into Reed's eyes, penetrating with her own the goodness of the love she saw there. They had known passion, a fierce enchantment which had been indescribable, and would again, but this was stronger, sweeter, *good*. He watched her, waiting, but not for long, his expression said. He had waited too long as it was. Seven years and in that time she had achieved all that she had set out to achieve. Seven years and in a few nightmare hours it had all been lost again. Browhead. Did it still stand? Her flock. How many survived? Her farm, her pride, her satisfaction in what she had carved out for herself in this hostile land, among these hostile people. It was all gone and amazingly, did it matter? Her life was here, with this man. Reed Macauley.

He held out his hand to her and she took it submissively. He smiled, knowing it would not last, her submissiveness, his teeth a white slash in his heavily bruised face. He led her into the church and up the aisle, moving through ankle deep water in which prayer books and footstools floated, until they reached the altar steps.

"Kneel," he commanded her and when she did, knowing what was to come, he knelt beside her. They made a

strange sight, Annie Abbott and Reed Macauley and yet
the beauty in them, in their eyes and softly smiling faces
was very real.

"Now say after me," he began.

They were hand in hand, looking, Phoebe screeched at
them, like two lovers wandering in the sunshine beside a
summer lake. Had they no thought for anyone but themselves, for God's sake? Her voice became even more frenzied as she scrambled over tumbling rocks and great fallen
trees, ready to knock their two silly heads together in her
wild fear. She and Charlie had thought Annie had drowned
and really, she might have come up and told them she was
still alive. She had the baby under one arm, bouncing her
about like a half-filled flour sack which Beth submitted to
amiably enough, and behind her was Charlie, his strained
face breaking out at the sight of them into that wide,
endearing grin they knew so well. Neither seemed surprised to see Reed and why should they, for did not the
most amazing things occur in Annie Abbott's turbulent life?

Yes, yes, Upfell had been saved by some fluke which
had sent the main torrent racing to Chapel Beck and not
in the direction of their farm. Of course it was flooded and
there was some damage . . . Long Beck? They didn't
know but as it was higher up the valley perhaps, but for
God's sake, did it matter? Jesus Christ, did it matter?
They were alive. They were all alive and unhurt . . . when
they had seen Browhead, not that there was much left
of it. Dear God in Heaven, did Annie know? They had
thought. . . .

Here Phoebe began to cry inconsolably, a great precipitation as immense as the one they had just survived, burying her face in the soft neck of the startled baby.

"Phoebe . . . Phoebe, darling. . . ."

"Give over, Annie Abbott, don't tha' say 'owt or I'll land
thi' one. I were right worried. . . ." she wailed, her normal
guarded reserve breaking down in the face of her vast
relief.

Wordlessly Annie put her arms about her friend, the

only one she had had before Charlie came, and they stood clasped together, the baby between them, watched by Charlie and Reed, themselves inclined to blink rapidly and clear their throats a time or two.

They wept in one another's arms, Phoebe and Annie, in sorrow for what had gone and would never be replaced, for Cat and Natty and perhaps Browhead; in thankfulness for what was left and in sudden joy when two bedraggled forms crept hesitantly over the gouged out enormity of what had once been an ancient oak tree. They hesitated for a moment, Blackie and Bonnie, then raced ecstatically across the sodden ground towards the two women.

"Now then, don't tha' go puttin' tha' great muddy paws on my skirt," Phoebe remonstrated tartly to the two animals, "oh, an' that cat's sittin' skrikin' on top o't'wall back at Browhead. 'Appen tha'd best go an' see to it, Annie Abbott."

WHEN MORNING COMES

Here's to the child and all he has to teach us.
Proverb

For my grandchildren who are my joy,
Daniel, Adam and Natalie.

1

The man was deep in thought, his dark head bent, his brow furrowed. He seemed to be studying his boots as they scuffed through the rich layer of leaves, russet and gold, orange and tawny pink which carpeted the woodland floor. Though he was not aware of it in his brown study, like the boy he used to be, he was kicking and shuffling his feet through the leaves, enjoying the rustling sound they made. It had been a particularly fine summer with less rain than was normal in this part of the country and the leaves were dry and crackling, satisfying, if subconsciously, that feeling he had known as a lad.

He was considering Miss Charlotte Gibson. He had been considering Miss Charlotte Gibson for the best part of the summer and the problem was that half of Fellthwaite, including the lady in question and her mama, were aware of it, though naturally they were too well bred to let it be seen they had noticed. That was the trouble with living in a small, close-knit community. You couldn't sneeze without it coming to someone's attention, who then told you, and everyone in Fellthwaite into the bargain, that you were in for an awful cold! Having paid Miss Gibson a certain amount of attention at several functions, and had her to dine a time or two, with her parents, naturally, at Howethwaite, his family home, he was well aware that speculation was rife in the district. She would make a splendid wife, it must be said, since she had been trained for it from the day she left the nursery. It was well known that she was already an excellent hostess, brought up to it by her mama who was one herself. Mrs Gibson, who was the great-niece of a baronet, was well accustomed to entertaining men of high rank, not only from the gentry, but the aristocracy from which her own family came, and Miss Charlotte Gibson was sensible of her position and proud of her own worth in the marriage stakes. Her father, Mr Arthur Gibson, had vast wealth, come to him from many of the businesses which thrived in the district of Furness and Windermere. Copper mining, the manufacture of gunpowder, the mining of iron in High Furness, the quarrying of slate round and about Coniston, several farms which were rented to tenant farmers, not to mention coal from the coalfields in the west which stretched from Cockermouth to Whitehaven. He owned a bank in the centre of Ambleside and it was rumoured that the interest he earned from the loans he made kept his wife and daughter tricked out in the exclusive, and expensive, Paris fashions they were to be seen in about Fellthwaite, Ambleside and Grasmere. Ball gowns and afternoon dresses, at the right time, of course, walking outfits, outfits for their carriage exercise, dinner gowns, three-piece costumes, tea gowns and cartwheel hats trimmed with feathers, flowers, ribbons and vast amounts of lace and tulle. Charlotte was Arthur's only child and the gentleman who took her to wife, and there were many who were eager to do so, would have at his disposal, when Arthur had gone, an enormous fortune and the added bonus of the beautiful Charlotte Gibson herself.

James Buchanan sighed deeply and then shook his head, irritated with his own foolish indecision. Charlotte would make a splendid wife and partner. She was young, healthy and capable of bearing many fine children, sons among them, and really he didn't know why he was dithering about as he was. He needed a wife. He knew without being told that Mr and Mrs Gibson favoured his suit, for he was as wealthy and well bred as themselves, but they wouldn't wait for ever and if he didn't look lively they'd give her to some other, equally well-endowed gentleman.

He had driven from his home near Skelwith that afternoon, following the lane which led towards Ambleside and was on his way to see a client, the Reverend Edward Dean. It seemed the rector, whose church lay on the outskirts of Fellthwaite, had come to the conclusion that it was about time he made a will and James, who was a solicitor with a thriving practice in Ambleside, had been asked to call on him. The rector was a man in his fifties and though, as far as James knew, in the best of health, it seemed his own mortality had come into question, as it does when one is past one's middle years, and his thoughts had turned to putting in order his worldly affairs.

James couldn't have said why – perhaps because he was early for his appointment, or maybe the breathtaking beauty of the autumn day, or even the magnificence of the brilliantly hued woods through which the lane cut – but whatever it was it had made him brake sharply, bringing his motor car to a stop just off the lane and under the trees. He had his dogs with him, both trained to sit quietly on the back seat while he was driving; with a murmured word and a click of his fingers he ordered them out. They stood, trembling with anticipation, their intelligent hazel eyes looking up at him, each with a paw raised waiting for permission to run free. They were big, handsome dogs, labradors with ebony coats which gleamed like wet coal. Their ears twitched and so did their noses, since there were dozens of scents to tantalise them and when he indicated with his hand and a soft murmur that they might go, they bounded away like two children let out of the schoolroom.

He knew exactly how they felt. But then the life he led, the career he followed was his own choice and he could blame no one but himself if he was tied down for the best part of each weekday with legal matters, problems brought to him to solve by the less affluent of the district of Windermere. He had chosen to study law at the University of Edinburgh, though he was a man of considerable means and had no need to seek employment. The three sons of Alexander Buchanan, Johnny, Harry and Job, had inherited equal shares in Alex's business enterprises, which were many and lucrative, and when Johnny, James's father, had died his share had come to James. His cousins, Ben, Andrew and Alex Buchanan ran the Buchanan Copper Mining Co, the Emmerson Gunpowder Manufacturers near Elterwater and a bobbin manufacturing mill at Staveley, the latter two coming to the Buchanan family through marriage. His fourth cousin Paul was to be a doctor. With the income that came to him from the shares he had in these concerns, and others that he had set up himself, James Buchanan was that envied being, an independent man. He had no need to go each day to his office in Ambleside and if, sometimes, he longed to put on a pair of sturdy boots, throw a haversack on his back and head for the long climb to Scafell Pike, to Helvellyn or the majestic peaks of Skiddaw, he had no one to blame but himself if he was unable to do so.

Lifting his head he breathed deeply, the air slipping like dry white wine down his throat and into his lungs. He could smell woodsmoke and the rich earthy aroma of the woodland where already the dying vegetation was beginning to rot down, ready to turn itself into the nourishment needed for next year's growth. Between the trees he caught a glimpse of the breeze-rippled waters of the lake, like moving silk, the flame of the autumn sun casting vivid colours of gold and rose and apricot across it and up on the fells at his back purple shadows were beginning to fall. It was not yet cold down here in the valley bottom but soon Coniston Old Man would wear its first fluted cap of snow, the whiteness creeping slowly down as winter approached.

The dogs had vanished into the rustling sea of bright copper bracken which carpeted the floor of the woodland on either side of the rough path. Leaves were falling as a small breeze tore them from their frail hold on the branches of the trees and when, smiling whimsically, he held out his hand, one spiralled down to land delicately on his outstretched palm.

There was a dog barking somewhere, not his, for this was the high, excited bark of a terrier, a small dog, and he hesitated since he did not wish to have company. He would turn back here, he decided, call his dogs to him and return to his motor car, for his appointment with the reverend gentleman was almost due. He abhorred unpunctuality since it seemed to him to smack of contempt for another's time and it would take him ten minutes to motor from here to the rectory.

Placing the tips of two fingers between his lips he gave a low but piercing whistle, one his dogs would hear but would be barely discernible to the human ear. He waited, his tall, lean frame lounging comfortably against the narrow trunk of a silver birch tree, both his hands pushed deep into his trouser pockets, one leg bent at the knee with his foot resting on the whitish bark.

He was not considered to be a handsome man, though there was certainly something about him that seemed to appeal to the ladies, other gentlemen had noticed. Of course, ladies were known to be romantic, intrigued by anything that did not fall into a category they could immediately recognise, though why they should consider it romantic to be sombre and grave, reserved and somewhat unapproachable the gentlemen could not fathom. His countenance was compelling, strong, unsmiling, but one that drew the eye to it, both male and female, though as yet none had caught his. To the female he promised something they could not understand but knew they liked, to the male a suggestion of mocking arrogance which told them he was not a man to be meddled with.

This was James Buchanan.

He had left his hat in the motor car and his dark,

chocolate hair was revealed to be thick and curling, needing to be trimmed every week if it was to be kept in any sort of order. Even now it grew vibrantly, tumbling to his frowning eyebrows and catching in the collar of his coat. He was clean-shaven, his amber skin glowing with good health. His eyes were quite beautiful, wasted on a lad, his old nurse used to tell him, the colour the softest grey, like the underside of a dove's wing, set in long black lashes. His jaw jutted implacably, his mouth was set firm, though a lift at each corner hinted at hidden humour. He was confident, vigorous, with a well-marked sense of his own infallibility, for James Buchanan had been looking after himself ever since his mother and father had drowned when the ice on Lake Windermere on which they were skating had given way. That was eighteen years ago. He had been sixteen years old at the time. His two uncles – brothers to his own father – and their wives, and his Aunt Amy, had done their best to keep a tight rein on him, even demanding that he take up residence with one of them, but he had refused to be tethered and, since he was a big lad with a mind of his own even then, self-willed as all the Buchanans were, they left him alone. They were all cut from the same cloth, Job and Harry Buchanan, their sons and their nephew James, for in their veins ran the rich and tempestuous blood of Alex Buchanan and his wife Christy Emmerson, who were legends in the district of Furness and Windermere and beyond.

James was visibly annoyed when not two but three dogs scampered out of the undergrowth to his whistle. The third was no more than a puppy.

"What the devil have you got there, you idiots, and

where in hell did you get him?" he exclaimed, pushing himself away from the tree.

The dogs, all three, wagged their tails energetically as they circled him, the puppy almost swinging himself off his feet in his ecstasy. He leaped up at James's knee, nearly doing somersaults in his efforts to reach his hand and James could not help but smile. The Border terrier, for that was what he was, was so small he could comfortably walk, or rather dart, beneath the bellies of his new-found friends. He had a short, rough, wheaten-coloured coat and eyes that were dark, with the keen expression of an animal that has been bred to drive the fox from its lair.

"Dammit, where in hell have you come from?" James muttered irritably, for he could hardly abandon such a young animal. The dog studied him, his tail slowing somewhat as though he were getting ready for a game, but already James could hear the sound of voices, children's voices and he heaved a sigh of relief mixed with exasperation.

"Dammit to hell . . ." He bent down and with a disgruntled gesture picked up the puppy which licked his face affectionately, and tucking it under his arm began to walk in the direction from which the voices came. His own dogs, subdued now that they had sensed his mood, padded silently at his heels.

"Thimble . . . Thimble . . ." the voices called, getting closer as he pushed his way through the crisping sea of bracken. He could hear the lilting sound of water tumbling across rocks coming from ahead, for you could not go far in this land of the lakes without stumbling across a ghyll, a beck, water erupting from the very ground under your feet. It gushed down runnels to join streams which foamed like spilled milk, making its way from hills and mountains to flow into lakes and tarns.

The puppy under his arm who went, apparently, by the absurd name of Thimble, lay there docilely, aware it was futile to struggle, knowing with the instinct animals and children have who means business and who does not. This man did!

They did not hear him as he stepped out on to the soft floor of the clearing, nor see him, for they were casting about on the far side of the rushing beck, calling the dog's name with increasing anxiety. There were six of them, four girls and two boys, all somewhat bedraggled, their feet bare, as though the loss of Thimble had interrupted some watery but exciting game.

"Thimble, you damn fool, where have you got to?" the smaller of the boys shrieked piercingly in the way of the young who cannot speak below a full-throated roar.

"Percy, you know Papa does not like you to swear, and need you scream so loudly? I'm sure you've damaged my eardrum, particularly as you were standing no more than six inches from it."

"Sorry, Luce, but that's not swearing, really it isn't. If you wanted I could really swear. I heard Bibby say—"

"That's enough, Percy, and if Bibby knows what's best for him he'll watch his tongue."

"Don't be daft, Luce, there isn't a cat in hell's chance you'd get someone to work like the old codger does and without wages too. When was the last time he was paid, tell me that? It's no wonder he swears so much and if he wasn't nearly a hundred he'd be off tomorrow."

It was the second boy who spoke, a tall, dark, good-looking lad of about thirteen or fourteen, James thought, scrawny yet, but already showing signs of breadth to his shoulders. In fact they were all handsome children. They made a charming group, decently but shabbily dressed, the boys in patched knee-length trousers in a particularly unsuitable shade of cream drill with open-neck, navy blue jerseys, long-sleeved and with a collar. The sleeves were pushed up to the elbow, the jersey hanging out of the trousers. The younger girls were in navy blue serge with sailor collars which had a row of white cotton braid round the hem and cuffs of the sleeves, again pushed up above their elbows. Their skirts were hitched up and tucked carelessly into the elastic of their sensible navy blue knickers.

"Now you're at it, Edward," the older girl challenged. "What you said was a swear word and is it any wonder if Percy thinks it's all right."

"Hell's not swearing, Luce. Hell's a place and Papa mentions it every Sunday from the pulpit."

"That's different and you know it."

"Ooh, girls!" Edward shrugged his shoulders and sighed in deep exasperation.

The fourth girl was not at all like the others, either in colouring or in looks, and he noticed with half his mind that she had a limp, but the girl who had rebuked Percy and Edward was quite the loveliest thing James had ever seen. Dark, like the boys, like them all, but her hair, where the sun caught it, had the glossy sheen and colour of a horse chestnut, similar to the ones James had collected from these very woods and played with as a lad. It had evidently started out that morning brushed smoothly back from her forehead and plaited, a single plait which, where it still retained some order, was as thick as his wrist. Three-quarters of its lower length, which fell over one shoulder and across her breast to her waist as she bent down to peer for some curious reason into a rabbit hole, presumably after Thimble, had come unravelled, curling vigorously at its end, and in the midst of this vibrant glory a scarlet ribbon dangled. Long wisps curled about her face and neck and there was a limp white flower of some sort pushed behind her ear. She wore a muslin blouse with a tucked front and a high neck, and a separate skirt with several deep flounces about the hem, both garments in white. Somehow James had the feeling that her outfit had not been made for her but had been skilfully altered to fit her. Like the other girls she had tucked the skirt up in some fashion and her legs, white and shapely, the ankle fine-boned, the foot slender, were revealed.

Hanging carelessly from the knotted branches of an ancient oak were six pairs of black stockings and in a jumble beneath it six pairs of black boots.

They had evidently been building a dam, for a neat line of rocks and stones had been laid from one side of the stream to the other. The water had already begun to rise at the back of it and there were small branches, twigs and leaves and a tangle of brush caught in it. A little brown grebe alighted for a moment, taking advantage of the children's momentary absence, then flew off with some wriggling insect in its mouth.

"I'll give that blasted dog the hiding of his life when I

find him," the older boy was heard to hiss as he poked about with a stick in the undergrowth.

"You'll do no such thing, Edward Dean. He's only a baby, and let me tell you he's more damned sense than you had at the same age." The eldest girl's ban on swearing evidently did not apply to herself. She straightened up and threw back the burnished plait, and her young breasts, full and rounded, strained against the muslin of her blouse. The peaks of her nipples were clearly visible and though James was certain she would be wearing some sort of under-garment beneath the blouse he could have sworn he could see the dark shadow of the areola about them. To his shame he felt his manhood stir and warmth spread up into his belly. She was tall, nearly as tall as he was, he would have said. He was quite mesmerised by the womanly magnificence of her, by her flushed and girlish face which was at such odds with her mature body.

His own dogs, one on either side of him, pressed against his legs waiting for his command and the one in his arms, a young dog who had exhausted his store of good behaviour, began to wriggle ecstatically, unable to contain his excitement at the sight of these people of his. It was as though he had been parted from them for a week as he struggled to get to them.

"Is this what you're looking for?" James asked, his voice brusque. "Don't you think in future it might be advisable to keep such a young dog under closer surveillance?"

At once six astonished faces turned towards him and he had time to note that they each, except the girl with the limp, had brown eyes of different shades, though none was like the eldest girl's, which were the exact colour of old whisky. They were identical in shape and size, though, with thick brown lashes surrounding them, but it was to the eldest girl he spoke and it was at the eldest girl his whole male interest was focused. Her skin was a creamy white but flushed at the cheekbones with her exertions, without a flaw to mar its perfection. Not a freckle to blemish the satin-like finish, only, as he watched, a small indentation at the left-hand corner of her mouth, the lips themselves giving the impression that they had been bruised to a rosy pink by a lover's kiss.

They looked at one another across the stream but though he appeared to have addressed his question to her it was not she who answered.

"Thimble," the younger boy shrieked, the sound going through James like a grating saw, "where in hell's name have you been?"

"Percy, what have I just told you?" his sister rebuked him, but her heart wasn't in it. It was an automatic response to the child's swearing. She was staring with great interest at the tall figure of the well-dressed gentleman in whose arms Thimble was struggling. She had thought them to be quite alone in this quiet part of the wooded inlet which led down to the lake and this man's appearance had rendered them all speechless with surprise, except for Percy, of course, who it was difficult, if not impossible, to shut up. She couldn't have said with any degree of rationality why they were struck dumb, for they were not a family who were shy or self-conscious, or even had any proper regard for the conventions of the day which said children should be seen and not heard. Papa, and Mama when she

.was alive, did not believe in the repression of a child's normal inclination to high spirits and she was well aware that some of Papa's parishioners considered his family to be out of hand and in need of proper parental control, which dear Papa seemed unable or unwilling to apply.

The dog in James's arms let out an agonised yelp, indicating that he wished to be reunited with his people on the other side of the stream. The eldest girl laughed, a laugh at once high and joyous and Charlotte Gibson, who had a precarious hold on him at best, was sadly driven for ever from James Buchanan's mind.

"The little devil. I don't know what on earth we're going to do with him."

"A bit of training wouldn't go amiss," James remarked dourly.

"You're right, sir, but he is such a nomad it is hard to get a good grip on him. He has gypsy blood in him, I suspect, if a dog can have gypsy blood. We found him on Elsie's bed only this morning with a bone as big as himself which he'd stolen from Bibby's dog and how he'd got the thing up the stairs will for ever be a mystery. Where did you find him, Mr Buchanan? We were so busy with the dam, you see" – indicating with an airy wave the crumbling construction in the stream – "that we didn't notice he had gone. Of course he is only a puppy. Mr Henley gave him to us. He breeds them for showing, you know, and this one didn't come up to scratch, though only the good Lord knows why for he's a charming fellow, don't you think so?"

She gave him a smile of such brilliance and good-will James had to work hard at forming an answer.

Like some callow youth faced with his first encounter with the opposite sex he seemed to be lost for words.

"That is not the description I would have used," he managed at last, his voice cold to cover his incredible loss of composure. "You really must train him to remain at your side," glancing down at his own obedient dogs who sat beside him without movement except for their eyes. "He is likely to get into trouble if you don't." He placed the struggling puppy on the ground whereupon it leaped into the water and floundered to the far bank. It was seized upon by the younger boy who clutched its wet, wriggling body to his own already soaked chest, kissing it with a passion of childish love.

James did not notice. He was too busy watching the girl. "You called me by name," he said shortly. "You know me? I'm sorry but you have the advantage of me." His natural good manners were returning. "Have we met?" Though it didn't show in his face the thought in his head was that he would surely have remembered if they had.

"Fellthwaite is a small town, Mr Buchanan, and your family, having been here so long, I suppose, is well known, whereas we are comparative newcomers. Yes, I'm afraid we're that dreadful species known as *offcomers*, and I do believe we shall all be in our dotage before we are considered to be residents of the town." She beamed as though the thought worried her not a whit. "Papa has been rector at St Silas's for the past six years. Only Percy here had the good fortune to be born here, the rest of us coming from a village near Buxton. A good friend of Mama's was related to the Forsythes – you know them? – of Dalebarrow Hall.

Squire Forsythe had the living of St Silas's in his gift and offered it to Papa."

She bent her head for a moment and her slipping hair hid her face but James saw her throat work, then she looked up at him, her eyes a pale gold dewed with tears.

"Our mama died when Percy was born, Mr Buchanan."

The six of them moved closer to one another as though to give support in what was evidently a great sorrow.

"I'm sorry," he answered gruffly, not knowing what else she expected of him. Apparently it was enough.

"Thank you," she said simply. "Now I really must apologise for not making proper introductions. These are my brothers and sisters. This is Margaret who is twelve." She smiled lovingly at the tall, awkward young girl who bobbed a polite curtsey. "Margaret is my right-hand man, Mr Buchanan and I don't know what I should do without her since . . . since Mama went . . ."

"Oh, Lucy . . ." the girl said in smiling exasperation.

"No, Margaret, it's true." She turned and took the hand of the third girl, a small but just as lovely version of herself who eyed him with a degree of shyness. "And this is Emily who is eight and equally indispensable."

The child bobbed her own curtsey, none of them seeming to wonder at the incongruity of their bare legs and feet which were turning to a mottled blue and pink with the icy coldness of the water they had just been splashing in.

"And this great lanky lad is Edward. Edward is nearly fourteen and if – well, we hope – that is, Papa hopes he will go to . . . to a decent school soon." She stopped abruptly at a sharp look from her brother.

"Sir." The boy bowed his head respectfully and James took his eyes from the girl for a moment to return the bow. Unconventional they might be, this flushed, dishevelled and decidedly damp family group, but at least they were mannered.

"This, of course, is Percy." What more need she say, her laughing expression asked him. "He is five and a scamp," but we love him dearly just the same, she had no need to add.

After a quick glance at Percy, which was all that was necessary in James's opinion, for he was not a lover of children, he returned his gaze to the oldest family member, unaware of the soft gleam in his velvet grey eyes which another woman, a more experienced woman, would have recognised.

"And this is my dear friend Buffy Tyson," drawing forward the slight girl with the limp.

"Miss Tyson," bowing slightly in Miss Tyson's direction. "And you are . . . ?"

"Lucy Dean, sir." She bobbed a quick curtsey as she had been taught as a child.

He did not know why but he did not like the "sir", for it told him that Lucy Dean, probably no more than eighteen or nineteen, thought James Buchanan, who had just turned thirty-four, to be an old fuddy-duddy of the past generation, which he supposed he was.

He was not wrong. Lucy studied him in that unselfconscious way she had, which often disconcerted those on whom her intense gaze fell. He was an attractive man, she would not deny that, despite his age, but his unsmiling, sombre expression was, in her opinion, enough to quell the most light-hearted, giving them cause to cast back into their memories for some misdemeanour they might have committed. He was soberly dressed in a morning suit of dark, business-like grey, with a single-breasted waistcoat of the same colour, and a wing collar. Totally out of place for a stroll in the woods, she would have thought, though he did have his dogs with him. He wore no hat and a shaft of afternoon sunlight burnished his dark hair to the rich gloss of mahogany.

"Miss Dean, a pleasure." He bowed his head then straightened suddenly, since he had just become aware that these must be the children of the very gentleman he was to see that afternoon.

"Your father is Edward Dean, Miss Dean?"

"He is indeed, sir. Do you know him? Are you a member of our church? I don't believe I've seen you there," twinkling as though the very idea of Mr Buchanan sitting through one of her father's sermons amused her enormously.

He did not return the smile, for James Buchanan worshipped no God and kept to no high-toned principles except those of honesty, decency and the belief that, as he interfered with no man, no man should interfere with him.

"No, Miss Dean, it's just that I'm to see your father this afternoon on a matter of business."

"Business?" She was clearly surprised and if James had made the acquaintance of Edward Dean he would have understood why.

"Yes." That was all he said, for it was not his custom to discuss his clients' affairs, even with that client's daughter.

"What on earth about?"

"Miss Dean, you must ask your father that."

"I shall, Mr Buchanan, and at once. Come, children," sweeping her brood up with the efficiency of a no-nonsense nanny. "Dear God, I hope and pray he is not about to invest money; not that we have any, you understand . . ." Suddenly aware that she was perhaps revealing too much of her family's business to this perfect stranger, she picked up her skirts and leaped into the shallow water, wading across with a great scatter of sun-filled diamond sparklets that flew about her in twin arcs.

"Come on, Edward, Margaret. Percy, don't drop Thimble, will you, darling. Perhaps Edward had better carry him until we get home. Why did we not bring his lead? Really we are the most disorganised people I know. Now, get your boots and stockings on. Yes, yes, I know your feet are wet, Emily, but just for once you may dry them on your skirt."

All the while she was talking, with a total lack of self-consciousness, she was pulling on her own stockings, hopping from foot to foot as she did so, then sat down on the exposed root of the oak tree and donned her ankle-length boots. Tying the laces about her slim ankles, unaware – as he was himself – of James's fascinated gaze, she stood up and stamped her feet then put her hands to the back of her head, the movement lifting her full, rounded breasts again, making James catch his breath and the blood to run warm in his veins. With a deft twist she re-plaited her heavy hair for an inch or two then, retrieving the scarlet ribbon, tied it in a bow. The plait fell to her buttocks. Instantly she was about her sisters, tweaking this and adjusting that, pushing a vagrant curl behind an ear and smoothing down the skirts of their mid-calf dresses.

"There," she said, her expression declaring that the most critical onlooker would find nothing amiss with the Dean children. She had overlooked the drooping white flower which was still caught in her own hair.

"Allow me, Miss Dean." To his own amazement he lifted his hand in what could only be described as a dream-like manner, and removed it, startling her with his closeness so that her eyes darkened to a clear chestnut brown. The pupils widened dramatically and he noticed there was a fine black line round the iris. She smelled of something fresh and sweet, something he could not recognise but would never forget.

"Thank you, Mr Buchanan." Her tone was polite, the tone used when one spoke to a gentleman, or lady, older than oneself. "Now then, if you are bound for the rectory perhaps you would care to walk with us." It was clear that the idea found little favour with her, since he was so serious, a condition the Dean family did not care for.

"Thank you, Miss Dean, but I have left my motor car on the edge of the wood so you see . . ."

He got no further. The effect his words had on the elder boy was electrifying. From polite boredom he exploded into life, cheeks blazing with colour, eyes blazing with the golden light of vivid excitement.

"You . . . you have a motor car, sir?" he breathed reverently.

"Yes." Again his manner was brusque, for he guessed what was coming.

"What make?" the boy asked.

"A Rolls-Royce," James answered reluctantly.

"Not . . . not a . . . a Silver Ghost?"

"Yes."

"Gosh, did you hear that, Luce? Mr Buchanan has a Rolls-Royce Silver Ghost."

"Really." Lucy was evidently not as impressed as her brother.

"It can do seventy miles an hour, sir, did you know that?" Edward went on, clearly under the impression that Mr Buchanan could have no conception of the jewel he had in his possession.

"I believe so, though I have not yet got up to that speed, not on these narrow lanes."

Well, you wouldn't, Edward's pitying glance told him, not an old man like you, but all he said was, "Oh, sir . . ."

He stood there, speechless with wonder and James sighed in defeat. He admitted to himself that it would be very pleasant to have the lovely Miss Dean sit beside him in the front seat of his elegant new motor car, but to take the lot of them, including the three dogs, was not something he relished, but how could he get out of it with the boy's beseeching eyes gazing into his.

It seemed he couldn't. Much against his will he said curtly, "Perhaps I might offer you a—"

"Oh, sir, would you?" The boy was overcome with some deep emotion. "I'd be eternally grateful. I've never been in a motor car, you see."

"This is most kind of you, Mr Buchanan."

During the short walk back to the vehicle Lucy Dean lagged behind with her sisters, her friend Buffy and younger brother, holding the hands of the two youngest, talking ten to the dozen, the four of them, laughing, pointing out to each other some wonder that they all seemed to find quite marvellous. A flock of butterflies dancing in a patch of sunlight, called, he heard her tell them, "speckled woods". A "great spotted woodpecker" drumming against the trunk of a hornbeam, and the antics of a daring dormouse playing acrobat in the branches of a tree. At his side Edward beseiged him with questions and bombarded him with information, for it seemed the young man was a passionate lover of the motor car, particularly the Rolls-Royce, and meant to have one at the earliest possible moment. He knew every nut and bolt that held it together. When they reached it he circled it in wondering silence, touching with gentle hands the polished windshield, the black hood which was folded down, the lights, the distinctive radiator with its diminutive mascot, the 'Spirit of Ecstasy' perched upon it and even the spare wheel. James tried to curb his impatience but the boy's rapt admiration would not be hurried and he could do no more than stand and watch.

He did at least have her sit beside him on the short journey to the rectory, the wriggling and alarmed Thimble on her knee, while behind him his own dogs fought for space with Edward, who hung over his shoulder shouting instructions, with Percy who was as white as tallow with excitement and with the three girls who, now that they were actually aboard and going at the incredible speed of fifteen miles an hour, were not at all sure they liked it.

She did, though, Miss Lucy Dean. Her face was flushed to a rosy pink and her eyes shone like newly minted golden guineas. Her hair came loose again, whipping back from her face in a long shining banner of silken chestnut, her ribbon gone, and it was perhaps then, a mere half-hour after he had met her, that James admitted to himself that he must have her for his own.

2

"I think that's the best I can do, sir, bearing in mind that . . . well . . . there is very little in the way of assets. This house belongs to Squire Forsythe and it seems that from your stipend, with your family to support, there will be little hope of putting something aside for them . . . when you are gone. Forgive me, I have no wish to be morbid but that is the purpose of this visit, is it not? To make a will. To . . . to provide for your family in the future?"

"Yes, that is it exactly." The benign and exceedingly courteous gentleman on the opposite side of the meagrely burning fire beamed triumphantly. "You have it in a nutshell, Mr Buchanan."

"But, sir . . ." How did one address a parson, James wondered, placing his cup of tea on the low table beside him, a cup of tea which, had he not been told what it was, could have been washing-up water it was so weak. And how did one tell an obviously unworldly gentleman such as this one that the making of a will did not necessarily guarantee the beneficiaries of it security for the future. "All my worldly possessions to go to my children, with my eldest daughter in charge of it, of course," was all very well and good but if you had no worldly possessions, which seemed the case with the Reverend Dean, it was hardly worth the paper it was written on.

The rectory was a square Georgian box, very plain, very bare, the passage which led from the front to the back cool and dim, the long windows of the room he was shown to opening on to a surprisingly well-mown lawn. The work of the cursing Bibby, no doubt. In fact the grounds in which the house stood were quite magnificent, well kept and lovingly tended even if the gardener, or so it appeared from the conversation he had heard earlier, had not been paid his wages for weeks. He evidently took great pride in his work, for the flowerbeds, even this late in the season, were rampant with colour, mixed borders of antirrhinum of red and yellow and pink, long-legged chrysanthemum with cheerful daisy-like blooms, yellow-centred and white-petalled petunias, showy with all the colours of the rainbow and, at the back of the borders, the great height of delphiniums in a rich, gentian blue. The borders led away like ribbons along the velvet lawn, turning the corner to the back of the house. Clinging in glorious profusion across the whole of the front of the house was a curtain of Virginia creeper already changing from the green of summer to shades varying from creamy yellow and pale orange to russet and gold and flaming scarlet.

The front door had stood wide open as James drove the Rolls-Royce along the neatly raked gravel drive and up to the wide, shallow steps. There was no one to greet them as the occupants leaped from the motor car and tumbled inside the house. At least the children, including Miss Lucy Dean, and the dogs leaped.

James's well-bred, well-mannered animals, galvanised by the sense of whipped-up exultation with which the Dean family seemed to confront every happening, even the simple act of arriving home from an outing, cavorted about the gravel drive with the puppy as though they themselves were the same silly age. He could hear the children inside the house shouting someone's name, and one could have been forgiven for thinking that they had been away for a month instead of a few hours. Only Edward hung about the vehicle, still in a maze of rapturous delight, still proclaiming to James on the finer points of the engine, the speed available and the consumption of petrol as though James were the grateful passenger and he the owner. Did Mr Buchanan know, for instance, that only two years ago a Rolls-Royce had run from London to Edinburgh, covering just under twenty-five miles to the gallon, and not only that but had achieved seventy-nine miles an hour at Brooklands? It was a sorry day for the motoring world, he said sadly, when Mr Rolls was killed when his aeroplane crashed, and that was another thing. Did Mr Buchanan think that flying would become . . . ?

He might have stood on the steps for ever since there was no manservant or housemaid to show him the way. He was just about to ask the boy, who still stood in a preoccupied daze, where his father might be found when Lucy, filled with apologies, hurried back down the passage.

"Oh dear, Mr Buchanan, what must you think of me. I seem to have forgotten my manners . . ." as we forgot *you*, her youthful expression seemed to say. "Please, do come in. Papa is waiting for you in his study. Will you bring your dogs in with you?" looking over his shoulder to where the labradors, the puppy swept up and carried away by Edward, sat side by side on the gravel waiting to be told what they were to do. "Oh, look at them. Are they not splendid? Do you think we might eventually train Thimble to be so obedient? No, I don't think so either, since we none of us has the patience."

Pointedly he ignored her last remark with the contempt it deserved and said instead, "No, they will stay outside, Miss Dean, providing they are in no one's way. If you are expecting carriage callers . . ."

She broke into helpless laughter, so rich and joyous he felt his own mouth tug at the corners, though he had no idea why she was so amused.

"Callers! Good gracious, no, Mr Buchanan. We are not a bit social here. Mama used to . . . to visit Papa's parishioners, those who were ill or in need and Margaret and I often go for a chat with old Mrs Jenkins or Mr Langley who worked in the garden before we came, but no one calls, not now. Not that we mind, you understand and of course Papa is too busy with his butterflies – he collects them, you know – to bother about it. No, we are . . . Oh, Lord, I'm babbling, aren't I. Buffy says I do that a lot, babble, I mean, but I seem to have so much to say and cannot get it all out fast enough. Do you find that, Mr Buchanan? You do! I don't believe it." She smiled impishly. "I'm sure you are just being polite. Well, if we don't get to Papa before he forgets you are here he is quite likely to wander off down the garden in search of a wall brown he spotted the other day. So, please come this way, Mr Buchanan and I'll send Elsie in with some tea."

She led him along the passage towards the back of the house where sunlight streamed through the open garden door. He watched her as she walked ahead of him, outlined by the bright golden light, wondering if she was aware of the effect she had on the male sex. Her back was straight, long and supple and she moved with the ease and elegance of a cat, her bedraggled skirt swaying with each movement of her hips. Jesus, she was a rare one, so innocent and yet with the sensuality one would only expect to see in a much older woman. So beautiful and yet so totally unaware of it.

The doors to the rooms on either side of the passage stood open and as he passed them, used as he was to the deep luxury of his own home, he was aware that each one was bare and spartan. It was all achingly clean, achingly barren, with no more than a strip of worn carpet along the passage and an ancient grandfather clock ticking sonorously against the wall.

Flinging open a door with the exuberance he had come to recognise as a feature of the Dean family, she stood back to allow him to enter.

"Mr Buchanan's here, Papa," she called out from behind him, then, when James stopped abruptly, confused since the room was empty, she cannoned into his back. For a delightful moment he was concerned with the matter of turning to steady her, of telling her courteously that, no, it was not her fault, that really he should be more . . . careful. He was quite bemused by the nearness of her. Her perfume, whatever it was, was in his nostrils, her hair, still drifting in silken swathes about her face and shoulders was under his hand and it was all he could do, to his own consternation since he had never been an impetuous man, not to pull her into his arms and kiss her surprised, parted lips until she screamed, which he was certain she would not do. Not Miss Lucy Dean. Land him a backhander more like, if he was any judge of character. Afraid of very little, he would have thought. The backbone and defender of her family, its support and mainstay since, it seemed to him, her absent father, after summoning James here and being told that he had arrived, had wandered off like a careless child. Not a man to be relied upon, James mused, and was it any wonder his family was as wild and unconventional as it was.

"Oh, for heaven's sake, where has he gone now?" Lucy asked no one in particular, certainly not him who, though he had kindly given them a lift home in his motor car, meant no more to her than any elderly gentleman who was owed respect. She darted across the room to the French window which led out on to a wide stretch of lawn backed by trees clothed in early autumn colours.

"Papa, Papa, where are you?" she yelled vigorously. "Oh, there you are," as a tall, spare gentleman in a clerical collar rose from a bench at the side of the lawn. "Now, dearest, I told you Mr Buchanan was here and I've ordered tea."

"Mr Buchanan?"

"Yes, Papa. Come to help you make your will, you have just told me, though why you should think such a thing necessary is beyond me at your age. You are years and years off needing it and we all agree that if we—"

Pulling herself up short, suddenly remembering James standing politely at her back, she continued

29

breathlessly, "Do come in, Papa, and let me introduce you to Mr Buchanan. We have already met, Mr
Buchanan and I. In the woods, which I suppose is not
a real introduction . . ." but what did that matter, her
shrug said. "I did tell you, dearest."

She cast a somewhat despairing glance at James,
who stepped forward to clasp the reverend gentleman's hand. From somewhere in the house he could
hear a female voice warbling a familiar tune slightly
off key.

> Early one morning,
> Just as the sun was rising.

And another complained that if that "dratted animal"
didn't get out from under her feet she'd hand in her
notice that very day. How was she expected to put
dinner on the table by six when every minute she was
terrified she might fall over it and Elsie was driving her
mad with that song so would she kindly give over.

Lucy tutted. "I'd best go and see what's troubling
Mrs Hutton," she said, but a timid knock at the door
interrupted her. A little maid of about twelve, as
fragile as a sparrow and as shy as a fawn, popped
her head round it, a tray balanced precariously in her
stick-like arms.

"Thank you, Elsie," Lucy said to her, smiling warmly,
"that will be all," as if the puny child had imagined she
was to play hostess. "I'll pour and then I must go and
see what the children are up to." Mrs Hutton and her
problems seemed to have been forgotten. "I'm doing
my best to teach Emily the fundamentals of fractions
but as I'm not too sure of them myself it's an uphill

task." She did not explain what possible use Emily might have of fractions. "We have no governess at the present moment, Mr Buchanan." She said it airily as though one were expected any day now. "So while Papa does his best with Edward and Percy I'm tackling the girls, but really, they are all quite . . . well, I wouldn't say wild, but they are not scholarly, are they, Papa?"

She smiled lovingly at her father and he smiled back in like fashion as though neither were unduly concerned with the children's lack of education since, this being their faith in life, something would be bound to turn up before too long. Besides, it was much more important to be well mannered, cheerful and willing, to keep a good spirit and be kind to those less fortunate than oneself than to know how to divide one number by another.

James held the door for her, bowing slightly as she left the room and for the next half-hour he and the reverend gentleman discussed the state of the Dean family's finances. At least James did, for Edward Dean seemed to imagine that, having told the solicitor how he wished to dispose of his worldly goods, whatever they might be, the matter was resolved.

James steered him back time after time from such subjects as butterfly-collecting which was the Reverend Dean's passion; a pair of bullfinches which had nested in his garden hedge last May, since it seemed bird-watching was another; the quaintness of the local dialect which he and his dear wife had found hard to understand when first they settled in Fellthwaite, and did not Mr Buchanan agree that October was the most beautiful month of the year in the district of the Lakes.

"Indeed . . . er . . . Mr Dean, but perhaps if we could return to the question of your will."

"Of course, my dear fellow. My mind seems to wander these days, particularly when the subject is not one of a cheerful nature. Now, what else can I tell you?"

"Have you, forgive me, perhaps shares in . . . well, the railways, for instance?"

The reverend gentleman looked bewildered. "The railways?"

"Yes, I have some myself and—"

"Have you indeed?" He smiled amiably, having not the faintest idea what they were to do with him.

"Yes, I just wondered whether you . . ."

"I'm afraid not, Mr Buchanan." The rector was genuinely sorry he could not be of more help.

"Did . . . was your . . . perhaps your wife left something?"

"Left something?"

Surely no man could be so artlessly ignorant of the ways of the world as this one?

"Perhaps for the children?" James prompted.

"I don't think so, Mr Buchanan. I know she gave Lucy, my eldest daughter, if you recall . . ."

"Yes, sir."

". . . a very pretty pair of earrings but I'm sure they have no particular value, only in as much as they were her mother's."

"Of course. How charming . . . well . . ." James looked round the bare room as though searching for inspiration. It was as well scoured and polished as the passage. It contained a large, square table with a Bible on it and at which, or so it appeared, the Reverend Dean wrote his sermons, a couple of glass-fronted bookcases crammed with crumbling books of great antiquity, a skeleton clock ticking on the mantelshelf and, on a small table beside the rector, a chessboard set out with ivory chessmen. A game was obviously in progress and James wondered who the players were. Two faded, red brocade chairs in which they sat and from which the stuffing had almost gone, stood on either side of the fireplace. There was a copper coal scuttle in the hearth with no more than half a dozen small pieces of coal in it, evidently to be eked out with care.

Set out on a table beneath the side window where they caught the northern light were a dozen glass cases containing hundreds of mounted butterflies.

James shuddered. He would have liked to discuss Miss Dean's earrings and indeed Miss Dean herself since there was so much he wanted to know. He had heard no talk in the district regarding her, nor any interest shown her by a young man but then, though she was quite, quite exquisite and evidently well bred, there was no money and young men, unless they themselves had considerable wealth, must marry an heiress.

The reverend gentleman, though the soul of courtesy, was beginning to fidget, presumably on pins to get back to his collection.

"So . . . you will draw up the necessary documents, will you, Mr Buchanan? I presume I will have to sign something?" His smile reminded James of Lucy. "If you like I could call in to your office when I am in Fellthwaite which would save you the inconvenience of coming to the rectory again."

James's mind worked swiftly, formulating ideas on how he was to see Miss Lucy Dean again. He knew no one who was acquainted with her, otherwise he would have met her at some function or other. It seemed probable she did not mix in society, the gentle, backwater existence in which she and her family lived, and the signs of reduced circumstances he had seen in their home not lending themselves to the round of social gatherings the women of his family indulged in. There must be some way in which he could get to know her better and his shrewd brain would find it, but in the meanwhile he must keep alive the small beginning they had made today and the only way to do this was to meet her on her own ground, it seemed.

"Not at all, sir. It would cause me not the slightest inconvenience. In fact I am passing this way on Friday to another appointment so if I may I will call in then. The rough draft will be ready for your consideration. After lunch, perhaps? Say about two o'clock?"

Again the reverend gentleman looked somewhat confused as though he were not really sure of the legal implication of a "rough draft" and James was just beginning to think he might be either hard of hearing or slow-witted when the furious sound of dogs barking came in through the open window. It was some distance away but getting closer and mixed with it were the angry screeching and squawking of hens, raised excited voices, children's voices, and over it all the thunderous sound of a man provoked beyond endurance.

"Get them bloody dogs off my 'ens, yer young 'ooligans," the voice roared and Mr Dean turned wondering eyes in the direction of the garden.

"Dear me, what . . ." he began, then stood up and moved hesitantly towards the open French window.

James did the same, doing his best to show no more than polite interest though he was pretty positive that the barking, deep and throaty, came from his own dogs. There was accompanying them the hysterical yipping of Thimble who sounded as though he were not at all sure he was having a good time but didn't know how to stop.

They all came hell for leather round the corner of the house with the speed and full-throated roar of the London to Glasgow express. The hens were first, beating their wings in frenzied madness, leaping in the air, feathers flying, then running when they hit the ground, jerking up again with their necks stretched out before them. They were a beautiful colour, a rich, glowing russet brown, their combs and wattles a clear scarlet. There were a dozen of them, Rhodes, James thought, though he knew little enough about the farmyard. They seemed not to have the sense to make for the safety of the trees but ran madly wherever they were driven. They were followed with ecstatic delight by his own two dogs who he had last seen sitting placidly by the front door. Their tails were lashing, their eyes were alight with joy, their mouths were grinning idiotically, for really this was the best game they had ever been allowed to play. At their heels, his own little legs pumping nineteen to the dozen, his wheaten coat a blur across the vivid green of the grass, was Thimble.

James groaned inwardly.

"Thimble ... Thimble, you little devil, will you come here?" a female voice shrieked, high with laughter. "Edward, what are those two belonging to Mr Buchanan called, d'you know?" the voice, which proved to be Margaret's, demanded. "It's awfully difficult to get them to take any notice when you don't know their names."

At Margaret's back were Edward, Percy and Emily and close behind lumbered a well-built, red-faced man in an overall and brandishing a garden hoe.

"I don't give a bugger what they're called, I'll throttle the lot o' them," he was telling the world. "They've dug up me cabbages an' trampled all over me sprouts an' if them 'ens ever lay again it'll be a bloody miracle."

"Don't let Papa hear you swear like that, Mr Bibby," Margaret told him reprovingly as she did her best to corner Thimble, who ran between her legs and nearly had her over.

"I'll 'ave that pup's 'ide, an' them an' all," the incensed Mr Bibby shrieked, aiming his hoe at one of James's dogs. It caught him on the rump and he squealed and James felt the irritation in him turn to anger. It seemed to him that wherever they went and whatever they did the Dean family created havoc, which was all very well and nothing to do with him except when it affected something which belonged to him. He could not abide cruelty to animals and what the gardener had done, no matter how he was provoked, had a nasty streak in it. His dogs had been trained to sit, to stay, to lie down, stand up, to walk to heel, and for the past six months, despite being less than a year old, had been exemplary in their behaviour. Now, what with free-roaming hens, an excitable and totally untrained puppy, four shrieking children, not to mention the maddened gardener, they had totally lost control and forgotten all they had been taught, and in a way it was his fault.

"Excuse me, sir," he said politely to Mr Dean, no sign of the storm brewing inside him. Gently putting the reverend gentleman to one side and stepping from the French window, the cold thunderclap of his voice brought them all, even, it seemed, the deranged hens, to a standstill.

"Holmes, Watson, come here to me," he told the dogs in a tone of voice which brooked no argument, knowing, as his voice cracked across the lawn, there was really no need for such a show of force. He was allowing his own ill humour, and not just with this mêlée, he was honest enough to admit, to blur his usually clear mind. Miss Lucy Dean had, from the moment he had first clapped eyes on her, flushed, dishevelled, her hair rippling in a polished curtain about her, her great golden eyes catching the very sunshine in their depths, bemused him, bewitched him, cast a spell about him from which he could not shake himself free. It confused him, penetrating the reserve which was his nature, and it took the form of raging at his dogs on whom no blame could be laid.

They were all completely bewildered by it, children and animals alike, though Bibby seemed well suited, looking round and nodding as though to say at last here was someone who could put a halter on this lot.

"Here to me, now." James's voice was harsh as he pointed at the ground in front of him and, both quivering and moving their tails placatingly, the suddenly silent black dogs padded obediently across the lawn and stood where he indicated.

"Sit!" They sat.

But Thimble was not so polite. Bouncing like a ball,

his teeth flashing, his eyes glowing, his tail wagging, he raced across the grass and began to leap all over the unfortunate Holmes. Holmes, his anguished eyes on his master's face, though it took a great deal of self-control, ignored him.

Bending down, James swiftly picked up the wriggling, excited puppy, holding him round his plump body with hands of steel, his face glaring directly into that of the dog.

"Behave, I say." His eyes were fierce and compelling. He gave the puppy a small shake and, surprised but not hurt, Thimble whimpered and became quiet. "You are an ill-mannered cur and if you were mine I'd—"

"But he is not yours, Mr Buchanan," a cool voice said, "and I'd be obliged if you would hand him to Edward."

"They was playin' 'avoc in my vegetable garden, Miss Lucy, an' all three need a good 'idin' in my opinion. If it 'adn't bin fer this gempmum 'ere" – Bibby nodded in an aggrieved fashion at James – "Gawd knows what'd 've become of them there 'ens."

"Thank you, Bibby, that will be all."

Lucy Dean had appeared from some doorway further along the house, probably an outhouse, James thought, for she wore an overall and had a large wooden mixing spoon in her hand. What she had been doing with it was not immediately obvious, that is until the hens all surged in delighted anticipation towards her, cackling their goodwill, their fright forgotten. It seemed this was something they recognised and James guessed that Lucy had been cooking up the scraps on which they were to be fed. Her indignation at James's handling of her dog was plainly displayed in the stiff turn of her head on her neck, by the high colour at her cheekbones and the flash of temper in her golden eyes.

"Lucy, my dear . . ."

"No, Papa, Thimble is only a puppy and—"

"And will remain so until the end of his days, Miss Dean, unless some farmer shoots him when he finds him worrying his sheep."

"You are being melodramatic, Mr Buchanan." She raised her head higher and waved her spoon. "He was harming no one."

"'E'd 'ave 'ad them bloody 'ens, beggin tha' pardon, Miss Lucy."

"There is no need to use language like that in front of the children, Bibby. You know my father does not care for it."

"Beggin' tha' pardon, Reverend, Miss Lucy, but them 'ens is – *was* – good layers as tha' well know an' Gawd only knows what they'll be like now. Useless, I reckon, after a fright like this 'un."

"Thank you, Bibby, but as you can see they have come to no harm. Now, I'm sorry if Thimble and . . . and these two" – with a disparaging wave of her spoon at James's quivering dogs – "have damaged the vegetable garden. It was unfortunate that . . . that Mr Buchanan's dogs were left unattended and—"

James, to his horror and amazement, found himself to be quite incensed, interrupting her rudely.

"Miss Dean, my dogs, if not interfered with, will remain where they are put until I tell them to move. If yours is not stable enough to be let loose in the garden then he should be kept on a leash."

What the bloody hell was he babbling on about, he wondered desperately and why did he feel the need to argue with this beautiful, spirited girl and all over a storm in a teacup? This was, of course, nothing to do with his dogs, the part of his mind that looked on coolly told him. So what was it about? his previously untouched heart asked him sardonically. You are making a fool of yourself, you who are normally so cool-headed. His dogs had, for a moment, lost control of their manners, and so, it appeared, had he. They were not used to hens, nor even children. His cousins, who all lived in and about Fellthwaite, Ambleside and Skelwith, had dozens of children between them, or so it seemed. He had lost count of the times he had been included, reluctantly on his part, in family christenings, in Christmas festivities where Ben or Alex's, Anne, Janet or Christine's offspring had squealed like hordes of piglets and raced about in what seemed to be senseless circles. His dogs had been left at home then, or, if the family event took place at Howethwaite, though he did his best to avoid it, were shut safely away from the excited hysteria that seemed to be the prerogative of the young. He always vowed at the end of such visits that when he had children they would be as well behaved as his dogs, or at least as well behaved as they had been up to today!

"Thank you for your advice, Mr Buchanan." Her voice was icy. "I shall bear it in mind. Now, if you will excuse me I was making the hens' feed and as you can see they are eager to be at it so I'll say good-day to you, sir."

She was turning away, dismissing him, since he had proved such a tedious boor, her manner said, but he would not allow it. When he spoke again his voice was as icy as hers though he tried his best to keep it polite. He knew he was making a poor showing and he cursed his own nature which was to be aloof, and his temper which could be quick. But somehow he must become better acquainted with Miss Lucy Dean and he knew he was not going the best way about it. Acquainted for what purpose was not really clear either at the moment, he only knew he must find some way to show himself in a better light than the pompous, self-opinionated fool she obviously thought him to be.

"I am just arranging with your father . . ." His voice was harsh, angry, truculent almost, and they all, including Bibby, turned to stare at him. The children, Edward with the squirming Thimble in his arms, Percy who was declaring loudly that he thought the whole thing had been great fun, didn't Emily agree, had been about to go back to whatever it was they were doing before Thimble had teased Holmes and Watson into lunacy. It really had been a good game and quite harmless since everyone knew what daft creatures hens were and the children couldn't understand what Mr Buchanan was making such a fuss about. Lucy was clearly displeased with him over something and now Mr Buchanan, as annoyed as she was, had something further to say, it seemed.

"Yes, Mr Buchanan?" Lucy's eyes narrowed suspiciously in that way they were all familiar with, a sort of warning that told them they were only a fraction away from going too far. "You have not yet finished your business with Papa?"

"Indeed we have, Miss Dean, but—"

"Perhaps you have something further to say on the bad manners of our dog who you clearly believe led yours into mischief."

James felt the irritation goad him and he spoke through clenched teeth. "No, Miss Dean, though I must say if I had him for a few days he would—"

"No doubt be as submissive as yours?"

"Well behaved, I would call it."

"Dear God, sir, you really will not give up, will you?"

"Nor you, Miss Dean."

She lifted the spoon and the spellbound audience were amazed when, for some reason, Mr Buchanan began to laugh.

"Really, Miss Dean, I do wish you would stop brandishing that implement in my face. I meant neither you, your brothers and sisters, your courteous father, your gardener, your hens or your dog any harm but I have the distinct feeling that if I don't behave myself you might give me a good paddling, just like the one my nanny administered when I misbehaved."

They watched, entranced, even Bibby, to see how Miss Lucy Dean, whose temper was quick but whose heart was warm, would respond. Would she unbend and begin to laugh, sharing the joke, or would she give Mr Buchanan a further demonstration of how haughty she could be? They were inclined to think the former, for the dimple at the corner of her mouth appeared for an instant and her lips moved in what might have been a smile.

"Lucy, my dear," their papa suddenly interrupted, just as though the past five minutes had gone by him unnoticed, hens, dogs, children, all some sort of passing parade that had nothing to do with him. "Mr Buchanan has been most kind and helpful. Though I know it upsets you to talk of wills, it really is necessary and now it is done and we can forget it. Put it behind us. Mr Buchanan has it in his capable hands and I have only to sign the papers when they are ready. You have no idea what a weight it has taken off my mind." He turned to smile genially at James. "I thank you, sir. Now I have matters to which I must attend," making them sound as though the good of the entire country depended on his judgement, "so I'll leave you in my daughter's capable hands."

If James was astonished it did not show, for by now he was becoming used to the Reverend Dean's eccentricities. He held out his hand, saying as he did so, "Then I shall look forward to seeing you on Friday, sir. The documents will be ready then. I trust you can find two witnesses?"

"Witnesses?"

"Yes, sir. Your signature needs to be witnessed by two people who do not benefit from your will."

"Really, of course, how silly of me." He looked vaguely about him as though two such persons might easily be found hiding behind a handy bush but his daughter came swiftly to his aid. She put a hand on his arm as though calming a troubled animal and he turned at once to smile with relief into her loving face.

"Mrs Hutton will do, Papa, and Mr Bibby."

"Will they, my dear?"

"Mr Buchanan?" She turned her polite gaze on him for confirmation.

"Yes, of course."

"There, then that's settled." The Reverend Dean let

out a great sigh of relief. "Now then, Lucy, will you see Mr Buchanan out. I must get on." Turning, he drifted back into his study, closing the French windows on a troublesome world.

Lucy handed the spoon to Margaret then turned to James, indicating that he was to re-enter the house through the door which led to the narrow passage. Her manner was still curt. She did not speak and he had not the faintest notion of what was in her mind. The face, which had been so open, so sparkling with good humour and joy, had closed up, turned against him and he was at a loss to know why. Admittedly he had been his usual forthright self on the subject of her dog, but surely she had not taken offence at that, at least not enough to keep up this icy restraint she had pulled about herself.

The dogs leaped into the back seat of the motor car and lay down, still subdued and she watched, her face quite blank as he climbed into the front.

"Until Friday then, Miss Dean," his face as expressionless as hers.

"Until Friday, Mr Buchanan," she answered coolly and he wondered why he had the impression she believed he had tricked her into something, what he couldn't imagine, against her will.

James Buchanan sprang up from the armchair in which he had been sprawled and sauntered in what he imagined was a casual manner across Franny Buchanan's drawing-room carpet. He placed both hands palm down on the windowsill and peered through the open window to the long stretch of immaculate garden beyond it. The sky was the lovely, tender blue of autumn and the sun spread its serenity across it. The paths were carefully raked, leaves which were beginning to fall removed one by one by the Buchanan gardeners and the flowerbeds glowed with michaelmas daisies, dahlias and chrysanthemums. There were bees at work and a few painted lady butterflies drifted through the still air. James wondered idly if the Reverend Dean had any in his collection.

Frances Buchanan, who was the wife of Alex Buchanan, James's cousin, was not deceived by his air of carelessness, watching him with amused interest. He evidently had something of great importance, at least to himself, weighing him down and she waited patiently for him to divulge it. It was a Sunday, a day when James normally would be found climbing some mountain or other in that solitary way he had but today, for some reason best known to himself, he had turned up in her drawing-room with no explanation nor excuse. He had accepted tea and listened to her chatter but it was very evident that his mind was not on twelve-year-old Henry Buchanan's threat to run away from the well-known public school to which all the Buchanan boys had gone, nor Franny's plans for a dance she meant to give shortly. The possibility of rain did not concern him at all, the last thrown in to test whether he was really listening, which she knew he wasn't.

He sat down again and absent-mindedly accepted a third cup of tea, sipping it with so little enjoyment it might have been hemlock, then, putting his cup and saucer on the table beside him, he stood up and prowled about again. He studied some prints on the cream-painted wall, then fingered a small sculpted copy of Degas's ballet girl which stood among others on a low table by the window. When he sat down on the stool in front of her piano, opened the lid and cast a haunted look at the keys, Franny stopped what she realised was just babbling and lay back among the cushions on her chair.

For several minutes there was silence but he did not appear to notice. He leaned his left forearm on the piano top and picked out a small tune with the index finger of his right hand, his brow deeply furrowed, his mouth clamped tight, his eyes a pale unfocused grey.

She could stand it no longer. "James, if you continue like this I swear I'll scream out loud. For God's sake, leave that damned piano alone and come and and tell me what you are doing here and why you are in such a state. Oh, yes, you are. I've never seen

46

you like this before and if I didn't know you better
I'd think—"

"Do you know a family by the name of Dean?"
He turned and interrupted her so brusquely she was
startled. His voice was harsh as though he were angry
about something, something he could do nothing
about. It was not like him, for he had his life in a pattern
of smooth routine which suited him to perfection, or so
he would have everybody believe, but this, whatever it
was, had him coiled like an overwound watch.

Franny was astonished. To give herself time to think
she leaned over and took a cigarette from an engraved
silver box on the table beside her, lit it and inhaled
deeply.

"No, should I?"

"They're . . . he's a rector."

"A rector! James, can you see me with—"

"There's a daughter."

"A rector with a daughter! My God, James, am I
to—"

"If you make one of your clever remarks, Franny,
I swear I'll hit you." His voice was savage with the
bottled-up emotion he was doing his best to hide
and which was warning her that he did not care to
be trifled with. This was serious, important to him
and he was in no mood for her usual facetiousness.
His mouth was clamped tight and his thrusting jaw
was clenched with a ferocious determination to be
calm, and though she was besieged with the longing
to question him, to know more about this rector's
daughter, for the moment she had the good sense to
keep her mouth shut. She raised one finely plucked
eyebrow questioningly and waited.

"They're . . . a decent family. A good family, if you get my meaning, but poor as church mice," he said at last, shooting her a fierce, none-of-your-smart-remarks look from beneath his lowering brows. "Reverend Dean has the living at St Silas's, given him by the Forsythes. Dalebarrow Hall, you know, so you see they have decent connections. I met them . . . the father, on some business last week and it struck me that . . . Goddammit it to hell, Franny. I'm not used to this."

"Used to what, James?" she asked him innocently.

"Don't take that tone with me, woman," he snarled. James Buchanan was an important, well-respected gentleman, not only in Fellthwaite but in the legal profession and had never in his life had the misfortune to be pinned down, squirming, and in a position where he had to play a part that he found downright uncomfortable. He did not beg favours, he gave them if he thought them worthy. He asked no one for their help, and any problem he might have he solved himself. His dignity was suffering and he did not like it, neither did he like Franny Buchanan's sly smile. He was a proud man, proud of his family name, self-reliant and private and to be brought to begging from his cousin's wife to help him in the matter of . . . of . . . Jesus, what was it he wanted? He wasn't absolutely sure himself. He only knew that from the day he met her, Lucy Dean, in all her young, innocent, untouched loveliness, had come between him and everything that up to now had formed his pleasant, harmonious lifestyle. She was in his night dreams and his waking moments, thoughts of her interrupting the flow of his words during the day to the consternation of himself and the men with whom he did business. He could not get her out of his mind. He had not seen her when he visited her father with the documents concerning his will, and had been appalled by his own feeling of devastation at her absence.

"Is . . . your daughter not at home, sir?" he heard himself asking the reverend, the yearning in his voice obvious at least to him, like some lovesick school-boy hoping to catch a glimpse of the object of his devotion.

"No, I believe she and the children have gone to . . ." Edward Dean struck his forehead with the palm of his hand. "Now where was it she said they were going? Dear me, my memory is appalling, Mr Buchanan. You must forgive me."

"No matter, sir." And indeed it did not matter, for if she was not here where he could see her it did not seem important where she was.

So, in his usual forthright manner, he must do something about it. Hell's teeth, he couldn't go about like this, could he? He must either put her completely out of his mind and resume his courtship of Charlotte Gibson, or take steps to get to know Lucy Dean; and since as a bachelor he could not ask a motherless young woman to his home, which was without a hostess, he must ask Franny for help. He could have confided in any one of his cousins, Anne or Christine or Janet, all married to well-set-up gentlemen, or to his male cousins' wives, Joan or Frances. The first four were conventional, straight-laced and concerned only with how things would look. So he had chosen Franny because he thought she would understand since she was the most – what would he call her? – sophisticated, worldly, uninhibited by the prejudices of their class with nothing to hold her back like the reputation of her children since she had none. He thought he could trust her to carry the thing off without revealing that it was at his behest that Miss Lucy Dean was being invited into their social circle, and besides, he could think of no other way to get what he wanted which was possession of the Reverend Edward Dean's beautiful daughter.

"I want you to take her up, Franny." His voice was abrupt as he rose from the piano stool and returned to his chair. "She comes from good stock and apart from a sad lack of cash is a most suitable young lady. She will not disgrace herself. She is a lady, clever and bright and you will find her ... quite delightful."

"As you evidently do and what I would like to know is what you have planned for this paragon?"

"That is my business."

"No, it's not. Not if I'm going to get involved."

James shook his head, giving a fair imitation of a beast tormented by flies. His face was dark and stormy and he turned away as though he didn't know how to deal with her obvious disquiet, a disquiet he shared, for he had no idea how this was to proceed. He only knew he had to see the girl again, talk to her, get some idea of ... well, what? God, he wished he'd never clapped eyes on her, really he did, for he would have been so much more in charge of himself with Charlotte Gibson as his wife.

"And another thing to consider," Franny went on, "is will she be interested?"

"Christ, Franny, you're not to tell her it was me put

you up to this." He was aghast, leaning forward to glare into her face.

"I don't mean that, James. I mean won't she be surprised to find herself being called upon by a woman she doesn't know?"

"Of course she won't. Ladies call on one another all the time. They . . . well, they call to welcome newcomers and . . ."

"She's hardly a newcomer from what you tell me."

"Oh, you can deal with that, Franny. You know how such things are done. She's only a girl and won't be able to resist." His voice was full of confidence.

"A girl, you say? How old?"

"I suppose . . . nineteen." He looked somewhat shame-faced, but then was it not the custom for a gentleman to wait until his thirties, or even his forties, and then to take a young bride with plenty of childbearing years ahead of her?

"Young, James. You're thirty-four. I'm not implying that she's too young but may you not find her . . . well, her girlishness too immature for your sophisticated tastes?"

"Not this one, Franny." His voice was quiet and very sure.

"Well, I suppose you know what you're doing. And as you say she won't be able to resist. After all, you are the county's most eligible bachelor."

He frowned, his expression telling her he did not care for the implication that the lovely Miss Dean would take him only for that reason. "You'll do it then?"

"It might be fun." Franny lit another cigarette from the stub of the first and James watched her with faint distaste. He did hate to see a woman smoke and he was surprised at Alex for not stopping her. He certainly would not allow it in any woman of his.

"This is serious, Franny. I'm . . . well, it's serious and I hope you act in a proper manner. Miss Dean is a lady of some refinement and breeding and—"

"Oh, get off your high horse, James. You can be a real prig sometimes. I've said I'll do it and I will, and I shall be the soul of discretion, not to mention decorum."

James Buchanan was not the only one to own a motor car in Fellthwaite. Just the same, when the dashing little Austin Ten two-seater drew up with a flourish and a spray of gravel at the front door of St Silas's rectory the day after James's talk with Franny Buchanan, those congregated there could not believe their eyes. To their knowledge the rectory drive had never before known the roar of the combustion engine, the blare of a motor-car horn or the screech of brakes and now, within the space of two weeks two such machines had thundered up the drive.

Mr Buchanan's Rolls-Royce was a gleaming silver. This vehicle was bottle green, its panels decorated with fine bands of gold, its hood, which was down and tucked away in a sturdy cover, black, and at the rear was a railed space for luggage. There were polished brass lamps and hub caps, black leather seats but the most amazing thing, at least to young Edward Dean and old Bibby, neither of whom had a great opinion of the female sex, was that it was driven by a woman. They were all even more shocked by the way she was dressed.

They were riding their bicycles round and round in circles on the carriage turning space, shouting with laughter as was their habit, totally ignoring Bibby's roars to be careful with his bloody gravel which he had just raked, even Miss Lucy, who surely at her age should know better, as daft as the rest. They had assembled for a ride over to the Roman Station south of Ambleside which Lucy was interested in and a sorrier bunch of machines Bibby had never clapped eyes on, he had remarked gloomily when they were first dragged up the drive. If they got them hooligans to the gate he'd be surprised, he had told Mrs Hutton as he drank a cup of her almost black tea preparatory to making a start with the oiling can. Oiling can! They weren't fit for anything but the scrap heap which was where they had come from in the first place and had it not been for Master Edward's know-how and knack with a spanner, with bits of odds and ends of nuts and bolts, old spokes and lengths of wire, they would never have been resurrected. Not one under twenty years old, falling to bits and held together by perseverance, cork and glue, as Bibby's old dad used to say when faced with some ancient farm machinery. Somehow the young rascal, with Bibby's help, of course, and a bicycle manual which he'd picked up in a book-shop in Ambleside, had made them comparatively roadworthy. Miss Lucy's was in the best condition, a Lady's Rover with a basket on the front, a spring saddle, a plunger brake and a dress cord to protect her skirts from the spokes. Miss Lucy, who needed her machine for shopping errands and such, since it was a long walk to the grocer and butcher – and they bought in small quantities for monetary reasons – used hers several times a week, but this morning, it being a fine golden day, they were off on some shenanigans Bibby wanted nothing to do with.

They all came to a screeching halt, mouths agape, eyes wide, machine crashing into machine, falling about like drunken sailors as they did their best to keep their balance, staring in wonder at the apparition which climbed from the motor car.

She wore knickerbockers! They were full, pleated round the waist and gathered into a band under the knee, below which were gaiters buttoned down the side. Her serviceable jacket of tweed was short and belted and she had on what looked like a gentleman's shirt with a tie. She wore no hat and her pale blonde hair, blown about by the speed of the machine she had driven, was carelessly tied back with a black velvet ribbon.

"Good morning. Am I speaking to Miss Dean?" she called out. "Lovely day, isn't it? I see you are about to make the most of it so I won't keep you. I just felt it was about time I called on you. I know you have lived in the neighbourhood for a while but better late than never, I say. I was hoping to meet you and perhaps invite you to come to one of my afternoons. I'm sure you will like my friends. Mostly ladies of the district who would be delighted to make your acquaintance. My name is Frances Buchanan, by the way." She grinned disarmingly. She was perfectly at ease, seeing nothing unusual in a woman dressed in trousers driving a motor car, nor in the fact that it had taken her six years to welcome newcomers to the area. As though to emphasise it she leaned her bottom on the bonnet of the Austin, drew out of her pocket a gold cigarette case and lit a cigarette with a lethal-looking lighter made of some base metal and dragged the smoke deep into her lungs. Folding her arms across her breast she narrowed her chocolate brown eyes against the sun's rays and studied them all one by one.

"Well, is no one going to speak?" she asked as the silence drew on, raising a fine blonde eyebrow and blowing out a perfect smoke ring at the same time. It was evident that Edward was vastly impressed.

Lucy was clearly amazed, but pulling her amazement about her she did her best to be polite as she had been taught. "How kind of you to call, Mrs Buchanan," she stammered, "but I'm afraid you are wasting your time. I am far too busy looking after my family to go about in company."

She knew she sounded rude, which was unforgivable, but she could think of no other way to discourage the astonishing Mrs Buchanan, who, it seemed, had taken it into her head to draw Lucy Dean into her well-bred circle of friends. Why, she didn't know and it certainly did not occur to her that James Buchanan might be at the back of it. Why should it? She had met him only once when he called on her father. A man almost as old as her father, at least it seemed so to her and his connection with this woman did not enter her mind. Now all she had to do was persuade Mrs Buchanan that Lucy Dean was perfectly happy with her own way of life, that she had no desire to receive or make calls as women like Mrs Buchanan did. Lucy was not a "company" person. She had no company manners and Mrs Buchanan must be made to understand that, for she did not want her coming here again with her bright smile and outlandish clothes which she knew would shock Papa if he saw them. Lucy had no wish to mix with "good" people though she knew she was one herself, for her mama had been a lady. No, Lucy loved long walks on the fells, cycling with the children, romping about the orchard and meadow at the back of the house. She was happy messing about with Bibby's hens, getting her hands dirty in the soil of the vegetable garden where she and Bibby were experimenting with the cultivation of globe artichokes, and to prove it she still had soil under her fingernails no matter how hard she scrubbed them. She had no style, as she believed it was called. Look at her today in her oatmeal flannel skirt and an old cream shirt of Papa's, her strong walking boots and thick, hand-knitted brown woollen stockings, her hair tied back into a twisted rope of tangled curls; but she was gloriously happy. There was a picnic in the basket at the front of her bicycle and the day stretched out before them, splendid with golden autumn sunshine, with the hyacinth blue of the sky.

But Mrs Buchanan was not put off by her rudeness, it seemed. "Miss Dean, you disappoint me. I believe it is the custom to ask a caller to take tea." She smiled composedly, telling Lucy that she was not to be turned away so easily.

Lucy was suddenly ashamed of her lack of manners. Her mama, who was surely watching from that gentle heaven where she now dwelled, would be appalled and she was just about to stammer an apology when her father's voice from the top of the steps interrupted her guilty thoughts. She turned to him in surprise, for it took more than a caller, when they had one, that is, to winkle him from his study. Standing beside him was Buffy and, bewildered, Lucy realised that she must have overheard the conversation at the front of the house and gone to fetch him.

He did his best to avert his eyes from Mrs Buchanan's knickerbockers.

"Mrs Buchanan, it is Mrs Buchanan, isn't it, or so Buffy told me." His voice was gentle and courteous but there was a core of something in it Lucy had not heard before.

Mrs Buchanan turned and went up the steps. "Reverend Dean. How do you do. A lovely day, is it not?" She held out a hand and shook his briskly.

"Indeed it is, but why are you standing here outside? Lucy, show Mrs Buchanan into the drawing-room and . . . well, I'm sure Buffy could manage some tea . . . or . . . Do come in, Mrs Buchanan."

Lucy's face was a picture and Franny Buchanan made a mental note to tell her that if she was to get on in society, as it seemed James intended her to do, she must make an effort not to let her every thought show so plainly. It appeared to have on it a mixture of consternation, irritation and plain indignation that her papa had so summarily spoiled her plans for the day, and she was right.

From where she stood Lucy could just make out a small corner of the lake, the deep blue sky mirrored in it and a small boat turning, its white sails like the wings of a gull. She could smell the sweetness of the bracken and fern and could picture the sheep trods up which, when they had finished with the Roman Station, their booted feet would climb. In her mind's eye was the tawny tapestry of autumn Lakeland spread out below right down into the vale where Grasmere lay. Fine waterfalls misted with silver spray, the strength and beauty of conifer and rowan. High fells where they would walk all day long without meeting a soul except for a taciturn shepherd and his dog and the scattered sheep they guarded.

Now, with a few polite and astounding words her papa had spoiled it all. It needed a whole day to enjoy the outing they had planned and by the time Mrs Buchanan had left the day would be half over.

The Reverend Edward Dean, his life sadly diminished by the loss of his beloved wife five years ago, had retreated from harsh reality and the responsibility of bringing up his children and, though he was was sorry about it, it was beyond his scope to change it. He could do nothing to ease his loss except become immersed in his obsession for catching and adding to his butterfly collection, and, in a lesser degree, bird-watching. He loved his children but without Evelyn had not the faintest notion what to do with them. So he did nothing, leaving Lucy to muddle through as best she could. She did it very well. She had a practical streak in her come from her mother and though she regretted her brothers' and sisters' lack of a decent education, particularly the boys, what she could not mend she put to one side for later.

But deep in Edward's consciousness was the niggling suspicion that Evelyn would want to see, at the very least, her three daughters decently married and how were they to manage that if they did not go about, as was their right, in the society from which he and Evelyn had come. Lucy was eighteen and went nowhere without a line of her brothers and sisters straggling behind her like a mother duck with her ducklings. She was a beautiful and intelligent young woman and would make a fine wife, though how he would cope without her he didn't dare think. But that must not stand in the way of his doing his duty by her. He had no idea what Mrs Buchanan was up to but if it was to lead to the sort of social life Evelyn would have wanted for her daughter, direct her to people who would guide her in the right way of doing things, introduce her to young men of good family and thereby ensure that all three of his girls had a chance of making a decent marriage, then he must do all he could to bring it about. And if this strangely dressed woman who had so astonishingly and belatedly come to call could help him then so be it.

The boys, well, they must wait, though for what he didn't know.

They sat and drank tea and he let Frances Buchanan do most of the talking. His eyes were drawn again and again to her knickerbockers and gaiters, though he politely did his best not to stare. The cigarette she had been smoking when he first saw her beside her motor car had been stubbed out in the gravel before she entered the house and thankfully she had not lit another one. They discussed the weather, at least he and Mrs Buchanan did, since Lucy was tight-lipped at the waste of her day. They talked of Mrs Buchanan's love of motoring and motor cars, though he scarce understood her remarks about cylinders and chassis, about supension and mileage and of her intention to enter a race at a place called Brooklands if she could persuade her husband to buy her a twenty-five hp Talbot racer like the one that had taken the record in February of this year. One hundred and three miles in just sixty minutes, imagine that, if he could, until he began to wonder if he was perhaps being a little precipitate in entrusting his daughter to a woman such as this.

"Well now, Reverend Dean," Mrs Buchanan said at last, placing her cup and saucer, the contents of which she had hardly touched, on the table beside her, "shall we get back to the reason for my visit. I have been meaning to call for a long time. My mother-in-law was acquainted with your wife, did you know that? Oh, yes," when the reverend gentleman looked astonished, "and I thought it was about time I called on her daughter now that she is of an age to . . . enjoy society. I am holding a small dance at my home next Saturday. Nothing formal, I might add, and I'm sure she would enjoy it." She ignored the look of frantic appeal on Lucy Dean's face, since she had promised James she would do this. Besides, she didn't care if the girl wanted to come or not, or if she enjoyed it or not. She was keeping a promise, that was all, and it was up to James to do the rest.

"I have no children of my own," she went on, "and if I had they would be too young, but I do love to dance so I borrow my nieces and nephews. My sister-in-law, Janet, Janet Gunson, that is, has four handsome sons. Job is eighteen and the eldest. They have lots of friends, young friends, so I thought, well, other members of the family will be there and a few close friends, so do say you will join us, Miss Dean."

Lucy turned to her father, her expression anguished. Surely he did not mean to force her to go to this dreadful affair of Mrs Buchanan's. Dancing which,

she supposed, meant waltzes and . . . and the tango
– was that what it was called? – and whatever else was
fashionable at the moment, was something she knew
nothing about. She could remember as a child – how
long ago it seemed – she and Mama briskly circling
the nursery, their arms about one another, laughing
helplessly, which she recalled her mama did a lot of,
and performing what she supposed must have been
a polka, but she had forgotten the steps of even that.

No, she would hate it. The guests would all know
one another, for they were a big family. Young men
and women acting the giddy goat, which she and her
brothers and sisters did all the time, she admitted it,
but the idea of witnessing perfect strangers enjoying
themselves in such a way, and worse still being asked
to join in, was a horror to which she would not submit.
Though she had not been among young ladies of her
own class she was pretty sure they would not relish
putting their white hands in the soil as she did, soil
mixed with manure, kneeling beside their gardener
as she did, planting globe artichoke off-sets. Would
they know what a dibber was and how far apart to
plant? Could they discuss how to cook up hens' mash
on the saddle-room boiler; how many greengages and
damsons, cherries and pears they could expect on the
trees in the orchard; the best way to milk a goat; how
to keep a cow, which Lucy longed to do since the milk,
and cheese and butter she would learn to make from
it would be invaluable in stretching out her papa's
pitifully small stipend. If Mrs Hutton would let her
she would have tried her hand at bread-making, at
preserving fruit, at making jam from the rich harvest
of plums, which she thought would be immensely

satisfying and yet here was Papa evidently prepared to plunge her into a round of social activities which she knew she would loathe. It seemed, from what he and Mrs Buchanan were discussing, she was to be fetched next Saturday at seven thirty sharp by Mrs Buchanan's chauffeur and be taken to Grange House on the other side of Ambleside where dancing and a buffet supper were to be held.

For a moment or two Mrs Buchanan was distracted by shouted laughter outside the drawing-room window which looked out on to the front drive. Holding up her hand in a peremptory fashion, well used to being obeyed, she strode to the window and her expression changed to one of deep annoyance.

"That boy is sitting in my motor car," she exclaimed, menace in her voice. "And why are those children making such a commotion?"

Lucy stood up and moved to stand beside her, and sure enough there was Edward in the driving seat of Mrs Buchanan's vehicle and, what seemed to make it worse, he had on her driving goggles. He was not touching anything, simply sitting there in a dream-like state, no doubt imagining that he was roaring round the track at that place Mrs Buchanan had mentioned.

And it seemed Thimble had escaped from the kitchen and made hotfoot for the front drive where he could hear his people's voices. His "people" were doing their best to catch him, making it into a game, as they did everything, and threatening Mrs Buchanan's shining motor as they chased him round and round it.

Mrs Buchanan opened the window and her voice might have been heard in the centre of Ambleside, directing them to take that animal to the back of the house and if that boy would get out of that motor she would be much obliged. They obeyed without a murmur, proving that all they needed was a bit of discipline which they obviously weren't getting at the rectory.

She and Lucy resumed their seats and Lucy resumed her protest.

"I really don't think I can be spared, Papa," she said desperately, though she could think of no good reason why not at such short notice. If she had known this was to happen she would have made damn sure she had a watertight excuse, but now all she could do was bluff and bluster, conscious that she was fighting a losing battle. Mrs Buchanan was very determined and Papa was putty in her hands. She was quite amazed that he was taking such an interest, was so agreeable to all Mrs Buchanan suggested and it was not until they were alone that he told her the reason.

"Have you ever considered what your life would have been like had your dear mama lived, Lucy? How different it would have been? From the age of thirteen you have looked after us all, managed the household and even, with very little help, brought up your brother who was a newborn infant. You have had no childhood to speak of, no young, carefree girlhood."

"Oh, Papa, my life is as carefree as a bird's," or would be if you refuse to allow Mrs Buchanan to interfere in it.

"Maybe it is, or you imagine it is, but you are a young woman of refinement, clever and bright and beautiful and . . . Lucy, my dear, I must say it, you are . . . ready for marriage."

She shook her head vehemently. "Oh, no, Papa, not yet. Not for years. The children need me, you need me and I cannot desert you. Besides, I'm sure all the young men I would be compelled to mix with next Saturday will be as brainless as . . . as . . ." She paused, running out of words.

"Yes, my dear? As what? Have you some member of the male sex with whom to compare them, these young men? You know only myself and Bibby, Edward and Percy, some of my parishioners and we can hardly be described as typical examples of—"

"I know what they will be like, Papa. All they will talk about are . . . are what I consider to be trivialities and I for one will be bored rigid by it. I won't fit in, dearest. Mrs Buchanan talks of having fun but I have no idea what she means by that. They will be strangers to me. I don't know how to do all these strange-sounding dances they do now and, Papa, you know I will hate it. Please, please, don't make me go. Please, I couldn't stand it."

He had to smile. She was so passionate, this lovely daughter of his. About her family, her care of them and the servants, of him and indeed anyone who asked for her help. She would go to any lengths to give support and comfort to people less fortunate than herself and Mrs Hutton had been heard to declare the lot of them would starve the way Miss Lucy tried to feed every tramp and vagrant who knocked at the kitchen door. Give them the food out of her own mouth, she would, ready to do anyone a good turn and taking under her wing any lame duck that passed by.

Swiftly she knelt at her father's knee, her face flushed with entreaty, her hair tumbling about in a way that was familiar to Edward, for hadn't Evelyn's done the same? Her eyes were deep golden pools of entreaty and he could feel himself wavering. He didn't want her to become a part of the social scene, not because he was afraid it would spoil her but because he could not imagine his life without her in the house. He did not want her to meet eligible young men, to find one that suited her, to marry and leave them, for in a way it would be like losing Evelyn all over again. How would they manage, he and the children, without her warmth, her laughter, her blithe spirit which led them through so many tangles? Who would play mother to Percy or do their best to make sure Edward had a chance at a decent school? The girls needed her companionship, her guidance, her protective love, her leadership and yet she deserved her chance, must have her chance of a suitable marriage, for what else was there for her in this world of which she was a part? He could not hold her back and if she needed to be persuaded, even pushed, then he must do it for her own sake. The Buchanans were an old and wealthy family and to be befriended by one of them could do only good, not only for Lucy but for his other children.

"Papa, please," she whispered directly into his face. "Don't make me go. You know how I will despise such . . . such affairs. I won't understand their . . . their manners . . ."

"You have lovely manners, child. Your mama saw to that."

"I don't mean that, Papa. I mean the way they go about things. I shall do everything wrong."

"No, you will not."

"And I just don't know what to talk about if sensible conversation is forbidden. I've never met people like Mrs Buchanan before and . . . well . . . I just don't want to become involved."

Her papa stroked her hair with one hand and with the other took hers in a warm clasp. His face was kind, calm, certain, and, though he could see she was very near to tears, his voice was firm with unusual resolve, he who had never been resolved about anything for a long time.

"I'm sorry, dearest, but I must insist. It is what your mama would have wanted for you," and that was that as far as Edward Dean was concerned.

"This is all your fault, Buffy Tyson," she ranted later, absolutely beside herself with rage. "If you hadn't fetched Papa to the front door I could have refused her, politely, of course, and Papa would have been none the wiser."

"Isn't that dishonest, Lucy Dean? I would say so, deceiving your papa who wants nothing but the best for you."

"I wish you'd mind your own business. It's not you who has to play silly party games and prance about the floor in the arms of some callow youth who can't find his way round the room let alone up to the high fells."

"There are more important things in life than tramping the fells, Lucy."

"Is that so? Well, I can think of none."

"You are being silly and you know it. Your papa knows best."

"Does he?" Lucy's voice was savage. "Well, I'll tell

you this. I refuse absolutely even to try and enjoy it. I shall sit in a corner and speak to no one and never get asked again and that, Buffy Tyson, will be the end of my social career!"

4

It was the next day and Lucy was still bemoaning her fate.

"I haven't the faintest idea what I'm supposed to wear, Buffy, and even if I knew I'm sure I wouldn't have it in my wardrobe. What do ladies put on for dances? Really, I can't imagine what prompted Mrs Buchanan to invite me, just out of the blue, so to speak, or even to call in the first place. She said her mother-in-law was acquainted with Mama but I can't remember Mama ever mentioning it, can you? It is very baffling. We're not her sort. We don't move in her circle. We don't move in any circle and I can't imagine why she should take it into her head to ask me to a dance in her home."

"But why shouldn't she? Your mama and papa are of the same class as she is and I'm sure you'll fit into any gathering of her friends. I'm only surprised you have not been invited out before this."

"We don't know anybody, that's why. Only Papa's parishioners and there's not a party-goer among them. I just can't imagine what Mrs Buchanan is thinking of, asking me to Grange House."

Lucy's voice was fretful and she twisted and turned

in her chair as though she were doing her best to escape from a situation that was not at all to her liking.

"So you keep saying but this isn't solving the problem of what you are to wear on Saturday. Have . . . would you consider wearing something of your mama's? There is a trunkful of gowns in the attic and I'm sure between us we could contrive an outfit that would be suitable. What is the fashion nowadays?"

"Lord, Buffy, don't ask me. As long as I'm warm and clean in the winter and cool and clean in the summer that's all I ask. If you haven't the wherewithal to buy new dresses you don't take a great deal of interest."

"I suppose not."

The girl who spoke smiled a little. She was sewing a button on a shirt and she bent her bright head, using her strong white teeth to bite the thread, at the same time keeping her eyes on Lucy who had sprung up to stare moodily through the window.

The scene beyond it was enough to make the most cheerful feel moody. A mantle of fine rain drifted across the garden, blurring the trees that surrounded the house. It draped itself in moving folds about the heights of Loughrigg Fell and Ivy Crag, the clouds from which it came dangling darkly beneath the lowering sky and rolling down from the tops in a grey swathe. The contrast to the vivid autumn sunshine of the previous day, when every peak from Loughrigg in the west, Rydal in the north and the Hundreds to the east had been sharp and clear against the endless, cloudless blue of the sky, was quite amazing. Then the fells had been ablaze with the colour of dying bracken, rich and russet, with red-berried rowans, with the whiteness of bent and grasses and the breathtaking purple carpet of the heather. Blackbirds had clattered in the hedgerows, the call of sheep could be clearly heard in the sharp air and the slender birches surrounding the silver blue lake had dipped their autumn leaves into its unruffled surface.

Now it had all vanished in the grey mists which drop so suddenly on the district of the Lakes, setting the Dean children to squabbling and sulks, since they did not care for the tasks their older sister had set them. They had no interest in doing the page of sums she had found and copied from an old arithmetic book belonging to her mother, who had also tried to instil some learning into her children, nor the composition, to be called "A day on the fells", she had commanded them to write. They would rather be out, they had argued, even if it was raining and they couldn't understand why she was so concerned with this foolishness, since she was usually as keen to escape the house as they were.

They had not yet realised, and neither had she, how the invitation from Mrs Buchanan had confused and upset her. It had thrown a pebble into the smooth pond of her life which, though that life was threatened with anxiety at times, mainly over money, was always contented and peaceful. It had sent out ripples which widened and washed up against her normal blithe confidence. A part of her had no wish to go to Grange House, to become involved with the cream of Windermere society in which Mrs Buchanan moved, and at the same time, being young and spirited, another part was curious to see how that society spent its time.

Those who attended her father's services were not young for the most part. Going to church on a Sunday was a habit they had formed when they were themselves children, taken there by their parents. It was a way of life going back to Queen Victoria's reign and before, one not easily changed by those who had grown up in it. But now, in these modern times of motor cars and flying machines, of telephones and electricity and all the other twentieth-century idiosyncrasies, it gave them a sense of security to keep to the old ways and going to listen to one of Reverend Dean's gentle sermons was one of them.

It was the only world Edward Dean's children knew, though it was becoming very evident that at least one of his brood was moving into the twentieth century and would not for long be content to remain in the smooth flow of the nineteenth which still claimed his father. Young Edward's fascination with the motor car and flying machine, and his oft-repeated declaration that he meant to devote his life to the design, creation and care of such things caused his father some heart-searching. A mechanic! That was the term used for the lads who spent their days with their heads under the bonnets of motor cars. A mechanic. His and his lovely Evelyn's son a man who did nothing but tinker with engines. It was unthinkable and so, in his usual fashion, he did not think about it. After all Edward was not yet fourteen and must first go to a decent school, a school where gentlemen went, though again how this was to be achieved had not yet been revealed.

Lucy turned and sat down on the broad window seat, her back to the window. Though her eyes wandered round the familiar bedroom where she had slept for the past six years she did not really see it. Like the long-skirted grey woollen dress she had on it was completely without adornment, and like the rest of the house, as though to make up for its deficiencies in comfort and embellishment, it had been subject to a great deal of scouring and dusting and polishing. There was a single, straight-backed chair on which her companion sat, a battered wardrobe, a washstand on which stood a plain white jug and basin, and a narrow bed. Everything was white from the counterpane to the curtains and walls except for the fireplace – in which no fire had ever burned – made of cast iron and ferociously blackleaded. The bare floorboards gleamed with polish. Beside the bed the room's only claim to comfort was a hookie mat made of hessian and scraps of material from the family's cast-off clothing.

The young woman sitting with Lucy went by the name of Elizabeth Tyson and she had been a part of the Dean family for the past ten years. She thought she was about the same age as Lucy but as the poorhouse where her mother had died, leaving Elizabeth at the age of seven or eight to fend for herself, had no records, it was hard to say. She and her mother had arrived in Buxton on a bitter day in January, struggling through the snowdrifts which were a feature of the Peak District, her mother already racked with the dry, hacking cough which was to kill her. Who knows what might have become of her, she often mused, had Mrs Dean, wife of the rector of a small parish church a mile or so out of town, not herself been stranded by the snowstorm that day.

"That child cannot possibly be expected to lift that sack of potatoes, Matron," for barely before her mother was cold they had set Elizabeth to work. "Not with that leg. It is beyond her capabilities."

Those were the first words Elizabeth heard Mrs Dean speak. Lovely, soft-voiced, sweet-faced Mrs Dean who had taken Elizabeth home to the rectory, fed her, bathed her, tucked her into a warm bed, kissed her goodnight as though she were one of her own children and didn't seem to care that one of Elizabeth's legs was shorter than the other. There was no name-calling in Mrs Dean's home. No "gimpy" nor "hoppy", only the endearing diminutive of "Buffy", based on the infants Margaret and Edward's unsuccessful attempts to pronounce her true name of Elizabeth. She had been part of the household since. Everything Lucy was taught, which wasn't much in the way of academic subjects, so was Buffy. She could read and write and play the piano. She could sew and embroider beautifully, surpassing Lucy who got her silks in a tangle and her seams crooked. But for the first eight years of her life Buffy had lived among North Country men and women and no matter how hard Mrs Dean tried she could not erase their long-vowelled accent from Buffy's voice. She was and yet she was not a servant, helping in the kitchen, cleaning, even scrubbing when Mrs Hutton was run off her feet by the reverend's lively family, but at the same time she was a member of that family. Obsessively loyal to those who had taken her in, eternally grateful, devoted to their welfare, she would have died to save any one of them a moment's hurt. In fact when Mrs Dean was swept away on a tide of her own blood at Percy's birth she had howled her pain and anger at the injustice which had taken such a lovely, much-loved lady and left unworthy Buffy

Tyson. It had broken her heart, but in the shared sorrow and support for one another, the comfort given to one another by the warm-hearted family, she had recovered, as they had, and her love from then on had been given to Lucy, who took her mother's place in the home and in Buffy's wounded heart.

Buffy was not pretty. For one thing she was painfully short-sighted and wore wire-rimmed spectacles which hid her one claim to beauty which was the size and shape and lovely colour of her long-lashed eyes. They were green, a deep sea green which in some lights turned to aquamarine. Her skin was as white as milk and scattered across her face, her chest and arms were hundreds of small golden freckles. Her hair could be described as no other colour but ginger and was tightly curled in corkscrews about her small head. Her mouth was the vivid red of strawberries, wide and serious, for Elizabeth Tyson had had little to smile about in the formative years of her childhood. The top of her head came just to the level of Lucy's shoulder. She wore a plain navy cotton dress with a white apron, its bib frilled across her small breasts, but no cap since she was not thought of as a maidservant. There was no name to describe nor had she a given task in the household, so she provided service wherever it was needed. Companion and friend, playmate and nurse, comforter and adviser, scullery maid and cook at times, since Mrs Hutton was getting on and Elsie, though willing, was barely capable of deciding for herself which brush should be used to sweep the yard and which to clear the hearth.

"Come on, Lucy," she said, her freckled face serious, "don't just give up. You've been invited to this dinner and you've no choice but to go. If you don't enjoy yourself you don't have to go again, that's if they ask you."

"You know I hate all that polite stuff, pretending to be interested in the silly things girls of my age talk about. I shall be bored to tears."

"Oh, give over, do. You're just mad because for once you've got to do something you don't want to do. You have things far too much your own way, my girl."

"That's not true, Buffy." Lucy glared but her friend took no notice.

"Yes, it is. Now get your bottom off that window seat and let's scoot up to the attic and see what's in your mama's box." Her brisk voice suddenly became soft. "You don't mind . . . I mean will it upset you to see your mama's dresses and things?"

Not one for sulking, Lucy took Buffy's hand affectionately as they moved towards the open door, accommodating her long stride to Buffy's lopsided limp. Her voice was low and sad as she squeezed Buffy's hand.

"No, I know Mama would want me to look my best. I think, if she had lived, we would have been invited to many such occasions, for Papa would not be . . . as he is. So I must not let her down."

She did look her best, they all agreed. They were all there to see her off, Bibby and Elsie and Mrs Hutton with Buffy beside her papa, watching with pride and a kind of fascinated awe as a uniformed chauffeur handed her into the back seat of Mrs Buchanan's rich blue Vauxhall which Edward said was called a Prince Henry and would Lucy look at the flutes along the bonnet. It was almost as splendid as Mr Buchanan's Silver Ghost!

"'Ave a lovely time, Miss Lucy, dear," Mrs Hutton called out, ready to sniffle, for it would have been grand if Mrs Dean could have lived to see the beauty her daughter had grown into.

"Bring us something nice to eat, Luce," Percy begged her. He should have been in bed but with the usual disregard for rules the family applied, he was still hopping about in his nightshirt, Thimble clasped to his chest.

"Don't miss a thing, Lucy, promise. Emily and I want to hear about everything, positively everything that happens and what all the ladies are wearing. And the dances. Try and remember how to do them so that you can show us when you get back."

"If you get a chance will you have a look at what make of motor car they're driving, Luce. Just a general idea, you know." Edward prowled round the Vauxhall, his face cast in one of brooding concentration. He ran a finger along the shining surface of the bonnet and peered at its tyres as though fully expecting a puncture. The chauffeur watched him anxiously. He did wish the little bugger would leave it alone, for if there was a scratch on it it would be his fault. He'd have liked to tell him to clear off but with his father watching he had to show restraint.

In her mother's trunk Lucy and Buffy had found, among other garments, a lovely dress of white mousseline with flecks of silver in it. Around the low-cut neckline was an edging of silvery lace and at the waist a broad sash to match. They did not know it but it had been made for Evelyn Dean at the turn of the century, a simple gown with a fluted skirt which had about the hem a broad band of silver ribbon. This Buffy had cut off and made up into a silver rose which, when Lucy's hair had been brushed up into a full, rather loose style framing her face, was placed in the coil at the back of her head. The dress fitted her as if it had been made for her, if perhaps a little short, but then dance frocks at that time had been worn just clear of the ground. Her mother's pearl drops swung in her ears.

To her own surprise she found herself admitting later to Buffy that she had enjoyed Mrs Buchanan's dance at Grange House. Not that she would like to make a habit of it, she stressed. They were all a bit . . . brainless, the young people, Mrs Buchanan's nephews and nieces and their friends, but, again to her own surprise, she discovered that dancing was good fun and, what was even more astonishing, she had a talent for it, or so all her partners told her.

From the moment she was admitted by the poker-faced butler and greeted by Mr and Mrs Buchanan she sensed that this was not going to be as dull as she had expected. For a start you could tell this was a party for young people. There were shouts of male laughter coming from a room off the wide hallway accompanied by girlish shrieks and giggles, the strains of lively music and what sounded like the stamp of feet on a bare wooden floor. It promised a definite air of youthful high spirits which drew her into the house more enthusiastically than Mrs Buchanan's smile of welcome.

"Come in, Miss Dean, come in and join the fun. We've just begun a two-step which is guaranteed to break the ice. It's called Alexander's Ragtime Band.

Have you heard of it? No? Already the evening's developed into what my grandmother would have called a 'reet merry-neet'. 'Lish as day-old lambs', they all are, as the saying goes. She was a Dales-woman born and bred, my grandmother. I remember her as a wrinkled face beneath her lace and ribbon cap. Stern, but with a twinkle in her eye which said, providing it was not offensive, she liked a joke as well as the next person. She was as outspoken as I am which is probably where I get it."

Lucy realised Mrs Buchanan was talking to put her at ease, to get her over the doorstep and into the house without too much strain. Mr Buchanan, who reminded her of an amiable, shambling bear he was so big and dark, stepped forward and with old-world courtesy, though he was still only in his thirties, kissed her hand, smiling in a way that reminded Lucy of someone, though for the moment she couldn't think who it was.

"Miss Dean, I'm so glad you could come, and take no notice of my wife. She'll be telling you next we're to eat tatie-pot and clapbread at supper. She is very proud of her northern heritage and sometimes labours it to death."

"There is nothing wrong with tatie-pot, darling. I've eaten it many times as a child before my grandparents Graham began to go up in the world. We were not always as you see us now, Miss Dean, or at least my family weren't. Now then . . ."

Slipping her arm through Lucy's, she drew her across the hall towards the doorway from where the sound of merriment came. A male voice begged someone to "Watch where you're putting those enormous feet, lad," and a female's, high with excited laughter, informed him that it was her feet which were being punished, not his. They did not stop dancing as Lucy was ushered into the room.

It was a large room. Once it had been two but Franny Buchanan, on her marriage to Alex, with her love of parties, dances, balls, anything that smacked of fun, had persuaded him to demolish a wall and make it into a room big enough to hold such entertainments.

Grange House had been bought for them as a wedding present by Alex's father, Harry Buchanan, and was situated in its own five acres of gardens to the south of Ambleside. There were fields all about it, with a drive that led from Borrans Road up to the house. A big house suitable for a family with many children but in the eight years of Alex and Franny's marriage none had come along. Her mother-in-law said sourly at first that it was Franny's love of riding that prevented her from conceiving and later that it was the fault of that contraption she drove about in, referring to her smart little Austin Ten motor car. She had even proffered her own carriage and horses in the hope that a more gentle way of getting about might do the trick. It had not.

The carpet of what was usually the formal drawing-room had been removed, the chairs, sofas and low tables pushed back against the wall and, to the music of a lively record played on a gramophone housed in an exquisite wooden cabinet made in the style of Chippendale, a crowd of young people were energetically throwing themselves about the room, or so it seemed to Lucy. They were now dancing to the tune which came from the most successful show in London, "Hello Ragtime", arms and legs flying, their faces flushed, their eyes bright with laughter. With the enthusiasm and vigour only the young possess it had become an overheated romp, to the alarm of several mamas who watched.

"As you can see, Miss Dean, there is little decorum at my parties and my sister-in-law is not happy about it," nodding her head in the direction of Mrs Angus Gunson, once Janet Buchanan, who was watching disapprovingly as her son Job steered an over-excited Marion Mossop about the polished floor. She was the mother of four of the young men dancing. "She is not at all pleased by the high spirits of her sons, nor their partners. Now then, let me introduce you to some of the young people not dancing."

"Thank you, Mrs Buchanan," Lucy managed to gasp, the first words she had spoken beyond the initial greeting at the front door. Her eyes were wide and startled, her mouth open in a small O of astonishment. She and her brothers and sisters made a great deal of noise in the old nursery at home. They laughed and became over-excited in some of the games they played, but the sheer volume of noise here, the shrill chatter of the ladies not dancing striving to be heard over the din, the bright lights which must be electric, she decided, the warmth, the colour of the dresses of the young ladies who were whirled about the floor, quite took her breath away. There were groups of young people lounging about the edge of the floor, the gentlemen in immaculately tailored evening suits, the ladies in the very latest fashions, for they were all from wealthy, or, if not as wealthy as the Buchanans, old families from the neighbourhood.

Colours were strong this year with no pastel tints,

emerald, cerise, saxe blue, mauve and sulphur yellow being very popular. The gowns were generally of a one-piece design, straight and tubular with a tunic or overdress, scooped-out necklines and short sleeves. Waists were high with a look of the Empire line about them. Bead fringes were common, and gold and silver embroidery and sequins. The fabrics were lovely, soft and drifting, very flattering, chiffon and gauze, lace, net, silk and voile.

But the most enchanting, the most expensively dressed was Miss Charlotte Gibson, and James Buchanan, to whom she was chatting, wondered what demon of mischief had made his sister-in-law invite her here to the same party as Lucy Dean. He, naturally, had known Lucy was to be a guest, having engineered it, but Charlotte had been something of a shock and his face, though quite without expression, seemed set in intransigent lines which only Franny understood.

She smiled sweetly as she introduced Lucy to the other guests.

"Mrs Mossop . . . Frederick, and that is Marion on the floor . . . Roderick . . .

"Mrs Askew . . . Rosalyn, Louise, Roger . . . Douglas, of course, away at school . . .

"Mrs Kendall . . . Aurora, Gregory . . . Mrs Kendall's other children too young . . .

"And, of course, my brother-in-law, James Buchanan whom you have already met."

"Good evening, Miss Dean."

"Mr Buchanan." An inclination of her smoothly brushed head which he returned.

"Oh, and do forgive me, this is our charming Miss Charlotte Gibson."

."Miss Gibson."

"Miss Dean." With no more than the coolest nod Miss Gibson, who knew a nobody when she saw one and did not care for the competition with her own good looks this newcomer threatened, took James Buchanan's arm and led him away, reluctantly on his part, towards her hostess's conservatory, saying she had a fancy to see Mrs Buchanan's orchids which were well known to be the finest in the district.

The young people, especially the gentlemen, welcomed Lucy as though she were come from another species they had never before met, one which was enormously entertaining for, not caring a jot whether anyone might disapprove of her carelessly light-hearted behaviour, she flung herself into the festivities with the enthusiasm she showed at home, where nobody cared. She did a square dance with Job Gunson who, at eighteen, thought he was God's gift, being handsome as well as rich; an eightsome reel partnered by Frederick Mossop who, when the music stopped, told her she was the most beautiful creature he had ever met, and rippingly funny, which she thought he meant as a compliment. She even attempted the latest tango with Roger Askew. Did she know, he asked her breathlessly, that the German Kaiser had banned the dance, and the two-step, saying they were not "proper", but Roger could see nothing wrong with either, could she, doing his best to appear older than his seventeen years.

There were lively polkas, the steps of which she remembered from Mama as soon as the music started and Gregory Kendall's boyish arms came eagerly about her. The St Bernard Waltz, the valeta and the lancers in succession, sharing her favours between Frederick Mossop, who liked to be called Freddy, he told her, Job and Lawrence Gunson, Roger Askew and fifteen-year-old Will Gunson, who had the impertinence and nerve of a fox, his infuriated brothers told him.

It was not until after supper that she was approached by Mr Buchanan, Mr James Buchanan, that is. She was surrounded by young men all clamouring to be allowed to fetch her another plate of mayonnaise of fowl, or perhaps tongue, or would she prefer raised game pie, for she certainly had a good appetite. In fact none of them had ever seen a girl enjoy her food as she did, they said, and it was a wonderful sight! She felt like howling with laughter, really she did, at the idea of someone simply enjoying their food being considered wonderful! But then half the things they said to her made no sense. Had she been up to London to see George Robey, "The Prime Minister of Mirth" at the Hippodrome? No! Good heavens! But hadn't she heard that the old king, yes, King Edward that was, had loved the music-hall and went, apparently, to visit in secret, but of course now it was quite proper to go, even among the upper classes. She really must make a point of seeing him; no, not the king, the Prime Minister of Mirth, the next time she was there. Now would she care for more fruited jelly, or perhaps a meringue, ice-cream or a custard in a glass, while all about her the young ladies and their mamas whispered behind their hands, or their fans, that they had never seen a lady eat such enormous amounts, which was surely a sign of bad breeding. Franny Buchanan had vouched for her pedigree, saying she was of good family but really, would she act like she did, and eat like she did if her people were of the respectable class?

They seemed to make a path for him through their youthful masculine circle as he approached her, younger men showing respect for an older.

"Miss Dean." His voice was quite without expression and his face showed none of the turmoil which seethed inside him. He had just spent an hour or more sitting beside Charlotte and her mama, Charlotte already preening in what was an annoyingly proprietorial way, listening to their description of the splendours of Paris and the fashion houses from where they had just returned after viewing the styles which were heralded for the spring. He had brought them supper from the magnificent buffet and a glass of champagne each with which to wash it down but as someone, Franny he suspected, put on a record of a slow and dreamy waltz he stood up abruptly. Charlotte smiled expectantly then her mouth dropped open when he asked her politely to excuse him and walked, bold as brass, across the shining floor to where Miss . . . Miss . . . whatever her name was, was sitting. Her face flushed with outrage and only her mama's warning hand on her arm stopped her from standing up and stamping her feet as she had done so often during her childhood.

"Miss Dean, as this is a waltz and therefore more suited to my old bones, may I take you away from your . . . admirers for five minutes? That is if you have had enough to eat?" One dark eyebrow rose questioningly though no smile warmed his face.

She was visibly startled. "I'm sorry but I don't know how to waltz, Mr Buchanan. Besides, I'm—"

"Nonsense, Miss Dean, it's the simplest thing in the world. 'One, two, three; one, two, three,' and away you go."

Without further ado he took her hand and almost pulled her from her chair and, short of making a small scene, she had no choice but to stand up and move into the centre of the room with him. They were the only couple on the floor.

The hubbub in the room ceased, for in every mind, except perhaps that of Miss Charlotte Gibson, was the thought that they really did make a handsome couple. Both tall with an excellent physique, his so completely male, hers so womanly. Both dark and graceful with a sort of dynamism between them which, though perhaps not evident to them, was clearly apparent to the onlookers.

"Now then, Miss Dean." Their faces were almost level and this time he smiled, an incredible smile which lit his sombre face. His eyes were narrowed and his lips curled back across his startlingly white teeth. Lucy felt her heart do a little flip in her breast and her breath caught in her throat and she wondered giddily what on earth was wrong with her. "I'm going to put one arm about your waist like this," he went on. "You put your left hand on my right shoulder and your right hand in my left."

"I do know the position, Mr Buchanan," she said coolly.

"I realise that, Miss Dean, having seen you dance with so many young men. I'm only telling you this so as not to startle you, you understand." His eyes gleamed with mischief. "Now" – when she was fitted, in her opinion, indecently close to his chest – "I shall move my left foot forward and you will move your right foot back."

"I'm not a complete idiot, Mr Buchanan," she hissed through clenched teeth, conscious of the hardness of his thigh just for a moment against hers. His male virility, which was nothing, *nothing* like that of the young men she had danced with tonight, made her feel decidedly peculiar. And why did he hold her so close, for heaven's sake . . .

"I'm holding you close, Miss Dean, so that you can feel the rhythm of my body, if you'll forgive the impertinence, in time to the music and also where I am to lead you. Now then, let your feet move to the tempo of the music. It has, by the way, the foolish title of 'Oh, Oh, Antonio', but nevertheless is wonderful to waltz to, don't you agree?"

Could he read her mind? she thought wildly as she stumbled and, had it not been for his firm hold on her, would have fallen. His breath fanned her right ear, for she kept her face averted from his and his gloved hand seemed to burn right through the back of Mama's silvery dress.

"'One, two, three; one, two, three,' and turn . . . smoothly, Miss Dean."

"I'm trying, Mr Buchanan."

"No, you are bobbing up and down like a cork on a pond. Try to relax. I'm not about to press my embrace on you, delightful as it would be, Miss Dean." His mouth was twitching. "After all, we are attempting to waltz before a room full of people. There, let your shoulders go . . . and turn. That's better, in fact that is much better. Now, if Franny will only put on the record again, or another like it, I will have you an expert within half an hour."

He was a good dancer. Steady as a rock and yet light on his feet with a wonderful sense of rhythm, and to her amazement she found she could follow his steps quite easily and was even beginning to enjoy it. She didn't know what it was but there seemed to be some harmony linking them, a sense of shared timing, a graceful flow which soon had them drifting round the edges of the floor as though their feet were winged and they shared one flight. She didn't want it to stop and when, for the third time, Franny, at a small signal from James, again put on "Oh, Oh, Antonio", she was content to continue their dreaming progress round the room.

"Oh, come on, Aunt Franny," voices were protesting, "let's have something a bit more lively," and it was with some reluctance that James Buchanan and Lucy Dean stepped away from one another as another two-step began. He bowed.

"That was perfection, Miss Dean," he told her in a voice so soft no one but she could hear it. "If only all young ladies had your grace and rhythm."

"No, it was thanks to you, Mr Buchanan. Now I shall be able to go home and teach Margaret and Emily." Her face had a strange unfocused quality about it as if she still dwelled in that enchanted world into which the lovely strains of the music and the shared delight of the waltz had spun her.

"Indeed you will," smiling wryly, "but for now, would you care to sit and drink a glass of champagne with me?"

"I'm not at all tired, Mr Buchanan. I find I could dance all night."

"I'm sure you could, Miss Dean, but I would be glad of a chance to engage you in some idle conversation if you could bring yourself to put up with it."

She frowned and he felt again that sensation which he had never known before he met Lucy Dean and which involved a curious movement of his heart, a quickening of his breath and something he could only call a bloody foolish weakening of his knees. She was so direct, an enchanting directness which he had always thought was not a part of the female character.

"What do you call idle conversation?" she asked him. "I'm no good at this 'small talk' they all seem to feel is so necessary at a party."

"Oh, no, not small talk, just anything that takes your fancy, except fashion which I warn you I know nothing about," though he'd heard enough about it in the last hour!

"That makes two of us, Mr Buchanan. In fact I seem to know nothing about anything that other young ladies find so fascinating. Not that I know what that is, you understand, so I suppose that's why."

"What do you like, Miss Dean? What do you like to do?"

"I like pictures and I wish I had some." Her tone was regretful. "I enjoy the art exhibitions when they come locally and I love to read."

"So do I. Now who is your favourite painter?"

"Oh, that's easy. I have no particular favourites among them but the French Impressionists . . . well, I could stand in front of Monet's *Woman with Umbrella* for hours on end."

"I'm the same about Renoir's *Near the Lake*. Now what else pleases you?" he went on autocratically.

"I love walking and climbing as high as I can."

"So do I. We have much in common, it seems."

"Do you really like climbing?" She was clearly startled.

"I'm not quite so decrepit as you seem to think, Miss Dean. I often put on a pair of stout boots, a few sandwiches in my rucksack and climb up to . . ."

"Where? Where? What is your favourite?" Her bright interest intoxicated him.

By this time he had manoeuvred her into a chair in a quiet corner of the room with a glass of champagne in her hand and, after warning her sternly, as though she were a child, not to drink it too quickly or it would go to her head, encouraged her to tell him all he longed to know about Lucy Dean.

"You tell me what you like to read first then I'll tell you where I like to climb. Is that a deal?"

She smiled then leaned back in her chair, putting her hands together and bringing them to her lips as she considered the question, staring out over the heads of the dancers, for by this time supper was over and a military two-step was being performed with more enthusiasm than grace. Franny Buchanan was always generous with her champagne and as Olivia Askew murmured to Laura Kendall, there'd be tears before bedtime if Marion Mossop drank another drop. The young men, those dancing and those lounging about the room, constantly turned their heads in the direction of Lucy Dean and James Buchanan, wondering what a spiffing, fun-loving girl like Miss Dean was doing with an elderly gent like Mr Buchanan, or Uncle James as some of them knew him. She was talking nineteen to the dozen, but so seriously they really could not believe she was having a good time.

Should they rescue her? Job muttered to Roger, but James Buchanan was his mother's brother; of the next generation and it might be thought ill-mannered simply to go up to them and ask her to come and dance. Aunt Franny had put on a record of what was very new and called ragtime, again from the London show which was transforming the world of popular music, and everyone's feet were tapping, even those of the older guests.

"Mr Buchanan," she was saying, "I really have no one preference. There are so many I love. Jane Austen, of course, and Charlotte Brontë. I adore *David Copperfield* and Dumas's *The Count of Monte Cristo* but . . . yes, I think I must say Tolstoy's *Anna Karenina*. I know it is a story of adultery but how can one pass judgement on those sad lovers. Anna is so . . . so . . ."

"Rebellious, Miss Dean?" His lips curled up in what she was beginning to recognise as humour.

"Oh, not just that. Courageous, maligned . . ."

"Aah, maligned. You have some sympathy with her then, Miss Dean? Perhaps because she was married to an older man. A beautiful young woman . . . ?"

Lucy found she was quite intrigued by this unusual man and also that she was enjoying their conversation enormously. It was the most sensible she had engaged in this night. The gentlemen seemed to concern themselves only with the fox-hunt they were to take part in the next day and the ladies what they were to wear at a charity ball to be held in Fellthwaite Assembly Rooms in a week or so.

She leaned forward confidentially and those watching held their breath, for it seemed she might put her hand on James Buchanan's knee.

"Oh, no, Mr Buchanan, I don't think that signifies. I don't think age counts if two people truly love one another."

"You are a romantic, I think, Miss Dean."

"Am I, Mr Buchanan?"

"Indeed you are and none the worse for it, I'd say."

There was a gleam of something in James's velvet grey eyes which might have been a reflection from one of the many lamps that stood about the room, or it might have been satisfaction, but before Lucy could even wonder about it, Franny's voice broke into the small circle of agreement that had developed between Lucy Dean and James Buchanan, breaking the slender thread which had linked them together.

"Now then, James, I cannot allow you to commandeer Miss Dean any longer and don't glare at me like that," a remark which bewildered Lucy and infuriated James. "There are half a dozen young men dying to dance with her."

"But does she want to dance with them, Franny?" James's voice was as smooth as silk but his eyes had narrowed and turned to the leaden grey of pewter.

"Now you know that's not how it works, James. Besides, there are more than a few young ladies who would be delighted to take a turn round the floor with you."

Franny could see it in his eyes and the way his lips firmed that he was longing to say, "Bugger the lot of them," but he was a guest in her house and he knew his duty. He stood up reluctantly, conscious of a horde of eager, younger men at his back.

He bowed to Lucy. "Perhaps the next waltz, Miss Dean, or would you like me to show you how to tango properly?" His look was severe as though she were badly in need of a lesson or two. Her own expression was bewildered but all she said was, "Thank you, sir."

They had all gone, Marion Mossop, as Olivia Askew had prophesied, tearfully begging Mrs Buchanan to believe that she had had the most wonderful time of her life. The young men were beseeching Miss Dean to tell them when they would dance with her again and would she consider coming with them on the fox-hunt tomorrow? They were to meet at the Fox in Chapel Stile and they would be overjoyed to see her.

They were nonplussed and suddenly speechless when she told them gravely that she attended her papa's services on Sunday.

Only James remained after standing with Alex and Franny to see her into the Vauxhall, to her great astonishment, his eyes dark as the night as they looked into hers.

"Until the next time, Miss Dean. I have yet to tell you what my favourite climb is and perhaps, if you are agreeable, we might do it together?"

"Oh, yes . . . of course . . . yes. Well, goodnight."

They sat, the three of them, Alex, Franny and James, in Alex Buchanan's study before the warm glow of the applewood fire, sipping a whisky nightcap apiece, and it was quite five minutes before anyone spoke.

"So, James Buchanan, you realise, do you not, that

you have lost all hope of winning the hand of the charming Charlotte?"

Franny, her shoes kicked off, her feet resting on the broad back of Alex's black and white English setter who lay, head on paws, before the fire, smiled roguishly through her glass at her brother-in-law.

He smiled back, a lazy, satisfied smile, and she thought how attractive he was and if he had not been her husband's cousin she would have done her feminine best to take him as a lover.

"Do you know, Franny, I find I can't care very much about that."

"You made it pretty obvious, old chap." Alex's voice was slow and deep. "And what, if one might be so bold as to ask, are you to do about the luscious Lucy? You also made it clear you were . . . shall we say smitten by her charms, which I must say are quite splendid."

"Now look here, Alex." James's face had turned to thunder. "I'll have no slurs cast on Miss Dean, nor sly innuendos regarding her charms." His voice was menacing. "What I am to do about her is my business and mine alone and—"

"Then you are to do something, James?" Franny put in, her voice soft, her eyes narrowing, her expression one of keen interest.

"Again, that is my concern."

"Which means you are," Alex burst out incredulously, "otherwise you'd deny it at once."

"Will you two stop trying to make me say something which . . . Goddammit, just because I spend a few minutes talking to a beautiful girl does not mean I am to . . . to . . ."

"Yes, to what?"

93

James sprang to his feet and the dog lifted his handsome head and looked at him reproachfully, then replaced it on his paws. His eyes swivelled from one person to another then came to rest adoringly, unwinkingly on his master.

"This is bloody ridiculous. I'm off," James proclaimed. In his voice was a ring of bluster and yet uncertainty as though he were revealing too much of his inner thoughts; then, just as suddenly, he sat down again. Franny and her husband exchanged glances.

James sighed then took a steadying sip of his whisky before he resumed speaking.

"I suppose it will be all over Fellthwaite, Ambleside and Grasmere by morning what a fool James Buchanan made of himself over a pretty face, but you see, she's not just that to me. Granted she is a beautiful young woman . . ." He paused and across his face flitted an expression Franny could only call fatuous, then, shaking himself as vigorously as a dog coming from water, as if he were throwing off some enchanted picture that was bemusing his mind, he continued, his voice soft.

"But she is not just beautiful. She has a mind of her own, unclogged with all the rubbish young ladies of the day seem to find appropriate."

"We noticed that, lad. Calls a spade a bloody—"

"Alex," Franny warned, but it seemed James had retreated again into some secret bewitched world where Lucy Dean had unwittingly thrust him and did not notice.

"She's bright and clever. Her brain is as sharp as that of any man . . ."

"Dear sweet Christ," Alex muttered under his breath.

". . . and given the chance she could become . . . well, anything she set her heart on. She's forthright, I grant you that. I call her honest. She's sensible, practical and, unlike many girls, has no airs and graces and false pride. She has a sense of humour and, if you'd seen her with her family you would know at once what love and loyalty she gives to them. She has lived in a cloistered world, even more so than most girls of her class, but she is not pedestrian. I have never met anyone like her."

He lifted his head and glared as though to dare either one to argue with him.

"I know I have done Charlotte Gibson a grave injustice. I have given her and her parents reason to believe that I might be considered as a serious suitor. I suppose the whole district was aware of it and will call me a bastard of the first order for my ungentlemanlike behaviour but I can do nothing about it. I have offended them, I know I have, and if I could apologise I would but it would hardly do to go round there and say I'm sorry but I no longer wish to press my suit – what a stupid expression – since I now find I'm—"

He stopped speaking abruptly. There was a silence filled with awkwardness and Alex fidgeted, uncomfortable with his cousin's evident emotion.

Franny sat up, putting her feet to the ground. She drained her whisky glass then placed it carefully on the low table beside her and said quietly, "What are you to do then, James? About Miss Dean, I mean? It seems there is something on your mind."

"I will call on her father tomorrow . . . No, he will be busy, it being Sunday. On Monday then, I shall call and ask his permission to – hell's teeth, it sounds so bloody trite, stilted – to pay court to his daughter, and I'd be obliged if you'd keep it to yourselves for the moment."

Alex sat up slowly, his face slack with shock. "You mean to marry her? That gauche, unpolished child, that naïve, unworldly, unsuitable . . . Oh, she's lovely, I grant you that and no doubt your bed will be sweet with her in it, but, James, lad, she won't do. Not for you. You need a woman to run your house. Confound it, you can't mean to marry . . ."

"I do and if you say one more word against her I'll ram your teeth down your bloody throat."

5

The Reverend Edward Dean was surprised and not a little annoyed, since he was busy cataloguing some new butterflies when Elsie, clearly overwhelmed by the importance of the visitor in the hall, piped that there was a Mr Buchanan to see him.

"What does he want, Elsie?" the rector asked her and she shook her head wonderingly, for would a fine gentleman like Mr Buchanan confide in kitchen maid Elsie Blount the reason for his visit.

"Nay, sir, that I couldn't say."

"Is . . . is he alone?" though what that had to do with anything Elsie failed to see. He was a funny old stick and no mistake, was the rector. More like a lad than a grown man which was why Elsie was so at ease with him. He never shouted or made her feel stupid but spoke pleasantly, politely, almost as though Elsie were as good as he was but she never, and never would, take advantage of his goodness and kindness. She knew her place, did twelve-year-old Elsie.

"Yes, sir, all alone. Them dogs of 'is is safely i'n't motor fastened wi' a lead ter't door 'andle. 'E's got top up an' all as it looks like rain."

Failing to see the significance of this remark the reverend gentleman looked about him vaguely.

"Yer remember last time," she prompted.

"Last time?"

"Aye, them dogs an' Thimble caused a right old rumpus. Made sure it don' 'appen again, Mr Buchanan 'as."

"Mmm . . . well . . . I see . . ." though he didn't, Elsie recognised that.

"Is my daughter at home, Elsie?" he continued. "Perhaps she could speak to Mr Buchanan."

"No, sir, she an't childer've gone ter see old Mrs Seaton." She nearly added, "poor old soul" for a visit from the Dean family was like being invaded by the hordes of China. Not that Elsie knew anything about the hordes of China but she'd been in the nursery one day when Miss Lucy had told the children about them. "'Sides, 'e ses 'e wants ter see thi' particular like."

Edward Dean sighed. "Show him in then, Elsie."

Elsie sketched a curtsey. "Rightio, sir. Will I fetch tea?"

"I suppose you'd better."

Though November had just whistled in on a bitter wind straight from the North Pole, or so said Mrs Hutton, shivering by the kitchen fire, there was little warmth in the Reverend Dean's study. There were several pieces of coal in the grate flickering bravely against enormous odds, but there might as well have been no fire at all for all the heat it threw out, or so James thought as the rector waved him politely to a chair before it. Reverend Dean still held a sheaf of papers in his hand just as though the moment his visitor had gone he would at once resume whatever he had been doing and therefore it was not worth putting them away.

Tea arrived, hot certainly but so weak James was positive he could see the roses painted on the outside of the cup through the liquid. Nevertheless he drank it valiantly down. Neither he nor the rector were *au fait* with the customs, so important to the ladies, of calling on one another, of taking tea, or not taking tea, all the protocol which one generation passed down to another, and so they sipped and told one another what an extremely cold day it was and expressed the hope that the approaching winter would not be too fierce. It usually was, of course, up here in Lakeland, snow making its appearance soon after Christmas, or sometimes before, with great drifts reaching the eaves of the low cottages so that folk were snowed in for weeks on end.

Edward Dean did his best to be courteous, wondering in his detached way what on earth had brought James Buchanan to his home again. It was nothing to do with his will. That was the first thing he had asked as he had shaken Mr Buchanan's hand, but no, that had been signed, witnessed and was all in order, Mr Buchanan assured him.

There was the clatter of feet on bare boards as someone ran upstairs singing a chorus of "O God our help in ages past" which James supposed was appropriate considering whose home this was, then clattered down again. A door opened and a cheerful voice, possibly that of the skivvy who had let him in, proclaimed, "I found it. It were in Master—" The rest of the sentence was cut off as the door banged to again. Even the servants in this house appeared to behave as ebulliently and with the same amount of noise as the family who resided here.

Edward Dean, his repertoire of small talk exhausted, began to fidget, doing his best not to let Mr Buchanan see his impatience to be back with his butterflies.

At last his visitor drew a deep breath, like a man about to dive head first into murky waters, and began. "It was kind of you to see me without prior arrangement, Reverend Dean, but I felt I should speak to you first before approaching your daughter. It is customary, I believe, in the circumstances, and I would like to do this thing properly." He drew in another deep breath and let it out gustily.

"This thing?" Clearly Edward Dean was mystified, not only by the content of Mr Buchanan's conversation but by his reference to his daughter.

"Yes. It's a matter of some delicacy and I hope you will bear with me." He cleared his throat and scowled. "I have never done this before, sir, so I beg you to forgive me if I seem somewhat precipitate."

"Of course." The rector smiled encouragingly though he had not the slightest idea what Mr Buchanan was getting at.

James steadied himself. He had come here on an honest mission, one not undertaken lightly and he wished to make a good show of himself. What he had to offer was worthy of any young lady's consideration. Without false modesty he knew himself, along with his cousins, Paul and Andrew, both still unmarried, to be an eligible man in the marriage market. There were a dozen young ladies in the district about Fellthwaite, Ambleside and Grasmere from whom he could pick a wife. He was a very wealthy man. He had a magnificent home, servants by the score and, not to put too fine a point on it, was endowed with reasonable good looks. In other words he was a good catch. He had property and businesses in many parts of the Lakeland and beyond. His forebears had given service to succeeding monarchs in the protection of the borders against the wild, marauding Scots and for this they had been rewarded and allowed to retain their rights as landowners, calling themselves Estatesmen, shortened to Statesmen. They were proud men, those who farmed in Cumberland and Westmoreland, true yeoman class since the days of Elizabeth. They were well-educated men for the most part, gaining degrees at the university of their choice, in engineering, the law and medicine since his cousin Paul had just qualified as a doctor.

"Is . . . is Miss Dean at home, sir?" His voice softened as he spoke her name.

"Oh, it's Lucy you want to see." With great relief the rector stood up, his eyes already straying to the sheaf of papers in his hand.

"No, sir, no. It's about Lucy . . . Miss Dean, that I'm here." James's face which, in his dealings with men of business never gave away an inkling of his thoughts, remaining cool, self-controlled and smooth at all times, revealed his anxiety now. He felt somewhat foolish, which he didn't like and yet at the same time his heart raced and his throat was dry. He wondered why, since he had never suffered with nerves. It was a measure of the effect Lucy Dean had on him, he supposed, and the sooner this was settled the better he would like it.

"Aah." Reverend Dean sat down again slowly and a frown began to crease his face.

"Yes. This is a . . . complex situation and one I'm confident you will treat with discretion. I appreciate that Miss Dean and I have only recently become acquainted but I . . . my feelings for her are . . . Sir, I would like to get things . . . finalised as soon as possible." He paused, then began again. "I am a well-set-up man, sir, and I have the means to give a good life to the lady who becomes my wife. I'm thirty-four years old and I know Lucy . . . Miss Dean is only eighteen or nineteen but I'm healthy and good for years yet so . . ."

Edward gasped. "You are saying you want to marry my daughter?" He fell back in his chair, every vestige of colour leaving his face. It was apparent that he was not only surprised but badly shocked.

"I do, sir. And may I add . . ." James looked down at his hands which he had not realised were tightly clenched, then up again at the rector and in his eyes was an expression the Reverend Dean instantly recognised. He had seen it twice before: in the lovely golden depths of those of his Evelyn, and in his own reflection in the mirror when he thought of her.

His colour came back and he smiled. "Yes, Mr Buchanan?" His voice was very gentle.

"I have never said this before, sir. I have never felt like this before but . . . well . . ." God, why was he acting like some callow youth confessing his first love, and the truth was, that was how he felt. And yet it was not so, not really. He was a mature man. His feelings for Lucy, though so new, were strong, rooted deep, true and steady and enduring, and as a man he could only say so. First to her father, then to her. He took a deep breath.

"I . . . I have a high regard for your daughter, sir. I can give her far more than material things. She will be safe with me, and cared for. I will not part her from her family. She will, of course, live at Howethwaite," he added hurriedly, the enchanting image of Lucy Dean – Lucy Buchanan – moving about his home, sleeping in his bed, temporarily silencing him, then he went on. "But she can come here as often as she likes: every day if she wishes. Her family will not suffer. You will not suffer her loss, sir, for I give you my word—"

Edward Dean raised his hand, looking in surprise at the papers there as though wondering where they had come from, then he returned his kindly gaze to James.

"Mr Buchanan, Mr Buchanan, please, let us both stop and catch our breath. I will admit to you that it would give me the greatest pleasure to see my daughter, all my daughters, safely and happily married to a good man."

James began to smile, thinking the battle won, his breath easing out on a great sigh of relief. He had the rector's approval and that was a great step in the wooing of Lucy Dean, but the reverend gentleman had not yet finished.

"But there is someone else who should be part of this . . . these arangements and that is Lucy herself."

"Of course, but . . ."

"So until I have spoken to her . . ."

"Of course, sir, I understand that."

A gust of wind rattled the windows and the curtains lifted dramatically and James, with that part of his brain not totally involved with his courtship of Lucy Dean, had time to speculate on the necessity of getting the frames fixed as soon as he and Lucy were married. A handful of sleety rain followed the wind, and smoke billowed from the chimney carrying particles of soot, which settled in the hearth. By God, the sooner he could get her out of this crumbling old rectory and settled in the warm comfort and luxury of his home the happier he would be. He had been reasonably warm when he entered the room but now his feet were solid blocks of ice and he had to stop himself from blowing into his cupped hands and flapping his arms like a duck about to fly.

There was a long and pregnant silence. The rector in his preoccupation had gone so far as to place his papers on the table next to him. He pulled at his lower lip as though deeply perplexed, staring into the fire which, if something wasn't done about it soon, would go out completely. James waited and at last Edward Dean looked up at him.

"Mr Buchanan, I can make no promises except to say that I will speak to Lucy first. She will . . . she has no idea . . . It will be a shock to her. She is very dear to me as she is to us all . . ."

"I appreciate that, sir."

"But I cannot say what her answer will be."

"But . . . do you approve of me as a prospective husband?" A thrill ran through him as he spoke the last word.

Edward Dean looked surprised. "I cannot say that either, Mr Buchanan, since I barely know you. Oh, I am aware of your family, which is well respected in this area. You seem to be a . . . a decent man, forgive me if

I'm blunt. And you are certainly endowed with more than your share of life's fortune. You have treated me courteously and though, from what I hear, you have no need of it, you have honourable employment. But I am ignorant of your character, your nature. I know you are not a church-goer . . . no, oh, no, please" – holding up his hand as James would have interrupted – "that is of no concern to me. Some of the most devout can be hard family men and the opposite can apply. All that concerns me is Lucy's happiness. She is not an ordinary young woman, Mr Buchanan."

"I realise that, sir."

"She is very like her mother. Put her with a man who would not appreciate and understand her unique qualities and I do believe she would wither away like blossom on a branch. She needs to live in . . . warmth. Do you know what I am saying, Mr Buchanan?"

"Yes, sir, I do. Loving warmth."

"Exactly."

"She will be loved and cared for, sir. She is very . . . dear to me."

"I am beginning to believe you, Mr Buchanan."

"Then may I . . . ?"

"You may try, Mr Buchanan, but if I see that your attentions are not pleasing to her I will put a stop to them. Is that fair?"

"It is, sir, and thank you. Now, if I may, I would like a word with Miss Dean. No, please, sir. I only mean to ask her, and perhaps Edward, or indeed any of the children who would care to come, if they would like to do some hill walking before the winter truly sets in. Perhaps up to Loughrigg Fell from Ambleside. Miss Dean did say she liked to walk and climb."

"Indeed she does, and if I'm not mistaken that is Lucy and the children now. They have been sick visiting."

From a chilly peace the house seemed to explode into a noise which at once gave the feeling of warmth and movement as though those who invaded it had brought their own heating system with them. James could hear his own dogs barking at the front of the house and was glad he had had the foresight to leash them, for it seemed whenever they encountered the Dean family their manners deserted them.

"We're absolutely starving, Buffy," he heard young Edward bellow, just as though whoever it was he was addressing were in Carlisle. "Has Mrs Hutton made those scones she promised?"

There was a murmuring which James did not catch.

"Well, I could eat a dozen," a younger voice added, "with strawberry jam and cream."

"Fat chance of that, lad."

"And don't be so greedy, Percy Dean," a prim young girl's voice admonished him, probably that of . . . Emily, was that her name?

A faint scream sounded from the kitchen as the Dean children advanced on its occupants and another voice, a young woman's voice, told them to behave themselves or she'd tan the lot of them. There was much laughter at this remark followed by silence as a door banged to, though James was convinced he could hear the shrill tones of Thimble beyond it.

Suddenly the study door was flung open and Lucy Dean burst in with the force of a whirling dervish, glowing, red-cheeked, her polished chestnut hair tumbling about her neck and dangling a bright blue ribbon.

She looked absolutely glorious, James had time to decide, shining with joy and good health, due no doubt to the brisk gallop she and the children had been forced into in order to beat the sleet which was now lashing against the windows, then she saw him and her jaw dropped, whether in amazement or dismay he could not tell. It was evident that she and her brothers and sisters must have come into the house through a back or side door or she would have seen his motor.

"Papa," she had been just about to say but changed it to, "Mr Buchanan, what on earth are you doing here? We weren't expecting you, were we?" she asked him accusingly.

James sprang to his feet as she entered the room, that stern look almost of disapproval darkening his face, and not for the first time Lucy wondered what she had done to displease him.

"No, Miss Dean, I was passing and took a chance on Reverend Dean being available. Just a small matter I wished to discuss with him but now I must get on, if you'll excuse me."

Lucy looked enquiringly at her father but it seemed he was not about to explain and neither was Mr Buchanan.

"I see," she said, though she obviously didn't.

"Will you see Mr Buchanan out, Lucy?" Papa asked her, making no attempt to take his guest's hand but nodding politely as he took his leave.

At the front door James hesitated. The hubbub in the kitchen continued, threaded with the shrill barking of the puppy and he wondered if there was ever peace and tranquillity in this house. It was all very well to be full of high spirits. It was one of the things about Lucy that drew him to her but the constant commotion would drive him mad, he told himself, and if he could manage it he would keep the visits of Lucy's family to his own home when they were married to the minimum. In the meanwhile there was still something he wanted to ask her.

"Miss Dean, do you remember at Mrs Buchanan's dance you told me you liked to climb?"

"Yes." She was clearly puzzled.

"I was wondering whether you would like to attempt Sergeant Man with me tomorrow. If the weather is fine, of course," he added hastily, "and you are not otherwise engaged."

Lucy, still looking puzzled, studied his face, noting once again that he seemed to find it hard to allow even the smallest smile to light his face. He was so serious, so stern, like a forbidding schoolmaster who was dealing with a recalcitrant pupil. And yet his eyes were soft, like grey velvet, she thought, set so beautifully among thick brown lashes. They really were his best feature and, though he was probably not aware of it, revealed feelings which his stern face did not. Not that she recognised what those feelings were but they were obviously of a kindly nature.

She smiled, her sweetly shaped mouth, which looked as it had on the first day he met her, bee-stung with kisses, parting over her even white teeth.

"Yes, I would, Mr Buchanan. Thank you for asking me."

"A pleasure, Miss Dean. Perhaps nine o'clock if that is not too early for you?"

"That would be splendid, Mr Buchanan."

"Until then, Miss Dean." He bowed, ran lightly down the steps, climbed into his motor car and roared away up the drive.

"Well now, Papa," she said as she returned to the study. "What was all that about? With Mr Buchanan, I mean? Not another legal matter? Surely you are not considering changing your will?"

"No, child, not my will, but something to which I must give a great deal of thought."

She was astonished. "Why, Papa, what can you and Mr Buchanan have discussed that causes you so much concern? We're . . . we're not in trouble, are we?" Her expression turned to one of anxiety and her father smiled and held out his hand to take hers.

"No, dearest. No trouble, but a problem I must wrestle with for a day or two. I promise I'll discuss it with you then."

James Buchanan was seriously dismayed and not a little put out to find not just Lucy waiting on the steps for him the next day but her brothers and sisters as well, not to mention the damned dog. But with his usual talent for hiding his feelings, whatever they might be, he politely helped them to cram themselves into the motor car, pushing aside poor Holmes and Watson who had had the back seat all to themselves. The two big dogs found, to their mortification and sad loss of dignity, that they must perch on the children's knees while the scrap called Thimble crawled over everybody, which nobody but James's dogs seemed to mind. Lucy sat next to James.

Their passage through the town excited much comment among the people who were that morning out and about in Ambleside. Well, you could hardly miss that enormous machine which James Buchanan drove at such terrifying speeds and when it was filled with singing children and barking dogs you would have to be deaf and blind not to notice. Who were they? You could see the open-mouthed wonder in the eyes of those who stood and stared as the Rolls-Royce thundered by, though the two ladies who were just about to enter a rather smart bow-fronted shop in Market Place knew exactly who was being driven by James Buchanan.

Charlotte and Mrs Gibson had made an early start that morning. It would be Charlotte's birthday in a week's time and she was to have a party to which James Buchanan was not invited, though others of his family were. Though her new evening gown had been made for her in Paris when she and her mama visited there, she had taken a fancy to see what Miss Medlock, the cleverest and most stylish dressmaker in Ambleside, had in stock. Miss Medlock dressed the ladies of the district who had not the wealth, or perhaps even the inclination, to travel to Paris for their clothes. Her silks and laces were superb, her taffetas glorious, her gold brocade, her fans and muffs and sheer, pale, silk stockings, her sashes and belts much in demand. Her broderie anglaise was of the highest quality, her bead fringes, her fur trimmings, her ropes of pearls, her gloves of kid, suede and silk, some short with two buttons, some long with twenty, her stoles and boas and parasols and indeed all her splendid merchandise was of the very best quality and much sought after by her customers. She employed two clever milliners besides her seamstresses, who made hats of every shape and size, in the latest styles, naturally, hats with wide, turned-up brims of beaver, plush, velvet and straw, toques of velvet, tam o' shanters and berets, Juliet caps sequined for evening wear and bandeaux with or without feathers or plumes. Her millinery was as chic as the outfits she designed and made, and those who knew her and were dressed by her could not for the life of them understand why Miss Charlotte Gibson had to go to Paris to be clothed. Just to be able to say she did was the general consensus of opinion among the ladies, since Miss Medlock's creations were just as stylish.

Charlotte and her mother watched, like the rest, their mouths hanging open as the Rolls sped through Market Place. James raised his cap to them as he swung on to the Rydal road. The motor was travelling at some speed by the time it passed Armbroth Hall where Janet and Angus Gunson and their four sons lived. The song the occupants had chosen for some reason was "Rule Britannia" and the sound of it rang out on the air even after the motor car had disappeared round the bend.

"Well, did you see that?" Mrs Gibson gasped unnecessarily, clutching her daughter's arm. "It was that dreadful Dean girl and, one presumes, her brothers and sisters. What can James be thinking of, making a spectacle of himself in such a way? And to tip his cap at us, too, as if he didn't want us to miss him. As if we could. You would think a gentleman in his position would—"

"Be quiet, Mama." Charlotte spoke through gritted teeth. "There is no need to carry on about it." Her face had turned bone white except for a streak of red temper high on each cheekbone, a sign her mother recognised with some trepidation.

"But, my dear, what is he doing consorting with that girl when he could have had the daughter of—"

"That's enough, Mama. Not another word."

"But he has belittled you in the eyes of—"

"Mama, I swear if you say another word I shall strike you, right here in the middle of Ambleside. And let me add that what James Buchanan has done to me will not be forgotten."

Mrs Gibson's face became even more bewildered. "What on earth are you talking about, child?"

Charlotte's voice was vicious. "I shall make it my business to see that he and that . . . that woman suffer for humiliating me as they have done. I shall find out something; anything, I don't know what. There must be, there *will* be a secret one of them wishes to keep hidden. No, I don't know what, Mama," as her mother would have begged her to tell her what she meant. "But I shall find it out, and, I don't care how long it takes, I shall humiliate them as James Buchanan has humiliated me. All our friends were . . . were aware of his interest in me and now . . . Dear God in heaven . . ."

"Charlotte, please darling, someone will hear you." Mrs Gibson glanced round in anguish. She and Arthur had had a terrible time with their daughter ever since Franny Buchanan's dance. Tantrums, screams of tearful rage at being deserted by James for that shameless vulgarian, and in front of all their friends, too. She would not be treated like this, she had shrieked and her papa must drive over to Howethwaite and tell James so. In her mind, as it had been in others', it had been only a matter of time before James Buchanan would speak for her. A spring wedding, she had planned. A honeymoon in Italy. She would be Mrs James Buchanan, mistress of Howethwaite which, though not as grand as her parents' house, was old and venerable and at the same time filled with the luxurious comforts she had always known. Now it seemed that James's attention had been captured by the appallingly dressed, appallingly mannered daughter of a local rector, and to prove that it was to be taken seriously, by the rector and by James's family, he had just driven past for all the world to see with the rector's lot stuffed in the back of his motor car and the rector's daughter preening herself beside him. Charlotte had hoped that by omitting him from the guest list for her nineteenth birthday next week he would come to his senses; realise that he was being punished, cast out from the Gibson circle and, seeing the error of his ways, return penitent to throw himself on her mercy. She would make him grovel, then forgive him charmingly, and her plans for him would proceed. Now it seemed he did not care and she wanted to kick and scream and break something as she had done as a child.

"They will pay for this," she hissed, taking her mother's arm with fingers which pinched cruelly and hurrying her towards the Salutation Inn corner where their carriage waited.

"But we have not done our shopping," her hapless mother protested.

"Damn the shopping. I want to go home."

Meanwhile, on the road beyond Ambleside, the Rolls Royce, its occupants either singing or barking, continued steadily along the north side of Rydal Water where the birches, bright and delicate among the heavier foliage of beech and oak, larch and ash, lined the shores and inlets. Autumn colours fading now but still beyond description as the blueness of the sky and water merged. On past Grasmere Lake, through Town End where Dove Cottage stood and on to the village of Grasmere itself.

"Will she be able to manage it, d'you think, sir?" Edward asked presently. Even he, staunch devotee of the magnificent motor car and the wonders which lay beneath its bonnet, looked somewhat strained as he hung over Lucy's shoulder. He had wanted to sit beside Mr Buchanan, two motoring enthusiasts together, but Mr Buchanan had been most insistent that Lucy sat next to him, since he could not stand the thought of talking engines and miles per hour with a squirt like Edward all the way up to where they were to get out. Edward had sighed but took it in good part and he and the others, with the three dogs, had no option but to cram themselves in behind.

"Manage what, Edward?" James was always patient.

"The climb to Goody Bridge, sir."

"Oh, we shan't go that far, lad. I'll leave the motor in Grasmere and we'll set out from there."

It was a splendid day to be out, a clear day with the light spreading along the summit of Sergeant Man. Below them as they progressed through the waist-high valleys of autumn bracken they could see the brilliance of Rydal Water, a silvery calm as sunlight travelled across it. On wild days it would be rippled with fast eddies blown by the wind but today it was as gentle and soft as silk. It was edged with reeds, and groves of silver birch added magic to a scene already superlatively lovely and the intense green of the little pastures between created a mosaic of colour that beggared description. The waterfall which cascaded from Easedale Tarn, the run called Sour Milk Gill because of its similarity to sour milk as it scrambled down the mountain, thundered on their right, the spray from it misting about them and scattering them with diamond drops.

They paused at Easedale Tarn itself to give Percy a rest, sitting in quiet contemplation of the scene before them, their backs to the trunks of trees, comfortable in the softness and vivid, multicoloured carpet of the fallen leaves, the dappled surface of the peaceful tarn having almost a hypnotic effect on their bemused senses. A low and solitary rock pierced the glassy smoothness and standing on it was a heron, patient, motionless, silent as a sentinel, its yellow eye following the movement of a brown trout in the water and James wondered out loud at seeing the bird so high on the fell. Even the dogs, which had raced madly hither and yon in a euphoria of delight, lay still, their tongues hanging from their panting mouths, their sides heaving.

"I'll put Holmes and Watson on a leash here. You take Holmes, Miss Dean, as he's the quieter of the two and the boy can take Watson. And I'll see to this little ruffian," advancing on the unsuspecting Thimble.

"Why, Mr Buchanan? Why must they be leashed? There are no sheep hereabout," Lucy protested as she reluctantly took Holmes's leash from him.

"Because I'm going to teach Thimble – God what a name," shaking his head in mystified disbelief at whoever had christened him, "some manners."

Instantly Lucy bristled at the slur cast on the puppy's name. "What's wrong with Thimble, may I ask? It was because he was so small that we called him that, and anyway, can it be more foolish than Holmes and Watson?"

James frowned, evidently not caring for her criticism. "Perhaps you're right but that's not the issue here. The puppy must learn to walk to heel and there'd be no chance at the moment that he'd behave with my two capering about. Now don't look so woebegone, all of you. Anyone would think I was going to give him a thrashing. I promise I won't hurt him but I must be firm."

It did not take Thimble long to become aware that he had met his match in James Buchanan. For the first ten minutes as they followed the rocky path up through the endless bracken beyond Belles Knott, named the Matterhorn of Easedale because of its sharp peak, to the stretch of grass which lay below Codale Tarn, the dog pulled and pranced and whined to be free and each time James steadied him with a jerk and a sharp word.

"Oh, not so hard, Mr Buchanan," Lucy begged, but he would not give in.

"Miss Dean, unless we persevere you will have a dog who will be a puppy all his life. He is not hurt, only infuriated at being made to do what he doesn't want to do. I'd be obliged if you'd drop behind so that he can't see you. When we get beyond the tarn I'll let him off."

Thimble dragged along disconsolately after that, evidently deciding he might as well submit to it. All five Deans were vastly impressed but also relieved when Mr Buchanan decided that Thimble had had enough for one day but they were to continue with the lessons each day, he told them, with little hope that he would be obeyed, until the pup would walk beside them, even without his lead.

They all agreed that it was a grand day. Progress beyond Codale Tarn seemed to be barred by slanting tiers of rock but Mr Buchanan said that they would come very soon to a remarkable grassy shelf, wide as a road, running up from the foot of Lang Crag, affording a simple way to the easier ground above. Percy was tiring and when, at the summit marked by a stone cairn, they had eaten the simple lunch each had brought and had a rest, James packed his rucksack and rose to his feet. To their surprise he instructed the small boy to climb on to a waist-high rock. Percy, bewildered, did so, then, on being told arbitrarily to "hop up, lad" found he was on Mr Buchanan's broad shoulders from where he had the best view of them all. They could just make out, turning in a slow circle, the high, shrouded peak of Skiddaw to the north, Helvellyn, High Street, Loughrigg Fell, Coniston Old Man, Scafell and High Raise, range upon range of rolling fells stretching out to the far horizons, vivid and silent except for the call of a flock of whooper swans spreading their wings across the waters of Rydal far below.

James and Lucy did not talk much, at least to each other. She could hear him pointing things out to Percy as he strode ahead of them, the child on his shoulders. Edward and the two girls, being strong, healthy, well nourished and used to exercise, did not tire easily, even the girls making nothing of their hampering, calf-length skirts though Emily was heard to say that when women got the vote, which could not be long now, she would ask them to pass a bill allowing females to wear breeches like their brothers.

Lucy studied the strong line of Mr Buchanan's jaw which was just visible beneath Percy's clinging hands. She could see the uplifted corner of his mouth and the lean plane of one cheek and, as he glanced down at the rocky littered path, carefully placing his feet, the long curve of his dark eyelashes. His hair, which was uncovered since he had left his cap in the motor car, was a thick, untidy thatch of dark curls, not helped by Percy's careless handling of it. Strangely he didn't seem to mind and she mused on the two sides of his nature. He had been an undemanding companion, not exactly cheerful but patient and instructive, since he was a Dalesman born and bred and seemed to know every rock and beck, every plant and bird and, what was most satisfying to Lucy, appeared to find the company of her brothers and sisters bearable.

They were a tired but satisfied group as they tumbled out of the Rolls at the front door of the rectory just as the light was beginning to fade. The sky was still luminous but the trees pressed close to the square, ugly house and James wondered how long it would take him to woo and wed Lucy Dean and get her away from these dismal surroundings.

"Will you come in, Mr Buchanan," she was saying. "Perhaps a hot drink?"

The others had gone in after thanking Mr Buchanan most profusely for a splendid day, calling to Mrs Hutton that they could eat a horse if she had one to spare, but Lucy lingered on the step. She had no idea of the lovely picture she made standing with the soft light of the newly lit lamps behind her. It outlined the slipping mass of her hair, forming a golden halo through which the light shone. It darkened her eyes, which were in shadow, to unfathomable depths and touched tenderly the strong line of her waist and hips.

"No, I'd best be off. Now mind what I told you about the pup. Every day on the leash."

"Yes, Mr Buchanan," she dimpled, and bobbed a curtsey.

"I want to see him walking to heel the . . . the next time we meet." Whenever that would be!

"Yes, Mr Buchanan, sir."

"No shirking now. Remember what I told you."

"Yes, sir, I will, sir."

He was stern with her but she could see he was ready to smile. "It's been a first-rate day, Miss Dean. Perhaps we might do it again."

"I hope so, Mr Buchanan. The children did so enjoy it."

"And you?"

"Of course. It was kind of you to take the time and trouble."

He had been leaning on the bonnet of the motor, his arms crossed, watching the mass exodus of the children and Thimble, speaking firmly to his own dogs who would have followed. Now he moved slowly towards her and, she didn't know why, she felt tension move with him, almost an excitement which stirred in her as he looked up at her from the bottom of the steps.

"Perhaps next time," he said quietly, and she felt the most incredible sensation of being drawn down the steps towards him. "Perhaps we can do a more strenuous climb but it would mean we would have to do it just the two of us. I'm sure Edward could manage High Raise, which is what I propose, but I could not look after two of you. It would mean ropes and equipment, you see, for there are crags to be climbed. And it would have to be before winter sets in. What d'you say?"

He was asking her a very simple question which required a simple, "yes, please" or "no, thank you," but there seemed to be something odd in his manner, the way he stood so casually, one foot on the bottom step, his hands in his jacket pockets, confident and easy and yet as tense as a tiger about to spring. She found herself to be quite intrigued by it, intrigued and confused and yet what was there to be confused about? She supposed it was because Mr Buchanan was taking so much trouble to be kind to her and her family and she couldn't imagine why. How many gentlemen would be willing to be cluttered up with children and dogs and all the paraphernalia that a day out with them involved? He had a kind heart, she told herself. He was a good man, if somewhat reserved, and yet so were other men in Fellthwaite but none had taken an interest in the Dean family as he was doing. Why wasn't he married? she wondered, the question, coming from nowhere, surprising her, an attractive and wealthy gentleman such as he. And why, for heaven's sake, was she dithering and vacillating over what was merely an invitation to go climbing with him? She had told him of her interest in the activity and, knowing she could not do it alone, or with the children, he was inviting her to accompany him since he was keen on it too.

"You seem to be hesitating, Miss Dean. Don't you trust me?" He began to frown.

At once she was full of contrition. "Of course I do, Mr Buchanan. I was just wondering why . . ."

"Why what, Miss Dean?" His voice was expressionless.

"I would sooner put my trust in you than any man I know, Mr Buchanan," she told him seriously, meaning it, "and yes, I would love to come."

They shook hands like men, hers warm and strong in his.

"Thank you again. I'll wait to hear from you then." It was as though they were businessmen bidding one another farewell after a satisfactory deal had been struck and for a moment he was disconcerted. Then he recovered, for was this not what he wanted? Friendship to start with, then trust and a growing ease between them which would turn to something deeper.

"Soon, Miss Dean. It's November already and . . . well, I'll call you."

"Call me?" a questioning note in her voice. Her hand was still in his and he was more than happy to leave it there.

"Telephone you, if I may. I have several meetings this week—" He stopped speaking as she began to laugh. "What?"

"We have no telephone, Mr Buchanan. We have no electricity, let alone a telephone. Surely you know that? And is that the thing to say? I'll call you! How extraordinary."

For a moment he was nonplussed, as though the idea that in this day and age, since it was almost the end of 1913, there were houses still without the wonders of electricity, at least in his circle of acquaintances, was very novel. Then he shook his head at his own stupidity, smiling in wry amusement.

"I'll get in touch with you by carrier pigeon then."

"Mr Buchanan, you do make me laugh. I'm so glad you make me laugh." And on this note she took her hand from his and went indoors, laughing as she did so as though she spoke only the truth.

6

"He wishes to marry you, Lucy, and there is nothing wrong in that. His intentions are honourable. He spoke to me the other day and told me of his feelings. He has been a gentleman in all this and I respect him for it. He has been . . . a friend."

"Yes, friends, that's what we are, Papa, but no more. We have met only on – what? – two or three occasions, so how can he know that . . . how can he have decided that . . . that we should be married? That there is enough between us to . . . to lead to a stronger feeling. I'm sure I've given him no encouragement to make him believe . . . Good Lord, if I'd known, guessed, I would have . . ."

"Why are you so angry, child? There is nothing to be angry about. He has done the proper thing. He is a decent man but if you cannot accept what he offers then he will leave you alone."

"Oh, yes, Papa, that's what I want. To be left alone."

"You do not wish to become his wife?"

Lucy looked horrified. "Of course not. I don't want to be anybody's wife, not until I fall in love. And besides, Mr Buchanan is so . . . old. I really cannot imagine why he has picked on me."

She really couldn't see it. She really didn't know her own worth, her beauty, her sweetness, and her love of life that had drawn James Buchanan to her, her father realised, shaking his head. She was genuinely bewildered that he had chosen her, and it showed in her distraught manner.

"There must be dozens of girls who would be more suitable," she went on desperately. "You know what I'm like, Papa. Far too outspoken for folk like the Buchanans who demand of their women that they be demure and soft and without an opinion of their own."

"Mrs Frances Buchanan doesn't strike me as being like that, dearest, and neither would you have to be."

"Papa, do you want me to marry Mr Buchanan?" she asked him quietly.

"Only if it is right for you and only you know that, Lucy."

"Then that is the end of it. I don't wish to marry Mr Buchanan."

Even to her papa it was very evident that Lucy, just by the way she said Mr Buchanan, not James Buchanan, nor yet James, was somehow insulted by James Buchanan's offer. She thought of him as a man of another generation. Someone who a person of her generation addressed by his surname with the prefix Mr in front of it. He had asked her to be his wife but the idea was not something she could even contemplate with any sort of composure. She was, in fact, quite appalled, just as though Bibby, or old Mr Henley from where Thimble had come, had had the presumption to imagine that Lucy Dean, who was eighteen years old, would consider him.

She was huddled in the depths of the sagging armchair which stood to one side of the fireplace in Edward Dean's study where Edward had summoned her. Her feet were tucked up beneath the hem of her skirt, her arms wrapped tightly about her knees. Her father sat opposite, grave and preoccupied. There was the usual sullen fire smouldering in the grate. Beyond the window the rain lashed down and the trees thrashed wildly in the accompanying wind, what old Bibby called a "rheumatic" wind which cut through the valley, plaguing his old bones. He was at this moment huddled up to the kitchen fire, his knees almost in the flames, a pork pie in one hand and a glass of ale in the other, "them bairns" safely tucked out of his way in the breakfast-room with Buffy Tyson in charge of them and their voracious appetites, playing some board game they favoured, and good riddance to them, cheeky little hooligans.

"Lucy, can I give you some advice," her papa asked her hesitantly. Although he was hesitant, his usual vague manner was missing. It was his practice to drift pleasantly through the days, leaving everything to his eldest daughter who seemed to thrive on it, cheerfully taking on what should have been his responsibility, but this was different. She would never get another offer like this and in his floundering way he wanted her to realise it. He would not press her, naturally, nor belabour her on how advantageous her marriage to James Buchanan would be, not only to her but to her family, but perhaps if they talked it out she would come to realise herself how suitable it would be. She was loved. That, of course, was the most important factor. She would be safe and so would his other children, for James Buchanan was not the sort of man to see his wife's brothers and sisters wanting.

"Lucy," he continued, "I'm a firm believer in not making hasty decisions," knowing as he spoke that he made none. "I really think you should give this offer . . . yes, I know he hasn't made it yet," as she looked up in surprise, "but he will and I feel you should give it some consideration."

"No, Papa, I cannot."

"Why not, child? You will live in a way which is your due. You are . . . well, I know it sounds silly in this day and age, but you are a gentlewoman, Lucy. Your mama was a great lady and Mr Buchanan can give you so much. He will take care of you."

Lucy propped her chin on her knees and stared stubbornly into the feeble blue and green flames of the fire.

"I can take care of myself, Papa. I'm no weak and foolish maiden who needs a gentleman's arm if she steps out of doors. I'm strong and sensible. Besides, if I married it would interfere with . . . well, you might as well know, Papa, I am very interested in the Women's Social and Political Union. You know of it? Yes, of course you do. There is to be a branch in Ambleside and I wish to . . . to become involved."

"Lucy, I'm not sure your mother would have approved."

"Oh, Papa, no harm will come to me. I just feel that women have rights, just like men and I'm sure Mama would agree with me."

"Well . . ."

"So now you see why I haven't time for marriage. I can look after myself . . ."

"I know that, dearest, but have you any idea how hard life could be if . . . well, I shall not say another word about it after this. I will not try to persuade you except to say that, of all people, I know the joy of a good marriage."

Lucy turned to glare at him and he wondered why she was so horrified. "Papa, it is not the same at all. You and Mama loved one another. How can you compare what you and she had with what Mr Buchanan and I would have if we married? I do not love him and I cannot marry a man I do not love."

"Of course not, child."

Her voice was very sure as she continued. "Papa, it's no good. I have . . . I have enjoyed Mr Buchanan's company on the few occasions we have been together. For an older man he is quite . . . interesting. We found we had one or two things in common when we talked at Mrs Buchanan's dance and I admit he loves the fells as much as I do but that is no basis for a marriage. You must know that. No, it is impossible. He is, I'm sure, a good man and will make some woman a splendid husband but I'm afraid it won't be me. He is not unpleasing to look at and, so they tell me, very rich and I'm sure he will have no trouble finding—"

"Lucy, you must not make light of Mr Buchanan's feelings for you in that way. You speak as though they were no more than a boy's passing fancy for a pretty girl. He struck me as being quite sincere and I feel that . . . should you refuse him he will not take it easily."

Lucy looked contrite. "I'm sorry, Papa, I did not mean to."

"I know that, child, so let's speak of it no further. You are absolutely certain that . . . ?"

"I am, Papa."

"Then we will say no more on the subject though I feel that not only will you lose Mr Buchanan's friendship but that of Mrs Buchanan who, I believe, has invited you to dine next week."

"Yes, she has, Papa but—"

"There will be no more socialising with the Buchanans from now on. You realise that. It would put Mr James Buchanan in an impossible situation. Especially when it becomes known that you have refused him."

Lucy looked distressed. "Oh, no, surely not, Papa. I will tell no one if you don't and Mr Buchanan is hardly likely to . . ."

"Dearest, you know how servants talk."

"But not ours, Papa, not ours."

"Well, let us hope for the best."

"And I don't care about going out into society, Papa. I find it does not matter to me in the least. I don't speak their language and they don't speak mine."

Edward Dean sighed. "Well then, that is the end of the matter. There is just the question of speaking to Mr Buchanan, Lucy." Her papa looked at her sadly. She returned his look, startled.

"Speaking to him? I don't understand, Papa."

"You cannot believe that you can just leave him dangling without a yes or no, child. He has asked my permission to court you which I gave on the understanding that should you find his attentions unwelcome he would be . . . informed and leave you alone."

"Then . . . you could do that for me, couldn't you, Papa?" she begged him anxiously, her face strained.

"Lucy, the man has behaved entirely properly. He has done exactly what he has said he would do. He has acted responsibly and you must do the same. He has dealt with both you and me courteously and must be treated in the same way. I shall let him know that you are aware of his interest and ask him to call when you can explain how you feel. It is only fair, Lucy."

"Oh, Papa." She found herself flinching away from the awkward picture of herself and Mr Buchanan in a room somewhere speaking of a marriage which she must refuse. She wanted to run away from it, forget she had ever met him, that all this had never happened. Go back to the relaxed and happy atmosphere of the carefree life she and her family had dwelled in over the years, but before she could do that she must speak to Mr Buchanan. Oh, dammit, why couldn't he have been satisfied with the way things were? Why did gentlemen always want . . . other things, again shying away from what those other things might be. Was it impossible for them to be merely friends with a member of the opposite sex? It seemed so and tomorrow or the next day she would be forced to tell him so and cast him from her life, she thought with a heavy heart as she slowly climbed the stairs to her own room. She needed to be alone for a little while to put all this chaos in her mind into some sort of order, though never before had she had the slightest inclination towards orderliness. She supposed she must prepare some words, those she believed a lady used when refusing a proposal of marriage from a gentleman, but really, that was not her style. She knew herself to be brutally frank and honest, hating deception, pretence and speciousness. Come right out with it, that was how she did things, but she could not be like that with Mr Buchanan. He was worth the truth and would want if from her, the truth that she did not love him in a way a woman loves a man.

A tap on the door cut into her reverie, telling her that her privacy was ended. It was Buffy and Lucy was not surprised, for Buffy had been her support, her friend in need, her critic, her conscience sometimes, ever since Mama had died. Unassuming but always there when she was needed. Sometimes it was no more than how to coax another pound of shin beef from the butcher whose bill was still unpaid, and at other times, like now, a crossroad in Lucy's life when she needed to speak of which path to take. Not that she was undecided about that. She had made up her mind and would not change it, but it might be helpful to talk it out with Buffy who had a good heart in her breast and a good head on her shoulders.

Buffy closed the door behind her, standing for a moment to study the disconsolate figure in the chair before the empty grate. It was bitterly cold and though both women had automatically thrown a shawl about their shoulders as they mounted the stairs to the icy regions of the upper floor, they were shivering.

"Your papa asked me to come in case you needed . . . something," prepared to give whatever it might be without stint. Buffy limped across the bare wooden floor and sat down on the end of the bed, waiting.

Lucy sighed and frowned at the same time, looking down at her fingers which were twisting and twining about themselves. Buffy reached out and placed her own hand on Lucy's and at once the quiet calm which was Buffy Tyson's nature lapped itself about Lucy Dean.

"He wants to marry me, Buffy. Mr Buchanan."

"Well, don't say it as though he'd asked you to commit murder, Lucy. A decent proposal of marriage is something most girls long for, and anyway, I'm not a bit surprised."

Lucy looked up at her in amazement. "You knew?"

"It was written all over him, lass, for all to see. How he felt about you."

"Well, I didn't see it. Why didn't I see it? Come to that, why didn't you warn me? I would have sent him away with a flea in his ear, I can tell you."

"Why? It's not a crime for a man to fall in love and want to marry, Lucy. And why are you so mad at him?"

"I'm not . . . mad with him, just disappointed." Lucy jumped to her feet, throwing off Buffy's restraining hand and strode to the window, pulling her shawl more closely about her. Her breath misted the glass and she rubbed it with the corner of her shawl.

"It's getting worse," she said absently, referring to the rain which pelted against the window.

"I can see that. The children are going wild being shut up in the schoolroom."

"I might take them for a walk."

"Don't be daft. You'll get soaked, and don't change the subject. We were talking about Mr Buchanan who seems to me to be a perfect gentleman and would make a splendid husband."

"Yes, perfect. For some woman he would be perfect, Buffy, but not for me. He says and does all the right things but I hardly know him. I'm sure he has all the . . . qualifications and I'm sure any woman would give her right arm for such a husband. I believe he has a . . . a gentleness underneath that gruff exterior and yet he is strong. He shows a sort of arrogance which says that no one, man or woman, will ever be his master. He'll be no woman's puppet, Buffy."

"Is that what you want then, Lucy? A puppet whose strings you can pull?"

"Don't be stupid, Buffy Tyson." Lucy's voice was flat. "When I marry it will be to a man I can respect. One who has all the qualities . . ."

"You have just described in Mr Buchanan."

"Oh, Buffy, leave me alone, please. I don't want to hurt him if he really does love me, which, by the way, he has shown no signs of doing, at least to me, but I have no choice. I don't love him. Besides, I couldn't possibly leave Papa and the children, and all of you. I am needed here and here I must stay."

The rain, which had begun early that day, and with a squally wind to help it, had begun to dash itself with increasing force, the wind howling directly at the back of the house. It became so heavy that by the end of the day a racing slick of water flowed like a small beck down each side of the house, cascading into the front garden and on to the lawn where it had begun to form a wind-tossed pool. The drumming of it on the roof could be heard distinctly even by those on the ground floor and Mrs Hutton moaned that she feared for the windows. They were rattly old things at the best of times but if this kept up she was convinced they would give way and the rain flood the house.

By morning, not having had a wink of sleep, she declared, she was even more fearful when she saw the amount of water that had collected about the house. It was still bucketing down, sweeping in a great impermeable curtain across Loughrigg and at the back of the house, the Hundreds, blotting out the high peaks until it seemed the very skies, black and surly, were pressing down on their heads. The fast-racing rainwater carried muck and mud, ripped out heather and gorse bushes and the bodies of many small fellside animals, depositing them in an appalling heap on the front lawn, and the water began to inch up the front steps of the house. Already at the back kitchen door Bibby had stacked bags of soil to prevent the kitchen from flooding, all the while bemoaning the fate of his "veggies" which were under six inches of water and with no sign of it letting up. It was almost as dark as at midnight and the only one enjoying the spectacle was Edward who longed to get out in it, fight the elements, though with what in mind he was not awfully sure.

After his Trojan effort with the sandbags Bibby settled himself by the fire declaring that, "Ah's gaan' nowhere an' the bloody 'ens'll 'ave ter fettle fer theirsenn." He worked his bum more comfortably into Mrs Hutton's chair by the fire and that's where he stayed for the rest of the day and the night, toasting his toes and telling anyone who was interested that there were plenty more sandbags in the stable if they were needed for the back door. If it got up to the windows, well, there was nowt he could do about that so best not to get in a mish-mash about it.

The following day it had stopped and the tidal wave of rainwater had receded and, sorry in a way since he had enjoyed the rest, Bibby, with the help of them hooligans, began to clear up his garden. His grandson, a strong lad of thirteen who sometimes helped him out after school with heavy jobs, lent a hand. He was surprised, and so was Bibby, when a command came from the reverend that he wanted a note delivered at once to Mr Buchanan of Howethwaite.

He was at the rectory within an hour of the note being delivered.

"I came at once, sir." His voice was eager, filled with hope, for the note had implied it was to do with Lucy. He had discarded his caped overcoat and knee-high rubber Wellington boots at the front door, handing them to an excited Elsie, for those in the kitchen had got wind, as servants do, that "something was up". Padding in his stockinged feet, he entered Edward Dean's study. They shook hands and Edward indicated that he should sit, appearing not to notice that his guest had no shoes on his feet.

It seemed, now that James was here and seated with as much comfort as the old chair and the meagre fire afforded, the rector did not know where to begin. It was a measure of his distress that he felt compelled to pick up the heavy brass poker and plunge it into the centre of the coals, for normally he would scarce have noticed if the fire was in or out.

He cleared his throat and passed his hand over his thinning grey hair, a picture of a man in some confusion and it was at this precise moment that the first small twist of doubt struck at James Buchanan's gut, though he did his best to ignore it, for the unthinkable was . . . unthinkable! He did his best to be patient while the rector hemmed and hawed and commented on the weather, hoping he had not had too tiresome a journey from Howethwaite until at last James could stand it no longer.

"You said you wanted to speak to me, sir. Is it about Miss Dean?"

Looking vastly relieved that the reason for James's visit had been so quickly reached, Edward Dean became calmer, then nodded his head.

"It is, my dear fellow. I spoke to her of our conversation."

"And . . ." James leaned forward eagerly.

"She is waiting for you in the small parlour. You know where it is?"

"Yes, sir." Before the two words were out of his mouth James was across the room and through the door.

Edward sighed sadly. So ardent, so joyful in his need at last to put before Lucy the gift of his love. His patience had been rewarded, it was written in his face and now he was to speak the words, about his feelings, about marriage, about the happiness to come for himself and Edward's daughter. Dear Lord, help him to bear the pain of his rejection, Edward prayed, his heart heavy for the man.

In the kitchen Mrs Hutton, Bibby and Elsie, who was filled with a great sense of her own importance, for had she not relieved Mr Buchanan of his coat and boots, debated on how long it would be before the wedding took place. They'd seen it coming, of course, they told one another, for no man took the trouble to be nice to a lady's brothers and sisters, as he had, unless it was serious. It would certainly take a burden from the rector's back, which was not strong at the best of times, to have a wealthy son-in-law and make a difference to them bairns who needed a bit of discipline.

"Throw another shovel of coal on't fire, Elsie," Mrs

Hutton instructed her handmaiden, in anticipation of better things to come.

The door to the room was ajar. James knocked softly and at Lucy's command, entered.

She was sitting, her head bowed as though in deep thought, by another of the Deans' lacklustre fires. She had a quilted shawl about her shoulders and he had time to gloat in his mind that soon, in the warm, fire-lit comfort of the rooms, every room at Howethwaite, she would no longer need such a thing.

She looked up as he entered, smiling, half smiling really, as though it were no more than her duty as a hostess to welcome him as a guest. He stood on the threshold and found his mind wandering from the images of her resting by his warm fireside to the consideration of why she looked so pale by her own. Her flesh was always a creamy white with little colour except when there was excitement in the air, or during vigorous exercise, but now she looked strained with shadows beneath her eyes. Her soft mouth quivered and she took her full lower lip between her white teeth. She was so exquisite. In this one girl was the promise of all he desired. She breathed exhilaration into what he saw now had been a sterile life, stimulating not only his body, but his mind. She gave him energy, inspiration, hope, captivating his senses and he could scarcely believe that the moment had come to claim her.

"Miss Dean . . . Lucy." His voice had never been so warm, so soft, so loving, allowing her to hear for the first time the depth of his feelings for her.

"Mr Buchanan." No more.

"Your father said . . ."

"Yes, yes, I know. He told me . . . I would have . . . well, we could not ask you to come sooner . . . the rain . . ." Her voice trailed away.

"I'm here now. May I sit down?"

"Oh, of course. I'm sorry . . . will you have tea?"

"I think not."

"Very well. You managed the walk then?"

"As you see," smiling at her, his eyes clouded with some buried emotion.

If only he would not smile that whimsical smile of his. If only he was not such a . . . a good person, so decent and honourable. If only there was something nasty she could focus on, something to shore up her ebbing determination and let her get through this without weakening. Not that she would weaken. She knew without a shadow of doubt that she could never marry this man, or any man while the children needed her, but she liked him and it was very difficult to hurt someone you liked deliberately. The expression on his face was unreadable and she knew he was making a decent effort to keep it neutral but his eyes, the grey of them pale as silver, not a cold silver but with a warmth in them, changing as she watched them, as they watched her, to pale misted smoke and they revealed exactly what James Buchanan wanted of her.

He took a deep breath. He supposed it was up to him to begin. Before she could answer he must ask the question so best get it over and then . . . and then, by God, he'd kiss that paleness from her cheeks, remove that drooping frailty from her lips, bring her alive as he had dreamed of doing for weeks now. God almighty! Was that all it was? Weeks! He felt as though he had been in love with Lucy Dean for all his adult life.

"You know why I'm here, Lucy, don't you? Your father has explained . . ."

"Oh, yes, Mr Buchanan, but . . ."

"No, let me speak, then. Well . . ." He took a deep breath and leaned forward in his chair so that they were almost knee to knee. He looked boyish in his haste to tell her of all that had been confined within him for so long. Ardent, and tense with his ardour, and excited too, like a lad about to have granted a youthful desire long denied him, compelling, oh, yes, and very attractive. The suave self-control of the mature man he was had melted away like mist before a breeze.

"Lucy, you know my feelings for you, don't you? No, let me finish. I've had a . . . a deep regard for you since we met in the wood. You have something in you that calls to something in me and though I don't fool myself that you feel the same way at this very moment, well . . . I think we would do very well together. I am a wealthy man. Not that I think that would matter to someone like you, but I could keep you and your family safe and . . ."

"Mr Buchanan, please don't . . ." Her cry was agonised.

James Buchanan frowned. "Don't, Lucy, but I must. I must tell you of my feelings and, of course, though I doubt it concerns you, your father will want to know that I can keep you in comfort, even luxury. You will want for nothing."

James Buchanan was an intensely reserved man who went to a great deal of trouble to hide his true feelings. He needed a wife and he thought Lucy Dean needed a husband, if only to see to that wild family of hers, but there was more, much more to him than that.

He had, under the forbidding aloofness he showed to most, a heart capable of a great romantic love. Not romantic in the manner of a tuppeny novelette but a love which wanted to, and had, put a woman, this woman, into a secret place where only he could reach her. Not hide her away, God forbid, but have the knowledge that she was committed to him, in her mind, in her soul, in everything she was, as he would be committed to her. He had, almost without knowing it, wanted, needed a woman who could give this to him and he believed he had found it in Lucy Dean. She would make him a perfect wife and, by God, he would make the perfect husband for her.

"Mr Buchanan, please, don't go any further."

"Lucy . . . ?"

"It will only make it worse for you when . . ." She was deeply distressed. "You see . . . I can't . . . That's why I asked you to come to tell you . . . I can't . . ."

"Lucy," he said again, his voice almost a whisper.

"It's out of the question, Mr Buchanan. I'm sorry."

He must have misheard her. The words she had spoken were there, in his head where his brain recognised them but they made no sense. She had not understood. She had mistaken his meaning. She thought he was saying something else. She . . . she . . . Dear sweet Christ . . . She sat there in her innocent sexuality, her eyes huge and dark with shock and . . . and . . . there was no sense to it.

Then, suddenly, there was. Then he heard them, her words of rejection and with them the hidden capability to love, to feel, to give, shrivelled and died inside him. He felt as though he had walked . . . run . . . full tilt into a brick wall that he had not previously noticed.

A wall that had not been there a moment ago. He could actually feel its impact as it slammed him back in his chair and from a great distance he watched her hand rise and reach out to him in alarm. From somewhere far away, it must be up on Loughrigg Fell it was so far away, he heard her speak his name in what appeared to be anguish and she stood up as though she would cross to him.

"Mr Buchanan, I'm so sorry." She was actually weeping though he couldn't think why. He didn't know where to hide from her. She had shattered his belief in himself, broken down the fortifications that all men have inside themselves so that he had not even a bit of blanket to pull up over himself in defence. He was defenceless. She had done it and yet it was not her fault. It was his own. He had taken it for granted that a love as great as his must generate it in her, but now it was finished, and so was he. God, what power a woman has over a man, he remembered thinking as his mind fell into a mercifully numbed state.

But she must never know. She must never know the full ferocity of his agony. He must have some shred of dignity to get him through the next few minutes.

He stood up, his face as grey as the ash in the hearth, then turned jerkily, making for the door, making for the escape route which would get him away from her pity, from her compassionate tears which she was shedding because she had hurt him so. Where had that bloody girl put his coat and boots? He didn't know, nor care. He'd walk home without them if needs be.

Jesus . . . oh, Jesus . . . he couldn't just blunder about like this. He was a man who had asked a woman to marry him. No, he hadn't even done that. In her eagerness to have it over and him out of her sight she had refused him before he had even got the words out, but he must not let her see his pain and sense of rejection.

He turned back to her and his face, the expression on it and in his eyes so blank she shrank away from him. His smile was terrible, turning his face into one of those gargoyles which adorn old buildings.

"Well, I'll get off then."

"Mr Buchanan . . ."

"I don't think there's anything further to be said except I'd be glad of my coat and boots."

"Of course, but, Mr Buchanan . . . please . . . won't you . . . ?"

His voice was harsh, icy, excessively polite. "I think not, Miss Dean."

By the end of the week it was all over Fellthwaite and Ambleside and even further – the servants' grapevine saw to that – that James Buchanan, after toying with the affections of the rich and beautiful Miss Charlotte Gibson, and then discarding them, had been refused in his turn by Miss Lucy Dean. Well, it served him right was the general opinion, for you couldn't do that sort of thing and still call yourself a gentleman, could you? That kind of behaviour would always find its just deserts, and, by God, he'd got his. Two young ladies, both as lovely as the day, one rich and one exceedingly poor and because of the way he'd gone about things he'd ended up with neither. A well-respected man was James Buchanan, who'd made a right fool of himself and no mistake and there wasn't a man nor a woman, especially a woman, who didn't have a bit of a chortle. How are the mighty fallen, they told one another, for it was believed in the area that James Buchanan was a prideful man and this would bring him down a peg or two.

"He'll be mortified, Alex. Dear God, how is he going to show his face in society after this?" Franny Buchanan was genuinely distressed, for she had a soft spot for

James which had nothing to do with the fact that he was Alex's cousin, though that counted too. Franny Buchanan had a soft spot for any man whom she considered might make a good lover. She loved her husband dearly but Frances was one of those women, and there are, of course, men the same, who are not satisfied with one partner. Since her marriage eight years ago, and even before, she had taken to her bed, or more precisely, a discreet bed of her choosing away from her home, many young men who took her fancy and she would have liked James to be one of them. She had never approached him or let it be known in any degree that she was available to him, since she knew the kind of man he was. His loyalty to Alex would have prevented him from taking up any offer she might have made to him and so she had made none. Nevertheless he was dear to her and though she had considered any alliance between him and the Dean girl would be disastrous from the start, for, in her opinion, he needed a more mature wife, a more discreet wife, a more conventional wife, she was aware that his suffering now would be a burden to him. He wouldn't allow it to show, naturally. How much wiser it would have been on his part to take the well-brought-up, well-trained Miss Charlotte Gibson, he was no doubt thinking. The same age as Lucy Dean but many years older in the sense of becoming a wife, a hostess, a mother to any children they might have, than the delightful and unconventional daughter of the Reverend Edward Dean.

"It's his own bloody fault, darling, and I for one have no sympathy for him," her husband told her, taking his knife and fork to his breakfast sausages, bacon and mushroom. "You and I both told him what a bloody fool he would make of himself but he wouldn't listen to us. D'you remember? After that dance of yours? Great God, she's no more than a child and it showed in her behaviour."

"She's about the same age as Charlotte Gibson and you thought her a marvellous choice. But then she's worth a lot more than the Dean girl." Though Franny agreed with him she still couldn't help but defend not only James but the lovely girl over whom he had lost his head.

"That has nothing to do with it, Franny. Charlotte would have been much more—"

"Yes, yes, I know." Franny sighed irritably, watching her husband stoking up for the day, which always set her off on the wrong foot. She usually had breakfast in her room but today she was up early since she meant to call on James. Not that she expected to get anything out of him except a bitter demand to be left alone, but she must make him see that he could not hide away and nurse his hurt pride, which she expected played a large part in his disappointment. With Christmas coming and all its attendant parties and dances he must force himself to be a part of them, if only for the sake of all of them and to scotch any rumours that he had a broken heart, and she meant to tell him so.

She did her best. His clerk told her he was occupied when she strode into his offices in Church Street but, with that high-handed refusal to be dictated to which the gentry have, at least in the clerk's opinion, she swept past him and into James's rooms, telling him over her shoulder that she and Mr Buchanan would take coffee.

James was sitting in his high-backed chair apparently staring at the mostly horse-drawn traffic in the busy street beyond. She could see nothing of him except his arms resting on the arms of the chair, as he had his back to her, but even when she burst in on him he did not turn round. It was a dreary day, with low sullen clouds hanging greyly across the fells and even down to the rooftops of the town, but though the room was dark and chill there were no lamps lit, nor had a match been put to the fire laid in the grate.

"Good morning, James," she said brightly, not yet having decided what her plan of action would be. A pretence that nothing untoward had happened? Casually cheerful perhaps? Sympathetic? Brisk, ordering him to pull himself together? Whatever it was she wasn't going to do it addressing the back of his head.

She was shocked when she walked round his desk and stood in front of him. It was a week now since word had filtered slyly through the community that James Buchanan had been rejected by Lucy Dean. Got his come-uppance, as they said, and it appeared from the expression on his face they were right. He was just as immaculate as always. A sparkling white shirt front gleamed beneath his double-breasted waistcoat and his well-tailored, dark grey business jacket. His trousers were of a dark grey pinstripe and his tie was black. He was freshly shaved. His hair was neatly brushed, though she noticed it needed trimming. Indeed he looked as he always did for a day's business. It was in his face that the change in him showed. The flesh was the colour of the underside of a mushroom, not exactly grey and not exactly brown but a mixture of the two and his eyes were set in liver-tinted hollows. The eyes themselves, in the fraction of a second before he realised she was there, were a dull pewter, dead and unseeing.

"James?" she said hesitantly as though unsure it really was him, though of course she knew it was and at once he looked up at her, then swung his chair to face the desk, straightening his back and lifting his head aristocratically. He reached for a pen and a sheaf of papers that lay on the desk and began to put a scribble or two on the top page.

"Franny," he answered politely. "To what do I owe the pleasure of your company at this time of the day? I was under the impression you liked to breakfast in bed and rise at your leisure. It must be something important to bring you out so early." Despite his mild politeness the tension in him was very evident.

"Well, we haven't seen you for a week, none of us. It's not like you to be so reclusive so I told Alex I would pop in to . . . Oh, dammit, James, why pretend? It's all over town that . . . that you have been . . . Oh, for God's sake, James, you know what I'm talking about. I just came to see—"

"To see what, Franny? If I was still in the land of the living? That I'd not slit my throat or my wrists or whatever it is rejected suitors do? Well, as you see, I am surviving and none the worse for the experience, though I can promise you it will never happen again, so I'd be much obliged if you'd push off and let me get on with my work. And I'd also be obliged if you would keep your nose out of my affairs. It's nothing to do with you or anyone."

"It was my concern when you wanted me to 'take

up' the Dean girl. I believe that is the expression you used," she cried hotly. "Then you were very keen for me to stick my nose in."

"That is finished and done with, as well you know so I'd be glad if you'd take yourself off to whatever it is you do with yourself all day. I am no longer interested in . . . in . . ." It seemed he was unable to bring himself to speak Lucy Dean's name. "It's over so kindly leave me alone." He had never been a man for smiling a great deal but in his eyes had been a glint of humour, a certain softness, a glow of warmth, despite their colour, which said that he was a man with a heart. That was gone now, leaving a coldness, a distancing of himself from others, an inaccessible resolution which told Franny Buchanan, sadly, and indeed anyone who tried to get near him, that he was not to be approached and those who attempted it did so at their peril.

Franny studied him compassionately. He was holding on to his composure with the tips of his fingers, a man come close to a cliff edge, and it was taking all his strength to prevent himself from plunging over. Like most men who have never had a woman touch their heart, when it happens it is like a tornado that picks them up and whirls them along and, if they are not careful, smashes them down again with a force that can cause serious damage. Apparently he had never considered that Lucy Dean would not want him. All his adult life he had had women flocking to his side and he had come to believe that he had only to beckon and the one he wanted would smile and say, "Yes, please". Not only his heart had suffered but his pride, and he was defending himself savagely.

"James, you're not going to—"

"What I'm going to do is my affair. Certainly not yours or any other member of my family so kindly remember that and if anyone asks, which I'm sure they will, tell them to mind their own bloody business. And you can leave me out of any future hospitality you intend to—"

"James, please, you surely don't mean to hide yourself away from now on. There are dozens of suitable girls who—"

"Stop it, Frances." His voice was heavy with menace and for the first time a wave of colour washed beneath his skin. "Don't say another word. Just get out and leave me alone."

"James . . ,"

"I'm warning you. If you don't leave now I swear I'll make you leave with force. Go home and get on with—"

"But it will look so obvious if you suddenly stay away from the . . . Christmas will be here soon."

"Sweet Jesus, d'you think I give a . . . a damn about that," he snarled. "Now take yourself off and leave me alone."

November bludgeoned its way into December on a ferocious vortex of gales that swirled up and down the valleys and fells, tearing up trees by their very roots, whipping at the bracken and gorse with such force they could not keep a grip on the earth. The streets and gardens were littered with the flotsam for days and it was not until the middle of December that calm came and with the calm, the snow.

It began with a flurry of flakes floating on the grey air about lunchtime, then, as though to match the storms at the beginning of the month, swept in violent eddies across the invisible fell slopes. The light faded rapidly so that by mid-afternoon, as the slanting snowflakes thickened, it was almost as dark as full night, the storm enclosing the Dean household in a solid and ferociously moving curtain. Nobody could move out of doors, not even to fetch the milk from the farm further up the lane, and Bibby declared they'd all have to drink their tea milkless since there was no way he was going out in this. Had Mrs Hutton seen the state of the yard, for God's sake, just as though Mrs Hutton were pressing him to go out in it. Window deep, the snow was and until it stopped they'd all have to stick indoors. As soon as he could he and them hooligans would be out there to clear it, he told her, placing himself, his pipe and his out-of-date copy of the *Fellthwaite Packet* in the chair by the fire and prepared himself most pleasurably to sit it out.

The children were shut up for two whole days and Mrs Hutton pronounced that if she had to go through it again with them children racing about the house, surging into her kitchen and out again in some game of their own making, shrieking and carrying on like them dervishes she'd heard were to be seen in some heathen part of the world, she'd hand in her notice. Why in God's name the reverend couldn't control them was a mystery to her. She knew what she'd do if they were hers, she told Bibby savagely in one of the lulls in the madness, and he'd give her a hand, he told her.

Christmas came and went, very much like all the other Christmases the Dean family had known since their mother died. Money, of course, was the biggest problem, but they managed a scrawny turkey, bought on Christmas Eve in the market, one of those picked over and rejected by careful housewives or house-keepers and Mrs Hutton mackled together a plum pudding, for if there was one thing they had plenty of it was plums. Miss Lucy, bless her heart, managed a small gift for every member of the household. Not the toy train Percy had beseeched Father Christmas to bring him, nor the handsome book on motor cars Edward had seen in the bookshop window in Ambleside, but, as Mrs Hutton tearfully said to Bibby, there was always plenty of love and fun to go round in the family.

"Aye, too much bloody fun," he sniffed, as racing feet thundered over his head in a game of what Miss Lucy called Sardines.

Lucy was in Ambleside when she saw him. She was making her way to the corner of Church Street where it ran into Market Place with the intention of picking up a copy of the *Suffragette*. There was a young woman who sold them there and, though it cost a precious penny, Lucy managed to buy one now and again. The woman, no more than a girl really, worked in the office of a local gunpowder mill and was an ardent member of the Women's Social and Political Union and she and Lucy often discussed the enormous differences between the WSPU, as it was called, and the National Union of Women's Suffrage Society. The latter was all very well as far as it went but it did not go far enough in their opinion. It did not put up its fists and fight, not like the Women's Social and Political Union which Lucy longed to join. She was a firm believer in women's suffrage and had been a fanatical follower of the WSPU ever since she had been old enough to understand its aims. She entirely agreed with the war they waged on the government and if she hadn't the children and Papa to care for she'd be window-breaking, setting fires, marching, demonstrating and hunger-striking with the rest. She wanted justice for all women, she told anyone who cared to listen, including Bibby who said he'd never heard such damned nonsense in his life and she should be ashamed of herself, a lady like her, wanting to get mixed up with a lot like that. What was wrong with it? she asked him hotly. She wanted equality with men under the law, and equal wages. There were 50,000 members of the National Union of Women's Suffrage Society and only 5,000 of the WSPU, but those 5,000 were doing more to further the cause in a few short years than the former had done in nearly fifty. Christabel Pankhurst who, last year, had advocated an even more violent policy of militancy, was her idol and her opinions on the infamous Cat and Mouse Act, passed only this year, drove them all mad in the kitchen at the rectory as she swept them along on tales of mass meetings, demonstrations, and legalised torture, which was, after all, only what the force-feeding of suffragettes in His Majesty's prisons could be called and which frightened Mrs Hutton and Elsie to death. Mad, they all were, in Mrs Hutton's opinion and the lot of them should be at home where they belonged.

He was walking towards her and for a ghastly moment she felt herself spin into panic, dithering on the possibility that she might dart into a convenient shop doorway and so avoid coming face to face with him, but he had obviously seen her. The sudden tightening of his mouth, the narrowing of his eyes as though he viewed her very person with loathing, the lifting of his proud head, all spoke of his bitter renunciation of any friendship there might have been between them and if he were not a gentleman he would have cut her dead. Instead he raised his hat courteously and in a voice as cold as death said, "Good morning, Miss Dean," then passed on.

She found she was trembling without the faintest notion why, since she had done nothing wrong. It was not immoral, or illegal to refuse a gentleman's offer of marriage though she could see why Mr Buchanan might feel rebuffed by it. Well, rebuffed seemed a mild word when one put it in the context of the splendid Mr Buchanan and she supposed that he, perhaps more than many men, would take it hard to be turned down flat. She had known that one day they would come across one another again. Fellthwaite was a small town and Ambleside not much bigger, so it followed that though they would never meet in the home of a mutual friend since they had none, and certainly not at Grange House or any other home of the Buchanans, who had dropped her like a hot coal, this was bound to happen.

"You look very pale, Miss Dean," said the young woman who was unsuccessfully doing her best to persuade the passers-by to purchase a copy of the *Suffragette*. Her name was Letty Hodgson and her family, respectable and frowning on her involvement with the women's suffrage movement, lived in a small house on the edge of Ambleside. But though her father threatened to give her a good hiding if she continued to go against his justified parental authority, Letty was undaunted, standing wherever there might be a crowd and calling out to all who would listen that the crimes against her sisters, those who were being ill-treated in His Majesty's prisons, should not go unpunished. She and Lucy often exchanged a word and smile, sometimes a more lengthy conversation about Lucy's longing to do more for the cause.

"Well, if you want to give me a hand selling these newspapers, Miss Dean, I wouldn't mind," Letty had said and Lucy had pondered on whether she might.

Today, as though the encounter with Mr Buchanan had stiffened her resolve, she didn't know why since her concerns were nothing to do with him, as she put her penny in Miss Hodgson's hand and took her copy of the *Suffragette*, she asked diffidently, "Did you mean it when you told me you would like a hand selling your papers, Miss Hodgson?"

"Indeed I did, Miss Dean, and please, won't you call me Letty." Though Letty Hodgson was not the lady Lucy was, since her father was not a gentleman like the Reverend Edward Dean, it seemed Letty saw nothing odd about two women who were, after all, longing to fight for the same cause, calling one another by their christian names.

Lucy bobbed her head smilingly, not shy nor even awkward but somewhat amazed at the unconventionality of Miss Hodgson.

"I'm . . . Lucy."

"Well, Lucy, if you take half of these newspapers and walk up to the Salutation Inn there's a spot there where you'll catch those going in and out of the hotel, besides those passing by. And if anyone asks you you'll know what to say."

"About . . . about what?" Lucy gulped as she took a small armful of the newspaper.

"About the cause, naturally. From what you've said to me you know as much about it as anyone I know and if you can catch them without their men some of the women are interested." Letty gave her a cheerful grin as she thrust a copy in the face of a bowler-hatted gentleman, begging him to buy one.

"Get out of my way, young woman, or I'll fetch a policeman," he bristled, pushing both of them to one side.

"See what I mean? But don't be put off," Letty told her.

"I'll try . . ."

"Perhaps when we've done you'd like to come to our place in Compston Street and meet the others. It's not much, just one small office but we call it our headquarters."

"The . . . others?"

"Oh, yes. There's more than you and me engaged in this campaign, Lucy. Well, good luck. See you in half an hour or so."

It was her voice, calling out in desperate but well-bred tones that drew the attention of James Buchanan to her as he made his way back to his own office via Market Place. There she was, dressed in an extremely shabby but well-pressed tweed walking costume of oatmeal and brown, the neck high, the waist neat and fitted over her womanly hips, the skirt just touching the tops of her black buttoned boots. On her head was a brown velvet tam o' shanter, clinging for dear life to the tumbling masses of her hair. The sun shone and was caught in its burnished depths and put a liquid gold in the deep brown of her eyes. In her arms was a bundle of newspapers with which she struggled as she was jostled here and there. She was attracting a great deal of attention since not only was she very beautiful, which drew the men to her like flies to a honeypot, but it was well known that she was a rector's daughter and he could hear the remarks, some of them bordering on the offensive, about the appalling state of affairs when a lady should act as she was. They could perhaps understand the poorer class of girl, who after all knew no better, getting involved in such carryings-on but a lady and the daughter of the rector into the bargain! That seemed to make it worse.

Before James could even consider what he was doing, what it meant, or even how it looked, he had marched across the crowded road, narrowly missing the wheels of an enormous dray, pushed his way through the crowd of delighted men and taken her arm in a grip which, for a moment, terrified her. She was so hemmed about and so alarmed by her own inability to speak with a loud voice, let alone beg these people to buy a copy of her newspaper, she did not see him coming, and as the hand which had her arm in a bruising fist whisked her almost off her feet and beyond the crowd, she dropped her papers.

"Stop . . ." she shouted to whoever it was that held her. "My newspapers."

"Be damned to your newspapers, Miss Dean, and I'd be obliged if you'd pick up your feet and walk properly instead of dragging along like a bad-mannered child."

She recognised him at last and was so astonished she allowed him to carry her several more yards before she began to struggle to detach his hand.

"Let go of me," she hissed furiously, conscious of the stares of the people going by. "What on earth do you think you're doing? You have no right . . ."

"Only the right of a gentleman assisting a lady to recover her senses and her dignity. Great God, I've never seen—"

"Do you know, Mr Buchanan, I don't give a damn about your sensibilities and I'd be very glad if you would allow me to take care of mine. I . . . I am to become a member of the Women's Social and Political Union and as a member I am helping to sell our newspaper." She said it with enormous pride. Her eyes were huge and burning with fervour and her cheeks were banners of bright carnation excitement. She had never felt so alive, her manner said, and though she had been overwhelmed outside the hotel she wouldn't be again. Oh, no! Now she knew what to expect. She'd speak up and tell them all, men and women, what their aims were, those of them who were members of the WSPU, since she meant to join as soon as possible. This very day, in fact. She didn't know what she might be found to do to help the cause, here so far from London or any of the major cities, but she and Letty and the others – the others, oh, Lord – could spread the word if nothing else. It was almost like being one of the disciples that Papa preached about from the pulpit, going among the people and telling them about the wonders that women's suffrage would bring.

That is if Mr Buchanan would leave go of her arm.

At last he did so, his face inscrutable, his eyes as dark and ominous as Lake Windermere on a stormy day. They were without expression, for he did not wish to reveal the awful truth which was that he had just discovered he still loved Lucy Dean with all his heart and soul and man's body and always would. Distance and time had not blunted it and he felt the despair racing through him, for what was he to do with the rest of his life without her in it. He had spent the last weeks becoming more and more reclusive, despite his family's pleas to come to this or that affair where he was certain there would be a dozen pretty young women paraded for his inspection. He could not face the idea of taking up Charlotte Gibson again, even if she would have him, which seemed doubtful for there was a rumour to the effect that his cousin Paul, young Doctor Paul who would need all the money he could lay his hands on to get himself a decent practice, was showing an interest in her. And she in him, it appeared.

"Well . . ." Lucy said, somewhat abashed by the strange look on Mr Buchanan's face, wondering why, now that he had totally disrupted her first attempt to help the cause, he just stood there with what she could only call an empty look on his face. She found she couldn't simply walk off, which was strange, but just as suddenly that familiar look of brooding bad temper smouldered in him, filling the emptiness and his words were biting.

"You'd best be off home, Miss Dean. Your father would not care to see you in such a predicament."

"I am not in a predicament, Mr Buchanan."

"Yes, you are, but that is your affair, as you said, and I'm sorry if I discommoded you in any way. I won't do it again. Good-day, Miss Dean." Tipping his hat, he turned and walked away.

Letty was not there when she returned to the corner

of Church Street, to Lucy's surprise. She waited for about fifteen minutes but Letty did not return. She wondered what to do. Should she try and find the WSPU headquarters in Compston Street, which she knew comprised a long row of small terraced houses in one of which, presumably, the WSPU went about its business, or should she go home and come again tomorrow? She knew that Buffy, at least, would wonder where she had got to and she really must go and collect her bicycle which she had left propped against the side of a shop in Lake Road.

She was just about to walk away, deciding that perhaps it would be as well if she made her way home, when a male voice hailed her.

"Are thee t'lass what were with the one sellin' them there papers?" it asked.

She whirled about to confront a large gentleman whom she recognised. He had a bright red and cheerful face and had evidently just crossed the road from his fish shop on the corner, still wearing his soiled striped apron and a straw boater.

"Yes." Her voice was hesitant since she wanted no more confrontations with angry members of the opposite sex.

"She's bin arrested."

"Arrested!" Lucy was appalled, for what crime could decent Letty Hodgson commit that would put her in the hands of the law?

"Aye. Disturbin' the peace."

"Disturbing the peace," she repeated foolishly.

"That's right. Some chap didn't like 'er pushin' that there suffragette paper in 'is face so 'e fetched a constable."

* * *

"I just don't know what to do, Buffy," she agonised. "Should I go to the police station and plead for Letty? Ask them to let her go since she was doing no harm at all. I was there. I can vouch for her. I just can't bear to think of her in a ... a cell. I wonder what the sentence is for? ... What did the fish man say ... breaking the peace? No, *disturbing* the peace. Heavens, it could have been me, for there was no peace on that corner by the Salutation Arms. Oh, Lord, poor Letty," almost wringing her hands, "what can I do to help her?"

"Nothing, and if you ask me you'd be better off leaving the whole thing alone. Your papa would have a fit if he knew what you had been doing. It's all very well believing in a cause like the WSPU does but to get caught up in such unlady-like behaviour is appalling."

"Oh, Buffy, do shut up."

"No, I will not. Your mama—"

Lucy's face became cold. "Please be good enough to leave Mama out of this. I'm amazed at you, really I am. And you know my views on women's suffrage. In fact I believed you thought as I do."

"I do, but not when it brings your name into disrepute. It will upset your papa, you know it will."

Lucy's face crumpled. "Oh, God, Buffy, I know it will. What on earth am I to do? I can't just leave poor Letty to rot in gaol."

"She'll hardly do that, Lucy. Her family will be informed."

"Dear God, that makes it worse," Lucy wailed. "Her father is set against it and said he'd give her a hiding if she continued."

"I doubt that, Lucy. Now let's sleep on it. In the morning you can confess to your papa and if I know him he'll go down to the gaol with you and speak for her."

8

There was no need after all for Lucy and Edward Dean to go down to the police station in Ambleside the following day, for a note was delivered to Lucy saying that Letty had been released the night before into her father's care. She was to appear at the Magistrates Court and would probably, as this was her first offence, be released with a caution.

"There you are, Lucy. You had no need to worry after all," Buffy told her in great relief and was surprised and offended when Lucy turned on her like a tiger.

"No need to worry! Oh, I admit the immediate threat has been removed but I can't just ignore Miss Hodgson's predicament and get on with life as though she had never existed. I feel . . . I feel as though she befriended me, trusted me. She went out of her way to let me know she had been released which was kind of her and so I feel I owe her . . . well, something. Besides, I still have those copies of the *Suffragette* to sell," which she had retrieved. She gnawed at her thumb, which she was wont to do when she had some problem that might take a bit of solving and her delicate eyebrows dipped in a frown.

"Lucy!" Buffy was outraged.

It was a bitterly cold January day, bright with a hard frost. The trees and shrubs beyond the frost-glazed window were outlined in silvery tracery against a pale pink sky as the sun struggled to get through the fine layer of mist. A great flock of rooks and starlings swooped across the lawn then up over the roof of the house before coming to rest in their hundreds on the white branches of the denuded trees. Robins, their red waistcoats brilliant against the dazzling rime, pecked at the grass but there was little of sustenance at this time of the year. And yet in a sheltered corner of the garden, struggling for life between the roots of the great oak tree, were pale primrose, polyanthus, winter aconite and snowdrops. The usual weak fire flowered in the hearth of the Deans' small parlour and both girls were wrapped about with a shawl apiece, their hands encased in the woollen mittens Mrs Hutton turned out by the dozens of pairs. Each of the children wore them in the house and so did the Reverend Dean, for there was no worse fate than fingers ablaze with chilblains.

"Lucy! You're not trying to tell me that you mean to go and stand at that place again," for Lucy had told her all about the altercation outside the Salutation.

"And why not, pray? If Miss Hodgson – Letty – is brave enough to do it then, as a member of the WSPU, which I mean to be, surely I can do the same. But I feel that I should, that I *must* go and visit her in her home first." She turned a fierce glare on her friend and lifted her head defiantly as though challenging Buffy to argue with her. Buffy ignored the gesture.

"Oh, Lucy, you might make it worse for her with

her father, not to mention your own. Could you not
. . . well, send Edward with the newspapers and a
message. I feel you might get her into even worse
trouble than she already is."

"Not if I explain to Mr Hodgson that it was my
fault."

"How on earth do you work that out, for heaven's
sake?"

"Well, I was there when the gentleman became
cross. Perhaps seeing two of us made him . . ."

"What absolute nonsense." Buffy drew herself up to
her full height, which came to about Lucy's shoulder
blade, getting ready for a further battle, but Lucy was
already striding towards the door.

"It's no good, Buffy. My mind's made up and no one
can change it for me."

Only your papa, Buffy thought sadly, but the Reverend
Dean had kept to his bed this morning, saying he
thought he was in for a cold and would stay there,
at least for today, with two hot-water bottles and a
supply of honey, glycerine and lemon mixed in hot
water, taken up to him hourly by the faithful Elsie.

"I'm just going out for a half an hour, dearest," Lucy
told the watering eyes and red nose which peeped
over the top of the piled-up blankets in her papa's
bedroom. "Oh dear, that's an awful cough, Papa,"
as the Reverend Dean hacked harshly into the cold
air. There was a fire burning in the grate – Lucy had
insisted on it despite Papa's weak protestations that
he was as warm as toast and she was to stop fussing
– but it did little to warm the bare, chilly room. At least
it gave the appearance of a bit of cheer, doing its best
to flicker bravely.

"I really think we should send for the doctor, Papa," she told him, anxiously putting a hand on his feverish brow, but he twitched away, saying in his mild way that he was perfectly all right and would she stop worrying and go and do her errand.

"Well, if you say so, but if you're no better when I get back I shall send Edward to bring Doctor Hayward."

It was a bit tricky, Lucy found, cycling between the deep and frozen ruts of the lane down to Lake Road. Even there it was hazardous, for a thick layer of hoar frost gave no sign of melting in the weak sunshine, turning the surface into an ice rink. She skidded and slithered her way through Fellthwaite and on to Ambleside, her breath wisping away like smoke in the thin air. Her tam o' shanter wobbled precariously on the top of her roughly swept-up hair and her face, red as a poppy, was buried in her father's warm winter scarf. She called out to several tradesmen who were guiding their horse-drawn carts carefully along the treacherous road, and they all agreed with her that it was not a good day to be out.

By the simple expedient of knocking on several doors – and having one shut in her face when she told the woman who opened it who she wanted – she found the house in Compston Street in which the WSPU had their headquarters. Well, you had to laugh, said the bright-eyed girl who let her into the tiny room, the very idea of this, waving a thin airy arm above the table, two chairs and a chest of drawers, being the Ambleside division of the Women's Social and Political Union, though she thought the posters on the wall made it more exciting, didn't Miss Dean agree. One said, "What women may be and yet not have the vote," with five positions listed: mayor, nurse, mother, doctor or teacher and factory hand. Underneath was printed: "What a man may have been and yet not lose the vote," detailing convict, lunatic, proprietor of white slaves, unfit for service and drunkard. Another depicted a woman in knight's armour with the word justice on her breast. She was bearing a sword and a banner. There was a third, all of them done in the distinctive white, green and purple of the suffragist movement, of a woman holding aloft a newspaper on which the words "Votes For Women" were printed. Lucy felt the tears come to the back of her throat, for it was all so splendid and brave, this one small room, or so it seemed, and the women who worked in it for the cause and if they would have her she would be proud to join them.

"Edwina Lawson's my name," the slender young lady said, sticking out her hand, "but everyone calls me Eddy. My father has the chemist shop on the corner."

Lucy, slightly breathless, first from her ride, then from her exertions along Compston Street followed by Eddy's enthusiasm, grasped it ardently, for she had never met such . . . well, smiling to herself, she supposed Mrs Buchanan's lot would call them "spiffing girls"! First Letty and now Eddy.

She explained why she had come and was relieved to hear that Letty had been released with a caution. Yes, her father had been absolutely livid – oh, do sit down – but that wouldn't stop Letty. She was used to arguments with her father, who threatened to throw her out if she didn't stop all this damnfool nonsense but so far he had not done so. Her own father, who was more liberal-minded, believing that women such as his sensible daughter, who had more intelligence than many men he knew, should be allowed the vote. Not until they were twenty-five, though, Eddy said cheerfully, but she supposed it was a start and better than nothing. Anyway, as long as it did not interfere with her duties in the shop he allowed her to continue her campaigning. Women were proving their strength in fund-raising, propaganda, organisation and publicity stunts, though as yet he had not been tested on that one, Eddy laughed. She had a few ideas up her sleeve if Miss Dean was interested. There were several occasions when they might make their presence felt, she told the open-mouthed visitor. The Rushbearing ceremony in May, for one, and the May Queen procession for another. Then there was the Grasmere Sports when she and several of the others meant to demonstrate in some way not yet decided that the Votes for Women movement was not confined to the big towns and cities.

"Letty means to have a dinner-hour meeting today at the gates of the factory where she works if you'd care to go along and listen to her, and only today we received a range of purple, white and green 'Votes for Women' merchandise which we shall sell with our newspapers. You know, of course, that green, white and purple are our colours, don't you? There are lovely sashes. Would you like one? That is if you're to join us. You could wear it when you take up your stand outside the Salutation," eyeing the sheaf of newspapers still clutched in Lucy's hands, "that is if you mean to . . ."

"Oh, yes . . . oh, yes, please, I do. I mean I really want to join. At least . . ." She bit her lip, for it seemed that the very first time – or did yesterday count as that? –

she was to be asked to help she had to refuse. "You see
. . . my father's ill. My mama died when I was a girl and
there is no one but me to look after the household. I
have two brothers and two sisters younger than myself
so you see . . ."

"Of course, Miss Dean."

"Lucy."

"Of course, Lucy, you go home and look after your
father. It was good of you to come and enquire after
Letty. I'll tell her you called and then, when you can,
come again. There's always someone on duty and I can
promise you we'll find some work for you to do."

It was to be several weeks before Lucy could get
down to Compston Street again. Her papa had a
dangerous and weakening bout of pneumonia which
kept him in his bed for over a fortnight, and then in
his room, huddled over the poor fire which was all
Lucy could afford, for another week. The prolonged
coughing, so agonising it shook his thin frame like a
sapling in a high wind, had strained his heart and the
doctor, filled with compassion for the poor young lady
who was already overworked and overwrought with
the financial needs of her family, his bill among them,
told her he would need a long rest with good nursing
for several more weeks. He must on no account think
of taking up his duties, not until the warmer weather
came, and in this Lakeland climate of treacherous
changeability, that could be any time up to May.
Thank God for Buffy, was a constant cry on Lucy's
lips, for she knew she would not have got through
without her. Margaret, brave and uncomplaining, took
turns to sit with Papa during the day but Lucy and Buffy
shared the night vigils and they both smiled, when it

seemed the Reverend Dean was on the mend, to see
what scarecrows they had become.

"Oh, for a bit of sunshine on my face, Buffy, and a
good long walk on the tops. I feel like some desiccated
old crone who has not breathed fresh air for weeks."

"It's been weeks, Lucy, and if you want to go, you
go. Your papa is sufficiently well to leave to Margaret
and me. But promise me you will go up to the tops
and not to that office in Ambleside. You know how
I feel about that."

"I promise."

And so it was in the second week of February when
the air was still crisp with frost and the ground hard
and solidly frozen that, donning sturdy boots and tying
herself about in a warm shawl, Lucy Dean set off to
climb to the top of Loughrigg Fell. Loughrigg was one
of the lesser heights of Lakeland but enough for Lucy
to tackle on this first day out after being confined to
her father's sickroom for so long. She decided on the
ascent from Ambleside, riding there on her bicycle,
leaving the children behind with the promise that they
would all go the next week, or at least as soon as they
were able to leave Papa alone with Buffy.

It was a climb of just over 1,000 feet and two and a
half miles of walking. It was a glorious winter morning
with the sun rising through a pink mist, delicately
tinting the sky and the tops of the fells, which were
still shrouded with a fine layer of snow. The trees
were stark and black against the ethereal loveliness
of the gradually awakening day and Lucy drew in deep
breaths of it, filling her lungs which had for so long
been thick with the smells of the sickroom. The sun
turned to gold as it rose above High Street in the east,

lighting the tip of Scafell Pike, the summit of England, and turning the waters of Windermere far below to a silent sheet of exquisite gold.

Her boots crackled against the frosted bracken and stiff grasses, the sound snapping in the air like a dry twig broken across a man's knee. She paused just below the peak and turned to look back, her heart stirring painfully with the perfection of it, of this land she had come to love so well. The blue of the sky hurt her eyes and the glittering diamond symmetry of the frosted trees dazzled her heart and it was perhaps this which blinded her for a moment to the presence of the man who rose from a rock above her. He stood, etched against the sky, tall and dark and silent, forbidding as an eagle ascending from its nest and for a moment her heart jittered in her breast until she recognised him.

"Mr Buchanan, I did not see you there," she said quietly, for it seemed a sacrilege to speak out loud in such a heavenly place.

"Miss Dean, I beg your pardon. I did not mean to alarm you. I'm just about to leave." His face was set in lines which were quite unreadable and she wondered if anyone had ever got to know this man who could hide his emotions so cleverly. His expression said he was neither pleased nor displeased to see her. It was a matter of sublime indifference to him whether she stayed or went.

"Please, Mr Buchanan, don't let me drive you away."

"Miss Dean, believe me, you could not do that if I wished to remain. Good morning." He bowed coldly. He was not wearing a hat and the rays of the sun put streaks of chestnut in his dark hair and lit his velvet grey eyes to ice crystals. Somehow he managed to avoid looking at her and she wondered why he felt the need to do so since his every gesture, his aloof bearing, conveyed to her that he found her presence distasteful.

"Mr Buchanan, I . . . I have wondered . . ."

"Yes, Miss Dean?" Still turned away from her, he stopped, studying with what seemed to be great interest the fox head on the top of his walking stick.

"I regret . . . that is to say . . ."

"Please, Miss Dean, I beg of you, don't tell me of your regrets, for I don't wish to know of them." His voice was harsh. "What is in your mind, if it concerns . . . past indiscretions, is of no interest to me. I don't look back, only forward and I advise you to do the same."

Without once turning to look at her he strode off, taking the path towards the Grasmere Cairn, his tall figure upright despite the slope of the land and she did not see the tremble which shook his frame nor the spasm of pain which twisted his face into what might have been a smile but was not.

She sighed then sank down on to the rock he had recently vacated, wondering why she felt so sorry that she and Mr Buchanan could not have parted friends, but then she supposed a gentleman's pride would not allow him, after being rejected as a husband, to be no more than a friend. She watched him until he disappeared beyond the bracken which ended at Loughrigg Terrace, taking the path which led him through the wood and on to Grasmere.

She did not know that he had her in his mind's eye all the way down through Deerbolts Wood. He could still see that shining look of innocence which was particularly hers, that look of bewilderment in her great brown eyes that she should have earned his dislike to such an extent that he could not bear to talk to her; how could she know that the exact opposite was true? And yet at the same time he cursed the day he had ever set eyes on her, that never-to-be-forgotten day when he had been, for the last time, a man without care or heartache. He loved and wanted her still and in his despair at knowing he would never have her, when Alex and Franny Buchanan called on him that evening to make sure he had received his invitation to the best-publicised event of the Ambleside calendar and, more importantly, that he was to accept it, he received them with a mood little short of boorishness.

Mr and Mrs Arthur Gibson had been delighted to announce on 14 February – such a romantic day – that their daughter, their beautiful daughter Charlotte, was to marry Doctor Paul Buchanan. An engagement party was to be held at their home, Ravenscourt, and the élite of Ambleside society was invited, including Mr James Buchanan, whom Charlotte was determined must be made to see what he had so casually thrown away. She had not loved James Buchanan just as she did not love his cousin Paul but James had been the greater catch and she had the distinct feeling that her friends and her mother's friends believed that she was "making do" with his cousin. She was resolute that they must be made to see that they were wrong. A great party in the enormous, glittering richness of her father's home would be the ideal way in which to demonstrate to them that this was a "love match", that she had had a narrow escape when she gave up James in favour of Paul, and though she was well aware that she was being married for her money, she did not care. Paul Buchanan was of good family, a clever young man on his way up, and with the help of her father's money and her own vital talents as a hostess, she meant him to get to the very top. She'd show James Buchanan and that strumpet who'd had the effrontery to turn him down, though why that should matter she couldn't quite understand, even in her own devious mind.

"Well, old fellow," Alex began, as Franny had instructed him, in a casual, not a word about the Dean girl sort of way, "and how are you this cold evening? Well, I hope. Didn't see you at the fox-hunt yesterday. We missed you, didn't we, Franny?"

"Indeed we did, James. It was a damned good day. The hounds found the scent just after daybreak. I bet the beggar, with the hounds in pursuit, covered sixty miles. A rare cunning beast, that one."

Fox-hunting in the fells is as much a necessity as a sport and bears little similarity to the colourful ritual which takes place further south. Few huntsmen wear the pink coat and black hat of the squirearchy, and to follow the hounds one requires, not a glossy, well-groomed hunter but a stout pair of boots and a stick, for fell packs are followed on foot. Most of the huntsmen are farmers but many of the local gentry looked on it as a day's sport and the Buchanans had always taken part for as long ago as any of them could remember.

James was sprawled in a deep armchair, a glass of brandy in one hand and a cigar in the other. His chin was sunk on his chest and he stared joylessly into the leaping fire with the same unconcern for the fox's doings as the two labradors at his feet. Alex and

Franny exchanged a quick glance which asked what should be said next.

"Yes," Alex went bumbling on, just as though James had answered him. "Mind you, Franny and I didn't manage that, did we, old girl? Kept up until lunchtime then had a bite to eat in the—"

"It's no use, Alex, I'm not going and that's that. It's beyond me why you can't bloody well leave me alone. I'm bothering no one—"

"I don't know what you mean, James," Franny cut in.

"Yes, you do. You're here to try and persuade me to go to this bloody do at the Gibsons for her and Paul. Well, if he wants to take her on, good luck to him, though I must admit I pity the poor sod."

"James, it's family. You must go. Paul is your cousin and this is an important moment in his life. The Gibsons are influential."

"Franny." James's voice was very weary. "I don't give a —— for the Gibsons," using a word of extreme obscenity.

"Here, steady on, laddie," Alex protested. "That's no way to speak in front of a lady."

"No, I apologise, Franny. It was extremely bad manners and I'm sorry, but you see I am so bone weary of being pestered to 'snap out of it', to 'stop being so bloody sorry for myself', and similar expressions meant to bring me to my senses. But the thing is, I have not lost my senses. I just seem to have lost the ability to caper about and make a fool of myself as the rest of you do."

"Now look here, James, that's enough. We didn't come here to be insulted."

"Why did you come here, Alex? I can't for the life of me work out why it is so important to you that I give up this ... this rather pleasant quiet time I am enjoying and attend all the madcap things you get up to. I find I like staying at home."

"Rubbish!" Franny's voice was curt. "You were always glad to come for dinner and to attend the madcap affairs, as you so quaintly put it, before that damn Dean girl got her hooks into you."

"That's enough, Franny." James sat up so abruptly he spilled his drink down his shirt front. His voice was heavy with menace and his eyes glittered in the firelight. Both dogs lifted their heads and turned their devoted eyes on him, alarmed at the tone of his voice, but he touched each one with his foot and they lay down again, shuffling about until they found the most comfortable position on the rich Indian rug.

"It's true, James, so don't deny it. She seems to have warped something in you and—"

"That's enough, I say." James's voice thundered through the warm calm of his study and both dogs leaped to their feet. "If you've had your say you had better leave. I shall send my congratulations to Paul and Miss Gibson but that's all and I'd be much obliged if you, and indeed the rest of the family, would leave me alone."

"James, please, we worry about you ..." Franny began but he cut her short with a peremptory gesture.

His voice had softened. "Don't, Franny. My heart is not broken or anything as foolish as that. It's just that ... well, I'm getting older and ..."

"Fiddlesticks, James. You're in your prime and there

are several young ladies who would be glad to prove it to you."

"Franny, stop it. If I need a young lady then I'll find my own. Now the pair of you push off."

Lucy didn't know what it was that woke her. There was no particular sound to disturb the absolute quiet. Thimble wasn't barking or the hens cackling, which they were in the habit of doing when disturbed, perhaps by a fox. In fact it was so still she could hear the fast beat of her own alarmed heart. The bed creaked as she shifted in it, then, reaching for her shawl she pulled it closely about her before getting out of bed. The floor was icy to her bare feet and in the starlight that shone through the uncurtained window she could see her own breath steam about her face. With shivering hands she struck a match and put it to the candle, then looked at the dainty fob watch which had belonged to her mother and her mother's mother before her. It was three thirty.

Well, something had wakened her and she'd not be able to get back to sleep until she found out what it was. She wouldn't be a bit surprised to find that it was Thimble after all, for he had a naughty habit of leaving his basket in the kitchen and scampering up the uncarpeted stairs to snuggle in with Percy and Edward, who shared a room and a bed in this cold weather, at the back of the house.

She was right. He raised his head apologetically, his eyes bright in the candlelight, his tail moving hopefully as he lay in blissful ecstasy between the two sleeping boys. She touched the dark hair of each of her brothers, then patted the dog, smiling her permission for him to stay.

In the large, icily cold bedroom at the front of the house the girls were twined about one another beneath a mound of bedclothes, their dark heads close together. Emily muttered in her sleep, then, as the candlelight fell on her, smiled and said Thimble's name quite distinctly.

Her father's door was closed. She put her ear to it and was relieved to hear the quiet on the other side of it. That dreadful wheezing breath which had plagued him for weeks now had slowly eased and with the help of the honey, glycerine and lemon approved by the doctor, who liked the old remedies, he had been sleeping well.

A light sound at her back made her turn quickly and the candle almost blew out. It was Buffy, bundled as Lucy was in a shawl, but on her feet she had thoughtfully put a pair of the woollen socks Mrs Hutton turned out with the mittens.

"Is . . . everything all right?" she whispered, placing a loving hand on Lucy's arm, a comforting hand as though already her instincts told her it would be needed.

"Oh, yes. All fast asleep. I don't know what woke me."

"No, nor me. Is your papa . . . Is he . . . ?"

"I haven't looked but I think I might just have a peep at him."

"I'll come with you."

"No. You wait here."

But it was Buffy who held her up and Buffy who pleaded with her to be quiet, for her cries would frighten the children, she said, as they gazed into the open but dead eyes of the Reverend Edward Dean.

The funeral was not well attended. It was March now and a late but icy "bottom wind" blew straight down between the fells from Siberia, or so the old folk told one another, and it was enough to keep them indoors. Most of the Reverend Dean's parishioners were elderly or even downright ancient. Besides which, he had not been what might be described as popular since he was, though a kindly man, somewhat inclined to be reserved. It was as though his mind were elsewhere and his sermons were vague and not to the taste of those who liked a bit more substance to their weekly admonishment to heed the word of the Lord. To make matters worse he came from down south, an "offcomer" who had been given the living through his connections with the squire's family at Dalebarrow Hall and though a nice enough chap, not really one of them.

They made a pathetic little group, the reverend gentleman's family. All in black right down to the youngest, a boy of five or six, a passing farm labourer, whose old mam attended the Reverend Dean's church when she was able, reported to her when he returned for his dinner. The girl, his eldest, God only knew how she'd managed it, for it was well known the family was penniless and would be in worse plight when the new rector came, for where were they to go? The servants, one old man, one old woman and a lass of about twelve, stood at the graveside with them while the chap who, it was rumoured, was to take over the living, committed the body to the earth. None of them was crying, he told his mam when she asked, which was strange, for you'd have thought that the girls at least would have shed a tear, but they just stood close to one another, holding one another up, it seemed to him, white-faced and silent and when it was over and the parson had hurried off to something more important, they walked in a close-knit group up the path and through the trees to the rectory.

He was not to know, that inquisitive labourer, that Lucy Dean had managed decent mourning for her family by the simple expedient of throwing every outer garment they possessed into Mrs Hutton's enormous boiler, the one in which she did the weekly wash but to which black dye had been added. For a couple of days, while the dyed garments dried and were pressed ready for wearing, they stayed indoors, not even venturing into the garden, for Lucy was determined that every respect must be shown to her beloved father. The boys had black caps, but Mrs Hutton delved into her wardrobe and found several old black bonnets which, being a frugal woman, she had kept, "just in case" and on the day of the funeral, from the top of their heads to the tips of their black boots, they presented a picture of a family in deep and grievous sorrow, which was what they were.

It was a week later when they were visited by

the squire's agent who, though he was filled with compassion for the frail and lovely girl who greeted him courteously and even asked him to take tea, was forced to inform her that the new rector would be taking up his post on the first day of next month and would Miss Dean, therefore, make arrangements to be out of the rectory by then.

"Of course, sir." By her calm manner and perfectly controlled voice one would have thought she had several places to where she and her family might go, and perhaps she had, for surely there were relatives? But he didn't think so. Not from the gossip he'd heard about the estate. Both her parents had been only children, so it was said, and relatives were in short supply.

She was very quiet that evening as she sat with Buffy in the small parlour. Of course, they had all been quiet since her papa's death, and in the seclusion of their home they had wept together for him, despite the brave front they put on for the rest of the world to see. As Mrs Hutton said to Bibby, she'd never seen such fortitude, the poor lambs, and what was to become of them, that's what she'd like to know. Indeed, burying her face in her apron, to Elsie's great consternation, what was to become of them all, for who would want to employ an old woman in her sixties and a man even older. Their Elsie'd soon be fitted up, being young and, thanks to Mrs Hutton, well trained but where would her and Bibby go, tell her that if he could.

"'Ere, 'oo are thi' callin' an old man," Bibby cried in high dudgeon. "Aah can still do a bloody good day's work wi't rest of 'em," but he knew she was right. What he did in the garden of the rectory he did at his own pace, and when he felt like it. He was helped by his grandson and by them 'ooligans, for despite the way he went on about them they were good-hearted kids. True, he hadn't had a week's wages since he could remember but he lived snug across the yard in the rooms above the old stable and ate as well as royalty on the vegetables he himself grew. Mrs Hutton was a dab hand with a spoon, a pan, a few herbs and that old oven in the kitchen and could make a grand meal out of a bit of mutton, making it taste like the tenderest cut of lamb. Aye, comfy he was and settled and where, like the rest of the family, was he going to fetch up now?

Lucy said the same thing to Buffy, though in different words.

"We have to be out of here by the month end, Buffy. Squire Forsythe's agent was very sorry but he had been sent to . . . let us know, he said. The new incumbent and his family, quite extensive, I believe, want to be in by the first of the month so it means we shall have to find somewhere else."

"Yes, I see." Buffy's heart quailed and she could feel it thump quite frantically against the black wool bodice of her mourning dress, but she held her head high and her back straight against the chair. She did her best, like Lucy had that afternoon when the agent called, to give the impression that there was nothing to be troubled about, that they would soon find a place of security, but within her desperation surged, as it did in Lucy, for where were four adults and five children – for what else could you call Elsie who Lucy would never abandon – to find a home and the wherewithal to support it and those who would live beneath its roof.

"I must find a home for the children, Buffy, you know that," as though Buffy was giving her an argument. "And then there's Mrs Hutton and Bibby and Elsie. They are my responsibility now, you understand that?"

"Yes. If there's anything . . . anything I can do. I'm a hard worker, you know that."

It was as though Buffy had not spoken. "I have a week." Her calmness was frightening and Buffy knew she was still in the black space into which her papa's death had thrown her and yet her mind was working clearly. It was up to her to find them a place of safety, she knew that, and Buffy's heart contracted in love and pity.

There was only one answer, of course, and they both knew it.

"There's a young lady to see you, sir." Dimity Blamire was so excited she almost forgot to bob the customary curtsey which her position as housemaid to Mr Buchanan demanded. Not that he'd notice, not if she appeared without her cap and dressed in a feather boa, she thought, and when he peered round his newspaper at her she could see he hadn't really heard her. Not properly.

It was Dixon's day off and so, by the greatest good fortune, it had been Dimity who had answered the door. She was dressed in her afternoon uniform of a black cotton dress over which she wore a crisp white muslin bibbed apron which tied at the back of her waist in a huge bow, the ends of which fell to the hem of her floor-length skirt. On her head a pretty white muslin cap trembled and though Mrs Burns, the housekeeper, was very strict about such things, a tendril of dark and glossy hair escaped it and drifted on to her neck.

"What?" he muttered irritably. It was a Sunday and almost into April and though it was a fine day he had not thought it worth the trouble to dress himself in his walking boots and outfit and get out on to the tops. He could hear through the half-opened window the sound of a chiff-chaff which had nested near the house and smell the wild daffodils and the great mass of golden catkin which hung about the willow tree near the pond, and something stirred in him. Something which had been dormant all winter but which somehow, more and more these days, he found he was inclined to let slip away since he had come to the conclusion it wasn't really worth the bother. He must make an effort, he kept telling himself, for he was fast becoming a recluse. Had it not been for his legal practice he believed he might not go out of the house at all. At first he had walked the fells for weeks, alone but for the company of his dogs, high above the "intakes", roaming the heights with the hardy sheep, glad to be away from those who pitied him, and, he was inclined to think, laughed at him for his foolhardiness. It had been his only pleasure until, one day, he had met Lucy Dean on the peak of Loughrigg Fell and even that was now denied him.

Dimity waited, longing to nudge him into some sort of response. She was almost hopping from foot to foot in her eagerness to see the visitor in and get back to the kitchen to tell them who it was who now sat in the straight-backed chair in the hall and who had asked to see their master, but until he came from his reverie and told her what she was to do about it she could only hang here in a dither and wait. She knew who it was, of course.

"A young lady, sir."

"What young lady, for God's sake? And what in hell's name does she want? Can't Mrs Burns see to her?"

"Oh, not that sort of young lady, sir. A real lady. To see you." Dimity beamed her encouragement.

"What does she want?" James Buchanan's heart did a little flip as though some instinct told him who it was who was waiting to see him, but at the same time, encased in the ice put there months ago by Lucy Dean, it told him not to be such a bloody fool. Nevertheless he raised himself from the lounging position he had been in after his Sunday lunch, put the newspaper to one side and glared at the housemaid.

She was not daunted. "I'm sure I couldn't say, sir."

"Well go and ask her."

Dimity was shocked. "Oh, I couldn't do that, sir. She's a lady," and as such not to be approached with such a rude question by a mere housemaid.

James steeled himself to ask the question, already guessing the answer, calling himself all kinds of fool, for his mouth had gone dry and his heart was banging quite furiously in his chest. He hated her for having this effect on him and his voice was almost a snarl.

"Who is she?"

"Miss Lucy Dean, sir."

His heart did a somersault. "Tell her I'm not at home."

"But, sir, she particularly noticed the motor car on the drive and when she asked I said you—"

"You stupid girl. Well, you can just go and tell her to be on her way."

"Oh, sir . . ." Dimity looked ready to weep now.

James Buchanan stood up and strode to the window with the savagery of an enraged tiger, looking out over the soft spring loveliness of his garden and in his heart he despised himself for his cowardice and for his treatment of the maidservant. He was afraid. He was afraid of Lucy Dean after all these months. He was afraid of the hurt and the loss of his pride, the loss of his dignity and the belief, which he knew was not so, that wherever he went people were pointing at him and calling him a fool. He couldn't bear to suffer it again. Twice he had seen her: in Ambleside on the day she had been selling newspapers for that damned suffragist movement, and then on the top of Loughrigg Fell when she had tried to engage him in conversation. He had nearly given in to her then. Her flower-like beauty combined with that enchanting grace, not just of figure but of spirit, had almost unmanned him. She had looked at him with honesty and candour, with the unexpected earthly common sense which her life with her father had given her and using every atom of strength he had he had turned his back on her, walked away from her and now she was here in his hall asking to see him and again he was afraid.

"Show her in," he told the maid curtly.

James Buchanan's home, Howethwaite, stood with its back to the wind-ruffled waters of the River Brathay. It was a big house built 300 years ago, the original farmhouse scarce more than a huge kitchen with a scullery off and a bedroom or two above, but over the generations bits and pieces had been added here and there until it could now be called a manor house, unrecognisable as the building it had once been. There were still the original pantries, a dairy, a laundry, an enormous, modernised kitchen plus a butler's pantry and a housekeeper's sitting-room.

On the ground floor to one side of the wide, glass-panelled front door was an elegant drawing-room, big enough, once the carpets were carefully rolled back, in which to hold a dance. On the other side of the hall was a dining-room, well able to seat thirty or more guests, a small, pretty sitting-room at the back of the house for the mistress's use, a study for the master and a library complete with a billiard table.

On the first floor was a modern tiled bathroom and half a dozen large bedrooms stretching across into the extension put on by James's own father, joined together across the front by a wrought-iron balcony on to which the long bedroom windows opened. The second floor had another bathroom, as luxuriously appointed as that on the first floor and used when guests were in residence, and at the back of these and in the roof space, with dormer windows looking out over the back towards Colwith Woods, were the women servants' bedrooms. At the end of the extension James's mother had had built a delicately soaring glass conservatory which opened on to the side garden. The house was painted white and had a blue slate roof. The windows were flat and square, the whole presenting a picture of solid, enduring patience coupled with a serene and ageless beauty.

If Lucy was dazzled as she sat in the wide sunny hallway waiting to be summoned into the presence of James Buchanan, or shown the door, whichever he decided, she did not show it. She had lived for the whole of her life in what could only be described as spartan conditions. Her mother, though Lucy was not aware of it, had brought some pretty pieces of furniture, a picture or two, some good crystal and Meissen chinaware to her marriage to Edward Dean but, over the years, to pay an enormously overdue butcher's bill, the servants' wages, to purchase warm, winter clothing for her growing children, these had found themselves in the salerooms and auction rooms of Buxton and Lucy had no recollection of their existence. She had become used to bare walls and empty fireplaces, uncarpeted wooden floors across which their boots snapped smartly, old chairs and wobbly legged tables, and the sudden explosion of colour and warmth and sunlight streaming through wide polished windows, the smell of fresh cut flowers overwhelmed her. She gazed at a portrait which hung above the fireplace of an exquisitely beautiful woman in a low-cut blue silk dress. She had hair the colour of the chestnuts she and the children gathered from the woods and her eyes were a pale velvet grey, reminding her of someone, though she could not bring to mind who it was.

"Will you come this way, miss," the pretty little housemaid beseeched her, smiling and bobbing and doing her best not to appear too excited. She led Lucy along the hallway, turning left into another until she came to a doorway which stood open. She knocked on it, then stepped inside.

"Miss Dean, sir," she announced importantly, then, at her master's thank you, scampered off as fast as her legs would carry her in the direction of the kitchen.

He was leaning with one arm along the mantel-piece, a cigar in his hand which, though she was not aware of it, trembled slightly. He was casually dressed, since he was not expecting visitors, in a blue polo-necked jumper and a pair of dove grey breeches which showed off the athletic leanness of his figure. His knee boots were well polished. He himself was well shaved and he looked exactly what he was, a gentleman enjoying a lazy Sunday afternoon rest from the exigencies of business. The strain he had suffered over the past months did not show in his face. In fact he looked the picture of health with no care in the world beyond the annoying prospect of spending half an hour with an unwelcome visitor.

Lucy, still as a doe which scents danger but is incapable of avoiding it, stood hesitantly in the door-way and waited. She was like a black wand, slender and ready to sway in the path of any stray breeze, her face pale but composed and James felt the sad loveliness of her hit him hard in the chest, but nothing of it showed in his face.

"Miss Dean?" he asked enquiringly.

"Good afternoon, Mr Buchanan. It was good of you to see me."

"Not at all." His voice was polite, nothing more, and he glanced at his watch as though to show her he was not a man who had time to spend gossiping. "May I offer you my condolences on the death of your father," he asked her civilly. "It must have been a grave shock to you."

"It was." Her eyes were steady but they became moist, soft golden brown pools of grief, the emotion in her difficult to contain.

He hardened his resolve, for this was not the time to weaken. He had not wanted to see her and the sooner she went the sooner he could get back – crawl back, some unwanted sneering thing inside him said – into the lonely life he had chosen for himself.

"Won't you sit down?" he asked her, for after all he was a gentleman and she was a lady, but his hostility was very evident and he hoped she could see it. He wondered what the devil she was doing here, hoping to God it was not for a handout, but his own knowledge of her told him Lucy Dean was not one to go begging.

"Thank you." She swayed towards the chair he indicated and sank down, her back as stiff as a ramrod, her bonneted head . . . Dear God, where had she got that monstrosity which covered her hair, drowning her white face with its huge old-fashioned brim and high crown. Somehow it made her seem all the more vulnerable and he swore under his breath at his own helplessness at being moved by her frailty.

"What can I do for you, Miss Dean?" he asked her brusquely, again looking at his watch, for he really did not think he could stand much more of this. Let her tell him what it was she had come for and be done with it. Whatever it was he would agree to it. A loan to tide her over. Jobs for her servants, who he was certain she could no longer keep. In fact where was she to live, now he gave it some thought, for the living had died with her father and . . .

"I came to see if the kind offer you made me last year was still available, Mr Buchanan. If it is I find I . . . would be willing to . . . to take it up." Her face had whitened even further as she spoke and even though she was seated, she swayed a little.

"Offer?" he asked dazedly. "What offer?"

"I believe it was an offer of marriage, Mr Buchanan." Her eyes gazed steadily somewhere over his shoulder, huge and somehow frightened and for a moment he felt compassion wash over him, for it had taken enormous courage on her part to come to him like this, then it was replaced by a savage anger and he had to whirl away from her in order to hide it. He wanted to crash his fist on the mantelpiece and swear obscenely, since it seemed she had come to offer him what he had asked for months ago. She was telling him that, distasteful as it was to her, for the sake of her family – oh, yes, it was that, there was no doubt of it – she was willing to sacrifice herself and take up the position, as if it were one of housekeeper or laundry maid, that she had turned down so rashly before Christmas.

Lucy sat impassively and waited. She felt very calm and yet inside her there was a small flutter of something she knew to be fear. Fear not of this man and what he would do to her, but that he might do nothing. That he might turn her out, tell her he was no longer interested and if he did she had no idea what she was to do next. There was always the poorhouse – was that what it was called? – she supposed, or perhaps she could go to the squire and beg a cottage on his estate. She and Buffy might get employment in service somewhere. Buffy was very clever with her needle, but then what was to happen to Mrs Hutton and Bibby and Elsie and who would take care of the children while she and Buffy ... Dear Lord, dear Father in heaven, don't let him turn his face from me, let there be something remaining in him that is willing to forget what happened between us . . .

He turned slowly and she was amazed at the expression of amusement on his face. He was actually smiling as though at some absurdity. He drew on his cigar, the smoke swirling about his head as he blew it out, continuing to lounge indolently to the side of the leaping log fire. His dogs, now that she was seated and their master was happy about it, settled themselves at his feet. When he finally moved he had to step over them. He sauntered to the window and looked out over the garden, putting his head out and sniffing appreciatively, or so it seemed, at the spring fragrance that hung there. He had all the time in the world now, he appeared to be telling her, and whatever Lucy Dean had done to him she was about to pay for it. Still she waited impassively, her fate and that of her family in his hands.

"So, you have decided that my . . . attentions are welcome after all, is that it, Miss Dean? Now that you have nowhere else to turn, no other person in the world who can help you out of this dilemma your father's death has plunged you in," cruelly ignoring the small distressed sound she made in the back of her throat, "you have changed your mind and elected to, despite your aversion, become my wife?"

"If you are still interested, yes, Mr Buchanan." Her voice in no way said she was humbled and he thought he had never before seen such bravery. She didn't love him, probably didn't even like him much. She hated the way his family lived, the conventions and rules, the etiquette that had to be observed in their strata of life, which was in direct contrast to the careless way she and her family had lived in the rectory, and yet she was ready to submit to it all, all that she despised, for the sake of her brothers and sisters, for there was no doubt in his mind that they would be part of the bargain.

"And what if I were to tell you that I am not, Miss Dean, what then? Would you trail round all the eligible bachelors of the district offering your very delectable self to anyone who will have you, or will you—"

"I would like an answer, Mr Buchanan. I am willing to marry you, and yes, it is for the sake of my family, for I can only be honest with you. I . . . I seem to have something you want."

"Wanted, Miss Dean." His voice was brutal and she winced.

"Very well, if that is the case I will waste no more of your time." She rose to her feet and her hands went in a pathetic gesture to her comical bonnet, setting it straight. A wisp of her silken hair drifted from beneath the brim to her forehead, for the bonnet was far too big, and she brushed it away with a hand which was trembling violently. He wanted to go to her, put his arms about her, tell her she had nothing . . . nothing, ever, to worry about again. That he would look after her until his dying breath, and her bloody family, but he could not do it, of course. She had wounded him deeply, wounded his pride and his self-esteem, damaged his standing in the community and he could not forget it. It stood between him and what he felt for her and he was not willing to chance it again.

"Not so fast, Miss Dean." His mouth curled at the corners and again she was astonished, for she knew it to be a satisfied smile that played there. And then it came to her. He was playing with her like a cat will play with a mouse, cuffing it almost affectionately as it makes a dash for safety, then pinning it down once more. A game the cat enjoyed, for it was its nature, but a sorry day for the mouse, and she was cast in the role of mouse.

But her name was Lucy Dean. Destitute she might be but she was not about to allow this man to treat her like some . . . some street woman who had come to offer her wares, for a price. She had dealt with him fairly last year. She had been courteous, even distressed by her inability to accept him and she did not deserve his contempt, for that was what he was showing her.

"Mr Buchanan, I would be glad if you would stop this . . . this . . ."

"Yes, Miss Dean? This . . ."

"This charade. If you no longer wish to marry me then say so."

"I do not say so, Miss Dean." In his eyes was a hard glitter of ice, silver grey and quite dazzling, but it was not meant to allay her fears, she knew that.

Nevertheless, "Then you do wish to marry me?"

"I did not say that either." His face was smooth and amber-tinted, totally without expression and Lucy died a little, for where else was she to go from here? But again the pride and strength she had drawn about herself since her mother died and her father had retreated into his shell of grief came to her rescue. The bonnet rose and the ridiculous black feather on it bobbed. Her back was very straight as she made her way towards the door which the maid had closed behind her.

"I'm afraid I have wasted your time and my own, Mr

Buchanan. I shall have to make further arrangements to protect my family and I have only until the end of the month to do it in, so I'll bid you good afternoon."

"What other arrangements, Miss Dean?"

"That is my concern, Mr Buchanan. Now, if you will summon your maid I will—"

"Miss Dean, may I ask you what you intend to put into this . . . marriage? If it is to take place, that is?" His voice was like silk and she turned, bewildered.

"I'm not sure I understand."

"Oh, I'm sure you do, Miss Dean. You know what a married woman has done to her each night in her husband's bed, surely? Does the . . . bargain include that?"

Her face changed from bone white to poppy red and her lips trembled but she did not hesitate. "I will be your wife in every way that you need, Mr Buchanan. That is my part of the . . . bargain. Yours is that you will look after my brothers and sisters, until they are of an age to look after themselves. Would that be satisfactory?"

"Perfectly, Miss Dean. I will call on you tomorrow to make the arrangements."

"Thank you, Mr Buchanan. Good afternoon."

He was trembling so violently after she had gone he had to sit down in a chair or he would have fallen. His teeth clicked on the glass of brandy he had poured himself but in him was a tiny bud of hope which he had not known for many months.

Her voice was without expression as she spoke. "We are to be married in three weeks' time." She ignored Buffy's gasp of amazement. "Mr Buchanan will arrange it all."

"Not . . . not in your papa's church?"

For a moment the mask of calm on Lucy Dean's face slipped. "Dear God, no! It is to be at St Mary's on the Kelsick Road." The curious woodenness returned and she continued in a lifeless voice. "Apparently Mr Buchanan's family worship there. He wants it to be . . . smart, the sort of wedding to which his family is accustomed. White, of course, for all young ladies of good family are married in white, with Emily and Margaret as bridesmaids. He thinks Edward would be old enough and a suitable choice to give me away and there will be a reception at Howethwaite afterwards. He asked me if I had any preference for a honeymoon. I said I didn't, but would leave it to him. I have never been anywhere, Buffy, so how could I choose? And we have no need to fear . . . eviction. Mr Buchanan will see to it. 'Arrange to have your family and servants moved to Howethwaite in the next few days and you must stay with Franny.' She is, well, you know who she is . . . until . . . Apparently she will know everything I will need in the way of . . . a trousseau. It seems I must have one. He will pay for it all."

"Darling . . . darling . . ." The endearment was a measure of Buffy's deep distress, for she was an undemonstrative young woman. She and her mam had had no time for it in the fight for life they had known. Before her mam had lost hers there had been a deep affection between them, just as there was between her and Lucy Dean, but it was not her nature to make a show of it. Now, the unnatural numbness with which Lucy told her of the plans Mr Buchanan was to make for them all affected her deeply.

"I know I must marry some time, Buffy, and Mr Buchanan is a . . . he will be kind, I'm sure, and there are the children . . ." which explained it all. If she was alone, or just had Buffy to protect, they would be off somewhere, probably to London, to get a job, perhaps with the WSPU, and her life would be wonderfully exciting, worth while, special, but the slump of her shoulders said that it was not possible so she must make the best of it, which was all any woman in her position could do.

"He loves you, Lucy, I told you that months ago, and with time . . ."

Lucy turned to her in surprise. They were sitting before the parlour fire which, to the servants' astonishment, had been banked up to enormous proportions. They were to do the same with their own in the kitchen, she had told them mysteriously, and they were not to worry about the future. It was all taken care of, as they would be taken care of, and though they trusted Miss Lucy with their lives, they were dubious, for what were they to make of that remark. Not worry about the future when their very home was to be taken over by another family at the month's end. What did she mean? What was to happen to them? Who was going to pay for the coal which, delightfully, burned halfway up the chimney, and the hamper, come from the local provision merchant, which had been delivered at the back door by a most polite, one might almost say servile messenger on a bicycle only an hour since. Meat pies and hams, chickens and eggs, though they had no need of those, a shoulder of lamb and a leg of pork, a whole salmon, in fact enough food to keep the Dean household for a week.

Yes, Miss Lucy had said vaguely, it had been delivered to the right address and would Mrs Hutton prepare something for the children's tea. The children, fed for the last month on eggs and more eggs, on bread and jam, both of which Mrs Hutton made herself, on porridge, on dishes made up mostly of potatoes and vegetables, all delicious and cheap, had been ecstatic, only Margaret showing a dubious face, for where had it come from. She was the closest to Lucy in age and was a practical child. She knew that such things didn't grow on trees, as Mrs Hutton was wont to say, but for the moment she kept her counsel and allowed Edward and Emily and Percy to enjoy what some guardian angel had provided.

Now Lucy considered the strange statement Buffy had just made, considered it as though it were a puzzle someone had just presented her with, a small frown on her ashen face.

"I don't know what love is, Buffy, between a man and woman, that is. Oh, Mr Buchanan informed me that we would share a bed and I think I have some idea what he is to do to me in it . . ."

"Dear God, Lucy."

"There is no use feeling sorry for me, Buffy. I have to face the fact that there is no other way open for me. He will pay for Edward and Percy to be properly educated, he said so. A governess for the girls. He is to come over tomorrow and explain it all to me. I am to be here at ten o'clock to receive him. I believe there are certain legalities . . ."

"Lucy, darling, I cannot bear to hear you talk like this, as if it were no more than deciding what the menu is to be for Sunday lunch."

"To me it is no more than that, Buffy. Now I must go and . . . and break the glad news to the children. Edward, at least, will be pleased."

"Edward?"

"To have a Rolls Royce in the family, of course."

"You're to marry the girl who turned you down last year and not only that you expect me to have her here, in my home, until you do. Well, all I can say is that you've a bloody nerve and I'm surprised at your lack of pride, James Buchanan, really I am. You know she has accepted you only because of her changed circumstances, and everyone in the valley will believe the same."

James Buchanan's face was unreadable. "It does not matter to me what anyone believes, Franny. Lucy Dean" – her name came easily to him now, Franny noticed – "is to be my wife and there is nothing that can change that."

"You're off your rocker, old boy," Alex growled, the

first words he had spoken since the dreadful news had been broken to them. "She'll be nothing but trouble."

"Why is that, Alex?" James asked mildly enough. "She will be my wife and as such will have a position to keep up. She will do as I tell her," which is more than can be said for yours, he almost added.

"But why, old chap, for God's sake, why? What in hell's name has she got that a dozen much more suitable girls couldn't give you? Why this obsession with her? She has two arms and two legs and all that goes with—"

"Be careful, Alex, that you don't say too much. I am to marry her and no man will insult my wife."

"Dear sweet Lord, I can't believe it." Franny was still grappling with the audacious request James had made of her to have the Dean girl in her home, to lead her through the ways of a society wedding, to see she did the correct thing, bought the right clothes, said the proper words to the proper people. She must be married from a decent address and what better than hers, he was telling her and yet, why not. It might be fun. She was always ready for something different, something perhaps the others might not agree with; besides which, she was between lovers at the moment and had nothing else to divert her. And though she had not really considered it in any great depth, she realised now that she had liked the girl. She had spunk, did Lucy Dean. You only had to see the way that old dodderer of a father she had, had acted. Dead now, of course, but when he was alive Edward Dean had had no life in him and it had been left to Lucy to bring up her family and run the household. But with him dead the small income, his living at the house which belonged to the squire, had died with him, which was why Lucy had accepted James's offer. The surprising thing to Franny was that he had made it again. For the past few months he had brooded morosely in his lovely home, refusing all invitations, snapping at her when she went to winkle him out, almost growing old before her eyes and yet here he was looking as he had always done. Attractive, debonair, a curl of humour at the corner of his undeniably sensual mouth, looking, she was inclined to think, like the cat that has just been offered a saucer of cream.

James watched her for a moment, then, smiling, walked to the window, satisfied, for her expression told him she would do it. His bride would come, a proper bride, a Buchanan bride, from this charming house. It would be seen as a mark of favour in the town and make Lucy's progress in his society so much easier. There was no one more suitable to help Lucy Dean through the difficulties that lay ahead of her than Franny Buchanan, whose position in society was assured. James was an influential man and his wife, when seen to be approved by the Buchanan clan, would find her way smoothed by the patronage of Mrs Alex Buchanan.

The worst moment, Lucy believed it firmly at the time since she had no way of looking into the future, was getting the children settled in their new home. The girls were tearful and bewildered, begging her not to leave them, and Percy declared that he would run away back home at the first opportunity.

"You can't, you silly beggar. The new rector will be there and his boy will be sleeping in your bed,"

Edward told him ungraciously to hide his own fear of this new environment. He didn't know whether to be pleased or sorry that Lucy was to marry Mr Buchanan, and he was worried about the difference it would undoubtedly make to their lives. Would Lucy become a grand lady dressed in silks and furs, for he knew Mr Buchanan was very rich, or would she be as she had always been, fun-loving, carefree, ready to join in any game, most of them devised by herself? Would she still romp with Thimble and take them for long walks up on the fells or would Mr Buchanan take up all her time, stealing her away from them? There was talk of going to school and how was Percy to deal with that, telling himself that Percy's welfare was at the forefront of his mind, not his own misgivings.

"Darlings, you know I will always be here for you, don't you? Though I shall be Mr Buchanan's wife I shall be, first and foremost, your sister. You are my first concern. We shall be together every day, I promise you, and apart from living in these rather luxurious surroundings, which you must admit are quite splendid, things will be exactly as they have always been."

"Except for Papa," Percy said gravely.

"Papa will always be with us, sweetheart. He and Mama are looking down on us now, watching over us."

"But they're not here, Lucy," Emily breathed, looking anxiously round the large, airy but unfamiliar room, flickering with firelight, which was to be theirs. Not a nursery, of course, for they were too old for that but a room in which they could keep their own things, play their own games, read, eat their meals and generally consider it to be theirs and theirs alone, Mr Buchanan had told them. Margaret and Emily were to have lessons here with a daily governess, a young lady by the name of Miss Bradley, who would be driven in from Ambleside and who would teach them all that a young lady of their class needed. A little geography, French, English composition, poetry, the Scriptures, history, some arithmetic, and, of course, all the artistic accomplishments such as drawing and painting.

Lucy had not liked the idea of her brothers and sisters eating here, at least not all the time, and as soon as she and Mr Buchanan were married she meant to discuss it with him. They were well mannered and could be trusted to dine with adults, at least Edward and Margaret, and she would not have them banished to the far reaches of the second floor where they were to live. Two of the bedrooms up here and the bathroom were to be used by them, Edward and Percy sleeping in one and Margaret and Emily the other. Not to share a bed as they had done at home – the rectory, she must remember that, the rectory was no longer their home – but having a bed each. The rooms were well furnished with thick, springy carpets on the floor, heavy velvet curtains at the windows to keep out the icy winds which often whistled down the valley and a good fire burning in the grate, for Mr Buchanan was inordinately generous, not just with her and the children, but with his own servants who, in many folks' opinion, were spoiled rotten.

"It will be all right, you wait and see," she told them, trying to draw the four of them into her arms and it was a measure of Edward's insecurity that he allowed it. She had told them that Mrs Hutton and

Bibby had been found a small cottage apiece in a corner of Mr Buchanan's grounds and they could go and visit them whenever they wanted. Wouldn't that be nice? And Elsie was only downstairs. She had been put to work in the kitchen which, it seemed to Lucy, was already over-staffed with six maids working in it, not to mention a cook, a housekeeper, a butler and God only knew how many more. But that was not her concern. She was to leave her family here, leave them in strange surroundings and be taken, driven by Mr Buchanan's chauffeur in the Rolls Royce, to Mrs Buchanan's house, Grange House, where she was to stay until the wedding but, she promised them as she kissed them a tearful farewell, she would be back first thing in the morning to see that they were all right. They were to be good and obey Buffy who was to look after them and sleep in the room next to Margaret and Emily's. They were to eat well and sleep well and not to worry, for she would always be here to protect them. Did they understand?

Gravely they said they did, coming to the top of the stairs with her and watching her all the way down, even Thimble who stood with his head on one side, evidently wondering what the devil was going on.

Mrs Buchanan put her in what she called the "apricot room" which was very pretty, and very warm. It had evidently been decorated and furnished with Franny's impeccable taste, for it was all pale colours, apricot, green and sand, the furniture of rosewood so light and delicate Lucy was afraid to touch it. The pale green velvet curtains at the window were swathed and tied back with ribbons of silk and there were flowers everywhere, the fragrance a delight. Spring flowers but all the right shades of apricot, cream, peach and gold to match the décor. There were brushes and combs and mirrors lying on the dressing-table, exquisite in silver. Lucy had never seen anything so lovely, so feminine and for a moment the woman in her delighted in it, savouring the idea that this sort of comfort and warmth would for ever be hers. But there is a price to pay, a small, defiant voice said inside her and when she turned to Mrs Buchanan her face was as expressionless as it had been, except when she was with the children and Buffy, for the past week.

There was a bathroom next door, she was told, which she was, of course, to consider her own. Would this suit her then? Mrs Buchanan asked her, an ironic smile on her face, for had she not seen first hand the lack of comfort and warmth at the rectory. They dined at seven, she added, but if Lucy would like to come down earlier she and Alex would be . . .

"I would – if it's possible and not putting anyone to any trouble – I would like to eat here."

"No, my dear, I'm afraid not. James was most particular that you should start as he means you to go on."

"I am still in mourning for my father, Mrs Buchanan. Surely . . . ?"

"I'm sorry about that, Lucy, and I do wish you'd call me Franny, since we are soon to be . . . related, but James thinks—"

"Mrs Buchanan, please."

"Is that all you have to wear, Lucy?" Franny viewed Lucy's shapeless black gown with some distaste, not at all softened by her appeal. It was Franny Buchanan's belief that when disaster struck you didn't just give in to it, you damn well took it by the throat and twisted it to suit yourself, and she was determined to see that James's bride, who she knew to be strong, did just that. She was sorry for the girl, but she was here for one purpose only and that was to be transformed into a bride fit for a Buchanan. Franny guessed that the dress was shapeless because of the weight Lucy had lost in the last weeks but that would soon be remedied and tomorrow she and the girl were to be taken to Miss Medlock's in Ambleside and there Lucy Dean was to be fitted out with a trousseau suitable for the young queen James evidently saw her to be. Everything she could possibly need from the skin out, for every possible occasion from the moment she got out of the bed she was to share with him until she got back into it, again with him. No expense was to be spared, he told Franny and if Lucy protested her protests were to be ignored. He wanted her to be the most elegantly gowned young matron Ambleside, Fellthwaite, Grasmere, indeed the whole of Lakeland had ever seen.

The first hitch, if you liked to call it that, occurred the very next morning. Lucy had dined with the Buchanans as she had been commanded. She ate a little of everything that was put before her, as young ladies of breeding were expected to, her manners faultless. She refused wine, drinking only water. She smiled only at the butler who served her, who was clearly startled, and at the footman who helped him. When spoken to she answered politely, but apart from that sat like a statue, staring ahead of her into the soft candlelight. There had been electricity installed at Grange House but Franny still liked to dine by candlelight and the effect was very lovely. Flowers and shining cutlery, flawlessly glinting crystalware, white damask tableware and Franny in a gown of quite stunning style, a scarlet chiffon so fine and clinging it was transparent and under it she wore a scarlet, fitted, tube-like underdress. There was a scattering of crystal beads at the neck and hem and her maid had cleverly arranged some in her hair so that it looked as though raindrops sparkled there. Her satin slippers had been dyed to match her gown and beside her husband, resplendent in his black and white dinner suit, the effect was dramatic.

Lucy scarcely noticed, nor was even aware of the contrast in herself to Franny Buchanan and would not have cared if she had. The young footman, when the butler was out of earshot, carried back tales to the kitchen of what a "guy" she looked, and he only hoped when madam had finished with her she would look more presentable.

"You shut your mouth, you fool," Cook hissed sharply, for she was a kindly soul who had heard something of the hardships the young miss had suffered.

"I was only saying . . ."

"Well, don't. See, help Agnes with them pans if you've nothing else to do."

The table had only just been set in the breakfast-room and the food had certainly not been brought in when she appeared like a slender black ghost at the breakfast-room door asking for a piece of toast and a cup of tea. They were not to bother with anything else since she was going out.

"Going out, miss," the same footman gasped, for it

was well known, as is always the case in big houses with many servants, that she was to be driven into Ambleside to be fitted out with a new wardrobe.

"Yes." Lucy sat down at the table and waited.

"But . . . well, miss . . ."

"Is there a problem?" she asked him distantly, not meaning to be haughty but anxious to get to Howethwaite to see how the children were. She had barely slept for worrying about them, though she had been warm and comfortable, and very clean after the bath the smiling little maid had drawn for her and the white lawn nightdress, presumably one of Mrs Buchanan's, she had been put in.

"No, but . . ."

"Yes?"

"Are you not to go into Ambleside, miss? The motor has been ordered for ten." It was not yet eight o'clock.

"Yes, but that is later, I believe. I have an errand to do first."

"An errand?"

"Yes."

"But the motor is—"

"I shall not need the motor. I'll walk."

"Walk, miss?"

Lucy stood up abruptly and the footman fell back. She looked so determined, her face set in harsh lines as though she had a problem of the utmost difficulty to solve. Should he run and fetch Mr Barrie, who was hardly out of bed himself yet? Short of physically tackling the young lady how was he to stop her just walking off and then what would madam do? Liked her own way, did madam, but then so did this one, it seemed, as she left the room, ran lightly up the stairs, coming down again struggling into an old black coat which his own mam would have been ashamed to be seen in.

"I won't be long," she told him as he hung about at the foot of the stairs, still not having made up his mind whether to go for Mr Barrie or not.

"Very well, miss," he said lamely before walking slowly up the hall to inform the rest of the servants that their guest had gone off – where, how the hell did he know? – without any breakfast.

The children were pathetically glad to see her. The same pretty housemaid who had answered the door the last time let her in, her face a picture at the sight of who was on the doorstep, and as Lucy ran up the stairs she passed maidservants on their knees with their brushes or energetically polishing the banisters. They all watched her go with open-mouthed wonder.

She stayed for an hour, just long enough to have some breakfast with them and to listen to their tales of this or that wonder, or this and that problem, all of which she reassured them would soon be solved. Buffy was with them, comforting and familiar and, drawing Lucy to one side, she was able to tell her that they had slept well, for she had checked on them through the night, though the girls had slept in the same bed, as had the boys. Thimble, already bearing the instincts of a family dog, had also shared the night with them all, moving from one bed to another in his determination to protect "his people" in these strange surroundings.

"They're fine, Lucy, really. You're not to worry. Don't forget both Mr Buchanan, and Mrs Buchanan at Grange House, have a telephone and I promise, though I don't know how I'll get the hang of the blooming thing, to telephone at the first sign of trouble. And you can telephone here if you want to speak to me or the children. Get the telephone number before you go. I'm sure Mr Buchanan won't mind."

"Buffy, what would I do without you? You've set my mind at rest. I thank God for the day when Mama found you, and now I suppose I'd better go or Mrs Buchanan will be sending a search party out for me, though I'm sure she knows where I've gone."

He was waiting at the foot of the stairs when she reluctantly left. His face had its usual stern, unsmiling countenance but there was something in his eyes which told her she was not to be chastised. A softness that he did his best to hide. She had no idea what it meant, for his mind was a closed book to her, but she sensed he was not displeased with her.

"They'll be all right, you know that, don't you, Lucy? They are your family and as such . . . they will want for nothing."

"I must see them every day." Her voice was abrupt. "They have been with me; they miss me and are in a strange place and I must make sure they are . . . happy."

"Will you be happy, Lucy?" he said with a suddenness which made her blink sharply. What on earth did he mean by that? Her mind was at rest that she had found a place of shelter and security for them. A home, good food, schooling and all the things her papa had never been able to give them. Except love, of course. He had given them, and her, that in abundance and she must take his place.

She said so and was bewildered by the strange

feeling that some light that was flickering inside him had gone out. She didn't know what to make of it and if she did, could do nothing about it. She was prepared to keep her side of their bargain, as it seemed he was to keep his and that was all that mattered, surely?

"Of course, and now Baxter will run you back to Grange House. I have telephoned Mrs Buchanan to say you are here. She is waiting for you."

"I can walk."

"No, you can't, Lucy, and when you want to come here to see the children, or me, you must ask Mrs Buchanan's chauffeur to bring you. It is only correct. You cannot just saunter about."

"You mean like Lucy Dean used to do," she said bitterly.

"Exactly. Now, will you have some breakfast with me before you go?"

"No, thank you."

It was as though she were telling him that she would take up her duties on the day they had specified, two weeks on Friday, 21 April, and not a moment sooner.

She made a beautiful bride, everyone agreed, even the Buchanans who were prepared to criticise her at every turn for what she had done to James. She wore the white her bridegroom had insisted upon, a dress of straight simplicity, silk net over chiffon which rested on her hips and hung in pleats to her ankle bone. On her hair, which Mrs Buchanan's maid had dressed back into a smooth bun was a Juliet cap with a veil attached which fell at the front to her breast, but fluted, so that at the back it reached her calves. She carried a small posy of white rosebuds, freesias and baby's breath. Her brother did well. He was almost as tall as she was and in the grey morning coat and striped trousers his new brother-in-law had tricked him out in, he made a handsome foil for the fragile beauty of the woman he led down the aisle. At their backs were her sisters, both in white, simply dressed with tiny wreaths of rosebuds in their hair. Why was it, the congregation wondered, that they gave the impression of being a close family group to which no one else was admitted? Even her younger brother, a lad of about six, walked ahead of her, carrying her wedding ring on a velvet cushion. They appeared to be protecting her, the lovely floating bride, hemming her in, and when they reached James Buchanan seemed reluctant to stand aside for him.

They wept inconsolably, except for the elder boy, when she and James climbed into the Rolls Royce which was to take them on the first part of their wedding trip, and so did the bride. They clung together in a most embarrassing way and had it not been for the little crippled girl who came to prise them apart they might have all been swept into the motor with James and his new wife. Not that James Buchanan was the sort of man to stand such nonsense, and it was seen that he spoke sharply to the new Mrs Buchanan. Her lovely head drooped and there were more than a few who remarked that it was not a very auspicious way to begin a marriage.

At the end of May Lucy Buchanan had her nineteenth birthday and to celebrate it and to show her how much he valued her she was given an exquisite bracelet and necklace to match by her husband. The set had been specially made for her. Tiny pearls, two rows linked by a chain so fine it looked like a cobweb on which droplets of dewed pearls hung. He also gave instructions to his housekeeper that a party was to be held in his wife's honour at their home, Howethwaite, to which a hundred people, friends and relatives, were to be invited, since he wanted to show off his beautiful, elegantly dressed young wife.

Though they had been married for six weeks he continued to make love to her every night and sometimes in the morning as well. The new Mrs Buchanan had become accustomed to it, though she could not say she cared for it. It had been painful the first time, though she felt certain, how she did not know since she was ignorant of such things, that he had made a decent effort not to hurt her.

"Do you know what it is I am to do to you?" he had asked her that first night after she had spent half an hour sitting up in bed waiting for him.

"Oh, yes," she had answered, anxious to have it over and done with so that she could turn away and go to sleep. She had expected an immediate assault in the dark, the lamps turned out, but he had left them on, sitting down on the edge of the bed and looking at her in the strangest way.

"You are the most beautiful thing I have ever seen." His voice was musing and his hand lifted a tress of her long hair and put it to his face.

"Thank you," she answered politely.

"So, here you are and you must be afraid."

"Oh, no, I am not afraid, Mr Buchanan," lying fiercely.

"So, you mean to be brave and suffer it without a word, is that it?"

"It seems I have no choice. Please, don't think me ungrateful since you have done all you said you would do. Now it is my turn to—"

"Is that how you see it, Lucy? Your turn to pay your dues?"

"Not at all," but he knew she was not telling the truth. For a moment he felt the devastation creep over him, but then what else had he expected? In the past she had been more than honest with him so could he expect her to be anything else now? The ceremony today, though it had altered her status, had not altered her heart, which certainly did not belong to him.

"Come, let's be honest with each other. This is a . . . an arrangement which suits us both. You want security for your family. I want a wife, someone to run my home and entertain my guests, and naturally, soon, I hope, children."

If he had expected a reaction he was disappointed.

She sat straight-backed in the bed, not lounging in any way against the piled-up pillows, her face slightly averted.

"So, have you nothing to say in answer," though what he hoped for he didn't know.

Suddenly she was angry. "Oh, for God's sake get on with it, Mr Buchanan, or are you to chatter all night?"

He laughed out loud then, the first time she could remember him doing so. "You're a rare bird, Lucy Dean, and you're right. I'm eager to see what I have bought . . . oh, yes, I know I have bought you, my darling, for the price of a home for your brothers and sisters you have sold yourself to me and so I'll have a look at what I've paid for."

"I don't know what you mean," she said coldly.

"Yes, you do, so off with that nightdress if you please." He put the tips of his fingers on her shoulder and she flinched away but he took no notice, running them down her arm and back again to her neck, tracing the outline of her ear, aware all the time of the rigidity of her body but ignoring that too.

Lucy could feel the red-hot flush of embarrassment move to every part of her when, with what she did not recognise as an anxiety as great as hers, he lifted her arms above her head and drew her nightdress from her. She had regained a little weight in the few weeks before her wedding and her breasts were full and rounded, the nipples, rosy and flushed, standing proud. He had not even kissed her yet except for the chaste peck at the altar; now, slowly, he put his lips to hers, enfolding them, caressing them, parting them in some curious way, his tongue brushing against hers while his hands went to her breasts. She closed her eyes and held her breath, for she felt as though she were being devoured, by his mouth and by his hands and if she kept perfectly still and made no protest surely it would soon be over, this humiliation, but James Buchanan was a skilled lover and one who liked to please not only his own need but that of the woman to whom he made love, and he wanted more than anything to please his bride. He had shrugged out of the dressing-gown he wore and, to her horror, was clasping her naked body to his own, savouring her, with his mouth, his tongue, his fingers, which found every private part of her cringing body.

"This might be . . . painful," he told her when at last some crescendo appeared to be approaching, and it was, for a moment later the pain of penetration lanced through her. His body was nailed to hers, shuddering in what must be agony, she had decided, only too glad when, at last, it seemed to be over.

"Don't be alarmed," he told her, breathing hard. "It will be easier next time. In fact I'm determined you shall like it. Now, go to sleep." He put his arms about her possessively, one hand cupping her breast and at once fell into a deep sleep. She did her best not to mind, telling herself that she would get used to it, that it was what she had promised him, but if only she could ease herself away from him, put some space between his hard, warm male body and hers, which felt as though it had been tossed upon storm waters and thrown up on a rocky shore. Was this to happen every time they got into bed together and if so how was she to bear it? She knew that it was just a small part of marriage, that there would be many blessings to balance it, to make up for the indignities she had suffered tonight. She must dwell on them, not the crushing arm which lay across her body, the heavy breathing of a man beside her, the hand which, even in sleep, seemed to fondle her breast. She must remind herself of the grammar school in Ambleside which Edward was to attend and which she had won from Mr Buchanan who had wanted him to go away to a boarding school. The concession she had begged for Percy who was, in her opinion, too young for the grammar school and for the time being was to share Margaret and Emily's lessons. She must keep her exhausted mind on the warm, well-made clothing she had bought for them, pretty dresses for the girls, stout new boots for the boys, on the good and plentiful food they ate and the warmth and comfort in which they now lived. They were safe and she must be glad of it. The price she was paying was worth it. Mr Buchanan was right. It would get easier.

The party was not the success that James had hoped for and she knew it was her fault. She felt the hush fall on the room the moment she entered it on James's arm. Around her neck and on her wrist was the expensive birthday gift from her husband which they'd all heard about. She wore a gown of shimmering loveliness which clung to her magnificent, long-limbed, full-breasted body like a second skin. There were those among them who had the fanciful idea that she put them in mind of an Amazon queen. The gown was a simple sheath which, though it did not show either in her manner or James's, had been put on twice this evening, which was why they were a trifle late. Dimity, who was now her lady's maid, for Franny said she must have one, had been sent packing by her master, her face as red as a poppy, for she was well aware of what he had in mind for her beautiful mistress. An ice maiden she had looked like and James Buchanan had sworn that this time he would thaw her so that she would melt into his arms like the true woman he knew her to be but, once again, she had submitted willingly enough to him then calmly shrugged herself back into her gown, asking his help with the fastenings since she could hardly summon Dimity to do it again, she told him coolly.

Her guests looked at her critically and could find no fault, for there was no doubt she was a gorgeous young creature and, the gentlemen at least, wished they could be in James Buchanan's shoes, or rather his bed for a night or two.

There were not quite the hundred James had envisaged but everyone who had been invited had come. They wouldn't miss this for the world, they told one another. The debut, so to speak, into society of the girl who had earned herself so much notoriety during the past few months. The girl who had turned her nose up at James Buchanan and then changed her mind!

The élite of Ambleside society was there. The Mossops with their son Frederick and their daughter Marion, remembering her, they gushed, from Franny Buchanan's dance where she had so enchanted them all. The Askews, with Rosalyn, Louise and Roger; the Kendalls with Aurora and Gregory, and the Grahams with their eldest, Rose. And standing somewhat aloofly, for they could not forget the slight to their daughter last year, the Gibsons, with Charlotte clinging possessively to the arm of her fiancé, soon to be husband, Doctor Paul Buchanan. A pleasant young man who, James was of the opinion, and had said so to Lucy, almost making her smile, would be eaten alive by Charlotte the moment she had him up the aisle.

There was Ben Buchanan, the eldest of the cousins and his comfortable wife, Joan, who could always be relied upon to be kind. Anne Mounsey and her prosperous farmer husband, Thomas and Christine Scott and her husband Douglas. Alex and Franny, Janet and Angus Gunson and Andrew Buchanan, who she was meeting for the first time, the only one still unattached, smiling wickedly into her eyes as he kissed her cheek, which, as a cousin, he was entitled to do, he told her, winking at James. For the first time Lucy felt a tremor of real warmth run through her.

Eight cousins, counting James, male and female, who were descended from Alex and Christy Buchanan and there was not one among them who was not dark-haired and attractive as their grandparents had been, only the colour of their eyes differing, some a soft velvet grey come from their grandmother, others the vivid blue, a sapphire blue from their grandfather.

She had met them before, naturally, for Franny had given a family party when Lucy stayed with her prior to the wedding, but this was the first time they were to see her as Mrs James Buchanan, wife and hostess and how would she shape up, they were dying to know. The gentlemen bowed over her hand and the ladies smiled graciously, distantly kind, since she was related by marriage to them after all, treating her as though she were a miss from the schoolroom despite the magnificence of her white bosom which the low-cut gown showed off to advantage. They were inclined to be critical, at least the womenfolk were, for they had had high hopes of Charlotte Gibson who was one of them, or at least her mother was. They were all well dressed, the women, if not fashionably, then expensively so, the gentlemen in full evening dress consisting of a dinner jacket, single-breasted and unbuttoned as was the mode, a black bow tie, gleaming white shirt front, pleated, and a waistcoat with short points. They were drinking the latest cocktails mixed by Dixon, the Buchanan butler. A glass was pressed on Lucy and she tasted it, enjoying the pleasantly fizzing sensation that rushed to her head. She took another sip and was instantly disconcerted and not a little annoyed when her husband took it from her, murmuring that there was to be champagne later and she was not to drink cocktails since she was not used to them. A fruit juice for Mrs Buchanan, he told the hovering footman. He smiled pleasantly as he said it, sipping his own drink and looking round the somewhat astonished group who had witnessed the exchange.

It was as though a small imp, a wicked and angry imp, entered Lucy's brain, needling downwards and though it was not painful it was hot and rebellious, taking over and defying the grateful state of impassive obedience in which Lucy Buchanan had dwelled ever since she had known that her beloved family were to be safe. She had never been a girl, or young woman, to be dictated to, for she had been the virtual head of the Dean household ever since her mother died and all decisions made had been hers. Now, for almost two months she had done her best to please James Buchanan and his family, resolute in her determination to succeed. The imp said to hell with it!

"I think I could manage another, James," she said, signalling to Dixon who, up to now, she had allowed to intimidate her. "I'm hardly likely to become intoxicated on one, am I, or even two if I feel like it. After all, it is my birthday. My nineteenth so I can hardly be considered a child," especially after what you do to me at least once a day, her flashing golden eyes said into his.

"I think not, my dear." He was beginning to scowl and his eyes became icy grey slits of annoyance. "These are very strong, made to Dixon's own recipe and will go at once to your head."

"And why shouldn't they, James? As Lucy says, it is her nineteenth birthday and by God, it's a few years since any of us, at least this generation, had one of those."

It was Franny, of course, a rebel herself and always willing to aid another. She took a small gold case from her bag, extracted a cigarette, allowed James to light it for her and inhaled deeply. She was wearing the most ravishing dress of gold chiffon studded with crystal beads and had a gold satin underdress beneath it caught at the ankle with narrow crystal insertions. It was very low cut, showing the swell of her small breasts almost to her nipples and Lucy, ready to laugh almost fondly at her rescuer, hoped to God they would not fall out. A long chiffon scarf with tasselled ends drifted about her bare shoulders. Her pale gold hair had a centre parting and was brushed into a heavy coil on her neck. About her forehead was a band of crystal set on gold satin. She was not a pretty woman but her style was such that no one noticed it. She was twenty-eight, childless, sophisticated and could be malicious if put out of countenance.

"Thank you, Franny, but I think I know how my wife should behave," James began but Franny merely grinned audaciously at him and, taking Lucy by the arm, led her away to where Andrew stood leaning indolently against the wall, his eyes on Lucy's splendid bosom as they approached.

"Don't be so stuffy, James," Franny said over her shoulder. "You were young once yourself, or so they tell me."

James Buchanan, with the gritty control which had been part of his nature for many years and which he was to perfect in the future, became even more rigid. He turned a tight smile on the group with him, then, bowing politely, showing none of the emotion which surged through him, begged to be excused for a moment.

She was flirted with by all the gentlemen, particularly Andrew who had no lady to restrain him, passing from one group to another and all the time sipping, first the cocktails and then the champagne which Dixon opened at a signal from James. He had her firmly by the arm again by then, his face inscrutable, his eyes as cold and dangerous as a snake's in his brown face and Franny was heard to say in an aside to her husband that the "child" was in for it when they had all gone home.

But she couldn't help it. Franny just loved to stir things up a bit, to make trouble, even for someone of whom she was fond. To throw a live squib into a gathering which needed livening up and this, now that James had Lucy firmly anchored and drooping at his side, seemed to be proving to be one of those. They were having supper, a buffet supper set at small tables in the enormous drawing-room and afterwards there was to be dancing. There was a throb of conversation humming about the room and the tinkle of instruments as the small band set up in readiness. There was some laughter, especially from the corner where Andrew Buchanan and several other young ladies and gentlemen were sitting. Nevertheless from the table she was sharing with her husband, James and Lucy, Franny's voice could be heard by everyone in the room.

"And what is your opinion of the women's suffrage movement, Lucy? I believe you are interested in their cause?"

The result was electrifying. It was as though a hand had reached inside her and flicked on a switch, like one of those that were placed on the wall beside the doorway of each room at Howethwaite and which so fascinated her. Her head came up, her slumped, bored shoulders squared and her eyes became a clear golden yellow, like a leopard's, the enlarged pupils black as sable. She turned with such force she knocked over a glass of champagne which Dixon leaped to retrieve but she did not even notice.

"My opinion," she cried, a clarion call which silenced every voice in the room. "My opinion is that they are quite marvellous, Mrs Buchanan . . . er, Franny, as I'm sure is the opinion of every woman who has a brain to think with." She glared about her as if defying them to deny it. "The National Union of Women's Suffrage started it but it needs fighters to achieve our aims, like those in the Women's Social and Political Union which I long to join."

Every face in the room turned expectantly to James, waiting breathlessly for his reaction to this staggering statement.

"We want equality and—"

"We? Mrs Buchanan?"

She did not know who spoke and she did not care, for here was something she could talk about at last. She was not interested in so much of the tinkling chatter which the women of James's society indulged in. They talked of people she did not know, plays she had not seen, books she had not read and places she had never visited. She would die for the cause, she told the frozen-faced and silent figures who sat or lounged about the room, just like Emily Wilding Davison who had thrown herself on to the racecourse at the Derby last June. She knew the suffragette movement did not meet with everyone's approval but surely . . .

Slowly she became aware of the vice-like grip on her arm, a grip so fierce she could feel the flow of blood to her hand become cut off and pins and needles attacked her fingers, and with it her torrent of words came to an end. By their silence and by the pain James was inflicting on her she was made to realise just how far she had gone to break every rule of society. The flush that washed her lovely face died down but she did not subside. Not her. Not the newly married Mrs James Buchanan, despite the appalled shock she saw in every face, at least those of the ladies, for the gentlemen were quite bowled over, wondering whether the enthusiasm she showed over this damn fool nonsense ever transferred itself into James's bed.

She tossed her head with a lofty gesture which

brought a shower of curls tumbling in charming dis-array about her ears, and grinned. "Oh dear, I have set the cat among the pigeons, haven't I?"

His rage was quite killing when eventually it could be let out in the privacy of their bedroom.

"Get out," he snarled at the terrified Dimity, who ran for her life, believing fearfully that her mistress would be sporting a black eye the next time she saw her. They had all heard in the kitchen about the show their young mistress had made of herself, spouting on about those dreadful women suffragettes, or so Mr Dixon had said, and the repercussions were just about to begin, it appeared. There'd be ructions the minute Dimity left the room but she daren't linger, not even to save her mistress, of whom she had become extremely fond. Oh, she did hope he wouldn't hit her!

"Now then, madam, what do you mean by upsetting my guests . . . *your* guests, with all that claptrap you spouted downstairs. I've never heard such bloody nonsense in my life and I'd be obliged if in future you'd keep it to yourself. Particularly when we have company."

"I was asked a question and I answered it. Was I supposed to—"

"I'll be having words with that bloody woman tomorrow. This is all her fault."

"That bloody woman, as you call her, has been extremely good to me and anyway, I was glad to be able to talk about something of real interest instead of that bloody rubbish."

"And I'd be obliged if you would refrain from swearing. It is not becoming in a lady."

"Dear God above!" She was as incensed as he was

now. "Why is it perfectly permissible for a man, a gentleman, to use the word 'bloody' and not—"

"You know perfectly well what the difference is." James's face was expressionless, carved in amber-tinted stone but his eyes were wild, brilliant with a dangerous, frosted grey. He stood in the centre of their softly lit bedroom, his hands clenched into tight fists which pressed against the sides of his upper legs. He was self-assured, completely certain in his masculine world that he would have his own way, arrogantly believing that it was a wife's duty to do as her husband did, think as her husband thought, and the havoc that pounded inside him was not allowed to show.

"This is what the suffragette movement is all about, isn't it?" she said slowly, as though a light had just been shone on some tricky problem which had not been quite clear to her up to now. "It is not just fighting for votes for women. It's for the rights of women. The right to be equal with men."

"Don't be so bloody ridiculous, Lucy."

"No, I cannot turn my back on it."

"Turn your back on what, for Christ's sake?"

Her jaw clenched as tight as his fists and she turned away from him as though she were no longer concerned with his petty tyranny. This was the first time they had argued, fought over anything, for he had denied her nothing, even over the question of the boys' schooling. She was as shocked as he was by the bitterness of their quarrel but it was not in her to give up, and he was the same. Well, it made no difference. Already, after only a few weeks of marriage, she was bored to the point of tears by the domesticated routine she was supposed to take up as a young matron. She did not want to be consulted each day by Cook on her preference for this or that menu for dinner or luncheon. She was not concerned with whether the windows had been cleaned properly or the kitchen floor scrubbed, if that was supposed to interest her, so she totally ignored her duties as the mistress of the house, believing that between them, Mrs Burns the housekeeper, Mrs Bunting the cook, and Dixon the butler, could manage things far better without her interference. James had been well looked after for many years and it certainly didn't need her half-hearted and reluctant involvement to keep up their standards. The house was run like a well-oiled clock under their supervision. The meals were splendidly cooked and served promptly and her only concern was for Elsie, though she realised that it made things no better for the little scullery maid to have her constantly asking after her. She had even made the grave mistake of going into the kitchen and talking to her, questioning her on her duties, for the child was only twelve years old and had had a poor start in life. She knew she had made an error by the way Mrs Bunting drew herself up and took a stance of offended righteousness before her ovens; yes, *her* ovens, as this was *her* kitchen and not a place where the mistress of the house was expected to show herself.

She kept away after that, making discreet enquiries from Buffy who, slowly, for she was neither a servant, nor a member of the family, was finding her feet at Howethwaite. Buffy had made a friend of one of the housemaids, a girl of her own age, and, as Buffy described her, plain, sensible and discreet, and was able to report that Elsie was fine and dandy. Not that Fanny, as she was called, was prepared to pass on tittle-tattle from the kitchen, Buffy was made to understand.

Though Buffy was against it, Lucy would not hear of giving up the long talks she and Buffy had. She and Buffy had been friends for many years and Lucy was not prepared to give up that friendship, no matter what the change in their circumstances might be, she declared stoutly. Buffy had been her help and support through many bad times, she told her, and if Buffy wanted to see her, to come and sit in Lucy's drawing-room and talk to her, then she should, and if Lucy needed to go up to the schoolroom, as it was called, and chat with Buffy and the children, then she would and no one, not James, not society, not the somewhat disapproving servants, would stop her. By God, she said, it was a damn sight more entertaining than the chitter-chatter of the ladies who called on her in the way society ladies did, and the only thing that kept her sane.

She had been taken to task by James, who had been complained to by Miss Bradley, for going against her during lessons by whisking them and Percy away on a walk up to Stockghyll Force and on another bright May afternoon to the top of Wansfell Pike.

James had not been too hard on her, understanding that the lives of the Deans, all of them, which had been unfettered by authority for so long, were now vastly different, but she must realise that if they were to have any sense of discipline and the education that had been so lacking in their lives, then she must leave them alone during lessons. At the weekend they would all get in the Rolls Royce and he would take them wherever they pleased, not realising in the newness and softness of his love, and the fulfilling of it, that it was precisely this they did not want. They did not want Mr Buchanan. They wanted Lucy and the old ways they had known before Papa died, and so did she.

She had tried to understand and be patient, but this with the suffragette movement was not something she was prepared to abandon.

She said so, and was alarmed by the savagery in his voice.

"I'm warning you, Lucy, this has got to stop. I will not have my guests insulted as you have done this evening. You are my wife and—"

"And so I'm to be allowed no opinion or views of my own."

"Not if it means airing them at parties to people who don't want to hear them and are offended by them. D'you hear? You are to keep your beliefs about the damned suffragettes to yourself in future. Follow the example of the other ladies and talk about . . . well, whatever it is they talk about but the word suffragette is not to be mentioned in my presence again. Is that understood?"

He had forbidden her to speak of it again but not for a moment did it occur to him to forbid her to go to the suffragette headquarters in Compston Street.

The first Lucy heard of the trouble in Europe was at the WSPU headquarters in Compston Street where she intended to go as often as she could, which meant, of course, when she could get out of the house without some domestic trivia interfering with her plans. Some days, of course, when she could not avoid it, she was compelled, because of her position as the wife of James Buchanan, to visit Franny, or one of James's other female relatives on the interminable round of "calling" which was the practice of ladies of their social class. They told one another they were only doing what they saw as their duty in shaping James's young and somewhat unconventional wife into the kind of lady they themselves were, putting themselves out in their efforts, for they felt they owed it to James. Often enough, during the period of what was known in their circle as "afternoon calls" when the ladies were either called upon, or called on other ladies, they would be told that she was out. Simply that! Out! Dixon, his face managing to be expressionless and yet at the same time sorrowful, could not even say where she had gone when asked by Mrs Joan Buchanan, or Mrs Janet Gunson, or Mrs Anne Mounsey, for one minute she was there in her small sitting-room at the back of the house and the next, vanished and only she knew to where.

It was hard work, for plainly she was not interested in becoming "one of them" but they struggled on, for surely, very soon, James would get her with child and she would be forced to confine herself to the suitable activities they themselves followed. It was known she was very fond of walking, or even fell climbing and had been seen once or twice on that ancient bicycle of hers in Ambleside, but where she ended up was anybody's guess. They would have been appalled if they had known.

They were delighted and quite astonished to see her at the headquarters of the WSPU in Compston Street.

"Lucy ... oh, I beg your pardon, should I call you Mrs Buchanan now?" Letty cried, seemingly none the worse for her brush with the law. They had all heard of Lucy's splendid marriage and might she not now be, in her elevated position, different to the young girl who had offered her services several months ago?

"Lord, no! I'm only sorry I haven't been able to call sooner but ... well, my father died, as perhaps you know. I ... married Mr Buchanan and, naturally, have had to get my brothers and sisters settled in their new home, which took a while, but the fact that I'm married hasn't altered my interest in the suffragist movement. I'm still eager to help in any way I can so, if there's anything, anything at all ..."

Her voice trailed away uncertainly as she became aware that she and Letty were not the only ones in the room. There appeared to be at least half a dozen other women, young women, crammed into the small space which was now furnished with not one but two tables, on one of which two of them were clacking away on rather ancient typewriters.

Or at least they had been until she walked into the room when every head turned to look at her. She was clad in the smart cycling outfit she now, as Mrs James Buchanan, could afford to buy. The short jacket was in a very fine, pale grey wool, the lapels edged in caramel and the ankle-length skirt had an inverted pleat down the centre of the back, the inside of which was lined again with caramel. The buttons fastening the jacket and those on the sleeve were covered in caramel-coloured satin. She wore a silk scarf at her neck and a small, caramel-coloured beret skewered by an unstable hatpin to her slipping hair. She looked quite enchanting, flushed and eager, and the women stared, mesmerised as most plain or ordinary women are by such loveliness.

She smiled shyly at each one, wondering why she should feel shy. Perhaps because this was so important to her, so new, so sacred almost and these young women already had a kind of mystique about them that made her at the same time feel envious and humble. They were working girls, the decent but plain clothes they wore told her that, probably from a farm or a factory. They appeared to be addressing envelopes and wrappers. One was carefully turning the handle of a machine with a roller which, as it revolved, printed some message on to a sheet of paper. There was a stack of newspapers piled at the end of the table where the girls were addressing envelopes, tied about with string which Letty had been about to cut and Lucy could see that it contained copies of the *Suffragette*, probably just come off the London train.

The last woman, a bit older than the rest, very obviously came from a different background. Though she was painfully thin, gaunt even, and though she smiled politely, her manner was uncertain and her movements weak as she reached for a pile of envelopes which the other girls had addressed. It was her clothing, obviously expensive and well made, if ill-fitting, and a certain manner the other girls lacked that told Lucy she was a lady. The daughter of a gentleman in fact. When she smiled at her Lucy saw that one of her teeth was broken.

"We're always glad of help, Lucy, and believe me there is always something to be done. Those handbills, for instance. The ones Connie is printing. They need to be handed out by the weekend. Outside the railway station at Windermere is a good spot and at the gates outside the grounds after the football match on Saturday. In fact anywhere there's to be a crowd. Connie and Isobel, this is Isobel," indicating a tall, ginger-haired girl with a mass of freckles across her nose who looked up from the envelopes and smiled again at Lucy, "and that's Connie," nodding at the young girl on the printing machine who bobbed her head at the elegant Mrs Buchanan, "will go up to Windermere and to Bowness, but Edwina, she's not here by the way since she was needed in her father's shop. I believe you met her the last time you were here. Well, she's looking for some help at the match at Grasmere. It's only a couple of local teams but there'll be a big turnout and wherever there's a crowd we aim to be there. And there's to be a procession in

Fellthwaite in a week's time, something to do with a Rose Queen, Sunday school, you know the sort of thing and there's bound to be a good crowd."

"This Saturday, you say?" Lucy's face creased with anxiety and she wondered how on earth she was possibly to elude her husband on a Saturday, a day on which he expected her to be home to entertain him, and also and more importantly, the day Miss Bradley did not come for lessons and Edward was home from school. The children would be looking forward to spending some time with her, which was really not a problem since they would think it no end of fun passing out the propaganda handbills, but escaping from James might be more difficult.

Her glance wandered round the office as though looking for illumination. There had been shelves put up since last she was here and they were stacked with books, of what sort she didn't know. To the pale brown wall there had been added a notice-board on which dozens of pieces of paper were pinned, including a map of the area. It seemed the Ambleside branch of the WSPU was getting organised. There was even a small fire flickering in the grate and on the wall, added to the posters she had noticed the last time she was here, was one of Christabel Pankhurst and above the mantelpiece a framed photograph of Emmeline Pankhurst.

"But first, before you decide, won't you speak to Anne?" Letty put her hand on the pale young woman's shoulder and in the gesture was pride and awe, some tribute she seemed to be paying her, and a deep affection. "Anne is up here to recuperate. She has just been released from prison."

There was a deep and reverent silence and for the first time Lucy noticed the small purple, white and green brooch pinned to the young woman's lapel, shaped like a broad arrow, which proclaimed she had been imprisoned for her beliefs.

"She needs some rest and the sort of food that will give her back her strength, don't you, Anne, and so we are proud to look after her. She is staying with Edwina and is supposed to remain in bed until lunchtime but she insists on coming over here."

"Please, Letty, don't go on so. I'm feeling much better and besides, I'm only sitting here sorting envelopes." Anne laughed, and as she did so Lucy could see that her mouth was half healed at the corners as though she had suffered some injury. She turned to Lucy and held out her hand. "I'm Anne Longman and it's a pleasure to meet you, Mrs Buchanan."

"Lucy, please." Lucy was ready to kneel down and pay homage to this woman whose body had been violated in the cause for other women. She felt a great need sweep over her to break down and weep for her suffering. For what Lucy saw as her nobility of purpose and for her cheerfulness and fortitude in the face of it. Would she, Lucy, be able to laugh and carry on with her life if she had been subjected to the indignities, no, the cruelties which had been imposed on Anne Longman? She hoped so, that is if she was ever allowed to fight for the cause, which seemed unlikely in the state of marriage that now tied her down.

"Oh, Miss Longman—"

"It's Mrs, Lucy, and please, call me Anne."

"*Mrs!*" Lucy gasped. "Does your husband not object to your involvement in the movement?"

"No, he doesn't. I'm one of those fortunate women whose husband does not think women have second-class brains. He is an active member of the Men's League for Women's Suffrage and supports us one hundred per cent in our fight."

"When . . . what . . . where . . ." Lucy was longing to hear more but she felt she could not pry into the obviously painful experience Anne Longman had suffered, but it seemed that Anne was, if not happy to tell her, then felt she owed it to them.

"I was involved in the riot, as they called it, at the Constitution Hill gate of Buckingham Palace. We were attempting to get our deputation in to the king with a petition but he refused to see us, so we marched on the gates. Our object was to demand votes for women and to protest against the torture inflicted on us in prison. We were met by ranks of the police, both mounted and on foot, who brutally ill-used us, and I mean in a sexual way, Lucy." Her voice was quiet and detached as though she were telling them of some happening on the other side of the world which had not affected her in any way.

Connie, who could have been no more than seventeen, had begun to weep silently.

"Dear God . . ."

"He did not come to our aid, Lucy. Mrs Pankhurst tried to but an inspector carried her bodily away to a waiting motor car, taking her off to Holloway. We tried to climb the gates of the palace but the police were too strong for us. Sixty-six of us, and two men, were arrested. We refused to give our names and so we were allotted numbers when we came before the magistrate at Bow Street. I was number thirty-six," she said simply. "We were dragged and kicked and . . . well, eventually bound over. I received a month's hard labour and, when I refused food and water I was . . . forcibly fed. That's where I got this broken tooth." She smiled to show them and reached for another bundle of envelopes while the other young women, who, they told themselves, would die for the cause that was so important to them, wondered if they could be as stoic, as calm, as accepting of what was almost rape.

"Mrs Longman . . . Anne, if there's anything I can do . . ." to help you, to help the brave women who fought alongside you, to help this cause which had become almost holy to her, Lucy wanted to say but her throat was clogged with suppressed tears and she wondered despairingly if she was ever to be of service to them if the smallest thing was to reduce her to tears. Not that what Anne Longman had suffered was small, nor her recounting of it, but it seemed to Lucy that to be of any help, to be the sort of woman the movement needed, you had to bury all emotion and go coolly to war; was Lucy Buchanan capable of that with her tendency to feel so desperately the sympathy which, though worth while, clouded the mind which had to be clear?

"My dear, we all want to help and only a few weeks ago I would have encouraged you, all of you," looking round the silently respectful circle of young women, "to march, to break windows, to set fires and do any kind of damage, to property, not to people or animals, you understand, that would move our campaign forward, but I think we are going to have to put aside our struggle in what could be a greater struggle for mankind."

Lucy looked about her at the faces of the other young women to see if they had understood Anne Longman's last remark but it seemed they were as bewildered as she was. Give up the struggle! Give up the struggle, she seemed to be saying, and after all she had suffered in its cause! What on earth could she mean? But Mrs Longman placidly continued to put the envelopes in neat piles, apparently the only work they would allow her to do.

"Mrs Longman . . . Anne," Letty began, her plain face creased into lines of worry, for surely poor Mrs Longman must be deranged. Had she suffered more in prison than was shown on the surface? Beside her broken tooth, her torn mouth and the damage to her lungs and heart which five periods in gaol had caused, was her mind broken, too?

Anne Longman sighed and looked up at them. "I'm not saying you must shut down at once, for it might not come to it but it seems likely, or so my husband and men he is acquainted with are saying. I know you are planning a meeting at – where was it? – Millan's Park, a week on Saturday, and that you are hoping to have a well-known speaker. No, I'm not about to say her name lest it get about and she is arrested, but I think it likely it will be the last."

"The last?" It seemed they could not get to grips with what she was saying, let alone what she meant by it and again she sighed.

"You will have heard of the assassination of the Archduke Franz Ferdinand last month, will you not?"

Yes, they all nodded their heads in agreement but what, in heaven's name, was that to do with the WSPU, their young, anxious expressions asked. None of them was well educated, not even Lucy, for her education had been sketchy at best. They could, of course, read and write, but the details of what went on outside their small world, unless it was to do with the WSPU, did not greatly concern them.

"That shot was considered a challenge to Austro-Hungary's position as the ruler of Bosnia."

"Bosnia?" one of them whispered in a total state of stupor.

"Yes. It is a challenge to its prestige as one of the Great Powers and there will be repercussions."

"Repercussions?" It was as though they could, in their lack of understanding, only repeat whatever Anne Longman said.

"Yes, military repercussions. Relations between France and Germany are not good and now this Balkan unrest has exacerbated the situation. It is the belief of gentlemen with whom my husband is associated, and indeed in the world of business, that that shot fired in Sarajevo will be the first to ring round the world. There are, of course, many instabilities in European society, far too many to enumerate here, but when they erupt, as it seems they are about to do, there will be war."

"War, between who?"

It did not seem to matter who asked the question.

"A European war in which Britain will be involved, but come, we must not cross the bridge until we come to it, as they say. Let us hope it will blow over and in the meanwhile we women must continue our fight. Pass out your handbills, send your letters, have your meeting next week and pray that I am wrong."

The children were so excited she was afraid it would

be noticed by the servants, or even by James on the Friday evening before the Saturday she and Edwina were to bicycle to Grasmere to the football match.

"But what are we going to do there?" Percy, who had never been to a football match in his life, whispered in a voice that might have been heard in the next room. "And why is it a secret?"

How could she tell them that if James heard about the expedition he would put a stop to it, probably confine them, and herself, to the house and her efforts to help the WSPU would be seriously impeded. Already she knew that her visits to Compston Street were risky, for he could put a stop to those as well if he found out from his cousins that his wife was very rarely where she was supposed to be.

She and James had settled into a polite but somewhat uneasy routine in those first weeks of their marriage. James was an early riser, sometimes leaving their bed at six in the morning so that she was allowed a blissful couple of hours without his dominating male invasion of it and he spent many of his evenings in his study with what appeared to be a mountain of paperwork in front of him. She was still awkward and uncertain in his nightly embraces which were often prolonged and, on his part, accompanied by the most astonishing heaving and groaning, but she found if she lay still and let her mind drift off to some pleasant place, perhaps the top of Loughrigg Fell, or even to the office in Compston Street, she could accommodate him without any undue stress.

Not once did it occur to her that her performance, or rather lack of it, might not suit her husband.

"I know women aren't supposed to like it, ladies,

that is, but I had hoped that . . . with time you might learn at least to hide your distaste," he said brusquely to her one night as he rolled away from her submissive body.

She was astonished, sitting up in bed to stare down at him, her naked body shielded by the mass of her tumbled hair. She looked quite glorious, her flesh flushed and rosy, though she was as untouched by what had just happened as a virgin. James felt his heart constrict with his love for her. He had been tolerant, knowing that what he did, no matter how much care he took to please her, did not touch the core of her, that sweet centre of a woman which comes alive when a man loves her. He had accepted her stoicism, believing that if he was patient, one night when it was over she would not turn away with a small sigh of relief as she did now but would cling to him, stretching languorously in the aftermath. One night he would awaken that slumbering sexuality which he was certain lived within her. He was painstaking in his effort to please her body, to please her unawakened heart, to please the woman in her with his caresses, his hidden love which she knew nothing about. Surely, even if she did not love him with her emotions her ripe young body would instinctively respond to his, but so far the best he could hope for was that she would not yawn as she turned away from him. It was becoming too much for him. He sometimes thought he would leave her alone, sleep in another bed, find a mistress to slake his thirst which never seemed satisfied but then, how would she conceive a child which he hoped might turn her to him, bind her to him.

"I don't understand you, James," she said to him

now. "Am I not . . . not more than happy to . . . to make love in our bed?"

"Is that what it is?"

"What d'you mean?" She was clearly perplexed.

"I mean, Mrs Buchanan, that what we do in this bed has nothing to do with love." He lay on his back, his arm across his face, his hard, muscled body spreadeagled, one knee slightly bent. He was a fine-bodied man and she had become used to him and to his nakedness, but for one inexplicable moment she had a strange feeling that she wanted to . . . to lean over him, to put a hand to his face, to remove his arm from it and see what he was hiding underneath. Then it was gone, that feeling, and indignation came to take its place.

"I have not deceived you, if that's what you're saying, James. I have never professed to love you, nor you me. It seemed that it was a marriage of convenience. Convenient to us both. Have you changed your mind? Though if you have I don't see what we can do about it."

"No."

"Well then, we must go on as we are. If there is . . . well, something you wish me to do . . . more than I do now . . . in bed, I mean," ducking her head in some embarrassment, "then please tell me."

"And you'll see what you can do to gratify me, is that it?"

"Well . . . yes."

"Thank you, my dear, that is most generous of you but really, don't trouble yourself. It is of no consequence."

"Well, then . . ."

He rose suddenly and strode across the room to the fireplace where he kept a box of cigars. Taking one from it he lit it, leaning indolently in his nakedness against the mantelpiece, then, reaching for the silk dressing-gown which he had flung over the chair, he shrugged into it. His face was shadowed though a lamp was lit beside the bed, for he would not make love in the dark like some peasant, he had told her, and she could not read the expression in it.

"I'm not tired," he said abruptly. His efforts had not only not satisfied him, he was telling her, they had not wearied him. "I'll go downstairs for a while."

She sighed and shrugged as he left the room.

And so, like conspirators in a plot that was to change the world as most knew it, she and the children were able to creep down the back stairs the next day disturbing no one except young Elsie who was on her knees at the kitchen fire raking out the ashes. She started violently as they giggled their way into the kitchen, leaping to her feet and spilling them on Ivy Bunting's rag rug on which no feet but Ivy's were ever allowed to rest. Ivy's chair, the rockers of which just touched its edge and where Ivy "took the weight off her tootsies", rocked vigorously as though Ivy had just sunk into it and Elsie squeaked in alarm.

"Oh, miss, you didn't half give me a turn. I thought it were Mrs Burns, though she'd not be about at this time of the morning."

Lucy put her finger to her lips. "Ssh, Elsie, not another word," though there was no one yet up to hear another word. "We're . . . we're off on an adventure so not a whisper about seeing us, d'you hear?"

"We're going to a football match, Elsie," Percy told

her excitedly, doing his best to hold the squirming little body of Thimble who, though nearly a year older than when James Buchanan had first set eyes on him, was still just as daft.

"A football match!" Elsie's eyes were round as saucers. "Eeh, well, I never . . ."

"But you're not to tell anyone, Elsie," Edward, who had been given instructions on his part of the day's proceedings, informed her importantly.

"What time's kick-off then?" for it was barely six fifteen in the morning.

"Oh, not for hours yet but there's a lot still to be done."

"I see," though Elsie clearly didn't.

Mass football matches between Lakeland villages were a common custom and the annual battle between the Rovers and the Wanderers was to take place on a wide stretch of ground on the shore of Grasmere Lake.

They were quite a little procession, she and Edwina, whom they had picked up in Ambleside, Edward and Margaret, Emily and Percy on their brand-new machines. At least she and the children were on new bicycles, for with his characteristic generosity, or was it indifference, James had told her to go ahead and buy them something decent since he was ashamed of the contraptions Bibby and Edward had so ingeniously put together. Edward's had a big basket on the front where Thimble, for all the world like a guide directing his party, sat and stared ahead of them.

They arrived in time to sit with the rest of the crowd and eat the picnic which, the night before, Buffy had prepared for them, having been let in on the plans, though she could not agree with them, and telling the servants that there was to be a picnic the next day. It was not a lie. She just was not to divulge where it was to take place.

The match was in full swing when they began to move about the noisy crowd handing out the handbills on which was printed "Votes for Women" and in smaller letters the information that there would be a suffrage meeting and demonstration next Saturday at Millan's Park, Ambleside, at which a well-known suffragette was to speak. The men, for there were very few women interested in the free-for-all which the match rapidly turned into, took the handbills without looking at them, most of them stuffing them in their pockets, peering round the two women and, strangely, the children who handed them out, for they were blocking their view.

"Votes for women," Edwina cried above the uproar and Lucy, taking courage from her, did the same and even Margaret took up the cry.

"Nay, tha' should be ashamed," one man retorted, "a little lass like thee. Get 'ome ter tha' mam."

"She's in heaven," Margaret answered shortly, to the man's discomfort, moving on to the next outstretched hand. The men were quite flabbergasted by the sight of pretty little girls like her and Emily passing out the leaflets and were inclined to take them before they were aware of what they were.

"Votes for women," Lucy shouted, taking no notice of the pushing and shoving that was beginning to take place and when she fell into the mud that the struggling players had churned up she took the first hand to reach out to help her.

She looked up into the appalled face of Ben Buchanan.

13

"I don't hold with it and I never will," Ivy Bunting declared stoutly to her crony, Maud Burns. "I don't hold with what them suffragette women get up to and I reckon they deserve to be behind bars, but to see the young mistress dragged by the scruff of her neck . . ."

"Oh, hardly, Mrs Bunting."

"As near as makes no difference, Mrs Burns. Up all them stairs, Dixon said, and her tripping up on each one and begging him to stop and let her get her breath and them children all crying, especially them little ones and that damn dog yapping its daft head off. Dixon said—"

"Mrs Bunting, this is really none of our business and besides . . ." Mrs Burns nodded her dignified head imperceptibly in the direction of the kitchen maids who were standing about clutching mixing bowls and saucepans, spoons and baking pans, their mouths agape, excited by the commotion though as yet they were not sure what it was all about. They had been busy at the tasks Mrs Bunting had set them in preparation for Mr and Mrs Buchanan's dinner when it all started.

Actually, if they were to be accurate, it had started at breakfast-time when it was discovered that not only Mrs Buchanan, but the children had mysteriously disappeared. Gone on a picnic, their companion – what else could you call her since she did no work in the house? – Miss Tyson said when asked by Mr Buchanan, who was in a right paddy, according to Bridie, his face as black as thunder and on it an expression which boded ill for their mistress. There was a whisper, a very quiet whisper since Mrs Burns didn't care for gossip, that the master had not spent the night where he usually spent it, which was in the mistress's bed, so what were they to make of that, they asked one another, in whispers, of course, and when young Elsie, who got on with her work and rarely offered an opinion about anything, reared up and told them to mind their own business they could not have been more surprised if the kitchen cat had spoken.

"'On a picnic?' says the master, glaring at Miss Tyson as if it were all her fault," so said Bridie who was in the schoolroom at the time seeing to the coal scuttle. "'Where on a picnic and why wasn't I told about it?' says himself, and 'I'm sure I don't know, sir,' says Miss Tyson. 'It is not my place to inform you of Mrs Buchanan's whereabouts,' she says, bold as brass. 'Is that so?' says the master. 'Well, in future see to it that you make it your business.' 'I can't do that, sir. I'm sure if Mrs Buchanan wished you to know she would have told you.'

"Glory be to God," said Bridie to the fascinated group of open-mouthed maidservants, smoothing her snowy white apron over her ample hips. She was all puffed up with a sense of her own importance at being the bearer of such exciting news. "Didn't I think the master was goin' to land her one, him looking so wild, so he was, but I've got to hand it to her she stood up to him, the spalpeen, and didn't he storm out o' there like the divil himself was after him."

Cook came upon them then, huddled in the scullery where none of them but Elsie should have been, and gave them the rounds of the kitchen, and since then they had hardly been able to get on with their work, constantly looking towards the kitchen door which led into the hall as they waited for news, wondering where Mrs Buchanan and those imps had got to.

Oh, yes, after being quiet and somewhat fearful at first in the home their sister's marriage had transferred them to, Mr Buchanan's new family had become imps again, reverting to their usual natures which was to be cheerful, noisy, teasing, always under your feet and invading the kitchens whenever they felt like it, begging for Mrs Bunting's chocolate shortbreads which, they said, were the best they had ever tasted. That Percy was a grand little lad, full of mischief, inquisitive and good-natured, and now that he had settled himself in, the pet of them all. The little girls were more subdued, but with lovely manners and willing to hold a conversation with any of them, seeing no difference between the servants and themselves, which Mrs Burns didn't like, of course. Master Edward was at school during the week and they hadn't really got to know him as well as the other three but at the weekend he often led his brother and sisters into some devilish prank or other which would involve a great deal of noise, laughter, usually muck and often water, like the time they dammed the stream which ran at the back of the house. It had overflowed into the rockery, causing havoc and tormenting Clapcott, the gardener, into threatening to give his notice in at once. They built "dens" where they shouldn't out of the wood he was sawing and chopping into neat piles for the winter fires, invading the mounds of branches and rubbish that he had stored after pruning ready to be turned into compost, for there was nothing ever wasted in his garden. They were harmless, the tricks they got up to, but sometimes Mr Buchanan, who was not used to such noise and exuberance, was heard to remonstrate with them, asking could they not find some quieter, less destructive pastime, because if they couldn't he could certainly find one for them. Perhaps a book in the schoolroom which was out of hearing of his study and had Edward done his homework? But they looked at him as though he were mad for suggesting such a thing on a lovely day like this and so did Mrs Buchanan. Even his own well-behaved dogs had got out of hand, racing round the garden in a barking circle of madness, no doubt spurred on by that Thimble, who even Mr Buchanan despaired of and who was as undisciplined as the children. Edward had discovered some great adventure books in Mr Buchanan's library, read apparently by Mr Buchanan as a boy, though Edward found it hard to visualise such a thing, boys' tales that were good, patriotic yarns. One was *With Roberts to Pretoria,* by G. A. Henty, which he and the others, under his direction, of course, played out in the gardens and woods surrounding Howethwaite. They were all cast in the roles of the brave heroes in the book, even the dogs, and the hullabaloo when the natives' uprising was in progress was enough to waken the dead, Mrs Bunting said faintly. And then, naturally, when the heroes and natives were hungry, for didn't adventures give you a tremendous appetite, they were inclined to invade her kitchen on the lookout for "rations".

At other times it was the Boxer Rebellion in China with Edward as the brave Sir Claude MacDonald who had held the garrison at Peking for fifty-five days, with Percy as his trusty captain and the girls, their hair in pigtails, as the dastardly Chinese. There was the Relief of Ladysmith, in which battalions of the Border Regiment, stationed at Carlisle, took part. They were events that happened over ten years ago but they still thrilled small boys the length and breadth of the land with their daring and excitement and the greatness of the British, which they were proud to be.

Was it any wonder then that Mr Buchanan shut himself up in his study with the door closed and strict orders that he was not to be disturbed, which was probably why he didn't miss them until the morning was well on. The empty chair at the breakfast table in which Mrs Buchanan usually sat was not commented upon and Dimity had her own theory about that. She had not seen Mr Buchanan leave his wife's bedroom the night before, nor Mrs Buchanan's escape this morning but it didn't need a detective to realise that only one body had slept in their marriage bed!

The arrival of Mr Buchanan, Mr Ben Buchanan, in his dashing blue, Prince Henry Vauxhall, the motor car overflowing with what seemed to be a dozen children, plus Mrs Buchanan, brought their Mr Buchanan to the wide front door where he elbowed Dixon aside as

though he were no more than the gardener's lad.
Mrs Buchanan looked as though she'd been dragged
through a hedge backwards and then across a muddy
field, Win, the parlour maid reported. Win had just
been about to tackle the dining-room table ready
for dinner when the motor car drew up and, hoping
Mr Dixon wouldn't spot her, she hung around in
the dining-room doorway to see what was to happen
next.

It was plain Mr Buchanan was so stunned he didn't
know what to say, but only for a moment or two,
then his voice rang out, carrying to the far corners
of the house, the garden and even into the bit of
woodland where Clapcott and Bertie, who was his
lad and learning the trade, lifted their heads from the
wood they were peacefully sawing and stared at one
another in amazement.

"What the bloody hell's this?" James Buchanan
roared and for the space of a second, perhaps two,
Lucy felt her heart falter in her breast. Then Emily
began to cry broken-heartedly since Mr Buchanan
was an imperious figure who did no more than nod
when she happened to pass him on the stairs and she
was frightened by the sheer volume of his bellow. It
was hard to recall sometimes that day when he had
taken them all up on to the fells, carrying Percy on
his shoulders, telling them about the plants in the
verge, the birds in the sky, smiling a little as though
he were enjoying it as much as they had done. That
was before he and Lucy were married, of course, so
perhaps that was where the difference lay, though she
didn't understand why.

Lucy drew her protectively to her side. "There's no

need to yell, James," she told him calmly. "It can all be explained but first I must get out of these clothes."

"Never mind that, woman. Where in hell have you been in that dress? You look as though you've taken part in a rugby scrum."

"In a way, I have, James, but can we not discuss this in private?" she asked him patiently, dabbing with her little lace handkerchief at the mud on her dress, fruitlessly as it happened.

James ignored her. "Ben," turning to his cousin, "can you explain to me what my wife is doing in your motor car on a Saturday afternoon with her gown, which I'm sure wasn't cheap and which I'm also sure I paid for, totally ruined?"

"Oh, no, James, it can be sponged clean and—"

"Will you stop babbling, Lucy, and explain to me what has happened to you?"

"I will if you'll let me—"

"I . . . I found her in Grasmere, old chap," Ben interrupted, looking uncomfortable as though somehow it might be his fault but he felt so bloody sorry for James who, against all their advice, had taken this young, independent and strong-minded woman as his wife. He would never forget his sense of shock and outrage when he saw who it was who was handing out those damned suffragette handbills, and she wasn't even *his* wife! And then to fall so ignominiously in front of Frank Askew and Edwin Kendall who, like himself, were keen on watching the Lakeland village football matches, and naturally it would be all round the district by morning that the newest member of his family was showing them up once more. The party when she had been so forceful about women's rights had not been forgotten!

James whirled about, his hand to his forehead, then, spotting Win in the doorway of the dining-room, snarled at her to get back to her duties, ready to vent his spleen on whoever got trapped in his line of vision. This wasn't a bloody peep show, he told her as she scuttled away, and would someone stop that bloody dog from barking or he'd have the thing shot.

At once Percy joined his sister, exploding into tears, wailing in terror, clutching the excited Thimble to his chest and dripping enormous tears into his fur. Margaret was trembling, leaning against Lucy, who was doing her best to hold her family in her arms and Edward, braving the lion who roared on the step, moved forward courageously, somewhat in the manner of Roberts of Pretoria.

"There is no need to shout at Lucy, Mr Buchanan. We have done no wrong. My sister, as a member of the Women's Social and Political Union, was passing out handbills, and we were helping her. It is not against the law."

"Is it not? You know the law then, do you, lad? Have you heard of disturbing the peace which is an offence for which the offender can be given a prison sentence? But you see that is not the issue here, though that is bad enough. Your sister is also my wife and she knows my views on suffragism. She also knows that, as my wife—"

"But, sir—"

"Damn you, don't interrupt me when I'm speaking."

"I was only going to say—"

"I would be much obliged if you would say nothing. Take your brother and sisters up to your rooms and stay there until I send for you."

"Stop it, James. How dare you speak to Edward like that." Lucy's face was brilliant with anger and her eyes had narrowed to pure slits of gold, venomous as a lioness whose cubs are in danger. "It is not his fault. If there is any fault it is mine but I won't admit even to that. I was merely—"

"Hell and damnation, woman, will you be quiet? Can you not see that you are no longer Miss Lucy Dean whose father allowed her to do as she pleased. You are Mrs James Buchanan, a woman of some standing in the community since you are my wife. We are an old, respected family and I will not have you cavorting about the countryside as you did before you married me."

"And I rue the day I did that."

He stood there as though he had been struck by a bolt of lightning. Every drop of colour drained from his face and for a second Lucy felt remorse race through her, since she did not mean it. She was not unhappy with James, since he was good to her and the children, if aloof. He gave nothing of himself, his inner self, to any of them, not even her and only for those few moments in their bed when he totally lost control was he not in cool command of himself. He did not care what she spent, on the house if she fancied anything new, he told her, on her clothes which, as his wife, must be tasteful and expensive, on the children – which was the best of all – new shoes, bicycles, pretty dresses for the girls, books and toys and games, and he did his best to accustom himself to the uproar which often invaded his previously quiet home. Even Thimble was tolerated in the schoolroom where he was learning to lie peacefully on a rug until the children were free to romp with him, and in Percy or Edward's bedroom at night. His own dogs were not allowed upstairs, sleeping in a tumble of legs and tails at the foot of the stairs where he and Lucy left them at night, waiting for him when he came down to breakfast. He had made many concessions to accommodate her family, many compromises and she would always be eternally grateful to him.

"I'm sorry," she whispered into the dreadful silence. "I didn't mean . . ."

As fast as it had left the blood rushed back into James's face, even seeming to leak into his fine grey eyes, but he had himself clamped tightly, his lips, which had been inclined to snarl in temper, folded into a rigid line of restraint. He spoke through them almost as though they were stitched together.

"Thank you, Ben, I'm much obliged to you. Give my regards to Joan." Ben was dismissed and he knew it and what's more was glad to go.

"Right, old chap. Perhaps we'll see you for dinner one evening?"

"I'm sure you will."

Ben climbed awkwardly into his motor car and it was plain he was not quite sure whether he should bid farewell to Lucy but he decided against it in the circumstances. He drove off quickly, leaving the tense, frightened group huddled in a protective circle about one another and up on the step his cousin James who, he told Joan later, he was sure meant to beat the living daylights out of his beautiful young wife.

Then, "You heard what I said, Edward. Take your brother—"

"Please, James, don't punish them. They only did what I asked them to do. They are not to blame."

"Will you allow me to speak, madam. You and I will have this out in private but they cannot just hang about here while we do so. I am not about to punish them as I am perfectly well aware that whatever it was they did you put them up to it."

"Oh, yes," she told him eagerly, "so please—"

"Then they will go upstairs now."

"May I not . . ."

"You may not."

"But what about our bicycles? They were left . . ."

"They will be collected."

Without another word James moved down the steps and took her arm, just above the elbow. She did her best to resist, to cling to her brothers and sisters as though still wanting to protect them against whatever it was James was to do to them, but he was too strong for her, dragging her up the steps and into the hallway where they followed in a pathetic straggle. Dixon still hovered there lest he be needed. He had not been dismissed by his master, after all, and besides, Mrs Burns and Mrs Bunting would be agog to hear what had happened. He would not deign to speak to the maidservants, of course, or even Fallows, the footman, but they would all know about this within the hour.

"Please, James, there is no need . . ."

"It seems there is every need, Lucy," he told her as she pulled back from him but he continued his steady progress up the stairs where she was forced to follow him, tripping on the hem of her ruined gown until even Dixon felt sorry for her in her humiliation.

The door to their bedroom closed with a crash and the children, continuing to weep as though their hearts were broken, gazed up the stairs. Not until Miss Tyson limped hurriedly down to collect them did they move.

James released her arm the moment they were alone. He walked to the window and stared out sightlessly but not by the flicker of an eyelash or a tremble to his voice did he allow her to see the pain she had inflicted on him with her admission that she was sorry she had married him. It had been as though she had viciously thrust a serrated knife into his heart and then, for good measure, turned it round in the wound. He felt as though he were bleeding to death inside. He had always known that she did not love him but their life since their marriage had been relatively pleasant, and she was his. He lived on hope that one day, he would be hers. Now that they were alone the madness had left him and he wanted to turn and plead with her not to go against him but he must not. He must be strong, upright, dignified, the master of this house and of her. He loved her with a devastation that was crippling him but he must draw back from it or he would go insane.

He leaned for a moment more against the window, his hands on the windowsill, then turned to her, his composure complete. He was almost undone once more, for she stood with her back to the door, her hand on the door handle as though ready for a quick getaway should he turn violent, but her golden eyes were fixed on him with a defiance which told him he had really not won a victory here today.

Nevertheless he must let her know that this with the suffragette movement could not go on.

"You must stop this, you know that, don't you?"

"Stop what?" Her eyes held his steadily.

"Don't pretend, Lucy. You know what I mean. As my wife you cannot associate with these women and their movement."

"Why not? There is nothing immoral in it. It is something in which I believe. I always have done and you knew that when you married me."

"I must confess it did not enter my head that you would become a member. I did not even know that there was a branch in this area. Nevertheless, you must finish with it. I do not believe, like a vast number of other men, that women should have the vote."

"Why not, for God's sake? What are you afraid of? That we will take over the government?"

"Now you are being ridiculous, which just proves my case that women should—"

"I won't give it up, James. The moment you go out of this house I shall cycle down to Ambleside and do whatever they ask me to do, whatever I am able to do."

"No, Lucy, you will not."

"How will you stop me?"

"I will stop you, believe me. There are the children . . ."

She looked at him, aghast. "You would blackmail me with my own brothers and sisters? You would stoop so low?"

"I will do whatever I have to, my dear. So, now, will you dress yourself for dinner."

"James, I beseech you . . ."

"No, don't."

"I won't be—"

"Yes, you will, Lucy. I am the master in this house and my word is the word that is obeyed."

"Damn you to hell, James Buchanan. I hope God strikes you dead and that you rot there for eternity."

"I probably shall, my dear. Now, shall we get ready for dinner?"

No one knew what went on in the bedroom the master and mistress shared but it was as though whatever it was had been accepted by them both, for they came down to dinner together in full evening dress, though it was noticed the mistress's face still bore signs of strain. Her gown was of barley-coloured georgette, which was the very newest fabric of the year, a beautifully draped but very simple style in which she looked quite glorious. She wore no jewellery and her long, creamy neck was graceful, the stalk on which her lovely head swayed as she nodded smilingly to Dixon and Fallows. The bodice of the gown was cut very low and Dixon noticed that she had a gauzy scarf tucked about her shoulders and into the neckline which rather spoiled the effect. The master must have insisted on it, he whispered later to Mrs Burns and Mrs Bunting, for he swore it would have revealed more of her . . . ahem . . . bosom than was modest.

He was right, for when he turned from the sideboard where he was serving the first course he nearly dropped the plate of Dover soles *à la crème* in her lap. She had removed the scarf, flinging it to the back of her chair with a movement of pure defiance. Though the master's lips tightened, he said nothing.

On the following Saturday, the day on which Lucy had planned to go to the rally that was to be held in Millan's Park in Ambleside and where a notable member of the movement was to speak, among others, she was prevented from doing so by the fact that this was the day on which Miss Charlotte Gibson was to marry Doctor Paul Buchanan. Even she, despite the defiance she had flung in James's face the week before, could not refuse to go since this was a member of the family who was to be married. Besides, she had the feeling James would simply have taken her arm as he had done last week and dragged her there.

Charlotte Gibson looked simply magnificent in her wedding gown which must have cost the earth, the lady guests whispered to one another. Her bridegroom, who was as handsome as all the Buchanans, seemed somewhat unnecessary beside her as she bowed from a carriage drawn by four white horses, as they drove away from the church where the bells pealed out to let the world know that Miss Charlotte Gibson had herself a husband at last. The wedding breakfast was meant to overwhelm and overawe the guests, some of whom were of the nobility, and it did that all right, spread out in a marquee on the lawn at Ravenscourt. There were silver trays overflowing with champagne, mountains of confectionery, a wedding cake weighing at least a ton, Franny whispered to Lucy, making her laugh, the whole spectacle decorated with sprays of white roses and white and silver satin ribbon. The ladies were elegant in their wedding finery of georgette and silk, satin and velvet, on their heads enormous flower gardens of roses of pink and white. Parasols twirled, as the weather was kind and the sun shone from a cloudless blue sky, and all Lucy could think of was the rally at Millan's Park, of Letty and Eddy, of Connie and Isobel and Betty, and of Anne Longman who was, if she was strong enough to speak, to tell the massed crowds what she had suffered in prison.

But instead there was Charlotte, Mrs Paul Buchanan, a plain gold ring on one hand given her by her husband and a diamond cluster on the other, given her by her father. She circled among her guests with quite royal composure, stopping even to speak to the James Buchanans, allowing her triumphant gaze to travel up and down Lucy Buchanan as though she were surprised to see her in such an unbecoming outfit. She would show them, her gaze seemed to say. She would be the most successful young hostess in the district and if Lucy thought she had caught the most eligible bachelor in Ambleside, Charlotte meant to show her that she was mistaken.

She was surprised and more than a little peeved when Mrs James Buchanan turned away in total disinterest, even stifling a small yawn. A yawn Charlotte Buchanan would not forget!

14

"Is there going to be a war, James?" Lucy asked her husband on 29 July 1914.

They were eating breakfast, just the two of them, for this was not one of the days when he allowed the children to eat with them.

He had been quieter than usual since the conflict which had erupted on the day Ben brought her home from Grasmere, more distant, less inclined to engage her in conversation at mealtimes and sometimes she thought he forgot she was even there, as now, surprised when she spoke. The question of her brothers and sisters and their banishment to the schoolroom for meals had been one that had been a thorn in her side from the day she and James were married, but just recently, ever since the fierce dissension over her involvement with the suffrage movement, she had kept what she liked to call "her head down", reluctant to arouse more disharmony between them. When she had suggested that, perhaps on a Saturday when the children had no lessons, they might all breakfast together, he appeared to be amenable to the idea, providing they were well behaved and didn't chatter. After all, they had to learn to take their meals with adults at some time in their lives, but it was not a success. The girls and Percy were intimidated by him, and Edward resentful, for he could not forgive Mr Buchanan's treatment of his sister on that fateful day. They were so silent James told them that unless they had something to say they might be excused.

They had fled like rabbits let out of a cage and so far Lucy had not repeated the experiment.

He glanced up from the newspaper he was reading and regarded her as though he were wondering if she was capable of understanding even if he explained it to her.

"I am aware that there is some trouble – in the Balkan, is it? – and that hostilities have been threatened for weeks," she continued. "Yesterday the Austrians declared war on Serbia, so what does that mean?"

If he was surprised that she had such a grasp of the situation he did not show it. He put his paper down and looked at her in that cool, quizzical way he had, a look that seemed to ask some question though he himself did not know what it might be. He sighed, unaware that he had done so, and certainly not attributing it to the deep sadness that welled up in him whenever he looked at this beautiful, intelligent young woman he had married. He knew that she had again been to the WSPU headquarters which he had learned was in Compston Street, but only once, presumably to tell them that she could no longer help them, since her husband was forcing her to give it up by threatening her with some retaliation to her brothers and sisters. Not that she would tell them this. She was too loyal, even to him, and he was filled with sorrow that he had been forced to act as he had. He had had no choice, he knew that. The wife of a Buchanan could not go round acting like some shop girl or factory worker, displaying herself in public, holding herself open to public ridicule and humiliation. Oh, he knew that there were many ladies, real ladies with titles, who championed the cause, but he was appalled that their husbands allowed it.

She looked quite glorious. Breakfast was a casual meal at the weekends and they were both dressed in the casual country clothes that were customary among their class. Franny Buchanan had persuaded her to learn to ride and, finding to her surprise that she enjoyed it and what's more was good at it, she had had a stylish outfit made which was not at all what James's family thought was suitable. She refused absolutely to wear the shapeless apron skirt over breeches which was considered suitable, or the divided skirt which was the fashion, for ladies at any rate. She wore what he himself wore, specially made breeches with flaring wings and vigorously polished chestnut brown riding boots. As a concession to her sex and James's dignity, she had agreed to wear a slightly longer well-fitted tweed jacket, and a stunning little bowler hat. Before she went to the stable she was to have her hair smoothed into a net snood by Dimity so for the moment it was loose about her face and shoulders, falling down her back to the seat of the chair. Her jacket was flung carelessly on another chair and her breasts strained, nipples hard and proud as cherry stones, against the fine silk of her shirt. James had made love to her last night, and again this morning, for no matter what she thought of it, he could not get enough of her long and lovely body, but even so he could feel his own breeches becoming extremely uncomfortable as she leaned across the table for another slice of toast. He wondered, and not for the first time, why, in all these months, she had not conceived. God above, he had played his part, and so, he supposed, had she, opening herself to him willingly whenever he asked it of her, but in the three months since their marriage he had not got her with child.

It seemed he was making some decision, his face thoughtful, his eyes looking at something only he could see, then he spoke.

"I think there is, Lucy. Only a week ago the Austrians sent an ultimatum to Serbia demanding that anti-Austrian propaganda should be banned in Serbia and that the man behind the assassination of Archduke Franz Ferdinand be found and arrested. Well, to put it simply, there were disagreements too numerous to mention and yesterday the Austrians declared war on Serbia."

"But how is that to affect us, and the rest of Europe?"

"That remains to be seen, but I'm afraid it will be like a row of dominoes, one toppling another, country after country until we are all involved."

James was right. The next day, 30 July, Russia mobilised. Sir Edward Grey, who was the British Foreign Secretary, asked both France and Germany if they would observe Belgium's neutrality, to which France answered in the affirmative. The Germans remained silent and the Belgians ordered that mobilisation should begin the following day. On 1 August it was France's turn.

Bank holiday Monday, 3 August, was hot and still, and in England crowds of holidaymakers sweltered under a shimmering haze of sunshine which reddened their skins and peeled their noses, in blissful ignorance of the fact that Germany had declared war on France. The following day German forces marched into Belgium. The British issued mobilisation orders and the British Ambassador in Berlin told the Chancellor that unless Germany withdrew its troops by midnight their countries would be at war with one another.

The Germans did not withdraw. It was war.

Six days later on 10 August the government released all suffragette prisoners on the understanding that there would be no more violence.

Despite what her husband might say, that day Lucy walked into Ambleside, making her way to the WSPU headquarters in Compston Street. She had read the news in James's copy of *The Times* but the report had said little else and she was eager to get more details.

She took the path through the small wood at the back of Howethwaite, dressed in her stout walking boots and a dark green gaberdine divided skirt that was easy to stride out in. Her shirt was cream, a crisp lawn with a high neck and a pleated front. The sleeves were long and narrow and she unbuttoned the cuffs and pushed them up her arm, leaving them bare to the elbow. Around her waist was a broad leather belt, narrowing it even further and displaying her graceful, womanly hips.

Leaves were already beginning to fall, drifting in slow spirals to rest on the mossy ground as they waited for winter, but the great beech trees were still heavy with foliage. She gazed up into the great limbs spread above her head and the layer upon layer of the branches cast a deep shade over her bare head. She carried her hat, a straw boater which she would put on when she reached the town. She could hear the musical sound of running water, purling and trilling from the beck that ran towards the river at the back of the house. Crossing the bridge that spanned the river, she continued up Clappergate until she reached the town, forgetting to pull down her sleeves and put on her boater, turning heads as she strode out, and drawing comments from one passer-by to another that James Buchanan's wife was still as unconventional as when she had been the Reverend Edward Dean's daughter!

She found Letty and Edwina industriously packing up the contents of the small room in which Lucy had hoped to achieve such great things in her own fight for the cause. The small printing press, the typewriters, all were consigned to cardboard boxes and the papers and books and posters were stacked in neat piles awaiting their turn. Already the room in which so much emotion had been aroused, emotions of hope and determination and unswerving dedication to the cause, looked strangely lifeless and Lucy supposed sadly that there were hundreds of such rooms and offices up and down the country, setting aside their own fight to take part in the much bigger one that was at hand.

"Aah, Lucy, there you are," Letty said somewhat distantly, for none of them had completely understood why she had so suddenly dropped the work for which she appeared to have so much enthusiasm. "Come to help?"

Lucy sensed the mockery but ignored it. She knew

Letty had been disappointed in her and would have given a lot to explain that it was not her doing but she felt Letty would not sympathise so she let it go.

"I came to find out what's going to happen, Letty."

"You mean to the movement? Well, as you can see we are disbanding this branch and obeying orders to take up war work and war relief work. Those who persecuted us now need our support and so Emmeline and Christabel have stopped campaigning for the vote and intend to throw themselves into anti-German propaganda and recruiting women war workers for the Home Front." She lifted a box and threw it furiously into a corner as though she would dearly love to do the same with Emmeline and Christabel!

"What does that mean?"

"It means that women are to take over jobs to free the men who are to fight."

"To fight?"

"Dear God, Lucy, are you not aware that already the BEF, the British Expeditionary Force, has sailed for France? Yesterday, in fact, and as far as we know could already be fighting. They are going to need women to be nurses, ambulance drivers, women for munitions and . . ."

"How do you know all this?" Lucy gasped.

Letty clicked her tongue in exasperation, pushing Lucy to one side and reaching for a pile of handbills, handbills which would no longer be passed out wherever a crowd massed.

"It doesn't take a great deal of imagination, Lucy, to know that where battles are, men will be wounded. As soon as this is packed up Eddy and I are off to volunteer."

"Volunteer?" Lucy felt she was involved in some strange play in which everyone but her knew their lines.

So far Edwina had not spoken but now she turned a grave look on Lucy. "We were sorry when you said you felt you could no longer support us earlier in the year but ... well, we realised how difficult it must have been for you, having a husband and a family, but surely Mr Buchanan would not object to your doing some kind of war work. That is what Letty and I mean to do. Nursing. We are to go to the General Hospital in Carlisle tomorrow where we are to begin our training. They're taking us as paid probationers since neither Letty nor I can afford to work for nothing as the VADs do."

"VADs?"

"Voluntary Aid Detachment. They're organised by the Red Cross and the Order of St John and, as you might imagine, they are recruiting girls from middle and upper-crust families." She pulled a face, not of derision but of acceptance. "As neither Letty nor I come from that sort of background, the sort of background where our families can support us, we must train as nurses. We've already been interviewed and as we're both over twenty-one we are to begin immediately."

There was a deep silence except for the rustle of paper and the click of their heels across the wooden floor as Letty and Edwina got on with their task of closing down the Ambleside branch of the WSPU. There was a firm resolve about them, a calmness that Lucy envied, a certainty that come what may they were to be a part of this fight the British people had on their hands and she wished with all her heart that she could do the same. Throw off the restraints that bound her, not just to James who was her husband and who, in the eyes of his world, owned her, but the responsibilities of Edward and Percy, Margaret and Emily, but it was not possible. She had a duty to them, laid upon her by her mother, and then her father, and she could not abandon them, no matter how well cared for they might be without her, and take a train with Letty and Edwina to what she knew would be the greatest experience of her life. She was not even sure that, had she not had her brothers and sisters, a woman could just march off to war without the permission of her husband. There might be some law forbidding it and so what was she to do?

"What can I do?" she asked the two busy young women who really had no time for her now. They turned to look at her, kindly, as they might a child who has offered to side the table, or help with the washing-up and she knew they thought her helpless, hopeless even. But as they considered her thoughtfully, like two grown-ups faced with a difficult child, she felt an unshakeable belief enter her heart, a sureness, a fixity of purpose that seemed to tell her that there was something she, Lucy Buchanan, could do, something that might not be as demanding as Letty and Edwina's new cause but which would fulfil this call to arms that was sweeping the country.

"I'll find something," she told them firmly. "I don't know what but I'll find something. I wish you luck, both of you, and when the war is won, we will get on with the battle we are putting aside for the time being. We can't let fifty years of fighting for universal suffrage go to waste, can we?"

* * *

YOUR KING AND COUNTRY NEED YOU

A CALL TO ARMS

An addition of 10,000 men to the Regular Army is immediately necessary in the grave National Emergency. Lord Kitchener is confident that this appeal will be at once responded to by all who have the safety of the Empire at heart.

So said the posters which began to appear several days after war was declared. The response was overwhelming. Recruiting offices all over the country were at once deluged with volunteers and by the end of the month 750,000 young men from every walk of life had joined up. Many of those who volunteered were to become officers, receiving their commissions on the strength of certificates granted by the Officer Training Corps of the public schools and universities they had attended. One of these was Andrew Buchanan; another was his cousin, Doctor Paul Buchanan.

The retreat from Mons, as they were beginning to call it following their defeat on 23 August, came when the BEF fell back south, suffering heavy casualties and pursued by the Germans.

The Battle of Le Cateau was next followed in October by the first Battle of Ypres but it seemed the Allied Forces were in a race to the sea and the German troops could not be stopped.

"I wish I could go," Edward told them all gloomily day after day as the news of the retreat was reported in the newspaper, his attitude saying that, given the chance, he could turn the fortunes of the BEF right round in no time.

"So do I," added Percy stoutly and they were both open-mouthed with admiration when Bertie Clapcott, who, it appeared, had enlisted on the quiet since he was only seventeen and knew his dad would have stopped him, received an envelope with OHMS on it telling him to report to the Drill Hall in Penrith the next day.

"'Ere, this is a nice how-d'you-do, an' no mistake," Clapcott was reported to have said and as for Mrs Clapcott, it seemed she had ranted and raved and threatened to "stop his gallop if Clapcott didn't", whatever it cost her, but it did no good. Bertie took the train to Penrith with a dozen other cheering, excited young men, the first to go from the district, but certainly not the last. Over the next weeks it began to be noticeable that young men were fast disappearing from the district, their places being taken by women. Farmers were stunned when young women in breeches and smocks and broad-brimmed hats turned up to work on their land. Land-girls, they called themselves and they weren't the only ones. It was coming to something, one old chap said indignantly, when that Mrs Owen took over her husband's job as gravedigger when he went away to the front. It wasn't right and proper, and he wasn't having some woman digging his grave, which he expected to be put in any day now, the way things were going.

Lucy was at Franny's when the idea came to her, neat, not exactly planned down to the last detail, but an idea none the less.

It was almost the end of November and the casualties from the front were beginning to flood the hospitals all over the country. Almost 90,000 men and officers had been killed or wounded since the beginning of the war and the lists in *The Times* grew day by day. The ladies still carried on the custom of calling despite the war. Well, standards had to be kept up, hadn't they and besides, it was convenient to use the time not just for calling on one another but to do something for the war effort. Rolling bandages seemed to be something they might be good at, at least until they were informed by Joan Buchanan, who had a friend with a husband at the War Office and so should know what was needed, what else they might pursue. Comforts for the troops, perhaps, knitting socks and scarves and those strange things soldiers wore on their heads in the cold weather. Not that any of them had ever knitted a line in their lives. A bit of fine embroidery was all they had been taught but they were willing to try if someone would just show them how.

Mrs Charlotte Buchanan was there that day, resplendent in an outfit her husband had certainly not bought her, the last to come out of Paris, she was devastated to tell them, where she and Paul had spent their honeymoon. Where, would they tell her, was she to buy her clothes if she could not get to Paris and her clever French couturier? She knew that Miss Medlock was gifted, casting a supercilious glance over the oufits of her new relatives by marriage, particularly Lucy Buchanan who had on her riding breeches, a woollen jumper and what looked like a checked jacket of her husband's. She'd decided to ride over, she had told them all, ignoring their shocked faces which she did more and more these days, pleasing herself, her expression seemed to say. She and Jacob, who was groom at Howethwaite, were to put her brothers and sisters up on the ponies James had bought them, since she had been a good girl over the WSPU, he had told her, though she did not mention this last, and she must dash off soon, for lessons in the schoolroom would be over and they would be expecting her.

Charlotte smoothed down the lustrous silk of her afternoon gown, her hand caressing the lovely garment, her smile of self-satisfaction very evident, then, for want of something better to do, proceeded to admire the diamonds sparkling on her fingers. Her devastation over the cessation of visits to Paris for her wardrobe did not seem to stretch to her husband's decision to become an army doctor, nor the fact that he was to leave a week on Friday for a military hospital in London and then on to the front, she told them casually.

"Dear God, he kept that quiet," Franny said, blowing smoke through her nostrils, then leaning forward to tap the ash from her cigarette into the cut-crystal ashtray.

"Oh, he seems to want to be 'in on it', as they say and as a patriotic wife how can I object? I certainly don't want one of those hussies to accost him in the street with a white feather."

"So you'd rather he risked his life?"

"What can I do, Lucy? It is his decision."

"But he can be 'in on it' by remaining in this country and treating the casualties in a military hospital."

Charlotte shrugged as though to say what was a wife to do.

"Aren't you afraid for him, Charlotte?" Lucy asked her curiously, for she really did not think she had ever known a more heartless, thoughtless, mindless young woman. She had taken a liking to Paul, the youngest of the Buchanan cousins. He was often at family affairs where she sought him out to speak to him, for he was diffident and shy. As James had predicted, his beautiful and rich young wife totally dominated him and she wondered whether it was this that had prompted him to volunteer for active service.

"Oh, not at all. He will be well behind the front line, after all. They are desperately in need of doctors, so I believe."

Charlotte held the strip of bandage with which she had been fiddling for the past half-hour as though even that simple task were beyond her well-bred, undomesticated fingers. She gave Lucy the condescending and imperious look which she turned on her servants in the house her father had bought her and Paul as a wedding present.

"Mmm, and can you wonder when you see the casualty lists?" Franny retorted shortly, evidently agreeing with Lucy about the lack of feeling in Charlotte Buchanan. "They're also short of nurses, stretcher-bearers and ambulance drivers. In fact, I'm thinking of going myself. I can drive a car so I'm damn sure I can drive an ambulance."

They all turned to stare at her in horror, Anne and Joan, Janet and Christine and Charlotte, speechless and frozen into poses of open-mouthed disbelief, all, that is, except Lucy who smiled at Franny with great affection.

"Oh, Franny, how wonderful."

"Never mind being wonderful, you silly girl," Joan declared. "I've never heard of anything so foolish in my life. Good God, Franny, you're nearly thirty and . . ."

"What's being nearly thirty got to do with it, Joan?" Franny's voice and face were frosty. "Anyway, it's nearly twenty-nine and if I feel like a little adventure then that's my business. I've applied to the Red Cross and been accepted. I have to do a course in first aid and motor mechanics, would you believe, but I can see no problem there."

"Problem! What about your husband? Does he not count as a problem?"

"It's because of Alex that I'm going. He's too old for active duty but he's been offered a post in . . . high places. They were delighted with the offer of his services and expertise and so he is to go up to London by the month's end. We're taking a house there so that when I can get home from France he'll be with me."

Franny turned a defiant look on them all and lit another cigarette while they continued to gape at her with growing consternation, all except Lucy who leaned forward to take her hand.

"I admire you, Franny. I think you're marvellous and I only wish to God there was something I could do. James is adamant—" She broke off, aware that she was saying too much to these women who believed, as she did, that matters concerning one's husband were not discussed with others.

Franny patted her hand soothingly, for she knew full well how James hemmed his young wife about with rules and conventions. She often wondered that Lucy put up with it, for if anyone was a fighter it was Lucy Buchanan. She had given in meekly about the WSPU which had amazed Franny but then, who knew what passed between husband and wife.

"Something will turn up, Lucy, you'll see. Something you can do at home. Who knows . . ."

It was then that the idea came to Lucy, as certainly, as surely as the feeling that had come over her when Letty and Edwina had told her they were off to Carlisle to be nurses. The WSPU must be put away for the duration of the war, and who knew how long that would be, but until then she must find something to occupy her, something worth while, a challenge to her mind and heart and soul which were stagnating in the life she led now.

And now she knew what it was to be.

She couldn't wait to get home. Her mare, which she had called Rose because she was so pretty, was brought round to the front steps from the stable and as the ladies watched her in obvious dismay, for what were they to make of the girl, she leaped into the saddle and, putting her heels to Rose's side, raced off down the drive towards the open gateway.

"I do believe if the gate had been closed she would have jumped it," Joan remarked disapprovingly.

"I believe she would, Joan, and where was she off to in such a hurry? I don't know, girls today . . ."

She left Rose by the front steps, her reins adangle, calling for Dixon to send for Jacob and was the master in?

"Indeed he is, madam. He's in the study." She was surprised by the look of gratification on Dixon's face. Though he did his job to perfection, Dixon's face had never been known to display anything more than total inexcitability in all the time she had known him, but now he seemed to be ... what? ... suppressing some emotion with the greatest difficulty, but she had no time to discover what was bothering him, if anything was.

She could barely contain her exhilaration as she flung open the door, hurling herself into the room with something like the enthusiasm she had once shown at her father's house.

"James ... oh, James, I've just come from Franny's and while I was there I had this wonderful idea. It needs your approval, of course, but ... but ..."

She did not immediately recognise the figure which rose from the fireside chair, a tall, erect, quiet figure of a soldier. A soldier in the uniform of an officer and when she did she was bewildered by the swooping anguish that struck at her heart.

James Buchanan told himself that he had volunteered for patriotic reasons but he knew in his heart it was not true. He had volunteered simply to get away from his beautiful young wife.

He could pinpoint the exact moment when he had recognised what was in his heart and what he was to do about it. He had come home unexpectedly and, still then with the hope that had flowered when she agreed to marry him, finding her not in her sitting-room had gone to look for her in the place where he realised she was most likely to be. He had opened the door of the schoolroom; it had been a cold day at the beginning of October, and a generous fire burned in the grate and there she was in an armchair in front of it, Percy and Thimble on her lap as she read them a story. It was *The Jungle Book* by Rudyard Kipling. The others were there, Edward building something at the table, Emily busy with a doll's house he did not remember seeing before, Margaret and the maid, Buffy, as Lucy called her, both sewing what looked like baby garments.

They had all looked up as he stood for a moment in the doorway and in a way that shrivelled something inside him, the life went out of the room. But what went straight to the core of him like an arrow from a bow was the way in which Lucy's face, so warm and flushed and radiant as she rested her cheek on Percy's curls and read the story, altered, the coldness that settled in her eyes as they looked questioningly into his.

His heart, and he loathed himself for saying it since it sounded like some trashy novel and not the thinking of a mature man, right then and there knew it could stand no more of the pain of her indifference and, as they all waited politely for him to say what he had come to say, and leave, his decision was made. He was forced into accepting the finality of it. It was not that he meant to go to war and get himself killed. Nothing dramatic like that. It just seemed a perfect escape route from this appalling sadness she had brought into his life and one that would be accepted by her, by his family, by the community, since what more natural than that a man should go and fight for his country. His law practice would still be there when he came back – if he did – and his wealth from his many investments, from the Emmerson Gunpowder Works and the Buchanan Copper Mines would still continue to come in. Probably doubled if the demand for gunpowder continued to grow. Lucy and her family, his home, with her in it, would go on as before, those under Howethwaite's roof cared for while he was away.

The strange thing was he had begun to believe she was settling down, if not to her married state, then to the life he had given her at Howethwaite. She appeared to be contented. The servants had taken to her, for though she allowed no liberties, she was fair and honest and let them get on with their work without undue interference from her. Mrs Bunting continued to cook meals she chose to cook since she was an expert, Lucy told her, and needed no prodding from her, meaning herself. She would be guided by her, she told the cook, when it came to dinner parties which, though she did not care for herself, she had come to accept she must give as part of her "bargain". Mrs Burns was in charge of the female servants and Mr Dixon the males and, as they had been at Howethwaite a long time as housekeeper and butler, knew the routine of caring for the house and serving the Buchanans in a way she never would. She was not domesticated, she told James right at the beginning but she could tell when a table top had not been dusted or a window polished, which, God forbid, should ever happen at Howethwaite.

Her delight in what she could give her family had been evident from the start and her gratitude to him was constantly acknowledged. She never failed to thank him warmly for the allowance he had made her, more money in a week than she had seen in a year at the rectory, and what it allowed her to do for the children. Edward was showing a great interest in mathematics, science and the growing technology of motor cars and flying machines, and was doing well at school. In the spring Percy was to start at the same grammar school. He had accepted Howethwaite as his home and the servants as part of his family and they had taken a real shine to him, quite enjoying the new excitement four children generated in the house. The girls were growing up, Margaret as lovely as Lucy, inclined to be quieter but seemingly content with Emily and Miss Tyson as a companion. He knew

Lucy spent a lot of time with them, particularly now as they were learning to ride as she had done, and the house seemed to wrap itself about them, cradling them as it had cradled many generations of Buchanans. It was as though the ghosts of those past children, himself among them, were glad to see the rooms filled again with shouts of laughter, the barking of dogs, the arguments, the racket boys make and in the middle of it all moved Lucy, his love, safe and established in her position as his wife and mistress of Howethwaite, content with her lot, if not with him.

He had just come from his tailor in Ambleside where his uniform had been especially made for him. He looked well in the khaki, the gleaming riding boots, the polished shoulder strap and belt, the leather holster in which was a revolver, but he had intended to take the lot off before she came home. His peaked cap with the badge of his regiment on the front lay on a side table. He supposed he should not have put the uniform on in the first place but the tailor had wanted to make absolutely sure that Mr Buchanan, Captain Buchanan, was as well turned out in war as he was in peace. James had been impatient to get home so he had not bothered to change back into his civilian clothes, roaring back through Ambleside in the Rolls and within the hour he was certain that every inhabitant would know that James Buchanan had answered his country's call to arms.

He didn't know why but he had intended telling her later that night, perhaps after he had made love to her for what might be the last time. He had not told her before because quite simply he could not stand the thought of days of seeing her happily moving about their home despite his imminent departure, since she was too honest to pretend it mattered to her. He was to take the train tomorrow for the training camp.

It was two weeks now since he had travelled to Carlisle to enlist in a battalion of the Border Regiment, his certificate granted by the Officer Training Corps of the school he had attended, sixteen years ago now, entitling him to a commission. In that time he had watched her, looking for some sign that might give him hope that she would perhaps be sorry to see him go, but there was none. He was not awfully sure what he expected, since she did not even know he was going. She had been exactly as she always was. Polite, ready to chat across the dinner table if he wished, willing in their bed, but as distant as the brilliance of a star in the firmament. He knew he had turned her against him when he had refused her permission to join the WSPU and particularly in the way he had enforced his refusal. He realised now that it had been outrageous to threaten her sisters and brothers, and, truth to tell, he had no idea how he would have carried it out. It had been a blind, hitting out with the only weapon he had against her, for he knew without a shadow of a doubt that if she had been alone, without responsibilities, she would have told him to go to hell. Well, be honest, she wouldn't have married him in the first place!

She might have run into a brick wall, or an invisible glass window, she stopped so suddenly. For a second something passed across her face; he didn't see it and if he had it is doubtful he would have recognised it. Lucy herself didn't know what it was that struck her so forcibly, but so swiftly come and gone it might never have happened.

"James?" she said questioningly, as though she couldn't quite believe it was really him.

"The same." He smoothed down his jacket and tried to smile jauntily, for if she laughed he wanted to be ready for it.

"James, what have you done?"

"I should have thought that was pretty obvious, Lucy."

"But I don't understand."

"What don't you understand?"

"Why you've enlisted. You had no need to."

"An old codger like me, you mean? I know what's in your mind, Lucy, so there is no need to protest. I am a married man of almost thirty-five and conscription will be a while coming."

"Oh, it will all be over soon, James, or so they are saying and will not come to that."

"Do you really believe that, Lucy?" He turned away from her and walked to the window and she had a moment to study his tall, athletic figure which the uniform fitted so admirably, displaying the hard lines of his body beneath it. He certainly did look very attractive, she thought detachedly. He had even had his troublesome thatch of hair cut short and it lay brushed smoothly to his head. His skin was suntanned still, for she knew he went walking up on the hills and the sun and the wind had put a good colour to his face. He did not turn as he spoke.

"Will you be all right on your own, Lucy?" he asked her, his voice detached and cool. "I mean looking after things here until . . . until I come back."

"Of course I will, James. Don't worry about us," she answered cheerfully, little realising what she was doing to him. "We shall manage. There are many women all over the country who are to be left when their husbands go to war. Charlotte for one." And if a nincompoop like Charlotte Buchanan can manage then I certainly can, her voice seemed to say scornfully.

"Yes, I heard that Paul was to go. And Alex is to take up a highfalutin' post in London. Andrew has joined the same regiment as me and is to travel with me tomorrow so the whole business will be on Ben's shoulders. He told me that Joan is determined to give him a hand, God help him."

"No, I think Joan will make a fine second-in-command. Pity she can't go into the army, she'd have the war organised in a week."

He turned back to her and smiled, the usual distant look of preoccupation on his face, his eyes clear and cool.

There was a catch in her voice as she spoke. "You've heard that Franny is determined to go to France and be an ambulance driver?"

He sighed. "Yes, but then Alex has no control over her whatsoever, more's the pity. But I must admit if anyone can do it, Franny can."

"And that only leaves me," she went on breathlessly.

His face tightened imperceptibly, but she saw it, for by now she had begun to read her husband's expressions, at least those he allowed her to see.

"Yes?" he asked quietly.

"May I put something to you, James?" she begged eagerly. "It's an idea I had . . . well, I went down to the WSPU. I know I shouldn't but I wanted to find out what was to happen. You know that we are giving up our fight for now . . ."

"We . . . ?"

"I cannot give it up in my heart, James, surely you know that. Though I have not been to Compston Street since you . . . you told me not to, I am still a believer, but that is getting away from what I was going to tell you. Two of the girls were there, clearing up, and they told me they are to go to Carlisle to train as nurses."

His face hardened and he straightened his back and shoulders as he stood away from the window. About his mouth a thin white line appeared as he compressed his lips and his eyes grew cold and grey as frost on a pool.

"Oh, don't worry," she said, seeing it, "I am not fool enough to think I could go."

"Though you would if you had not your family?"

She hesitated and her own eyes grew bleak. "Yes."

"Even if I told you not to?"

"Yes. I'm sorry, James, but it is not to come to that. What I want to do is . . . they are already overflowing, the hospitals, I mean, with our casualties from the front, and I've heard that the government would be glad of any help it can get in the way of accommodation. Now, I'm sure we could convert Howethwaite, with your permission, of course, into such a place and then I could help. Oh, I so want to help, James, and this is the only way I can think of, and still remain at home where my responsibilities lie."

There was a deep silence. Lucy's face was pink and her lovely golden eyes glowed with fervour as she looked into her husband's unreadable face. She had thrown her bowler hat on to a chair and pulled off the snood in which her mass of hair was stuffed. It fell all about her, rich and rippling, the light firing copper glints from it. Her lips were like poppies, parted over her perfect white teeth and she gazed at him beseechingly, her heart exposed, for she wanted this and only he could give it to her.

He could feel the distaste rise in him but he fought it down. Howethwaite invaded by strangers. His lovely home where he had lived all his life, where his ancestors had lived, stripped of the beautiful things his parents and grandparents had gathered about them. Wounded men lying in every room, the smell of infection, death perhaps, and in the midst of it this woman who he loved beyond reason and from whom he was running away, possibly to his own death.

"James, don't deny this to me, please. Women all over the country are going to be doing jobs to free their men to fight. Did you know that Mr Owen the gravedigger has gone and that his wife is taking his place, and that there is to be a lady chemist at Lawson's? Now I cannot take over your work and would not want to but I think I would be a good nurse. I would not be a proper nurse, of course," she added hastily as he frowned. "A nurse's aid, I think they call it, but it would give me the opportunity to help in this war. Please, James . . . please."

"What about the children and the servants?"

"Oh, I have been thinking about that all the way from Franny's." Her face was alight with enthusiasm and he wanted to take her in his arms and crush her to him, tell her he could not bear the thought of other men having her compassion when she had none for him. Kiss her into subjection, into a submissive wife who would willingly stay at home and wait for him to come back home to her. He wanted to remember her in this deep comfort he had given her, just as she had been for the past seven months, not moving about a crowded ward in a white uniform smelling of disinfectant, putting the hands which had never, ever touched him unless forced to in the sexual act on other men.

"Well?" he demanded shortly.

"I would turn the dining-room, the drawing-room and the conservatory into hospital wards. We could probably get at least twenty beds in each one. My sitting-room could be made into an operating room or whatever they call it and your study—"

"Not my study, Lucy. Let's have that understood."

"Very well, some rooms at the back of the house could be turned into small bedrooms for the nurses and doctors, and the children and I would have the upstairs floor. The servants' bedrooms would not be touched though there will be empty ones if needed. The spare bedroom would be my sitting-room and—"

"You have it all arranged, it seems," he interrupted coldly.

"Yes. If you will allow it."

"And the servants? How are they to manage all this extra work?"

She sighed sadly. "I'm afraid some of them won't be here much longer, James. You know that Fallows and Tom Baxter are to go, don't you?"

"Yes, Tom is going to put the Rolls up for the duration and I have a feeling the horses will be commandeered for service."

"Yes, I'd heard." Her face was sad, for she had

enjoyed the few months of riding she had known and had grown fond of Rose. Perhaps the children's ponies would be spared but then Jacob, who was in his fifties, would be all that was needed to see to them.

"And three of the maidservants have been told that there is money to be made in munitions, besides which they also want to help the war effort, so there will be room and to spare. Whoever is left can help Mrs Bunting and I'm sure the War Office will send staff to look after their wounded."

He made love to her that night with a tenderness and a passion he had never shown before. It was as though, knowing it might be for the last time, he drew from her, and from himself, some instinctive emotion which let him forget the past and the future and be James Buchanan simply loving his wife. He did not speak as he drew her close, drifting over her with barely any sensation, moving so slowly and feelingly she could sense something in him that had never been there before. His hands seemed to float about her body, soft as down, but ready to be hard with male sexuality. He cupped her buttocks, pulling her in to him and for the first time she was surprised by the sweet flickering which began somewhere in the pit of her stomach, a flickering which was ready to flare into a bright fire. He smoothed her back and she had the feeling that he had gone somewhere else though his hard body remained close to hers. Her breath drew in on a deep sound, almost a moan and her hips, of their own volition, pressed against his. Her breath was soft against his throat, getting faster and faster and when the explosion occurred somewhere inside herself she heard her own voice call out a name that was unintelligible.

For the first time she did not want him to turn away from her as he usually did. Her body was filled with the most delightful sensations, feelings, needs, stirrings which made her want to sigh and stretch like the tabby in the stable yard when the sun fell on her, but with James's back firmly presented to her as it always was she felt she could not. She had not the faintest idea what had happened to her and James appeared to be totally unconcerned with it, so what was she to do? She could not question him about it, could she, since it might be something he did not care to talk about, but really, it had been quite delightful and she wished she had the courage to touch his shoulder and ask if they might do it again!

Sighing, she turned on to her side and within minutes was sound in the sleep a well-satisfied female knows after lovemaking.

James stared into the darkness and his soul knew the meaning of the depths of hell. Tomorrow he was to take his life and remove it from this woman, this woman who had for the first time responded to him, who had gone with him to the far places of the enchanted love he had longed for, but it was too late. She had met him, woman to man, equal in their desire for one another and he did not know why. Nor, to be honest, did he care now, for it was all too late.

They kissed on the front steps, more for convention's sake than anything, a brief touch of their lips, for the servants were watching and waiting to say goodbye to their master, Mrs Bunting with her apron to her eyes, Dixon dignified but obviously moved and Mrs Burns keeping a stern eye on the maidservants who would, she was sure, lose total control and weep over one another with great enjoyment. He shook hands with them all gravely, his face shuttered so that not one of them could see what was in his heart.

"Good luck, sir, good luck."

"You'll not be long away, I'm sure, sir. We'll soon have them Huns on the run." This from Clapcott whose Bertie was at that mysterious place called the front, wherever it was.

"I'm sure we will, Clapcott."

He crouched to fondle his dogs' heads, looking deep into their intelligent eyes and Holmes whimpered mournfully as though he knew what was to come.

Mr Andrew, Captain Andrew, had driven over from Yewdale Park, where he had said goodbye to his parents, in his dashing little sports car which made Edward's eyes pop out on stalks, and was to drive them both to the railway station in Windermere. He would leave the motor there to be picked up by his mother's chauffeur. Edward longed to say *he* would pick it up right willingly, for he knew how to drive now but, glumly, he knew he would not be allowed. They stood in a line, the Dean family, Lucy with her arm across Percy's shoulders, smiling with all the appearance of a group bidding farewell to a guest who they would see within the week, ready to dash back indoors and resume whatever they had been doing before he interrupted it.

Andrew's kiss, and the one he received back from Lucy, had been warmer than his, and Andrew's arms had held her for a moment too long, but then Andrew was known for a charming rogue and a ladies' man.

"I'll look after him for you, Lucy," he shouted,

waving his hand as they roared down the drive. They were never to see Andrew again.

By Christmas the house had been inspected and found to be suitable for the needs of thirty or so wounded men. The equipment, thirty-six iron beds and everything else that would be required for the nursing of wounded soldiers had been delivered by the year's end. New Year's Day found Lucy and Buffy, alongside Gertie and Elsie, the only maids still in service at Howethwaite, scrubbing floors with buckets of water into which carbolic acid had been added. Even the walls had to be disinfected to the Hospital Board's high standard ready for the first arrivals which, they were promised, would be soon but it was not until after the Battle of Neuve Chapelle on 10 March that they arrived.

Lucy would never forget that day. She had felt a strange restlessness, a need to be about something and yet everything that could be done, was done. She had fiddled with the crisp white sheets that were tucked like envelopes on each waiting bed and studied the "wards" to see how she could make them more comfortable for the soldiers. She was wrapped around in one of the capacious aprons she had taken to wearing and which she had borrowed from Mrs Bunting, much to Mrs Bunting's disapproval.

"You don't want to be wearing that thing, madam," Cook remonstrated with her, for Mrs Buchanan was a lady, despite her efforts with the scrub bucket, and ladies did not wear aprons all day long.

"I never know when I might have to do some dirty job, Cook."

"Well, if you do you just send for Gertie or Elsie, madam. They can do any dirty job that needs doing."

She could not settle to anything, wondering why, and so, throwing a warm cloak over her apron, for it was still cold despite being April, she had gone for a walk. She had received one of James's strange letters that morning, written on Good Friday, which spoke of giving the men a holiday that day and of a service by a visiting clergy in a field. They had sung hymns, he told her, and would she thank Mrs Bunting for the splendid food parcel she had sent. The men had been most appreciative, especially of the chocolate shortbreads, and the shirts Lucy had forwarded were most welcome but could she manage a few cigarettes? It was short, formal, as though he were writing to the rector's wife thanking her for her kindness. Not a word about the children, or Howethwaite, and certainly not about her.

It was in her pocket as she took the road towards Grasmere. At the Knoll she left the road, striding out across the rough pasture until she came to the river. Spring was always later arriving in Lakeland than the rest of the country and it was still cold; nevertheless she took off her boots and stockings and stepped into the shallow water, gasping with shock as the icy water bit into her flesh. On the far side she dried her feet on the hem of her skirt and put on her boots, then began the steady climb through the trees until she came to a clearing where the sun struck and spring flowers were in full bloom. Wood anemones and primrose and violets, as shy and lovely as only they could be, lifting their faces to the sunshine. A yellow Brimstone butterfly hung in the sheltered air and for a moment her papa was there beside her. She could hear his voice, gentle, as he had been, and a great longing for him came over her.

She sat for almost half an hour, dwelling on the past as she looked down at Rydal Water, the sun touching it with such brilliance it hurt her eyes. It was as smooth and soft-looking as silk but even as she admired its beauty the surface of the water changed, ruffling as a breeze caught it, lapping to the edges of the lake, distorting the mirrored reflection of the trees which grew around it. She thought about James and Andrew and Paul, all in France now, and of the other young men who had come, khaki-clad, to say goodbye to her. Job Gunson, Janet's eldest son, nineteen, a boy still, but wild to get over there before it ended. Frederick Mossop, Roger Askew, Gregory Kendall who had all danced with her at Franny Buchanan's party, so long ago and yet it was only yesterday. And Franny herself, roaring off defiantly in her little car, as eager as they were to get to the front. Dear Franny, abrasive and outspoken, a troublemaker some would call her but willing to be her friend if she wanted it.

For the last four months nothing much seemed to have happened at the front and those at home had begun to wonder why their boys were out there at all. The last Battle of Ypres had taken place in November, weighted down with mud and casualties, but Ypres had not fallen.

It was not until March that it had been reported that, following a massive bombardment, General Haig's 1st Army had attacked the village of Neuve Chapelle. British casualties were about 13,000, it was said, and a telephone message to the newly converted hospital at

Howethwaite of impending arrivals had come through two days ago.

A convoy of ambulances was rolling up the drive as she came through the gate, and she began to run.

As the weeks passed she wondered what she had done with her time before Howethwaite opened its door to the flood of casualties which seemed to flow, via the clearing hospitals in the south, into her care. That was how she thought of it though her part in it was, as yet, very small. Her care! She was caring for the sick and the wounded and it was as though God had given her, at last, the very job she had been designed to perform.

She wasn't in charge, of course, far from it, and she had to take orders from Sister Colyford who had at first treated Lucy as she would any society lady who was acting out the part of Florence Nightingale, which, in Sister's opinion, many were doing. Playing at it. Dressing up in well-tailored nurses' uniforms and sitting about holding the hands of officers, those not too badly wounded to be objectionable, naturally. Like Mrs Buchanan's cousin-in-law, for instance!

There were no officers at Howethwaite but nevertheless Mrs Charlotte Buchanan came over in her papa's motor, a splendidly elegant chauffeur-driven Mercedes which was, in many enthusiasts' opinion, the best car in the world, dressed in an immaculately tailored, enormously expensive and beautifully fitted nurse's uniform the like of which Sister Colyford had never in her life seen. Their Mrs Buchanan met her at the door.

"Charlotte, this is a surprise, a welcome one, let me tell you, for a helping hand is always welcome. You have come to help, I take it, and may I say how charming you look in your uniform." The touch of irony in Lucy's voice was not lost on Sister Colyford though it went right past Mrs Charlotte Buchanan.

"Thank you, Lucy. I thought, with my husband at the front and all these poor boys . . ." She actually put a wisp of handkerchief to her eyes. "Well, I consider it my duty to help those who have been unfortunate enough to . . . I'm sure you know what I mean."

"I do indeed, Charlotte, and you could not have come at a more opportune time. We are expecting Doctor Yates at any moment. An emergency operation so the stillroom, which has been converted into an operating theatre, must be scrubbed down with carbolic. Pennington and I" – indicating a tall VAD who was armed with a bucket and an ominous-looking scrubbing brush – "are just about to start. We would be grateful for a bit of help."

Charlotte smiled and inside her, where it still rankled that Lucy Dean had taken the man Charlotte Gibson had earmarked for herself, that small growth of malevolence that had been festering for almost two years increased a fraction.

"Scrub . . ." Her voice rose in horror. "I thought perhaps . . . flowers or writing letters. I'm not sure Paul would want me to scrub the . . . the operating theatre." Her voice grew stronger. "In fact, it is not the kind of work I am used to at all."

If she had ever done any work in her life, Sister Colyford, who was pretending to be busy with the post which had just been delivered, thought with amusement.

"Well, Private Andrews in the conservatory was asking if someone could write a letter for him to his mother. He lost both his hands when a land-mine blew up, you see, and, of course, if you could stay on and feed him at lunchtime we would be eternally grateful. Any help we can get, from anyone, is most welcome."

Charlotte had turned the somewhat peculiar colour of dirty flour as every vestige of the rosy flush she usually wore drained from her face, then it hardened and she drew herself up in stiff rage. She was not only insulted to be asked to consort with a private, a man from the underclasses, but one with no hands and she would not forget it. She was a lady and ladies could not be expected to do what working women did. They were not brought up to it and when her father heard of this it would be woe betide the unladylike wife of James Buchanan who was, after all, nothing more than a . . . a . . . Well, she didn't know how to describe her standing there with that odd smile on her face, that smile which she had begun to recognise as contempt. She would not forget this, she swore it, nor the insult James had paid her by marrying this woman instead of her.

But she had not done yet. She had come over to Howethwaite for a purpose other than to offer her services to Lucy Buchanan. In fact, that was secondary to the real reason. An excuse, if you like, to call on Lucy legitimately without seeming too obvious.

She had come to hurt her, to "get her own back", though she would not describe it as such to anyone but herself, for past insults, or if not insults, then grievances.

"By the way," she said, her voice gloating. "I had a letter from my husband this morning. He has some leave and will be home next week. It seems James has a week too but, as I'm sure you must know, since the journey is so difficult he has decided to spend it in Paris. I'll bring Paul over to see you and perhaps give you some news of James."

She turned on her heels and flounced triumphantly, there was no other word for it, down the steps, calling for Giles, the chauffeur, who had wandered across the lawn to have a word with one or two of the wounded lads who were sitting in the garden.

Mrs Buchanan put out her hand – Sister Colyford and the VAD both saw it – and put it on the door handle but neither of them noticed that she gripped it so hard her knuckles turned white.

Mrs Buchanan's other female relatives were not quite so forthright. Mrs Gunson and Mrs Mounsey and Mrs Scott came over, not dressed as Mrs Charlotte Buchanan had been, but prepared to help out in some genteel manner, since the hospital was a Buchanan contribution to the war effort and they felt they owed it to Lucy. They were prepared to sit with a soldier, read to him or perhaps play some board game to take his mind off his suffering. They would, of course, have been happier to associate with an officer as all their menfolk were of that rank but, since there was none, they would make the sacrifice. After all, they were accustomed to speaking to gardeners and footmen and so on, giving them orders, so it should not be too difficult to hold a conversation with a non-commissioned soldier. Ask him about his family and life before the war, if Sister knew what they meant. Yes, Sister knew exactly what they meant and she supposed it might perk up a badly wounded chap to speak of his wife or his mother and home.

Sister Colyford soon found that Mrs Buchanan and her companion, Miss Tyson, were not like the other ladies and so she began to treat them as though they were probationer nurses, answering the hundreds of questions they put to her and allowing them small but responsible duties, recognising their trustworthiness.

Before Howethwaite could be considered to be a hospital in the true sense of the word there had been acres of floor to be scrubbed, miles of skirting board to be attacked with a small brush and carbolic soap, windows to be polished to a high gleam, as though they weren't already spotless, a somewhat offended Mrs Burns retorted acidly, the kitchen converted into one that could cope with preparing meals for over fifty people and it was she and Buffy, with the help of two girls from Ambleside, who had done it, apart from the kitchen, of course. That had been arranged by the medical authorities. Howethwaite hospital, as the locals were now proudly calling it, as though they had had a hand in its creation, was to be run like any other military hospital. Because of its size there was no resident doctor; they had to share the services of Doctor Yates who moved between three other establishments in the area similar to Howethwaite, one of them a converted church hall which took only con-valescent cases. He was summoned wherever he was needed in an emergency but the experienced nursing staff were more than able to take over the running of the wards and to nurse the soldiers who were in their care. There was no matron since Sister Colyford was a nurse with twenty years' experience, and under her were four fully trained nurses and three VADs. Lucy and Buffy were called nurses' aids by the others and were expected to perform any onerous or dirty job they did not themselves care to do. It was frustrating at first to be given orders by a seventeen-year-old girl who, because she possessed a first aid certificate was considered superior to her and Buffy, but they were learning all the time, standing at the elbow of Nurse Cartwright or Nurse Bickerstaffe while dressings were done, injections given, and wounds cleaned, and even, when Sergeant Collins's injured leg became gangrenous, standing with a bucket in the makeshift operating theatre to receive the amputated leg!

It was at the end of May, several weeks after their second intake of wounded had arrived which now meant they were full, that Lucy found herself lying on the floor of the sluice-room which she had just scrubbed. It had once been Dixon's pantry where he had decanted wine, supervised the cleaning of the silver and glassware and plate, and performed the important task of dealing with bills from the wine merchant and generally overseeing the running of the house. His work had been drastically cut when his master went away, for entertaining on the scale of before the war was practically non-existent, and now he shared Mrs Burns's small sitting-room next to the kitchen.

The war and the subsequent departure of so many of the servants to the call of their country in its hour of need had brought out of retirement two of Lucy's old servants, and glad to help they were, they said, especially Bibby who, he told them all, was sick to death of sitting on his bum and twiddling his thumbs all day. Mrs Hutton, still with plenty of work left in her, though she had enjoyed the rest, she told Miss Lucy, bless her, trudged over every day from her small cottage beyond the greenhouses to give a hand in the kitchen. She couldn't do heavy work, she told them, but if she could sit down to it there were many jobs, once done by Win or Fanny or Bridie, she could manage nicely. Shelling peas for the patients' dinner, for instance, preparing the veg, mixing and stirring and generally giving Mrs Bunting a hand, for feeding thirty-six wounded soldiers and seven nurses, not to mention the family, three times a day took a bit of doing. There was many an argument between Mrs Hutton and Cook over the finer points of producing gravy or making an arrowroot blancmange that the poor wounded chaps in the wards could cope with, but on the whole they got on well enough.

Old Bibby had received a new lease on life when he was called upon, or rather pleaded with, to give a hand to Clapcott who sadly missed the services of his Bertie. The government was asking for flower gardens and lawns to be turned over to the growing of vegetables and though Bibby's back was not what it was, or so he was fond of telling them at frequent intervals, he picked up his spade and tackled the job with some enthusiasm, not taking orders, mind, for wasn't he a competent gardener in his own right, but, like Mrs Hutton, glad to be doing something for the war effort.

She didn't know how she'd got on the floor. She was alone and she thanked God for it, since if one of the others had found her there would have been no end of a fuss. She knew she was working harder than she had ever worked in her life. She fell into her bed every night, descending into a stunned sleep so vast and depthless she had a job to drag herself out of it in the morning but she knew deep inside her where she firmly refused to look that it was not tiredness that had made her faint. It might have added to it but the true reason was the life growing inside her, the life James had left behind when he drove away last November. She had buried the knowledge, wrapping herself in her capacious apron which would have hid the fact that she was carrying twins it was so roomy and, knowing they would try to stop her from this work which she loved so passionately, she had ignored every symptom that told her she was pregnant.

She picked up the pail full of reeking dressings which she had brought into the sluice – when? – perhaps fifteen minutes ago, she couldn't be sure, ramming it upside down hard into the rubbish bin which was already half full, then moved carefully to the steriliser, putting her feet down with the precision of a marching soldier. It was as though she had to concentrate hard on keeping her balance, keeping her head clear, her back straight, an untroubled smile on her face, for she meant to hide her condition for as long as she could. She knew nothing about babies, before or after they were born since Buffy had performed the more unpleasant tasks of bringing up Percy. This one meant very little to her only in as much as it might prevent her, or at least force Sister

Colyford into preventing her, from carrying on with her nursing. She had felt some movement inside the growing swell of her belly and, not knowing what it implied, deliberately ignored it. She felt well. She had never ailed a day in her life and she wasn't about to start now, just when she was doing something important, so the baby must await its turn! It was almost into June so she supposed she must be six months pregnant. It was also apparent to her that had she still been wearing the stylish clothes she wore before the hospital opened, she could not have got away with it. As it was, under her apron, she had to leave her skirt gaping with a big safety pin holding it in place.

She walked slowly along the bright hallway towards the open front door, pausing at the top of the ramp which had been laid for the easy movement of wheelchairs and stretchers, conscious of many eyes on her. Some of the men were well enough to be pushed outside into the garden in long, flat, wickerwork stretchers on wheels. They were recovering from the dreadful wounds they had suffered in the trenches at the Battle of Neuve Chapelle in March and would, some of them, be well enough soon to return to the front. They were part of the deluge of 100,000 soldiers wounded in the first few months of the war and had been shuttled along a casualty line beginning at the front with basic first aid performed by the Royal Army Medical Corps; to clearing stations a few miles behind the front line where they had received emergency medical treatment, were put in ambulances which took them to the ambulance trains and on to one of the military hospitals. The more seriously injured were shipped home. These men at Howethwaite had been in a hospital down south but when the second Battle of Ypres had brought another 60,000 casualties pouring into wards already at bursting point, these "old" casualties, half healed and not in such desperate need of nursing, were sent to hospitals further afield.

Half a dozen of them lay in the shade beneath the trees, their wheeled beds in a precise line, for Sister Colyford liked things tidy, the dappled sunshine giving their thin, suffering faces a veneer of health. One or two sat in wheelchairs and, at a small table, four were playing some card game. In the midst of them was her family, for she had decided from the start that she could not forbid them to mix with these soldiers who were so pitifully grateful for any little attention, particularly from a pretty girl. Margaret was reading to them, *Robinson Crusoe* which many of them had never heard of. They were ordinary working men, plumbers and postmen and clerks who had answered their country's call and look where it had bloody landed them, they were inclined to think. Already the gloss of high ideals and fervent patriotism had worn off, tarnished by what they had suffered and seen others suffer and Lucy was aware that none of them wanted to get better and go back to war.

Thimble was lolling on Corporal Holden's knee, his tongue hanging from his mouth in the heat, his eyes screwed up in ecstasy as the corporal's hand caressed his rough head. Thimble was in heaven with the fuss he got from all the soldiers, many of whom had a dog at home just like him, they said wistfully. James's dogs sprawled at the corporal's feet.

Emily, listening to the story, was resting her head

against the knee of a soldier older than the rest, a quiet, fatherly chap with a full moustache and a pipe between his teeth. He was Sergeant Collins whose leg they had cut off and who was to go home to his own little girl soon, thank God. Emily was making a daisy chain, and on the grass Percy practised handstands with great enthusiasm, entertaining the men who, Lucy was positive, gained a certain healing from their contact with the children. Only Edward was missing, but soon he would come cycling furiously up the drive from school to talk to whoever would listen to him about motor cars or aeroplanes or some other mechanical marvel.

Though they had been watching the soft, girlish beauty of Margaret Dean as her voice murmured the story, in unison their eyes turned to Mrs Buchanan as she came down the ramp. Miss Margaret was a treat to look at, they would all have agreed had they discussed it, and was as sweet-natured as an angel, longing to help ease their pain, you could tell, but Mrs Buchanan was something they could not describe, some wordless thing that dwells inside all men who have a dream, a fantasy of the woman they will love, and as she approached there was a deep collective sigh from a dozen male throats. Not that they would aspire to think of Mrs Buchanan in that way, for she was so far above any of them it almost felt like blasphemy. Each of them had some small story to tell – not that they did, for it was precious to them – of Mrs Buchanan's face bending over them, perhaps in the dark of night and how she knew she was needed was a mystery to them, but there she would be, a hand to your brow, smoothing back your hair like your mam used to when you had a nightmare and by God, they had plenty of those.

"Who wants a cup of tea?" she asked cheerfully, walking towards them in that kind of swaying manner that mesmerised them. There was a blooming about her recently, a lovely flush, a gloss of good health, but they were simple men, simple soldiers who, most of them, being young, knew nothing of women and they did not speculate on the reason. She was married to an officer who was at the front, a soldier like themselves, and so they treated her tenderly, respectfully and with great affection. Most of them were half in love with her, and Sister Colyford said privately to Nurse Bickerstaffe that she attributed some of the more spectacular recoveries on the wards to the almost madonna-like beauty and care she gave to them.

"Pity she can't be a full-time nurse, for she's a natural."

Cups of tea were wheeled out on a trolley and handed round by Margaret and Emily, while from the drive Edward shouted a greeting, standing up to cycle in order to put more pressure on the pedals and get there the sooner.

Behind him, but cycling much more slowly, came the telegram boy.

She was to be ashamed later of her sense of deep relief that the yellow envelope the boy held out was addressed not to her but to Mr F. Clapcott. She was conscious of the awful silence about her, for these men were well aware what the telegram boy and his envelope meant to their families at home. The poor lad was detested and yet he was only doing his duty, as she must do hers.

They watched her walk away, her head high, and softly Margaret began to weep for she had seen the name on the envelope. Private George, called Georgie by the others, put out a hand and took Margaret's in his, patting it clumsily as her head bent on her tears.

"What is it?" Percy demanded shrilly, afraid, though he didn't know what of. "What's happened? Who's the telegram for?" He had just done a perfect handstand, walking for at least a yard on his hands before toppling over, and he was irritated that no one seemed to have seen it. Edward knelt down beside him and put a brotherly arm about him and all the while Emily continued to make her daisy chain, for this was the first time the war had struck personally at them and they must find a way through it.

"Give me the book, lass," Sergeant Collins said quietly to Margaret. "I'll read it fer a bit. There, there, lass, don't fret. See, come and sit close ter me an' us'll find out what that there Man Friday's got up to. But before yer do, pour us another cuppa, there's a good lass," and Margaret was comforted by the simple task and the kind heart of a soldier who had witnessed more things than any man should be asked to witness, but still had compassion for the pain of a young girl.

Clapcott was turning over the soil at the side of the house where, to his sorrow, he had been forced to sacrifice the lawn into which he had put nearly thirty years of his life. It had been a grand lawn, like bloody velvet what with all his coddling of it and he was saying so to Bibby and Licky Thripp who, as odd-job man with not a lot to do now, helped out wherever he was put.

"I've fed that lawn better then me own babby," he was saying, stopping a moment to relight his pipe and for a moment Lucy wanted to throw the telegram away. She didn't know what was in the envelope; perhaps Bertie was wounded or a prisoner of war, or even missing, which would give them all a bit of hope but something inside her seemed to say she knew this was not so. Just at this precise moment, to Clapcott his son was still alive, still the cheerful lad who had grinned impishly and marched off to war saying he wanted to see a bit of the world before he settled down like his dad, and now where was he? Dear Lord, spare Clapcott and Mrs Clapcott, who are part of this family, the pain of . . . Oh, dear, dear God . . .

He turned and was about to smile and nod, for they were all fond of their master's lovely wife, when he saw what was in her hand. She didn't realise she was doing it but she was holding the hated envelope away from her, towards him, and she watched as the life drained away from his face in terror. Bertie was Clapcott and Mrs Clapcott's only child.

Bibby and Licky Thripp moved away respectfully and both removed their caps as though already they knew they were in the presence of death.

"I'm sorry, Mr Clapcott," Lucy said helplessly, holding out the envelope, but Clapcott began to shake his head as though in denial that it was for him, refusing to take it while further down the row they were digging Bibby and Licky sighed pityingly.

"Eeh, Mrs Buchanan," the gardener moaned, "eeh, I can't . . ."

"Would you like me to open it for you, Mr Clapcott?" She put a gentle hand on his arm, stroking it a little, her lovely, white-capped head bending towards him, her face filled with compassion.

"Aye, would thi', lass?"

When she had told him his son was dead, killed in action, she put her strong young arms about his bowed shoulders and held him, weeping with him as she led him towards the cottage where Mrs Clapcott was baking him an apple pie for his tea in cheerful ignorance of what was to come.

They couldn't believe it, really they couldn't, they told one another in the kitchen. Not that cheeky little lad who Mrs Bunting, Mrs Burns and Dixon had known from birth. He was a little tyke and no mistake, but sweet-tempered and honest and since he left school a good worker beside his poor pa. What were they to do, the Clapcotts; they must go over at once, one of them, to see if they could help, but it seemed the mistress was there and would stay as long as she was needed. She'd looked real bonny these last few weeks, which was daft really, for she'd always been bonny, and her tender pity for the men in her care had amazed them all. They'd thought the master had made a mistake when he married a girl of eighteen and brought her and all them children back to Howethwaite but would you look at them now, especially her, a family they were proud to serve. She'd proved times she was worth anyone's respect and affection and if anyone could help them poor Clapcotts it was her.

She came home just after midnight, her face calm but as grey as the ash in the kitchen fire. They'd not gone to bed, for it was as though they'd lost one of their own family and there had been frequent outbreaks of weeping, from Dimity who'd often been teased by the cheeky young lad, from Elsie who had had hopes of Bertie though she'd not let on and who couldn't seem to come to terms with the realisation that she'd never see him again. She had cried noisily on Mrs Bunting's deep bosom, setting Dimity off. Dimity had a sweetheart at the front, a handsome lad who had been groom to old Mr Harry Buchanan from Oak Bank and Bertie's death had finally brought the awareness that he, like Bertie, might never come home and if he did, perhaps he might be in the state some of those poor chaps at the front of the house were in. Dimity didn't do much "maiding" these days, since Mrs Buchanan never went anywhere to need it. Her hair, which she kept threatening to cut, was brushed each morning by Dimity, who insisted on it, and pulled back into a neat coil under her nurse's kerchief, a sort of square which was wrapped tightly about her head with the points down her back.

She was exhausted and so she was careless.

"I'll come up with you, madam," Dimity told her sympathetically. "A nice bath's what you need and when you've had it straight into bed with some warm milk."

"Oh, Dimity, I really . . ."

"No, madam, I mean it. Now come along, up them stairs and off with that apron and I'll run your bath."

She was unfastening the broad ribbons that held the apron round her waist even before she reached the door which led out into the hall. She was stunned with sorrow for the Clapcotts who had finally fallen into an uneasy sleep, and with her own aching tiredness. She held the apron in her hand as she turned to say goodnight to the servants, who were themselves on the move now she had returned, and her profile was silhouetted against the light from the hall.

For a second or two she wondered what was wrong with them, all staring in consternation, then, when Mrs Bunting began to smile, a smile of such joy it lit up her kindly face, she knew what she had done. Her hands went defensively to her belly where the child kicked, unconcerned with the world's woes but she said nothing.

Mrs Bunting did though. "They say as one life goes another comes to take its place. God bless poor Bertie and God bless this new 'un."

They drove her wild with their protective solicitude, not only the servants who now considered her to be their exclusive property, for was she not to bear a child, a Buchanan child, the first in the house since the master himself had been born thirty-five years ago, but the nurses and patients as well. To the afflicted soldiers it was as though, in this world of madness that was killing and maiming human beings in their hundreds of thousands, the coming of a new life, which, now that they knew about it, they could see growing almost before their eyes, gave them a sense of continuation, of the bountiful goodness of Mother Nature who had nothing to do with the carnage at the front. Mrs Buchanan, in her new role of mother-to-be, was an image they carried into sleep, an image which in some way took them back to their own childhood and their own mother who was the comfort and blessing given to children. They were like children again, some of them, in their pain, calling out for "Mam" in their delirium or sleep, and Mrs Buchanan, though it was said she was only twenty, was everyone's mother in her new role.

She fought it like a tiger, the restrictions they tried to put on her.

"You cannot possibly continue your duties on the wards, Mrs Buchanan," Sister Colyford told her in that imperious tone which frightened VADs and nurses alike, as Lucy had known she would which was why she had kept her condition hidden.

"And why not? I am aware that I must no longer lift heavy buckets."

"Or heavy men, my dear. You are in your sixth month."

"I know that, Sister, but that does not mean I am an invalid. There are many tasks I can still perform and, believe me, you nor anyone else will stop me. This is my house and I shall do in it exactly as I wish."

Lucy straightened her back and squared her chin and shoulders, the movement thrusting forward the bulge of her child. She still wore Cook's enormous apron over her nurse's uniform but her pregnancy was very obvious and those who had worked with her for all these months, especially Sister Colyford who should, as a trained nurse, have known better, were amazed that they had missed it. Of course she carried herself so well, so gracefully, and she was tall and womanly with splendid breasts and hips, like a young Juno, and so it was perhaps not to be wondered at, but that made no difference to Sister Colyford.

"And these are my wards and my patients and I will not have you here among them. They will be embarrassed."

"So, none of them have seen a pregnant woman before, Sister, is that what you're saying and will shriek and faint away as spinsters did in Victorian times? I refuse absolutely to be kept from them and anything I am still capable of doing for them, I will do."

They were both strong-willed women and everyone on the wards, – the soldiers betting on the outcome with Mrs Buchanan winning hands down – in the gardens and the kitchen could hear them going hammer and tongs, though Sister Colyford, for the sake of her dignity, was doing her best to remain calm. Lucy had no such scruples.

"I knew this would happen the moment you found out."

"And none too soon, if I may say so, Mrs Buchanan. Do you want to harm the child?"

"Of course not, but if I am careful . . ."

"Perhaps your husband might have something to say on the matter. This is, after all, his child too."

For the fraction of a second an expression of doubt, doubt and something else that Sister could not put a name to, slipped across Mrs Buchanan's mutinous face and her eyes clouded.

Ever since Charlotte had told her that James had chosen to spend his leave in Paris rather than come home, Lucy had brooded on what it might mean. She could not say it distressed her, since she knew that she and James were both aware that they were not as other husbands and wives were. They had struck a bargain over a year ago and she had more than kept her side of it, as he had. She was to bear his child which she supposed would please him and she had also supposed, in one of her infrequent letters, she should have told him about it, but she had been afraid that if she did the very thing that was happening now would be forced upon her.

And yet she was sorry in a strange way that he had not taken his leave here, in the home where he had been born, where he had grown from childhood to manhood and she hoped it was not because of her. Why he should avoid her, if that was what he was doing, she couldn't imagine, and she decided she was being silly to think so, but it had unsettled her, upset her in a way, for it would have been . . . What? What would it have been? She didn't know what she meant, where her thoughts were going, only that they were not happy ones.

"Mrs Buchanan, may I have your word that you will do as I ask?" Sister Colyford was saying. "It is my responsibility to look after these men and if you should . . . have an accident you know how it would upset them. They have a high regard for you, you know that?"

There was a catch in Lucy's voice as she answered. "And I have a high regard for them, Sister Colyford, which is why I would like your permission to—"

"No, Mrs Buchanan, I cannot."

"I was just about to say may I still continue to . . . nurse them, not physical nursing but . . . something that will help them to recover. It might be only helping them to tie their ties in the morning but I must feel I am . . . Please, Sister, don't ban me from the wards."

"Mrs Buchanan, as long as you promise not to do more than tie a tie, read a letter or a book, arrange flowers . . ."

"In other words what all the other so-called society women are doing?" Lucy's voice was low and bitter but she knew she must have regard for this woman's position and also the wellbeing of the patients. If she was to take a tumble and lose the child it would put some of them back in their recovery, she knew that.

There was a new illness, although some in the War Office did not call it that, to which the medical people gave the name of "shell shock". Men whose nerves had been pounded into insensibility by the continual noise of the barrage that apparently went on and on for hours before they went "over the top" – they were all learning the jargon the Tommies brought back from the front – and it was this along with the constant fear in which they lived that was driving some men to the brink of madness. They had one such in a separate ward, a small room at the back of the house since his cries disturbed the others. He had not been seriously wounded, a piece of shrapnel in his calf that had been successfully removed, but it was his mental state that gave cause for alarm. He must be tiptoed round, for any sudden noise, a door banging, the barking of James's dogs, sent him off into what Mrs Bunting called "the screaming abdabs" which gave her the creeps, really it did, poor lad. He even slept under his bed and it was soldiers like him who must not be distressed.

"Nevertheless, Mrs Buchanan, will you promise me, until your child is born, that you will take no unnecessary risks. I will not ban you from the wards but if anyone reports to me, and they will all, staff and patients alike, be watching you like hawks, that you are not keeping your promise I will take steps to have you removed."

If Sister was in high dudgeon over what she saw as sheer irresponsibility on Mrs Buchanan's part, the Buchanan ladies, who came over the moment the servants' grapevine revealed the news, were speechless and totally baffled, they told her, by her foolish negligence. Charlotte was to come later with Paul – had she heard that he was home on leave? – and would, no doubt, add her disapproval to theirs and they were, of course, quite sure she was to give this all up and leave it to the professionals. What would James say if he knew that she was still nursing, and then there were the men who were not gentlemen after all and it was not proper that the wife of one who was, a pregnant wife, should be continuing to mix with them and on and on until at last, standing up and sticking out her stomach for them all to see, she told them they must excuse her since she was tired and if they were to see Charlotte would they beg her to come on another day since she did not feel up to any more visits.

They left, somewhat put out, for they had not told her half of what they had intended telling her. After all, they all had borne a child and it seemed to them she was badly in need of their advice.

Lucy stood at the window and stared out into the thin drizzle that had started overnight. The garden was empty except for Licky Thripp who walked across the lawn on some private business of his own. She had seen him earlier with Mr Clapcott, who had resumed his duties as soon as he could, leaving Bertie's grieving mother in the care of her sister from Birmingham. He needed to be doing something, he had told Lucy, and his sister-in-law was a kind soul and would look after Mrs Clapcott as well, if not better than he could. It was all he could do to manage his own grief, just yet at any rate, and Mrs Clapcott was even worse.

Lucy sighed deeply, watching some blackbirds having a good wash in a puddle of water beneath the window. Their wings flapped, their heads bobbed and their feathers were wet and spiky. The rainwater flew about in a mad arc and the birds were totally unaware of the man standing under the gnarled oak tree that crouched at the gate leading into the vegetable garden. It was a soldier by the look of it, simply standing under the dripping spread of the tree watching the birds, as still as an animal trapped by a predator, cornered and terrified and unable to escape.

Lucy narrowed her eyes and peered at the figure through the rain, which was coming down faster now, dashing against the window of her sitting-room and running in growing rivulets. Who on earth among the wounded men was capable of walking round from the front of the house, where the wards were situated, to the back and why had no one noticed him? He had no overcoat on and she could see that the blue hospital uniform the men wore was darkening with rain.

Suddenly she recognised who it was. Swiftly she reached for her old cloak which she kept handy in her sitting-room and, throwing it about her shoulders, opened the French windows that led on to a small terrace lined with pots of herbaceous flowers. There were steps leading down to the lawn, which was next on the agenda for the growing of vegetables, and though she was quiet as she moved across the sodden grass she knew he had seen her by the sudden tightening of his body and the tic which developed in his pale cheek as she drew near. He took a step backwards, then another until his back was pressed against the trunk of the tree, putting out his hands as though to ward off some unimaginable horror and Lucy's heart moved with pity.

"It's only me, Rory," she said quietly. "I saw you

watching the birds. I was too. They make a comical sight, don't they? But it's awfully wet out here. Why don't you come into my sitting-room and we'll have some tea. I don't know about you but I'm ready for one. My husband's cousins' wives – heavens, what a mouthful – have just left and I feel like a wrung-out rag. They are full of good advice on what I should or shouldn't do. You know I'm to have a baby, don't you?"

His gaze fell slowly to her swelling stomach and she saw him relax, the awful rigidity of his tall, slender body slipping away. His shoulders slumped and his hands fell to his sides. He moved away from the tree trunk, just one small step, but Lucy was encouraged to take one to meet him. He did not seem to mind.

Rory Cameron was an unusual soldier in as much as he did not come from the working-class background of the other enlisted men. He was what was known as "officer material", for he had been educated at a well-known public school and had gone on to Cambridge. His family had an old and respected name. His father was a wealthy man from somewhere in Surrey, a stockbroker, and it had been hoped that Rory would go into the family firm but the war had put a stop to all that. Lucy had never actually talked to him, except to soothe him when his nightmares came, but she knew he had the drawling, well-bred accent of the privileged class into which he had been born. He had the appearance of a thoroughbred horse among a herd of sturdy work ponies, with an athlete's build, tall but pared down to the bone, a long, lean body without substance and a face that was almost too handsome. Had it not been totally and undeniably male it might have been described as beautiful. His hair was a pale silver blond, thick and heavy and his eyes were the deep blue of a cornflower.

"Will you come with me, Rory?" She smiled and was rewarded with a further relaxing of his muscles. "I would be glad of your arm across this wet grass, if you wouldn't mind," she went on, shamelessly exploiting her condition and at once his gentleman's manners, which had been bred in him since the nursery, prodded him into immediate action.

"Of course, Mrs Buchanan," he said, almost leaping out from beneath the tree and smiling in return. Her condition did not seem to embarrass him, rather the opposite, for it overshadowed his own fears and gave him, for that small period of time, a crutch on which to lean. Not that he leaned on Lucy, far from it, he almost carried her across the grass, saying, in a solicitous voice, "Now mind where you put your feet, Mrs Buchanan. It is really quite hazardous and those steps are covered with moss. Let me get the door. No, don't leave go of my arm just yet," until at last he had her where he wanted her, which was in her armchair by the fire, her cloak carefully hanging over a chair back.

"Is that comfortable?" he begged her to tell him. "Would you like to take off your shoes? They look wet to me," and before she knew what he was about he knelt at her feet and with gentle hands undid the buttons on her stout shoes and drew them off her feet. He placed them by the fender, then sat back and grinned up at her.

It was like a miracle, a transformation, the merry twinkle in his lovely blue eyes, the creases in his cheeks where, in the past, he had done a great deal of laughing, the white perfection of his teeth in a face that was tinted now with colour.

"Rory, you make a better nurse than I did and I shall tell Sister Colyford that if ever she needs a hand, you're her man."

"Dear Lord, she'd reduce me to jelly the moment she came into the ward. I've heard her." His voice rose to a light falsetto. "'Nurse Bickerstaffe, why is that soldier lolling on his bed and as for the casters, they are a disgrace and I'd be obliged if you would straighten them at once.' But I must admit she does her best with me and I'm not easy to deal with."

It was said with total ease and candour and if Lucy had not seen for herself the dreadful shaking, the blankets under his bed where he hid from the nightmares, heard him cry out a name which sounded like "Mama" she would not have believed this was the same man.

"Ring the bell, will you, Rory, and we'll have tea." He did so and when Elsie, who had been promoted to the dizzy heights of parlour maid by the desertion of Win and Fanny and Bridie, popped her frilled cap round the door, she couldn't believe her eyes. There was Miss Lucy relaxed and smiling in her armchair, her belly out to here – this *sotto voce* to Cook so as not to offend Mr Dixon's sensibilities – and the soldier, the *mad* soldier, sitting on the floor at her feet.

"Tea, please, Elsie," she was told, "and will you ask Mrs Bunting if she could rustle up some of her chocolate shortbreads. I'm sure Private Cameron would love to taste one, wouldn't you, Private? Let me

tell you they are the most wonderful biscuits you have
ever tasted."

"I bet they're not as good as the ones my mother's
cook used to make. I can remember when we were
children, my brothers and me, stealing them off the
wire tray where Cook had put them to cool. We didn't
half get a wigging, I can tell you."

"I couldn't believe it, really I couldn't," Elsie declared
in an awed voice. "There he was, as happy as Larry,
chatting away to the mistress and no sign of his shakes
or anything. Eeh, that Miss Lucy," she continued in a
fond voice, "she could get round anyone, her."

He stayed with her for an hour and when Sister put
her head round the door to see if Mrs Buchanan had
seen him he told her to "Bugger off, Sister, there's a
dear," with an impish smile on his face that took any
insult out of his words.

"Well," Lucy said later to Buffy, "I might not be able
to give Sergeant Collins a hand with his stump or help
Nurse Bickerstaffe with rounds but I seem to have got
through to poor Private Cameron." She smiled with
enormous satisfaction, believing in her naïvety that
just one little chat with her had cured him of his
shell shock.

She heard him yelling for someone to "get your
bloody head down unless you want the thing shot
off", a couple of hours later, followed by Sister's firm
tread as she hurried to his room with an injection. Lucy
followed her, waiting until she knew the injection had
taken effect. He was asleep, drugged and motionless,
but his face had the marks of tears and she felt
that compassion that she seemed to have in such
overflowing abundance for these men who, most of

them, would have to go back to the hell that had sent them here.

He spent a part of each day with her from then on, feeling, it seemed, that she needed his arm to go the smallest distance. He did not mix well with the other men, not because of the difference in their class but because of the difference in their injuries. His were not visible. His mind had been damaged and that didn't show as their wounds showed and though they were sympathetic since they had gone through exactly what he had and knew what he had suffered, they had not reached that fine line between sanity and madness which had affected him.

When Lucy walked in the garden or through the woods he went with her, guarding her every step and she had not the heart to stop him, feeling that here, at last, she was doing some good, giving him a reason for his very existence at that dreadful moment in his young life.

It was a lovely day towards the end of July and the heady scent of the roses, which Clapcott nurtured with the deep concern he gave to any growing thing, drifted over the roof from the front of the house to the back where she was walking in the shade. Her step was slow and heavy now, for she was near her time, and he followed her hesitantly, on his face an expression of great concern.

"I hadn't seen you on the ward today, Mrs Buchanan. I wondered whether you were ... unwell." Quite naturally he took her hands and held them out to the side, looking down with great gentleness to her swollen belly. "It won't be long now, will it? I asked Sister and after a lot of waffling, as though she did not think it quite proper for a gentleman to ask after the health of an expectant mother, she told me that there were only two weeks to go now. I had hoped to see the baby but I . . . I may not be here."

She looked astounded and her hands clutched his tightly. "Not here?"

"No, they say I am recovered and so . . . I am to go back." A shadow crossed his face but he managed to grin. "I *am* better, I know that and I believe I have you to thank for it."

She looked even more astounded. "Me!"

He led her to a quiet corner of the garden which, as yet, had not been dug up for vegetables. There was a seat there, an old wooden bench which was in need of painting and with great care he helped her down on to it. He flinched as Thimble came tearing round the corner, not barking but going somewhere at great speed, but he remained calm. Somewhere they could hear the sound of the children laughing and she knew they were messing about with an old perambulator which had been dug out of the attic and in which, presumably, James had been trundled about as a baby. It would do fine for the new little 'un, Licky Thripp had told her earnestly but Mrs Burns had been horrified, for the thought of putting "their" baby in such an ancient contraption was not to be considered. Instead the children had taken it over, Edward informing them that he meant to put a motor on it if he could save up enough money and didn't they think a motorised perambulator would be enormous fun. James's dogs were barking, as they did now at every show of excitement and Lucy wondered idly what he would say when he got home. They were as wild and undisciplined as Thimble was but, she told herself, they had a great deal more fun.

"I felt . . . improved after that day we talked in your parlour, Mrs Buchanan, though I have had relapses. But these few weeks with you and the thought of the new life; Christ, I hope you don't think me indelicate, but it has given me something. I don't know how to explain it, Mrs Buchanan."

"Dear God, Rory, can you not call me Lucy after all this time."

He flushed like a boy. "May I?"

"Of course you may."

"There was something I wanted to ask you. A great favour. You see I have come to . . . well . . ." He managed a boyish grin. "I wondered if you would mind if I wrote to you, from the front, I mean. Oh, I write to my parents and they write to me but my father cannot forgive me for not taking a commission."

"Why didn't you?"

"I wanted to fight the war the men fought. I know that sounds highfalutin', even pompous, but I felt the need to . . . get away from the things my father thought so important." He grinned. "I was always a rebel, Lucy, doing the opposite to what was considered proper, so I enlisted on the day war was declared and my father has never forgiven me for it. That is why he has not been to see me here. Not a son who was cowardly and could not face up to his responsibilities. I have three brothers, all officers in a swank Surrey regiment, but . . ."

He looked down at his hands which were gripping one another in what seemed to be an agony of embarrassment, but she knew it was not that which had him in such turmoil. She put hers out and covered his and at once they stopped twisting about one another and relaxed. His fingers entwined with hers and she could feel her strength flowing into him and he smiled.

"There, you see what you do to me. One touch and you cure me of my bloody jitters. I wish I could put you in my pocket and take you back with me. You know, don't you? You know that I love you."

"Yes, I know, Rory."

"Do you . . . mind?"

"It is something every woman should treasure, the offering of a man's love."

"But it can come to nothing."

"No, Rory, but I would like it if you wrote to me. We have become friends and one does not like to lose touch with friends."

"Will you write back?"

"Yes."

"Promise."

"I promise."

Somehow all the men knew the exact moment that Mrs Buchanan's pains began and among the married men who had children there was much conjecture as to how long her labour would be.

"My old woman was two bloody days wi' 'er first," one offered, lugubriously, lighting a Woodbine and dragging the smoke deep into his lungs.

"Nay, don't say that. Poor lass. I wish . . ." another said wistfully and they all knew what he wanted to say. There was not one among them who would not have suffered their own injuries all over again if it saved the lovely Mrs Buchanan her pain.

" 'Appen it'll be quick. She's a big strong lass."

" 'appen."

Lucy lay with her legs apart and her knees up, the mound of her belly jutting up so high she could barely see over it. She swore through gritted teeth that she would never go through this again. She had never felt so humiliated in her life, for Doctor Yates, who had been on duty at the time, had his nose almost inside her. And as if this wasn't bad enough she was suffering the most appalling pains which came at frequent intervals to tear her apart with a ferocity that appalled her. When would the damn child come, for goodness sake? She had been in labour quite long enough for several babies to be born and here was this old fool telling her, "Bear down . . . push . . . push now, there's a good girl," when every movement was torture. She was splitting apart and this had been going on for hours now and she didn't think she could take much more.

She said so weakly. Sweat stung her eyes and ran into her hair and someone – was it Buffy? – ran a damp cloth round her face.

"You're doing very well, my dear. When the next pain starts take a big breath and push."

"It's all right for you," she managed on anguished breath, but doing as she was told, trying to get rid of the round and heavy rock that was jammed inside her. It was breaking her open, tearing her tender flesh, wave after wave of pain until, with a surge which she was convinced was her life's blood, the rock slipped out and it became not a rock but a baby's head and she let out a long sigh of relief. The doctor was smiling with great satisfaction as though it had all been down to him and Buffy began to make foolish cooing sounds as the child was wrapped about in a towel and put in her arms. She didn't feel like asking what it was.

"Well done, Mrs Buchanan," Lucy heard Nurse Bickerstaffe say before she slipped into a lovely sleep which she hoped would last for at least a week. She deserved it!

They could none of them sleep that night, telling one another it was the heat, or the pain of their injuries, or that bloody dog barking its fool head off in the stable, though they all knew it was none of these things. When dawn broke, and Nurse Bickerstaffe bustled down to tell them that Mrs Buchanan had a beautiful baby girl, the cheer could be heard in the kitchen where the servants were keeping their own vigil.

There was champagne that day, the day Alice Buchanan was born, the day Rory Cameron was driven away and the day that Captain James Buchanan was promoted to major, though he did not celebrate with champagne. He did not celebrate at all.

Lucy Buchanan wrote dutifully to her husband to tell
him of his new daughter, saying in the letter that she
hoped it would not be too long before they met, he
and Alice. Did he like the name? She was sorry not to
have conferred with him on the choice but Alice had
been her grandmother's name and Christina, which
was Alice's second name, had been his grandmother's.
She made no apology for not writing more often; this
was her first letter since telling him he was to be a
father three months ago. Alice was quite beautiful,
she said, dark with pale grey eyes like his and not a
scrap of trouble and the children adored her.

She did not mention that the soldiers did too.

"I don't hold with it," Mrs Bunting told anyone who
would listen to her, even Mrs Buchanan who she
thought had lost her mind, the daft things she did.
What Mrs Bunting didn't hold with she was not afraid
to disclose. "Them poor men I feel sorry for, I really
do, but to let them have a hold of that poor little
mite is more than I can bear to think of and I'm
shocked and disappointed in the mistress. And that
there Sister ought to know better an' all. All them
bandages and what-not an' that poor chap wi' only

his eyes showin'. Eeh, I've a good mind ter write ter the master."

When Mrs Bunting was upset, as now, she reverted to the speech of her childhood, which had taken place in Bolton.

"Fancy, babby not even a month old and 'er passed round like a parcel from bed ter bed." She shook her grey head in bewilderment and Mrs Burns patted her arm comfortingly, entirely in agreement with her. They had been overjoyed at the birth of Miss Alice and amazed at the splendid and speedy recovery of the mistress. Too speedy in their opinion and that of the other Buchanan ladies who were on her doorstep the very day the baby was born, ready with their advice and opinions on the upbringing of this newest addition to the Buchanan clan. Even the old people, the remaining grandparents, though not of Alice, of course, Mr Harry and Mr Job and their wives, all as spry as week-old lambs, Mr Harry, at sixty-nine, and Mr Job, a year younger, did her the honour of paying her a visit, since this was, after all, James's first child. They poked the baby and told one another that she was the spit of old Alex, their father, and yet she had their mother's eyes. A real Buchanan and no mistake.

Lucy was not quite sure how she felt about Alice. She was glad she had arrived because it meant that she, Lucy, could resume her duties on the wards. She was keen to be involved with every aspect of nursing, not only on the three wards but in the operating theatre, she told Sister Colyford, and now that she was herself again, meaning without the burden she had dragged about with her all those weeks, she intended doing just that. She hoped to find a capable girl to look after

Alice, which would leave her free to get on with her hospital work.

But when the time came she found, for some reason, she couldn't just give Alice over to another woman. It was strange really, for she had not expected this placid little scrap who had been put immediately into the family cradle, the one in which even Alex Buchanan, Alice's great-great-grandfather had slept, to attach herself so firmly to something in Lucy which she had not known existed. On Sister Colyford's advice, Sister Colyford having come from a large working-class family which thought such things to be entirely normal, she fed the infant herself, finding she had plenty of milk and quite enjoying the silent communion, except for the small grunting sounds of pleasure which came from Alice, growing between her and her daughter. Alice was left in the schoolroom with Margaret and Emily and Miss Bradley when Lucy was on the wards with instructions that they were to come for her at once if an emergency arose. She slept in her cradle or simply lay watching her own pink fists waving in the air and at the slightest sign of boredom on her part Margaret, Emily and Miss Bradley quarrelled over whose turn it was to pick her up.

Percy had started going to school with Edward now, both of them riding their bicycles along the country lanes and into Ambleside. He missed Thimble, he said, but otherwise it wasn't too bad. There was a splendid chap called Dickinson the same age as he was; oh, yes, they all called one another by their surnames. He was Dean Minor, of course, and he and Dickinson got on like a house on fire; in fact, if Lucy was agreeable and would telephone Dickinson's mother, he would like to have his new friend over to tea one day. That's if Lucy could pick Dickinson up, for Dickinson's father was at the front and his mother didn't drive their motor which was put away, like Mr Buchanan's Rolls, until the end of the war.

"But I can't drive either, darling," she told him, holding him in her lap before the fire. He was seven years old now but still liked a cuddle, though she was careful not to do it before the others, for his dignity might be damaged.

"You could learn, Luce."

"Why can't Mrs Dickinson learn then?"

"Oh, she's too old, but I bet you'd have the hang of it in no time. Edward'd teach you."

"Edward?"

"Oh, yes, you know he's been able to drive for ages, only he's not old enough yet."

The seed of the idea had been put into her head and it began to take root and grow. She could be found in the garage now and again, circling the Rolls Royce which was carefully wrapped up in tarpaulin, a thoughtful expression on her face. She was not sure about Edward but she was sure there would be someone who could teach her.

Alice was eight weeks old when James came home on leave, almost a year after he had left.

Lucy was helping to dress the leg wound of a young private, no more than eighteen she was certain, who was doing his best not to scream out loud as Nurse Bickerstaffe, a pair of forceps in her hand, swabbed out the deep and appalling hole in his leg. It ran from his knee down to his ankle, probably two inches deep, and the nurse, who had to be brutal to clean it with the lysol, kept on murmuring like a litany, "Not much more, old chap, soon be over, old chap," while the young soldier clung to Lucy's hands, his eyes fearful holes in the ghastly grey of his agonised face, his gaze never moving from hers. There was a smell coming from the wound, a smell familiar to all those who treated these dreadfully injured men. After all these months Lucy could recognise gangrene when she smelled it and saw it and it lay deep in the young soldier's leg where cutting could not reach.

"Don't let 'em tekk it off, Mrs Buchanan," he hissed through teeth which were clamped together so tightly the bones of his jaw stood out, white and rigid. Lucy bent over him, ready to gather him into her arms if necessary. She had a perfume, something James had given her in the early days of their marriage and she wore it on the ward, for she knew it pleased the men who knew only the smell of lysol and carbolic and all the other aromas of sickness which could not be prevented. Her hair, which she bound back with her nurse's kerchief, despite the pins and combs Dimity tucked into it, still had a tendency to slip out in curling tendrils, to Sister's disapproval, and now one drifted across the boy's face, touching his cheek and he relaxed and smiled through his agony.

It was this that met James Buchanan's eyes as he stepped slowly into the hall and looked into what had once been his elegant drawing-room.

Along both walls, and even in a line down the centre of the enormous room were beds, each one filled with a bandaged man. Arms, legs on pulleys controlled with a mass of wires, heads that were totally encased in white, hands, faces with slits from which eyes peered and mouths gaped, and when he turned and looked into what had been the dining-room it was the same. The beds were close together with only a locker standing between each one and along the windowsills beneath each window stood a mass of flowers in vases and somehow he knew they were his wife's doing. Some of the lockers had a photograph standing on them: a family group, a wife, a sweetheart. There were trolleys draped in white gauze on which were kidney-shaped dishes, instruments, bottles of disinfectant, pads of dressings, cotton wool and hypodermic needles in disinfectant. The wide doors at the far end of the drawing-room opened on to the conservatory, through which even more beds could be seen and from it came the sound of a gramophone playing the soldiers' favourite song of the moment.

"It's a long way to Tipperary, It's a long way to go . . ." warbled a female voice, but from the conservatory, apparently unaware that they could be overheard, several male voices parodied.

> That's the wrong way to tickle Mary,
> That's the wrong way, you know . . .

There were several wheelchairs in which blue-uniformed soldiers sat, some with one leg, some with none, and in the midst of it was his lovely wife who had haunted his dreams and filled his heart with pain and rejection for two years now.

He had been slightly wounded at the Battle of Loos which had begun on 25 September. There had been heavy casualties at Neuve Chapelle earlier in the year and the disaster at Gallipoli had decimated not only British troops but those from Australia and New Zealand; but those in command, who must know what they were doing, or so the men in the trenches said with deep irony, began the attack at Loos on the 25th. The infantry had scrambled out of their trenches and headed across no-man's land in a haze of gas and smoke, gas which was later to turn on their own men, and it was then that the bullet went cleanly through James's upper arm and knocked him out of the battle. He had walked back to the casualty clearing station with scores of other walking wounded, carrying one young lad on his back and repeatedly telling the others to get on their bloody feet and follow him. His wound was clean, the bullet having gone right through, and as he had not been in contact with the filth through which his men staggered, it was easy to treat.

"Aren't you due some leave, Major Buchanan?" his commanding officer asked him and when he said he was, he was told to get on the convoy and take himself off until his arm had healed. He had come from London where most of the hospital trains arrived and, still with the convoy of wounded, had been brought north, since the hospitals in the south were no longer able to take any more casualties. The ambulances were gathered on the drive behind him.

An orderly pushed him unceremoniously aside, calling out to the nurse who stood beside Lucy that there was a fresh batch of wounded for her, though fresh was hardly the word to describe them for they had come straight from the trenches and had been on the move for several days.

At once other nurses appeared, led by an older one in a frilled cap and a small cape which evidently denoted her rank as a sister.

"How many, Corporal?" Her manner was brisk and not at all disconcerted.

" 'Ow many can yer take, Sister? We got abaht thirty, I reckon. I'm to share 'em out among the three 'ospitals up 'ere."

The sister turned to Lucy and said crisply, "Can you manage any more beds, Mrs Buchanan? I know the authorities delivered some a few weeks ago for emergencies but . . ."

"They're in the tack-room, Sister. I'll get some help and fetch them over. The mattresses are stored in my sitting-room upstairs. They can be put . . . let me see . . ." James saw his wife look round her, her eyes narrowed in concentration. "We could put some in the hallway and a couple at the end of the conservatory. Say about a dozen."

"Very well, bring in a dozen, Corporal, and put their stretchers down wherever you can find a space. The beds will be ready for them in half an hour. Is there a doctor with them?"

"There is, Sister, an' 'e ses 'e knows these parts. Name of Buchanan."

The dozen men, who had appalling untreated wounds, apart from the bit of rough first aid they had received at the clearing stations, were dumped on the floors with the mud and filth of Flanders still on them. One was screaming but the rest were grey and silent, deep in shock. Not for several hours did Lucy and James Buchanan take stock of one another in the quiet back reaches of her parlour. They had passed one another a dozen times in the sorting out of the men and the treating of their wounds, for James was soon caught up in the drama and could not stand idly by and watch those slips of girls, the VADs and his own wife, tussle with stretchers and heavy men who had to have their stinking uniforms cut from their damaged bodies. He had been helping Paul on the journey, Doctor Paul Buchanan, who was to return immediately to the war zone when he had delivered his broken cargo.

"Go and have a bath and spend an hour with Charlotte, man," James had told him. "And that's an order." And as Paul was a captain and James a major he had smiled, kissed Lucy and left, for by this time Doctor Yates had arrived. With the increasing number of wounded pouring into the hospitals about Ambleside and Windermere there were now three doctors, all elderly men brought out of retirement but better than nothing, and they had had to learn fast the treatment of wounds that they had never, in their entire medical careers, expected ever to see.

"Well, Lucy, you seem to be keeping busy," were the first words her husband spoke directly to her. "I'm surprised you have the time with a new baby to care for."

On the attack from the first, though it was not so much attack as a form of defence, for he could not seem to get his bearings around this lovely, calm, madonna-like woman who he had noticed, even in the madness of the past few hours, every man in every bed followed with his eyes. Though he would have given ten years of his life to put his arms around her and lay his weary head on her breast, it did not show in his expressionless face. His manner was cold, though inside the beating of his heart was so loud and fast he was certain she would see the movement of it beneath the stained jacket of his uniform.

"Oh, James, have you nothing else to say to me after all this time?" she asked him sadly.

"Such as what, Lucy? I knew, of course, that Howethwaite was a hospital now but I had no idea you were so totally involved in it. May I ask where my daughter is? In whose care have you put her while you play Florence Nightingale to these men?"

It had appalled him to see her continue treating the young soldier whom she had been holding when he had entered the ward. That alone had driven him to the point where he could have torn her from the bedside and struck the man who lay in it but, naturally, he had not done so, but later, when the first wild rush was over, he had watched her place maggots, a hateful mass of wriggling maggots, into the open wound on the soldier's leg, his own stomach ready to heave and yet she had done it calmly, holding the boy's hand when it was done, brushing back his fair hair and telling him that if she could help it he would not lose his leg.

"They . . . they won't fall into the bed, will they, Mrs Buchanan?" the boy asked valiantly.

"No, Freddy, they won't do that. They will eat the badness from your leg and then it will heal. Now go to sleep."

"I know you can't stay with me, Mrs Buchanan, not with all this lot to see to," restlessly tossing his feverish head upon the pillow, "but will you come and . . . see me, later?"

"I promise, Freddy."

"You promise too much, Mrs Buchanan," he heard the sister say to her as she passed. "You can't be with them all, all the time."

"I can do my best, Sister. As we all do."

Now she spoke to him in the quiet voice, the calm and soothing voice she had developed over many months of dealing with fractious men.

"Alice is with the girls and Miss Bradley, James. Would you like to come up now and see her? She is ready for her feed so I must go."

"Her feed?" His shuttered face revealed none of the antipathy he felt at the thought of some infant at his wife's breast, at that lovely rosy nipple, the white, full flesh which had given him so much delight.

"Yes, I am nursing her myself so you see she is not totally neglected. Perhaps you would like to inspect her for damage?"

"I think a bath first, if such a thing can be had," for the thought of his daughter gave him no pleasure and he was in no rush to make her acquaintance. He was not fond of small infants and this one, though it belonged to him and to Lucy, was surely the same as all others. He could not seem to care overmuch, though he knew he should, but over the last months his mind had begun to shut itself off to so many things – sights, sounds, smells, emotions, fears that he had to endure – and so, like many other soldiers, he put them from him, or at least did his best to put them from him in order to get from one day to the next without going completely mad.

"Of course, I'll get Dixon to—"

For the first time he showed some signs of pleasure. "Dixon. Good God, is he still going?"

"Of course, what did you think had happened to him? That I had turned him out because we no longer give dinner parties?" Her voice was sharp. "Some of the maids have gone. Munitions, but Mrs Bunting and Mrs Burns will be delighted to see you."

There was the sound of frantic barking coming from the back of the house and James lifted his head eagerly.

"Holmes and Watson. I must go and greet them or they will wake the dead with their row."

"Yes, though I warn you they are not quite so well behaved as they were. Thimble's bad manners have rubbed off on them and not the other way around."

"I'll soon knock them into shape."

"How long will you be home?" They were like two polite acquaintances, thrown together after a long interval, their faces averted from one another, their thoughts hidden.

"Oh, a couple of days, I suppose," though he actually had a week.

As he was about to leave the room, his face warm with anticipation at the thought of greeting old friends, his dogs, his servants, all of whom meant more to him than she did, she asked him casually, "Why did you not come home in the summer? Charlotte told me you had gone to Paris. Paul was here for a few days . . ."

"That was why. I would have spent too much time travelling." He kept his back to her, his voice casual as though it mattered to neither of them.

"Paul seemed to find it convenient."

"Well, perhaps he was sure of a—" He broke off, aware that he was about to show something of himself that he preferred her not to see.

"Yes?"

"Nothing. Now, I'll have a bath and then if you would send one of the servants to let me know when it is . . . convenient for me to see the child. When you have finished your . . . her . . . meal."

"I wouldn't object if you were to come while she is nursing. She is your child, James, and I am your wife."

"So she is, and so you are. Nevertheless, please let me know a time that would be suitable to you."

He left the room and from the garden she heard the high-pitched excited barking of his dogs, frantic with joy. They had sensed his presence in the house but had been kept from him; now, in a frenzy of love, they were leaping up at him until, as she watched, they brought him down. He was laughing, his face creased and merry, his groans of remonstrance having not the slightest effect on them. All over the grass they romped and when, at last, he went across to the kitchen door and disappeared inside they howled dismally, flopping down in a great heap of misery.

She sighed, a long-drawn-out sigh which spoke of her own misery, for how was she to treat this husband who had come home from the war with what looked like hatred of her in his heart? She didn't know why. Surely it was not simply because she was nursing? Before he became a soldier they had rubbed along, not in the way married people did, at least not like her mama and papa had done but it had seemed to satisfy James. Now, for some hidden reason he was treating her as though she had seriously offended him and she didn't know why.

Taking off the square of her nurse's cap and undoing

the top buttons of her uniform, she moved slowly up the stairs to the first floor. She opened the door of her bedroom where, she supposed, she and James would sleep together tonight. She threw her cap on the bed with her stained apron then turned and walked out again, moving towards the stairs that led up to the children's rooms.

Edward and Percy were still at school but Margaret, Emily and Miss Bradley were sitting cosily round the fire. Miss Bradley had taught both girls to knit and they were engaged on long khaki scarfs that would wrap many times round the neck of some soldier at the front. Winter was coming and they would be glad of them, they had been told. They were making up a sort of a parcel of socks, mufflers and mittens, with thumbs only, though Miss Bradley was knitting the socks and mittens since they needed four needles and the girls weren't up to that standard yet. Buffy was helping, though she was not as good with knitting needles as she was with a sewing needle.

She was nursing Alice, her plain freckled face soft and loving as she crowed over the baby in her arms. She had helped, like Lucy, with the influx of wounded soldiers and there had been blood and filth on her apron but she and Lucy made it a point to change before they came to the schoolroom. The baby's head was pressed close to Buffy's breast and the silver grey eyes in her face, so like her father's, stared up in sharp concentration, then with a sort of jerk, she smiled, putting her whole body into it.

"Look, oh, do look, she just smiled. For the first time she actually smiled. She's kept it for the day her father comes home. The little darling. Oh, Lucy, just wait until Mr Buchanan sees her. Can he help but love her?"

Lucy did not answer but took her daughter from Buffy. She opened her bodice and put the child's open mouth to her nipple where Alice latched on with great eagerness. The girls watched for a moment but, used to the sight of their sister and niece, resumed their industrious and laboured tussle with the needles and wool.

He came an hour later. She had sent Buffy, an astonished Buffy, she could see, to tell Mr Buchanan that he might come up now, just as though he had to have an appointment, Buffy said later to Miss Bradley, with whom she had struck up a friendship.

The baby was in her cradle, sunk in the deep and infant sleep that comes after feeding. She lay on her back in the pretty white lawn nightgown Buffy had made and embroidered for her, her arms flung up above her head, since no one had told Lucy that young babies should be wrapped like a parcel before they were put into a cradle. If the Mrs Buchanans could have got to her there was no doubt they would have been horrified at what they would have seen as Lucy Buchanan's careless handling of James's daughter. She had not even been christened yet and her, meaning Lucy, a rector's daughter.

There was pink ribbon threaded through the yoke of Alice's nightdress and about the cuff. She had been bathed and her dark hair lay in a fat, glossy curl from her forehead, across the pulsing fontanelle to the crown and in swirls about her ears and neck. She had the soft button nose and the pouting rosebud lips of the new baby and her satin cheeks were pink with health. Her dark eyebrows arched delicately over her closed eyes which had the long fine eyelashes he himself had as a child. Unlike his wife, he fell in love with his daughter the moment he set eyes on her.

"Well," Lucy said ungraciously, expecting some criticism. "Does she suit?"

James was frozen to the strip of carpet which lay beside the cradle. His gaze never wavered, his eyes as frozen in their sockets as the rest of his body. Had someone asked him to speak he could not have done so, for the vulnerability of the child moved him to such depths of protective love he was totally overwhelmed. He had not expected it. The child's breathing was light and she snuffled as air passed through her small nasal passages and James Buchanan was enchanted.

Without thought, without asking for permission, he leaned down and with careful hands picked her up and settled her to his chest in the crook of his arm. He had changed into flannels and a clean, white, open-necked shirt and his daughter turned her face towards him and sighed in deep satisfaction and he could feel the tears begin to form at the back of his throat. She was his. This lovely child was his. To her he would give his love, the great swell of love that his wife did not want. Now, now he had something to bring him back to Howethwaite, something to get him through the horror of what was waiting for him out there in Flanders. This tiny child would bring him home.

They all stared at him in amazement, the two girls open-mouthed, for Mr Buchanan had never seemed to them, who were children, to be interested in children. Of course, Alice was his daughter which probably made a difference but would you look at him, sitting down in the chair Buffy hastily vacated, one leg bent and crossed over the the other knee, Alice comfortably resting in the crook of his arm and on his face an expression none of them had ever seen before. Thimble came up to him, willing to be friends, though he seemed to remember harsh words from this man and he put out his hand to fondle the dog's head.

"Should the dog be up here?" he asked his wife idly, never taking his eyes from his daughter's face.

"They . . . they all come up, James. The children are used to them and so Alice . . . well, I thought she must get used to them too."

"Of course."

They sat for five minutes, all of them exchanging glances of total bemusement as Alice's father touched her cheek and her eyebrows and seemed in no hurry to put her back in her cradle.

"You all go about your business," he said at last. "I'll stay here for a while."

"Well . . ." They looked at one another and shrugged, wondering what to do in this unprecedented moment of wonderment. Then, Lucy, with a gesture of compassionate understanding, for had she not seen the healing process her daughter worked on them when the soldiers downstairs held her for a precious moment, put her fingers to her lips and with a silent nod of her head, drew them all from the room, leaving James and Alice Buchanan alone.

James had intended staying two days at the most. He had meant to give Paul a hand on his journey up north with the wounded, and, for the sake of how it looked and to give the impression that he was like any other officer on a spot of leave with his family, depart for the front as soon as he was able. He would go to London, get lost in the mad frenzy of soldiers on leave from France, perhaps get himself a woman, get drunk, see *Chu Chin Chow* which was all the rage in London, eat at all the best restaurants and night-clubs and generally have a bloody good time until it was time for him to go back to the hell of the Western Front.

Alice Buchanan altered all that.

He made them smile, even the soldiers watching him from their beds in the conservatory which had a good view of the gardens, as he wheeled his daughter in her brand-new perambulator about the front lawns of Howethwaite, proud as punch and ready to show her to anyone he met. Licky Thripp told them in the kitchen he'd never seen 'owt like it. By gum, he'd got six bairns of his own, all grown up now and two of the lads at the front and he'd been fond of them. Well, a father was, wasn't he, but that there master of theirs took the bloody cake, if Mrs Burns would pardon his language. Queer as Dick's hatband, 'e was, but then perhaps that was what war did to you. Made you cling to what was at home and he certainly clung to that babby, by crikey.

"'E stopped me by t' wall side o't river. Scrafflin' about in that there lupin bed waitin' for 'er ter wake up, 'e said. Wanted ter show 'er t' ducks, would yer believe, an' 'er no more 'n eight weeks old. 'Look at 'er, Licky,' 'e ses ter me, in't she t' most beautiful child you've ever clapped eyes on an' watch her smile. They say she first did it on t' day I come home,' 'e ses, 'an' I'm prepared to believe it. She never stops now, Licky, 'cept when she's asleep.' Aye, she were a right smiler now, an' no mistake, an' 'appen she did it fer't first time day 'e come 'ome but it was a bit of a facer ter see t'master what rarely did more than nod in yer direction, draggin' yer over to peer under th'ood o't baby carriage."

"I think it's lovely," Elsie declared stoutly, vigorously stirring the huge pan of vegetable soup she and Cook were preparing for the soldiers' meal. Elsie had come on a pace since she was the skinny little maid of all work who had answered the door at the rectory two years ago. She was fourteen and with the weight she had gained due to Cook's constant admonishment to "eat up, lass, there's not a pick on you," and the confidence which had come with her new position she was ready to tackle any suspected criticism of her master who had made all this wonderful change in her possible. Him and Miss Lucy, of course. She was still maid of all work, they all were, mucking in wherever it was necessary. There was nothing to be gained by Dimity arguing that she was a lady's maid and therefore it was beneath her to scrub out the sluice or polish the windows, nor in Gertie, who had been a parlour maid, refusing to do other than parlour maid's work. There was a war on and things were different and with the wards and the extra cooking it was a case of whoever was available, did it!

James was still home when Douglas Askew, and Janet and Angus Gunson's second son, Lawrence, came to say goodbye and at the same time get first-hand news of what it was like at the front, for that was where they were off, they said. They were wild with excitement and very conscious of the splendid officers' uniforms they both wore. Would Uncle James tell them about it? Lawrence's brother Job, who had been one of the first to go, was a real spoilsport, having nothing to say on the matter when he came home on leave and Freddy Mossop was the same. Roger Askew had been wounded in the recent Battle of Loos, they didn't know how badly, their young schoolboy faces gravely serious for a moment, and Greg Kendall was a prisoner of war, had they heard?

Uncle James was as uncommunicative on the subject as every other soldier they had spoken to and they left with no premonition of what was ahead of them. They averted their eyes from the unlucky chaps in the dining- and drawing-rooms, not because they were unfeeling but they could not visualise that anything like this could happen to them.

"Mrs Buchanan, will you get out of my wards and go and spend some time with your husband," Sister Colyford said to her in an exasperated tone on the third day of Major Buchanan's leave. There he was, marching about the place with his baby daughter, either in her perambulator, or held gently, protectively against his chest, his dogs close at his heels and really, Mrs Buchanan should be with him. A week's leave was very short and, yes, they could manage without her for a few days and she was to stop arguing.

It was one of those glorious autumn days when the world seems to stand still for a moment, reluctant to let go of summer and head into winter, gathering to itself for a brief day, perhaps the last, all the glories of the year. A warm, delicious calm and sweet peace brooded over the house, broken only by the voices of the children who had gone blackberrying along the hedgerows that bordered the woods at the back of the house and the sound of one of the ponies whickering from the paddock. Clapcott and Licky were picking apples and there was to be apple and blackberry pie for dinner, Cook had promised, when the master, Miss Alice asleep in the crook of his arm, wandered into the kitchen to show her off.

Lucy found him there, sitting at the kitchen table watching Elsie make pastry, peaceful and relaxed in a way she had never seen him before. She could not get over the way he was with the baby and said so a dozen times a day to Buffy, who was still her only confidante. She herself had found that as the days went by her love for her child, which had been of an uncertain nature to start with, became stronger, the bond tightening until she longed, at many times during the day, to run upstairs for a moment just to hold her in her arms. She couldn't imagine her life without Alice now but that feeling had not come spontaneously. It had crept up on her stealthily, multiplying, giving her a deep sense of fulfilment and joy she could not have imagined. Now, James felt the same, she knew he did, but his feelings, his love had surged at once into his heart. From the very minute he had seen his daughter, there it had been, whole, complete, unending, and it had amazed and yet at the same time delighted her. She did not love him, she knew that, but now his daughter would and it gave her a sense of repayment, of a debt paid that through all the years to come, through her, he would know the love of his child.

"Sister says I'm to have a day off, James." Her voice was diffident. There it is. If you wish for my company, I am yours, she seemed to be telling him, but if he didn't she would go away again and leave him to his deep contemplation of Alice Buchanan.

"Well, and what had you in mind, Lucy? A walk on the hills, perhaps, but I warn you I am not leaving my daughter behind."

They all turned to stare at him, Elsie and Cook, Mrs Burns and Dixon, who had been studying the master's wine cellar with a view to tonight's dinner. Dimity held a spoon from which cream dripped, since there must be cream with blackberry and apple pie and the richness of it dripped on to Cook's clean floor where the kitchen cat immediately set to with its rough and greedy tongue.

"Here, mind what you're doing with that cream, my girl." Cook was first to come out of her tranced state. The idea of walking on the hills with that babby and her no more than eight weeks old filled her with horror, just like when them soldiers with their terrible wounds were allowed to nurse the little mite, but who was she to argue, though her face said she'd like to.

The mistress laughed. "On the hills. That sounds wonderful, James. I havent been up there for weeks. Well, since before Alice was born and it's the perfect day for it; but I don't see how we can take Alice."

Cook relaxed and turned back to her oven but she might have known the master wouldn't be overruled.

"Why not? It's dry and warm and if Jacob and I were to put our heads together I'm sure we could find something in the tack-room, some harness, or a nose band or two that could be mackled together to make a carrying contraption. Like a rucksack I could put on my back."

Well! What next! They were to put that precious child in a rucksack and lug her about like some bit of climbing equipment. Cook stirred her gravy so hard it slopped over the side of the roasting dish in which the juices of the roast lamb had been combined with the cabbage water.

"Well, I suppose that would be all right, providing it doesn't rain."

"We could take an umbrella."

"And a picnic."

"With a bottle of wine."

"And James . . ."

"Yes?"

He turned to look up at her, the smile he had been bestowing on his daughter still there with a bit left over for his wife.

"Can we get the Rolls out? I want to learn to drive."

They made a right pair and it did all the men a power of good to see their Mrs Buchanan, with her officer husband and their baby daughter, setting out for the day in the major's splendid Rolls Royce which had been uncovered, brought out, the engine turning over as sweetly as though it had been used only the day before, given a quick polish, and filled up with a can of petrol Tom Baxter had put away for a special occasion.

The most astounding thing, beside all the other astounding things, was the sight of Mrs Buchanan in a pair of her husband's trousers with the legs stuffed into a pair of sturdy climbing boots. At least they supposed them to be her husband's, for she was tall, almost as tall as he was and where else would she have got them? Eeh, she was a right one, was Mrs Buchanan, they told one another admiringly. Holding the trousers up was a leather belt round her waist which was now back to the size it had been before the baby. She wore a shirt of some fine material with a jumper slung round her shoulders and as she climbed into the motor she turned and waved to them, laughing, her hair already all over the place and there was not one man there who would not have given ten years of his life to change places with Major Buchanan. The baby was settled on her lap, the two big black dogs were settled on the back seat, the major started the engine and with a fine flourish the beautiful Rolls Royce Silver Ghost thundered off up the drive.

They were to motor to White Moss, a spot where Grasmere Lake and Rydal Water met, not far but just long enough to turn the engine over, James told her, which would do it the world of good. They would park there and on the way back he would give her a brief driving lesson. There was nothing much on the road and she might as well plunge right in. It was no good chugging up and down the drive. If she was to learn she must do it on a proper road. And she was not to think that when she could drive she would be allowed to dash hither and yon because she wouldn't. The shortage of petrol would put paid to that but he agreed that in an emergency – meaning naturally, to do with Alice – it might be wise to have some means of transport.

They had decided in the brief preparation for the outing that to climb as far as Elterwater would be far enough, at least with the baby. That was when Lucy had put it to him that she would be more comfortable and *safer*, which was of paramount importance with Alice, if she was to wear trousers.

He was pulling his own corduroy breeches on at the time and he turned to stare at her in astonishment. For a moment he hopped about comically and Lucy wanted to laugh but she knew she mustn't. Alice was lying in the middle of their bed, her arms waving vigorously, her eyes fixed on a shaft of reflected sunlight which lay across the ceiling. She gave a gurgle, or was it just wind, but whatever it was it distracted her father from what her mother was saying and he leaned over her, fastening his breeches round his lean waist.

"James?"

"Did you hear that?" he asked, totally bewitched by this tiny creature who, a few days ago, he had never met.

"Yes, now what about the trousers? You have some old flannels in the wardrobe and I'm sure they'd fit me."

"Would they?"

"Mmm, so you don't mind?"

"Not at all," his indifference to whatever Lucy Buchanan did totally obscured by what Alice Buchanan did.

It worked quite wonderfully well, the harness, and Alice seemed to find it all quite acceptable, nodding off to sleep on her father's back as they climbed up through the bracken which was beginning to turn from the deepest green to the brown of autumn. The heather, which was a dense purple coverlet in the summer, was changing to umber and burned yellow. Sheep called and a dog fetching them in streaked across their path as it answered the shepherd's whistle. Rock ledges, fan-shaped screes, black rocks and the green pasture contrasted sharply in the brilliant sunshine and a warbling beck tumbled past, rowan-shaded, on its way to the lake. They stopped for a moment, shading their eyes to look across the land, the harsh fell land which undulated fiercely, range after range, as far as they could see, before vanishing into the heat haze on the horizon.

They didn't talk much. She mentioned that Charlotte Buchanan was to have a child in the spring, apparently conceived on Paul's last leave.

"God almighty, don't tell me he actually persuaded her to lie down and open her legs?" He grunted in disbelief then turned to share her shout of laughter, for he had never joked with her before, especially a crude sort of a joke which a husband would not normally tell his wife.

"That's all the men think of, did you know that?" He grinned at her.

"I don't believe it. How do you know?"

"Well, apart from being a man I have to censor their letters. One chap wrote to his wife . . . Good

God, I should not be telling you this ... It's not decent."

"Oh, do go on, James. I'm not the ignorant rector's daughter you knew two years ago, you know."

"No, you're not," eyeing her rounded buttocks appreciatively. "Well, he told her to get a good look at the floor because when he got home all she would see was the ceiling!"

For a moment she looked at him, at the deep, velvet grey of his eyes which were glowing with laughter then she began herself, listening as his voice and hers echoed about the hills.

She saw her husband sigh in contentment and within her was the hope that he would carry this, this beauty, the companionship they had so unexpectedly found, this love of his child who he was introducing to his land, back to the trenches with him. She, of all people, knew what he lived through. The tension of trench warfare, the terror of mutilation and death, the unceasing din of the artillery which could completely unhinge the sturdiest of minds. She had lived through it with soldiers who were in her care and who babbled ceaselessly in their nightmares of pals blown to smithereens before their eyes and other things that she did her best to forget, as they did.

They came at last to the small, gem-like lake of Elterwater, set among hummocks of enchanting trees, surrounded, but not forbiddingly so, by the mightier fells. Larch and birch and the crumpled deep yellow leaves of the oak to sit on and while Alice slept in the nest of her mother's jumper and her father's jacket James and Lucy ate the small pork pies, the hefty ham sandwiches, for a man likes something to get his teeth into, Mrs Bunting said, the almond cakes and chocolate shortcakes that the master had loved from childhood, all washed down with a bottle of dry white wine of Dixon's choosing. James drank most of it, for as Lucy said with studied casualness, she must feed Alice and they didn't want the child to be tipsy.

She hesitated when the time came, remembering James's command to fetch him when she had finished nursing but that was before he met Alice, and since then he had made love to his wife four times in their deep bed. He had seen her naked, fondled the breasts from which Alice gained her sustenance, put his own mouth to the nipple where Alice's had been, so was she now to turn prudish?

Holding the baby in the crook of her arm she bared her breast and at once Alice snuffled on to the nipple, her little mouth working ten to the dozen, milk dribbling from the corner of her mouth and for ten minutes, and then another ten on the other breast, James Buchanan watched his wife and child and it was not the child who captured his full attention. Alice was changed and put down in her little bed where she at once fell into a deep sleep under the watchful protection of the dogs, who knew their duty to this new, puppy-like creature, and when Lucy looked up to smile at James his eyes met hers with an intensity that made her heart skip a beat and her mouth dry up. A spark warmed her, like an arc of electricity from him to her, a touching of something inside her which was disconcerting but not unpleasant and when he reached out to her and took her hand she did not resist. Her shirt was still partially unbuttoned and her breast was only half covered and with his other hand he began to undo the rest, exposing it. His finger reached to touch her nipple. It was rosy, still damp from the child's sucking but at his touch it peaked and hardened at once. He looked up into her face, one dark eyebrow arched questioningly. He smiled and in her chest and throat something lurched in the most astonishing way. Her flesh shivered in delighted anticipation and without conscious thought her mouth reached for his.

He undressed her and then she undressed him, wordlessly, as though each was somehow aware that this might be something important to them and they were afraid to shatter it with the wrong words. Let their bodies speak, and their eyes. Hers had turned to an unusual light colour, golden brown, like amber in crystal, almost yellow as passion began to rise in her under her husband's sure hands.

For a moment she drew back, her hands pressing against his naked chest and at once he stopped, for this was not the first time James Buchanan had made love to his wife during his leave and she had responded as she had always done in the first months of their marriage, which was to be totally acquiescent, willing, but no more.

"I don't want a child, James," she gasped, for the last time she had felt like this, her body answering his with a strength which matched his, Alice had been conceived.

"You won't have a child, my love, I promise you," and under the deep blue bowl of the Lakeland sky, with the sheep bleating and the curlews calling and their child asleep beside them, James and Lucy took one another to a place of warmth and excitement and cherishing, and in his hard embrace their explosion of pleasure came at the same time.

When it was over she sat up, lifting her strong young arms above her head, her hands lifting her tumbled hair from the nape of her neck, arching her back, displaying herself for her husband's pleasure, and for her own. He turned her face to him and looked deep into her eyes and saw something there, he didn't know what, but whatever it was it made his heart sing with joy and hope.

He took her out without Alice on the following day, which was still warm and dry, letting her drive the Rolls up as far as Keswick, along the winding road in the valley bottom, below the towering heights of Helvellyn, which had a crown of low clouds, ragged and uneasy, and James forecast that the spell of warm summer-like weather would be over soon. They had tea in Keswick, again not speaking much but easy in one another's company, their eyes meeting, smiling, and Lucy wondered at this side of James that she had never seen before. He was allowing her to look into him, to see him, to know the sum and substance of the man who was James Buchanan, trusting her in a way that delighted her. Could it all be because of Alice? she wondered and was surprised when the thought sent a small frisson of disappointment through her.

On the way back they were jolted out of the almost dream-like state the day had wrapped them in by the sight of the gunpowder carts on their way to Windermere railway station from the Emmerson Gunpowder Works. There were twelve of them with a certain distance between each one in case of accident. The drivers walked beside them as a precaution but on the way back they were allowed to ride the empty carts. The procession, to which the last driver warned them they must not come too close, held them up for nearly an hour and when they got home there was a stream of servants, soldiers, nurses and even the children to tell her in a reproving tone that Alice was awake and crying for her tea. He raced up the stairs with her towards the sound of the indignant wailing which came from the top of the house, as flustered as she was to get the child to her breast, smiling in guilty relief at each other as they shared Alice's enjoyment. He knelt at her feet watching these two human beings whom he loved more than life itself, his lean face softened with emotion. His hand touched the curls on Alice's head, gently smoothing them back, then went to Lucy's wind-tossed, glossy mane and doing the same.

It was a Sunday and tomorrow he was to leave. The christening of Alice Christina Buchanan was to take place at the church of St Mary's in Ambleside where Lucy and James were married and for the first time since before the war the Buchanan family were gathered together and for the first time, in some amazing way, Lucy felt them to be *her* family.

Only Alex and Franny were missing and, of course, the young men of the family who were at the front. Charlotte was there looking exceedingly smart in a concealing gown the clever Miss Medlock had fashioned for her, though she was barely three months pregnant. She took full advantage of it though, clinging to some male arm throughout the afternoon, barely looking at Alice and certainly not holding her, since there was a possibility that the child might be sick on her. Paul had returned to the front the day after he had delivered his wounded, probably glad to do so, Lucy privately believed, since he would get no welcome from the self-absorbed woman he had married.

Janet Gunson and her husband Angus came, both with that strained and anxious look of those who had boys over in France, trying to talk to James, wanting to be reassured that Job, who had been home on leave but was totally uncommunicative, and Lawrence, who was really only a baby, his mother said, would be safe.

Ben and Joan, whose own lads were too young for soldiers, thank God. Anne and Thomas Mounsey who had all girls, again thanking the Lord though they had been disappointed not to get a boy. Perhaps it was as well, they now had told one another, and Christine and Douglas Scott, again with young children. The old people were driven over, bringing a magnificent silver christening cup which had been in the family for generations and which was to be held by Alice until the next baby was born, Mr Harry inclined to poke Charlotte Buchanan in the stomach and ask her why she was lolling about like an invalid.

They all exclaimed on the infant beauty of Alice Christina, passing her from one to the other in her lovely Buchanan christening gown. They were crowded into Lucy's upstairs sitting-room, for there was nowhere else to put them, perched on chairs that had been brought from here and there, marvelling over the behaviour of James towards his new daughter, telling one another that if they hadn't seen it with their own eyes, they wouldn't have believed the way he was acting, when there was knock on the door and Dimity peeped in.

"Oh, madam . . . oh, madam," she whispered, grief-stricken to be the one to deliver the loathsome yellow envelope that she held in her hand.

The silence in the room was total except for the murmuring of the child who was held in old Mrs Buchanan's arms, anxiously being watched by her doting father. Only Charlotte Buchanan seemed curiously unconcerned.

"Who . . . ?" someone said in a hoarse voice.

"Oh, God, Angus, I can't bear it."

James moved forward and took the envelope from Dimity's hand and she scuttled away as though she could not bear to hear what the envelope contained. He glanced at it, his colour draining away, his eyes turning in compassion to old Mr Job and his wife, Mary.

"It's for you; they must have sent it over from . . ."

Job Buchanan's voice was harsh and his wife began to cry the slow tears of the elderly, for they knew who it was, while, leaning in her husband's arms, Janet Gunson's breath left her body in a great sigh of relief.

"Open it, lad, would you?"

It told them that Captain Andrew Buchanan, dashing, laughing, impertinent Andrew Buchanan, had died of wounds received in the service of his country.

James left the next day. The flesh wound in his arm had healed enough to satisfy Sister Colyford who pronounced him, sadly, fit for active service. He walked slowly down the drive with his right arm round his wife's shoulders and his child in the crook of his left and all those who watched sighed for the sadness of his going.

Charlotte Buchanan listlessly crumbled a piece of toast, on her face an expression with which her parents and the servants at Ravenscourt, her parents' home, were very familiar. It meant that something that she wanted to happen hadn't happened, or something she didn't want to happen, had. She wanted something and so far whatever it was had not been given to her; there was nothing more certain, as they all knew, than that she would move heaven and earth to get it.

Charlotte was staying with her parents at the present moment, the present moment having stretched from the day her husband "abandoned" her, marching off to war which he had no need to do since he was a married man, to this day in December a year later.

And then, of course, there was this baby, the bearing of which she couldn't possibly manage on her own in that big house her papa had given her and Paul as a wedding present. No one could expect her to, surely, and though she was aware that other women coped on their own with their men gone to war she had always had her papa to look after her and had no intention of changing that situation just because she had a husband.

Where had it all gone, she often brooded, her lovely bright dream of being the perfect hostess, the smartest, most fashionable young matron in the district and the answer was it had been blown away by the winds of this stupid war, the reason for which she couldn't imagine and didn't care to know anyway. And to top it all she had had to suffer the indignity of Paul insisting on doing "that" on his last leave, putting her in this appalling condition and she would never forgive him.

She could remember her wedding night with a clarity which never diminished, and her horror and shock, when he had intimated to her what he wished to do in the double bed in the smart Paris hotel where they had honeymooned, would never leave her. Take off her nightdress, he had demanded, as he had taken off his dressing-gown, standing before her totally naked with some great, thick, throbbing spear standing out from between his hairy legs and which he intended sticking into her. She had wanted to scream and hit out at him, the beastly man who was now her husband, but instead she had hissed that if he came an inch nearer she would get up, get dressed and take the boat and train back to Ambleside. He was to sleep elsewhere, she didn't care where but it was not in her bed.

Paul Buchanan, a gentle man who liked peace and tranquillity, wondered why he had allowed himself to be married to this selfish, heartless creature with the magnificent body of a woman and the mind of a petulant child. She had been indulged from birth by her doting parents and, having been thwarted in her attempt to marry his cousin James, who, he smiled sadly to himself, would not have been denied her bed on his wedding night, had swooped on him with the avarice and speed of an eagle. He was not a wealthy man since he had no head for business like his father, his uncles and cousins, and the small income that came from the few shares he had in the Emmerson Gunpowder Factory was certainly not enough to keep him until he established a practice in the area. He was honest enough to admit to himself that that was why he had married Charlotte, though, of course, the idea of getting into bed with her and having that splendid body at his disposal had been a further incentive.

His wife was still a virgin when he enlisted four months after their marriage, which was probably why he did it. They lived in their newly built and magnificently furnished home, which she had grandly named Buchanan Hall as though expecting a dynasty to come in the next generations, Charlotte settling down with great expectations of being a wife, in name only if she had anything to do with it, and hostess. She gave dinner parties and tennis parties, croquet parties and dances, swathing through Ambleside society as she had always imagined herself doing until suddenly, there was no society there to entertain. Wives, oh, yes, daughters, school friends, her female cousins by marriage, but who wanted strictly female company or that of elderly gentlemen and youths, too old and too young for the army whither the rest of the male population had gone. Even her servants deserted her, parlour maids running off to higher pay and shorter hours in munitions, her butler enlisting, along with her chauffeur and gardener.

"Mama, can I come home for a little while?" she had

beseeched her mother, tears in her beautiful eyes. "It's so lonely at the Hall without Paul," and her mother, who had no idea of the state of affairs between her daughter and her son-in-law, agreed at once.

"Of course you can, darling. It will be quite like old times," her mother had gushed.

"It's lovely to have you here, sweetheart," her besotted father said at every meal, for he had missed her idle gossip, her childish chitter-chatter at the table, her lovely wheedling when she particularly wanted something from him.

Paul Buchanan, who had seen things and suffered things he would not care to describe to anyone, let alone his empty-headed wife, got into bed with her as he had always wanted to on his first leave. Though he had tried to be gentle, her strugglings and whispered commands to stop this filth at once, whispered since she did not want her parents to hear the disgusting noise Paul was making, turned the encounter into what he could only describe as rape and which she swore would never happen again. To be fair, with perhaps another man, an experienced man who would have known what to do with her, she might have been different, but that one night in her husband's bed, and the consequences of it, a child to be born in the spring, turned her mind from petty resentments to a bitter determination to get even with the woman who had stolen the only man Charlotte believed could have made her happy. That was how she saw it. Though it was her husband who had taken her against her will and made her pregnant, in a twisted way she turned it round until it was the fault of that bitch James had married

It was nearly Christmas and she was six months pregnant and if she could have destroyed the life inside her without danger to herself or harming her reputation as the leader of society she meant to be when the damned war was over, she would have done, but she couldn't and so she gritted her teeth and let her parents cosset and coddle her, pet her and spoil her as they had always done, while waiting for the child to be born.

She looked hideous, she knew she did, huge and bloated and totally unable to wear any of the lovely clothes she had had transferred from Buchanan Hall to her parents' home. She was ashamed to be seen in public because not only did she look quite appalling with her swollen body and puffy face but because people would know that she and Paul had performed the obscene act which had made her like this. She had not been out anywhere except to droop round the garden of Ravenscourt since the christening of that brat of Lucy and James's. That event which had ended with such drama, she supposed she might even say tragedy, for she had been quite taken with Andrew Buchanan who had always flirted with her and admired her with his eyes which she had enjoyed. The christening party had made her all the more determined to find some way to make Lucy Buchanan suffer for what she had done to Charlotte. She had seen the way James looked at his wife, they all did, recognising it for what it was even if his wife didn't, and his devotion to his daughter, which was the most astonishing thing they'd ever seen, they told one another, and it boded well for the marriage when James finally came home, they all agreed. Not if she'd anything to do with it, she thought viciously, eaten up with jealous envy.

"Papa," she said now, turning an angelic smile on her father.

"Yes, poppet." Arthur Gibson looked up from *The Times* and turned his fond gaze on his daughter, wondering for the thousandth time how in hell he and Edith had got this exquisite creature who was their daughter. Edith was pleasant-looking, he supposed, but then he'd not married her for her looks but for the wealth which had come with her from her father. He himself was not exactly ugly, but this child of his was like some exotic flower growing among the pretty but very ordinary blooms in a cottage garden. She turned heads wherever she went with her fair loveliness, the splendour of her full-breasted figure, which stunned the male sex to open-mouthed awe and the female to open-mouthed envy. Oh, he knew she was a handful, she always had been, but she'd only to look at him as she was doing now with those glorious eyes of hers and he could deny her nothing. He had been furious when his son-in-law enlisted, deserting Arthur's lovely Charlotte, Paul's wife of no more than a few months and he had told him so, but secretly he had been delighted when Charlotte had come home to stay for a while and he'd be sorry when her husband returned from the front. He was looking forward to having a grandchild – at least the bugger had done something right – and would make sure his lass had all the support she needed during her pregnancy and when the time came for the birth.

"D'you know anyone at the War Office, Papa?" she

asked him innocently, popping a piece of buttered toast into her mouth.

"The War Office?" He laughed and put down the newspaper, wondering what the hell was in her pretty head now.

"Mmm. You have so many contacts I just thought you might."

He looked from her to his bewildered wife then back to Charlotte again, his expression asking Edith if she had any idea what the child was getting at because he certainly didn't. The War Office, indeed. Was it to be something to do with her husband? Did she want him to pull a few strings, which he could certainly do, and get Paul Buchanan back from the base hospital in France where he was stationed?

"What makes you ask, darling? Is it to do with Paul?"

"Oh, no, Papa." A faint look of distaste passed across her face. "I . . . well, I have been hearing the strangest stories; rumours, I suppose you'd call them, not that I believe them, of course, but I was wondering . . ."

"Rumours? About what?" Her father's voice was sharp.

She picked at the piece of toast on her plate. She was trying to eat as little as possible in the hope that not only would it perhaps starve the baby, making it smaller and, it had been whispered to her by her maid, easier to deliver, but prevent herself from putting on more weight.

"I hardly like to . . . It is so fantastic it can't be true but, well, it's about Lucy Buchanan."

Edith Gibson looked up quickly from the good breakfast she was tucking into. She and Arthur liked to start the day right with a breakfast of bacon and eggs, sausage and tomatoes and mushrooms. She came from a family who rode to hounds in the winter, shot grouse and partridge in season, were keen on tennis and sporting parties, and you had to have a sound constitution to do these things so a decent breakfast was essential.

She looked keenly at her daughter and her mind went back to the day, two years ago now, when she and Charlotte had been in Ambleside and James Buchanan, with the Dean family clustered round him in his motor car, had roared by, all singing at the top of their voices. Well, perhaps James had not been singing, for he was not that sort of a man, but the rest had, Lucy Dean and her sisters and brothers. Charlotte had been seized by a fury so violent Edith had had to restrain her from rushing after the Rolls Royce and screaming what her mother knew to be her jealousy for all the world to see.

They will pay for this. Those had been Charlotte's very words but surely she had not meant . . . She could not possibly still be harbouring . . . Not after all this time . . . no, it was not possible. She was well aware that her daughter liked to get her own way, and always got it, for how could any parent deny this lovely child, this lovely child who was sweetness herself, when she was not thwarted! She had always been difficult to handle, having hysterics to the point where she and Arthur had been afraid for her health, which was why they had given in to her since she was an infant.

"Lucy Buchanan?"

"Yes. It is really very silly but she is rumoured to

have formed an attachment for . . . one of the soldiers in her care. I was told by—"

"Great God, what a thing to say. One of the soldiers in her care! Why, they are only ordinary working men, not even officers," as though, had they been this would have made it palatable.

"I know, that's what I said . . ."

"Who told you this, child?" Her father's voice was threatening, not towards her, naturally, but towards the person who had put such a nasty thought in his daughter's head.

Charlotte's expression turned truculent. She was not used to having her word questioned, especially by her father. She had not expected him to ask where she had her information from and if she had to tell him that it was from a servant who was friendly with a servant who knew someone who worked at Howethwaite and had reported the story of the "idiot" who had been in Lucy Buchanan's care, when she was pregnant with James's child too, she knew her papa would not like it.

She did what she always did. The tears that she could command at will brimmed to her eyes and at once her mother and father both stood up and rushed to her side. She must not be upset, they told her, not in her precious condition and her papa was sorry he had taken such a firm tone but really, it hardly seemed the sort of . . .

"Perhaps we could find out who he was, Papa, that was why I was asking you about the War Office," she sobbed against her papa's chest, "and that should tell us whether the talk is ridiculous or not." She did not explain why and nobody asked.

The two parlour maids, who were too old for war work and had been serving breakfast, exchanged glances. She was a troublemaker was Miss Charlotte Gibson and had been the bane of their lives ever since she was born, which was how long they had served the Gibson family, but this was the end, really it was. To accuse Mrs James Buchanan, who, it was reported, was a saint, giving of herself night and day to those poor wounded soldiers up at Howethwaite, of having an affair with one of them, was . . . well, of course, they were not to know what went on up there and perhaps . . . Mr Buchanan was away and there was no one to . . . and she was known to be unconventional, had been right from the start, if the stories they had been told were true. They found it hard to believe, their exchanged glances and lifted eyebrows said, but still, was there smoke without fire?

"I'll find out who he is, darling, and that will put paid to this nasty rumour. Old Reggie Withers owes me a favour for that surplus deal I put him on to. He'll have the lists, whatever they are . . ." Arthur said vaguely, patting his little girl's shoulder and begging her not to cry. He couldn't bear to see her cry, he told her, watching as she was led away by her mother who thought a rest on the bed was called for and perhaps her forehead rubbed with cologne.

"The chap's name was Rory Cameron, Private Rory Cameron," he told his daughter a few days later. "A shell shock case, apparently, but he's back in the trenches now. Still unstable, his record reports. Reggie says he comes from a good family in Surrey with a mother who has landed connections, and he can't imagine why the damn fool refused a commission but . . ."

"Yes?" his daughter said, leaning forward eagerly.

"He has left a document which says that on his death he wants a certain Mrs Lucy Buchanan to be informed."

Lucy missed James and she was astonished by it. After all, she barely knew him. He had been Mr Buchanan to her for a long time, though she had persuaded herself to call him James. He had been a stranger sitting at the dinner table night after night, polite, sometimes even charming. A tyrant, she had believed him to be, even cruel when he had refused her permission to join the WSPU and threatened her family with some dire consequence if she disobeyed. A hard male body in her bed, demanding her submission and something more, which she had not understood then, but she did now. Oh, yes, smiling secretly to herself, she did now. A generous man who carelessly told her to spend what she liked on her family. A generous man with his money but not with himself. A humorous man, she had believed, though it was a side of himself he had not allowed to reveal itself to her very often.

But he had been none of these things and yet all of them during the few days they had spent together with their daughter and she had been strangely delighted with it, and with him. He had made her laugh. He had made her slumbering body come alive. He had been gentle and rough in his lovemaking, and tender and humble in his gratitude for the lovely child she had given him. His pain at leaving, not just Alice, but herself, had been very evident. What a complex man he was, with so many facets to his nature, most of which she thought were still buried within him.

His letters came regularly, week after week, telling her not of his love, for he knew it was too soon for that, but of his love and pride in his daughter. She must promise to write as often as she could, he implored her though he knew she was busy. Would she send him photographs of Alice? Buy herself a decent camera, a Kodak or a Brownie and record every phase in her development, her every mood. He could hardly stand the thought that he was to forgo so much of her growing-up. He missed her so, she was his precious scrap and any woman with more insight into the ways of a man's love for a woman would have recognised at once that James Buchanan, though he loved and missed his child, was not speaking of her when he poured out his heart in his letters. He and his men ate well, he wrote, when they could but it was bully beef stew mostly, bread and cheese and jam, and sometimes even butter. They had an ounce of cold ham for their breakfast, a mug of tea and half a loaf, but if she could include some chocolate, Oxo cubes, peppermint drops, Camp cocoa, and writing paper and envelopes in her parcels they would be very welcome. It was very cold now, he wrote to her and he'd be glad of that thick woollen underwear he wore for climbing in the winter and she was to tell Margaret that her scarf and mittens, the technique of which she had mastered, were superb. He was billeted at a farm, he couldn't say where, but it was very comfortable.

She was so glad, she wrote back, imagining him in a clean bed and getting some fresh farm food, and he hadn't the heart to tell her that when they were not in the front line he and his men lived with the farm animals, sleeping in straw. Both armies were firmly entrenched for the winter and it seemed stalemate had been reached. He didn't know when he would get leave, but the photographs she sent him of Alice were wonderful and did she think she could get someone to take one of herself, perhaps with Alice, and send it out to him. He couldn't believe Alice was sitting up already but then he'd known from the start that their daughter was quite exceptional.

She first noticed the odd behaviour of the shopkeepers in Ambleside, and even one or two of the shoppers, just after Christmas. They all knew her now. She was not only the wife of one of the most prominent men in the town, but a man who was fighting for his country in France. She was also the woman who had opened the hospital of which they were so proud, if not a nurse, then a nurse's aid and what she did for those young men was to be greatly admired. They liked to nod and smile at her as she passed, gratified when she smiled back, which she always did for she was a gracious young woman. She didn't often drive the Rolls Royce, for petrol was very short and when there was any shopping to be done she rode in on her bicycle, often taking Margaret with her. Margaret was growing up, at almost fifteen, ready to become a young woman, longing to help on the wards, which Lucy had promised she would think about when she was fifteen.

They had just dismounted, leaning their bicycles against the side of the chemist's shop when two ladies, both of them known to her by sight, after a start of what looked like embarrassment, tipped their noses in the air and walked past her as though she didn't exist. They continued up the street past the chemist's window, pausing to look into the draper's next door where they turned to look at her, their heads together. When they saw her staring at them in amazement they hurried on as though afraid she might accost them.

"Well, what's got into those two?" she asked Margaret but Margaret had noticed nothing untoward, for she did not know the ladies concerned.

Lucy shrugged and pushing open the door of the chemist's shop went inside.

"Good morning, Mr Lawson," she said to the elderly gentleman behind the counter. "Have you heard from Edwina recently? I believe you told me that she was to go to France. How brave of her. Has she gone yet?" She smiled her lovely warm smile, eager for news of the friend she had made in the WSPU.

"Not as yet, Mrs Buchanan," Mr Lawson said stiffly.

"But she is well?" She raised her eyebrows enquiringly, wondering what was the matter with everyone today. Those two women looked as though they had a pole up their backs and now Mr Lawson had his mouth buttoned so tight he could barely speak.

"Thank you, yes."

"Is anything the matter, Mr Lawson?" she asked him, wondering why he was avoiding her gaze. He was normally full of Edwina's exploits in the nursing field where she had done so well, but today he passed her her purchases and gave her her change with barely a nod of acknowledgement.

"Not a thing, Mrs Buchanan." And that was that as far as Mr Lawson was concerned. He had been polite but no more. Mrs Buchanan was a customer and customers must be treated civilly but if the rumour which was being whispered and which had even reached the church where he was a sidesman were true he had no wish to be more than that.

They did their shopping. Wool for more socks and scarves and mittens. A length of material for nightdresses for Alice who was growing so fast they couldn't keep up with her. A bag of pear drops for Cook and some tobacco for Mr Clapcott. Only small items, for the rations for the men and staff were delivered by the army. Several times Lucy was conscious of sly looks and whispers though most of the people to whom she spoke did reply.

She was surprised when she got home to find a note from Charlotte Buchanan begging her to go round and take tea with her if she could spare the time. She was so bored and, naturally, in her condition she couldn't go out but she had had a letter from Paul and James was mentioned in it and she also thought that Lucy might like to hear a bit of news Charlotte had of a friend of Lucy's.

A friend of hers? Was it perhaps Franny who wrote now and again in that laconic way she had, making light, even fun of what Lucy was sure was a difficult and dangerous job, but then why would Franny write to Charlotte whom Lucy knew she couldn't abide, calling her a silly simpering child without a thought in her head that was not put there by someone else.

She didn't want to go so to make the outing more congenial she drove to Ravenscourt, where, apparently, Charlotte was staying with her parents until after the birth of her child. She didn't quite trust this

invitation, she didn't know why. She did know that
Charlotte was no particular friend of hers though she
had no idea why she thought so. There had always
been this feeling of antipathy, of undercurrents that
ran deep and hidden in Charlotte which was strange
when one considered the shallow nature of the woman
who had married the nicest Buchanan of them all, in
Lucy's opinion. Nicest in the best sense, that is. Kind,
sensitive, thoughtful, so unobtrusive that it took a
while to recognise and appreciate his quiet charm,
Paul was far too good for her and she shuddered
to think of him living the rest of his life with such
a woman.

"Will you come this way, Mrs Buchanan," the
Gibsons' pompous butler said, leading her from the
overheated hallway, which was rich with pictures
and ornaments and the expensive folderols Arthur
Gibson liked to exhibit to show off his wealth, into a
drawing-room which was even warmer and there was
Charlotte reclining on a velvet-covered chaise-longue,
cushions at her back, the colour of her full gown
exactly toning with the colour of the velvet.

"Oh, Lucy, there you are. Do come in," she trilled
with the false sincerity that told Lucy she disliked Lucy
as much as Lucy disliked Charlotte, so what on earth
was she doing here?

"Send in some tea, Edwards, and please, Lucy, do
sit down by the fire. I would ask you to take off your
hat but I see you're not wearing one. Is it . . . windy
outside?" her eyes straying to Lucy's tangled hair.

"No, it's just that I came in the motor. I had the top
down," Lucy answered shortly, wondering how much
of this she could stand.

"Really, at this time of the year?"

"I like to feel the wind. Now then, what is it you wanted to see me about?" indicating that if Charlotte had time on her hands she certainly did not.

"Well, I hardly know where to begin." Charlotte's voice was silky and for some reason Lucy felt the hairs on the back of her neck rise.

Lucy drove home in a state of dazed confusion, unable
to shake off a feeling of impending disaster, though
of what sort she couldn't put into words, unable to
make head nor tail of her own emotions which were
so mixed up she felt she would have to have an hour
or so on her own somewhere to unravel them. Her
first thought had been for James. With this sweet, slow
blooming of something between them which she was
not prepared to risk, a tentative softness, a tenderness
even, which she knew was as precious to James as it
was to her, she was aware that she must find some way
to break it to him before someone else did, probably
Charlotte herself.

One thing was certain, she had made a bitter enemy
this day.

She barely remembered the journey home, winding
her way through the main street of Ambleside, along
Clappergate and over Skelwith Bridge, turning into the
gates of Howethwaite without recognising how she
got there. There were several ambulatory wounded
in the garden, most on crutches, making a brave effort
of stumbling about the gravel paths, and others in
wheelchairs pushed by the VADs, getting some good

air into their lungs, as Sister Colyford was fond of saying. Doctor Yates's Cowley motor car, his choice of colour never failing to amaze her, a vivid scarlet, was parked at the front steps and she wondered who it was that needed his attention. Perhaps the young private who was so ill with the dysentery that was sapping what little strength he had, not to mention the stomach wound he had suffered when a sniper's bullet got him, he was not expected to live through the day. Eighteen years old, poor lad, and kept calling piteously for his mother. She had been fetched from Manchester and sat by his bedside holding his hand, murmuring over and over again in her broad northern accent, "Theer, theer, lad, theer, theer, Mam's 'ere," and he had quietened, so perhaps there was a chance for him.

She parked the Rolls in the garage, shutting the big doors behind her then turned and sniffed the air, she didn't know why. There was just a strange feel to it, a sort of waiting, a hushed expectancy that she knew from experience heralded snow. The clouds, heavy and grey, sat ominously low on Loughrigg Fell and the image of James strengthened in her mind. These hills and dales and uplands were what symbolised her husband more keenly than anything else, for she knew how he loved it all. It was his heritage, the feeling for it come from generations of Buchanans and Emmersons and all those before them. She had had a letter from him only this morning written several weeks ago, saying the weather was cold enough to freeze the . . . well, he had quipped, he wouldn't tell her what part of his person might be affected but she had smiled, for by now she was beginning to recognise the sharp humour, the sense of the ridiculous which James had kept so well hidden from her. It was as though he trusted her, which was a curious thing to say, with a private side of him no one else knew and it pleased her. They were going down the line, he told her, and he had put on the good warm underwear she had sent him, since there would probably be a lot of hanging about in this war which seemed to have come to a full stop with the winter weather. He did not elaborate and she knew there were many aspects of his life as a soldier which he, and all the rest of them, officers and Tommies alike, shared with no one but each other.

There was nobody about in the hall. Through the open doorway of the ward she could see Doctor Yates bending over the bed of the young soldier and the rest of the wounded were quiet, as though suspecting they were in the presence of death. The soldier's mother had her head bent over the face of her child, stroking back his hair and occasionally kissing his brow as Lucy did when she was soothing Alice. Her heart constricted in compassion for the boy's pain and the mother's sorrow and she wondered furiously when this bloody war would be over and they could all resume the peace and content which surely all God's creatures were entitled to. She felt like dropping to her knees and breathing a prayer for them all, right here on the bottom step of the stairs and she was troubled suddenly by thoughts of her father. He had brought them all up to pray to God, to attend church and to help the afflicted, and since she had come to Howethwaite she had only attended to the latter. Dear Papa, would that suffice? she asked him gently and her heart was soothed, for she thought it might.

Those on the ward did not notice her so she continued quietly up the stairs to the sanctuary of her own room. There was a small fire, for they were not short of fuel, so taking off her warm winter coat and throwing it on to the bed, she sank into the chair, leaning forward, her chin cupped in her hands, her elbows on her knees, staring sightlessly into the flames.

Charlotte had taken her time, drawing out for as long as she could, Lucy was well aware, her enjoyment of the moment. Paul was well and had spent Christmas, at which time he had a few days' leave, in a château behind the lines, she had prattled. She seemed to be totally unaware of exactly where her husband might be. France, Flanders, they were all the same to her. The only place she knew in France was Paris because that was where she and Mama bought their clothes. Paul had told her the name of the place but she couldn't quite recall. Had James mentioned it? They had spent only an hour or so together, she babbled on, for as Paul was arriving for his few days' rest, James was just leaving. Wasn't it a shame that they could not have spent more time together, just as though they were holidaying on the continent, which was a fashionable thing to do and their paths had crossed. How strange that James had not mentioned it, she couldn't resist saying as though her husband never kept anything from her.

"My letters were held up over Christmas," Lucy answered curtly, ready to tell Lucy to damn well get on with whatever it was she was drivelling on about, girding her loins, so to speak, ready for the blow she was by now convinced Charlotte was to aim at her.

"And then there is the news that a school friend of mine has just become engaged . . ."

"What?" Lucy was caught off guard by the sudden change of direction the conversation had taken.

"Oh, I'm sure you've heard me speak of Joanna Clarkson," Charlotte said archly, sipping her tea from the fragile bone china teacup, the tea service of which the Gibsons had especially made for them with what looked like a coat of arms painted upon it. She had not moved once since the tea tray was brought in, her legs, crossed at the ankles, stretched out on the chaise-longue before her.

"I can't say I have," Lucy answered shortly.

"I went to school with her and when she wrote to tell me she had become engaged to Aubrey Blane, Captain Aubrey Blane of the 1st Battalion, the Surrey Regiment, I immediately thought of that poor young soldier you nursed last year. Wasn't he in a Surrey regiment?"

Lucy felt the shiver begin somewhere inside her. She wasn't sure exactly where but it rippled outwards, touching her skin with feathers of alarm. She could feel the fine hairs on her arms lift and she put her cup and saucer down very carefully before she answered.

"I'm not at all sure I know."

"Oh, yes, there was quite a lot of talk about him in Ambleside since he was the first case of . . . do they call it shell shock? . . . that had been reported."

"I was not aware that his case was known about in Ambleside." Lucy's voice was stiff with suppressed fury. "And I fail to see what it has to do with anyone, apart from the medical staff at Howethwaite. Besides which he was cured and has since returned to the front."

"So Joanna tells me."

"What in hell's name has it to do with this Joanna, whoever she is?" Lucy felt her control slipping but Charlotte merely smiled.

"She had it from Aubrey who is in the same regiment, you see. The soldier, I believe she called him Rory Cameron, comes from a decent family, but then, I suppose you know that, don't you."

"What has this to do with anything, Charlotte?" Lucy's voice was filled with contempt. "He was nursed at Howethwaite and then went back to the trenches. As far as the hospital was concerned that was the end of it and why your friend and her fiancé are bandying his name about as if he had something to be ashamed of, I can't imagine. He was wounded, a wounded soldier who was put in our care."

"Oh, quite, but I believe, or so Joanna tells me, he formed an attachment for some lady round here and—"

"Your friend Joanna seems to know a hell of a lot about . . . about this soldier and where she gets her information . . ."

"There is no need to be offensive, Lucy. I am just telling you . . ."

"What are you telling me, Charlotte?"

"That he is corresponding with some lady, some woman . . . whatever, in these parts, a lady of whom he is very fond and I just wondered if you knew who it could be? Was he visited by anyone while he was with you?"

"Charlotte, really! I am not prepared to sit here and discuss a perfectly decent young soldier who your friend happens to—"

"Apparently he is still having these . . . attacks, or so Aubrey told Joanna. They seem to think he is merely trying to get out of the trenches by any means he can. A cowardly—"

"He is not a coward. He is afraid, like they all are but he still remains to do his duty, which is not the action of a coward and anyway, how does Aubrey come by this information? About the letter-writing, I mean."

"That's what I'm telling you. When he goes off his head, which he apparently does with great frequency, Corporal Cameron" – there was a sneer in Charlotte's voice on the word "corporal" – "babbles about the woman, calling for her. And then, naturally, Aubrey, being his captain, has the job of censoring his letters and . . ."

"And, of course, you and Joanna having found out what that name is, you had me over to tea to tell me all about it."

"Well, it does seem strange."

"There is nothing strange about it, Charlotte." Lucy rose to her feet with great dignity, turning to look for her coat but Edwards had removed it. "I do correspond with Rory Cameron but there is nothing in my letters that my husband couldn't read." She did not tell Charlotte that the same could not be said about Rory's letters to her, but then she probably knew that anyway. They were filled with his love for her, every line and page a joyous enchantment overflowing from his heart. As long as he could write to her, describe to her his feelings, have the hope and rapture of her letters, her thoughts, her friendship it was enough for him to get through each day. He loved to hear about Alice. It kept him sane, or as sane as any other soldier in the insane world in which some of them managed to survive. He knew she would never be his, never. She was married to a fine officer and had a child but the letters, that bond her letters created, gave him a reason to go on, to cling to life and when it was all over . . . well, that was something none of them could visualise.

"So James knows about the corporal then? He knows you exchange letters with a man in the ranks."

"Dear God, Charlotte, what in hell's name has his rank got to do with it? Are you saying that if he were an officer it would be quite proper to correspond with him? I've never heard such nonsense in my life, so I'll be going. I'd be glad if you would ring the bell and ask that butler of yours for my coat. We're extremely busy at the moment."

"How brave you are, Lucy." Charlotte smiled slyly. "I'm sure I couldn't do what you do and I'm sure Paul wouldn't want me to. After all, there are women to do these—"

"Shall I tell you something, Charlotte? I don't give a damn what you think of me, brave or otherwise and I've thought for a long time, in fact, ever since he married you, how sorry I am for Paul. And how this child of yours will fare with you for a mother doesn't bear thinking about. No, don't bother with the butler. I'll find my own way out."

Lucy was surprised and delighted when, having been brought from the ward where she had been dressing the leg wound of a cheeky-faced and impudent young soldier from Liverpool because she had a visitor, she found that visitor was Franny Buchanan.

"Dear God, what a bloody get-up," were Franny's first words as she grinned at Lucy's astonished expression, but nevertheless her embrace was warm and affectionate. "Mind you, mine's not much better," looking down ruefully at the drab skirt and tunic she had on. It was dusty and stained, worn at the cuffs and collar but Franny wore it as though it were a designer gown from Paris, her head proudly set on her shoulders, her back straight. Her hair had been cut short in the newest style but Lucy had the feeling she had not done it to be fashionable but to be tidy without trouble.

"When did you get home? Is Alex with you? Where are you staying, surely not up at Grange House?" which had been taken over as an officers' convalescent home for those fleeing the Zeppelin raids in London. Lucy's words fell over one another in her eagerness to speak.

"No, darling, not at Grange House. I thought I might beg a bed from you. It's that or the mother-in-law and I don't think I could manage even one night with old Phyllis. I'll go round. Is the Rolls still in action? Oh, good, I'll do the rounds and visit the relatives then I'm off back to London. Alex will be expecting me tomorrow or the day after at the latest and I've only got a week's leave. The first I've had since I went, I might add. Now, what about you? You don't look too good. Dear Lord, we're all working ourselves into an early grave but you . . . what is it? Not James?"

"No. Come upstairs into my bedroom. I've no sitting-room now, I'm afraid. There are patients in every corner and apart from the children's rooms we have all had to make sacrifices."

"The children, and the child? I'm looking forward to

meeting this paragon who, so everybody tells me, has tamed James Buchanan. He tells me she is—"

"You've seen him?" Lucy clutched at Franny's arm, almost overbalancing her as they walked up the stairs. "When? When did you see him?"

"Ah-ha, do I detect something in the lady that was lacking on her wedding day? Why this sudden urgent need to hear about the man you married simply to gain a home for your brothers and sisters? Don't tell me that perhaps your feelings have become warmer?"

"Don't tease me, Franny. Have you seen him recently?"

"Yes, I have and he's . . . well, but, darling, won't you give me a couple of hours. I'm dead beat and if I don't sleep I shall simply fall over and drop into an unconscious state at your feet."

"Of course, and perhaps a bath?"

"Lucy, if you asked me at this moment to choose between the crown jewels and a bath, the bath would be it. If you could see what we have to put up with in France . . ." She stopped suddenly and her face closed up. She put her hand through Lucy's arm as they walked along the broad landing. "As though what we have to put up with is important." Her voice was bitter. "Those poor blokes . . . well, you will have seen them here, I'm sure." She sighed raggedly, running her hand over her short cap of curls. Her face was strained now that she had stopped smiling, a curious grey colour, the tiredness seeping from her so that she drooped against Lucy's shoulder.

Within fifteen minutes she was bathed and, wearing one of Lucy's nightgowns, asleep like one dead in Lucy's bed.

It was almost midnight when she woke. Lucy had just come off the evening shift and was exhausted herself but she curled up in the armchair before the fire and, dozing a little, waited for Franny to wake. She knew there was something Franny had come here to say to her. Franny was not so fond of her relatives that she would come all the way from London to Lakeland just to look them up. She had travelled for hours on a slow train filled with troops, soldiers with the mud and filth of France still on them, desperate to get home for a few precious days, young men no longer young as Franny was no longer young. Lucy could not have said why that thought came to her but it was in Franny's face. Not lines or wrinkles but a certain detachment, an unwillingness to be involved in anything but the job in hand. Lucy could only think of the word *crippled* though Franny was unmarked. She had appeared to be mentally drained and Lucy knew, who had seen it in men in her care, that in the eighteen months since the war began Franny had met death so often, seen bodies torn, bloody, mutilated, gassed, burned, blinded, and to survive it was turning in on herself, holding herself aloof from life itself. It was how it was affecting them all, those who suffered it.

They talked quietly. They went up to the nursery and peeped at the beautiful Alice Buchanan, like a rosy cupid with the bloom of babyhood on her rounded cheeks and her eyelashes, so like James, curled tight on her sleeping eyes. Franny admired her politely, saying it was no wonder that James loved her so, then withdrew from the room.

"So, my dear," she said at last, "what's this I hear about you and one of the soldiers in your care? I don't believe a word of it, of course, so don't look so alarmed. I know you and one of your chief assets is your honesty which wouldn't allow you to cheat on James, but there is something . . ."

"Dear sweet Jesus, what have you heard?" Lucy was aghast, though she had been expecting something of the sort. "I knew you'd come to tell me something dreadful and I thought—"

She stopped as though a fist had been driven into her stomach, expelling all the air from her body and every vestige of colour drained from her face. She put out a blind hand and Franny took it with great compassion.

"He . . . knows, doesn't he?" Lucy whispered, her voice stricken with a savage pain which came at her from nowhere. "He's sent you."

"No, you should know better than that, darling. That's not James's style at all. He doesn't even know I'm here. I had the devil's own job to get out of him what was wrong. He looked appalling. I've seen him a time or two since he was home on leave and if he'd been a woman I would have said he positively glowed. Daft, isn't it, but that's how he was. In the middle of all that horror, he was calm, patient, unhurried, as though he had something inside him that was protecting him from it all. The men – his men – looked to him for support and leadership. They loved him, Lucy, because he gave them something they could not find themselves. Jesus . . ." She bent her head and Lucy thought she was weeping but when she lifted it again she was dry-eyed. "He's lost that. I saw it at once and asked him . . . He wouldn't tell me at first. Said to mind my own bloody business, you know how he is, but I got it out of him. He'd had a letter from a 'well-wisher', a bloody well-wisher. Can you believe there are people so evil in this world? To take a soldier's sanity, his peace of mind when it's all he has to cling to. To tell a man fighting for his life that his wife is unfaithful to him. Who would do such a thing? Who? I can't believe it."

"Oh, I can," Lucy said softly. "I know exactly who sent that letter. I was going to write to him myself."

"Lucy!"

"No, not to speak to him of an affair but to . . . to tell him that I was writing to a soldier. I only knew that it was common knowledge – that others were aware of it – today. Charlotte Buchanan has a friend who's . . . Oh, God, Franny, it's a long story. I nursed him, you see, Rory Cameron. Shell shock. He seemed to find some peace with me and so Sister Colyford said I was to spend as much time with him as I could. Quite simply, he fell in love with me."

"Who wouldn't, my dear?" Franny took Lucy's ice-cold hand in hers, then reached to smooth back her hair in a gesture that could only be called maternal.

"I was so sorry for him, Franny. He was a boy, no more, gone straight from university like so many of them to the trenches and he just couldn't take it. But he survived and was sent back. He begged me to write and I knew that if I didn't he would go out of his mind for ever or he would run away and be brought back as a deserter and shot. So I wrote. My letters were those of a friend to a friend, I swear it. I spoke of Alice. Great God in heaven, I was pregnant when he was here and on the day he left Alice was born so how in hell . . ." She began to laugh harshly and Franny shushed her, stroking her trembling hands.

"You and James were . . . lovers when he . . ."

"Oh, yes, we were. I had hopes and I think he did that when he came home . . . We don't write love letters, I don't know why."

"Seeing that you love one another?"

There was a long and agonising silence and Franny watched as the truth slipped tenderly into Lucy Buchanan's confused mind, clearing it, warming it, burning away the last shredded mist of indecision.

She sighed, almost hopelessly. "Yes."

"Then you must write and tell him. Not just of this correspondence with Rory, but that you love him. You must give him back that magic something which kept him *and* his company from going under. This war is going to last a long time, darling, a hell of a long time and anything you, or any woman, can give to her man to keep him alive, to give him something to fight for, such as coming home to you, must be given without stint. I've seen it over there, darling, and . . ."

Franny's face crumpled and that devilish cheek that had driven her female relatives to distraction was gone without trace. She had always had a charm of spirit, a streak of defiance against authority, against convention, against the rules that governed her society and though they all loved her they all sighed with exasperation when she did outrageous things like buying a motor car and wearing the only knicker-bockers seen in Ambleside. She had marched away to war like the men of her family, her head high, her grin wide, her expectations of a bit of "fun" in the dull world in which she had up to then lived showing in her seething determination to do her bit. And it would be fun! Driving an ambulance! Well, hadn't she always loved motoring? Hadn't she always loved the unexpected, despised safety, but even her great capacity for bearing a burden had not prepared her for the suffering she had witnessed in her search for adventure.

"I shouldn't speak of it, not to you who have a man you love there but it is quite appalling, Lucy. Even when they're not fighting Germans, they're fighting the cold, the mud in which a horse can sink without trace, the lice and rats, the dysentery, the sheer bloody boredom of waiting for something to happen and when it does the terror that comes with it. That Rory of yours – I'm sorry, I don't mean that how it sounds – is not the only one who is going off his head. Most of them cope somehow but it is with the help of men like James. Now James is . . . Dear God, Lucy, you must write to him and explain. About this Rory, I mean. He needs to know you are . . . well, I wasn't going to tell you this but whoever wrote that letter to him implied that . . . Alice might not be his."

Lucy moaned deep in the back of her throat, putting her hand to her mouth as though to keep some dreadful sound inside her. She was shaking so much she seemed in imminent danger of collapsing, the horror of what Franny was saying sending her thoughts into a series of disjointed images which flew about so quickly she could not get a grip on any one. Charlotte's simpering face . . . she must have already written to James even before she summoned Lucy to . . . Mr Lawson, so that was why he was so . . . and those women, people she knew in Ambleside . . . sideways looks . . . she understood it all now. It had been . . . someone had spread it round. James, James, how could you believe? After that last time, up on the fells, the magical bond that had bound them together . . . She couldn't stand it, she couldn't go back to the way they were before. If she could only see him, go to France and see his face as she explained.

"Darling, don't look so tragic."

"Franny, it is tragic and I don't know how to put it right. What am I to do? What am I to say to him? And in a letter which is so impersonal? Dear God, I can't stand it, the thought of what he must have in his mind. I haven't heard . . . no, that's not true, I had a letter this morning but it was written weeks ago, before Christmas and nothing since. That is why, because someone . . ."

"That damned Charlotte."

"It might not be her, Franny," she said, trying to be fair. "I've had some funny looks recently whenever I've gone into Ambleside. Now I know why."

"Perhaps, but I'm damned sure it was Charlotte who wrote to James."

"But why? What have I ever done to her to make her do such a thing?" Lucy's voice was anguished and she leaned forward in her chair, her arms about herself as though she were in great pain.

"She's never forgiven him for preferring you to her and she's never forgiven you for taking him. She had him, or so she thought, firmly in her grasp, and I must admit we all believed he would marry her. But then he saw you and that was it. He's loved you from the first moment he saw you. You know that?"

"No, I didn't. I thought it was a marriage of convenience for both of us."

"And you've discovered that it wasn't?"

"Yes."

"Hell and damnation, I'd like to go over to the Gibson house and smash Charlotte's bloody perfect teeth down her bloody perfect throat."

"Can I hold your coat while you do it?"

Mrs Burns tutted irritably as she watched Elsie struggle with a great load of brightly shining copper saucepans, one piled on top of the other in such a totter she was having a great deal of trouble containing them.

"Girl, what have I told you, time after time, what I tell you all but will you listen, no, you will not. Lazy man's load, my mother used to call it. Take half of them to the shelf and then come back for the other half. And don't take all day about it. I want them ice-cream moulds rinsed and—"

"I only washed them this morning, Mrs Burns."

"Don't back-chat me, girl. I don't care if you washed them two minutes ago, I want them rinsed and wiped with a dry cloth. Yes, all of them. You know how those lads like my ice-cream and Sister says it goes down a treat for them what can't fancy much."

Elsie had to admit that the ice-creams, when set and turned out into the little fancy dishes Cook used to serve them, did look right pretty. Cook was clever that way. She made each one so that you'd swear they were real lemons, real apricots or apples or strawberries in a delicate pile, each fruit the exact shade nature meant it to be and the soldiers loved them.

She sighed, not because Mrs Burns had given her the rounds of the kitchen but because the atmosphere in the house, in the back and in the front, had changed dramatically since the New Year had come in. Of course, the war was dreadful and the columns of figures in the newspapers of the dead and wounded were dreadful too, but despite that they had all felt there was hope and optimism in the air, a feeling that they were sharing in the suffering of the men and doing their best to ease it. And that hope had been created by their mistress, fostered by her, nurtured along with her cheerful determination that they were all to do their best until the master came home.

It was very different now. Miss Lucy crept about like a stricken animal, haunting the front step for the sight of the postman and the letter from Major Buchanan that never came. No one knew why, that was the mystery of it. He was not wounded or dead, or Miss Lucy would have been told about it, but for reasons best known to himself the master had stopped writing and the light of life had gone from Miss Lucy's eyes like a candle blown out.

Lucy moved through the days like an automaton, doing what she had done for the past eighteen months but with no trace now of the spirit of resolution that had urged her to set up and run a hospital for non-commissioned men. Except when she was on the wards. Then she was the same as she had always been with the wounded men in her care, dedicated, patient, compassionate, encouraging, giving one hundred per cent of herself, day or night, so much so that Sister Colyford had a word or two to say about it.

"You must leave something for the others to do, Mrs Buchanan. You cannot be with the patients twenty-four hours day and night. That's why we have rosters and shifts. Nurse Cartwright tells me you sat by the bedside of Private Hardacre late into the night when you should have been asleep. It was not your shift and it may cause resentment in the other nurses if you interfere."

She had been summoned to the cubby-hole at the end of the passage leading from the side entrance of the house, the one Sister called her office and which had once served as a store-room for wellington boots, walking sticks, cricket bats, tennis racquets, umbrellas and mackintoshes and all the paraphernalia of the out-door pursuits of the Buchanans, and then the Deans. The miscellany had been whisked away to the large cupboard on the first landing, a walk-in linen cupboard and so crammed, every time the cupboard door was opened, falling out into a heap across the carpet, to the deep annoyance of whoever opened it. But they were so short of space, with rooms being cleared to accommodate the wounded any little convenient area, convenient for the nursing of them, that is, was pounced upon and this was one of them. The shelves were filled with bottles and jars and against the window was a small desk behind which Sister Colyford sat when she needed privacy to speak to one of her staff, such as now.

"I don't interfere, Sister. Frank's wound had just been irrigated and you know how agonising that can be. He knew he was to go through the whole painful process in three hours' time and quite frankly he was in such a state of dread I felt I could not leave him. Nurse Cartwright was very busy with the new intake and both Jones and Pennington were rushed off their feet. I was in no one's way and Frank became calmer."

"And that is another thing, Mrs Buchanan." Sister lifted her double chin, beneath which ribbons were tied and her dainty frilled cap bobbed. There was a neat pile of folders on her desk in which were the records of the new intake and Sister moved them determinedly from the left to the right as though to emphasise her need for order. Sister did not like to have her authority questioned. It was not that she was heartless but she ran the wards in the only way they could be run, and still function, and that was with a strict routine. She could not have people hanging about who were not performing some task, unless, of course, they were visitors come to see the wounded men, and there were not many of those since Ambleside was a long way from the places most of these young men called home.

"Yes, Sister?" Mrs Buchanan asked patiently. She was very quiet these days was Mrs Buchanan. Gone was that lovely laugh which the men listened for and instead was the smile, just as beautiful but so sad it broke your heart, it really did, but just the same Sister must do her duty.

"You cannot call these men by their christian names, Mrs Buchanan. We must have order. They are still in the army despite being wounded and it is protocol to call them by their rank and surname."

"Sister, I don't wish to be rude, but bugger protocol."

"Mrs Buchanan!"

"I'm sorry, that was uncalled for, but you see I cannot believe that to address a man by his surname can do him any good at all. It gives them a sense of identity to be called by their first names. They are human beings who are suffering, weary for their homes and their families who *do* call them by their christian names and if it helps them just a little bit to hear them then I shall continue to say them. They respond, Sister, to a small gesture of familiarity. It seems to give them a feeling that they are perhaps being addressed by their mother or sister or wife, or at least a friend and not the company sergeant-major. They are men again, not just soldiers when they hear their names. Oh, I know they call each other by their christian name, or a nickname most likely, but just the same I believe that what I do is helpful in the healing process."

Lucy had been just about to go on duty and she was dressed in the immaculate white uniform, high-necked and calf-length, the snowy apron and handkerchief nurse's cap which bound back her hair. Her face was flushed with indignation and a resolve not to be turned from what she believed was an intrinsic part of nursing, personal contact with the patient. They were always pathetically pleased to be given that extra bit of attention, reaching to the hand she held out to them, their faces smoothing, the grey lines of suffering leaving them for a moment as they warmed themselves under her smile. She could not give it up and her raised jaw and tight-lipped expression said so.

"I cannot treat them as though they were nothing but a gangrene leg or a stomach wound, Sister. They are young men, and some not so young who are equally vulnerable."

"Mrs Buchanan, if you will not obey me I shall be forced to put the wards out of bounds. If you defy my orders . . . oh, my dear . . ."

Suddenly Sister Colyford leaned forward and, putting out her hands across the desk top, took Lucy's, holding them firmly when Lucy would have pulled away. "I know that something . . . I don't wish to pry but one can't help hearing gossip; rumours about this and that and I know you have had some . . . My dear, I don't know how to put this, but you cannot let your personal life control your professional work. These men rely on you, on us all and if you refuse to follow the rules made by myself and the doctor, then you will become ill and be of use to no one. You are not a trained nurse but you are the best nurse's aid I have ever known. You have a way with the patients that seems to reassure them when they are in distress."

Where had she heard this before and who had been speaking, and about whom? The question went through her aching head and when the answer came to her the pain became worse, crashing over her eyes, round the back and into the nape of her neck with sickening force. Franny. Franny talking about James and the men in his company. He was – or had been until his faith and trust in her had been destroyed – he had been like that, just as Sister was describing and it was her fault that it had been shattered by some ill-wisher. Charlotte Buchanan, she was sure of it, though she could not bring herself to face her with it, for what would be the good. The damage was done. But it was Lucy Buchanan who had caused it in the first place by becoming too friendly with one of her own patients and, pitying him, had continued the friendship even when he had left her care. James's feelings for her had been too fragile to stand the blow and he had believed it, believed that there was more to it than friendship and that was almost the hardest thing to bear. Though she had written and explained what had taken place; how her feelings for the patient had been nothing but those of friendship and pity, James had not answered. He had just stopped writing. It was as though he had died, killed by shellfire, rifle fire, fire itself, mustard gas or any one of the dozens of horrors that the men in her care babbled about in their nightmares. Oh, she knew all about them. She had relived them time and time again holding the hand of a delirious man who spewed them over her like some putrescent matter but she could not deny them the relief it gave them. She lived with it, slept with it, worked with it until she thought it might drive her mad, not because of what it would do to her but because she knew exactly what it could do to James and the taut ferocity of her grief almost overwhelmed her. How was it that she had not known? she asked herself in the bitter depths of the sleepless night. How was it that she had loved James Buchanan and not known? How could it happen?

Even Franny could not help her. She had promised when she got back to France to try and find James and tell him of Lucy's feelings, of her terror that, thinking he had been deceived, he might become careless, rash, indifferent to bullets and shells and whizz-bangs. She had sent snaps of Alice and some of herself with Alice, willing to blackmail him emotionally into responding, but it seemed he was inclined to believe that perhaps the child was not his, and he had told Franny to sod off and leave him alone. Not a word for Lucy. No message, just an empty nothing as though she were not even worth denying, let alone answering.

"Thank you, Sister, I'll try, but you see, whenever a man calls out for someone it makes me feel better if I can believe that . . . should my husband . . . if he were wounded, there might be someone . . . a nurse who could hold his hand and comfort him a little. I do it for . . . not just for the men but for their wives and mothers who can't be with them. Dear God, I'm sorry, Sister," as she began to weep, broken at last on the terrible image of James wounded as these men were wounded.

Sister Colyford did not ask her to stay away from

the wards after that. If she was on duty and she saw Mrs Buchanan's slender figure leaning over a soldier who wept for his mother or called for "Annie" or "Flo", she did not interfere, for she knew Mrs Buchanan was working through this appalling thing that had come upon her in the only way she knew how.

The snows which had fallen early in January had cleared sufficiently to allow her to take the children for long walks through the woods and up on to the lower slopes of the fells. Taking the three dogs, she would put Alice in the harness James and Jacob had devised and, wrapping the children up in warm clothing, take them on the tramp, going as far as the untouched snowline where they stopped to breathe in the breathtaking beauty of the white, shadowed hills which rose up before them. Every tree stood sharp as ebony against the pale blue of the sky, their branches heavy with the patina of glittering ivory. The snow was pure, with no mark save that of the dainty paws of a fox which had come this way earlier. Below the snowline the shadows cast by the mountains were a deep purple in which ferns, bracken and gorse, not dead but withered, stood frozen in pearl and silver.

They were mesmerised for a moment but they were children, made for fun and merriment and soon the virginal snow was trampled as they threw snowballs for the dogs and even attempted a small snowman. Alice, who could just about sit up unaided now, watched, ready with her slow, baby chuckle, but soon deciding she wanted to join in this wonderful game, struggling in Lucy's confining arms until Lucy took off her jacket and sat her down on it, letting her scoop handfuls of clean snow which she promptly put in her mouth.

Lucy found a sheltered spot, and keeping her eye on Alice sat with her back against a snow-speckled rock watching the shadows of the clouds form a shifting pattern on the white hills. They seemed to hang in formation like sheep on parade, fat and fluffy, each waiting its turn to be off and Lucy moved back in time to that other day, in another world, when the sun was hot on two naked bodies who bonded together in love. James, her heart agonised, James! Why was I so blind? Why didn't I know that you loved me? It took Franny to open my eyes, to dash away all the stupid nothingness from my mind so that the clear shining light might be let in. A dozen things should have told her she anguished, but then she was not in love with him then and her heart took no notice. She was conscious that Margaret watched her, for her sister was fifteen now and though still a child in many ways was sensitive to the sadness in Lucy. She came now, leaving the others shrieking joyously in the snow, a child no longer, sitting beside Lucy, taking her hand, letting her know that though she was not awfully sure what was causing her such deep sorrow, Margaret was willing in any way she could to ease it.

Lucy confided in no one but Buffy. After the children were in bed and she was not on night duty, she and Buffy would sit before the fire in the homely comfort of the schoolroom and for hours, when she should have been sleeping, Lucy would talk, pouring out her sense of anguished loss and love for the man who, not believing – and who could blame him after the indifference she had shown him? – that she truly loved him had turned away from the dream, the hope they had begun to build together. At least, that was what she thought they had done on his last leave. Begun to weave a dream, to make small plans, if only in their minds, for the future. She had believed that something tender had taken root and was ready to blossom but Charlotte Buchanan, with the destructive hand of a spoiled child, had destroyed it, and she could not bear it.

"Even if I could see him, explain exactly how it came about, the friendship with Rory, I mean, I still cannot help but feel that . . . that if his love had been as truly strong as Franny seems to believe, he would have been prepared to . . . well, at least give me the benefit of the doubt, Buffy. He's known me for nearly three years and not once in all that time have I been dishonest with him. He never told me that he loved me, you see."

Her eyes were grown so huge they devoured the rest of her face and Buffy leaned forward, her own face harrowed by Lucy's pain. She had always known her friend was capable of a deep and abiding love. That some day there would be a man who would see it, know its worth, take it and give it back and now it had happened, that man and that love, only to be crushed in the havoc that was consuming the world.

"It will be over soon, Lucy, or so they say, and then James will be home and you can let him see the truth of it in your eyes. He has only to look at you, see what is in your heart and he will realise how unthinkable it is." Buffy tried to console her, knowing even as she said the words that they were no more than glass bubbles which would shatter at the slightest touch.

In January the First Military Service Bill introduced conscription for single men and those on the ward cheered, for it was about time those buggers who sat about at home got a taste of what they had suffered. They had heard of the young men who sat all day in the cafés of London, sipping coffee, smoking and playing dominoes while they had been sitting in rainwater up to their arses, slipping in the mud which could get you if you fell off the duckboard, crouching in minute dugouts which were little less than useless if a bloody whizz-bang decided it was your turn.

In February, 21 February, the tragic Battle of Verdun began. Verdun! "A place of execution" it was later called and that was what it was, for the Germans believed that if they could kill as many French soldiers as possible with their artillery they would break France's will to fight. Wholesale slaughter, it was reported as, and that was just what it was. Over the whole of the front, it was reported, to a depth of many kilometres the dance of dust and smoke and debris was scattered while thousands of French soldiers bent their backs to the storm, clinging together at the bottom of holes, most of which were no better than scratches in the ground. Dante's Hell, they were calling it, the sacrifice of nearly a million soldiers in one battle when it ended in December.

The men on the wards were quiet that day when the newspapers came through, for hadn't they been there themselves.

In May there occurred the first and last great engagement between the British and German fleets and although the British fleet suffered serious losses the German High Seas Fleet never faced them again.

On 23 June the British army began shelling the German lines along the Somme and it was said that the sound of the massive bombardment could be heard across the Channel in England.

At 7.30 on a clear, sunny and pleasant morning on the first day of July, the bombardment stopped. There followed a moment's silence then waves of British divisions went over the top. James Buchanan, Rory Cameron, Aubrey Blane, Job Gunson, Lawrence Gunson and Roger Askew were among them.

"Follow the flash," they were told, for each soldier had a tin disc on his back, glittering in the sunshine, to show their own guns where they were. "Follow the flash," they were told, but within seconds it was hopeless, for those at the front, all the young officers, were picked off like flies, disappearing in the dust and smoke so that there was no flash to follow. Soldiers who had been given orders to take a certain position marched into fierce machine-gun fire, falling in rows almost as though they were on parade. It became impossible to go forward without stepping on the dead and wounded, many of whom were mates and who were not only lying everywhere but were beginning to pile up, one on top of the other in hideous walls of suffering.

A field of craters formed in the strip of land between the two armies' trenches and soon they too were filled, not only with wounded men but with those who were terrified to leave their small safety and go on into the enemy's withering machine-gun fire.

The crater nearest to the enemy line where soldiers had not yet reached had only two men in it. The different battalions had been rehearsed on training grounds in the back areas of the trenches until every soldier in every battalion knew his part and exactly where he should be but the confusion, the smoke, the dust, the noise disoriented many and they just marched blindly forward, following the man ahead until he fell, then settling their sights on another. Often it was a soldier from another company.

One of the men in the crater was badly wounded. His uniform below his waist was soaked with his blood and his face, beneath the mud that coated it, was a dirty grey. It was impossible to tell his rank and what did it matter? They were all comrades in this hell on earth, two small parts in the 60,000 casualties that were estimated that day.

"Where are you hit?" the first soldier asked.

"God knows," the second one answered, laughing weakly. "Somewhere below the neck, I suppose, since I'm still conscious."

"I'll have a look, old chap. Do you hurt in any particular place?" which was a bloody daft question when you saw the state of the poor sod's legs.

"Nowhere, that's the bloody – if you'll pardon the pun – worry."

Shells thundered overhead from the German trenches and machine-gun fire rattled, the sound like the angry staccato swarm of bees disturbed from their hive, but nobody seemed inclined to join them in the precarious bit of safety they shared. There was water in the bottom of the crater and they both slid into it, the wounded man held firmly in the arms of the other. They both took a sip of water from one water bottle but it set the wounded man to coughing and still the blood pumped from him.

"Let me get this dressing on you. I thinks it's your thigh that got it," which was an understatement if ever there was one, and putting a dressing on what was left of him would serve no purpose except to make him feel something was being done. As gently as he could the second soldier pressed the dressing on to the gaping wounds of his fallen comrade, hoping to staunch the flow of blood. "As soon as there's a chance, which I'm afraid means when it's dark, we'll get the hell out of here, old chap. I suppose we should be going forward but to me that doesn't make sense."

"Nor me, neither. What is it the lads say, 'the higher, the fewer' meaning brains, and whoever thought up this fiasco must have none at all."

His companion laughed harshly. "I hadn't heard that one but it's the bloody truth."

Darkness did not come early for this was just past mid-summer but when it did, gritting his teeth to stop himself from screaming as he was moved, the wounded soldier allowed his companion to hoist him on to his back and edge up to the lip of the crater. They both peered over the top, like two bloody moles, one whispered to the other, then, standing up with one on the back of the other, they began to stumble towards the British lines, falling a dozen times over the bodies, some of them still moaning, of those who had gone down earlier in the battle.

"Nearly there, lad," the one carrying the wounded man gasped, and then the world blew up in his face and he fell into a hole as black and as deep as the crater they had just left.

The first news reaching British civilians about the battle was encouraging. Newspaper headlines declared "Great Day on the Somme", "Kitchener's Boys Make

Good" and "Swift British Advance", but gradually the truth, the real truth became known. Within a few days the rolls of honour, the lists of deaths and casualties began appearing in local and national newspapers. Among those listed as dead were Job Gunson, Lawrence Gunson and Roger Askew. It was learned that in just a few minutes whole towns in the country had been decimated. "It took two years for us to get here and ten minutes to finish us off," one private from a "Pals" battalion was reported as saying.

Trainloads of wounded men began to arrive from across the Channel and on 5 July one of these came to rest at Windermere station where a line of ambulances waited to take them to the three hospitals in the area. One of those to receive them was Howethwaite.

They knew they were coming, for they had been warned by headquarters to be ready but nothing had prepared them, even such experienced stalwarts as Sister Colyford, for the horror of what they found on the stretchers in the back of the ambulances. Lucy just had time to shriek to Buffy, who had come out on to the steps with Margaret to give a hand, "Get the children back to the schoolroom and keep them there, for God's sake, Buffy," and then it began.

They had known it was bad, for if "our boys" were being sent as far north as this what in God's name was it like in the south, but nothing, *nothing* had prepared them for the contents of the ambulances which lined the road from Ambleside waiting to turn into the gates of Howethwaite. They parked wherever they could find a space, jostling among the flower urns which Clapcott had planted with his usual display of geraniums and white lobelia and when there was no more room simply lifting the stretchers out and placing them on the gravel drive or the lawn, driving away to leave space for the next vehicle. On each stretcher was a soldier, some still and dreadfully silent, others tossing and mumbling, moaning, many of them, a collection of khaki rags, each one with a rough, blood-soaked dressing slapped on it in one spot or another. Not fresh blood but blood that had dried and clotted and was covered with filth and flies and mud and whatever nasty matter had been picked up and clung to them on the long journey from the trenches to the north of England. Orderlies shouted, harassed and so distressed by what they were being forced to do to this broken flotsam, they wanted to smash something. They had seen some sights in the last two years, they told one another, but this beat the bloody cake and what in hell's name was going on "up there", meaning the War Office, when they allowed such things to happen to poor, decent, hardworking blokes like these. They were not conscripted men, but volunteers who had answered the call of their country and it was a crying shame that they should have had this done to them. They hastily scrutinised the labels that were tied to each man, those that were red telling them that the soldier must be attended to at once, which was a laugh really when you considered how long the poor sods had been on the road.

They all helped to carry them in, even Clapcott and Licky Thripp, Mrs Burns and Mrs Bunting, Dixon and Elsie and Gertie and Jacob, for it was beyond the power of the nurses and the one doctor – though they had been promised another – to ease the men from the ambulances, or the gravel path and on to the hastily erected camp beds which stood wherever there was an empty space.

The men were, for the most part, quiet, for they were all deep in shock but there was an odd sound, a kind of sibilant rustling drifting on the warm, sunshine-filled air, and Lucy realised with stunned shock that it came from dozens of throats, lungs gasping for breath through the agony, the almost silent moans and retching of men who could endure no more but knew they must. She could feel the bile rise to her throat and she tried to draw shallow breaths, for the stink of war was appalling. Though by now she was used to wounds and even gangrene, her eyes slithered from the blood and bone of a wound that had come unwrapped. The men she had attended to in the past had been cleaned up when they got to her, strapped with pure white bandages, resting in white-sheeted beds. These men were not like that.

Her head began to spin and her stomach had a strong desire to spew forth what Sister had made them all eat before the men had arrived.

"You don't know how long it might be before you have a meal so get some of Cook's good soup inside you and you'll come to no harm."

Cook's good soup was heaving violently inside her and for a moment she knew she was going to faint but Sister's voice snapped in her ear, telling her there were two soldiers lying on one stretcher. Don't ask her why, she didn't know, but the orderlies had told her they wouldn't be parted and had put them at the foot of the stairs. Would she go and have a quick look at them. She had been told they were alive but who could tell. Already several had been taken discreetly round to the back of the house and laid out in the stables ready for interment. Come along, Mrs Buchanan, she admonished, looking at Lucy's bone white face, this is no time for squeamishness.

Mrs Bunting was there, sitting on the bottom step of the staircase, her face wet with tears, begging to be told why she couldn't give these . . . well, there were a few who would enjoy a nice cup of tea, surely, but that there Sister had said no and she thought it was wicked to deny them it. There was nothing like a nice cup of tea to pick a body up, then, realising the irony of a cup of tea helping these poor lads, she burst into tears, reaching for Elsie.

"Nay, Mrs Bunting, I'm needed here," Elsie told her sternly, reaching out a gentle hand to uncover the faces of the two men who lay side by side on one stretcher. A bit of khaki blanket was wrapped about them, hiding what wounds they might have, though Lucy could see blood seeping from the end of the stretcher on to the black and white tiles which had been discovered when the carpet was taken up.

The head of one was wrapped about in what had once been a clean bandage though by now it was foul with mud, days old, and the residue of blood from what must be a head wound.

The other was Rory Cameron, unconscious, with several days' stubble on his face. It was unmarked, young and boyish, but unmarked.

"We'll take the one with the head wound, Mrs Buchanan," the sharp voice of Nurse Bickerstaffe told her. "We'll lift him on to this stretcher and then you can help me and Pennington to carry him into the operating theatre."

She had been kneeling at Rory's side but it was as though, deep in shock as she was, some instinct got her on her feet and with Elsie and herself at the shoulders and Nurse Bickerstaffe and Nurse Pennington at his feet, they lifted the soldier on to a spare stretcher. His head lolled and he moaned beneath his bandages. He had had his arm round Rory Cameron and now, as they moved him, his hand fell limply from the stretcher and on the little finger was a signet ring Lucy had seen many times.

It belonged to James Buchanan.

23

There were dogs howling somewhere, a sound that seemed strangely familiar to him though he didn't know why. He didn't know anything really, and that was a bit worrying but there was nothing he could do about it except lie here on the bed and wait. He'd nothing else to do, had he, except wait patiently for the gentle hand that he knew was on its way. It was the only thing, that and her voice, that stood between him and the deep hole of blackness into which he was terrified to fall. In that hole which he had begun to recognise as sleep, or perhaps a state of unconsciousness, he was nothing, just a speck that floated mindlessly in space with no dreams or thoughts or memories, except one, and it terrified him, but when her hand touched him it gave him an identity of sorts and he felt calmed.

He could hear her progress up the ward.

"Andy, you're looking better. What, you've had a letter from Mavis? Well, that explains it. No wonder you've that grin on you. You look like a Cheshire cat. I'll be along presently to write your answer.

"Jack, did you sleep well? I know Sister was going to give you something . . . good, good. Yes, I'll bring her in as soon as she wakes up but I warn you she's trying to walk and is a bit of a handful.

"Sid, let me hold your hand for a moment. I know, I know, the pain is dreadful but your mother will be here today, had you forgotten? She'll make you feel better. It will be better soon, I promise you. Yes, I'll slip back as soon as I can."

He could not hear the soldiers' answers, just a murmur mingling with her compassionate voice. A clock ticked nearby and footsteps moved busily by the end of his bed. Someone was playing a mouth organ in the far ward, a conservatory, he had been told, in which those on the mend were put. Again a familiar sound to him who had heard the tune on the last day before . . . before . . .

> Keep the home fires burning,
> Though your heart be yearning . . .

There was the sound of a dressing trolley being wheeled past, and a nurse's voice telling another to slip to the sluice for a clean bedpan for Corporal Whittaker. He had come to know all the sounds of the ward, the sighing moans of men having their wounds treated, the squeak of the trolley wheels which he wished someone would oil, the rapid footsteps when some emergency arose, the rasp of a match on a matchbox as some chap lit a cigarette. The hiss of pain from another bed, the crisp voice of the doctor which subtly changed when he had to tell some poor sod that the gas gangrene was too far gone. The weeping and shouts of men in their sleep and the infectious chuckle of the baby which was brought in to the ward for a brief moment each day to cheer up the men whose own babies were far away. Apparently it belonged to one of the nurses, but he'd heard them say that it gave a small measure of comfort to men who had wallowed in filth and mud and blood and terror for days on end to be allowed to touch the pure, shining innocence of the child.

When it came he could not see the hand, at least no more than the vague shape of it. He could not see the owner of the hand either, for his face and head were heavily bandaged, but he knew and waited for its touch and for the gentle voice which called him James. He didn't know why. He supposed it must be his name, for the authorities would know who he was. He didn't much care at the moment. He knew her footsteps and her laugh, which was low and sweet as though it knew there were men about who could not cope with heartiness, but it was laughter all the same, like the ripple of the wind in the trees.

He knew the scent of her too, a fresh, sweet smell which, like the howling of the dogs, seemed familiar though again he didn't know why. She was a nurse, he recognised that, for she had the sharp, clean smell of carbolic about her, but underlying the hospital smell was that fragrance which tantalised him.

He could hear the rustle of her uniform as she came along the ward and something in him longed for her to hurry up with the chap in the next bed and get to him. Something urgent, compelling, something that would not wait, and without thinking he put out his hand to her and at once she was there.

"James, I'm here," she told him and immediately the urgency was gone and the tranquillity she brought washed over him and he sighed.

"I wish you wouldn't keep going away," he heard his own voice say fretfully, knowing he was being unfair, for all the men in the ward had as much call on her time as he did. He had been told he had been wounded, as the rest of them were, but it was only when she was with him that he had any peace.

"I'm here now," she whispered and he felt her breath brush the skin of his hand, and something else, warm and damp which was quickly brushed away.

"What is it?" he asked.

"Nothing," she answered him and though he was sure it was a tear he could not be certain and anyway, why should she be crying over him?

"Is Rory about?" he asked her, turning his head restlessly on his pillow as though he might see the only man he knew through the thickness of his bandages.

"No, he's been taken to the operating theatre again. His stumps are . . . need irrigating and the doctor wants to put him to sleep."

"Poor sod. Tell me when he gets back, will you, Nurse?"

"Of course, but in the meanwhile why don't you try and get some sleep?"

He turned his head away from her and sighed deeply. "That's all I'm ever told to do, Nurse, but . . ."

"What? What is it? Tell me and if I can I'll . . ."

"What will you do, Nurse, give me back my life, my thoughts, my memories?" He moved his body in the bed, twisting away from her and then back again. "Jesus, I'm sorry, I shouldn't say that, not to you who . . . but when you know only one person in the whole bloody world."

"I know . . . I know, James, but you will get it all

417

back, I promise you." Surprising him she lifted his hand to her face and held the back of it to her cheek and again he could feel a dampness there. Her lips brushed it and he felt his heart begin to race and for the life of him he didn't know why. She was a nurse, filled with a great compassion, not just for him but for them all. He had heard her in the night when he knew she was supposed to be off duty, moving along the ward, stopping to murmur to some restlessly tossing man, stopping to put her hand on his own brow though he could barely feel it through the bandages. Several times he had threshed up from the infernal depths of the blackness he was captured in, like a fish leaping from the ooze at the bottom of the ocean, to find her there, his hand in hers, her face close to his though he did not know how he was aware of this.

"James, I'm here," she would say with a strange break in her voice and he would be comforted.

"Don't let me go to sleep again," he would beg her, for he could not stand that blankness he tipped over into which contained, though he could not bring it to him, his past life.

"Why has Rory gone to the operating theatre again?" he asked her. Rory was the only human being in the world, in his life, his past and present, who he remembered. His life had started really when he had staggered across no-man's land with him on his back. He could remember the weight of him, the sighing rustling sounds of his moans at every jerking step, every fall and stumble. He could hear Rory's voice in his ear telling him to let him go but he couldn't do that, could he, and he had told him so, the silly sod. He didn't remember any more until he came to, lying on a stretcher among hundreds of others, the bombardment thundering over him and the bandage that had been slapped hastily on his face blinding him. He had begun to shout in panic but the voice of the wounded man on the next stretcher had reached out to him.

"Don't fret, old man," it said weakly. "We're in this bloody thing together. You don't think I'm going to lose sight of the stupid bugger who dragged me here, do you?"

"I must have been mad," he said, just as weakly.

"We all are in this bloody war."

"What's your name?"

"Rory Cameron. And yours?"

It was then that the black thing came down on him and swept him away on a tide of terror. There was something behind him that pressed against his present consciousness, pushing him and belabouring him and he wanted to turn and stare into it, sweep aside the curtain that hid himself from himself and see whatever it held, for it was his life up to the time he had carried this Rory Cameron to safety. But no matter how hard he tried it remained a vacuum.

He didn't even know his own name!

They had travelled together from that clearing station in France to this hospital, which he had been told was near Ambleside in the Lake District, and whenever they tried to separate them, he and Rory, he had yelled and screamed and tried to do the stretcher-bearers an injury, and for the sake of peace – and what difference did it make to anyone? they asked one another – they had kept the two badly injured soldiers, one an officer, together. They had even shared a stretcher in the ambulance up to the hospital, for by then Rory was off his head, twisting and turning and throwing himself about so that the only way to keep him from falling out of the bloody ambulance had been to hold on to him.

He sensed her leaning over him. Her elbows were on the bed and he wanted to let his body fall against her but instead he gripped her strong hand with his which was ridiculously weak.

"They're trying a new treatment," she told him. "Rory has gas gangrene in both his legs, or rather in the stumps, as you know, and the doctor doesn't want to . . . to cut again. This new thing is called hypochlorous acid. Drainage tubes will be attached to a large syringe and the liquid will be injected into the tube every three hours to irrigate the wounds of his stumps. It will be an agonising procedure but, if we don't do it, Rory could die."

She kept nothing from him. That was why he clung to her, he supposed. Some of the staff, and the men, too, treated him as though he were an infant or a lunatic because he could not remember . . . remember what had happened to him before this. They spoke over his supine body as though, having no memory, he also had no feelings, no adult mind and he'd had the devil's own job to force the doctor to tell him what was wrong with him. In fact had it not been for this nurse, who was his lifeline, as she was to many of the others, he would not have succeeded. The less you know the better was the attitude of the medical profession but this woman had stood beside him and fought the doctor on his behalf. He would never forget her. He might never remember his previous life but he would never forget her.

"Let me tell him who he is," she wept, clinging to the doctor's hands, flinging off Sister Colyford's attempts to restrain her. She knew Sister believed she was about to do the doctor an injury in her desperate state of fear for James, but nevertheless she could see no reason why her husband should not be told that he was in his own home, that he was with his own wife, with his own family about him, and during those first days she had said so at every turn. Every time Doctor Yates or Doctor Penfold came off the ward she would be there, hovering anxiously, resolute in her determination to accost him and talk about this one patient when the doctors had over forty others to see to. The doctors were patient with her but very adamant.

"Mrs Buchanan, we know very little about the human mind and if we just . . . just barge in and force on Major Buchanan the truth of who he is and where he is we might do untold harm. Here, on the ward, he is a soldier among other soldiers and that is familiar to him and for the present he can cope with that. Of course he wants to remember, to know who he is and where he comes from but we must go slowly. No, please, don't ask me why. From experience the medical profession, in these unusual times, has found that it is better to wait and see if the patient recovers naturally. That whatever is blocking out his past will simply drift away. There might be some dreadful thing, dreadful to him, that is, which is putting up a barrier to help him keep it at bay. It might be a . . . a physical wound, in his head, though we don't think so," he added hastily as Mrs

Buchanan swayed and turned the colour of her own nurse's apron, clutching at his arm for support.

"May I put his child in his arms, Doctor?" she pleaded. "He loved her so and it might . . ."

"Again you are trying to force him to remember, Mrs Buchanan. Has he shown any interest in the baby when you take her on the wards to visit the other men? They all want to pat her and talk to her, even hold her, and we know now that it does them untold good, but does your husband ask? No. Then we must not do anything which might precipitate him into something worse than his present state."

The memory of that day when James and Rory came home together would haunt her to the end of her days. Gallant little Elsie who had wanted nothing more than to help these poor broken soldiers, had staggered back in horror, turning to Mrs Bunting and falling into her arms, the pair of them crouched together on the bottom step of the staircase, the stretcher on which Major Buchanan had been placed left to fend for itself on the floor. Sister had lifted the casual dressing which covered James's face, saying she would just have a quick look at his wound and it was the sight of that wound which had knocked Elsie for six, as she was to say later, ashamed of herself and ready to apologise to anyone who would listen.

Whatever it was that had exploded in front of him, mine or shell, had taken the skin from his face as though someone had peeled it with a knife. There was shattered bone showing just below his right eye and most of his hair was gone. Had it not been for his ring they would none of them have known him. The wound had festered and it had turned Lucy faint and sick to see it but in her compassion and her love for this man whom she had come late to knowing, she sank down on her knees and took his filthy hand in hers. His eyes were open and he could see her, she knew that, thank the good God, but he said nothing, held in the deep shock that merciful nature sends to mend the injured. Would James Buchanan mend? her heart anguished. Her tears, of which she was ashamed, for what good would tears do her wounded husband, dripped on to the hand she held and his eyes moved to look enquiringly into hers but there was no recognition.

"Mrs Buchanan, please, we must take him," Sister's urgent voice had told her. "Let him go, my dear."

"I must come with him, please." She knew she was becoming distraught, hysterical and Sister moved round the quiet man and lifted her to her feet.

"No, you cannot. He needs immediate attention. That wound is . . . my dear, you have seen enough wounds to know that unless . . . Pull yourself together, Mrs Buchanan, and let us do our job. Go and help the others. There are uniforms that need cutting off and . . . well, you know what to do."

"Please, please, Sister, let me . . ." Her tears coursed down her face and on to the hands which Sister Colyford was holding and it was not until Sister's voice became harsh and commanding, telling her to behave herself and remember her training, that she let him go, watching the stretcher being carried along the hallway to the operating room where a queue was already forming. There were three doctors on three tables, surrounded by nurses and VADs and they would work the clock round, they were aware of that, and Lucy must do the same. She must let them do what they could for James while she put her quite considerable knowledge to work in the easing of the others. She was allowed to give injections now, to take away the agony for a while of a wounded man, to change dressings, to irrigate wounds and there were men here who needed these things. Let her do what she was capable of doing, she told herself, wiping her eyes and squaring her shoulders, for there was nothing she could do for James. Not yet.

"Lucy . . ."

The voice, so weak she could barely hear it, came from the stretcher from which James had just been lifted and for a moment, disorientated, confused, distraught as she was, she did not recognise it, or the pallid face that looked up at her from the floor. She knew who he was, of course. Silver blond curls clotted with blood and mud and what could have been manure, which she supposed was not out of the question since that was what the farmers had put on their fields before the armies of three nations tore them up in the bloodbath of war. It was that which turned so many wounds to the dreaded gas gangrene, they all knew that by now too. Pale blue eyes surrounded by long, fair lashes tried to smile at her from that filthy face and with a murmur of pity Lucy dropped to her knees again and put her hand to Rory Cameron's cheek. He turned his face into the palm and sighed in great relief and even contentment, as though he were safe now, for he was in the care of the woman he loved. He closed his eyes and for an appalling moment she thought he was dead but he opened them again and smiled that sweet smile she remembered so well.

"He . . . brought me back, Lucy. We were . . . in a shell hole together . . . I didn't know who he was, of course. Not until they read his . . . identity tags." His voice was barely a whisper rasping from his throat and she leaned over him tenderly.

"Don't talk, Rory. It's all right. There's no need . . . later, perhaps." She smoothed his hair, once thick and heavy and shining, from the sweated brow of his powder grey face, and she could feel the rigid strain of something in him begin to ease.

"I wanted to do . . . the same for him, my darling. I may call you that, mayn't I? I've always . . . longed to. I wanted to do it . . . for you because I . . ."

"I know, Rory, don't talk any more," for she could see he was hanging on to life by no more than a slender thread that threatened to break at any moment. He was exhausting his already badly depleted body in his effort to explain to her how he and James had come home together.

"Sleep, Rory, and when you wake I'll be there."

"Promise."

"I promise."

Then Clapcott, Licky Thripp, Jacob and someone she didn't recognise came to lift him up and take him to the doctors.

That had been six weeks ago and today, later in the afternoon, they were to remove the bandages from James Buchanan's face.

"We did the best we could, Mrs Buchanan, but he was . . . his face was . . . Well, we shall have to wait and see, won't we?" and she knew he was warning her that her husband might not look like the man who went to war nearly two years ago.

They wouldn't let her take him to a private room, her bedroom even, where she could nurse him. She had wanted to have him with her twenty-four hours a day and night, while she slept beside him in a truckle bed. He was an officer, which she didn't care about, and she knew he wouldn't either, and the rest of the wounded were ordinary Tommies, and by the military rules he should not have been with them, but again the doctors, who did not give a damn about protocol, fortunately, would not allow it.

"He feels a comradeship with these men, Mrs Buchanan. He is one of them. He has no idea who he is, whether he was an officer or not, it wouldn't matter, and to put him on his own would distress him immeasurably. Leave him with those he knows, the only ones he knows, especially Corporal Cameron. I'm sorry, Mrs Buchanan, if I seem heartless," for she had flinched away from his words. "They both owe their lives to the other and it seems fitting, at least to the major, that they should lie side by side in the ward."

She had bowed her head and though she wanted to weep and even scream that she would nurse her own husband if she wanted to, for who better than the woman who loved him more than life itself, she did as she was told.

Rory was lying in the bed beside his when the doctors came. He himself had only just come round from the anaesthetic and his face clearly revealed his shock and pain, his eyes huge in his thin face. His hair had been recently washed and it shone a pure silver blond in the sunshine that streamed through the window above the two beds. His head was turned painfully on his pillow, his eyes looking directly into

James's and for a moment Lucy knew these two had no need of her or indeed of anyone but each other. They had suffered together, gone through the hell of battle together, a battle from which Job Gunson, Lawrence Gunson and Roger Askew had not returned, and they were united in that mysterious bond which only another soldier would understand.

When he heard the sound of the screens being drawn round his bed James turned to glare at the nurse, or at least as much of a glare as he could manage with his face totally obscured by the bandages.

"Don't do that, Nurse," he snarled.

"But it is customary, James." They had all been told to call him by his given name in order to protect him from the chance of his being flung into the confusion and terror of being inadvertently told who he really was.

"I don't give a damn. Rory is . . . I don't want to. And where is . . ."

She knew at once what it was he wanted.

"I'm here, James," taking the hand he held out to her and gripping it firmly in both of hers. She wanted to put her arms about him and hold him safe, tell him it made not the slightest bit of difference to her what he looked like but naturally she could do none of these things. He was not her husband at this moment. But he still needed her hand in his.

"Right," he said briskly, doing his best to keep his hand steady in hers. "Let the dog see the rabbit."

She met Rory's eyes for a moment and in them was a message of love and hope and compassion. Rory Cameron would never walk again unless his stumps healed enough to fit him with two artificial legs. He would never know the blessings that awaited James Buchanan but he let her see that though he loved her, that he, Rory Cameron, loved her and wanted her for himself, he knew she belonged to James Buchanan.

The bandages came away quite easily and the doctor grunted in satisfaction. The whole ward seemed to be holding its breath, even men at the far end knowing that this was an important day for the poor bugger who was known simply as James. Was he to be as hideous as some they had heard of, men who were burned, or shot in the face, or had the clever doctor who, before he had retired to the Lake District, been a surgeon in the field of plastic, reconstructive surgery, and who had been brought back at the beginning of the war, been able to put his shattered face together again?

His hair had grown in the six weeks since he had been brought here, falling in that way she was so familiar with in a rough tumble of darkness across his forehead, and without thought, scarcely looking at the rest of him, Lucy brushed it back from his forehead, saying, as any wife would, "It's time you had a haircut, James."

He turned slowly towards her, looking up in surprise to her smiling face and there were his eyes, smoky grey and as soft as velvet, the lashes thick about them, uncertain but without the fear she had expected to see in them.

"You sound like my mother," he said, the first time he had made a remark that told them he knew he was a person like the rest of them.

It was then that Lucy looked at the rest of his face. It was the bright shiny pink of newly healed flesh, clean and smooth, with a mottled creasing of scars about his mouth and eyes and a puckering beneath his right eye where the doctor had mended the broken bone of his cheek. There was a lift at the corner of his mouth that would always be there but which might have been the start of a smile and a slight dragging down of his right eyebrow. She didn't see them or if she did it did not matter. It was James, that's who it was, the James she had loved for years, she knew it now, had known it for a long time, and it shone like a candle in her eyes. A candle flame that would never blow out.

He was blinking in the bright light, despite the drawn blinds, for though he had had eyeholes cut in the bandage they had been covered thinly with gauze. It was seven weeks since James Buchanan had looked at anything, another human being, and the first face he looked up into was that of the loveliest woman he had ever seen. A face so exquisite, so young and tender he felt he wanted to hide what he was sure was his own disfigurement from her. A face in which two golden brown eyes, deep and soft as old sherry, looked into his with an expression of . . . well, what in hell's name was it that was in her face? He was damned if he knew but it wasn't revulsion and he tightened his grip on her hand.

"God, you're a handsome dog," Rory croaked valiantly from the other bed. "None of us will have a chance now with Nurse Buchanan."

They saw his body relax though he still clung to the nurse's hand, glancing about him as though to catch any faint shiver of distaste which might come from one of them, but they were all smiling and the doctor looked like a dog with two tails, both of which he thought he might wag.

"Perhaps Mrs Buchanan's husband might have something to say about that," he joked, turning towards the nurse who held a mirror, not exactly eager to see what a guy he was but prepared to suffer it, he said to Rory.

He held the mirror and cautiously peeped into it but it was not what he saw there that relieved him but the expression of approval on Nurse Buchanan's face. Her great shining eyes beamed down into his, and she was nodding and he was not to know that, having seen his face, she was thinking that there was nothing on this earth that would stop her from bringing his daughter to see him.

"What d'you think?" he asked diffidently, looking not at the rest of them but into the lovely smiling face of the nurse, the one who had got him safely from there to here.

He was astonished and so were the rest of them when she bent her head and kissed him on his shiny new cheek.

She watched him from her bedroom window, his tall, thin figure erect and easy as he strolled down the grassy slope at the front of the house towards the group of men who had already been put out there by the nurses. He had lost a lot of weight during the past weeks, and his cheeks were hollowed out below the flat planes of his cheekbones but the exercise and the sun had touched his lean, scarred face with the amber tint that had been his before he was wounded.

He was pushing Rory in what they both called the "baby carriage", the wicker stretcher on wheels which the legless and those still recovering from serious wounds and unable to walk got about in. They were laughing at something one of them had said, James bending his dark head to Rory's silver pale one, and it was obvious even from this distance that their companionship was strong and important to them both. They wore the blue hospital uniform with its distinctive red lapels, James, the officer, indistinguishable from Rory, the corporal.

It was a glorious September day with that special crispness in the air which says that summer is almost over and autumn hot on its heels. The sun cast its benign warmth over the men and Lucy could hear their voices, accented with the brogue of Ireland, the burr of Scotland, the long-vowelled flatness of Lancashire and Yorkshire, the clipped chirpiness of the cockney and in the midst of it the well-bred drawl of James and Rory which the others seemed to find easy to accept. They might be of a different social class to the others but they were soldiers, damaged men just like them who had gone through the hell they had and their comradeship was total. They did not know who James was, nor his rank, apart from the fact that he was a soldier wounded in battle, respecting the loss of his memory, poor sod, for the doctor had impressed on those who knew him, only Sister and herself, the servants and the children, that for a while they must let him heal until, gradually, they were certain, he would find the truth of it himself.

Though the day was bright and cheerful none of them could forget that in the trenches the leaching of the nation's best blood went on relentlessly day after long day in the Battle of the Somme where so many of them had fallen and as far as those who followed it on the map could see, no realistic gains had been made by the British army. The previous month forty-nine of the new and unreliable tanks had been shipped over to France and on the fifteenth of the month they had lumbered monstrously forward with the leading infantry against the German army, three hours later moving through the third German line. It was the greatest gain since the battle had begun.

When the men heard the news they were as excited as schoolboys, telling one another that now they had the Hun on the run, but it seemed their elation was to be short-lived. From what the newspaper reports said there were too few tanks to make much difference and after the initial success the fighting had degenerated into its usual bull-headed contest for every inch of ground.

But they were out of it and for the moment that was all that mattered, though they felt ashamed to think so when they remembered all those still out there. Some of them who were recovering quickly, the strong and sturdy country lads and those who had been built up in childhood with nourishing food their mams had cooked and so had the strength to fight the infections, knew they would have to go back when their wounds had healed but most, and these were men who had lost limbs, or their sight, would go home to their families and thanked God for it.

James placed Rory's stretcher in a patch of sunlight then flopped down in a deckchair beside him. A card game was going on round a small folding table and several men on crutches were stumbling awkwardly along the neat path Clapcott and Licky Thripp kept swept and tidy. The flowerbeds were a vivid blaze of colour, the showy splash of dahlias and stock and zinnia, sweet william, peonies and pinks, and edging the lawns an eruption of lavender, its fragrance a delight to these men who had known the stench of war, the stench of the sickroom. They did not know the names of the flowers but Clapcott, who was anxious to talk to any man who might have known his Bertie, was only too happy to tell them about mignonette and rock rose, hydrangea and delphinium and the correct growing of them.

Lucy turned away with a deep sigh, the open window still bringing in the men's voices. Her bedroom was on the corner of the house and moving slowly from the window which faced west she leaned her hands on the sill of the second and stared sightlessly in the direction of Colwith Woods. They stretched from the winding river to the fell top, hazel and birch and rowan, and so exquisitely lovely at this time of the year as autumn approached Lucy felt the pain of it enter her heart which already ached in a continuous destruction. The grandeur of the fells never ceased to bewitch her, to overwhelm her, to hurt her in some strange way and she studied the great swathe of the bracken already turning from green to brown, the heather from purple to umber, her eyes ready to moisten with tears. She cried very easily these days. The dry stone wall at the back of the house, where a couple of ambulatory wounded were perched in peaceful silence had, during the summer, burgeoned with hedge parsley, dock and nettle, meadow cranesbill, ragwort and foxglove. They were slowly dying away now but over it all the sharp smell of aniseed from the sweet cecily drifted about the gardens so that she could smell it from here.

The old cast-iron fireplace that once had graced the bedroom when Alex and Christy Buchanan had slept here was gone and in its place was an unadorned white marble surround in which a small fire burned. A pretty French clock ticked on the mantelpiece next to a small bowl of late roses. Apart from the fireplace the room was exactly the same as when James's grandparents had occupied it. The flickering flames of the fire gilded to cream and apricot the white lace curtains and the plain white walls, putting a touch of rose in the soft velvet curtains and the two small bedroom chairs, into one of which she sank. The bed, which was enormous, was new, for James was a tall man and liked a bit of space, he told her when they were first married and it had been purchased. She had kept the white theme throughout, with a touch of colour here and there in cushions and the valance above the bed, though James had told her she might change anything she wished. But she had delighted in the pale rosewood furniture, the pale biscuit carpet, rich and deep to the foot and, apart from putting a picture or two on the walls, prints of the French impressionists which she loved, and her own personal brushes, combs and the toilet things her mother had left her, it was almost exactly as it had been a hundred years ago.

There was a tap on the door and at her call it opened and Buffy entered, Alice on her hip. The child, who was thirteen months old now and the pet of every man and woman in the house, with the exception of her own father, was wriggling to get down, shouting her displeasure at Buffy, for now that she was mobile she did not like to be carried.

"I'm just going down now and I wondered if you were coming," and perhaps this time James Buchanan might take more than a polite interest in the child, Buffy's face plainly implied, the child whose charm, laughter, innocence and total unconcern with the disfigurements the men had brought back from France was helping them to come to terms with their own particular horrors.

Looking at Lucy's bowed head, Buffy put Alice down and let her totter over to her mother's dressing-table and climb precariously up on to the stool before it. She reached for the hand mirror, jabbering at her own reflection, smiling and turning the mirror towards them so that they might see it too.

Buffy sat down in the second small chair and leaning forward took Lucy's flaccid hand in hers, her face filled with loving sympathy.

"Don't give up, Lucy, not now when he has come so far. He is almost himself again—"

Lucy laughed harshly. "Don't be a blithering idiot, Buffy. He is far from being himself again."

"Let me finish, Lucy."

"There is nothing more to be said. A man who does not know his own child, his wife, his home where he was born, a man who prefers the company of the man whose life he saved to . . . to any other, clings to him even as though . . . as though he were his lifeline."

"Perhaps he is, Lucy. Rory is the only person James remembers from his past. He *is* James's past and so James cannot bear to be parted from him. He wants to be Rory's legs. I don't know why, I suppose it gives him a purpose in life. All these men have something, a life, a family."

"So has James." Lucy's voice was low and despairing.

"But he doesn't know it, so he holds on for dear life to the one man who knew him before . . . before . . ."

"Oh, don't go on, Buffy, there's a love. I just don't know how much longer I can manage without babbling to him to . . . to wake up, as though he were some bloody princess in a fairy tale. I want to put Alice on his knee and say, 'This is your daughter who once you loved so much,' and me . . . he loved me as well, Buffy."

"He still does, darling."

"Then why doesn't he recognise it?" Lucy's voice rose in despair and the child turned anxiously, her eyes, so like her father's it was incredible, becoming clouded. She hesitated as though she would climb down and run for the safety of one lap or the other but Lucy quietened and Alice went back to her pleased contemplation of her own reflection.

"I've tried to explain to the children, which was the hardest thing I've ever done, especially Percy, that they must not talk to James about . . . about the days before he went away but I know they don't understand. He's lost all memory of those days, I told them and he must be left to find it again by himself, but Margaret wept and said it seemed brutal, that those who loved him must not help him. Percy wasn't even sure what a memory was and I know they are trying so hard. I can see it when I'm with them and James. Just the fact that they are to call him James and not Mr Buchanan as they used to is a mystery that puzzles them. I know that it will slip out . . . something, I don't know, perhaps about the motor car, or the walks we had and I'm convinced that that will be more harmful than this . . . this charade we must all keep up. And then there are the others."

"The others?"

"His family. They can't be put off much longer. He is their cousin and is dear to them. He has been home for almost three months and I am beginning to believe they think that I am holding them off for some purpose of my own. They are offended by what they see as my bloody-mindedness. They've always thought me a bit odd, Buffy, you know that. An unconventional rebel, undisciplined and not like them. I told Doctor Penfold that if James didn't recognise me how could he be expected to recognise Ben or old Mr Buchanan and so where would the harm be, but he seems to be obsessed with the idea that should one of them say anything untoward James might have some sort of relapse. It frightens me, this constant walking on a tightrope. Last week I heard Clapcott call him 'Mister James'. He was about to remind him of something that had happened years ago but he caught himself in time and fortunately James didn't notice."

"Darling, I don't know what to say, except that you can only take the doctor's advice. There are so many men whose minds have been disturbed. That Rory is still inclined to jump at any unexpected sound and that other poor chap . . ."

"Private Matthews?"

"Yes. He'll never get over the sight of . . . you know what I mean." Buffy's face spasmed in anguish.

"Yes, I know." Lucy's face was dark and brooding as she looked into the dark dread which haunted poor Private Matthews who had seen his own wounded comrades, fallen in battle, go under the tracks of the British tanks that had been sent to protect them.

"They all have their own private hell inside them, Buffy, and I suppose that is what James is hiding from. At least I pray that it is," she finished sombrely.

"What d'you mean?" Buffy leaned forward to look into her face.

"I'm hounded by the thought that . . ."

"What, darling?"

"That it might be that bloody letter Charlotte Buchanan sent him. The one that told him about . . . about me and

Rory. He believed it, that is what is tearing me apart, and is that what he's hiding from? Oh, Buffy," her voice was soft and frightened, "it's breaking my heart."

It was the dogs who got to him first and it was perhaps then that memory began to seep, like a dripping tap, drop by slow drop into James Buchanan's empty mind.

There were some children, relatives of the owners of the house, he was told, who spent a lot of time with the wounded men who were well enough to get about outside and when he became one of those, walking out into the bright sunshine pushing Rory in his baby carriage, it was then that he met them. The children and the dogs.

"This is Edward, James," Rory said, somewhat hesitantly, James thought, "and this is Percy, and these are their beautiful sisters, Margaret and Emily."

James nodded pleasantly, waiting for some reaction to his scars but when none came he managed a smile and though they all stared at him with great curiousity he supposed that was only natural. He was still a bit of a freak despite the process of healing that was taking place, with a sort of half smile always about his mouth whatever his mood, but it was better than a snarl, or so Nurse Buchanan told him during one of the delightful little interludes they spent together during the night when all the others were asleep and he was wakeful. Jesus, "one of their little interludes"! It sounded as though they got up to something they shouldn't but it was nothing like that at all. They talked. Mrs Buchanan's husband was an officer in the Border Regiment, she told him when he asked her, her face somewhat strained, reluctant to say more for some reason, and he did not press her, for he did not want to remind her of the terrors of the trenches. She already knew enough of that particular demon from the men she nursed.

The dogs, who he had never seen since it seemed, for the safety of the men who staggered about the front garden, they were kept locked up, were howling in that strangely pitiful way of animals who are distressed and he wondered why. He knew they were taken up on the fells by one of the outside chaps, the fellow they called Jacob who was, apparently, a groom. The children had ponies up in the paddock and he meant to take Rory up there to see them when he was able to get him into a wheelchair. Rory had once ridden to hounds, he told him and loved horses and these were only ponies but he thought he might like to see them. The children had names for them. Cornet, Oliver, Silver and Sally, they had told him shyly, but when he had asked them the names of the dogs that howled so painfully they looked away to Nurse Buchanan, awkward and stiff, the smallest boy ready to reach for her hand. She had changed the subject brightly, sending the children off back to the schoolroom where their lunch was waiting for them, she said.

Today the boy, the eldest boy called Edward, was messing about with a bit of something mechanical, deep in conversation with Sergeant Cooper who was interested in such things. It looked like an old clock and the pair of them were doing something with a screwdriver while the elder girl, Margaret, was reading to a group of young patients, only boys themselves, every one of them taking more interest in the lovely girl than what she was reading. Their eyes were unfocused with peace, their tormented bodies relaxed in their respectful contemplation of her young beauty, while Emily, who was younger, was making daisy chains, of which she was inordinately fond, one for each of them, she told them. The boy, Percy, was darting about the grass with a wooden sword, charging and retreating in some game of his own devising and along the flowerbeds Clapcott and his workmate placidly hoed the dark earth.

It was a beautiful garden, filled with the peaceful tranquillity that the old man who had created it and tended it for so long had brought to it. The terrace, the steps of which led down to the lawns, was lined with terracotta pots of yellow-eyed forget-me-nots and violas. There were benches on the terrace on which men sat enjoying the warmth of the sun on their faces. There were more benches in the shade of the old oak trees which had seen James Buchanan's ancestors stroll under their magnificent arch and at the bottom of the garden a bed of roses: cabbage roses, old white damask and maiden's blush almost overwhelmed them with their heady fragrance.

It was as though a whirlwind had been let loose on them and for several moments there was pandemonium as men in wheelchairs did their best not to be turned head over heels and others like Rory, in stretchers, cowered beneath their blankets, some of them beginning to whimper, for they were, for a moment, flung back into a world of fear. There was the sound of a furious barking, high-pitched and ecstatic, hysterical with joy, and before he could get to his feet they were on him, two enormous black forms, leaping and jumping and placing their huge paws on his chest and his shoulders, forcing him back in the deckchair until it collapsed beneath him. They would not let him alone, licking his face and ears and neck and any bit of flesh they could reach with their rough tongues, still barking in the shrill voice that dogs, even dogs as big as these two, take on when they are overcome with joy.

Strangely, he was not afraid. "Get off me, you devils," he roared and all the men fell silent, recognising authority, as it seemed the dogs did. Though it was evident it would take more than a few words, a barked command to calm them, they had begun to back off a little, enough to allow him to sit up. Still they huddled up close to him, whining now, their joy almost a pain, their strong tails nearly wagging them off their feet, and when he put an arm round each neck they simply shivered against him, their eyes rolling in silent adoration.

"Well, you've made a hit there, old chap," Rory said flippantly, doing his best to cover the total confusion that had fallen over the men. They had never seen the dogs before, and, as far as they knew, neither had James but, by God, it was evident they knew him. They were taking absolutely no notice of anyone else, even though young Edward and even Percy were doing their best to haul the pair of them off James.

"Get off, Holmes, you blighter," Edward was yelling, pulling for all he was worth at the dog's collar, while Percy was doing the same to the one he addressed as Watson, but with little success. They would not leave James's side and, being big, strong dogs, they were having their own way.

"Sit, sit, I say," James said quietly and at once, incredibly, they both sat, though it was very evident it would not be for long.

"You've certainly a way with animals, James," Rory drawled. "They must be well-trained beasts to obey . . . well, someone they are not used to, wouldn't you say?"

James was still sitting on the flattened deckchair, his arms about his bent knees, his eyes looking directly into those of the two dogs who were, though still sitting, inching nearer to him. They were doing their best to obey him but for three months now they had known he was home and, having been kept from him, they were not about to do it again.

From somewhere, probably the same gate that the dogs had forced open, another streak of canine activity raced, this time in the shape of a small, brown Border terrier, prancing and leaping at every seated man, excited beyond measure, until at last it fastened its small black nose on the scent of the man on the ground and, with a yelp of pleasure, swarmed all over him.

"Dear God, not another one," James groaned, beginning to laugh. "Where in hell's name have you come from and why am I the recipient of all this bloody rejoicing? Go and lick some other bugger to death and let me get to my feet," and at once they were all laughing and as Lucy ran across the lawn, Buffy hobbling behind with the protesting Alice in her arms, it was this sight that met her frantic gaze. She had seen it all from her bedroom window and after a frozen moment of horror had raced down the stairs and out of the front door, convinced that some dreadful catastrophe was to befall them all. But it seemed James saw nothing wrong in the three dogs singling him out and though she had distinctly heard Edward and Percy call the labradors by their names, James appeared not to have caught on.

She sat down in a vacant chair after dragging Thimble on to her lap where he settled placidly enough, for by now Thimble was three years old and though still a bit inclined to disobedience, was no longer a puppy. She watched James, the expression on his face just as it used to be with his animals, though she had to admit she had never before seen him romp with his dogs as he was doing now. They had him on his back again, and when Percy, who loved a bit of male rough and tumble, threw himself into the fray, rolling over and over on the grass, shouting with laughter as the dogs and James played, not only together, but with him, which was a bit of an eye-opener since Mr Buchanan had never played with any of them before, Lucy waited, holding her breath, for surely this must be the moment when memory would return to James Buchanan. She caught Rory's eyes and she could see the same anxious thought in them. There was no one more urgently in need of James's return to his own life than she was, but James was Rory's friend by now and was this commotion to slip that friend into some sort of appalling limbo from which he would never recover? Would the disturbance – God, what a foolish word to describe chaos – create more harm to James than the gradual return the doctor wanted, or would he suddenly turn to her, recognise her, and Alice, who was ready to join in what seemed like enormous fun, and . . . and what? Sweet Jesus, she didn't know. She couldn't think properly. She was fixed in a block of ice, in a cast of a longing so great it had set her into the pose of a statue, her face grinning in what she knew was a grotesque image of her own smile.

She turned to look at Buffy. Her heart was fluttering somewhere in her throat and her hands were wet with the sweat of terror. She wanted him back, God how she wanted him back, but she didn't want that return to harm him. What should she do, her expression asked her, but Buffy smiled comfortingly at her, then leaned to take her hand, pulling her from the chair. She led her across the lawn towards the side entrance.

"A cup of tea for everyone, I think, Lucy. Let's leave James with his new friends while you and I go and fetch it. Watch Alice, will you, Margaret," she said over her shoulder, her arm still through Lucy's.

"I'll keep my eye on her, Miss Tyson," Major James Buchanan called after her as his daughter, who was on the grass studying a daisy, crawled over to him, climbed on to his chest then sat on his face and chortled with laughter.

He was awake later that night as she made her way through the ward towards him. There was a moon and the light of it pricked in his eyes in the dark as he watched her walk to where he and Rory now lay in the conservatory. She had changed out of her uniform and for the first time he saw her in a dress, a becoming dress of some soft material, light and gauzy, the colour of which was extinguished by the pale moonlight. Her hair was brushed back and pulled into a loose knot on the nape of her neck, held there by a ribbon. He could smell that light, fresh perfume she always wore. Beside her, for the first time, was the small dog.

"I wanted to bring the labradors," she murmured as she reached him, smiling her lovely sweet smile, "seeing they made such a friend of you today but I knew they couldn't be trusted not to leap all over you again. Thimble is a bit of a nuisance at times but he is considerably smaller and I thought you might like to . . . stroke him."

If Sister saw her with a dog on the ward she would be in for it, she was well aware, but this room was for men who were on the way to recovery and there was little chance of infection. She lifted the little dog on to the bed and at once James's hand went out to it, fondling the rough coat. It was a contact with normality, with the world of peace, free from fear and the horror they had all known and, like the hand she held out to them all, a healer.

"What did you call him, Nurse?" He smiled and his teeth gleamed white in the darkness of his face. "I'm not sure that I should call you that, the way you're dressed. I haven't seen you before . . . out of uniform."

"His name's Thimble, on account of his size. And . . . I just felt like . . . dressing up."

She sat down in the chair beside the bed and waited. She didn't know what she expected. The conservatory, when it was turned into a hospital ward, had been cleared of all the lovely hothouse plants which a past Mrs Buchanan had put there many years ago. But since then, very gradually, Lucy had returned those that could be hung from the glassed arch of the ceiling: the pure white of magnolia mingled with hanging fern and ivy; deep pink, cerise and scarlet bougainvillaea with dark glossy green leaves flowed from their baskets, low enough for the men to see and smell but high enough to suit Sister's insistence on hygiene; camellias, the palest pink and, in a cage where it sang its head off all day, a small yellow canary. It was silent under its sheet now, sleeping with the men whose company it kept.

She knew he was studying her, as a man studies a woman, and she could feel the hot wave of blood beneath her skin, thankful for the cover of pale darkness that surrounded them. When he put his hand on hers which were clasped before her on the bed, she trembled and so did he.

"The dogs knew me, Mrs Buchanan, didn't they? All three of them." His voice was hesitant, unsure, wary, as though he were afraid of her answer. "Won't you tell me? Am I from round here?"

"I didn't know what to say, Doctor. He's not a fool and even in his present state he was aware that the dogs had recognised him and that being so it made sense to him to come to the conclusion that he had been here before. In fact, if the dogs belonged to Howethwaite in some way, then so did he. He knows he's not a servant, his own speech tells him that, and so what is he to this house? I could see it going through his mind, twisting and turning but he was also backing away from it. His eyes were fastened on mine, imploring and yet at the same time afraid, as though there were something he couldn't face."

"What did you do, Mrs Buchanan?" Doctor Penfold's voice was grave. He held one arm across his chest, resting one elbow against it, pulling at his lip with his other hand in a way she knew meant he was very concerned. They stood in her bedroom, for there was always a nurse on duty and so the only place Lucy had with some privacy was the lovely, fire-lit bedroom she had once shared with James. It was made even more cosy today as the bright fire leaped in the grate, for the rain sliced down across the hills and gardens of Howethwaite, darkening the room and putting a weight of moody depression on soldiers who had been, for several weeks now, getting about in the sunshine. There was a different feel to the wards when the sun shone through the long windows, but today it was morose and in the midst of the men James Buchanan sat beside Rory Cameron's bed in total silence, staring at the rain running down the windows, the pattern of the raindrops reflected in his blank face.

"What shall I do, Doctor?" Lucy begged Doctor Penfold. "He was on the edge of something last night, I know he was but he drew back so . . ."

"That's what worries me, Mrs Buchanan. He drew back, which seems to say he's not ready yet to face whatever it is that he's hiding from. I know he is to be awarded a medal for his bravery in bringing back Corporal Cameron and that on that day he must have gone through . . . well, what they all went through which was, we all know, sheer hell, but I somehow cannot believe that it is that which has done this to him. Of course, the shell exploding in front of him concussed him for a while, and who knows what damage that has left, but somehow I don't think . . ."

He watched as Mrs Buchanan, so lovely and vulnerable and so very frail all of a sudden, hung her head, putting both hands to her face. She was not weeping but her expression, what he could see of it, was stricken. She turned away and went to stand by the window, her back to him and he watched her, for he was convinced that there was more to Major Buchanan's loss of memory than the extremes of war that he had gone through. He had, apparently, been a brave and resourceful officer, a striking leader of his men and had been in the trenches since the beginning and not once in that time had he shown the symptoms of shocked terror that afflicted so many. So why, suddenly, had he slipped away into the dark recesses of his own mind, to a place where memory could not reach? If he himself was any judge of the human creature, which, having been a doctor for forty years, he was, Mrs Buchanan knew more than she was telling. He admired her enormously. For two years she had moved among badly wounded men, giving them unstintingly of herself, wearing herself to a shadow of the blithe, spirited girl he had heard she used to be, in the service of these men. She had made a home, a loving home for her brothers and sisters, protecting them from the worst of what the war was doing. She gave time and patient love to her child and supervised her servants and the running of the house and the hospital, and now she was forced to pretend she didn't know her own husband who was sitting beside the man whose life he had saved with a look of unutterable sadness on his face.

"Is there . . . something more, Mrs Buchanan?"

She stood for perhaps thirty seconds, staring out into the soggy landscape which yesterday had been golden with sunshine then she turned to face him.

"Yes," she said simply.

"Would you like to tell me?"

"I'm surprised you don't know. Everyone in the area does . . . did at the time. Before last Christmas. The gossips had a high old time of it."

"I don't listen to gossip, Mrs Buchanan."

"No, I wouldn't suppose you did." She sighed sadly, then moved to the fireplace and sat down in front of the cheerful fire. She picked up the brass poker which stood with a brush on a "tidy", poking the glowing embers with a listless hand, indicating to him that he should take the other chair.

He hesitated. "I haven't much time, Mrs Buchanan. I'm sorry, but that lad with the stomach wound . . ."

"Private Ernie Henshaw."

"You know them all by name, don't you, lass? They're real people to you."

"Oh, yes."

"I cannot believe that you have done anything, *anything* in your life that would turn your husband against you, Mrs Buchanan, if that's what you're going to confess to me."

"No, I haven't, but my husband believes I have."

"Aah . . ."

"Or should I say James Buchanan did and the awful, ironic thing is that it concerned Rory Cameron."

The doctor raised his bushy grey eyebrows in amazement and disbelief. "Rory?"

"Yes, he's been here before, did you know that?"

"Sister did say . . ."

"Shell shock. He was in a bad way, Doctor Penfold. Out of his mind but somehow, I don't know why, he seemed to draw strength from . . . from me."

Dear God, and could you be surprised, Richard Penfold thought. Her flawless beauty was what drew men to her initially, for they were human, male, and would find her irresistible, but what was not immediately visible was her true female compassion, her sweetness of spirit, the indomitable resolve of that spirit which she gave without stint to whoever asked it of her. They leaned on her strength, watched and waited for her, beginning to smile, even those who had suffered appalling wounds, as she came through the door. They drained her in a way, he could see that and yet she always had something in reserve for every man who needed her.

Her voice was sad as she continued, her face pensive as she gazed into the dancing coals. "They sent him back to the trenches, of course, and it was as he left that he . . . he told me that he loved me. He knew, naturally, that there was nothing for him. I loved my husband and my child and . . . well, he asked if he might write to me and if I would answer. He needed . . . something, Doctor, and if I could give it to him by the simple act of writing a letter, was I to refuse? But his letters were . . . love letters and someone heard of them. She knew the officer who censored them, you see. She wrote to James and . . . well, that was the end for him. He . . . we had only just begun to . . . realise our love. It was very fragile and he believed her letter and I am . . . I feel . . . I am certain that that is what he is blocking out. He clings to Rory, the very man I am accused of having an affair with and if he knows the truth . . . Dear sweet Christ, what will that do to him? I am torn in two. I want him to know me, and Alice, his home and family and yet I'm afraid that the knowledge, if it is because of me and Rory, will send him further out of reach."

"So what did you tell him last night?" Doctor Richard Penfold, though he was filled with painful sympathy for this woman, kept his voice steady and calm, not wanting her to know the grave doubts he had of her husband's recovery. Not that he knew a great deal about the mental wounds these men had had inflicted on them. Shell shock, or neurasthenia, and other psychiatric disturbances were a new condition never before studied by the medical profession and loss of memory was one of them. They knew that the human mind had a talent for shutting out what it could not cope with but they had no idea how to treat it, so they walked gingerly round the men who suffered it, hoping for the best, which was all they could do. Great strides were being made in the control of infection, the advancement of surgical techniques and wound control, the management of compound fractures, wound infection and the development of plastic, constructive surgery. They had plenty of patients to practise on, he thought bitterly, and there would be more as the war raged on but at the moment he was concerned only with this woman's husband

"I was stunned when he said that . . . about the dogs and he must have seen my hesitation," she went on. "Immediately he turned away, not waiting for an answer, saying he was tired and, in a way, dismissing me. He is on the verge of knowing, I'm sure of that, Doctor. Little things: he knows his way about the grounds, for instance, and . . . oh, I can't remember, but things he wouldn't know if he had never been here before. He looks at me with those piercing grey eyes of his and I swear he knows me, but then if that is so and he believes the tale about me and Rory, why does he still stick like a burr to Rory's side?"

"I don't know, my dear. I wish I did." A deep sigh accompanied the doctor's words. He rose to his feet, glancing at the clock. "I'm afraid I must go, Mrs Buchanan, so all I can say is that we can only carry on in this fumbling way until we learn more and hope that it is for the best. I have several colleagues in London and I think I might write to them and see if they can shed some light on what is the safest thing to do. Just waiting like this is unbearable for you, I know." He put a gentle hand on her shoulder. "Bear up, my dear, and pray."

"I do, Doctor, for all the good it does."

It was a week later when the discreetly black Vauxhall drew to a graceful halt at the bottom of the sweep of steps that led up to the open front door of Howethwaite. A smartly clad but elderly chauffeur got out and opened the door at the rear. As there was no one about to welcome them in the shape of a butler or footman, the old couple who had alighted, and the young woman who accompanied them, moved up the steps and into the wide hallway. The older woman carried a bunch of chrysanthemums, glowing in a blaze of bronze and gold, tied about with white satin ribbon.

"Where's the carpet, Job?" she asked in consternation, looking about her at the chequered black and white tiles of the floor. "What on earth have they done with the carpet? I can remember when these black and white squares were covered up by . . . oh, dear, who was it put the carpet down? Was it your grandmother, or perhaps Sara? She always hated the black and white squares, though I thought they were wonderful when we were children. I can remember playing hopscotch."

"Yes, dear." The stooped, white-haired old man patted her arm tenderly as they both peered round looking for someone to receive them as they were accustomed to being received, but there were only a couple of men in hospital blue, one on crutches, the other with one arm, the sleeve of his uniform neatly pinned up.

The young woman was icily beautiful, like a princess in a fairy story, the soldiers were inclined to think, staring in wonder at her magnificently clothed and curved figure and the enormous cartwheel of a hat perched dashingly on her silver pale hair. She looked quite magnificent. She had recovered from the birth of her son and though Paul had not been home since he had impregnated her, she had made a vow to herself that when he did, come home, she meant, there would be no repeat of the act that had got her that way in the first place.

Her blue eyes passed over the soldiers unseeingly as she peered distastefully along the ward on her right which had once been the splendid Howethwaite drawing-room. The rows of beds were filled with men wrapped in bandages, some with their arms held up on splints, others with a contraption of pulleys supporting a leg. Some of them were reading newspapers, others smoking a cigarette, talking to each other quietly about the Somme offensive which still dragged on and which was swallowing the thousands of young volunteers who had enlisted in Kitchener's New Army. Two nurses were bending over a dressing trolley, unaware that they had visitors and when the elegant and imperious figure of Charlotte Buchanan swept between the rows of beds, her skirts held so that they would not touch anything in this dreadful place, they were too astonished to try and stop her.

"Good morning, Nurse," she said, just as she might address one of her own servants. "I've come with Mr and Mrs Buchanan to see their nephew." The men in the beds stared at her in open-mouthed wonder. "I believe he is here and, in fact, has been here for several months. Mr and Mrs Buchanan have been very keen to visit him but . . . well, it seems Mrs Buchanan, Mrs Lucy Buchanan, that is, felt the need to keep them away. They lost their son a year ago so they are particularly concerned to visit James, so we would be glad to be shown to his room."

"His room?" Nurse Pennington gasped.

"Yes, his room." Her expression clearly said that she thought the nurse to be a half-wit and why she was in charge of seriously wounded men was a mystery to her.

"But . . ."

"Dear me, is there no one in charge here?" She swept haughtily past the nurses and their trolley, Job and Mary Buchanan hesitating in her wake. They were not at all sure they should be here, but Charlotte had been so insistent and it would be lovely to see James again. Especially after the loss of Andrew, their only son. They still had Janet and Christine, of course, but the added blow, a blow which had crucified their elder daughter, of the deaths of their grandsons, young Job and Lawrence, was one they could hardly contemplate. And now Anthony, just turned eighteen, had gone, breaking his mother's heart all over again. Out of her four handsome sons, poor Janet had only young Will at home and if this war dragged on he would be the next to go. He was eighteen next year and already talking of enlisting, though not where his mother could hear him.

It was at that moment Lucy Buchanan, who was

bending over the last bed in the conservatory ward where young Private Ernie Henshaw was clinging to her hand, his face grey with pain as his dressing was changed, heard the voice which, for a moment or two, she did not recognise, or if she did, at the very corners of her mind, she flinched away from in horror.

Rory Cameron was reading a newspaper to James Buchanan. There was only the one on this ward and several others were listening to Rory, trying to take their minds off the laboured breathing and harsh gasps of the boy at the end of the ward. James looked peaceful, the withdrawn expression that had hung about him for the past week gone for the moment. Rory was reading to them about the report of the poppy which was growing in the battlefields of Flanders. Legend had it that Genghis Khan, the Mongol warlord, had brought the seed of the white poppy with him in his advance on Europe during the thirteenth century. It was said that the white poppies turned red with the shape of a cross in their centre when they sprang up after a battle and certainly on the Western Front, for had they not all seen it for themselves, the scarlet poppy proliferated on devastated battlefields, particularly those of the Somme.

James's two dogs were sitting patiently on the step of the conservatory door waiting for him to emerge and take them up into the wood, a task he had taken over from Jacob since he had renewed his acquaintance with them, though it was very evident that his mind was still in a state of total confusion. It was as though he had come to some sort of crossroads in his condition and was not sure which path to take and so he stood there, waiting, no one was awfully sure for what, least of all himself. He was conscious that the dark veil which had hid something from him for almost three months was becoming lighter, not quite as opaque as it had been, and through it he had glimpsed vague shapes, sounds, smells which were familiar to him though he didn't know why. From his past life, he supposed, but still he hung back from it, immersing himself in the comradeship of the wards, the men on them, with helping Rory to recover. Rory would be measured for two false legs very soon, for there was no way he was going to sit on his arse for the rest of his life, he had laughed, and James meant to be there to get him up on them. In a way, Rory was his responsibility. He had brought Rory back from death and he meant to make sure Rory had the very best chance he could. One day, when he himself knew who he was and where he came from he would take Rory there and continue to look after him until the lad was back on his feet. He almost felt as though Rory were his son, for after all there were fourteen years between them.

Lucy had reached the chair he sat in at the same time as Charlotte and on her face was a look of such horror, Rory, who had looked up as the exotically beautiful woman approached, as they all did, for she was like a young queen, put out his hand, he didn't know why. To stop something, again he didn't know what, but there was a look of triumph on the unknown woman's face to match the horror on Lucy's.

"Lucy," she cried extravagantly, "how good it is to see you after all this time. And James, too. How are you, James? You certainly look well," though it was in her eyes for all to see, including James himself, that she did not really think so, not with all that scarring which, in her opinion, made him look like some freak in a show.

James rose to his feet uncertainly, the manners taught him as a child not forgotten. He was hampered by Lucy's closeness as she did her best to protect him from this woman who had damaged their lives so dramatically. It was evident she wanted to draw him away, tell him to run up to the schoolroom where he would be safe from fresh hurt, as she would one of her brothers or sisters, to get him away from further damage and if she had to put her arms about him, even carry him on her back, she would do so to save his sanity, which she was sure would be threatened if this woman had anything to do with it.

"James, oh, sweetheart, how lovely to see you," quavered Mary Buchanan from behind Charlotte, doing her best to get to her nephew and put her arms about him, but she hesitated when she saw his scarred face, putting her hand to her mouth in confusion. "It *is* James, isn't it?" She turned to her husband imploringly and put her hand in his and the lovely bouquet fell to the floor.

The room was in total silence, even the two VADs frozen to the polished floor in their dismay. James had been with them for nearly three months and though they knew, of course, of his condition, they had not the faintest idea who he really was. The doctors would know, and probably Sister Colyford, and until the amazing occurrence of last week when the Buchanan dogs had greeted him with such ecstatic joy had believed him to be from . . . well, somewhere, but certainly not about here. There had been talk on the wards, among the nursing staff and the men and now, from nowhere, here were three people, two of them related to him, come to visit him.

And would you look at Mrs Buchanan! If her eyes had been daggers that gorgeous creature in the cart-wheel hat would be lying dead at her feet pierced to the heart. She was pulling at James's arm and begging him to come away but he seemed to be fixed to the floor, staring at the three visitors in total incomprehension.

"Go away from here, Charlotte," Mrs Buchanan hissed venomously. "You have done enough damage already. There are men who are ill and need peace and quiet and . . ."

"Well, I'm certainly not going to upset them, Lucy, and I'm sure Mr and Mrs Buchanan wouldn't dream of it, would you?" turning to the bewildered old couple who still were not sure whether this scarred soldier was their James, though he certainly had James's build and, of course, his eyes. It was the eyes that decided them.

"Job, of course it's James. He has Grandmother Buchanan's eyes, can't you see? Oh, James, James, it's Aunt Mary and Uncle Job. We had heard you were home but were allowed no visitors so we kept away but Charlotte here . . ."

"Charlotte here had to come and stir up fresh trouble, is that it, Charlotte?" Lucy was beside herself with terror and rage, for how was this to affect James? "Not content in writing lies to my husband about Rory . . . Dear God, let me keep calm. James, see, darling, come away with me. Let's go into the garden, shall we?" She was doing her best to be calm, normal, pretending for his sake that there was nothing untoward about these people, though her face was stiff with shock. "Look, the dogs are waiting for you. Would you like to . . . to . . . would you like me to come with you to . . . oh, please, James, do come with me."

Rory Cameron was looking at James who was retreating further and further from this commotion that was washing over him in great crashing waves. Rory could see it, all the progress that had been made in the tranquillity of this house and this woman whose husband he was, the other men and their acceptance of him, the children, smashed into a million pieces by the gloriously beautiful woman who had the eyes of the devil in her face. She was smiling, turning to look at him now, fully aware it seemed to him of who he was, ready to twist further in the knife she had apparently aimed at James all those months ago when she must have written to him to say that his wife was . . . what? It didn't take much working out to realise that she had told him that Lucy was having an affair with a private, as he was then, by the name of Rory Cameron. No wonder James had gone mad with it, particularly when added to what he was going through at the front. It was all clear to him now. There had been no truth in it, of course, but this woman had made James believe it, totally devastating the man he had once been.

"And this is Rory Cameron, I believe?" Charlotte Buchanan's voice was a gentle murmur of politeness. "We had heard you were James's special friend after he had saved your life which, in view of what happened here while James was away, seems very odd, but then who are we to judge what a person will do, or not do, in times of war. Now then, we mustn't keep these brave soldiers from their rest, must we?" turning solicitously to look about her at all the brave soldiers who were listening and watching in fascinated silence, knowing something was being destroyed here but having no conception of what it was. She took the arms of Mary and Job Buchanan who were like children in her grasp. "Say goodbye to James," she was telling them and obediently they parroted her words, but as she turned to glide away up the ward taking them with her, every man and woman in the room, including her, felt the hairs rise on the backs of their necks as James Buchanan shook off his wife's restraining hand with a roar that could be heard in the schoolroom and sent Alice Buchanan scurrying for Buffy's protective arms.

But it was not at Charlotte Buchanan that his bitter rage was directed but at the man in the bed who had been, though he couldn't walk himself, his crutch for three months. Before they knew what he was about, any of them, even Lucy, who was totally unprepared for it, he had flung himself at Rory Cameron and grasped him round the neck.

"I'll kill you for this, you bastard," he screamed, squeezing his fingers deep into the slender neck of the defenceless man. Outside, disturbed by the uproar inside, the two dogs had begun to bark furiously, leaping and crashing against the door, for all they were concerned with was the safety of their master. All along the ward men began to shout, some of them to whimper, others trying to get out of their beds to go to the aid of the soldier who was being strangled by another, while Charlotte Buchanan, who had by now reached the door into the hallway, turned round for a last jubilant look at the chaos she had caused. The old people were horrified, calling out to James to behave himself, as though he were still a boy at school having a go at another. From everywhere medical staff were racing, seeing only James apparently trying to wring the life out of Rory Cameron, his friend and support, while at his back, *on* his back, screaming into his ear, Nurse Buchanan was completely unsuccessful in stopping him.

"A syringe, Sister," Doctor Penfold bellowed, medical professionalism thrown to the wind as he and several nurses flew down the conservatory ward, pushing aside anything and anybody who got in their way. It was total chaos as soldiers fell back on to their beds and even Mrs Buchanan was thrust on to her back as the doctor, Nurses Cartwright, Atkinson and Stephens, all big, strong women who were well versed in the control of obstreperous patients, began to haul on James Buchanan's arms. Sister Colyford appeared, carrying a syringe containing something she knew the doctor wanted, and without bothering with anything like antiseptic, or even the barrier of his trousers, plunged it into James's buttock. It took no more than a moment or two as he struggled to fight against it, and then, for there was enough in the syringe to fell a horse, she told a distraught Lucy later, then he grew limp and fell, though he was not aware of it, into the arms of the man he had been trying to kill.

They put him to bed in the same small room where once Rory Cameron had grovelled under the bed, locking the door and barring the window. He was still deeply drugged when Lucy and the doctor looked in on him last thing that night. When they unlocked the door the next morning he had gone.

The two big, black dogs moped about the stable yard, lying down for a brief moment then getting up to sniff miserably under the gate through which James Buchanan must have gone. They had been found shut up in the tack-room, which was not where Jacob had left them the night before, so it seemed evident, the authorities said, that Major Buchanan had put them there. An ancient greatcoat, a woolly scarf knitted by Mrs Bunting and a cap belonging to Jacob were missing, along with a raised game pie, a loaf of bread, a lump of the Lancashire cheese of which Mr Dixon was especially fond, and a bottle of whisky.

Buffy sat quietly and watched Lucy stride up and down her bedroom to where, with every room in the house either packed with children or servants, wounded men or being used for some purpose in their medical care, those who wished to speak to her came. The house was in turmoil, with Mrs Bunting and Mrs Burns tearfully telling one another in the kitchen that they had known no good would come of all this secrecy in the matter of Mr James and his loss of memory. Surely, if he had been given the facts, the facts being that Mrs Buchanan was his wife, that

Miss Alice was his daughter and Howethwaite was his home, he would have been far happier and none of this would have happened. It was unnatural to keep from a man his family and Mrs Bunting had told them all so, at least those in the kitchen, time and time again.

"Well, the doctors didn't seem to think so," Elsie ventured bravely. "I don't know the ins an' out of it, but . . ."

"Then I should keep me lip buttoned if I was you, young lady," Cook lashed out at her, and then was sorry, for Elsie was a good girl and as concerned as them about poor Mr James. Where could he have got to? they asked one another and Cook was comforted by the thought that he had on that warm scarf she had knitted for Jacob though Jacob was not best pleased about it, nor his coat which had gone missing.

"Yer should be ashamed of yersen, Jacob," she had cried, dreadfully upset. "How can yer begrudge him a bloomin' old coat when the master might be wandering them there hills, and in this weather, an' all," for it had turned cold and drizzly. "I'm only glad he took that pie, an' bread an' cheese wi' 'im an' the whisky'll put a warm fire in his belly, poor lad."

Lucy told herself the same thing, directing her remarks at Buffy who had not moved from her side since the discovery that James was gone. Smashed the window and forced back the shutters, he had and it was a wonder no one had heard him, they said, though Jacob did admit to hearing them dogs for a few seconds. They had settled at once and he had turned over and gone back to sleep. James must have had a key to the house since he had simply let himself back in and helped himself to the food from the kitchen. Oh, he had had his wits about him, there was no question of that, preparing himself for what lay ahead of him and really, were those the actions of a man who was out of his mind? Lucy demanded.

He had to report James's disappearance, Doctor Penfold patiently told James Buchanan's almost de-ranged wife, looking for confirmation to Doctor Yates who had just come on duty, holding her firmly by the upper arms as she tried to break away from him. Despite his age he was strong.

"No, oh, please, Doctor Penfold, no! Doctor Yates, tell him," for Doctor Yates had been the Buchanan family doctor for many years before he retired. "He's not a violent man, not usually. He was . . . not himself when he attacked Rory. He had been provoked by that bitch . . ." Her face spasmed with bitter hatred and if Doctor Penfold had not seen it for himself he would not have believed that Mrs Buchanan could summon up an expression of such malevolence.

She flung herself away from him and resumed her frantic pacing of the room, constantly returning to the window to peer out through the thin veil of drizzle that drifted across the empty garden. It was as though she might see him there, catch him before he flitted off again to some secret place only he knew of and she must be at the window or she would miss him. Her hair was wild about her, falling in a long cape of dark, glossy brown down to her buttocks, for she had been brushing it when Doctor Penfold had knocked on her door. She had on her uniform and the pristine whiteness of it was no paler than her face.

Buffy spoke for the first time, trying to catch her

friend in one of her demented whirls. "Lucy, calm down, darling. You must take a hold."

"Don't tell me to calm down, Buffy Tyson," she spat out. "How can I be calm when only God knows what has happened to him? I love him so much, you see, and I cannot forgive myself."

The two doctors were seen to bend their heads in enormous pity for the sorrowing woman, but it was Buffy who spoke again.

"Darling, it's not your fault."

"Maybe not but that does not make me less responsible. I should have stayed with him. I was not there when he needed me and . . ."

"Mrs Buchanan, don't torture yourself like this. It is not healthy. He must be found, and soon." Doctor Penfold put his hand on her arm but she shook him off violently and he backed away. Nevertheless he continued to speak. "We cannot have him wandering about in his condition, whatever it might be by now. No, I'm sorry, but it must be said. We don't know how this has affected him. He may be even more disturbed."

"He was alert enough to take some warm clothing and food which surely proves he was thinking coherently?"

"True. But as I said he must be found. He might be wandering about the fells, losing himself in some—"

"He would never get lost, Doctor Penfold. He knows these mountains like . . . like he knows his own garden. And if he wants to remain hidden there is no one, whoever they may be, who will be able to find him. He has been climbing and walking this area ever since he was a boy. I think he just wants time to . . . to think;

so won't you let him alone for a few days? Don't send the police out looking for him. Let him be. He loves these hills and if he could be given time, time to come to terms with who he is and . . ."

"He might still not know who he is, Mrs Buchanan."

"He knew Rory and what had been said about . . . us; that is why he attacked him, but he wasn't . . . wasn't . . . Oh, I know I keep repeating myself but he wasn't himself."

Lucy slumped down in the chair by her fireside, her head in her hands and felt the comforting hands of Buffy on her shoulders. She reached up and clung to one, keeping her eyes covered with the other. It was all she could do not to leap up and put on her stout boots and go shouting up on the fells for James this very minute and as soon as this lot, meaning the two doctors and the military policemen Doctor Penfold meant to call in, were gone, that's exactly what she would do. She could not believe what the doctor had told her gravely, which was, that by leaving the hospital without permission, James was technically a deserter, though it would not come to that, surely? He had been ill. The doctor would vouch for it and the authorities would acknowledge that fact and accept that as far as the doctors were concerned, he was not in his right mind.

But she did not believe it. Not for a minute. She had seen his eyes for a moment, just before he had leaped, like a man tackling another on a rugby field, on to the recumbent figure of Rory Cameron. They had looked into hers, a soft and smoky grey, the pupils narrowed to tiny black pinpoints, and in them was an expression of such love and joy, of wonder and remembrance she had been ready to lift her arms and enclose him in a miraculous embrace. It had taken no more than the fraction of a second, that glance their eyes had exchanged, then the veil had come down and his face had twisted in a snarl of jealous rage and he had turned to throw himself at the man he thought had taken his world from him.

"There is one other thing, Mrs Buchanan," Doctor Penfold told her hesitantly. She lifted her head eagerly and her hand clung like a vice to Buffy's.

"Yes?"

"Do you remember when your husband first came here and we took his belongings, his wallet and such like? We do that with all the men, as you know, but as soon as they are fit enough they are given back to them. We didn't give Major Buchanan his in case . . . well, he would have known at once who he was, or who he had been and . . . you know the rest, Mrs Buchanan. His documents were in Sister Colyford's office. Photographs of you and your daughter. They are gone."

The man in the long, shabby overcoat pulled his scarf more warmly about his neck and adjusted the peaked cap he wore, tugging it down more firmly over his forehead, then leaned his back against the pitted grey stone of the craggy outcrop behind him. He reached into his pocket and withdrew a packet of Woodbines, grimacing ruefully as he lit one, for it was his last.

"You'll have to do without now, old feller me lad," he murmured softly to himself, settling himself more comfortably into a slight crevice in the rock, trying to get out of the chilly wind which whistled straight from the North Pole, or that's what it felt like. His eyes moved slowly from one horizon to the other, glad that on this, his last day, it was fine and clear, for he knew he was saying goodbye to his home and the beauty in which it stood.

He was standing on the summit of Silver How, gazing down towards Grasmere where the intermingling of crag and conifer, juniper and bracken, was breathtaking in its majestic beauty. There was a mass of timber on the lower slopes and trees persisted even in the crags which fringed the summit, guarding waterfalls, Blindtarn Gill, Wray Gill and Meg's Gill, all the names as well known to him as those of his own family. His eyes roamed over the vale and village of Grasmere far below, and the lake itself. Rydal Water lay sleeping under a silken sheet, no wind today down there in the valley and even the upper reaches of Lake Windermere to the south could be seen and a small corner of Coniston Water. It was all spread out before him, this lovely land of his which he loved so well and he knew he would take it with him in his heart wherever he went. As he would take the woman he loved.

He had seen her again today with the dogs, and heard her calling his name and it had taken all his strength and resolution not to begin the mad run down the scree and slippery slopes the rain had left, to shout and wave and tell her he was here, to whip her into his arms and kiss her until her eyes were blinded with love and hold her curving woman's body which he knew so well against his and to hell with the consequences. She was so loyal and true to her promises, to those she made and those she had been forced to make, for he knew now that she and Rory had never been lovers and that Alice Christina Buchanan was his own child. He knew her and he knew Rory. Rory had been a stranger to him when he had picked him out of the funk-hole and carried him back to safety, but he had come to know him and to love him during the three months they had been together, three months which he remembered now, just as he remembered the whole of his life. He remembered her indifference to him, polite but still indifference, when they first married. She had been gracious with him, as she was gracious with everyone, even complete strangers, and only on that last leave of his had she become warm, responsive to his lovemaking. She had appeared to be sad when he left to return to France but then, perhaps that was the natural sadness anyone would feel to see a man going back into danger. Mrs Bunting had wept and so had that little maid, and to them he was just the master of Howethwaite. It was all an impenetrable mystery, a complicated web of "maybe" and "perhaps" but until he unravelled the complexities of it he could not stay in the same house with her.

They had been searching for him for three days now, the local police and the military police who had been brought in to find him, but he had evaded them easily enough. They had come high, the local men, looking in caves and old quarries, in worn-out mines and outcroppings, but none knew it like he did and so they had gone away, but not her!

She called his name again and again. The dogs were casting round, looking for his scent as she directed them but he had covered his tracks too well, wading in his bare feet through icy cold streams and keeping himself well hidden high above them. He had wept on the first day he saw her, for her cries were harrowing but he could not go back. Not now. He could not even explain it to himself why he should feel like this but he did. He must have time to . . . to get to know himself again. He must pick up his life somewhere and where better than in the place where he had lost it?

He watched her re-enter the belt of trees on the lower slopes, the dogs following her reluctantly, both of them stopping again and again to sniff at the air as though they knew he was here somewhere. He waited for an hour, wishing he had another cigarette as his eyes once more lifted to the hills about him. Helvellyn. Wansfell Pike. Loughrigg Fell. Pike o' Blisco and Pike o' Stickle and Gibson Knot. Loved and familiar names all of them and he printed them more firmly in his mind so that wherever he was he would only need to close his eyes and they would be there.

He looked again to the place where he had seen her disappear and his voice was infinitely soft, infinitely tender as he spoke.

"Goodbye, my love, goodbye."

Pulling his coat and scarf more closely about him he turned away and began the long walk across fell and mountain to Penrith and the railway station there.

She continued searching for many weeks, weeks after she knew it was no use, for he was either dead in a gully or long gone from the area. The womanly curves her husband had longed to hold to him that last time on Silver How had disappeared, eaten up by her grief and terror for his safety, and her positive belief that it was her fault. That she was to blame. That the guilt for this could only be laid at her door and it made no difference who spoke to her, gently, or harshly, as Doctor Penfold tried to do, she would stubbornly shake her head, then, putting on her stout boots and her thick, fleece-lined coat, would call up the dogs and set off again to search for him, or at least a sign that he was still alive.

She found it four weeks after he had gone. She had taken the dogs to the summit of Silver How, going up the rough track from Grasmere, moving between waist-high bracken and a jumble of boulders. There was a cairn, several cairns at the top and a huge outcropping of rock and it was here that the dogs went wild. They began to yelp and run round in mad circles, their noses to the ground, moving outwards in circles, almost talking to one another as Holmes lost the scent for a moment and Watson picked it up again. They set off in a northerly direction, still running with their black noses to the ground, casting this way and that and it was not until she bellowed to them to come back that they stopped for a moment to look back at her as though to ask her what the hell she wanted, for couldn't she see they were on important business. Their massive heads nodded at her and their tongues hung from their mouths and she could see they longed to be off but she put that sharp crack in her voice that James used to make them obey him and reluctantly they came back to her. They sat where she put them, side by side, constantly looking over their shoulders towards the north-east but by then she had seen the cigarette stub. Only a bit of a soggy end with a shred or two of tobacco still clinging to it, and when she pointed to it with a shaking finger both dogs nosed at it curiously then sat down and began to howl. Again they wanted to be off, moving along the path towards the Langdale Edge but she had them by the collar now, and as they sat impatiently once more she knelt down beside them, an arm about each strong neck and began to weep.

"He's still alive . . . he's still alive," she whispered into their ears. "He had a cigarette here and then began to walk . . . you've shown me the direction. Dear God, he's still alive."

She was jubilant for about a week, going about her work on the wards, ready to whistle and sing and the men elbowed one another saying that their cheerful Mrs Buchanan was back with them again, for they had all heard the good news. James was still in the land of the living, or at least he had been . . . well, they couldn't really say, and, when she began to think about it, neither could Mrs Buchanan, and it was then that the euphoria of finding the cigarette end and the reaction the dogs had displayed to the spot on the summit of Silver How began to wear off.

"I'm going to go back, Buffy," she said one night when she and her friend were sitting drinking cocoa in her room before going to bed.

"Go back where?" Buffy put her mug on the side table and leaned forward to look into Lucy's face.

"To Silver How."

"Darling, what is the use? James isn't there now and there seems no point in—"

"No, not now, but he was there, Buffy, and the only way I'm going to find out where he went to from there is to take the dogs and let them . . . just go. They'll find his scent and—"

Buffy was aghast. "Lucy, it's the first of November

474

tomorrow and the winter is beginning to close in. You can't just go tramping about on those fell tracks, sheep trods most of them, not knowing where they are going to lead you. Even Mr Buchanan . . ." meaning Mr Ben Buchanan who had been over with the rest of the family to remonstrate with her hotly over what they saw as her dereliction of duty in not consulting with them on the matter of her husband's illness. It didn't seem to concern them that she had been following Doctor Penfold's precise orders. They felt that it had been a mistake and to prove it look where it had led! Ben was the head of the family, for you could not count the old gentlemen, Job and Harry, and Lucy should have brought him over to talk to the doctors. The shouted argument had been heard on the wards and Sister had been forced to come up to her room, where they had all been perched on whatever seat they could find, to ask them to respect the men who were ill.

"Buffy, d'you think I give a damn what Ben Buchanan says, or any of them? The only one I had any respect for was Franny and as she's not here to put in her twopennyworth I shall make my own decision. I must go soon before the scent fades."

"Perhaps it has already done so."

Lucy put her mug on the hearth and in a great surge of pain leaned into her own arms and bent her head. Her voice was muffled. "Don't say that, Buffy, please, it's all I have to cling to. The hope that I might find where he has gone to. He might be working somewhere quite close by and I would never forgive myself if I didn't try and find him. Oh, Jesus, why did he leave me like this? Why did he go without speaking to me? Why didn't he give me a chance, Buffy? I know he loves me and I love him but something has sent him away from me and if I can't find out what it is I shall go mad."

"No, you won't, Lucy, not you. You're the strongest woman I've ever known and your dear mama and papa would be proud of you."

Lucy lifted her head and her eyes were blind with tears, dewed to a deep golden honey, the lashes round them spiky and separated.

"I haven't thought of them for weeks, Buffy. Not once. Even my child has retreated from me as though she realises that I am not really giving her my full attention when I should. Well, there is only one way to settle this." She lifted her tousled head and Buffy reached for her hairbrush and, standing up, moved behind Lucy's chair and automatically began to brush the thick, gleaming weight of her hair.

"You're going then?" Buffy's voice was fearful.

"Yes. I have to, Buffy."

But it seemed the harsh Lakeland winter had decided to thwart Lucy Buchanan's plans, for on the next day, just as Lucy was fastening the laces of her heavy boots, it began to snow, the first delicate flakes drifting down from the leaden skies Lucy had scarcely noticed.

There were not as many men on the wards now, as those who recovered and were sent either home or back to the front were not replaced, for the war had faltered into what seemed to be a winter lull. The Somme offensive was dragging on until, with the advent of winter rains which came in November, when the exhausted, hungry men could no longer drag themselves through the deepening mud, it died away

in disappointment and despair. The BEF was astride
the ridge originally occupied by the Germans but for
this ridge the British and the French between them had
lost in the region of 600,000 men. Time to call it a day
until the next battle, those high up said and the poor
tattered armies, on both sides, breathed a collective
sigh of relief.

"Damn and blast it to hell," Lucy swore when she
saw the snow. The time was ideal for her to take some
days off, for with the wards quieter she could easily be
spared, but with this snow, which even after half an
hour was beginning to drift, she could not chance it.

"I'll wait until tomorrow," she promised Buffy, then
went along to the schoolroom to spend some time
with her sisters and her daughter. Edward and Percy
had set off for school early that morning, riding their
bicycles at breakneck speed down the drive, turning
to wave at the men who watched them go, some of
them scarcely older than Edward.

"They'll not get far on them things," Sergeant Higginbottom remarked sagely, lighting his pipe and turning round to nod at the younger men. Sergeant
Higginbottom was a country man, a farm labourer
from Lancashire and knew the look of the weather
like no other man on the farm he had worked. This
wasn't no bit of a snowstorm, he promised them, and
them lads'd not be seen again today, which turned
out to be true, for just before the telephone lines
came down, dragged by the weight of snow, Mr
Joliffe, headmaster at Fellthwaite Grammar School,
telephoned to say that he was keeping Dean Major
and Dean Minor overnight and Mrs Buchanan was
not to worry about them. He and Mrs Joliffe would

look after them and send them home as soon as it was fit.

Those at Howethwaite did not see them for three whole weeks, though Edward was furious about it, saying that old Jollops was nothing but a Mary Ellen since he and Percy could have walked home after three days if they had been allowed.

"And wouldn't be able to get back," Lucy told him, raising her eyebrows with some irony.

"Well, probably not," Edward grinned, "but have you any idea what sort of food Mrs Jollops serves up? Dear Lord, I've seen Mrs Bunting put better stuff in Mr Clapcott's pig bucket."

The children had been quite devastated by James's disappearance. The two girls and Percy had wept bitterly, begging anyone who would listen to them, including the police who combed the area, to allow them to go too. They knew the hills, Percy said seriously from his manly position of just eight years old. James, as they had got used to calling him, had taught them all sorts of things like which side of a tree trunk moss grew on and things like that and if only he could be allowed to give them a hand he was sure, with Thimble and Holmes and Watson to help him, he would soon track James down. He had been incensed when Lucy had forbidden any of them to go out with her, saying it was better for the dogs to be undistracted.

"I wouldn't distract them, Luce, honest," he told her earnestly. "Please let me go with you," for Percy had found he had liked the new Mr Buchanan enormously. He was quiet and patient and of course they had all heard of his bravery in bringing Corporal Cameron back from the funk-hole. And his face hadn't been bad at all. At least Percy didn't think so. It was a bit puckered and a funny colour at first but nobody had minded, not even baby Alice.

The snow grew deeper and deeper, the next morning when daylight came, what there was of it, revealing the still solidly eddying curtain of it stretched from tree line to tree line. It reached up to the windowsills and covered the drystone wall that surrounded the house and it had taken Jacob almost an hour to flounder from his room above the stable to get something to eat in the kitchen and then to wallow back again to see to the ponies in their warm stalls. The men were quiet, absorbed with the sheer magnitude of it, for they were from cities like Manchester and Liverpool and Bolton and were only used to the poor stuff which fell there and which turned to grey slush the minute it hit the ground. When it stopped and the sun beamed from a hard blue sky, they looked out to the frozen, crystallised whiteness of trees and shrubs which were hung with a sparkling, breathtaking loveliness. Every branch and leaf was illuminated a thousand times over with a dazzling reflection from the sun's rays and they told one another in awed voices they had never seen anything like it before. They simply sat or lay in their beds and gazed at it in silent, stunned wonderment.

As they watched there was a great shout and the children erupted from the side gate, wrapped about in scarves and mittens and bobble caps, for by now Mrs Bunting's efforts with her knitting needles had become very creative. Margaret, at almost sixteen, was quite exquisite with that fresh and innocent look of a girl on the threshold of womanhood and the men were almost ashamed to find themselves watching her as she threw snowballs at the windows, making them flinch back for a moment as though the snow could reach them. The boy, Edward, was just seventeen and thought himself to be no end of a fellow but he was a nice lad and full of fun. He was busy in the construction of a snowman, for he liked to build things, did Edward, whether it be mechanical or something simple such as this. The two younger ones were pelting one another with snow, their faces a laughing poppy red and when Mrs Buchanan came to join them, waving to them all and laughing as she had done before James left, they all told one another wistfully that, given his legs, or his arm or even his sight, for the men who were blinded were having the scene described to them, they would be out there too.

Winter moved on with its inevitable mixture of snowstorms, aching days of bitter frost, of blinding sunshine and deep blue skies and it was not until April when the United States of America entered the war that the next blow came to break the already fragile heart of poor Mrs Buchanan.

The Battle of Arras, as it was later to be called, began on 9 April, the very day young Will Gunson left to join the Border Regiment into which all his relatives had gone and in which, on his eighteenth birthday, he had enlisted.

It was a bank holiday and the two boys were not at school, so they did not discover Edward was missing until nightfall. His bed had been slept in, for Elsie had made it, and that of young Percy, and in her fluster to turn out Mrs Bunting's and Mrs Burns's bedrooms, which she had been ordered to do by Mrs Burns, she completely overlooked the envelope with Miss Lucy's name on it which stood on the dressing-table propped against a pile of books. The room always looked as though one of them there shells had hit it, she had been known to say to Mrs Burns, even when they had lived at the rectory, littered with whatever them lads had been busy with when called away. A jigsaw puzzle half done, school books opened and scattered on the beds, an "airieplane" Mr Edward was trying to build, only a little one, of course; clothes strewn about though she had heard Miss Lucy tell them many times that they were to tidy up after themselves, for Elsie had enough to do without clearing their mess up, which was true.

They all ate in the schoolroom now. Lucy and Buffy and sometimes Miss Bradley before she rode home on her bicycle to Fellthwaite, the four older children and Alice. It was more convenient to bring up trays from the kitchen; besides, where else would they eat with the dining-room turned into a ward and the breakfast-room into a second operating theatre? Even James's study had gone, though Lucy had promised not to touch it, but with so many men needing peace and quiet, no room could be spared. All his books, the furniture, the horse prints which lined the walls, his guns and fishing rods, lamps, desk, chairs of glowing leather, his decanter cabinet, all had been carefully wrapped away and put in the attic with so much of Howethwaite's lovely things to await the day when they would be brought out and lovingly restored to their rightful place.

Edward was often at the last minute for his meals. He had so much to do in his busy day, not only his schoolwork, which would come to an end in August when Lucy prayed he would go on to university, but his hobbies, matters he was deeply interested in, first and foremost, of course, his love of things mechanical. The motor car, the aeroplane which was performing such useful and daring activities in the skies above the battlefields of France, and the contraption he was building in the tack-room which he swore would make Mr Clapcott's work with the lawnmower considerably easier.

Lucy sighed and indicated to the others that they were to start. Cook had made a splendid steak and kidney pie, the pastry crumbling, the steam rising and the smell which came from beneath the crust making all their mouths water as it was cut into. There was mashed potato, sadly without the knob of butter Cook usually mixed in with it, for butter was very short, and cauliflower done to perfection, for she did not like to see vegetables turned to mush with overcooking.

"Has anyone seen Edward in the last hour?" Lucy asked irritably, looking round the table at the intent faces of her brother and sisters as they tucked into their evening meal. Even Alice, who insisted on trying to feed herself with the spoon and pusher which had once been used by all the Dean family, was making short work of the plain but delicious meal. On the table where he usually sat Edward's meal was going cold.

"Well?" Lucy asked, exchanging a glance with Buffy, for Edward loved his food and though he might be late when time got away from him he always turned up eventually. Now, as they were about to lay into the apple pie and custard which had been keeping warm on the hearth, he had still not come and Lucy began to feel the creeping dread of something stir in the middle of her chest. She didn't know what the dickens it was but so many dire misfortunes had befallen this family she was frightened, which was silly, she knew, by the smallest thing that happened out of the ordinary.

They all shook their heads and picked up their spoons in preparation for the pie, even Alice waving hers to indicate to her mother that she was ready as well. She babbled something in her new-found vocabulary, for she was getting on for two years old now, something which might have been, "Pie, Mama," and, leaning forward in her high chair, banged in a peremptory fashion on the tray.

"Yes, yes, darling, it's coming." Lucy smiled, for a moment distracted from her small worry by the charm and loveliness of her daughter. If only James . . . if only, if only . . . How many times a day did she say that? she wondered, particularly when she was with Alice who had James's colouring and even in a strange way, the shape of his chin. She looked at Lucy, with James's eyes, a sparkling merriment in them, sometimes a turbulent rebelliousness which Lucy recognised as her own nature but her charm and sweet ways were being missed by the man who was her father, wherever he was, for he had vanished off the face of the earth as though he were dead and buried in it. He wasn't, Lucy was convinced of that, for she felt that her heart would know if his was no longer beating, but it was very hard not to throw a few things in a bag and set out to look for him. The thought was ridiculous, she knew that, for he could be anywhere, north, south, anywhere, so where was she to start? Sometimes when she lay sleepless in the night she became angry with him. Enraged that he should have done this to her and Alice, deserted them both and gone off on some private pilgrimage which had left her bereft and grieving. It was cruel of him, a cruelty which was not like him, but then he had suffered a great trauma and could he be blamed if he no longer thought in that precise and logical way which had once been his?

"I'd better go and look for Edward," Buffy said with an edge of anxiety in her voice and at once Lucy was aware that she was not the only one with a sense of something wrong. "You stay and finish your meal,"

Buffy went on. "I'll just go and ask the servants, or perhaps the nurses . . . he might have been on the wards; you know how he loves to talk to that private who was wounded on an airfield. He was going on about a Sopwith Camel whatever that is, the other day."

"It's an aeroplane, Buffy," Percy said, round a mouthful of apple pie.

"Don't speak with your mouth full, Percy," Lucy told him automatically and he subsided with a resigned sigh, which said he was only trying to help.

Buffy put the envelope in Lucy's hand, her face drained to the hue of suet, her ginger freckles standing out on her skin in tiny spots the colour of Cook's marmalade. Lucy's hand wavered, for it very badly wanted to refuse what Buffy was offering her and every child at the table stopped eating, even Alice, as though she sensed the bleakness that had swept over them all.

"It was in his bedroom," Buffy said simply.

"Well, I never saw it," Percy retorted defensively, ready to cry, it seemed, for these were days when the simplest thing could turn into a tragedy.

"It's all right, darling. It's not your fault." Again Lucy's response was automatic. She pushed her chair back from the table and stood up and they all watched her. Thimble, who had been stretched out before the fire, got to his feet and moved across to her, nosing her hand.

"Well . . ." Her voice was barely more than a whisper. "I suppose . . ." With a sharp movement as though she hated the thing and couldn't wait to get it out of her hand and on to the back of the fire, she ripped it open.

It was very simple.

Dear Luce,

I couldn't stand back any longer, not with all of them gone now. Will was the last. Then there's James, wherever he is and even Franny Buchanan and can I sit at home messing about with schoolboy stuff when I'll be eighteen this year and would have to go anyway. I'm hoping to get something with the . . . no, I'd better not tell you, for I know you'd try to bring me back. Give my love to the brats and say you forgive me.

Your loving brother,
Edward Dean

Not Edward, not her baby brother who had been her boyish support for as long as she could remember, even when Papa was alive. Not cheerful, good-natured Edward who had kept up the spirits of the men on the wards with his passion for making things, things he had shared with them, often bringing one of them back from the brink of hell with his innocent belief that they were as interested as he was in motor cars and aeroplanes and even the motorbike he was hoping to build himself when the war was over. He was no more than a child and someone, herself probably, for she could trust no one else, must go down to the railway station and find out where he had gone. What in hell's name were the military authorities thinking of taking schoolboys into their dreadful war, she demanded. She couldn't bear it, her voice becoming shrill, fighting Buffy off, until they brought Doctor Penfold to take her away, for she was terrifying the children. She'd had enough, she'd hissed at him, breaking away from his arms. She couldn't bear it, she repeated over and over again, and it was not until the wail of the baby and the gasping sobs of Margaret, Emily and Percy finally followed her down the deep well of terror into which she had fallen, that she managed to get a weak hold on to her flailing senses.

"I'm sorry, really I am. It was the shock. I didn't mean to frighten you all, darling," she told Percy who cowered on her lap alongside Alice, both of them fighting for space. Margaret and Emily were held in Buffy's strong embrace on the other side of the fire and at their feet Thimble licked any hand that came within his reach, his eyes dark and sympathetic. "But you see, Edward should not have gone . . . yet. He is not eighteen and besides he had not finished his schooling," as if that mattered, her bruised heart whispered, only his safety. If only she had him here, where he belonged, where he had been last night, lying his full length, which was quite considerable, on the floor, fiddling as usual with something or other, his face absorbed. Where . . . and how had he persuaded the recruitment centre that he was old enough to go for a soldier? But then he was a big lad, strong and well fed and with the war machine gobbling up men, and boys, like some malevolent and greedy giant, would they refuse him, for they needed more and more fodder to feed the monster.

"What will you do, Lucy?" Margaret quavered. "Will you bring him back? I don't want him to . . . to be like those men in the wards. I don't want him to fight."

"I wish I could go with him," Percy said defiantly, though he still clung like the small, frightened boy he was in the only really safe arms he had ever known. "I'd kill all those—"

"Don't, Percy," Emily shrieked, setting off Alice again and there was bedlam for several minutes as Lucy and Buffy and Elsie, who had been sent for to help, since she was part of their family from the old days, calmed them down. Doctor Penfold gave each of them, except Alice who had fallen asleep on her mother's knee, a small sleeping draught and it was not until they were all in their beds, Percy tucked in with Emily, that Buffy and Lucy were able to discuss what should be done.

Buffy spoke first. "I think you should call Mr Buchanan. He knows a lot of people, probably in the War Office, or wherever it is records are kept and they'd be more likely to help him. After all, it's his bloody gunpowder that keeps this war going." Buffy's voice was bitter and Lucy reached out to take her hand. She turned it over, looking at the small palm which still retained the rough calluses gained in her service to the Dean family.

"I honestly don't know what I would do without you, Buffy," she said in a low voice, "and I bless the day my mother brought you home to us. You're like a sister to me."

"Lucy . . ."

"And it follows that Edward is your brother as well as mine. I want to dash off to Windermere and see if he left from there and yet he could have gone up to Penrith, or even Carlisle. His bicycle has gone, Jacob told Elsie, but I know it makes more sense to let Ben Buchanan do the searching. Perhaps a few telephone calls is all that it needs. I know if James was here he would move heaven and earth

. . . Oh, God, oh, dear sweet God, don't take my brother as you took my husband. Buffy . . . Buffy, hold my hand, for I feel I'm going to fall into that deep black hole again. I love them both so much, and I have lost them."

"They're not lost, Lucy, only mislaid for the moment." Buffy shook her hand, trying to lighten the moment but Lucy wept again.

The Battle of Arras continued and in many places the British troops advanced triumphantly. The Canadians captured Vimy Ridge and the Australians broke through the dreaded Hindenburg Line which the Germans had built over the winter months, and the doughboys, the name given to the American soldiers, were coming.

April drifted into May and May into June and the war which had swallowed up Edward Dean guarded him jealously, for he was a brave soldier and a grand lad, those who shared his scrape-hole with him, a small burrow dug out of the side of the trench, told one another. He had had, like all the other young lads who came out with him, no more than a rudimentary bit of training, which, for all the good it did, was a total waste of time, and had it not been for them, old hands, some of the youngsters would not have survived a week. Though he was a big chap he was no more than a boy and his innocent cheerfulness in the face of terror provoked admiration in them and they adopted him as a kind of mascot. Aye, Private Eddy Fellthwaite was a good lad, a toff, they could tell that by the way he spoke, but he never held himself above them. All he wanted was to get posted to some airfield, for his passion was flying. He'd spend hours, when he could, of course, watching the tiny birds swoop about the skies, tracer bullets zipping among them like demented wasps, his face white, his eyes glittering as our lads gave what for to theirs, though sometimes it was the other way around. The trouble was, he told them earnestly, that with the movement of troops and the constant change of the position of trenches as advance or retreat took place, airfields were constantly being changed from one place to another, but he meant to see one, and if he could manage it, work among the aeroplanes he loved. One day, he told them, he would learn to fly and be up there with the other men of the Royal Flying Corps. His hero was Captain Albert Ball, VC, DSO, MC who, at twenty years of age, had shot down forty-three aircraft. He had been devastated, sobbing like a child when they had heard that Captain Ball had been shot down in his turn and, rough chaps that they were, they had held him in their arms and comforted him. They loved him and his tales, the old sweats, of whom there were not many left, and the boys, and when it was rumoured that they were to be on the march again, this time to the Messines Ridge that ran south from the Ypres salient, they jostled to march next to him, for he was their good-luck mascot.

They sang as they marched, even young Eddy Fellthwaite joining in the gruesome words that he had soon learned.

If you want to find the old battalion,
I know where they are, I know where they are.
If you want to find a battalion,
I know where they are,
They're hanging on the old barbed wire . . .

* * *

Lucy wouldn't leave Ben alone, even after weeks of telephone calls and urgent messages left on the desks of all the men he knew who were influential in the War Office and Foreign Office.

"I can't keep on and on at them, Lucy," Ben told her impatiently. "I've tried everybody. They've gone through the enlistment records with a fine-toothed comb and could find no Edward Dean among them. There is only one conclusion to be drawn, lass," softening, for this wife of his cousin's was wearing herself to skin and bone, not only trying to find that bloody young brother of hers, but James as well.

"Yes?"

"That he enlisted under another name."

Her face whitened and seemed to sink in on itself and he remembered thinking that if she lost any more weight she'd be a bloody skeleton.

"Oh, Lord," she whispered. "How are we to find him?"

"You're not, Lucy. There are many men in the army who enlisted under names that are not their own. God knows why. Perhaps men doing their best to escape from something."

"But not Edward," she cried. "He had nothing to hide from."

"Only you, lass."

She looked horrified and he went on hastily, "Oh, I don't mean that how it sounds, but he knew you would do your best to fetch him home and if he had gone in under his own name you might have found him."

"Oh, Ben," she whispered brokenly. "Why must men feel the need to fight?"

"They fight for what they believe in, Lucy."

"But it is so futile."

"Is it? You were willing to knock the block off anybody years ago who stood in the way of women getting the vote, as I recall."

They were in his office at the Emmerson Gunpowder Works beside Elterwater. It was the seventh day of June and across the Channel the Battle of Messines had proved an outright victory for the Allies though the couple in the office were not yet aware of it.

"But that was not the same at all, Ben. We were not willing to spill blood to attain our aims."

"Some of you were pretty violent, as I remember."

Lucy got up and moved to the window, still holding the cup of tea Ben's lady clerk had put in her hand. It was a fine day and the start of a long spell of good weather which again she and Ben were not aware would affect their troops in France. There was a turbulent area of activity going on in the yard as carts were loaded with the barrels of death the Buchanan family manufactured and Lucy shuddered. There were many women among the men, for the war had taken much of Ben's workforce.

"When will it end, Ben? When will they come home to us? Haven't enough of them died yet? Your Henry is sixteen now, so is he to be dragged into it soon? What about poor Janet and Angus? Three of their sons gone and yet young Will still breaks his mother's heart by—"

"He had no choice, lass. They would have conscripted him and let's pray to God that the bloody thing will be over before . . ."

"Before Henry goes?"

"Aye." Ben's shoulders slumped, for the image of

his tall, handsome elder boy marching off as Janet's lads had, put a cold ring of despair about his heart. They all grieved for Janet and Angus, who would never be the same again, even if Will was spared. They were like two old people whose lives were nearly done with, creeping about their empty home in bewilderment, the sharp-tongued, witty woman who had disapproved of this lass standing dejectedly before him, gone for ever.

The victory at Messines prompted those in the know to begin a new offensive at a place called Passchendaele at the end of July, for the weather was good. For two weeks the heaviest bombardment of the war churned up the land into a sodden mass of mud, for by now the rain had begun. A vast morass of craters appeared filled with water and it was across this that the British troops began their attack. Not deterred by the shattering losses on the Somme last year, the soldiers were thrown into battle as though they were invincible, and like the Somme, it was found that they were not and again the hospital at Howethwaite was crammed to the doors with men who had come straight from the trenches. Lucy looked for Edward among them, her heart almost exploding in fear, and at the end of each convoy, gasping with relief when he was not among them. Foolish, she knew, for even as the last one drew away she was aware that he could be lying dead or dying on some battlefield, or having his blood-soaked, mud-encrusted uniform cut off him as she was doing to the lad on the stretcher.

The telephone shrilled in the night and it woke her but she turned in her bed, ready to drift off again into the exhausted sleep her body craved. It would not be for her, she had decided, and when the quiet knock at her door brought her to a rigid sitting position in the bed she could feel her heart begin to leap like a fish on a hook.

Drawing on her robe, she opened the door and was surprised to find Sister Colyford there, immaculately starched as usual but with an expression of some anxiety on her face.

"What . . . what is it?" Edward . . . or James? Dear God . . . Dear God, would she ever know peace again, the thought flashed through her mind while she waited for Sister to strike her down with some appalling news.

"A telephone call, my dear, from a Mr Alex Buchanan."

"Alex . . ." For a moment she was astonished and vastly relieved, for what possible bad news could Alex have to tell her? He worked in London, certainly, but he had nothing to do with . . . with . . . what did he do? She couldn't even remember anyone telling her exactly what Alex Buchanan did for the war effort but she was sure it . . . Oh, God, please . . .

"Mr Buchanan wants to speak to you, my dear. I asked him what he wanted, for if it was . . . bad news I felt it should be told you by . . . by one of us," who are your friends after all this time. It was in the compassion on her face and in her hands which reached out to Lucy in case she needed something to hold on to.

The voice at the other end of the line was tinny and faint, fading and roaring suddenly into her ear in the most odd way. There were crackles and buzzes and for a while she had not the faintest idea what Alex was trying to say to her. She could feel Sister at her back, ready to catch her, she supposed, if the news proved to be too much for her to bear but when she at last heard the name she was so stunned she could not at first take it in. It was soldiers who were wounded, or killed, and those who were out there to help them just did not fall in battle, or so she had liked to believe, though she knew that was absolute claptrap.

Slowly she replaced the receiver, beginning to shake, allowing Sister to lead her to the chair that stood by the telephone.

"Who . . . ?" Sister paused delicately.

"It's . . . that was James's cousin in London." Her voice sounded hollow even in her ears and she could feel shock beginning to take her over but she must not give in to it, for she was needed and she must make arrangements . . . trains . . .

"Is it a relative?"

"Yes, his wife."

"His wife?"

"Yes, she's an ambulance driver . . . *was* an ambulance driver in Flanders. She was changing a tyre . . . Oh, Franny, how you laughed when you said you were to learn the . . ." She could feel an almost hysterical need to laugh herself, for she could clearly remember that day when Franny had told them in that droll way she had that she was to learn how to service her own vehicle, but she thrust it away, clinging to Sister Colyford's kind hand and being dragged back to reality by her wise eyes. She had waited for this telephone call for weeks, months, dreading it but expecting it daily, waited to hear a voice at the other end of the wire telling her that her beloved husband was dead, that her beloved brother was no more and not once had it occurred to her to give a thought to

Franny who was the most courageous woman she had ever known. Franny who had gone to Flanders for a bit of adventure.

"She was hit by shrapnel, Sister, and they are bringing her home. Alex has asked for me and I must go."

"Of course you must. I'll send for Miss Tyson to help you to pack and I myself will telephone the railway station to find out the times of the London trains. You did say London, didn't you?"

The journey from Windermere was long and wearying. At every station the platforms were crowded with soldiers but she had little luggage and she had been lucky at Windermere to find a seat. She felt quite strange in her elegant dress and flowery hat and she could see the men eyeing her as though wondering who in hell she was, travelling down to London in a crowded train looking as though she were off to Ascot. She had no conception of her own beauty but they had and she found one or the other of them looking at her as though she were some miracle that had come among them. They smiled when she did, shy with her but there was little conversation. These men knew they were going back into battle and that the likelihood was that they wouldn't ever come this way again. They were weary of war after three long years but when the train steamed into Euston station in the light of a chilly grey dawn they jostled with one another to lift her small bag down from the luggage rack.

She had never seen so many soldiers in her life and so many trains taking them away, while others brought back those who were no longer any use at the front.

The sound of marching feet drifted in to the station hall and she watched until they came into view, uniformed men moving steadily in columns of four, their heads held high, their shoulders erect, betraying no sign of their reluctance to go back to the trenches.

She managed to get a taxi-cab to Kensington where Franny and Alex's smart little house lay, though she had never been there, or even to London. A milkman clattered his way along the road and he eyed her with the same degree of astonishment the soldiers on the train had done. She moved slowly up the steps and rang the bell and when Alex, his face white and strained, opened the door, she fell weeping into his arms, the first tears she had shed for Franny Buchanan who had teased her and provoked her but who had always been her friend.

"She's being brought back today. I've arranged for her to go straight to a private hospital. After all" – Alex gave a shaky laugh, reaching for Lucy's hand – "she can't be expected to be put among all the other wounded soldiers, can she, though if I know my Franny, that's exactly what she would have relished. And she is a soldier, Lucy. She was wounded in battle just like all the other brave and broken men who are pouring back across the Channel. The hospital is quite near here and the sister in charge has promised to ring as soon as Franny arrives. I wanted to go the station and meet . . . meet her, but they advised against it. An ambulance will pick her up and take her to . . . to the hospital and then, when . . . when she is . . . when they can tell me . . . I am to go . . . Dear God, Lucy, what am I to do if she . . . They said, others said, that I shouldn't have let her go but you know Franny. When did she ever listen to anything anyone advised her? I couldn't stop her, wouldn't stop her, for like you I believe women, as well as men, must decide their own course of action but if . . . if she should . . . if she doesn't recover I'll never forgive myself."

"Don't think like that, Alex." Lucy was appalled to

see the anguish which had Alex in its frightening grip. They were sitting in a pleasant room furnished in the style of the new look the Edwardians had given to their drawing-rooms. It was lighter, brighter and less formal than the Victorian, elegant with a few simple pieces of furniture and pleasant chintzy fabrics, with unpretentious pictures on the plain walls which toned in with their surroundings. A white marble fireplace, in which stood an enormous vase of mixed flowers, occupied the wall opposite the long windows which overlooked the street, and above the fireplace was a vast mirror in a plainly carved frame. There were crystal light fittings on either side of the mirror and pretty lamps to match on the small polished tables of light English wood. There was a deep sofa in a shade of biscuit velvet and two chairs to match and the sun streamed across the pale patterned carpet, reaching up to touch Alex Buchanan's haggard face.

Lucy's heart, which was enormous in its compassion, went out to him and she leaped up, drawing him to his feet. She folded his enormous frame in her arms, drawing his head down to her shoulder where he rested his forehead. She knew he was close to breaking point, this big man who once she had described to herself as a shambling bear. Good-natured, even-tempered, wanting to please, that was the way she had always known Alex Buchanan, and to see him now, ready to weep over the woman who, though she loved him, had never been faithful, was almost more than Lucy could bear. If she could comfort him, reassure him, give him some of her own strength, though sometimes she admitted she had little left for herself, then she was ready to do it.

Alex relaxed and leaned his not inconsiderable weight against James's wife and felt the tension ease out of him. She once had been almost Junoesque in her young beauty, broad-shouldered, tall, full-breasted. All men's fantasy of the perfect woman. Though she was still tall, her eyes almost on a level with his own, now she was slender, frail bones at her shoulder blades, and yet he sensed something powerful in her transfer itself to him. He didn't know what it was. Perhaps it was to do with her upbringing in the house of a man of God where goodness must surely have rubbed off on her since that was what she was. Good! A simple word which had connotations of virtue and purity and Lucy Buchanan had these characteristics too, but she was far from being a prude, and very far from being the self-righteous paragon so many raised as she had been might be. No wonder James had loved her, he remembered thinking in a kind of disjointed way. Different she had been, when first Franny had invited her to Grange House, undisciplined and naïve, rebellious to their code but, by God, she was a rare bird, then and now, and when James came home from wherever the fool had hidden himself, she would make him a wife and a soulmate that any man could treasure. He had been right to send for her and not one of his other cousins' wives, for this woman's durability, which had been proved a hundred times in the four years since he had known her, would support and strengthen Franny's recovery as no one else's could. It did not occur to him to question Lucy Buchanan's own frailty and need of support.

"Alex," she was murmuring, her hand stroking his dishevelled hair and he felt the tears come to his eyes.

All night he had walked the floor of this room, waiting for morning and the moment when he would be told if Franny was to live or die. He had eaten nothing and drunk nothing but now Lucy was leading him to the sofa, sitting him down with that smiling grace she had, looking round for the bell and when she spotted it, pulling it vigorously. An elderly housemaid popped her head round the door, then, on seeing the poised and lovely creature who raised an imperious head as though to say, "What took you so long?" bobbed a creaky curtsey.

"Some tea, please, er . . ."

"Whittaker, madam." Whittaker came with the house which Alex and Franny had rented. Whittaker had been born and bred in London and when the family who owned the house and who had young children had moved to their country place in Derbyshire for the duration of the war Whittaker had been kept on here, with a scullery maid, an ancient cook and an equally ancient gardener, to look after the place and see to Mr and Mrs Buchanan. It had turned out very well, for Mrs Buchanan had taken herself off to Flanders, of all places, the minute she got here and Mr Buchanan had been out such a lot and, like all men, when he was at home scarcely noticed what went on, especially in the servants quarters. They virtually pleased themselves what they did and when they did it. Whittaker was not awfully sure who this haughty young woman was who was sitting on the sofa holding Mr Buchanan's hand, but it looked as though she might be a bit of a tartar by that glint in her eye. Used to having her own way, the elderly housemaid thought. Whittaker, who liked to know what went on in her own place, had overheard several telephone calls Mr Buchanan had made, and received, and they had all been astounded, and sorry, of course, though she shouldn't have been over there in the first place, to hear that his wife had been injured at the front and was to be brought home. So how was this young woman to be involved?

"And perhaps some sandwiches for Mr Buchanan." The young woman turned solicitously to the man beside her. "Have you eaten, Alex?"

"I don't remember," Mr Buchanan mumbled, and really, you couldn't help but feel sorry for the poor bloke, Whittaker said a few minutes later to Cook who had her feet on the fender in the kitchen, her stockinged feet to the fire.

"Well, 'oo is she then?" Cook asked, ready to enjoy any bit of a change so long as it didn't involve extra work for her. Mind you, if she had been a bit younger she would have gone with the family to Derbyshire, especially after that air-raid on London last month and then, blow me, another a week or two back. Twenty German aeroplanes, it was said, in the skies above London, bombs dropped and folk killed and injured and what was the world coming to when a body wasn't safe beneath her own roof?

"Eeh, I dunno, though she acts as though she were Queen Mary 'erself." Whittaker spread margarine on a thin slice of bread and reached for the potted meat, which was all there was in the house to make a sandwich with.

The telephone shrilled and Whittaker sighed, laying the knife on the table beside the bread board, turning towards the kitchen door and the hallway to answer it, but as she opened the door Mr Buchanan had beaten her to it.

"We'll be there at once, Sister," he was saying, while at his back the lovely young woman was straining her neck to hear what was being said at the other end of the line. "Is . . . how does she seem, Sister?" Whittaker heard Mr Buchanan say from behind the door where she hid, pulling a face at Cook to be quiet.

There was a small silence as Mr Buchanan listened to whatever was being said by the sister then, "Thank you, Sister. We'll be there at once."

Clinging to the hand of the young woman in the most peculiar way, Mr Buchanan flung open the front door, almost dragging her off her feet.

"We shall need a taxi-cab," Whittaker heard him mumble, then the front door slammed behind them.

The hospital showed none of the chaos the mass of suffering humanity brought from the trenches to Howethwaite and the other military hospitals up and down the land. It was a place of calm and order. The corridor was filled with sunshine, highlighting the exquisite polish on the floor put there by several hardworking VADs. Though the walls were painted a somewhat sombre green it was bright and smelled of disinfectant and on several polished tables along its length were bowls of flowers. A porter directed them to the ward they asked for and when they got there they were told to wait, since, the pursed-lipped nurse said, this was not visiting time, looking ominously at the ticking clock on the wall.

This was a general hospital, a civilian hospital and

in a tiny ward lit by a tiny lamp, for by now it was evening, Franny Buchanan lay, the sheets smoothed across her and tucked in in that strangling grip so beloved of sisters and nurses the world over. It was as though they imagined patients might escape if they were not firmly anchored to their beds. Lucy nearly smiled. Even if Franny had been feeling up to it she could not have moved.

She and Alex moved slowly across the threshold, their hands still clasped for comfort, their total attention on the white bed and the white face on the white pillow. Franny looked peaceful, too bloody peaceful, Alex was to tell Lucy later, for a less peaceful woman had never been born, her hair brushed tidily across her forehead and if they hadn't known they might have thought her to be asleep, uninjured. There wasn't a bandage to be seen but the bandages and the hurt were underneath the immaculate sheets, the hurt which, the doctor had just told her husband, would never allow her to walk again.

Alex had wept, again in Lucy's arms, but now he was dry-eyed, composed, ready, should his wife be conscious, to tell her to keep her chin up, old girl, and what the hell did she think she was doing, putting the wind up him like this.

She opened her eyes as Alex gently placed a kiss on her cheek, then, when she saw who it was, she smiled, doing her best to struggle out of the cocoon that held her rigid, wanting to put a hand up to him, to tell him that he was not to be upset.

"Don't try to move, Mrs Buchanan," the nurse on the other side of the bed warned but Franny Buchanan was not one to be told what to do, even now.

"Oh, go to . . . blazes, Nurse," she said. "I . . . want to give my . . . my husband a hug."

"Now then, old girl, behave yourself and do what the nurse tells you. There'll be time enough for hugs later."

A flirtatious smile wisped about Franny's pain-drawn face and Lucy felt a small cry of painful admiration catch in her own throat. "Is that . . . a promise, Alex?" Franny whispered, then winked in that wicked way she had, a slow wink, merely a small drooping of one eyelid, but a wink just the same.

"It is, and it won't be long, either," ignoring the small moue of disapproval on the nurse's face. Not that she objected to Mr and Mrs Buchanan's words, or what seemed a promise to one another that they would soon resume their . . . marital relationship, but her concern was that Mr Buchanan must not promise something that would, in all probability, never come about. Mrs Buchanan had been hit in the back by shrapnel from a shell which had exploded quite close by, killing a dozen of the wounded she was about to lift into her ambulance. She had been changing a tyre on her vehicle, it was reported, and though she had not caught the full blast, the shrapnel had lodged in her spinal column. In fact it was still there and it was imperative that she lie quite still until the doctor, who was a specialist in that field, could operate on her.

"Who . . . who's that with you, darling?" Franny's voice was barely audible. Her eyes wandered past Alex's bulky shoulder, doing their best to focus on Lucy's shadowy figure at the end of the bed.

Alex turned and the nurse frowned her disapproval again. Her patient must not be tired any more than could be helped and this was not doing her much good, but she supposed the husband was entitled to see his wife. She didn't know who the woman was but her face was calm and her eyes, as they met hers, told her that she would not be long.

"It's only me, dearest," and it was a measure of Lucy's love that she called Franny by the endearment her mama and papa had exchanged and which, up to now, had been used only for those of her own family. "I've come to keep Alex company. No, you must not speak. Not again. I'm a bit of a nurse myself now," managing a quirky smile, "and I know what's best for you and there's no need to raise your eyebrows like that. I'm staying with Alex and then, when you can be moved, you shall come to Howethwaite and I will look after you myself. Is that clear?"

"What a tyrant she . . . has become, Alex, but may I . . . say one thing?"

"No, you may not."

"I did not . . . come home alone, Lucy. Someone brought . . . me," and again her eyes moved but over Lucy's shoulder this time. "Look," she whispered.

Lucy wanted to turn but dared not. There was something warm and loving in Franny's eyes, something almost impish, as though she was pleased with herself and knew Lucy would be too. She knew there was something . . . someone of importance there, something that was to mean life itself to Lucy Buchanan and she was afraid to turn in case she had been mistaken in Franny's expression and it was not . . . not . . .

She sensed the movement behind her in the corner of the room as someone she had not even noticed sitting in a chair in the deep shadows stood up. A tall figure. A man. A quiet man, and when Alex gasped sharply, a gasp cut off in mid-breath, she found the courage to turn her head, looking for the first time in two years into the eyes, the true, knowing eyes of James Buchanan.

"We brought . . . one another . . . home, Lucy . . ." The whisper from the bed trailed away as Franny Buchanan lapsed into unconsciousness and the plain truth of their deep, enduring love stood between Lucy and James Buchanan.

"You must all leave now," the nurse told them firmly, quite put out by this show of emotion, feeling under the curve of Franny's jaw for her pulse. She had wanted the man in the filthy uniform with his arm in an equally filthy sling to wait outside while Mrs Buchanan's husband visited her, but he had flatly refused, saying he would deliver her to her husband and then he would go. Apparently he had been the same all the way through from the Ypres salient where he and Mrs Buchanan had been wounded. He had fought like a tiger any move on the part of the authorities to separate them, and so, after he had had his own wound seen to, they had let him be. He had been no trouble as long as he had his eye on Mrs Buchanan who was a relative.

They waited until they were outside the door before James and Alex fell on one another and pummelled each other's arms and back in that strange way that men have when they are deeply moved. They hugged and pounded and it was not until they were done that James looked at Lucy.

She looked back at him with a sort of drifting,

dream-like expression in her eyes, telling him that she was in no way put out that he should greet his cousin before her. She knew why, naturally.

"James." What else was she to say to this man who had broken her heart and yet had loved her as she had loved him? Oh, yes, there was no doubt about it now, since the day they met, though in her innocent girlhood she had not known it. She had loved him then, she loved him now and would never stop until they both died, which she hoped earnestly would not be for a long time but would be on the same day, for she could not bear to be parted from him again. Tonight, in the bed she and he were to share at Alex's house, make no mistake about that, she would tell him so, show him how it was, but it seemed she did not need to speak, for her eyes were soft and unfocused with the love she bore him. They were warm and deep and incredibly lovely, her smile welcoming him home where he belonged, for it was not her nature to bear a grudge. They had hurt one another badly but she loved him, it was all there for him to see in that one look and he fell into it as it cherished him, enfolded him in the knowledge that nothing would ever change in her heart.

She could see the strain run out of him, empty from him in a weary torrent. His mouth had been held tight and drawn in a grim line as though he could not remember a day when he had not been weary and in pain but now that day had come again, brought to him by her.

The wariness in his eyes was replaced by a drowned sweetness, a sweetness put there by her, by the shining knowledge that at last they were meeting as equals in their love. He smiled gently and his uninjured hand rose to cup her cheek.

"My love," he said softly and neither of them noticed as Alex Buchanan tiptoed quietly back along the corridor.

They scarcely noticed him when they got back to the house either, for he diplomatically slipped away upstairs to his room, leaving them to whatever it was they were to do. It was no business of his, though the servants, who were still up, were open-mouthed in wonder, gawping at her as the young woman, whose name turned out to be Buchanan, walked into the kitchen and demanded a fire in the rather small bedroom where Whittaker had decided she was to sleep. In fact, she said, since her husband . . . *husband* mind you, was to share it with her she rather wondered if there was a bigger room, with a double bed, please, where they might spend the night? Was there hot water, good, and the bathroom . . . yes, that would be splendid . . . clean towels, good, and she'd be obliged if the fire was lit at once since her husband, who had just come from the trenches, was cold.

The trenches! Well, that was a turn-up for the books and no mistake, though they could well believe it when they saw the state of him and would you look at her now. A bit different to the pale and peaky thing she had been earlier in the day. Now she was all shining eyes and flushed cheeks and looking as pretty as a picture and no wonder! She also wanted hot water in a bowl, she went on, scissors, any sort of antiseptic ointment they might have, carbolic and clean bandages. They could tear up a sheet if such things were not available, she told them, and they did not mind her high-handed manner at all now, for nothing was too good for a man who had been in the trenches.

She undressed him while his dreaming eyes studied her face, not looking away from her as her fingers unbuttoned and gently removed his tunic and then the rough khaki shirt he wore. She smoothed his chest and shoulders with wondering hands, making him tremble and his nipples peak, then she pulled off his trousers, and he obeyed her when she told him to stand or lift his foot. He was totally absorbed by her, by her hands on him as she removed his muddy, bloody – thankfully not his own – clothing, easing the filthy bandage away from the gaping hole where the shrapnel had hurriedly been dug out of him and which it had stuck to with dried blood. Thankfully there was no sign of the infection she had dreaded. The shrapnel wound was in his right shoulder which, naturally, meant as a right-handed man he could not perform any of the duties a private soldier was asked to do in the trenches. He could not dig a hole in which to shelter. He could not hold his rifle or draw a bayonet. He could not salute his officer or go over the top with the other lads so they had sent him home. He was no longer of any use to them, was he? Nevertheless he had no trouble getting his arms round his wife!

She cleaned the wound and expertly re-bandaged it, her professionalism not allowing her to begin what they both wanted, which was to make love to her husband and have him make love to her, not before she had tended to his wound.

She had put him in the bath, aware with her breath catching that though her husband's naked body was thin and undernourished, it still had the virile power to become erect with his need.

"Is this the kind of treatment I may expect when we get home, wench?" he asked her drowsily as she soaped his aching body with hands which were gentle but at the same time searching. He groaned a little as her hands found his penis.

"My love, I shall be no good to you at all if you continue with that, delightful as it is," he told her, so would she stop it at once and let him get out of the bath, for he had better things to do than succumb to her nurse's need to boss him about. Was she always to be as masterful as this? he murmured into her hair as she bent to dry his body and would she be careful with that bit . . . yes, there, for he had great plans for it later. He would have had her in the bath with him, he told her, bemused and bewitched by her, but as she had seen for herself, he had been covered in what could only be called . . . well, it was worse than filth, for he had not had a bath, or even a proper wash, since he couldn't remember when and why in the name of all that was wonderful, hadn't they done this before, he begged her to tell him, his breath catching in his throat as she began to remove her own clothes.

She found that though he murmured soft words and endearments throughout the whole joyful encounter, she couldn't speak. Her heart was too full. It was as though it were so filled with emotion it had cut off her ability to utter a word, to tell him how she felt, but it seemed her hands on his body and the adoration in her eyes as they met his was enough for him.

The firelight was a gentle glow on their naked bodies, turning them both to burnished gold as he began to tell her what had happened to him since he last saw her, but before that they had loved one another in the deep enchantment their need and their long separation had created. He did not hurry. His concentration was complete as he studied her body, the beauty of her breasts which he told her were smaller but he liked them just the same. He cupped them awkwardly, for his arm, which he had refused to allow her to put in a sling, stabbed him painfully as he moved it to lift his hand to her nipple. He turned her this way and that, telling her smilingly, wonderingly, that he must inspect her for change, satisfied when there was none, speaking with that loving humour he had kept well hidden for so long. He caressed her slowly, carefully, surely, smoothing his hands down the length of her slender body, not wishing to neglect any of the sweet sensations his hands and loving heart created, for himself or for her. He put his face against her flesh to smell the musky fragrance of her willing, female body, pressing his lips to every inch of her, groaning when his shoulder tore at him but refusing to stop. His hands slipped down her back and across her buttocks, moving to her flat belly and into the dark, mysterious bush between her thighs, making her sigh and stretch until his fingers found the sweet, moist centre of her when she began to cry out in need. They were overwhelmed by the sensual renewal of what they had known only twice before, glorying in this love that they had thought to be lost but which was found.

"I will never leave you again," he told her harshly as he thrust into the waiting centre of her.

"I wouldn't let you and if you try I will follow." She

gasped in exquisite pleasure and her body arched to meet his.

"I will never . . ."

"What, my love?"

"Love anyone as I love you."

"I know. I love you the same. Not grammatical but true." There was laughter in her voice but he silenced it with his mouth.

"Always?" he managed a moment later.

"Always."

"I'll kill any man who tries to take you from me."

"No one will."

"I know that now, my dearest love. And when morning comes . . ."

"Yes . . ." Her voice was no more than a sigh.

But he had put his head on her breast and was asleep.

They did not return to Howethwaite until the middle of September and when they did Lucy was already pregnant with her second child. Was it any wonder, she giggled to her besotted husband, when he wouldn't leave her alone for a moment, day or night.

"Do I hear a note of complaint in your voice, my darling," reaching out to put his hand on her leg, then beginning to slide it up beneath the hem of her skirt.

"James! Whittaker might come in at any moment. I know she takes an age to carry out an order, poor old soul, but if she brings the tea in and finds you with your hand . . . where it is, she'll possibly faint, or run screaming to Cook." She gasped and arched her back and her husband smiled complacently, ignoring her words as his fingers found that sweet place they could not resist.

"Put this shawl thing over your knee," he suggested, smiling with pure devilment, but Lucy pushed him away and just in time, for there was a knock at the door. It opened and Whittaker came doddering round it pushing a trolley on which were the teacups and saucers, the teapot, sugar basin and milk jug and the cakes, scones and biscuits Cook made in an endless orgy of activity in her attempt to "put a bit of flesh on that lad's bones", for it seemed that the whole household now revolved round the wounded warrior who had come back from the war.

Whittaker would report fondly back to the kitchen that "they were at it again" but they all thought it was lovely for a man and his wife to be so much in love. She gave her whole attention to the pouring of the tea, handing a cup to Major Buchanan with what could only be called a dimpling smile, though she hadn't a dimple in her. James took it from her and winked, and Lucy smothered a smile, for she knew the elderly housemaid was as under the major's spell as she was herself. It was not fair to the poor dear to tease her the way James did, but James insisted she loved it and perhaps he was right. She knew *she* did. She couldn't get enough of his attentions, his kisses, his whispered remarks in her ear on what he was to do with her later in their bed. Sometimes it was his hand reaching out blindly for hers as something from the war came to plague him in a way that told her she was loved and needed, and that he must touch her at once to reassure himself that she was really there. He needed protection, his hand told her, comfort, like a small boy whose mother has momentarily strayed from his sight.

He had nightmares. She would be woken from her own sleep by a voice chanting in her ear, a chant of fear which was very familiar to her, for had she not heard it a hundred times on the wards at Howethwaite?

"Don't go, Joe . . . Pass me my rifle . . . a dozen killed . . . poor old Dick . . . there's Alf with all his ribs broken . . . 5,000 bombs gone up . . . Oh,

God . . . Oh, God . . . Joe said he wouldn't last three weeks and he bloody didn't . . . his glasses blown into his face . . . poor sod, they've blown his balls off as well . . . Oh, God . . ." and in the way she had learned she would wake him carefully, shielding him from his terror, holding him until he quietened, then fell asleep again in the safety of her arms.

They had given him the Military Cross for his courage in rescuing a corporal on the Somme though when Major Buchanan deserted and Private Jimmy Johnson took his place it caused a great deal of confusion in high places when it was discovered he was one and the same man. Could he be described as a deserter when, strictly speaking, he was still serving bravely in the king's army and if not then he must surely be entitled to keep the medal he had won. There must be some sort of enquiry, they all agreed, some discipline taken against Major Buchanan, some punishment, but as he had now been medically discharged from the army with a shoulder which a shrapnel wound had permanently stiffened, what were they to do? He was thirty-eight years old, a married man with a child and really, they had enough to trouble them, for by now the army, which they had expected to break out of the Ypres salient and be halfway to the ports of Ostend and Zeebrugge, was bogged down in the tides and storms of autumn which was now upon them. The troops were still painfully inching upwards and onwards through the slough of shell holes and mud towards the village of Passchendaele, which was finally taken, but with winter upon them again it was going to be a hard push.

Sometimes, in the aftermath of their loving, when

he lay with his cheek against her breast, relaxed and at peace, he would talk about it, about the waste, the sheer bloody brutality, the slaughter of a whole generation of the country's young men, the irony, the humour, the simple bravery of them all, whether they be peers or peasants.

"I was having a quiet smoke among the men, I can't remember after which battle since they all became the same one, when I overheard one chap say to another, 'D'you remember halting here on the retreat, George?' His mate answered simply, 'Can't call it to mind somehow. Was it that little village in the wood down there by the river,' pointing to the desolate and empty landscape, 'or was it that place there with the cathedral and all them factories?' Do you see, Lucy, they were looking at nothing but an ocean of mud, shell holes, devastation for as far as the eye could see, but in their mind's eye they still saw what had been there once. They were wonderful men, all of them, and brave, for they go back again and again, even though they know what it is they are going to. They are always cold and wet and tired and yet they remain cheerful. They are mown down like wheat before a scythe, often getting no further than the parapet of the trench and the bloody officers, myself included once, keep urging them to get up and go on. Dear God, Lucy . . ."

"Don't . . . don't . . . you're home."

"But they're not, Lucy, they're not."

She knew she kept him with his head above water at times like these, above the stinking mud he dreamed he floundered in, holding him in her compassionate arms and gradually, as the weeks passed slowly by, she knew she was winning. She was one of the lucky ones and so was he.

They talked about Edward and again she cried in his arms for her little brother who had gone to "do his bit". Edward was not as ignorant of war as were many young men, schoolboys really, who marched away with colour blazing in their cheeks and their eyes shining with pride. He had seen in the wards of Howethwaite what war could do to a man and yet he had still gone.

One night, after a long silence in which James seemed to be making his mind up about something, he suddenly said, "I saw him, my darling."

She sat up in his arms, flinging her hair back from her face and stared at him, not knowing whether to be horrifed or glad. Edward had written to her. She knew the name he had enlisted under. It had caused her a wry smile, but he wanted her to write to him and so he had been forced to tell her. He spoke of the men he was with, Bert and "Rosie" and George, all men from the original British Expeditionary Force which must prove, or so she told herself, that if they could survive for so long there was hope that he would come back home again. He did not speak of the march to Ypres where the men lived in shell holes and were afraid to leave them, for the whole earth was ploughed up and the holes were filled with water and if the shells didn't get you the deep waters in the craters might.

"Where?" she whispered.

"On the road to Ypres. He was marching with his platoon. They seemed to be very attached to him, watching out for him, if you know what I mean, but he was in good spirits, Lucy."

"I want to bring him home, James. He's only a boy."

"No, he's a man now, and would not thank you for it."

"But he's not eighteen yet," she wailed.

"Oh, yes he is, in experience if not in years and you must leave him where he is, my darling."

"It's so hard . . . so hard."

"I know, my love, but we can only hope and pray that someone . . . perhaps your mama and papa are watching over him."

Comforted by the thought she fell asleep at last in the shelter of his arms.

He did not tell her that when he met Edward the boy was in a rapture of enchantment, for he was to report to an airfield behind the lines where his hopes of becoming a pilot might be at last fulfilled. Edward was a clever lad, well educated and with a gift for machinery, and when it became known to his officers they had done all they could to have him moved. It meant that he would transfer from the army into the Royal Flying Corps and would probably be sent home for his training, but it also meant, which was why James didn't tell his wife, that her brother's expectation of life once he became a pilot was seventeen and a half flying hours.

He was longing to return to Howethwaite to see his child but Lucy refused to leave Franny and he refused to leave her. And not only Franny kept her in London. She was sadly aware that Alex would simply fall apart if there was no one to share his devastation, to tell him constantly that Franny was a fighter and would come through this. To hold his hand each time he came back from a visit to the hospital, to see that he ate something and changed his underwear, for of everybody, including Franny herself, he seemed the worst hit by the tragedy.

Franny had had her operation and was out of danger now but there was no way she could be moved just yet, the doctor said. She and James and Alex went to see her every day but Alex was still in the war, though what good he was in his present state, Lucy often wondered, and could not spend as much time with her as he would have wanted, so it was up to Lucy to be with her as much as she was allowed.

It was on one of Lucy's visits when she had gone alone, that Franny talked of what the future held for her. James had gone to call on the mother of one of the men killed in his platoon. She lived somewhere in the warren of working-class streets near the docks where Fred's family had always worked and though Lucy had offered to go with him he said that he would rather go alone.

"His mother will want to talk about him, how he died, was he brave, did he speak of her when he was wounded, where his grave is, was it a nice funeral, that sort of thing, and she proably won't be able to do it if you're there."

"Why not? I have every sympathy for her."

"I know that, my darling, but you are so obviously not like her. It will inhibit her. You're a lady and she's just the mother of a simple working-class lad and besides . . ." He hesitated and bit his lip, staring sombrely out of the long window to the busy street beyond.

"What? What is it?" At once she was kneeling beside him, her lovely face passionate in her dedication to his welfare.

"I may not be able to lie as easily with you there."

She looked astonished. "Lie?"

"Yes, you see her Fred died by a bullet from the rifle of one of his own men." His face was livid with pain.

She put her hand to her mouth and leaned back on her heels. "Dear God . . ."

"He . . . hung on the barbed wire, you've heard the song, calling for his mother . . . for seventeen hours. We couldn't get to him, you see. We kept hoping the German machine-gun fire would finish him off but . . . it didn't and so . . . one of us . . . stood up and took aim and shot him."

"You?" she whispered.

"Yes."

"Oh, my darling, have you any idea how much I love you." She began to weep, laying her face against his knee. He lifted her up and cradled her against him, shushing her tenderly but his face was bleak with memories.

It seemed Franny Buchanan wasn't going merely to loll – her word – about all day when she got out of this bloody place, she told Lucy on that day. She didn't believe it when they told her she might not walk again and anyway, she meant to have a damn good try at it and if it turned out that they were right, then she was going to have a chair made, a motorised chair.

"Perhaps that lad of yours might be able to come up with something," she mused, gazing out of the window towards a stand of trees which were already beginning to lose their leaves. The lawn beneath them had a thin carpet of gold and amber and bronze and there was a chill in the air, a feeling that winter, the winter so dreaded by soldiers in trenches, was creeping inexorably closer.

"That lad of mine? Which lad?" Lucy was bewildered.

"Edward, of course. As I remember he was for ever fiddling about with bits of wire and a spanner. He was obsessed by anything mechanical. I can see him now sitting in that little Austin of mine, his face absorbed, his eyes sort of unfocused with wonder. Do you remember?"

Oh, yes, Lucy remembered. She remembered all those lovely days with her brothers and sisters, the long innocent days of their childhood, for she had been no more than a child herself then. Their "expeditions". The bicycles which Edward had cobbled together from bits and pieces of scrap and dear Papa, so wrapped up in his butterflies and his memories of his beloved Evelyn that they might all have cycled to John o' Groats and back and he would have smiled that sweet smile of his and asked them if they'd enjoyed themselves!

"Lucy." Franny took her hand and squeezed it gently, looking into Lucy's bent face. "He'll come home, darling, really he will, and when he does, he'll design me a chair with a motor on it so that I can get about the gardens and the house and then he can start on the Austin. I want to be able to drive and the vehicle will need to be adapted to my needs. Edward will do it for me so take that look of woe from your face and tell me how you and James are getting on. Aha, that brought a flush to your cheeks, lady, so I gather that everything is pretty good in that department." Her voice was low and sad.

"Treasure it, darling, and him, for it's very special, what you and he have."

The great day came when the doctor told Alex that as long as he promised that Mrs Buchanan was to go straight to the hospital where the other Mrs Buchanan nursed, then she could go home. She must have a well-padded mattress to lie on in the railway compartment and he himself would accompany her if Mr Buchanan could give him a bed for the night. He had already had lengthy telephone discussions about Mrs Buchanan's condition with the doctors in the Lakeland hospital but he wanted to speak to them face to face. Mrs Buchanan must be brought back to him – yes, he knew it was a long way – at regular intervals but she was healing nicely, at least physically, though he did not add this last to Mrs Buchanan's husband.

If the doctor was amazed at the reception committee Mrs Buchanan had waiting for her on the steps and spread out in the lovely autumn gardens of the hospital, he managed to keep it to himself as he supervised the tender lifting of her from the ambulance which had brought them from the station at Windermere. There were people everywhere. Men in wheelchairs, children doing cartwheels, women weeping and wiping their eyes on their aprons, dogs barking and racing round like mad things, so that he began to wonder if this was going to be the right environment for his patient to recuperate in.

Lucy was overcome, blaming her tendency to weep at the slightest thing on her pregnancy, as she climbed down from the ambulance. Margaret and Emily and Percy had her in a stranglehold the minute her feet touched the gravelled drive, laughing and crying and begging her not to go away again. Percy must show her the cartwheels he could now do, flying at once to the lawn where he proceeded to throw himself about in a mad arc of joy, his face beaming.

"Look, Lucy, look, Mr Buchanan," he cried, including his brother-in-law in his delight.

"I think I liked it better when you called me James."

"Look, James, watch me, watch me."

"I am, old chap, and when you've a minute to spare you shall teach me. I've always wanted to do cartwheels."

Percy was enchanted and when James opened his arms to him flew into them without hesitation, for it seemed this new Mr Buchanan was going to be enormous fun.

There were shouts of "Welcome home, sir," from Clapcott and Licky Thripp and even old Bibby who had brought Mrs Hutton across from the cottage they now shared. Mrs Hutton was Mrs Bibby now, and a prouder man never walked the earth, he was fond of saying to all and sundry. She'd done right well for them all, had Miss Lucy, but then hadn't he always said to anyone who would listen what a grand lass she was.

The two big black dogs frightened the life out of the doctor as they hurtled towards him but it was not him they were after but Mr James Buchanan who was swept off his feet, lucky to be standing on the grass at the time as they got him down and sat on him as though determined he would never escape them again.

"Get off, you daft beggars," he was yelling at them, just as he had a year ago but now he knew they were his dogs, that he belonged to them. And as for that mad imp, Thimble, he was no better behaved than when James clapped eyes on him four years ago and would need taking in hand, he told his wife, helping her solicitously up the steps which made Mrs Burns and Mrs Bunting, who were the ones shedding the tears, nudge one another and exchange a significant look.

Buffy was there and in her arms was Alice. A shy Alice who hung back for a moment, hiding her face in Buffy's neck, her finger in her mouth, but when Lucy held out her arms, Alice held out hers and in a moment Lucy was being besieged by a torrent of words which seemed to imply that Alice had missed her and she was not to go away again. There were open-mouthed baby kisses and strangling hugs and then the moment they had all waited for when father and daughter met one another for what was really the first time. She did not remember him, for a year or more is a long time in a young child's life, but she had been accustomed to sitting on soldiers' laps, to being petted and gently hugged by men who could not get enough of her infant sweetness and when James held out his arms she went to him willingly enough.

The moment was fraught with emotion. They all cried then, even Sister Colyford who had taken Lucy's hand in greeting but was swept into her affectionate embrace instead. Then they all turned to watch James and Alice.

"Darling . . . darling . . ." James seemed unable to say more than those words as the memory of his love for this child rushed back again and became real.

Alice turned away in his arms, directing her gaze at Buffy.

"Daddy?" she asked questioningly, pointing a plump finger directly into James's face.

"Yes, it's your daddy," Buffy told her. "Give Daddy a kiss."

Turning back to James, who was himself weeping unashamedly by now, Alice pursed her rosy lips and placed them gently on his cheek where the tears were. "Daddy cry," she said softly, then put her arms about his neck.

It was all too much for Franny Buchanan, who lay on the stretcher holding her husband's hand. She looked up and in that whimsical way of hers sighed heavily, theatrically.

"Well, I can't stand much more of this, really I can't. You'll have me in tears next and that would be a catastrophe. Now, will someone get me inside and, Lucy, will you ask that butler of yours if there's any champagne in the cellar, for I do believe this calls for a celebration. And there's no need to look at me like that, Doctor. It's my back that's injured, not my innards and a glass of champers would go down very nicely."

They moved slowly up the steps, the stretcher carried carefully by the ambulance driver and his aide, and there, at the top of the steps and just inside the wide front door, was Rory. He was in a wheelchair, the stumps of his legs sticking out over the edge of the seat. To Lucy's consternation Margaret flew up the steps beside her, standing at Rory's back, her hands on the wheelchair as though she were ready to take him wherever he wished. She was smiling, a lovely luminous smile that transferred itself from Lucy to Rory, who put up a hand which she instantly took.

"Lucy," he said quietly, clinging to Margaret's hand.

"Welcome home. We've missed you. And ... and James. How are you?" And in all their minds was the memory of that last day when James and Rory had been together and James had tried to kill Rory and what were they to make of one another now?

But James Buchanan had his daughter in his arms and his wife by his side, both of whom he loved more than life itself. Lucy was his now, totally and irrevocably, as was the child growing in her womb. He was whole and slowly healing the wounds of his mind and could he turn away from the man who had none of these things, though by the look of him and Lucy's sister things might be different one day.

"Rory. Good to see you, lad. And out of that bloody bed as well. We'll talk soon." He placed the hand of friendship on Rory's shoulder.

There was a great letting out of breaths on a sigh of relief, and though Lucy wasn't sure she cared for the way Margaret was fussing about Rory Cameron, she merely smiled, bending to kiss Rory's cheek.

"You look well, Rory. As James says, we'll talk later but now we must get Mrs Buchanan to bed."

"Never mind bed, Lucy Buchanan. I haven't had my champagne yet and here is Dixon with the bottle. Now then, Doctor, remove that sour look from your face and take a glass with me. Let's drink to ... to absent friends." Her face saddened, thinking of Andrew and the three sons of Janet and Angus and all the other young men who had gone so gladly off to war and would never come back, and for a moment they were all silent then Franny laughed, "and to happy homecomings," and with that special no-nonsense magic that was hers she had them smiling again.

There was just one more thing that Lucy had to do and the cause of it was her sister Margaret, or rather what had been done to Margaret.

They had been home a week when she had been startled by the sound of desolate weeping. She had gone up to check on Alice who was having her nap and intended, if Alice was still sleeping, to persuade James to walk with her up through the woods at the back of Howethwaite. It was a glorious winter's day with a light frost and a smoky, opalescent haze above the treetops. The grass was stiff with the cold and the path up through the gardens was like a ribbon of tawny brown, the bricks in it brushed with white. Just the day for a walk.

She could not at first identify where the weeping came from, or even who it was who was so grief-stricken. It seemed to come from the attic, the stairs to which were beyond the nursery door. Buffy would be in the nursery with Alice so, without going inside to check on her daughter, she moved slowly past it and climbed the stairs to the attic. Putting her head through the trap-door which had been left up she peered round, trying to pierce the gloom which was thick and heavy among the unidentifiable shapes, small, large, square, piled on top of one another or stacked against the wall.

The weeping continued, not loud but heart-wrenching in its poignancy. Lucy moved further up the narrow staircase and stepped quietly into the attic. Brushing past all the odds and ends of unwanted furniture which the years of Howethwaite occupancy had accumulated, she saw, to her horror, that it was Margaret.

She sat on the floor between two boxes, her knees up to her chest, her arms about her knees and her head resting on her arms. Her hair fell about her in a dark curtain, covering her shoulders which shook with her distress.

"Darling . . . oh, darling, what is the matter?" Lucy blundered into a packing case, knocking it to the floor as she rushed to get to her sister, flinging herself down beside her and clutching her in frantic arms. "Whatever has happened? Why are you crying? Tell me . . . dearest, I cannot bear to see you in such a state. You're not hurt, are you? Has someone hurt you?" though she was not certain what or who she meant, for who would hurt Margaret in this place where they all loved her?

"Has . . . is it to do with . . . Rory? Please tell me, dearest. Perhaps I can put it right. Dear God, I'll have no one upsetting you like this. What is it?"

Blindly, without lifting her head or responding in any way to Lucy's determination to have her arms about her, Margaret thrust a piece of paper into Lucy's hands, then with what seemed to be a movement of distaste, drew herself away from her, her head still hanging in despair.

"What?" Lucy reluctantly took the piece of paper, a sheet of good quality notepaper and glancing quickly at it saw that it had no address nor a signature.

"Who?" she said, foolishly she knew, but something was ringing alarm bells in her head, remembered alarm bells, though they eluded her for the moment.

She began to read it while Margaret continued to sob, though the storm was lessening somewhat.

It has come to my notice that you have become involved with a man called Rory Cameron and I am concerned that you might not know of his history, or that part of his history which involves your sister, Lucy Buchanan. Perhaps you are not aware that some years ago he had an affair with her and the child she passes off as James Buchanan's is, in fact, that of Rory Cameron. I could not have it on my conscience if you were to marry a man who will toy with the affections of two women, indeed two *sisters*, so disgracefully and felt it was my duty to warn you.

A well-wisher.

Lucy felt the nausea rise to her throat and for a moment she thought she would be sick, but it didn't last long, for hot on its heels came a rage so dreadful she wanted to scream and shout and fling herself about in a way a child will who is frustrated beyond measure. But she was not a child. She was a woman and this was her little sister who was weeping so broken-heartedly and all over what was a tissue of lies.

"Dear God," she hissed. "Dear sweet Jesus, is there no end to her madness. It was not enough for her to do her best to destroy James and me, now she is bent on doing the same to you and Rory. I can't believe it and really, Margaret," her voice stern and forbidding, "I'm surprised to find that you do."

Margaret had lifted her head and turned her swollen face to Lucy, her expression uncertain, frightened even, for she could see that Lucy was as mad as a wet hen, which was one of Lucy's favourite expressions. She brushed her long tangled hair back with a trembling hand then wiped her nose on her sleeve.

"Lucy . . . I didn't . . ."

"You didn't think, did you. That's what the trouble is, you didn't think this out or you would have come to the proper conclusion, which is that this letter is a load of . . ." Here she used an expression she had heard from James which was very rude and Margaret gasped.

"Do you honestly believe that that child downstairs, who is as dark as the night and with James Buchanan's eyes smiling out of her face, can possibly have been fathered by Rory Cameron? Margaret, I thought you had more sense. Rory is fair, fair-haired and fair-skinned and has blue eyes, and apart from that Alice is so like James in her ways it is quite uncanny. We've all said that, haven't we? Go on, admit it. Even the way she laughs. And apart from that, you who have known me all your life, can you believe that I could be so dishonest, so dishonourable, so deceitful that I could have an affair with a man while my husband was fighting for his life in the trenches? Have I ever told you a lie?"

"No . . ." no more than a whisper.

"Well then . . ." She took hold of her sister by the forearms and turned her fiercely to her. "Do you believe me or this . . . this sick person, whoever it is," though of course she knew, "and who is bent on making trouble?"

"Lucy . . . oh, Lucy, it's just that I love him so much and I do remember when you were . . . special to him."

"He was desperately ill, dearest. He needed something I could give him. Now you are giving it to him because you love him and believe me, he loves you. Can you not tell that?"

Margaret's eyes, though still wet with tears, had begun to shine and with a little cry she flung herself into her sister's arms.

"I'm sorry, Luce. Oh, Lord, I'm sorry. I should have known. Forgive me."

"There . . . it's all over now," Lucy said, knowing it wasn't. "Go and kiss Rory and then dare to tell me it isn't you he loves. Go on. Get out of here. Wash your face and brush your hair and don't let me hear another word."

James was doing what he had done ever since they had got home which was thoroughly spoiling his daughter when Lucy told him she had to go out for an hour. He could scarcely bear to have the child out of his sight and Lucy had told him she would become decidedly jealous if this went on much longer. What about her? she asked him plaintively, but he merely smiled and said her turn for spoiling would come later unless she would like to go up to their room now when he would spoil her until she screamed for mercy.

"D'you remember me telling you about that chap who wrote to his wife that she was to have a good look at the floor, for when he got home she would see nothing but the ceiling? That's how I feel, as I think I've demonstrated ever since I came home."

"Darling." Her smile melted his heart which he had thought would not be big enough to encompass both her, his daughter and the new little one to come, but it seemed hearts were designed to expand as and when necessary. This house was filled with love and affection as it had not been since before his own mother's death.

Margaret, who was sixteen now and quite old enough to know her own mind, she had told him and Lucy firmly, spent most of her time with Rory Cameron who, in his early twenties and come from a decent family, not that that mattered, she had added scathingly, was very suitable for the daughter of Edward and Evelyn Dean. It made no difference to her that he had no legs. Rory meant to have false legs fitted as soon as he could and she would have him up in no time at all. Yes, she loved him and he loved her and that was that, she had said, lifting her head defiantly, looking the image of Lucy, James thought, and Rory was a lucky chap. He knew Lucy had pulled strings to keep him at Howethwaite when really he should have gone to a convalescent home. He had become almost one of the family and everyone, including the children, had become so fond of him.

She drove the Rolls herself, telling no one, not even James, where she was going. She had put on her most elegant oufit which she only just managed to get into. It was what was known as a coat frock, double-breasted and buttoning down to the waist where a broad sash was tied. The skirt was slightly flared, ending six inches above her ankle bone. It had a definite military look about it and was made in a soft woollen material the colour of burned almond. Her hat was the same shade, close to her head, the small brim framing her lovely, serene face and had a ribbon the same coffee colour as her sash. She looked well and very, very fashionable.

He would see if madam was in, the high-nosed butler she remembered from the last time told her, gliding away to the door of the drawing-room, but she did not wait as he had asked her to, but followed on his heels as he tapped discreetly then opened the door.

Charlotte Buchanan might have been frozen to the same chaise-longue she had occupied over eighteen months ago. She was in exactly the same position, leaning back and flipping moodily through the pages of a magazine. There was a box of chocolates on the table beside her and as Lucy strode in she was just about to stuff one in her mouth. She had put on weight.

"Those won't do you much good, Charlotte, not if you're to regain your figure. I know it's hard after having a child but after all it is over a year since your son was born."

Charlotte Buchanan, for the space of five seconds, was struck dumb. The chocolate hovered at her lips as though she were not quite sure whether to pop it in or not, then, with what sounded suspiciously like an oath to the astonished butler, she sat up and threw it back in the box.

"What the devil are you doing here, you bitch?" The words were spat out with all the venom that had lain like a cancer inside Charlotte Buchanan ever since James Buchanan had married Lucy Dean. She turned on the butler. "And what the hell d'you mean by letting her in? You know my father does not like riff-raff in his house."

"But, madam . . ." the butler stammered, then, seeing that retreat was his best course, almost ran from the room.

"Don't worry, Charlotte, I can't stay long so don't bother with tea. My husband is expecting me home. As you will have gathered you did not succeed in parting us, and I'm happy to say he can't bear me out of his sight for more than half an hour. Yes, isn't it a marvel after all you tried to do to us? He loves me and I return his love and we are to have another child because of that love. I don't suppose you know anything about that since it seems to me that it is unlikely ever to happen to you. I can't say I lose any sleep over it except that it saddens me to know that Paul will never know what James and I have.

"But that is not why I'm here. James and I have resolved our differences, no thanks to you but it seems you are not satisfied with doing your best to destroy us, you are determined to destroy my sister as well with your hatred and envy. Yes, I believe it is envy that eats away at you and turns you into a malevolent shrew. You cannot bear to see anyone have what you wanted and couldn't get, and even after all these years your twisted little mind is still scheming on how to avenge yourself on me. Oh, yes, I am aware that it is me you want to hurt but you have not succeeded and never will. I will just say this. If we have another of your vituperative letters I shall take it to the authorities which will cause such a scandal your poor mother will not be able to hold up her head again. Do I make myself clear?"

Charlotte's face was a bright crimson and her eyes were slitted with rage. She stood up, then seemed undecided on what course to take, twisting her hands together in the lovely silk folds of her tea gown.

"Get . . . out . . . of . . . my . . . house."

"Your house. I thought this was your father's house.

Oh, I see, you are still his little girl, is that it? Dear God, I pity you, Charlotte, I really do."

She turned and before Charlotte could say another word, she left the room, swept through the door which the smiling butler opened for her, having heard "madam" get what for, she supposed, and ran lightly down the steps.

"Good day to you, Mrs Buchanan," he called after her as she started the motor and, as she turned into the road she began to sing.

"Rule Britannia, Britannia rules the waves . . ."

AUDREY HOWARD

ANGEL MEADOW

The Brody girls have always been a bit different from the rest of the folk in Angel Meadow, the appalling slum where their drunken mother Kitty is the lowest sort of prostitute. Then one day Kitty disappears from their lives forever – and this new crisis turns out to be a new beginning.

For Nancy Brody, only nine years old, makes up her mind that she will not see little Mary and Rose in the workhouse. Determined to find a better way to live, she gets work for them, at the Monarch Cotton Manufacturing Mill – and then sets out to better herself and her sisters. Saving every penny, working every waking hour, pushing her less-ambitious sisters to the limits of their patience and loyalty, Nancy succeeds. She becomes an employer herself, buying the cloth for her own factory from the Monarch Mill where she was once a labourer.

But happiness seems as elusive for Nancy as it was when she was a mistreated child. Though he once said he loved her, Mick O'Rourke has become Nancy's worst enemy, and seems determined to take a terrible revenge on her and her sisters. And Josh Hayes, the man who truly loves Nancy, seems to be destined to be parted from her . . .

HODDER AND STOUGHTON PAPERBACKS

AUDREY HOWARD

THERE IS NO PARTING

Callum O'Shaughnessy is Liverpool Irish.

Ninth child of a tumultuous, affectionate, mostly devout, sometimes too outspoken family. He has 'got on': working his way up by sheer hard work and dedication to be master of his own ship.

Maris Woodall's family know about ships as well. They own them. Along with their kin, the Osbornes, they live the comfortable life of the landed gentry.

Callum and Maris, from families that seem fated to meet and collide, are so different in class, experience and even age: ill-matched yet passionately attracted.

But, as the Depression years of the 1930s give way to World War, everything around them is in a state of violent upheaval that echoes, and may even swamp, their own stormy relationship.

HODDER AND STOUGHTON PAPERBACKS

AUDREY HOWARD

NOT A BIRD WILL SING

Though Poppy Appleton has grown up in ignorance and poverty, she grabs her chance of a better life with the kindly Goodall family.

At Long Reach Farm, Eliza Goodall teaches Poppy all the skills she would have passed on to her own daugher: the skills that would enable a young lady to become the mistress of a farm like Long Reach. And when the time comes for Eliza's son Richard to choose a wife, it seems only natural that he should choose Poppy.

But though Poppy feels nothing but affection for her new family, the only man for whom she has ever felt love is Conn MacConnell. And when he returns unexpectedly, Poppy has to choose between loyalty and love.

HODDER AND STOUGHTON PAPERBACKS

AUDREY HOWARD

THE SILENCE OF STRANGERS

Nella Fielden marries Jonas Townley believing he is the one man who deserves her hand and her fortune. The Lancashire colliery heiress, as proud and ambitious as any man, cannot believe the truth: that Jonas has married her for her money.

He tries to be true to her. But soon, his heart belongs to another woman: Nella's protégée Leah Wood, the girl from Colliers Row.

Torn between her loyalty to her protector and her love for Jonas Townley, Leah tries to be true to both. But she cannot cure Nella's broken heart – or avoid the tragedy that lies in wait for them all.

HODDER AND STOUGHTON PAPERBACKS

AUDREY HOWARD

A WORLD OF DIFFERENCE

Cosseted heiress Jenna Townley is used to getting her own way. And when she meets ambitious young Conal MacRae, she soon knows that this is the man she must marry, despite her father's disapproval.

Their courtship is fiery and their marriage passionate. But their happiness is threatened by tragic and sinister family secrets which refuse to be buried. Is Jenna destined to repeat her mother's tragedy or can she triumph over the past and keep both the Townley legacy and the man she was meant to love?

HODDER AND STOUGHTON PAPERBACKS

AUDREY HOWARD

ECHO OF ANOTHER TIME

Celie Marlow first begins working in the Latimers' kitchen when she is only ten, learning her art from kindly Mrs Harper. By the age of eighteen, she has become a talented cook.

Celie knows her place, and longs only to run a kitchen as skilfully as her mentor. Until she falls in love with the wrong man: Richard Latimer, eldest son of the house. And all their lives change with frightening swiftness.

Driven from her home, Celie finds unexpected success in a new venture with Mrs Harper – then loses everything once more. Thrown on to the streets of Liverpool, penniless and desperate, she will have to find her own way.

HODDER AND STOUGHTON PAPERBACKS